THE SUICIDE KING

THE FALLOCAUST SERIES BOOK 3

VOLUME 1 OF 2

QUIL CARTER

www.quilcarter.com

First Edition

978-1519638373

151963837X

This book is dedicated to Jon and Kristie. Jon, it's because of you finally deciding to read my half-finished *The Gods' Games* and *A God Among Insects* six years ago that got me back into writing, thank you. And Kristie, your continued support and friendship has been a light in my life. Thank you for not just being an awesome beta reader, but an awesome friend as well.

'All that you love will be carried away' – Stephen King – Everything's Eventual.

PROLOGUE

DRAKONIUS DEKKER CHEWED ON THE EDGE OF HIS biscuit and walked down the paved sidewalks of Skyland. He was grinning and waving at everyone who recognized him, and had even picked up a chocolate bar and a donut, which had both been quickly devoured.

It was dark out and balmy that evening, one of the first warm nights that Skyfall had seen in the year 232 A.F. The temperatures tonight promised a warm spring and summer, which was exciting enough for the orange-eyed cicaro. Drake was so thrilled with the evening in front of him, he had decided to wander around for a while to see where his feet were going to take him.

And why not? Master Silas was gone and Master Elish as well, even Sanguine was busy taking care of things and had told Drake to just do whatever he wanted. He had taken brother Sangy's words seriously and was doing precisely that: whatever he wanted.

What do I want to do tonight...? Drake glanced around and saw Big Shot looking into a shop with bright lights that illuminated televisions for sale. The half-raver had a surprised look on his face, and his eyes were wide and rather impressed. Drake liked Big Shot because Big Shot treated him nicely, he had convinced him to leave Jade and go and have fun. It had taken three thien guards, Luca, and a locked door behind him, to convince Big Shot to go, but it was worth it.

"Haven't you seen television before?" Drake asked as he walked up to Big Shot and looked into the shop too. The TV was playing a show about a man with black hair throwing spices on food and then going–

"BAM!" Big Shot said loudly after the TV man had exclaimed the same. He looked at Drake and smiled, though it was a crooked smile since his face was messed up from him being a raver for so long. He had a grey callous on the side of his cheek that stretched down to his jawline and a scar that split his eyebrow in half.

Drake laughed and nodded. "He's making food from China called chinese food. I can get the sengils to make us that. Do you want us to make that?"

Big Shot's eyes widened further. "China food? What about..." Big Shot's brows met as he tried to find the words. "Hamburgers? Jade liked hamburgers. Ketchup... King Jade got us to find him ketchup for the ground-up people. He was happy, smiled all the time when he had ketchup."

Drake snorted through his laugh and he looked behind his shoulder. There was an abandoned building behind them, boarded up and without anyone inside, but it was on the corner of a street and further down that street was a bar.

"We can get hamburgers with cheese on them. I can go in there and tell them what I want and I get it just like that." Drake snapped his fingers. "I can ask for anything extra and they give it to me too."

Drake hooked his arm under Big Shot's own and started walking right into the street. Big Shot swore and pivoted his feet as headlights and screeching tires suddenly filled the warm air but Drake seemed unfazed.

"They won't hit me. If they hit me they die," Drake said in his same cheerful voice. He squinted as the headlights shone into his eyes, but a moment later all of the car lights turned off. "And they know to shut off their damn lights too." Drake raised his middle finger at both cars that he had just walked in front of, and carried on with Big Shot to the other end of the street.

Big Shot looked behind him as the cars turned their headlights back on and continued on their way, though he was once again pulled by the arm down the street. "This place is owned by my brother Sanguine. I love Sanguine. This bar is called Sharky's and he has another bar called The Penguin which is our nickname for him because he's Sanguine the Penguin especially now 'cause he likes to wear fancy suits and stuff," Drake said happily. "We can get whatever we want. Do you want bacon? We can have bacon and we can have drinks and it's all for free 'cause of this." Drake reached into a small leather bag he was carrying, the same one that had his chocolate bar and pulled out a black wallet that looked to be made out of snake skin. He handed a black card to Big Shot.

Big Shot took it and stared at it, then his green eyes, now completely clear of their milky white film, travelled up to Drake. "This makes things free?" Big Shot smelled the card and licked it before his face scrunched. "Tastes bad."

Drake, of course, laughed at this. "No, read. See what it says? The silver writing right there and the chimera logo. See?"

Big Shot shook his head. "Brain still recovering. Master Elish says to me that eventually maybe brain heals and read again, write again, but for now, no, no, raver head."

"Oh, right," Drake said with a nod. He took the card back and looked down at it. "It says Drakonius Fennec Dekker which is my full name. This is a black card and it gives me whatever I want. Do you think you'll get one, one day?"

Big Shot shook his head. "I'm not chimera just King Jade's guard. He go, I go. He says he's..." Big Shot's eyes widened again. "He says I'm family. Maybe I will get card?"

"Maybe!" Drake said, his tone brimming with excitement over the prospect. He smiled at a bouncer standing with his arms crossed, the bouncer nodded back and held the door open for the two. "Do you have a real name or have you always just been Big Shot?" he asked as the two of them walked inside the bustling and noisy bar.

Big Shot looked around the bar and his mouth dropped open. He paused for a brief moment to take in the busy atmosphere around him, before Drake pulled him towards a booth with blue fabric seats. Still though, even when he was sitting, Big Shot continued to look around with a shocked expression on his face. There was a long wooden bar by the far wall with many liquor bottles sitting on glass shelves, glowing from a backdrop of blue-tinged LED lighting. Behind that bar was a handsome gentlemen with black hair that had blond tips. He was talking casually to several men sitting in booths with drinks in front of them.

And around Big Shot were many more tables, most filled with patrons and people behind and in front of him too. They were talking and eating food that had filled the entire bar with the smell of fried things, an aroma that made the half-raver's mouth water.

"Incredible," Big Shot said under his breath. He held out his hand as a waiter walked by with food and grabbed onto his apron. "You... what's that?"

The waiter took one look at Big Shot and his nose curled. He snatched his apron away from Big Shot. "We don't let diseased–" Then his eyes travelled to Drake and his sneering expression suddenly changed into a smile. It happened so quickly it was as if a channel on a TV had been changed.

"Prince Drake, how–"

"Finish your sentence," Drake said, his tone dropping several octaves. "We don't let diseased...? Go on, tell my best friend-in-the-whole-entire-world what you were going to say."

The waiter's smile remained plastered on his face like cheap gyprock, but his eyes were terrified and his pupils little specks. He looked at Drake then slowly those same eyes went back to Big Shot.

"Prince Drake... I was going to say we – we –" The waiter started stammering when he saw Drake reach into his leather bag and pull out a small rectangular object made out of smooth metal and plastic. Drake pressed a silver button on the side and a sharp but narrow blade shot out of it with a *shink*.

The chimera's orange eyes flickered up to the waiter and they flared with a dangerous glint, one that the waiter wilted under. "– we... we have crazy bread. Do you want a big plate of crazy bread with extra cheese and garlic, and butter dipping sauce?"

Drake's eyes lit up, erasing all hostility seen just moments ago, and he looked at Big Shot with a wide and beaming grin. "They have crazy bread! They have crazy bread! I WANT THAT! GET THAT! NOW!"

The waiter, looking visibly relieved, nodded. And while he had the chance, he turned around and disappeared.

"I could kill him if I wanted, in front of everyone," Drake said with a smug smile. "You can too now since Jade says you're family. I'm not sure if King Silas will be okay with that, sometimes King Silas is happy but sometimes he's really mean."

Big Shot nodded understandably. "King Jade the same. I the same when led the ravers. Good when good, bad when bad. I like being bad, seeing people scared... I like that. Jade liked that. I miss Jade. I hope head gets better."

Big Shot looked behind Drake when there was the sound of a tipping glass in the booth behind him. Big Shot scowled as a man with red hair swore and started cleaning up the mess with a clean dish towel provided to all patrons in lieu of napkins. Big Shot started at him for several more moments, but eventually when Drake started to speak, his attention turned back to him.

"I miss him too," Drake said with a sad nod, "and I miss King Silas and Master Elish and the others. Do you know me and Sanguine and Jade are the only chimeras in Skyfall right now? Isn't that neat? Sanguine is king right now. King Sangy. He'd be a good king but he's too sadistic to be king for long. He's kinda crazy sometimes he goes all..." Drake curled his fingers into claws and growled. "Like that."

Big Shot laughed before his eyes lit up once again when a new waiter, looking rather nervous, came over holding a large plate of bread sticks, heaping with cheese and garlic and all centered around a bowl of yellowy oil.

"Bring hamburgers too," Drake said, both of his hands now holding breadsticks which, moments later, got dunked simultaneously into the butter. "With cheese, lots of..." Drake's eyes went glassy when another waiter appeared with two tall drinks and hamburgers and potato fries.

"They really know how to kiss up," Drake said as he rubbed his hands together. "Eat as much as you want, even if your stomach hurts. I can show you a neat trick that I was taught. You can make yourself throw up and then you can eat all over again!" Drake grinned at this, even when Big Shot gave him a horrified look back.

"Make... yourself...? On purpose?" Big Shot asked.

Drake nodded vigorously. "I'm not allowed. I'm forbidden actually by Master Silas, but he's gone and Sanguine's king and Sanguine said I can do whatever I want. So I'm going to eat until I puke! Then eat MORE!" And at this Drake started shoving one of the breadsticks into his mouth as Big Shot watched him; the half-raver looking rather alarmed.

"I see why you need keeper," Big Shot said, his brow knitting and his face growing grave and serious. "You not allowed out alone often? Without master to tell you no?"

Drake looked up, his cheeks stuffed with food. He smiled and shook his head back and forth before grabbing a large handful of potato fries. Even with a mouth puffed out with food, he pushed more in and started chewing happily.

Then Drake stopped. He stared at Big Shot with an odd expression on his face... then he spat the food back onto the plate and put a hand up to his throat.

Big Shot stared at him as Drake clutched his neck and started taking in sharp gasps, then a moment later, he started banging on the table.

"Are you dying?" Big Shot asked. He glanced to the side and waved a hand. "Waiter? Chimera dying?" He looked back at Drake who was grasping the table cloth with a tense hand; he was starting to turn blue and his orange eyes were bulging with fear.

"You come back, right?" Big Shot looked around and waved his hand again, a look of unease now on his face. "You-you're one of the forever ones, yes? Um… chimera dying? Hello?"

The bartender looked over and immediately his mouth fell open. He dropped the glass he'd been cleaning and sprinted over. "Again, Drakey?" he hissed when he reached the table; his hasty running alerting the entire bar to the scene playing out in front of them. "Drake, get up. Get up!"

Drake, still clutching the table cloth with his eyes protruding from their sockets, gave the bartender a stricken look. The bartender grabbed onto the collar the cicaro always wore, and tried to pull him to his feet; but Drake only stood for a moment before he fell to the red-carpeted floor. Immediately the bartender started banging on Drake's back but after several minutes of thumping he stopped and swore loudly. The reason why was obvious – Drake was dead.

"Shit… too late…" the bartender said. He looked around and put a hand on his forehead, then turned to where a cluster of waiters had gathered. "Pat… run to the precinct and see if you can reach Ellis, or at the very least, one of the half-chimeras."

Big Shot shook his head and picked up a bread stick. "Not here," he said as he chewed on the end of it. "All chimeras gone but red-eyed one, sick Jade, and dead one."

The bartender looked at him as he rolled Drake onto his back. The cicaro's orange eyes were staring off into nothing, and his face was now blue with froth all around his pale lips. "All of them? Why?" Then suddenly he held up both hands. "Actually don't answer that. Please, please, don't answer that…" He looked behind him again. "Pat, go to Alegria then and tell a thien to get Sanguine. If they're all out of Skyfall besides Sanguine, Jade, and Drake… that means Jack isn't going to be coming for him." Then he looked back to Big Shot. "You're not a chimera, obviously. Are you okay getting home yourself?"

Big Shot waved a hand in a dismissive manner, still gnawing on the bread stick. "I'm from greywastes. I protect Jade. I need no keeper; that's truth." He then pointed to the rest of the food. "Put in bag, yes? I eat outside, too noisy here."

The bartender waved one of the waiters over, coincidentally the one who Drake had threatened with the knife. The waiter, without making eye contact, took the food and disappeared into the back.

When he came back with the bag, Big Shot nodded towards him. "Drake... comes here a lot, then?"

The waiter paused and let out a nervous laugh. "Uh... yeah... he – he does. Um, sorry about earlier."

Big Shot got up with the bag. "It's okay. I called worse." He stepped over Drake and looked down at him. "You know him well? It is true everyone has to do what chimera says?"

Another nervous laugh; the waiter looking like he'd rather be getting threatened with a knife again than talk about Drake and the other chimeras. "Y-yeah, but we know how to make him happy. He kinda... once you know how to make him happy, it's okay. He's Drake, all of Skyfall loves him. He's an angel compared..." The waiter paused before swallowing down his next comment. "I better get back to work. You're welcome here anytime."

"Okay." Big Shot took one last look at Drake before leaving with a shake of his head. "Chimera all crazy, make raver look normal. Throw up food and eat until die? We eat until bursting but we keep it down. Why throw up good meat?"

The half-raver walked back into the warm night, food in hand, and started heading to Olympus. Eventually he opened up the bag of hamburgers, potato fries, and breadsticks (minus the food that Drake spat up on) and started eating the fries.

"Hey..."

Big Shot stopped and turned around as a man jogged up to him. A sickly-looking man with a hollow appearance and unhealthy red hair that fell over grey eyes.

"Hey... can I talk to you for a moment?" the man asked.

Big Shot looked behind his shoulder to see who the man was addressing, but it was just him and several people walking down the sidewalk. It looked like the man was wanting to talk to him.

Weird, Big Shot said to himself, then shrugged. "Okay," he said. "Talk about... food? Ketchup is nice. My favourite, I think, is liver. What is your favourite?"

The red-haired man gave Big Shot a confused look, then shook his head. "No, not about food." His movements were odd, jerking and fidgeting. Big

Shot found himself taking a step back. "I wanted to ask you… what's wrong with Jade?"

"Jade?" Big Shot's brow furrowed. "Brain attack fucking up mind. Why ask?"

The man stared at Big Shot before saying back to himself. "Brain attack? You mean…" Then his tone dropped, his face twisting as if he had trouble processing information.

Maybe he half-raver too? Big Shot cocked his head to the side at this prospect and kept watching him.

Then the man with the red hair nodded to himself, as if the information had finally hit the right spots inside of his troubled mind. "That… the things he can do with his mind, is hurting his head?"

Big Shot nodded. "King Jade bad head. Almost died, now won't wake up. Now all chimeras gone. I protect him, no one comes near him with me. Why ask? What wrong with your mind?"

The man continued to stare at the ground, then he raised a hand and held it to the back of his own head. Big Shot's green eyes widened when he saw a large pink scar.

"It comes and goes, today is just a bad day for me," the red-haired man said.

But then his eyes became hostile. "Even that blond fuck is gone?" he asked. "He left Jade alone?"

"Blond fuck? Husband, you mean?" At this comment Big Shot's expression turned clouded, then he shook his head back and forth rapidly. "You call him that. You not friend of chimera… good day. Bye."

"No… wait… I didn't mean…" The red-haired man put a hand on Big Shot's shoulder, but as soon as his hand touched Big Shot's skin, the half-raver spun around and let out a loud and vicious hiss.

The red-haired man jumped back, his face stricken with fear and his body tightened like a wrung washcloth.

"Husband loves King Jade. I see this. Elish held him, carried him when was weak. I see that and I let husband around King Jade with no protest. He's no *blond fuck*. Good chimera, strong head, strong back," Big Shot said angrily. "Jade sick but not alone. Big Shot with him; I bodyguard and family. This is truth. Good day."

Big Shot turned around and stalked away from the red-haired man.

"Why hasn't he made him immortal yet if he's so sick?" the man called, but Big Shot just kept walking, his face creased in a scowl and his hand clenching the bag of food. He picked up his pace and made his way back to Olympus quickly.

When he walked through the doors of the skyscraper, he headed directly towards the elevator. Seeing him approach the secretary jumped up from her seat and fast-walked over to him. Big Shot knew why so he let her. He often forgot how to use the elevator.

"Where did you want to go, Mister Big Shot?" the lady asked with a kind smile.

"I see Jade," Big Shot replied. "Drake okay?"

The lady, with pulled back brown hair, nodded and pressed the correct buttons on the elevator pad. "Yes. Sanguine is in Alegria with Drake. He doesn't wish to be disturbed right now but he has him." Then she stepped out and inclined her head to Big Shot. "Have a good evening."

Big Shot nodded and laid a hand on her head. "Kah!" he said, and the elevator doors closed on him. He looked up and around and grabbed onto the railing as the elevator took him up to the infirmary floor; he still wasn't used to the motion.

Skyfall was a strange place but at least he was getting used to it, even if the chimeras and their customs made no sense at all.

"Kah!" Big Shot said with a smile on his face when he entered the infirmary. Jade was where Big Shot had left him, in the hospital bed with his eyes closed. There was a long tube going into his mouth and many wires hooked up to his body. It troubled Big Shot to see Jade attached to all of the machines; but the more of his mind he got back, the more he had accepted that this was for Jade's own good.

"Hello, Big Shot. I hear Drake choked and died again," Lyle said. The middle-aged doctor was sitting down beside a lamp reading from a text book.

Big Shot nodded as he took his seat beside Jade, three thiens now standing in the hallway with their bushmasters. He felt better knowing the thiens were there, King Jade always attracted trouble.

"Drake dies a lot?" Big Shot asked.

Lyle snorted as he chuckled and nodded. "My father Levi, the now mayor of Moros, and Drake were the same age growing up and they were good friends. He tells me it was difficult keeping him alive, Drake seems drawn to death like a magnet. Master Elish figures he's probably died about two hundred times by now. Would you believe he once chased a Frisbee off of Olympus? He probably chokes on his food at least ten times a year.

That's why he isn't allowed out often unless he's sneaky, and why he wears that I.D tag telling people to not feed him."

Big Shot opened up the food bag and put a breadstick in Jade's still hand. "I'm happy he only one like that. If Elish like Drake... would've killed him when tried to take back king. Bang bang in the head, no questions. When husband back?" Big Shot patted the hand that he'd put the breadstick in, but Jade was still.

"He... he won't eat on his own," Lyle said in a soft voice. "He's completely – I don't think..." Lyle got up and walked over to Big Shot as the half-raver shook Jade's hand, encouraging him to eat. "I don't think he's ever going to eat or do anything on his own again. Not until... King Silas makes him immortal."

Big Shot shook his head rapidly. "No, he eats when hungry. You'll see. Just not hungry yet, I guess."

Lyle gave him a sad smile before raising a hand and brushing Jade's long black bangs from his bruised eyes. "You say it differently, of course, but... you have no idea how much you sound like Elish right now." The doctor patted Jade's head and sighed. "I don't think... you two realize that this will be permanent and that... Jade's mind is gone."

But Big Shot only shook his head back and forth some more. "No... Jade's strong. Jade's been almost dead many times. He okay. He be fine... he has to be fine."

Lyle looked at him, but though it appeared that the retired sengil wanted to say more to Big Shot, much more, he remained quiet. Like when he was talking to Elish, he just nodded and forced an encouraging smile.

"Yes..." he said, patting Big Shot's shoulder, "maybe you're right."

CHAPTER 1

Sanguine

I RAN MY HAND ALONG THE RAILING AS I WALKED UP the stairs, a song that had been stuck in my head long enough for it to warrant a tune now on my lips. It was a happy tune – because this was quite the happy time.

I reached the top of the concrete stairs and opened the door to outside. Automatically I squinted from the bright sun but there was happiness in that too. The sun was out and there was a warm breeze this afternoon. It was May now and spring was back in Skyfall.

And oh what a beautiful spring and summer it was going to be.

Beautiful.

"Hello, friends," I said happily as I stepped out onto the tarmac roof. My eyes swept the top of the large skyscraper, and I smiled when I saw over two dozen crows perched in various places. Some on the benches, some on the raised garden beds, and others on the weather-stained statues.

As soon as the crows saw me they all started cawing and bobbing their heads, some even flapping wings in anticipation for whatever presents their master had brought them. They were smart creatures, smarter than your average crow and raven, and they knew when I appeared I brought with me the loveliest of treats.

"Hello, Sanguine," one of them said back.

I laughed and reached into my vest pocket. I pulled out a plastic bag full of seed and when the crows eyed the bag the cawing got louder. It was an orchestra around me now, a soothing song that gently drew out and caressed all of my past memories. Most bad, but when the crows were around during those nightmarish times… basements seemed lighter, touches kinder, masochism all the more painful.

I closed my eyes and took in a deep breath of the spring air, and when I opened them I saw the rows and rows of glistening red eyes watching me intently.

I always did love an audience. I opened the bag and started throwing the feed to the crows.

There was a flutter of wings, and all of the crows flew and hopped to the tarmac to eat their seed and the pieces of bread that I had thrown into the mix. The crows stayed close together, their wings flashing as they reflected the sunlight shining above them. They were clustered so tight they looked like a wound filled with beetles, shifting and churning as one organism, though with how tightly packed this murder was – they did seem like one creature at times.

"Got any food?" "Come here, Crow."

"Crow's coming. Crow's coming. Hello, Sanguine. Crow's coming."

I smirked and I shook my head. I grabbed a handful of seed and lightly tossed it to the birds, but when I reached in to grab another, I paused.

The smirk quickly turned into a smile when I heard the distinct sound of a plane in the distance. I walked to the edge of the roof and stepped up onto the concrete barrier that surrounded it. I put a hand to my brow to shield my eyes from the sun's glare, and looked to the east.

My heart skipped before my chest clamped a protective vice around it.

The Falconer was coming back; it was flying above one of the factory towns but I could see it. I was the tallest man in Skyfall right now from my place atop of Alegria and I had the best of views… yes, the Falconer was coming back.

I stepped down from the concrete barrier and walked past my still eating crows. I stood beside one of King Silas's iron rung benches and straightened my bowtie, before brushing a crow feather from the shoulder of my wine-coloured shirt.

This is it… please let this be it. I took in another breath, the cold air soothing my burning chest. *I have to break him out of there. No plans can move forward until I know he is safe and breathing the same crisp air that I am. I sold him out to protect Reaver, and now I must fix this.*

I'm sorry, Nero. I wouldn't have done it if I wasn't confident I would break you out quickly. I have allegiances I need to keep – and Elish is already going to be livid with me.

I exhaled and closed my eyes. With that sense now diminished, my hearing intensified, and as the low rumbling of the Falconer got closer, my pulse increased.

Don't hope... I shouldn't hope...

I can't help it. My chest echoed with the sounds of my thrashing heart, and to try and force it to slow, I closed my eyes and took in another deep breath. I had trained my body not to succumb to these physical reactions, but here I was feeling like I was going to pass out.

So much depended on who would be exiting that plane.

Forgive me, Elish. This was unexpected and I have no plans as to how I am going to explain this to Silas – I just cannot let Nero stay in there.

Just like I couldn't let his husband Ceph fall into insanity from the same fate.

I opened my eyes and looked up. I saw my crows flying around me, and more taking flight with every second that passed. They heard the Falconer was coming and they knew to get out of the way.

The crows were my comfort and now they too were fleeing, leaving nothing but flutters of feathers around them as they took off to find more food; or a place to catch the rays of the sun.

I walked from the bench to the yellow circle that the Falconer would land in the middle of. I stayed on the edge of the ring and watched the black plane's thrusters switch positions so it could land vertically; the intense heat from the black cylinders disrupting the air around it.

A moment later it landed with a thud, and the motor switched octaves and died.

And then there was silence; the unnerving and eerie silence that was only apparent when something assaultingly loud was turned off. It made me stand up straighter and swallow the lump that kept crawling up my throat like a determined spider.

Then the sliding door of the Falconer opened.

My lips pursed, my heart palpitated and shuddered, and in spite of myself, I dug my fingernails into the soft skin of my arms. An act of masochism that had always brought me comfort, even as a small boy.

There was a slam as the door closed and it was then that my heart dropped.

No voices of Garrett arguing with Elish. No tones of Jack making gilded remarks. No Silas who I had seen last in the greywastes.

It was just…

A boy of sixteen, lanky with black hair and vivid copper eyes walked out from behind the plane, looking pale and about to throw up.

"I did it," Kiki stammered. He looked behind him like he didn't recognize the plane he had just flown all the way back from the plaguelands. "S-Sanguine... I left them all behind. I left... S-Sanguine, I did it."

Yes, yes, boy, you did. I squinted as I smiled and inclined my head to the, rather frazzled, chimera teenager. "You did a grand job, Kincade. Shall we go see what our Nero is doing right now? I think he will be quite eager to see us."

Kiki looked at me, and though it hadn't seemed possible several seconds ago, the young chimera had achieved an even paler, more stricken look. Poor boy, he looked as if he was going to become sick right on the tarmac.

"Now?" Kiki whispered. He put a hand to his mouth; I could see the small raccoon ring on his finger. "Now? Really?"

I rested a hand on Kiki's shoulder. "Believe me, love. When you're locked in that monotonous hell with nothing to keep you company but your own slowly dying body and an abundance of caustic thoughts... now is even too late." I directed the boy towards the stairs and grabbed his hand. "Let's go, little one – let's go see how wide of a smile we can put on our big brother's face, yes?"

Kiki squeezed my hand and sniffed. "I miss him so much. Do you think I helped him, by talking to him and reading to him?"

"Yes, lovely," I said, our boot steps echoing off of the concrete walls around us as we descended the stairs of Alegria. "It always helped me and it always helped him."

Kiki turned to me as we descended the stairs. "You've been locked in concrete too?"

I could feel my body tighten at the question, and my mouth went dry. "Yes," I said, my dry mouth making my voice rasp. "I don't think there is a single immortal chimera now who hasn't been disciplined by King Silas at least once." I absentmindedly ran a hand along the metal railing, painted dark blue, and continued to walk down the stairs. "It is an especially cruel fate for me, and he knew this but still he didn't care... he used to care though. At least he was kind and the longest I've been locked away is a week, I think. If I was gone longer he made me forget, another thing he enjoys doing when he's especially cruel to me but regrets it."

Kiki's response to this was silence. But, really, what could he say back? He was sixteen years old and he only knew King Silas how he was now.

Not who he used to be… who I remembered him being.

And who I dearly wished he still was.

When we got to the bottom of the stairs, I paused. This floor was dreaded amongst the family, and the pulse quickening inside of me reminded me that I wasn't immune to this place either. If you took any of my brothers, whether it be Elish, our most stoic and controlled, or Jack, our most collected and morose, each one would not be able to escape the visceral reaction to stepping foot in this dark hallway, one that was bursting at the seams with the nightmares and past screams of our brothers.

Kiki took in a deep breath and squared his shoulders. The young chimera looked ahead and I saw him raise his chin high. He was trying to be brave and strong. I wondered in that moment if he even realized what the consequences would be for what we had done.

No, of course he doesn't, I said to myself as I walked down the dark hallway towards the double oak doors. *If he knew just what was in store for the both of us – he would have ran from me the moment I opened that wooden crate.*

But what can I do? Oh, tell me what was I supposed to do? That man inside the tomb yanked me from my own prison like he himself was pulling me from my steel mother. He delivered me to my new life, and it was him and him alone, who never gave up on me.

It was Nero who has done more for me than any family member, dead or alive. I am bound to that man and it is for his sake that I condemned myself to thirty years of slavery. It was for his sake that I said goodbye to my love. My Jack.

At this, I smiled, and looked into the dark room in front of us.

It looked like an indoor graveyard and in many senses that is exactly what it was. An open room with walls draped with black curtains, even the wall-to-wall windows that every floor in Alegria had were covered with thick fabric, held down to the ground by bricks or boxes. There was no light inside of this room because the living dead needed no light. What use did they have for the sun when their world was nothing but monotonous darkness and the roaring static that only the most deafening of silences could bring?

"Kiki… love," I said with my smile.

Kiki looked at me, the pupils centered inside his vivid copper eyes retracted when they saw the smile on my face.

"Take the curtains off of the windows and let the sun shine inside of our little crypt. I would like my lovelies to feel the sun shining on their faces when I pull them from their graves."

Kiki nodded and turned, then left the corner of my vision.

I looked at the six concrete tombs in front of me, five of them standing like forgotten sentries in what used to be Garrett's living room. So much happiness had once filled this apartment. So much laughter, joyful times, sex, good food, and drunken parties I myself had used to love attending. Perhaps one day it could be returned to its happy state.

I walked up to Nero's tomb and gently grabbed the black canvas that had been laid over the grey concrete. All of these coffins were draped with sound muting canvases when they were receiving no visitors, and Silas didn't want to hear their desperate screams.

At times it was those very screams that kept me loyal to my king. Deep in the middle of the night when I would lay cold in my bed full of loneliness, I would visit these chimeras and receive courage from them. Sometimes all it took was an agonizing, muffled moan to give me the strength to live one more day with the man that had become such a terrible monster at times.

I wish they could talk to me… I wish he hadn't gagged them. Oh, what I would've given to have someone to talk to some nights, I thought to myself as the thick canvas covering Nero dropped to the floor. I looked down at the large hand and felt a laugh come to my lips as it weakly waved to me. With a closed-mouth smile now wide on my face, I gently picked up Nero's hand and kissed it.

And it was in that moment that sunlight flooded the room.

"Come here, my lovely little raccoon," I said to Kiki. I looked to the light, my eyes squinting. I could see Kiki reach up to the top of the window to pull down a second curtain, and as it fell to the clean grey carpet more light shone in the room. It was odd to see the room light up, as if such a terrible thing had taken place here that it should only be viewed in its veiled shadow.

But no more… no more.

Kiki walked to me, and for the first time since seeing him, the cicaro himself smiled when he saw Nero's hand being held firmly in mine.

"He's alive?" Kiki whispered. He grasped Nero's hand too and when Nero gripped it firmly the shy smile turned into an excited grin. Just like that, the nervousness I had been seeing on the young chimera disappeared.

The reality of what was about to happen seemed to be hitting him.

If only he knew we would be doing so much more by the day's end.

"How do we do it, Master Sanguine?" Kiki asked eagerly. "How – how can we get him out?"

I patted Nero's hand and let go of it. I walked to what used to be Garrett's bedroom and Kiki followed behind me. I opened the door and heard the young chimera gasp when he saw what was inside.

"How did you get a sledgehammer in here?" Kiki exclaimed, his facial features quite animated.

The young chimera ran into the bedroom, covered in boxes and old furniture draped with dust-covered sheets. The room was dark, though the light from the living room had leaked in to cast some sunlight into the darkness.

"No one cares what I do, little one," I said, with a hint of acid in my words. "They're too busy chasing dark chimeras who hate them, and trying to prevent the northern greywastes from exploding. It has become quite easy to sneak around and a sledgehammer and several metal spikes are simple to hide in a storage room."

Kiki picked up the sledgehammer, but even though a stealth chimera had good muscles on them, he was unable to lift it higher than his waist. The hammer fell to the carpet with a low *clunk* and I took it from him.

"How – how long have you been planning this?" Kiki asked curiously. "As soon as Master Nero was encased?"

I shook my head and motioned for Kiki to pick up the metal spikes I had underneath the sledgehammer. "I have been taking care of the living dead for thirty years. Ever since Nero's husband was condemned to live in his confining madness." I sauntered back into the sunlight-bathed living room, walking through millions of little dust motes that were floating through the air. Though I was instructed to clean this floor once a month, the only chimera allowed to come and go as I pleased, it still attracted dust almost as much as the greywastes did. To my own inner amusement, I found myself chastising myself for letting it get so dusty. Even though I wasn't born a slave, old habits die hard, especially when they were still alive inside of me.

"Ceph?" Kiki said in a small voice. His eyes became troubled as he walked back to the square of concrete that held Nero. "I asked Nero about him once after Sid had mentioned him... Nero hit me and I flew across the room."

I walked over to a different concrete tomb. This one was old and worn and had been there for decades. I swung the sledgehammer and gently tapped it as I practiced my aim. "You would've been a cicaro to a much different man if Ceph wasn't encased in concrete only several feet from him." I nodded to my left and Kiki looked at the tomb that always held little red heart stickers. "He would've been... like he used to be."

A whimsical, almost longing smile crossed my face before I shook myself free of it. I licked my finger and touched the wet digit to the old tomb, making a mark. Then, with my tongue sticking out of the side of my mouth, I swung the hammer, with a little more force this time, and hit the exact location. The tomb didn't break through but it did make a loud *thunk*.

I smiled and nodded to myself, happy with my aim. "Well, little one... I think Nero has waited long enough." Then I walked over to Nero's tomb and touched it gently. "Nero? Close your eyes."

Nero, of course, didn't answer, but his free hand balled into a fist. I held the sledgehammer in both hands and addressed Kiki. "Put the spike in that small hairline crack," I instructed, motioning to a slight split in the concrete about three quarters of the way up it. "And hold the metal spike. Do not drop it."

Kiki paled at these instructions. He looked nervously at the long and rusted spike in his hand, the top of it flattened from being hammered before, then he found his bravery. He placed the spike in the concrete and held it firm.

"Now... close your eyes as well. If you flinch I will hit your hand, and unlike Nero and I... you will not grow one back," I said as my tongue stuck out of the corner of my mouth. I tightened my grip on the sledgehammer and spread my hands to get a better hold on it.

When Kiki's eyes were closed and his hand as far down on the spike as he possibly could get it, I mumbled a silent prayer to the universe and swung the sledgehammer towards the spike.

Vibrating pain rippled up my hands almost making me drop the hammer, but I managed to hang onto it and, to my surprise, Kiki did as well.

I grinned and nodded when I saw the spike embedded an inch into the concrete with two fissures now forming in three different directions. Kiki pulled his hand away and grabbed Nero's which was still being clenched hard into a fist.

"Master Nero... is the spike anywhere near your body?" Kiki asked loudly. "Can you–"

"One question at a time, little one," I said. "Is the spike near your body, love?"

The hand unclenched, there was white on his palm from the tightness of it. Nero shook his hand back and forth, which I knew meant no.

"Let's do this then," I said, not hiding the excitement in my voice. I raised the sledgehammer a second time and swung it against the spike. This time there was a loud crack and a large piece of concrete fell to the floor, exposing Nero's blue jeans, putrid-smelling and damp, but shifting with excitement.

And that same excitement was now ripping up and down my body like I had been struck by lightning. Using Kiki's excited cries as fuel, I raised the sledgehammer and did a sideways swing towards a large crack to the right of the broken off piece. This one ripped off a larger chunk and exposed a grey button-down and a nylon jacket.

"Fuck!" Nero gasped. A burly arm raised and with a bellow Nero pushed it against the concrete. With a quiver shaking my chest I swung the hammer, with less force this time, and helped him break it off.

Nero's sweaty, grey-stained face was exposed, his eyes squinting under the sunlight and his body trembling from the adrenaline. I watched him look around, seemingly in a daze, and quickly jumped out of the rest of the concrete prison. But as soon as his foot hit the ground, he fell to his knees with a strangled groan. My Nero looked like he was literally being born again, spilling onto the floor from a concrete mother to face a new world around him.

Kiki gave out a cry and motioned to run to him, but I raised a hand and gave him a sharp look, a look glaring enough to make the young chimera stop in his tracks. To barrel towards a chimera who had been locked up, even for a short time, wasn't a wise idea and that boy was no immortal.

Instead I knelt down in front of Nero and put a hand on his shoulder. "How is your mental state, my love? Are you okay?"

Nero took in several gasping breaths. "I... I just woke up a few hours ago. I'm okay," he said through his laboured breathing. He looked up as I started wiping his flushed red face with the sleeve of my blazer. "How...? W-why, Sangy? Silas... Silas will..."

I gave him a warm smile and shook my head, gently clearing away the concrete dust from his nose and mouth. "Because fifty-two years ago you pulled me from my own hell, after spending almost a decade looking for me. You know how much I love you, Nuky. You know I couldn't let him keep you there forever."

Nero's face dissolved; he threw his arms around me and held me tight. "Thank you, puppy. Fuck... thank you."

I put my arms around him as well and we embraced each other. Nero's hands so tight around my torso I could feel the breath being constricted inside of my chest cavity. "If... if only you knew what else I have been doing for you. If only you..." Then my eyes travelled to Kiki. He was still standing beside the dusty mess of concrete, the remaining shell now kneeling in its own broken innards. "Kiki played an important role in this, love. He was unwavering in his devotion to you. We have Silas, Elish, Jack, Garrett, Caligula, Nico, and Reno stranded near the plaguelands because of your little racoon. Let him give you a hug."

Nero looked over at Kiki and gave him a faint smile. He raised a dusty and sweaty hand and waved his cicaro over. "I smell like piss, vomit, and sweat, peaches, but if you want a hug..." Before the last words could come out of Nero's mouth, Kiki ran over to him and threw his arms around Nero. There was a muffled cry and Kiki buried his face into the crook of his master's neck.

"I love you," Kiki sniffed. "We need to get out of here. I got us a lot of money. We're going to run away far from here, so they won't get you."

"I don't think we have a choice..." Nero rubbed Kiki's head and kissed it, then looked back to me. "You really stranded all of them in the plaguelands?" Nero shakily got to his feet and started limping towards the door. "Sanguine... you're coming with me, right? Kingy, fuck... baby." Nero shook his head and a look of pain crossed his face. I felt my own throat go tight. "Kingy's going to concrete you, just like me."

I got up also and swallowed down the restriction threatening to shorten my breath, "I have a lot to catch you up on, love. We have a plan... I didn't do this without a bit of a plan in place. Sort of..." But when I saw Nero heading towards the door I stopped talking and crossed my arms. "Where are you going?"

Nero rested a hand on the door frame to steady himself. "I need to get the fuck out of here and shower, eat, and you need to tell me just what our plan is. Kiki... I need you to order a lot of–"

"Aren't you forgetting someone?"

Nero froze; his shoulders tightened and his hand on the door frame clenched.

"He's dead..." Nero's voice was a hushed whisper, a whisper that would've been inaudible if it wasn't for chimera hearing. "Let's... let's go."

"He's dead?" I smirked. I flicked a stray lock of hair from my eyes and tilted my head to the side as if my smirk was physically weighing my head. "Lovely, he's immortal. He's but–"

"He's dead!" Nero whirled around and cried, anguish flooding his face. His indigo eyes briefly travelled to the concrete tomb covered in heart stickers but he looked away, as if the sight physically burned him. "He's dead. He's dead, Sanguine. He's been in there for thirty years. He's c-c-claustrophobic, and he's insane by now." Nero ran a hand down his face as it crumpled. "Why you gotta bring him up, Sangy? You know he's gone. You know he wouldn't be my Cephy anymore. Why you need to – why you need…"

I quickly walked to him as Nero let out a strangled, devastated sob, but as I approached he turned around and started walking down the hallway.

I put a hand on his shoulder to stop him. "Follow me, love. I have something to show you."

"N-no, let me go," Nero choked. But I only shook my head and grabbed his hand.

I squeezed it. "It's only one floor down. Follow me. You'll want to see this."

Nero sniffed and shook his head no, but he followed me anyway. I walked my Nero down the dark hallway, only a streak of light from the apartment we'd just left lighting the way. Kiki followed us, and when I glanced at him from over my shoulder, I saw a curious, yet worried, look on his face.

We carried on down the stairs, Nero's sniffs echoing off of the stairwell, until we were in the hallway of what used to be Nero and Ceph's own apartment.

"Floor twenty-four. Where I lived with him during the beginning of our relationship," Nero said in a broken voice several octaves higher than his normal deep tones. "Why the fuck are you doing this to me, Sangy? I just… I just want to eat and get clean. I can't do this right now."

I shook my head and pushed the door open. I headed towards what had once been the living room. "You'll want to see–"

"See what!" Nero suddenly cried, his body tense and his fists once again clenched from his anguish. He stalked up to me and opened his mouth to unleash more of his agony, but then he paused to watch me grab a black linen sheet covering an object almost as tall as him.

I withdrew the sheet with a smile, revealing underneath it a metal IV drip, which still held in it a bag half-full of fluid.

And as Nero took a step back, I pointed to a thin tube that led up to the ceiling and disappeared into a small hole the size of a baseball, then underneath it was a small machine was hooked up and connected to the IV. I looked back to him and smiled proudly when I saw the flabbergasted look on his face. I had been imagining this scene for decades and I couldn't help but drink in his expression.

It was quite the expression too.

"What… what the fuck…?" Nero whispered. He took a step back and looked around the dark storage room but there was nothing out of place, nothing that gave suggestion as to what I had been hiding for thirty years. I had been careful to conceal everything as well as I could, and thankfully this was one room that everyone avoided, Silas included.

I took advantage of Nero's shocked state, and walked over to one of the cardboard boxes that were stacked on top of one another. I opened it and tipped it for Nero to see.

Inside were stacks of empty IV bags and small needles tipped with blood.

"S-Sanguine?" Nero said in a hushed voice. He walked on shaky feet to the box and picked up one of the empty bags, then his eyes travelled back to the IV drip and the small whirring machine. "What did you do?"

I smiled sadly. "I didn't just become his sengil thirty years ago because I knew Silas needed me, love. I did it to save Ceph from the insanity-inducing monotony I knew would claim him. For thirty years I've had him in a coma. Not even our white flames of death which can, at times, be maddening themselves, but asleep. Once a week I set up the IV, a slow drip that would last the entire week, and on Sunday, sometimes Monday, I would change it for him." Then I pointed to the machine. "This little thing pushes the fluid up since gravity would work against the IV. I made it myself."

A look of pure awe crossed Nero's face. He stared up at the ceiling, his mouth open and his head shaking back and forth. Never had I seen my Nero look so amazed, it warmed my heart and already my cheeks were hurting from smiling.

All of this, everything I have suffered through, it was all worth it just for this moment.

"For thirty years?" Nero whispered.

I nodded and rested a hand on his shoulder. "There were times I was resurrecting that he was without, but for the most part… your husband has been asleep, waiting for his prince to kiss him awake." I removed my hand from Nero's shoulder and grabbed onto the clear plastic tube. I gave it a yank and out popped a needle, the same kind in the cardboard box.

I let it fall to the ground. "What are you waiting for, love?"

Nero was still staring at the ceiling, seemingly stuck inside of my words and the emotions that were charging through him like an advancing army. "What am I waiting for?" Nero whispered. Then he shook his head rapidly, as if shaking away the overabundance of new information. "What am I waiting for?" A smile banished the shock on his face. He threw his arms around me and crushed me to his chest.

Then as quickly as he grabbed me, I was dropped, and with a hand on Kiki's head to give it a shake, he ran out of the apartment and into the hallway.

I laughed and walked past Kiki. "Let's go. He won't wait for us."

I followed Nero as my brother ran up the stairs, what weakness his body had from being trapped inside of his own tomb had vanished with the news he had just received.

He got to the twenty-fifth floor and ran down the hallway, Kiki and I both trailing behind. Then he sped into the still sun-filled room.

Nero grabbed the hammer and turned around with a grin on his face. "Okay, how do I do this without killing him?" he said with a laugh.

I grabbed the metal spike and gave it a flip in my hand. "The concrete will be brittle from it being so long. Don't use your full force or you'll crush my hands and I will have to kill you." I winked and put the spike into a crack in the concrete. "Swing, lovely."

Nero nodded, and he bit down on his lower lip. With his face creased in concentration, he swung the hammer sideways and hit the spike with a loud clang that echoed throughout the room.

The concrete split right down the middle, a putrid smell coming from inside of it like a broken rotten egg. But Nero didn't care. He slammed the sledgehammer, end first, into the crack like a battering ram to crack it open further. It must've been good-enough for him, because he gave the sledgehammer a violent throw and grabbed both ends of the split.

I winced when I heard the sledgehammer smash into something, but my eyes were too fixed on the scene in front of me. Nero, his teeth clenched and his face red, pried the two ends apart with all of his genetically engineered strength. A low cracking sound sounded and the shifting of rock, before a large slab of concrete fell to the ground, revealing inside of its center someone who looked nothing like the auburn-haired brute chimera who had been put into it.

Ceph's hair was stringy and stuck to his face, what had once been a short buzz cut was now down past his shoulders, framing a gaunt, hollow face that held a greasy but long reddy-brown beard.

"Cephy?" Nero choked. He put his hand up to Ceph's face; his own crumpling under the emotion he was feeling as he touched his husband's face for the first time in thirty years. "Cephy?" Nero leaned his forehead against Ceph's own. He sniffed and raised his head, then started patting his cheek. "Cephy? Look at me."

Ceph's eyes fluttered, then looked around in sleepy confusion.

And when they focused on Nero, Nero inhaled a shuddering breath and smiled. He framed Ceph's face and shook it gently. "Wake up, baby boy. Can you speak?" As the last chunk of concrete crumbled to the now dusty grey floor, Nero grabbed Ceph's underarms and pulled him from the shattered shell. He lowered Ceph onto the ground as Ceph's arm weakly rose to hold onto Nero's arm.

Ceph mumbled something as his eyes shot in all directions. For a moment, there was an anxious quiver in my heart. The way Ceph was looking around reminded me too much of how I knew I looked when I was in my own psychosis. A small fear gripped me that Ceph had fallen into insanity, even though he had been asleep, but a moment later that was dashed as a weak smile appeared on Ceph's dry and chapped lips.

"Nuuky?" he rasped, his voice scratchy but still there. The smile widened when Nero let out a sob and put his arms around Ceph. The brute chimera, one of the toughest and strongest of them all, broke down and started crying openly into Ceph's shoulder.

All I could do was stand there and smile; Kiki beside me with his own smile on his face. I knew that trouble and punishment were in store for me and the young chimera standing to my side. I knew that my actions would have a permanent impact on my life and that I had most likely burned a stable bridge I'd once had with King Silas.

But all of that wasn't important in this moment, because this was Nero's moment and Ceph's moment. And what nightmares would come from what I'd done... what blood I would have to give as payment... could wait until the darkness descended on me.

For now there was no darkness, only long overdue happiness – and Nero deserved this happiness.

I will take it as it comes, I said to myself as I watched Nero cry into Ceph. *In the greywastes we never planned out our lives because we didn't know if tomorrow would come. Now if there is one thing I know for sure... it is that I have a tomorrow. I can take that as my solace that King Silas cannot kill me... even if what he may have in store for me is worse than death.*

I looked over at Nero, who was now standing up with Ceph in his arms. Though the brute chimera was engineered to resurrect with their muscles and strong build, Ceph still looked weak and sickly in his husband's arms.

"If Kingy won't be back for a while, I'm taking him upstairs," Nero said, his face now tear-stained and flushed. "We both need to get clean and eat and... and he needs some time to wake up. He's still... still real drowsy." Nero sniffed and he looked at me. "I can't ever thank you enough, Sanguine. You know you have me forever. Come upstairs with us and we... and we can talk after everyone is clean and not smellin' like death."

I nodded and put a hand on Ceph's head as Nero walked past me. "That sounds good, lovely boy. Ceph... what would you like to eat?"

Suddenly to our left there was a loud crash, one that shook the floor underneath our feet. Our eyes turned towards the noise, and I knew we all held identical looks of shock.

Lying beside the sledgehammer was a young man with black hair covered in dirt and grey dust from the concrete. He was on his hands and knees and sharp, hyperventilating heaves were coming from him.

"Oh... shit," I heard Nero say. Oh shit indeed. The flung sledgehammer had more force behind it than any of us had thought.

We'd... we'd fucking freed someone else.

But who?

I looked around and got my bearings and realized that the shattered concrete pod was one I knew very well. Because it had been around since before I had come to Skyfall. The mysterious first prisoner that everyone told me didn't exist. Every brother I had asked had thought it was empty or that it held only bones inside. A mortal prisoner whose punishment was a death of suffocation inside of that shell of terror.

But no...

I ran to him and put a hand on his shoulder. "Are you okay?" I stammered. I looked back to Nero who still had Ceph in his arms, but all Nero had for me was a wide-eyed stare.

And when I looked back, I saw his eyes.

They were two different colours, one a dark blue, the other one onyx black, and what I'd thought was concrete dust was actually a frock of white hair nestled in with the black. He was strange-looking and...

... when he opened his mouth to give out a cry of confusion... I saw crooked bottom teeth, and though he looked like he'd be handsome at full health, I saw other oddities none of our chimeras had: a slightly wider nose, detached earlobes, fearful yet narrow eyes, and he had no eyebrows or facial hair, just red bumps like he'd pulled it out.

"It's okay... we won't hurt you," I said as kindly as I could, though I was shaking inside. "Just calm–"

The last thing I saw was his single blue eye turn black... before my own world turned to midnight.

I woke up to Nero shaking me awake and patting the side of my cheek. My eyes opened and I saw that I was inside of King Silas's apartment.

Immediately I looked around wildly. I jumped to my feet to search for the strange young man and it took me several moments to realize Nero was trying to calm me.

When I finally looked at him he had his hands out. "It's okay, Sangy," he said. His face was unsure, troubled even. "I woke up twenty minutes ago and we're all safe, Kiki too." He looked towards the door and cocked an eyebrow. "Um... we're going to go remake his concrete tomb after we get all cleaned up and, ah... we're not telling Kingy we just freed that dude. Okay?"

I looked at him, my mind hastily trying to knit together what had previously happened, but as if knowing what I was subconsciously doing, Nero shook his head.

"Don't fucking think about it because nothing happened, okay?" Nero slapped his hands on both sides of my face and shook it. "Hear me, Sangy? Nothing – happened – down – there. Okay? We didn't free no one. Okay? So don't even think about it."

I swallowed down the hardest lump in my throat before nodding. There would be no question as to why Kiki stranded some of our family in the greywastes, but we could hide the fact that we accidently freed that strange man.

Nero dropped his hands and let out a long breath. "We got a lot of shitty work ahead of us. We need to make that concrete tomb and... fucking hope he doesn't notice it looks new." Nero pinched the inner corners of his eyes with his fingers and shook his head.

"Where's Ceph?" I dropped my voice and looked around Silas's apartment, but then I saw that my bedroom door was partially ajar.

"He's still kind of confused and overwhelmed, so I put… put him in the closet in the dark. I, ah, didn't know what else to do and it helped you," Nero admitted with a look of guilt. "Kiki's in there with him. Fuck. Who was that?"

"I was hoping you knew and just didn't want to tell me," I replied grimly. "He was here before I was… I remember that tomb. Why doesn't he have a beard and long hair like Ceph? And his eyebrows… did he pluck them out?"

"That's exactly what he did," Nero said. He handed me an open beer. "When I woke up I saw fucking compacted black hair at the bottom. I think he had longer hair at one time because some strands were all thick and long. And his shell was open enough on the inside for him to be able to reach his face, so I'm guessing he pulled out his hair from stress. Poor fucking guy…"

"He's not… a first gen?"

Nero shook his head. "No. We have tons of baby pictures of all of us and our files all say it was just three embryos and when Ellis split from me there were four. I can see him faking files but you can't fake that there were only three steel mothers back then." But then Nero shook his head back and forth like he'd been reminded that it was him who had told us not to talk about it.

And my theories into my brother's inner monologue were correct, Nero raised his hands again and closed his eyes. "From here on out… we never ever mention him again. Okay? We'll lie… ah, fuck, I don't know, but we're wiping this from our memories, okay?"

I didn't like this. I wanted to know who that immortal was and why he had been in there since possibly before the first gen… but there was so much more on my plate right now… I nodded and agreed.

Nero let out a breath, a look of relief on his face. He clapped me on the shoulder before taking me into his arms.

"I love you, puppy," he whispered and squeezed me tight against him. "Thank you for everything."

I kissed his cheek back and gave him a smile. "Thank you, Nero. From seven years old to seventy… thank you for being someone I could trust."

CHAPTER 2

Elish

ELISH WATCHED THE ROAD AHEAD WITH EYES THAT only blinked when the dry air burned them. He just stared forward, putting one foot in front of the other as quickly as they could walk. They walked with confidence, as if well-aware of their destination, though that couldn't be more false. Elish didn't know where he was going, all he could do is walk southwest towards Skyfall, even if it was hundreds and hundreds of miles away.

Almost eight hundred, Elish said to himself in a desperate tone, a tone that was only allowed to be heard deep inside of his own thoughts. *I am eight hundred miles from him. Why did I leave his side?*

He's brain-dead because of me.

Killian is dead because of me, and Reaver will burn for twenty years.

He closed his eyes and pursed his lips. He held those lips so tight his teeth dug into them and threatened to meet through his flesh.

Was it worth it? Reno's voice screamed in his head; over and over it screamed, and every time it repeated, a new level of agony was laid on top of it.

"Was it worth it?" Elish repeated quietly to himself before slowly opening his eyes. There was nothing in front of him but the dirt-covered road, the medians with strips of rebar snared through, and…

Elish looked to his side and noticed a building that was fully intact.

It looks like we're at least out of the plaguelands. This is the first house I've seen without at least some char.

"Elish…" Garrett's voice called after an hour. He jogged up to him until they were walking side by side. "We're taking a break. Come rest with us."

"I am not stopping," Elish said in a dark tone.

"Please…" Garrett pleaded. "Reno's falling behind. He's exhausted and he won't sleep. Please, Elish. I need you to help me with him, I – I don't know what to do."

Elish stopped and looked ahead. He didn't want to admit it to himself but he knew he needed to rest. They had been walking for almost twenty hours now in a desperate break for the barriers of the plaguelands. Nico and Reno were both mortal and all of their radiation juice and Iodine pills were in the long gone Falconer. It had been hard to force Reno to leave, but eventually he did. Though the two of them needed to get back to Skyfall and quickly for more pills and anti-radiation therapy. Their exposure, even the short time that it was, was still high above the levels their Geigerchips could handle and they'd be soon getting sick.

Elish turned around and saw the others heading towards the intact house he had just observed. He followed behind them, with Garrett walking in sync with his own steps.

"I'm sorry," Garrett sniffed. "I… I didn't know what else to do. Silas had already given Sanguine the order to kill him and he was seconds away from stabbing him. I had to tell him."

"I trusted you to keep quiet," Elish said in a dangerously iced tone. "Killian is dead and Reaver is worse than dead because of you."

There was a pause as Elish stalked towards the abandoned house.

"My fault?" Garrett's voice was sharp and holding a layer of darkness that rarely saw light. "My fault?"

"Don't even start with me," Elish said, his own tone showing many beacons of warning.

But Garrett didn't plan on heeding any of those warnings; his green eyes were narrow and glaring with anger.

"If you didn't start this fucking rebellion in the first place, none of this would've happened. If you didn't have this stupid need to be top dog, none of this–"

"ENOUGH!" Elish whirled around and roared. Jack and Caligula, on the porch and looking on at the tense interaction, raised their eyebrows. "You will not patronize me about shit you do not understand."

But surprisingly Garrett stood his ground. However his stance was braced, as if expecting a physical blow as punishment for his brazen defiance. "Your husband is dying because of your foolish dream. Two innocent boys are dead, or better off dead, and our born immortal brother is dead. All because of YOU!"

"My husband would already be dead if it wasn't for me," Elish snarled, "and you wouldn't even have one. Know your place, you fucking coattail-clinging coward; I am not above taking back gifts."

Garrett's already angry face blazed; his lips pursed together and his head tilted just slightly to the side. "If you ever threaten Reno again…"

"I don't threaten, I promise."

"If anything happens to Reno, I will take back the gift I gave you by saving Jade after your order to kill him before he was born. I swear on my life, I will end that brain-dead little shit's suffering and–"

Elish raised a hand and backhanded Garrett so hard he flew sideways and onto the greywaste ash.

"If you ever speak ill about my husband again… it will be you I kill, not Silas," Elish said in a dangerous tone. "That… that I swear, Garrett. I will burn Skyfall for my husband, and I will burn the world if harm comes to him, and as the world turns to ashes I will stand on your bodies and the bodies of each of your lovers."

As Elish turned to walk towards the house a low voice could be heard.

"You sound like Silas, you know," Garrett said behind him. "I bet you don't even see it, do you? You're becoming the very thing you're trying to convince us to kill. You give us our lovers… and if we don't do what you want… you take them back."

Elish stopped, and with his fists locked and his shoulders tight, he slowly turned around.

"I am not Silas," Elish said in a cold whisper. "Enjoy your jabs, brother. You will never get the chance to say such untrue filth to me again."

"No, I won't," Garrett said as he got to his feet, a trickle of blood running down his chin. "Because we're done. I'm not helping this stupid rebellion, it already almost cost me Reno. I'm out, do it yourself."

"Very well," Elish said casually. Then, to Garrett's horror, Elish pulled out the small pistol he kept inside of his overcoat and walked towards Reno, who was huddled in a corner with his arms clasped over his drawn-up knees.

"Elish! NO!" Garrett screamed. He tried to pull the gun out of Elish's grasp but Elish whirled around, and with a quick swing of his free hand, sent Garrett crashing into an old, worn table. It splintered and broke, spilling Garrett onto the ground in a plume of dust.

Elish stood in front of Reno and raised the gun.

Reno stared back at him. His eyes were sore and puffy and his body an angry red from the heat of the white flames they had left behind.

The greywaster sniffed before his face twisted in agony.

"Just do it," Reno said in a weak whimper. He lowered his head and shook his half-silver, half-black hair slowly back and forth. "Please... just do it."

"Reno, no!" Garrett cried. The sound of wood and debris being shifted around was heard before Garrett dove in between Elish and Reno, his hands up in surrender. "Please, Elish, don't. He's been through enough. Don't hurt him."

Reno stared down at Garrett, then back up to Elish. "What the fuck are you waiting for, Ice Man? I got nothing – I got... I fucking got nothing. Just do it already."

"Don't – don't!" Garrett cried, tears starting to well in his eyes. "I'll align with you. I will... I... I was just upset. You have my allegiance."

Elish's eyes narrowed at Garrett before he put the gun back into his overcoat. "You will not get a second chance to backtrack." Then his eyes flickered over to Jack who was sitting beside Silas. The Grim had a piece of something charred in his hand and his mouth was moving up and down. The explanation was right in front of Jack, strips of Silas's black skin had been peeled away, showing off the ruby-red meat underneath.

"Stop eating the fucking king!" Elish snapped, and with a sweep of his robes, he left the terror-stricken Garrett and the indifferent, depressed Reno.

"It's all going to slough off anyway," Jack replied casually, like the intense confrontation in front of them hadn't even happened. Jack just sat there with his chin resting on his hand, chewing away. "I've dealt with many burnt chimeras before. You all might as well dig in. It's a free meal and we might as well save the meat we got from those slave bodies we found."

"I'm not proud..." Caligula walked over with a radiation-burnt Nico beside him. Elish swallowed the growl in his throat and stalked out of the abandoned and crumbling house and onto the porch.

Elish sat down on a sun-bleached bench and stared out into the greywastes, seeing nothing but grey terrain, rocks, and the dirt-swept road.

Everything looked the same in front of him, the greywastes never changed. He could only be twenty miles from Nanaimo Harbour and the scenery around him would be the exact same.

But he wasn't twenty miles from Skyfall… or a hundred, or two, or even five.

Eight hundred miles…

An hour after sitting on the bench in silence, Jack came out holding several aromatic strips of Silas's blackened skin. He sat down beside Elish and offered it to him. "Everyone inside is eating, even the greywaster. If you want to get to the nearest town, you should be eating."

Elish stared forward before grudgingly taking the flesh. He took a bite out of it and grimaced as he chewed. When he was done eating the overcooked meat, which tasted like burnt jerky, he let out a reserved sigh.

Jack noticed it. "Sanguine is watching over your husband, brother. He wouldn't let harm come to him; you know how much Sanguine loves him. We're already much too late returning, I bet he has a Falconer coming to pick us up right now."

Elish was quiet for several more moments before he finally spoke. "Sanguine is the one that put Kincade up to it. No one is coming for us."

Not only did a silence fall between the two of them but inside had also gone quiet.

"He wouldn't…" Jack said in a hushed voice.

"You actually believe that that timid little twink of a cicaro would have the balls to pull this off?" Elish said in a flat tone. "Do you not remember how Sanguine came to us? Who pulled him out of that coffin that pedophile greywaster had him in? Who searched for him when the entire family had given up? Sanguine would not let Nero spend an eternity in that concrete tomb and he has resorted to desperate measures to break him free, desperate measures even if they defy the allegiance I had with him."

Jack stared at him. "You – why are you telling me this?"

"Because I know Sanguine tells you everything," Elish replied coldly. "And it will now be up to you to keep an eye on Sanguine. I will not be punishing Sanguine for abandoning me in the greywastes because through him I can secure Nero. You will now be my eyes and ears when dealing with Sanguine. Understand me, Anubis?"

Jack turned his gaze away as soon as Elish looked at him. His own black eyes focused on the grey in front of them. "Why do you think I want this?" he asked simply. "I have everything I want. Juni is immortal and my life is simple and predictable, just how I like it. Why do you think an offer of chaos is one that I want?"

Elish's eyes hadn't left Jack's, even though the silver-haired chimera refused to look back.

"You are still in love with a slave," Elish replied simply. "I hold the keys to remove the slave from his collar. If you want Sanguine – you need me."

There was silence between them and in that silence Jack's head shook back and forth. "What if I don't want Sanguine as much as you think I do?" he replied back. "It's been thirty years and I've dealt with my feelings towards him. I wish for nothing but a simple life in my tower and that is good enough for me. I'm sorry, Elish. I would never betray you by telling Silas what I know, because I love and respect you, but... like you, I prefer the quiet life."

Elish turned away from Jack. "I thought I did once as well. Our more bloodthirsty brothers seem to have quite the effect on the quiet ones. My offer stands, I–"

"That's all you know how to do, isn't it?" a low voice suddenly sounded to Elish's left. He looked over and saw Reno standing in the doorway, his half-silver hair falling over a face filled with disgust. "Play your fucking games. You just got Killian and Reaver killed, you got Jade brain-dead, and still you're playing your fucking games? You disgusting piece of shit."

Elish rose. "We'll be continuing now. We've rested enough."

"YOU'RE GOING TO LOSE EVERYTHING!" Reno screamed, his voice breaking as Elish walked away from him. "You're going to fucking lose everything and all you'll have to blame is yourself. You disgusting fucking monster! Just stop! JUST STOP THIS!"

Elish kept walking, and he didn't look back.

"From where we are... it's going to take us weeks to make it to the nearest town," Caligula said that night. He was sitting beside the fire they had made with Nico sleeping beside him. Reno was finally sleeping as well, but only after receiving a well-aimed jolt of electricity from Elish when he had worked himself up into another frenzy. Garrett and Jack were resting also. "But I don't know what we're supposed to do when we're there." Caligula threw his melted remote phone onto the fire and shook his head. "I don't see a point in even going to a town unless you want to pray we find legionaries there. But even then… we're so far north and the Legion isn't as active around this area."

Elish looked up at the sky, grey clouds were covering all of the stars but the moon was showing its glow through the haze. "We'll eventually need supplies."

Caligula was quiet; he stared at the fire with his brow furrowed. "Dad should be looking for me by now. He was out when I left with Nico, and I had told Theo to go to the explosion with Sid and Grant…"

Elish's lips pressed. *And for all I know Kessler's severed head is burning with Reaver. There was nothing on that gasless quad we passed. However this is information I will not risk sharing with his son.*

"Theo might be aligning with Sanguine," Elish said to him. "You know as well as I do how obsessed Theo is with Sanguine and Jack. They're not here… which means someone told them not to go."

Caligula let out a hiss through his clenched teeth. "It doesn't matter. Eventually our family in the Dead Islands will return, even if Silas told them to wait. They'll find us, it might take a few days but they'll find us."

"The greywastes are vast and the northern greywastes all the more," Elish said bitterly. He looked around the darkness surrounding him. "I'm going to catch my four hours of sleep. Wake Jack up in two hours."

"Yes, Uncle Elish," Caligula said, before adding in an encouraging tone. "Dad will find us. Especially with what happened to Tim, he's been keeping a tight hold on me."

Elish stared at the fire; he saw Kessler's head burn in the flames. "Yes," he managed to say in a level tone, "hopefully you are correct."

Your father better hope he's burning with Reaver. Because twenty years of flames will be a mercy compared to what I will do to him for shooting my husband.

Elish laid down by the fire and rested his head on crossed arms. He closed his eyes and tried to imagine that he was back home in his bed with Jade beside him. Though every time he brought up his cicaro's scent, and the way Jade eventually crawled on top of him during the night to sleep splayed over his stomach, Elish's mind soon wandered to the darker corners. A place full of ideas on how to punish Kessler for what he did, and the eventual day he saw Silas die. It was those fantasies that eventually lulled him into a troubled sleep with the fire crackling beside him.

Little did Elish know, those same thoughts kept replaying in his mind after he'd drifted off. They grew and transformed and took on a life of their own, infiltrating and corrupting Elish's dreams and twisting them on their whim. Soon in Elish's dreams, he found himself in front of Kessler again, holding Jade's bleeding head in his lap.

"– put a bullet in the pet's head. Finish him off and make sure Elish sees it."

Elish's body suppressed a groan threatening to burst from his lips. His cold countenance forbidding such a naked display of feelings even when under the influence of sleep. Instead his fists clenched and his blood boiled as he was forced to watch the taunting and satisfied look on Kessler's face.

Elish found himself rising in that very dream, standing tall with Jade beside him. And with Reaver, the half-raver, and the deacondog to his left, they rained bullets on the legionaries around them, leaving their quads abandoned and their bodies for the scavengers, Kessler's included.

Quads abandoned... Kessler's headless body left to rot. I took the Falconer with Jade and the others and we never looked back.

Kessler would've had a remote phone on his person, and a 4-way radio.

Elish's eyes opened to the first hints of pink on the horizon.

"You certainly clench your teeth when you sleep," Jack said in a casual voice. "You used to sleep so soundly beside me too."

Elish quickly rose and looked around. To the East, the pink above him was turning into a deep but hazy red, the sun just beginning to peek over the horizon before it put on its cloak of ashes. It was early morning, extremely early morning.

"I'm leaving," Elish said simply as he dusted off his pants. "I can make better time without that greywaster slowing me down."

"I'm coming too," Jack said also rising to standing, but Elish put up a hand to stop him.

"I'm going alone," Elish responded. "You need to stay behind as protection. Caligula and Nico may be more than capable but they're still mortal. Keep walking southwest and don't stray off-course. If I find something before you do, I'll send help."

"And what if they find us first?" Jack said back.

"In a week I will be dispatching myself with a single bullet to the head," Elish said, his body now shrouded in darkness as he walked away from the campfire. "Silas implanted the alert back in my head six months ago so it will go off. If you're in Skyfall, come get me. If not, I'm still on the road."

"Elish... I really think we should stick together," Jack called back to him. Elish could hear him take several steps towards him before stopping. "Elish..."

Elish stopped and turned around. He paused for a second before walking back up to Jack.

The hopeful look that Jack had in his eyes soon vanished when he saw the strange glint in Elish's own.

"While I'm gone... it will be your job to keep Reno from poisoning the minds of the others," Elish said in a dropped tone. "I need you right now, Anubis. Report to me all of their conversations and make notes. I know you always carry pen and paper with you."

Jack looked at him strangely. "Elish, this isn't the time to affirm allegiances. We just need to get home and–"

Elish shook his head back and forth, a little too quickly for the usually collected and calm chimera. "No, I need you now. I think..." Elish took a step back and nodded to himself. "Yes. Once I get home and to my laptop, I can look over those hard drives. I can pick through everything and see if there is a way. There has to be a way. There has to be a way." Elish took another step backwards, he was still nodding to himself.

Jack stared, and as he stared at his brother an uneasy feeling started crawling up his throat like a cockroach.

"Elish, brother," Jack said slowly. "I... I think it's over. Whatever you had planned... I think perhaps... you should just focus on Jade and your life at home."

"NO!" Elish said sharply, his eyes turning to rock. "This wasn't in vain. They got the hard drives, they succeeded. I can figure it out. I can figure out the puzzle. There is still... there is still one more out there I can use."

"One more...?" Jack let that drag, though the insect in his throat was quickly breeding and multiplying. Something was inherently wrong with Elish; Jack had never seen him this... unstable.

"This wasn't a waste, this wasn't in vain," Elish said. "I need you right now, Anubis. Understand me? Watch them... do not let them stray. Okay? Do you understand me?" Elish's eyes pierced Jack's own and he found himself held by them, unable to move or look away. It was like those two violet diamonds were holding him for ransom, and the demand was only one simple word.

"Do you?" Elish snapped.

"Okay," Jack whispered. There was nothing else to say, Elish would take no other response from him. "I will keep an eye on them for you."

Elish nodded and turned around. He walked into the cold morning towards the direction he knew the Legion massacre occurred, trying to calculate how long of a walk it was going to be before he found the area. He knew it would be two weeks at least but there was a pit in his stomach that told him the family he was leaving behind were going to be wandering around for longer than that.

I will walk fast. I will make it home.

I will fix this.

The six stranded Skyfallers were but miniscule ants in a backyard of grey rock and pounded down ash. Small specks that blended in with the areas around them that stood as desolate and lost as their chances of rescue.

But there was a chance, Elish had his chance. It would be impossible for Kessler's ground zero to stay abandoned for long and if it was… the remote phone in Kessler's pocket would be Elish's saving grace and the quads his backup plan.

It wasn't much… but it was something.

Eight hundred miles from you.

I'm coming home, Jade. My parvulus maritus. And I will fix this.

CHAPTER 3

Reaver

I LOOKED AROUND THE DUSTY STORE, WALKING UP and down each of the aisles. My eyes were going in all directions but I was too close now to give up. It may be here, it may not be here, but really it was a fucking supermarket there was no way it wouldn't be here.

I glanced up and shot a dirty look to the equally dirty signs above me, hanging down on rusted chains like acrobats who had lost the momentum to deliver their charges to the safety of the platform. It looked like several of them had all-out failed, dropping the little victims and dooming them to spend their eternity getting covered in dust and debris.

I'd have to bring Killian back here to wipe off these damn signs, but for now it was just me alone with a blue basket filled with baking ingredients.

Laughter spilled from my lips at the audacity of it, but it's not like I fucking cared. No one was around to watch me make an absolute fool out of myself, running up and down aisles looking for cake mix.

Yeah, fucking cake mix.

I kicked a few boxes down and picked one up. I wiped it with my sleeve and tried to read the faded writing that was written on the box.

Cream of wheat... no, that wasn't cake mix at all, but I put it into my basket anyway because that would make good breakfast crap, then I carried on with my mission.

I couldn't believe what a sight this place was when I first entered it. Never in my life would I have ever thought I'd find an untouched store like this. It still had everything on the shelves just waiting for customers that would never come. A layer of thick dust now covered everything, but even the dust was different than the greywastes ash miles and miles from here. It was soft almost, and although it still stuck to everything, it fell looser and made for easy wiping. The shit that was preserved here was amazing, and even though I had been in about a dozen of these types of shops during the past several days, I still couldn't help but look around like a gobsmacked idiot.

The roofs were intact, all of them, even the light fixtures still hung from their wires. Sure the thin chains that held up the signs telling you which aisle was which had failed in a few places, but that was miniscule in the ways of destruction when it came to this place as a whole.

We could spend the rest of our fucking lives in the plaguelands. That thought alone made my heart shudder and a smile come to lips that I never thought would ever smile again.

I sprinted down the produce section which, of course, even the plaguelands couldn't save, and went down the next aisle. I stifled a victory cheer when I saw old bags of flour, grey and dripping dust onto the sandy floor, and started paying closer attention to finding my cake mix.

I picked up another box and wiped it off. I ended up sneezing on it and sprinkling the yellow box with my snot and spittle. Thankfully that was not cake mix but it was pretty fucking close: brownie mix! That would do, but I fucking wanted cake. Well, the closest thing I could make to cake with no milk and no eggs and old-as-fuck icing, but whatever, the little shithead wasn't going to be picky.

To keep myself entertained I started whistling as I looked, my ears always on guard but over the past few days they had become complacent. I hadn't seen anything in the plaguelands besides this weird deer-type creature that looked like something out of Killi's nightmares. I had been eyeing them up like Biff to a moth though, and had great plans for killing them and roasting them on the fire. Now that would be great, fresh meat. It had been way too long since I'd gotten to taste something bloody and fresh. At least we were skulking the borders of the plaguelands, I could still sneak into Melchai or one of the other bordering towns and take some flesh for myself. What were they going to do about it? Go ahead, fucking follow me into the plaguelands, bitch, see what happens!

I laughed again and grabbed all of the boxes of cake mix in case I fucked up the first couple of them, and after reading the instructions I started hunting for oil too. I wasn't sure if that shit would still be good but ten minutes later I had an odd browny-gold bottle of canola oil in my blue basket and I think I was set.

At least if my post-apocalyptic cake poisoned and killed me and Killian we'd come back.

I sprinted to the front of the store where I could see the dirt and dust-stained windows leaking sun into the Save-On-Foods I had been rummaging around in. There wasn't much light which was good, any more and it would've fucked up my night vision which I needed to find all of this crap.

I walked past the checkouts with their dusted tills and conveyor belts, grey but still holding the forms of what they used to be. The ash was like snow in a lot of ways, but this ash would kill anyone who didn't have immunity to the sestic radiation that was still at lethal levels around me.

Not like I had to fucking worry, or Killian for that matter.

"I'm back, baby!" I shielded my eyes from the grey sun above us as it temporarily dazzled my senses. When my eyes adjusted, I looked around until I saw my beautiful boy sitting in the shopping cart I had put him in.

I walked up to Killian and put the blue basket on his lap, taking care not to put too much pressure on the red fissures in his skin that were all that remained of what had once been an open and gaping wound.

I smiled at him and petted back what little hair he had left, his lifeless eyes staring half-open into nothing and his mouth slightly slacked. His lips had already healed back to a bright shade of pink and what blackened, charred flesh he'd had for an arm had shedded off days ago and was now growing back his porcelain skin.

I leaned down and kissed Killian's lips, leaving the smallest glisten of wetness on them, and with a smile, I started wheeling him back to my quad. Killian, of course, didn't say anything back but he didn't have to; his heart beating inside of my ears was the best answer he could give me.

This morning I had woken up to his heart beating. Every evening I would lay my head on it and listen for those small rhythmic beats, and at two hours before sunrise this morning, I heard them.

And so maybe I decided to celebrate a bit.

"I bet you're going to wake up tonight, Killibee," I said happily to him, thankful once again that no one could see me because I knew I looked like a fucking lunatic in that moment. "And when you do, we'll eat some birthday cake cause you're eighteen now!" I shook my head with a smirk. "I can't believe how old you are. I'm going to have to exchange you for a younger model soon."

I paused and looked around the deserted parking lot for at least a pity laugh but there was nothing. Assholes.

I pushed Killi through the parking lot and back to the quad. Since I didn't want to leave Killian alone in the house just in case he woke up (like fuck if I knew how immortality healing worked) I had just bungee-corded the shopping cart to the back of the quad. It had worked out pretty well, but a couple times I had gone too fast and he kinda, well, tipped over and rolled off of the road. I might've added a few more injuries to his already healing body... I don't think I will be sharing that with him.

I didn't want him to wake up alone. So sue me! We needed food!

Carefully (very carefully) I rode with Killian towed behind me back to the house I had chosen for us to live in, at least for the time being. It was a nice little rancher with a backyard that even had a rusted swing set (the chains were too rusty for one to swing on though, and, no, I didn't figure this out by trying to have a swing... I swear). It had two bedrooms and a nice, but completely destroyed, kitchen, and furniture that was preserved enough for us to sit on as long as there was a blanket over everything. The blankets were because the stuffing was a bit buggered and the fabric that covered it was all scratchy.

All in all it was pretty fucking fancy, and it was on a nice street with a bunch of other nice houses; probably about a ten minute quad ride from a highway that would lead us deeper into the badlands. I think Killian would be impressed with my choice of house. And if not? Well, we could move, real estate prices were excellent here.

I drove up the dusty grey road, black trees and leafless bushes around us. About a block up we had a river for us to drink from and I'd already gotten us quite a few containers of water. My Geigerchip had broken long ago but I had a feeling that if any non-immortal ever drank this water they would be glowing. It was good for immortal consumption though and I hadn't grown tentacles yet so that would be our life source. Plus those weird deer-things drank from it too, so when I eventually decided to start killing them it'd be easy pickings.

I picked up my resurrecting prince and carried him through the threshold of our new house. There was a living room to the left of me which had our blanket and sheet-draped couch and chairs, and a nice coffee table too for our drugs and stuff. The kitchen was to the right; I'd cleaned the counters so it was free of the dusty ancient crap but now it was covered in all of the things I had scavenged. Me and Killian's room was down the hallway with new blankets on it that I'd washed for us, and the spare bedroom had all of the shit Perish had loaded on the quad.

I kept all of Perish's stuff in that spare bedroom and had closed the door. I really didn't know how Killian was going to react when he saw it and I didn't want the triggers right in front of him. I knew eventually he'd tell me everything that happened between the two of them, but I just fucking wanted us to be happy for a while before we tackled it.

My mouth downturned as I unpacked all of the food I had scavenged. There was a lot of happiness inside of me, bordering on being giddy, but whenever I thought of what we'd both had to go through to get to this point... my stomach soured and twisted into knots. Killian had been on the road with Perish for months and I knew I was going to have to be the supportive boyfriend when he told me what had gone on.

I knew without a doubt that Perish had raped him at least once. I knew because I had found the evidence in that house before I unleashed my first sestic radiation pulse from the sheer agony of it. I had prepared myself for that already and had accepted that it had happened. There wasn't anything I could do about it... Perish was dead.

There was no part of me that was planning on telling him what happened while I was in Nero's custody. Those weeks of my life sat like an infected ulcer inside of me, and whenever my mind brushed on it, it opened and leaked its pus and fetid liquid all through my body. When I had been on the road with Elish, and then Jade and Big Shot, I'd managed to bury it deep inside of me. But my lack of people to talk to, and lack of distractions, had unburied that corpse and now it sat rotten. It was like it was waiting for me to bury it again but I didn't have the tools to do it without getting its disgusting, rotting stink all over me.

It had helped when I'd told Elish what had happened to me. I never said it to him but it had, and it had brought me closer to him too. He understood and... he'd even told me a story about something that had happened to him as well. I think that night, leaning up against those black trees on the Coquihalla, I had gone from just being Silas's assassin to being Elish's friend.

And I had considered him a friend, and not in the same way I thought of Reno as a friend... but someone that I actually saw as my equal, that I respected as someone I could learn from.

I... I really had liked my time with Elish. Things had been tense, and we had both been worried about our respective partners, but besides all of that... I'd fucking had a blast with him.

My lips pursed, even in my own mind thinking of that made me flush. Why? Because thinking of Elish would eventually lead me to the kiss we'd shared.

No, not just a kiss. I had been on the ground with my hand sliding down his pants.

I took in a deep breath and shook my head. We had our engineering to thank for that, he said. I guess I'd have to tell Killian that part at least, just because it wasn't well... the same as what Nero had done to me, and Perish to him. If I hid that from him it would mean I saw it as something else and I didn't.

When everything was unpacked, I moved Killian from the shopping cart to the living room couch and I laid him down with a blanket over him. I put my ear against his chest and found myself smiling when I heard his heartbeat again. Then, with a kiss on the cheek, I tried my best to make that stupid cake.

The first thing I did was put the hard-as-rock icing into a bowl and pour water in it, then some oil just because I had it. I set that on the table to try and... I don't know, dissolve? And I opened up two things of cake batter and poured some water and oil into that too. I mixed it up with an old rusty whisk, and when I tasted it I was rather thrilled that it tasted pretty good. Edible at least.

I walked to the back door, where a fire pit I had lit was. We didn't have any power here obviously but I had made a small brick oven which would have to do. I had harvested our bricks from the next door neighbour, which amusingly enough, had inside the house dried up, shrivelled corpses. Both of them were in the bed with a gun between the two of them. So it looked like the Jones's had committed suicide together. That was kind of sweet. I stole their gun though; they wouldn't be needing it.

That was another amusing thing about being in the untouched plaguelands. All of the corpses were still where they had died. I don't think there were any remaining pre-Fallocaust corpses in the greywastes, since the Fallocaust had happened so long ago. I guess eventually some scavenger got desperate or else the ash covered everything. I had seen shrivelled up, brown skeletons inside of buildings but even then you couldn't be sure if they were pre-Fallocaust or post-Fallocaust. Here there was no doubting the types of skeletons I was finding. It was like walking into some morbid museum. I couldn't wait to show Killian all of this neat shit. Who else got to experience all of this stuff? It didn't look like the rest of the chimeras ever cared to venture out there, everything was preserved the way it had been left.

While the cake was baking I stirred up the half-dissolved icing. It was all thick and tasted kinda stale but it was sweet. Killian loved sweet things and I had been hoarding candies for him which had preserved nicely in the plaguelands. My poor boy was skinny and sickly when I had seen him in the brief time before he had died, but I was hoping he would resurrect a little healthier. I didn't know how it worked though. I wish I had asked Elish more about this sort of stuff but all of my questions had been about how I, as a born immortal, worked, not so much a mortal made into an immortal.

Well, we had forever to figure it out at least. It had been five days since Silas had released that sestic radiation, five days since the lab had exploded. He had been healing quickly in my opinion at least.

In truth, I was going a bit nuts only having myself as entertainment. All I had to kill the days were books and scavenging, and scavenging had been difficult the last two days since I was worried Killian would wake up. Even before his heart started beating it was a concern because I just didn't know how quickly he'd resurrect after it started going again. The last thing I wanted was for him to wake up alone in a strange place. The kid was going to be terrified of everything enough as it was, on top of not knowing what the fuck was going on.

I really missed electricity, every book I found was shit or something I'd read a thousand times. If I read one more chapter of Harry Potter I was going to shove the sword of Gryffindor through my eye. Didn't these fucking people read anything else?

Forty-five minutes later (thanks to a wrist watch Perish had left for Killian which was mine now) I checked on the cake. It was a bit crispy but good enough, so I took it inside and poured the icing all over it to make it tasty.

I was slightly disenchanted by the fact that my icing immediately melted from the heat of the cake and then turned into a shiny glaze, but I wasn't Martha Stewart so I let it go. After everything was all settled in the baking department, I sat down in front of the coffee table and started preparing us both drugs.

It had been a difficult thing to do but I had only been swallowing opiate pills, no heroin or anything like that. The only reason I had for this was because I kinda wanted to wait until Killian woke up so we could take our first hit together. It would hit us both like it was our first time and it was something I wanted to share with him. And if he was all spooked and scared when he woke up it would be a good way to calm him down too.

So I prepared us both needles and laid them out on the coffee table and swallowed two yellow Dilaudid pills myself. No one would be surprised to hear that one of the first places I had raided, when coming up to my first town in the plaguelands, was a pharmacy. I had gotten myself a pretty good supply of opiates and even Xanax and Valium and their generic cousins in case Killian planned on flipping out more than I had prepared for.

I would miss my drug suitcase, just like I'd miss the other sparse possessions I'd had to leave behind, but it looked like we weren't at risk of running out of anything. We literally had almost the entire earth's supply of shit to keep us fed, drugged, and watered for the rest of time.

After everything was completed and I'd eaten myself a dinner of ramen noodles mixed with a can of flaked chicken, I sat down on the other end of the couch with Killian scrunched up beside me. I was reading some Conan comics I'd found and shoving gummy candies into my mouth. It was a peaceful evening in a land of grey, but unlike my life in the greywastes, I laid beside my boyfriend with the subtle confidence that it would stay quiet and peaceful.

And then my silence was broken.

It was just starting to get dark outside when I saw movement out of the corner of my eye. My head shot towards Killian and I bore witness to his mouth opening to take in a sharp breath. I stayed as still as I could, not knowing what to expect; I just stared at this frail boy as he started breathing on his own.

When several tense minutes had passed I, with slow movements, got up off of the couch and knelt down beside him. With a smile on my face, I raised a hand and brushed it over his pale skin, now showing a redness to his cheeks which highlighted his rosy lips. The colour had returned to his skin and it was now warm underneath my hand.

I couldn't believe it when I realized how nervous I was. The entire five, almost six days, of being out here my life had been waiting for him to wake up and look at me with those beautiful blue eyes... and now that it was about to happen I felt like a giddy teenager.

I forced down the vibrating nervousness with a deep breath and continued to lightly stroke Killian's chin. A part of me still couldn't believe that he was about to come back to me. I thought, as I held that dying boy in my arms, that he would disappear from my life as swiftly as he had come. That I would be bound to live an eternity only having the love of my life for several short months before the chaos had split us in two.

Now he was coming back... holy crap, he was coming back.

Did Killian feel this way the first time he'd watched me resurrect? At least I wasn't expecting him to go rampaging through the house chasing down Elish's cicaro with a butcher's knife.

I pulled my hand away when I heard a small whimper break through Killian's lips and watched intently, but with my heart a beating drum, as he moved his head to the side. His brow creased as he scowled but still his eyes were shut.

"Killi?" I whispered, the excitement in my voice made me smile wider. I was acting like such a giddy idiot. "Killi Cat? Open your eyes."

Killian scowled further before slowly... slowly he opened those blue eyes. They squinted a few times before focusing on me, and when they saw me, they widened.

"Reaver?" he whispered, an expression on his face so shocked it was like he was seeing a ghost instead of me.

I'd replayed in my head, many times, what our first moments together would be like. In some of my daydreams I kissed him, in other ones I held him tight to me and hugged him until I heard his bones break.

But all of those stupid fantasies washed away from me when he said my name. All I found myself doing was staring at him, feeling like his voice had wiped me clean of my senses.

He stared at me and I stared back, our eyes locked like two meeting laser beams. I was looking at him like I had just found him laying here only seconds before, even though I'd been waiting for this moment for almost a week.

I knew I had to say something. I knew I had to make my mouth move. Why wasn't my tongue doing anything?

Then finally I managed to grab a fleeting handful of senses, but it wasn't enough to make me form a complete sentence, or even say something loving to him. All that socially-inept Reaver's mind allowed him to do was stare at his boyfriend and say back:

"Hi."

Killian looked at me confused, then he slowly raised a hand and brushed it against my cheek. I smiled at him as he did this, and my own hand rose to lay on top of his.

"Hey, baby," I said to him in a soft voice. "Everything is okay, alright? Everything is just fine… are you feeling okay?"

Killian slipped his hand out of mine and looked down at it; he scowled again before looking at his hip which was covered in the pair of blue jeans I'd dressed him in. He put his hand on the area of his side that had been charred burnt before, once again, making eye contact with me.

My beautiful boy looked right into my eyes and I could see the confusion start to drip away, but it wasn't replaced with joy like I had been hoping.

The signs came in quick succession, one after another: the wider eyes, the tightened lip, the shuddering breath... and finally…

Killian burst into tears.

I was wondering how long I'd have until he cried. Honestly, I was surprised he'd lasted this long.

With a choked laugh, I gathered Killian up into my arms and squeezed him. In response Killian wailed into my shoulders, clinging to me like a baby monkey and clenching me to him so tightly I was sure he was trying to make us into one person.

"Shhh, it's okay," I soothed. I rubbed his back and let him unleash himself onto my shoulder. I knew he was just overwhelmed and confused. With me those emotions translate into rage and madness, but I knew on Killian it would manifest itself into tears. Pretty much every negative emotion Killian felt translated itself into crying. I didn't mind.

When he had soaked my shirt in tears and his crying had been reduced to whimpers, I patted his back. "All cried out?"

Killian sniffed, and even though I didn't know it was possible, he tightened his hold on me. "Where are we?"

"In the plaguelands," I said to him, keeping my tone gentle. "You're immune to the sestic radiation. We have nothing to worry about, no one can survive the radiation where we are."

Killian pulled away, his deep blue eyes red and puffy from crying. I recognized those beautiful eyes but damn did he look different. He was mostly bald now from the explosion and what hadn't fallen off was patchy and brittle. I think eventually we might just shave it off so he could start growing it new.

He was still beautiful though.

"I'm… immortal?" Killian said in a hushed voice. When I nodded at him his brow creased again, before his lip stiffened.

"Is Perish dead?"

I paused. I had been dreading that question… I didn't want to get into Perish. I wanted to enjoy the first few minutes of being with my boyfriend, without having to tell him that Perish had killed himself.

I honestly didn't know how I felt about that man. A part of me hated him with a fiery passion for what he had done to Killian, even though I know it was supposed to have been Sky's O.L.S fucking his brain – but another part of me wished I could've gave him a hug and told him thanks for… for doing what he had done. For giving me my boyfriend back, immortal.

Honestly my mind danced around lying to him, but I knew I couldn't. So I nodded and gently wiped the tears from the corners of his eyes. "Yeah, baby… Perish died. I'm sorry."

Killian was still as I rubbed away the tears, then to my surprise his eyes hardened.

"Okay."

I blinked and now it was my time to furrow my brow. "Okay?" That was a strange, un-Killian response.

Killian broke his gaze from mine and looked around the house. "Is anyone else with us? Does anyone know we're here?" He sniffed and slowly got to his feet. I watched him, the confusion clear on my face, but I remained silent. I didn't understand this subdued reaction but like fuck if I wasn't going to run with it. Denial did me a lot of bad after Leo and Greyson had been killed, but it had also saved me from literally having a nuclear meltdown.

I mean fuck, I still hadn't dealt with them dying… I think I was still in denial that my dads wouldn't be in Aras, waiting for us to come home. It didn't feel real at the time and it still didn't feel real now.

"No one knows we're here," I said, pushing that thought from my head. I stood up with him and put my arm around his side. "It's just us out here. Me and my Killi."

Killian let out a small breath; he had a tense and worried expression on his face. I thought he was going to say something but he just turned around and put his arms around me. I heard another sniff and felt him bury his face into my still damp shoulder.

"I knew you'd find me," Killian whimpered. "You came so far... how did you escape from the Legion? Aren't they looking for you?"

I shook my head but had to swallow down Killian's mention of my time in Kessler and Nero's custody. It was hard to think that the last time we had properly been together was in Mariano when we were going to sell Chally and charge the Ieon.

And now Chally was most likely getting skewered by both Reno and Garrett. Sengil to the friendliest chimera in existence and my good-natured best friend. Lucky fuck.

"I was rescued actually," I said to him lightly, and when he looked at me with surprise I smiled. "Reno, Caligula, and Caligula's boyfriend Nico, plus Elish. Reno was still injured from his time with those terrorists and he couldn't come... it was just me and Elish on the road for quite a while looking for you." I put a hand on his chin, rough from his prickly facial hair and kissed his lips. "Well, you and Jade."

Then Killian's face fell and I cursed myself for bringing Jade up.

"Jade? Oh... oh god, poor Elish," Killian choked. He held a hand up to his mouth and his eyes started to brim, but a glint of hope appeared when I shook my head back and forth.

"He survived," I said to him with a half-smile. Killian's face flooded with relief and I heard a faint whimper. "I'll tell you that fucking unbelievable story later. He... we got into some trouble and Elish had to take him back to Skyfall." I decided to leave out Jade's state at the time. "And that's why I continued on, on my own..."

"With Silas?" Killian whispered, then he shook his head, his face tense. "I... I need to just sit down and..." His lips pursed. "Use the bathroom... do we have one?"

I chuckled and kissed his head. "I remember pissing for a solid minute when I had been resurrecting for a long while. Just find a tree outside that's what I've been using, that and digging a hole. Why don't you go and when you come back, we'll shoot up some heroin and just enjoy some quiet."

The expression of shock on his face made me smile. "We..." Then his eyes travelled to the coffee table where he spotted the two needles. "Thank – thank you, baby. I really need to just... I don't even know if this is real."

I watched Killian run a hand over his bald head, barely showing the faint prickles of blond hair, and walk out of the door into our new neighbourhood.

I fucking missed that kid… I really fucking missed him.

I turned around and walked to the coffee table, but when I sat down on the couch with the drugs in front of me, I felt something hit my thigh. I looked down and saw a rounded black pebble resting beside my leg.

That was strange. I had been laying on this couch, sleeping on it too, and I had never seen…

A queasy feeling started growing inside of my gut when I picked up the round black object. I held it up to the window and turned it around in my hand before smelling it. It was plastic with a small silver band on the top and the tiniest of screw holes. What the hell…

Oh – *fuck.*

It was a fucking O.L.S.

My mouth dropped open but immediately my eyes travelled past the device to where Killian was. I saw him walking slowly towards a black tree unaware of the bombshell that had just been dropped on me.

How could I have not seen this thing? It couldn't have been on Killian's clothes because his clothes had been almost entirely charred off of him, and I'd changed him in new clothes Perish had packed. Where could it have come from?

Then I remembered back to when I had held him against me. The fist that I had originally thought had been clenched in pain. It had been locked tight the entire time he had been resurrecting and I'd thought nothing of it.

So if Killian had been holding an O.L.S… whose was it? He had eaten Sky's in front of Silas, hadn't he? Was it Perish's?

I turned the small pebble-sized ball of plastic around in my fingers and squinted to see if it had any writing on it, but there was nothing. All I knew for sure was that it was an O.L.S and it looked like that would be the extent of my knowledge.

But… I might know where to get more knowledge on it.

My eyes took me to the spare bedroom, where all of Perish's belongings were, and I swallowed down the curiosity burning my throat. Perish had packed a lot of shit on that quad, not just survival things for Killian, but what looked like years and years of research. He had CDs, those little stick USB things, a laptop, two knapsacks full of what looked like half-finished projects, and vials and vials full of serums and fluids, some in strange protective containers that required batteries, and all of which I had immediately zipped up and put in a corner. It was obvious from what was on that quad that Perish had been preparing to kill himself for quite a long time. This wasn't a suicide because Killian had shunned him or something like that – I think my brother was really ready to go.

If this was Sky's O.L.S…

Even the prospect of Sky's O.L.S still being viable filled my head and heart with many different feelings, and none of them were good.

A small, devious smile split my lips as Killian started walking down our driveway. I wrapped my fingers around the little device and allowed myself a fleeting grin that acted like a lit fuse to my mind. If I was in possession of the last shred of Sky that Silas had…

Oh just think of the havoc I could bring, just think of how much control I could have over him. It would be beautiful. The expression on his face, the moment his heart jumps when he realizes just what's in my possession.

My eyes closed and I felt a heat rush through my body. It was orgasmic, soothing, and wrapped itself around me like a ribbon made of the softest silks. Its voice was that of a lullaby that soothed the rough edges of my mind with songs that sung promises that only in my wildest dreams could I hope would come true. The promise to taste the anguish on Silas, to drink in his hysterical screams as I held that O.L.S in my hand. I wanted to torture him in so many ways, so many ways it made my mouth salivate.

"Are you tired, baby?"

And just like that, my sadistic and alluring thoughts of revenge and seeing the agony on King Silas's face disappeared.

I opened my eyes and saw Killian looking back at me, his hand clutching his forearm and his brilliant blue eyes gazing at me with an inquisitiveness that painted the most beautifullest of portraits on his face. My blond-haired boy who I had just gotten back after months of us being separated, who I had almost lost to death. The boy I had sworn to give up revenge for; the boy I had cried into when I had thought I'd felt his spirit float away.

The hatred that coated my body, fuelled by a need to see Silas suffer and driven by what he and some of my other brothers had done, drained from me like a plug being pulled on dirty sink water.

I smiled back at him and shook my head. Without him seeing, I slipped the O.L.S into my cargo pants pocket and walked up to him. I leaned in and softly kissed his lips and slowly wrapped my arms around his waist.

"Do you know how much I missed you?" I whispered to him. I inhaled his scent, and as I leaned my face towards his, he did as well, and we shared our first real kiss.

When I pulled away, I framed his face with my hands and just went over every detail. Looking at him made me wish I was an artist, it made me wish I had some sort of creative talent, because I wanted to freeze frame this moment, capture it forever.

He was just that beautiful.

I was tempted to tell him just what was going through my mind at that moment. I think he would be surprised with me. He knew how much I hated King Silas; Killian had just as much of a reason to hate him as I did.

But my hatred for Silas didn't outweigh my love for this perfect immortal boy in front of me. I wouldn't go back on the promise I had made as I'd ran behind King Silas towards that lab. I would give up my need for revenge to keep him safe. This would be no start of a mission to torture and destroy King Silas. No. I had Killian and we were safe in the plaguelands with everyone most likely thinking we were both dead. Or me as close to death as I could be.

And for all I knew King Silas didn't make it out of there and he was burning too. If that was the case, Elish would be king for the next twenty years and he'd be happy anyway. He could make Jade immortal and they'd have the life Elish always wanted.

And if Silas was alive? I don't know. It was no longer my problem. I had almost lost Killian because of Elish, Leo, and Greyson's foolish dream and I refused, flatly refused, to put him in more danger. Even if he was immortal his mind was still fragile and prone to his bouts of crazy; he didn't need the mental repercussions of going against Silas and the chimeras Elish hadn't secured.

So either Silas was burning or he'd be insane from sadness over losing Sky's O.L.S, both of those things were good enough for me.

I just wanted my Killi.

"Come on, baby," I said as I gently took his hand. I led him towards the couch and we both sat down beside each other. I picked up the nylon tie-off I'd found in someone's closet and started tying off Killian's arm. "I think we should get high out of our minds and just snuggle on the couch.

We can talk about anything you want, or nothing at all."

The left corner of Killian's mouth rose in a crooked smile. Poor little mister still looked sleepy and out of it. It was cute and it just made me want to take him into my arms again.

"Just promise me I'm not dreaming," Killian said in a quiet voice. "Promise me I won't wake up to Sky beside me, staring at me… wanting…" I put my arm around Killian when he shut his eyes and shuddered. I squeezed him to my side and shushed him, then kissed the top of his head.

"He's gone, baby boy," I whispered, though as I said that I felt the outline of the O.L.S in my right pocket. So dearly did I want to ask him if it was Sky's or Perish's. One I knew he'd be relieved to still have, the other he would make me destroy on the spot. "He's gone and it's just you and me. Until you eventually drive me insane and I go kidnap one of my brothers to distract you."

I watched his face to see if he was either going to smile at the comment or cry, my heart filled when the crooked smile came back.

"Who knows…" Killian said in the same timid voice. "We've been apart for so long, it's hard to remember what it was like when it was just the two of us." Then he looked up at me and the corner of his mouth rose higher. "But… I'm looking forward to being your boyfriend again and I think now…" He shrugged. "Now I think you'll finally let me be a boyfriend back to you, instead of just a kid you always had to try and save."

I opened my mouth to say something witty back, but I found myself closing it. Honestly I had never thought of that before. Killian was right, a large part of what our relationship had entailed, saving Killian, was now gone. We were about to enter into a whole new faction of our relationship.

Though as I looked at him, with his bald head, black-circled eyes, scrawny appearance, and of course, the needle sticking out of his arm. I knew that that day wasn't today. For now, possibly for the next two hundred years, he'd still be my Killi Cat. Someone who needed to be taken care of, but also someone who needed to take care of someone too. One day maybe he'd grow into an adult but that was in the future.

And even then, it would be mentally only… Killian was now stuck as an eighteen-year-old forever. Elish hated the idea of having Jade frozen as a teenager but I didn't mind. I couldn't see Killian any other way.

Then I smiled. As Killian pulled out the now empty needle from his skin, I rose to my feet and clapped my hands together with a crooked, toothy grin.

"And while that hits you, I'm going to get you some fucking cake!" And, just to solidify this strange, creepy new happy Reaver I was still myself getting used to, I started to sing to him *Happy Birthday*, Killian looking at me like I was insane the entire time.

CHAPTER 4

Sanguine

WHEN I SAW THE SIGHT IN FRONT OF ME, A SMILE immediately spread on my lips, and when Nero looked my way, grabbed the rubber duck in the bath water and squeaked it at me, I burst out laughing.

Nero was sitting in the Jacuzzi tub with Ceph facing him. Both of them were naked, up to their chests in bubbles, and surrounded by bath toys which I usually kept in one of the bathroom cabinets for when the younger chimeras were staying over… or when King Silas was drunk and in a silly mood.

My brothers looked absolutely foolish and it was wonderful. In that moment I wished Jack was here beside me, because surely he would be wanting to paint this unique scene. Two brute chimeras in a bathtub full of toys. I wonder if he could capture the emotion I was seeing in Nero's eyes.

And oh were Nero's eyes ever overflowing with love, love for this auburn-haired man in front of him. He never took his eyes off of Ceph for long. Even when Nero was picking up toys or looking at me, his eyes travelled back to that man like he was stuck in his gravitational pull.

King Silas had taught me to be strong. Jasper had taught me to endure. Jack had taught me to accept myself.

But Nero had taught me what true love was.

"Nero, you look absolutely foolish," I said with a casual smirk. I glided over to them and put my hands behind my back. "Do tell me we're going to give him a haircut and shave him?"

"Oh, definitely," Nero said. He picked up a bath mitt with a scratchy end, one that all little chimeras hated because it meant I was about to scrub their little bodies raw, and started gently washing Ceph's arm. "He's already smelling better. Do you want us to cut all your hair off, Cephy?"

Ceph, who had been quiet but alert, nodded his head slowly. "Yeah, just... leave a few inches, I think," he said, his voice deep but I could still hear the weakness in it. He was speaking normally and coherently though, and that was what I had been the most afraid of. It looked like my plan that had extended through the past thirty years had worked – Ceph hadn't lost himself.

"Do you have any plans on where you're going to go?" I asked. I heard movement behind me, and when I turned I saw Kiki peeking in with a shy smile. "Is the food here already, little one?"

Kiki nodded. "I have everything covered so it'll stay hot. How are you feeling, Master Ceph?"

Nero smiled and rubbed the bath mitt over Ceph's long and stringy hair. Ceph was completely covered in little white bubbles, but his red hair was breaking through the white like blood on snow. I didn't know whether it was his pale skin contrasting it, or perhaps the brightness of the bathroom lights, but Ceph just seemed unworldly to me, glowing and angelic even. He may be a ghost of pale skin, trembling hands, and a worn-out face, but there was something bright inside of him, inside of those green eyes and that luminous auburn hair that told whatever spirit harvester in the room that they could not claim this soul quite yet.

I picked up the second bath mitt. With Ceph looking at Nero, though with more than a dash of weary confusion on his face, I started scrubbing the dirt, sweat, and whatever else from his body. Kiki asked to help soon after, and together we spent the next half an hour cleaning Ceph to our specific standards. Kiki was Nero's sengil-cicaro and used to washing the greywaste ash, blood, mud, and sweat off of his body and I was as well, but thirty years of sweat and grime was a challenge; and oh did he ever need a shave.

After we were done, Nero rose out of the tub, dried himself off, and changed into clothing, he then came back and helped Ceph out too. Ceph, seeing the apartment for the first time in decades, continued to look around in awe, every once in a while mumbling and shaking his head like he was expecting to wake from this dream he had stumbled into.

But this was no dream, and I wondered if Nero had really grasped that yet.

We dressed Ceph in a robe and sat him down in the kitchen. I pulled up a chair in front of him with a plate of food on my lap and watched Nero, now standing behind him, start to snip away his shoulder length stringy hair.

"Do you remember what happened in this very kitchen over fifty years ago?" Nero said with an amused smirk, the scissors snipping away with movements made by a talented hand. Nero was the first one to cut my hair when I had arrived here; he was quite a talented hairdresser.

"I remember…" Ceph said in his deep but scratchy voice. His mossy green eyes found mine and he tried to wink. Oh dear, did that man look weak. I handed him two potato wedges and tried not to smile when he missed his mouth with them, hitting his cheek instead. His hand and eye coordination was horrible; I hadn't even thought of that.

Ceph managed to reach his mouth this time, but before he took a bite out of the potato wedge, he smiled at me. "I remember… it was a cake, wasn't it? You – you were trying to eat an entire fucking cake yourself."

Nero laughed but my cheeks only reddened. I was quite the mess back then. "Yes, I hope I gave you some amusing memories, dear brother. I remember that time in my life a little too clearly."

"How many new ones do we have, Nuuky?" Ceph asked. He took a small bite of the potato before the entire wedge disappeared into his mouth. It didn't seem to take him long to remember how good food was. Ceph, like all brute chimeras, had enjoyed eating immensely.

"Oh, fuck… dozens," Nero said with a laugh. "You've missed a fucking lot, puppy pants, but I'll fill you in once we get home."

"And do we know where home is?" I asked him. I hated to address the elephant in the room but I wanted to know what Nero's plans were. I think it was a way for my mind to make up for my own personal lack of plans – I really didn't know what I was going to do after they left. All of my concentration had been on breaking Nero and Ceph out of their prisons. Nothing else had mattered when I'd heard that Nero had been encased. Everything had been put on hold… Elish's plans, my plans for me and Jack…

Now I had broken out Nero and Ceph, and Nero and I had spent the last five hours mixing and pouring quick set concrete. Not for his and Ceph's crypts, but for that mysterious man we'd accidently set free. There would be no hiding what I had done.

Soon I would be sending the three of them off to hide, and I myself would have to stay behind to pick up the fallen pieces.

"I'm thinking of taking him into the plaguelands," Nero said. Half of Ceph's hair had been cut away now, only three inches of it remained. Nero looked at me and I saw his lips pale as he pursed them together. "Sangy... I can't let you stay here while we fuck off. You gotta come with us."

At this I shook my head. "I cannot run from him, Nuka. Silas loves me, you know he would never do anything permanent."

Nero took in a cautious breath and exhaled it out of his mouth. He continued to cut Ceph's hair and I continued to feed him.

"I know Kingsly loves you but... he was real pissed that I..." Nero patted Ceph's shoulder and I knew he didn't want to bring voice to what he'd done to Reaver. Not that Ceph would care, but it would lead away from the conversation. "He might take out the anger on you... or, well, I know he will."

"Nonsense," I said with a wave of my hand and a reassured smile; a smile that was as fake as my own confidence but I wore it regardless. "I'll be fine, lovely. You just take care of your husband and your cicaro, and don't worry about me."

The look that Nero gave me told me that he was unconvinced, but behind that look I knew he dearly wanted to trust that I had everything under control. He wanted to leave with Ceph and Kiki but he couldn't until he reassured himself that I would be okay.

I knew I wouldn't be okay but perhaps King Silas's anger towards me would deflect his attention from my brothers. Not just Nero, but his anger towards Garrett keeping the secret of Reaver's location from him too. Hell, maybe the family I arranged to have stranded will come back with Reaver in tow, and Silas will forget all of our disobedience for a while.

I kept my smile and handed Ceph half of a hamburger. "You just do what needs to be done. I will handle everything... I have brothers who will aid me if Silas decides to punish me."

"What if he encases you too?" I was surprised at the fear that laced Nero's words.

But it only made me push my confident stance. I shook my head before getting up to grab Ceph a napkin, he was still missing his mouth. "Silas would never do that to me. You know he... he would never do that."

"Kingy has been acting pretty nuts lately though," Nero pointed out. He tried to make eye contact with me when I walked back in with a hand towel but I refused it. "You've seen it... he's been driving himself crazy trying to get Reaver."

"And he went into the plaguelands to get Reaver," I said to him back. "For all we know he has Reaver, and he'll be content for the next hundred years. Love, we have no idea what happened in the plaguelands and Kiki has already told us everything he knows. We just don't know and I don't know either; all I know is that I have to get you, Ceph, and Kiki on a Falconer and far from here. I am king now and I have Skyfall to run and, like I said, I will not hide from him. Please..." I walked up to Nero and kissed his cheek, my nose filling with the smells of spice and shampoo from his and Ceph's bath. "Just give me one less thing to worry about and leave with Ceph and Kincade tonight. I'm going to try and come up with a plan, and in three day's time, once the concrete is hard enough and I've had time to scuff it up, I will start looking for the group myself."

My voice hung in the air before it was consumed by the silence of the room. I watched my brother, staring worriedly at the back of Ceph's head, take in a deep breath before he let out a sigh.

"I'm taking a remote phone and an Ieon," Nero said after the silence had been around us for at least a minute. "I'll turn the phone on every odd-numbered day at six for an hour. Even if I get a single ring from you I'll come back to Skyfall and get you. I don't care where he has you or what he threatens... just call me and let it ring once and I'll be coming. I swear on Cephy's life, you know I will."

I rested a hand on his shoulder and pecked his cheek. Though as my lips broke away from his prickly skin, Nero turned his head to me and the two of us joined in a deep kiss.

When Nero broke away he looked me right in the eyes. I hadn't seen that much apprehension and nervousness in decades. "You better know what the fuck you're doing, Sangy..." Nero said. "I know you love Kingy but I've been around him longer, and I know he's bordering on snapping again. You know what happens when he snaps..."

We all knew what happened when Silas snapped, most of us had the mental scars to prove it.

"I'll be fine," I reassured him for what seemed like the hundredth time. Perhaps this repetition was because I needed to reassure myself. "He cannot kill me and he would never put me in concrete." The reason why I was so sure of this was because of my own traumatic past. Silas knew what I had endured in the greywastes, and he knew the horrible consequence of triggering my psychosis. I had issues with my brain, and though a lot of those problems had been repaired when I had been made immortal, both from immortal healing and surgery, I still suffered lingering issues. Silas was ravaged with guilt over my past, and I was confident he would never do something that would exacerbate my problems.

"You've never seen him snap as bad as I have… and we're heading towards a big one, I know it," Nero said. "And if he finds out… what else I accidently did… freeing that dude…"

His voice trailed to nothing and only silence followed his words. We both stood in this silence and I knew he was thinking the same things that I was.

"Do you think… he's dangerous? I mean, Nero, he had… Silas, Valen, Jade's… empathic abilities…"

Nero bit the bottom of his lip. He tilted Ceph's head to the side, his haircut now finished, and started to trim his beard in preparation for shaving it. I stared at him, analyzing his face and wondering to myself if I was going to get a response. It looked like I was going to be kept waiting because Nero continued to cut off Ceph's scraggly beard without saying anything back.

I wasn't that impressed with his lack of response, but when the last thick patch of reddy-brown hair fell onto King Silas's granite floor, I found myself temporarily forgetting our troubles, and instead, smiling.

In front of me was the Ceph I remembered. Square face, dark green, inquisitive eyes, ears that stuck out just a little bit too much and a thick neck that Nero used to love to kiss and nip.

He was back.

"Hey, Cephy baby," Nero said sweetly as he rubbed the stray strands from Ceph's face. He gave his husband a playful smack on the cheek before grabbing his chin. "Fuck, I knew you were in there somewhere. You looked forty with that damn beard."

Ceph scratched his cheek and looked down at the hair that surrounded him. And there was a lot of it as well. The sengil nature that had branded itself into my bones over the last thirty years made me sigh at it, but then again, I was technically king so I would just make Juni and Luca clean it up for me. Those two had been enjoying each other's company, and bodies, with their masters gone and it was time for them to expend their energies elsewhere.

"I think I'm starting to... come back to reality," Ceph said as he rubbed his squinting eyes. "I just feel like my head is in a fog." He wiped both of his hands down his face and tried to get to his feet, Nero helped him. "It's really been... thirty years?"

"Yeah... but that's a good thing that you think it's been shorter, peaches," Nero said with a supportive smile. "I bet you'll be good as new in a few days and some quiet in the plaguelands will be the best thing for you."

Quiet in the plaguelands... now that sounded good right about now. What was I going to do when they left? I had been pushing down the apprehension rather well, but like a spider in an open glass jar it kept trying to crawl out.

I jumped when I felt Nero's hand on my shoulder. He sighed at this and rubbed it. "I haven't seen you this tense in decades. Please... please come with us."

My head shook and Nero sighed again. I put the plate down in front of Ceph, who was petting one of Silas's cats, and walked to the window.

It was dark outside and Skyfall in front of me was carrying on as normal. King Silas's people below had no idea that their king was stranded in the plaguelands, or that all but a small handful of chimeras were gone from the only radiation-free city in the entire dead world. They lived their simple lives and carried on as normal, whereas I was up here, as King Sanguine, watching the sand in my hourglass start to collect at the bottom.

But though the sand was eternal, never to run out, none of this mattered in darkness, none of this mattered when you had no eyes to see it, and here I was... facing the prospect of living my own concrete nightmare.

Not only had I freed Nero and Ceph... we'd accidently freed someone that Silas had kept secret from all of us.

He's going to do worse than kill me.

No... no, he wouldn't do that to me. I dismissed my anxiety with a deep swallow and found myself standing up straight, as if all of Skyfall were watching me through the window.

I stared out into the night, seeing the lights twinkle and the headlights go up and down the street like rows of soldiers holding torches. I tried to find peace in this lit-up darkness, but all I saw was my anxious reflection.

But then I looked past my reflection, to the living room behind me. I saw Nero with Ceph in his arms, arms that bound themselves around Ceph tightly. Nero's eyes were closed as he held him, and as my ears adjusted I picked up the rapid thrumming of his heart.

Yes... this is why I did it. I turned around and smiled at the two of them, then quietly walked to the couch they were both sitting on. As I approached, Nero opened his eyes and returned my smile.

"I'm going to take him to my apartment in Skytower and quickly pack us some things," Nero said, then he looked towards Kiki who had been the silent wallflower for most of the evening. "Kiki will be fine but I obviously can't bring Elliot, the radiation will kill him, so I'm going to tell him he can stay with Artemis and Apollo. You'll keep an eye on him, right?"

I nodded. "Yes, of course. The twins would be more than happy to have another sengil to ravage."

Nero smirked at this and stood up. "I'm going to try and think of a way I can get Kingy's favour back, so not only can I keep Cephy but I can stay out of the box as well. I'm not sure what yet, but who knows... if you have any ideas tell me, if not..." Nero shrugged. "I don't know. I just know he's never putting Ceph in there again."

Nero took Ceph's hand and helped him up, and I felt my own heart pitter-patter in my chest. There was a question that kept running to the front of my mind, but whenever I brushed a hand over it, it retreated like a sea anemone. Though if Nero was leaving now... I wouldn't get the opportunity to ask for quite some time.

"If there was a way to get Silas help..." I began as I followed Nero to the door. "... but it meant Silas would be gone for a long time recovering, and it would mean us... having to overpower him to do it, force him to take our help... would you?"

Nero froze at my words, and like they had brought with them the chill of the Arctic, everyone around me seemed to freeze as well.

Even me.

"You... I thought..." Nero turned around and I was shocked to see hurt in his eyes. "I thought you loved Kingy, Sam. You – you want him gone too?" The pain on his face broke my heart in two, and before he even finished his sentence, I was shaking my head.

"No... not..." How did he know this? Had Elish already spoken to him? "Not in the way you think. I don't want him hurt, or miserable, or encased in concrete… I want to get him help. I want…"

"What Elish wants… so Elish got to you? What the fuck did he promise you?"

"No!" I found myself saying back sharply, his accusatory tone digging up both guilt and defensiveness. "Elish did not *get to me*. If he got to me why would I abandon him with the others?" I swallowed down a bitter taste in my mouth. "I don't want to hurt him like Elish does. I love Silas dearly as I know you do. I want to get him help; I want to help him finally put Sky behind him and perhaps find someone for him to love, someone besides Reaver."

Nero looked at me skeptically; Ceph just looked confused and lost.

"Sangy… I know nothing of your plans but I've been hearing Elish's bullshit since the night he smashed Kingy's head in after Jade's party. I know Silas encased me in concrete but I fucking deserved it… and…" Nero looked at Ceph. "… if I hadn't been so scared of what state Ceph would be in, I could've given Reaver to Silas and I know Silas would've given me Ceph as a reward. All of this shit I did myself… none of this was Kingy's fault. It was me."

I took Nero's hand in mine and held it. "My plan isn't a plan, love. Elish wants to be rid of Silas and he thinks with some clever manipulating he can get the family to go along with it. But I know you, as I know Garrett, Jack, Ellis, and many others… we don't want Silas permanently gone; we love him and we see how sick he is. So tell me… if there is a way for us to… force him to receive our help… or if there is a way for us to find someone to make him happy… will you go against Silas's wishes for it? You know if we can find him a partner he will thank us, and we can all live with our own partners and be happy."

The skeptical look didn't disappear from my brother's face, if anything it only became more prominent.

"You know I am bound to Silas," I said to Nero, then I squeezed his hand. "As I am bound to you. Give me your word. Let me know I have you as an ally and I can move forward with this. If I know I have you… I can feel a bit more confident confronting the brothers Elish has already swayed to go along with me."

"But what can you even do?" Nero asked. "Reaver fucking hates him and the smart chimeras haven't been able to clone Sky. How can you say you can help him or send him away to make him well?"

63

Lies laced my tongue but Nero knew me and I wouldn't insult him by lying to his face. "I don't know yet..." When Nero groaned and turned from me, I pulled his hand back. "But I will figure something out," I said hastily. "I have been living with King Silas for thirty years and he's been my master, my lover, my king, and my friend, for almost fifty-one. I know his secrets and what secrets I don't know... I know where to find them. I can figure out how to help him, and I know I can find him someone."

"He doesn't want us," Nero said bitterly. "Elish tried and he got spat on for his efforts and he was never the same after. Silas doesn't see us as being good enough to be his lovers. He just wants Sky and Sky's clone hates him, and the smart chimeras can't clone another. That's it for the born immortals besides Perry, and Silas's fucked up Perish's mind so much he's gone retarded."

Then, like two wires were touching inside of my brain, each not realizing the other one was live, something occurred to me. It was something so obvious that I was sure my subconscious had been leading me there the entire time.

What if that man in the tomb was another born immortal...?

I dearly wanted to talk to Nero about my theory, but I knew that would be the equivalent of talking to a brick wall. No, no, I wouldn't get anything from Nero, perhaps this was information I would be having to find myself. And it looked like the perfect opportunity had fallen onto my lap.

I was alone, and I was king.

"Just promise me you'll always be my ally," I said to Nero. I raised his large hand to my lips and kissed it.

My brother's eyes softened for me and his hand slipped from mine to cup my chin. I followed his guidance until my lips found his again. He kissed me with a gentleness rarely seen between the two of us. When we were intimate it was masochism and sadism's finest hour; we rarely made love unless I was having a bad night with Silas and needed him, but right now he was treating me more like his husband than the one standing beside him.

"I love you and I will say again what I've been saying since you were little: No matter what happens, it'll always be the two of us. I would never go against you, Sanguine, and I will follow you into whatever darkness your psychotic and crafty mind leads you. I trust you more than Elish, more than Silas, fucking more than my own mind. But, Sanguine..." Nero let out a tense breath, like he had been holding something back the entire time we'd been talking. "… you have a bad habit of becoming a martyr." Nero looked to his side where Ceph was standing beside Kiki, both of them watching our interaction. "And I love you for it… you're so self-sacrificing it hurts my heart. But please, puppy, don't get involved with trying to fix Silas, because many have tried and… many have failed. And when you're in the fallout zone when Silas explodes from having his heart broken… people die, people get encased in concrete, just like Ceph did when Silas flipped out over baby Adler dying. If you're near him when he reaches that explosive point… Sangy, he'll wipe your existence from our lives. He'll–" Nero let out a frustrated growl as I started shaking my head rapidly back and forth.

"He wouldn't do that to me," I said simply, then I gave him the same reassuring smile I'd been conjuring since we'd taken Ceph out of his crypt. "I know what I'm doing, Nuky, I really do. I will find a way. I have Alegria and Silas's computers at my fingertips and a world of secrets I can uncover. I'm quite confident I can find something. If Elish can find a way to destroy him – I can find a way to heal him."

Nero didn't return my smile but I think he realized that was as far as the conversation with me would go. I didn't expect him to understand, only someone who had been living with Silas as long as I had would. I knew I could do this, and now more than ever, I knew that I had to.

Both for my family's safety and my own.

When Nero was in the elevator with Ceph and Kiki, I gave the two a hug and a kiss on the cheek and then turned to Nero.

"Every odd day at six," I said to Nero, reiterating his instructions for when the remote phone was on. "I'll call you when I come up with a solid plan to fix our king."

Nero nodded and gave me a bone-crushing hug. "Thank you for everything," he whispered as he embraced me. "You have me forever, every crazy, stupid idea. I'm yours forever for giving me Ceph back, and for keeping him sane for me all this time."

We pulled away and I patted his cheek playfully. "How could I do anything less? This time with Silas may have been hard, but in the end it will wield us many benefits. I know Silas and I promise you, Nero, we will fix him. We will make Silas the king we all knew when I first arrived in Skyfall."

"I… I trust you, baby," Nero said, though his tone didn't support the weight of his words. We were both holding our cards up to our faces and we were both bluffing our hands. "If he threatens you… if he hurts you or anything… call me, one ring and I'll come running, okay?"

I nodded and pressed one of the elevator's many buttons, this one for the roof. "One call." I nodded towards Ceph and Kiki. "Take care, lovelies."

"You too," Kiki said quietly and he inclined his head.

Ceph though, embraced me a second time. "Thank you," he said, his voice still weak and raspy. "I knew it was you stickin' those needles in my foot and… and thank you, Sanguine. I promise… I promise I'll be able to form better sentences when we see each other next."

I laughed lightly and kissed his cheek. "No worries, amor. You take care of Nero, and do tell me about your first time after thirty years, hm? I wish I could be there."

That quip got me a playful push out of the elevator, courtesy of Nero, and after several more goodbyes and I love yous… Nero, his husband, and his cicaro, were gone.

And when the elevator doors closed I breathed a shaky sigh of relief, but when I started heading back to the apartment I found my knees growing weak and my head filling with a hazy heat.

I managed to make it to the couch before the emotions overwhelmed me. I found myself burying my face into my hands and holding back shuddering breath after shuddering breath. I was surprised at my own visceral reaction, I hadn't realized what I was keeping in until my mind had deemed it safe for me to show the emotions.

And what was I feeling?

I looked around the empty apartment, my chest rising and falling as the rapid puffs of air escaped from my chest. My gaze took me in all directions, but what my mind kept looking for, I didn't know.

But when my breathing started to become all the more laboured and my lungs failed to fill me with adequate air, when my hands started to tremble and my mind started to swim in a pressurized haze of red… I realized that I wasn't looking for anything.

I was plunging head first into the first anxiety attack I'd had in a decade.

CHAPTER 5

Killian

"THAT IS WAY TOO MUCH FOR YOU, MISTER," REAVER chastised. "Just because you don't have to worry about overdosing doesn't mean you can use up all of our smack."

I playfully stuck my tongue out at him and continued to push the needle in and out of my arm, searching for a vein. The needle had an inch of the brown, tarry liquid, and beside me on the coffee table, was our small brick with a plastic bag full of disposable needles. The brick was about a quarter of the size it had been when I'd discovered it and was now covered in little pinch marks from us grabbing small amounts to inject.

"We have tons and tons of it somewhere," I said to him. I pulled on the plunger and saw a swirl of blood mix in with the heroin; I had found a vein. "We just have to know the right places to look. There must be a drug dealer's house somewhere. Do you know any cities around here?"

My boyfriend shrugged and popped a handful of sour candies into his mouth. He was wearing a bandana on his head today, a red one, and a brown button-down with his black cargo pants. He looked handsome, but he always looked handsome. "Somewhere around here. Everything was melted until I found these houses and I just stayed here until you woke up. I didn't want to take you too far, you were a real pain to haul around in the shopping cart."

I smirked at the thought of him pulling me around in an old shopping cart and motioned for him to take the needle. He liked injecting me; he had always gotten a small thrill out of it.

My eyes closed as Reaver slowly pushed the toxic brown into my veins. I gave a low moan and leaned into him, and he shifted himself onto the couch. I laid my head on his chest, and as the cold, icy drugs froze my veins, he started playing with my hair. Reaver had shot up only minutes before me and now was our time to relax with each other and enjoy the tunnel of comfortable, painless heroin that was like angels draping feathery blankets over us.

I groaned and took in a deep breath, ripples of comfort travelling up and down my body. I stayed in this cocoon of contentment and enjoyed the feeling of my boyfriend playing with my hair.

"I love you," I said after several minutes of silence.

"I love you more," Reaver said back. His hand travelled down to my chin where he softly petted it. I was shaved now but there was still a thin layer of stubble and several nicks where Reaver's hand had slipped while shaving.

It had been three days since I had woken up and the past three days had consisted of me and Reaver doing nothing but eating junk food, doing drugs, and snuggling. There had been no talking about what had happened while we were separated. No talk of Perish, or Elish and Jade; whenever I had touched on one of them, or had brought something up, Reaver would either put drugs under my nose or a needle in my arm.

Admittedly, it had taken a day and a half of him doing this before I actually clued in that he was deliberately distracting me, but after thinking about it I decided to roll with it and let him continue. We had been apart for months, and this time was a time for us to connect and just be happy together.

I still had questions. Oh did I ever have questions. I wanted to know what happened after Reaver had been taken in Mariano, and I wanted to know just how he and Silas had both found me at the same time – it was like they had been travelling together but they would never do that.

But on the other hand, I knew that if I asked Reaver anything, he would be asking me things in return – and I don't think I was ready for that.

At the mere mention of it, my heart gave a shudder and that shudder turned into a painful sting.

Perish…

"Are you okay, hunny bee?" Reaver asked kindly. He scratched my head and tenderly caressed it.

He must've heard my heartbeat quicken. "I'm fine," I said to him. I rested my hand on his and pulled it to my mouth to kiss it. "You know how heroin is… makes your heartbeat go nuts for a bit."

"Hmm…" Reaver said, sounding unconvinced. "Alright… want to do a few lines to help your high?"

He knew better; he knew where my mind was. I shook my head and rubbed my prickly cheek against his hand. "Nah, I'm getting pretty high. I'm okay." Though as I said this my eyes looked to the hallway, covered in a stained and matted carpet, and with corners full of powdered gyprock and plaguelands ash.

At the end of that hallway was a simple brown door with a golden door knob.

It looked unassuming and normal, like any other door, but inside held all of Perish's things. I knew this because yesterday I was checking out our house, and I had opened that door… I'd immediately closed it when I'd recognized the bags that were piled in a corner. Reaver, who had been outside cooking us fried corned beef and rice, had known what I'd done the moment he'd come inside. That earned me an extra hit of heroin and some china white to top it off.

"Okay," Reaver said back, and we fell silent as we enjoyed our individual highs.

But eventually I heard Reaver take in a big sigh, before he started drumming his fingers on my scalp. "So I was thinking…"

My heart jumped and at this, Reaver chuckled. "Ahh, he's thinking! Shit's about to go down," he mocked. I grunted and pretended to bite his hand.

"Nothing bad…" Reaver said. He let his voice trail before taking in another breath. "I think I want to find a town to buy a few things at."

I raised my head and stared at him in horror. "Go back to the greywastes?"

Reaver nodded and tried to encourage me to lay my head back down but I didn't want to. The thought of going back to the greywastes was terrifying. "What if someone sees us? What if Nero finds us again? We don't know how he found us in the first place."

Reaver shook his head and reached over to grab a cigarette. "I know how he found us. I was an idiot and I took the tracker off of the phone by accident. I'm pretty confident that they think you're dead and I'm burning. No one's going to recognize us if we just duck into Melchai for a night. We need more fuel for the quad and I want to try and get a generator."

I frowned at Reaver. "Melchai? That's where Hopper and the other slavers were heading…"

"And they're dead, right?" Reaver shrugged one shoulder. "The chances of us running into someone we know is zero and I'll scout it out beforehand anyway. I really want to buy some shit and Perish left you a lot of money. Don't you want a generator so we can watch television and have lights?"

"I just… want to be happy with the safety we have," I said, my voice small. "We just got our freedom from everyone… why are we risking it?"

I looked around our living room as silence took over the conversation. I had cleaned it the best I could and had swept the dirty carpet in the living room. There was brown panelling, slightly warped, around us, a sheet-draped blue couch we were laying on, two chairs and a coffee table. The television, of course, didn't work but I had dusted it off, and even put the VHS movies underneath the television stand and wiped off the VHS player and a Super Nintendo as well. We had a lot of electronics we could use and… I guess it would be nice to have lights. Reaver had theorized that maybe Perish could've given me chimera enhancements during my surgery but that hadn't been the case. And though I knew he had put something else inside of my brain, too much else had been going on for me to think about what it was.

My cheeks puffed as I let out a pensive breath. I wouldn't mind electricity but I felt like we were taking risks we didn't need to take, and doing things that didn't need to be done. Sure, no greywaster could survive in the plaguelands, but chimeras could, and those were the ones we had to watch out for.

We were fugitives, whether we wanted to admit it or not, and I wanted it to remain that way.

"I don't want to risk it," I said, my already small and submissive voice dragging lower. "Let's just… be thankful for what we have."

Reaver shifted himself up so he was sitting. I did as well and took a cigarette out of the pack he had on the coffee table. The house was always filled with the smell of stale tobacco from Reaver's smoking. He had been smoking a lot, one cigarette after the other usually.

Then I frowned as something occurred to me.

"Are you… are you bored?" I asked. "Is that it? Are you bored of it just being me and you?"

"No, don't be retarded," Reaver said. He looked annoyed at even the suggestion. "We just had all that shit to entertain us in Aras and even in Elish's base. I'm just used to it." He shrugged and looked around our house. "You like your books and I've already read all my comics. And it's such easy pickings here, I have already scavenged us enough food to last three months. I don't even need to sentry since no one can survive here... it'd be nice to, I don't know, at least have some TV and video games. We have so much money and didn't the slavers say Melchai had good farming? That's why they sacrificed the slaves? We could get fresh fruit and vegetables."

My eyes lit up at the prospect.

"We could have real meals with vegetables and shit like that," Reaver said. He had me and he knew it. I'd inadvertently bit the baited hook he'd dangled in front of me and now he was reeling me in. "Get some flour and you can make us bread and cake that doesn't taste like motor oil." I smirked at his comment, and at that, Reaver gathered me up into his arms and leaned his head against mine. "We could see if they have heroin too, but I know you'd be most happy buying a big bucket of strawberries or whatever the fuck they have. Right? We have like twenty thousand dollars; we could buy all their damn fruit and I don't even think it'd go rotten for a while in the radiation."

I grunted and pulled away from him. "Only if you promise to wear sunglasses and a hat... and you sneak around first and make sure there isn't anyone we know. I told you about what Perish said about Mantis and the flare gun." I remember Perish's instructions, before he knew that Reaver was on his way to get me. There was a chimera somewhere in the plaguelands, but Reaver had reassured me we were miles and miles away from where the laboratory was.

Reaver nodded. "You know I wouldn't put you at risk, immortal boy, not after we've been apart for so long. I'll go in there and we'll get supplies and leave, maybe come back in a few months when the fuel runs out or see if we can steal some solar panels or some shit."

I didn't feel convinced and he sensed this.

"We just need some stuff to get ourselves established and then we won't have to go back to the greywastes, ever."

To my own surprise, this brought its own wave of sadness. We hadn't mentioned him, or anyone else, besides in passing, but I felt compelled to tonight. Maybe it was the drugs or maybe the fact that we were going to return to the greywastes, but I had to say it.

"What about Reno?" I whispered.

Immediately Reaver tensed up beside me. I didn't want to look at him though.

"He has Garrett now," he replied quietly.

"But… he's going to think I'm dead, and you gone," I said and found my voice starting to wobble. "He's going to be devastated. We're all he has. We're really never returning – ever?"

Reaver shifted around. I finally did look over at him and saw he looked troubled and uncomfortable.

"We're not all he has anymore…" Reaver said, a hint of dejection in his words. "He has Garrett who loves him and they both have Chally to love maul. He's better off with Garrett in Skyfall then he ever would be with us. Even if there was some way for him to come here, he'd be the third wheel and it always made him sad watching us be boyfriends when he was alone. Now he has Garrett and he's like… living in royalty. I bet he doesn't even care."

This shocked me. "Doesn't even care? He loves us… of course he cares. And what about Silas hurting him?"

"Silas was in the lab when it exploded. He could very well be burning with me, as far as they know."

"I – I still…"

"No," Reaver abruptly cut me off. He licked his lips which I knew was from stress and stood up. He ran a hand over his bandana-covered head. "Reno's fine and he's happy, alright? He has Garrett and he's engaged. He's fine and… and Elish will be fine too."

"Elish?" I said slowly. "Since… when do you care about how Elish feels?"

Reaver walked over to his M16 and grabbed it, then put his jacket on. I watched helplessly as he got ready to go outside.

"I'm going for a walk… going to go see if there are any animals to kill. Get us… some meat," Reaver mumbled. "I'll be back."

"Reaver…" I said with a whimper. "I didn't mean to make you upset. I… just… Reno's, Reno's going to be devastated."

Reaver walked over to the front of the couch and I thought he was going to at least give me a kiss, but he just grabbed his pack of cigarettes.

"I'll be back in a few hours," Reaver said. He looked at me while he was walking away and stopped with a sigh. I sniffed when he doubled back and this time, he did kiss my cheek, then he walked off… and out the door.

My heart felt heavy for the rest of the evening, so I went to bed early after taking a few lines of china white. I fell asleep in our new bed, a big king size one, and woke up only momentarily when Reaver came home sometime in the middle of the night. I crawled into his arms and he held me close to him, and I fell asleep to his breathing.

The next morning I woke up to Reaver gently nudging me. I opened my eyes to his smirking face, his dark hair, now longer than it had ever been, falling over his black eyes.

"Come on, sleepy head. You've slept enough. Wake up," he said as he poked me in the cheek.

I grunted and batted his hand away. "Your fault for finding us a mattress so comfy," I mumbled with a big yawn. "Come back in an hour."

"I have drugs prepared," Reaver said in a singing voice.

Automatically I perked up. Reaver scoffed at this and left the room.

"You're just as bad as I was when I was a teen," he called as he walked down the hallway.

I sat up in bed and stretched, my joints snapping and cracking from sleeping for so long. I walked out in my boxer briefs and undershirt and saw he had several rows of white powder waiting for us.

"Well, unfortunately you're stuck with me as a teenager forever," I said to him, the springs on the couch squeaked as I sat down. I reached over and grabbed the cut up pink straw. "I hope you don't mind an eighteen-year-old as a boyfriend for all eternity."

"Nah, I'm not Elish, why would I care?" Reaver shrugged. I could see white powder under his nostrils, I guess he hadn't wanted to wait for me.

It kind of made me feel better that he said that, a part of me was worried he'd be upset that I wouldn't be a full adult. I myself didn't know how to feel about it.

I took my share of china white and leaned back to let the drip fall down my throat, but a moment later I heard a *thunk*. I looked to my left and saw my boots beside me, Reaver had thrown them.

"Put them on and follow me. I got a surprise for you," Reaver said. He grabbed his gun and walked towards the door. "Hurry up."

I gave him a skeptical look but did as he asked. "What is it…?"

"Follow me and you'll see."

My eyes narrowed suspiciously but once again I did what he said. The next thing I knew I was stepping out into the plaguelands, only wearing my underclothes.

Reaver walked ahead of me, and I tried to keep up though my boots weren't properly laced. He sauntered across the street and started heading towards our next door neighbour's house. A rancher like the one we were staying in, with almost the same layout except the inside was more destroyed than the one that Reaver had made up for us.

The plaguelands were remarkably preserved, and I was looking forward to Reaver taking me to one of the shops to scavenge things. The sestic radiation was an amazing preserver; I hadn't seen a house in either direction with anything worse than a sinking roof.

I kicked a rock and watched it bounce down the dirty road. Though the plagueland ash had covered a lot of the road, it was barely cracking, even the cars had remains of their paint jobs. I wasn't sure how much rain we got here but it couldn't be more than the sparse rainy seasons we had in the greywastes. We got two rainy seasons there, a short one in the fall before winter, or early winter, and our spring rains.

Finally, my legs caught me up to Reaver; he sure did walk fast. "Give me a hint," I said as I gently nudged him with my shoulder.

The corner of Reaver's mouth rose in a coy smirk. "The first morning I woke up to you beside me... I knew you wouldn't be up for quite a while and I was bored. So I went out and did something special that I knew you'd like... something really out of character for me since I usually hated doing nice things for people." Reaver started sprinting down the driveway of the neighbour's house and continued down the road.

I stopped and thought for a second, before it finally popped in my head. "You – you found a loader tub here?" I asked as I ran after him.

Reaver turned around and started jogging backwards. "Nah, I'm not that creative but..." He turned around again and started running towards a thatch of bushes, just dry sticks all weaved together like tumbleweeds. I followed him and soon my ears picked up the sound of running water, and, surprisingly, my nose actually found the smell of the water as well. It... it smelled like radiation; I was now getting really familiar with that scent. The smell of radiation was a light tinny aroma, easily missed and your brain ignored it most of the time, but when I made a point to sniff the air, I could smell it.

A huge smile appeared on my face when I walked through the tightly woven bushes and saw an incline leading to a river. Far to the left, I could even see a truss bridge that was still intact and well-preserved, with metal beams criss-crossed above it and concrete pillars below. It looked like this river had been around even before the Fallocaust.

"This is where I've been getting our water," Reaver called as he skidded down the rocky embankment to the river's shore. I could see a green grocery basket full of soap, just like when he'd taken me to the loader tub. "Can you smell the radiation on it?"

I nodded as I put one foot in front of me and started sliding down the steep incline after him, rocks and dirt piling up against the back of my boots as my skidding disturbed the ground. "I can. Can you imagine how quickly this water would kill me if I drank it when I was mortal and still affected by the radiation? It has to be really concentrated for it to give off an actual smell."

Reaver took his gun off and started unbuttoning his shirt. It was warm out today but every day seemed to have the same temperature. Warm enough that you didn't need a jacket, but barely; I usually wore one though because I got cold so easily. I wonder if there was even weather here?

"I'm glad our Geigerchips are broken," Reaver replied as he slid his pants down, revealing his black boxer briefs, the edges of them smudged with ash.

To my own humiliation, I felt myself blush, and to further drive in the embarrassment, Reaver noticed right away.

"Do you want me to stay dressed?" he asked, a strange look on his face.

"No, no," I said hastily. And to show him I was okay I took off my own shirt. "It's just... you know it's been a long time since..."

Now it was Reaver's turn to flush. He nodded and turned around to walk to the edge of the river. "Yeah, it has."

I was only wearing my boxer briefs now, blue ones for me. I walked up to Reaver and we stood side by side in front of the river. The water had a brown tinge to it but you could see the rocks on the bottom so it was clear. I leaned down and cupped some of it into my hand and drank. It was cold, colder than I thought it would be.

I put my feet in and started wading. "Why don't you grab some soap?" I asked, but when I turned around I saw Reaver already returning with the basket.

"When we get gasoline we can rig up some sort of water system," Reaver said. He started walking into the river with a bottle of Gillette body wash in his hand. "Maybe move into one of these houses nearby. It might be worth it for convenience." He walked into the deeper water before, to my surprise, he dived right into it. I shuddered at the thought of doing that myself but took several more steps into the brown-tinged river.

Reaver burst out of the water several feet away from me and gave me a grin, his hair, looking completely black, plastered against his face. He shook his head like a dog and started swimming in place. "Come here."

I shook my head.

Reaver lightly tossed the bottle of Gillette over to me. "Come on, you can soap me up just like you love doing. I haven't had a bath in months. I've died more than I've bathed. Come on and soap me up."

A huff of air escaped my nose but I started walking towards Reaver, the water climbing up my bare, pasty legs.

I yelped though when the water touched my sensitive area; there was nothing worse than cold water on your testicles. Reaver, of course, laughed at me... then to my annoyance he splashed water at me.

"Stop it. I just need a moment!" I said exasperated.

He splashed me again, this time a great deal of water got on my groin. I sucked in a sharp breath and threw the bottle of soap at him.

Reaver caught it with a chuckle and splashed me again.

"That's it. I'm going to kick your ass!" I declared. I jumped into the river, gasping at the cold and started swimming towards him. Reaver gave me a sheepish grin before raising both hands... and slamming them down on the water, completely coating my face.

I splashed him back and it was war after that. The two of us, like two kids, splashed and swept water at each other, laughing like idiots and grinning more than we had since I had woken up.

Then, feeling brave, I advanced towards Reaver, a mischievous grin on my face. He returned my look with a suspicious one himself, and started swimming backwards.

It must've been the playful mood between us because I was about to do something I hadn't even anticipated, or known I had wanted to do. But as soon as it popped into my head I had grabbed it and ran with it.

I could be spontaneous and devious too.

I took in a deep breath and dipped under the water. I opened my eyes and saw Reaver's pale legs and his black boxer briefs. I grabbed both sides of the elastic with my hands and started pulling his briefs off of him.

A heat centered in my chest when I saw his dick pop out of the briefs, soft and surrounded by untrimmed black hair but still the most beautiful one I'd ever seen. I pulled the briefs all the way off of him and rose to the surface with them in my hand.

Reaver was giving me a surprised look. I lifted up the black briefs and grinned, not knowing what had gotten into me but liking this brave side I was seeing in myself. I guess the last several days with him, and the relaxing we had done, had been good for my mind and my mental state, I was feeling better than ever.

"Why do you even need those?" I said with a coy smile. "You *are* my boyfriend." I swung the briefs several times before letting go; they landed on the river bank with a wet *splat*.

Reaver, still with a shocked look, just stared back at me. I don't think he knew what to say. So I decided to help him along. I put my hand on the small of his back and pulled him closer to me. Then, with his surprised face only inches away, I leaned in and pressed my lips against his.

Reaver let out a small groan and his lips parted; mine did as well, and we kissed deeply. Then, taking advantage of his open mouth, I slowly introduced my tongue and slid it across his front teeth. In response, his met mine, and like long lost lovers, they greeted each other and stayed intertwined as we kissed.

I didn't want to break away from him so I didn't. I raised my hand and grasped the back of his head. I didn't let him pull away or move from my lips. We stayed, with our mouths locked together and our tongues reintroducing themselves, for quite a while before I finally separated us.

Then my hand reached down. I wanted to feel what that kiss had done to him; I was eager to feel it hard against my hand. The fire that had started inside of my chest when I had seen it under the water had turned into a bonfire from that kiss, and it had already made my own dick stiff.

I tried not to feel disappointed when I still felt it flaccid. I joined our lips again so he couldn't see my face, and instead started gently stroking it. Though I didn't get that long to play with it, Reaver's hand soon found itself wandering and he pushed my own hand away to get easier access to my front.

Well… I really wanted to give him the attention but I let Reaver take the lead. He always had to be leader so I shouldn't be surprised.

And any reservations I had at him not letting me get him hard, were soon vanquished when he pulled my briefs away and started rubbing my penis with his hand.

"Feeling good?" Reaver asked playfully. I loved the glint in his eye.

"Yes!" I gasped. He chuckled before ducking back under the water. I looked down and took in a sharp breath, followed by a cry of surprise when I felt his warm mouth cover the head.

The pleasure overwhelmed me as Reaver sucked on the head of my dick, his tongue massaging the bottom and his mouth flexing with the suction. It was sending shivers down my spine and both relaxing and tensing up my body.

Reaver removed his mouth and surfaced but his hand was still on my dick, my foreskin now protecting the temperature sensitive head. He leaned in and kissed me, then took my hand and started swimming back to shore.

Even though Reaver and I had been intimate probably over a hundred times now since we'd began our relationship I still felt that apprehensive quiver in my gut. I found myself smiling and feeling my face go hot as he led me to the rocky shore.

Reaver got up and grabbed both of our towels and laid them down, though the tips of them were in the water. I laid down on top of them and propped myself up with my hands. And when Reaver kneeled beside me, I put an arm around his neck and pulled him onto me for another deep kiss.

Once again though, I tried to hide my surprise when I noticed he still wasn't aroused. I was hard as a rock, the head of my penis turning a deeper shade of pink now that it wasn't being cooled by the river water. It... didn't make sense but I couldn't ask him about it – nothing would kill the mood quicker than that.

And when I reached down to start stroking him to try and make him aroused, he only shifted away from my touch. He was making it as subtle as he could though; he wasn't batting me away like he used to do when he wasn't in the mood... he was being sneaky about it.

Was... something wrong with him?

Reaver was kissing my neck now, his hands all over me and in all the places I wanted them to be. Eager to feel more of him, I separated my legs and moaned when he started kissing lower and lower.

He got to my stomach, where he trailed his tongue along my navel, then down lower to my groin. I didn't have any pubic hair, save for a small spread of stubble from where it was starting to grow back. I told Reaver that it had fallen out from the radiation and the rest must've been burned from the fire, but in reality a lot of it was from me. On top of pulling my own hair out, I had been pulling it out from my groin too, tufts of it sometimes, from stress.

I gasped when I felt Reaver's tongue tease the slit of my dick and those past thoughts were vanquished. I looked down at him, one of my hands propping me up and the other stroking the nape of Reaver's neck, and watched the head disappear into his mouth.

"C-come and lay on your side," I said in between groans of pleasure. "I want to do you at the same time." I loved sixy-nineing with him; we'd done it for an entire hour once.

"Mm-Mm," Reaver said. He took the crown of my dick out of his mouth and ran a tongue up the shaft, then he pulled my foreskin all the way up and over the head, and over his tongue as well. I swore as he sucked on the loose skin and played with it with his tongue, I could see the outline of his tongue through the skin. "Close your eyes and just relax."

My teeth lightly clenched at this. I wanted to give him pleasure back. I wanted to taste his dick, to make him moan, make him feel good. Why wasn't he letting me reciprocate? I'd missed him too. What was –?

Another gasp, Reaver's tongue was travelling below my testicles. He tapped my foot as a signal and I held my legs back. My breathing started to become quicker, and when I felt him spread my cheeks apart, a moan of surprise and anticipation broke my lips.

His tongue started flicking my hole. I bit my lip as the pleasurable feeling started to take over and slay all of the worries and apprehensions in my head. If he was doing this to distract me then he knew what he was doing. Reaver had gone down on me like this before, but not often, and each time it drove me absolutely wild. He had yet let me do it to him but my mouth salivated at the thought.

I closed my eyes and put a bent arm over my face, the other one holding my leg back. I gave in to the feeling and let moan after moan roll from my mouth as Reaver licked and lapped my hole, occasionally spreading the area apart further to sneak a tongue inside of it. It always blew my mind how good this felt; how could it feel so fucking good? But it made me want more. I wanted him inside of me, with his body heaving against mine. I wanted the pain that quickly turned to pleasure, I wanted his moans and grunts in my ear… I wanted his cum.

But when my mouth moved to beg him to put it into me, I stopped. Though I ached for it, I literally ached to feel him inside of me, if something was preventing him from getting hard, whatever it was, I didn't want to put him on the spot. We would talk about it later, for now I didn't want to ruin our first intimate moment in months.

A sharp hiss escaped my clenched teeth when I felt his finger push inside of me. Then, as it eased itself in, his mouth was once again on my dick. He quickly got himself into a rhythm of sucking and stroking my shaft and moving the finger in and out of me, a rhythm that I knew would make me cum, and quickly. It was then I realized he wasn't going to make love to me on this beach, and that planted yet another seed of worry inside of my heart.

My own moans started coming closer and closer together. His mouth wasn't stopping and neither was that finger; it was like his mouth was gasoline with how much it was fuelling the inferno inside of me. It was blazing and raging, and at the same time, wrapping tight band after tight band around me, tensing and constricting until the eventual flooding and overwhelming relief.

And it was approaching... quickly. I found my hand grasping a handful of Reaver's hair as I moaned and cried in unison to his finger thrusts. In response to my pleasure, another finger pushed its way inside of me, the pain, reminding my body of how his cock felt entering me, triggering the beginnings of my orgasm.

"Third... third..." I cried, my mind temporarily blanking under the feeling. I was trying to tell him to put a third finger in. "More... put more in."

I cried out when I felt the third finger push inside of me. I pulled my leg back further and pushed my backside out. His mouth was like liquid bliss but it was what he was doing to me inside that was driving my orgasm. Fuck, I didn't want fingers... I wanted his cock. I needed his cock. Oh, fuck, why wasn't he pushing it inside of me? Automatically up to the hilt and fucking me without a moment for me to get used to it? Why wasn't he putting me on my hands and knees and riding me like I knew he wanted to, filling the riverside with the sounds of our skin smacking together and our pleasure-filled cries.

My fingers dug into Reaver's scalp. I took in a slow and shuddering breath, then shut my eyes, and let the orgasm take over me. Small moans fell unbidden from my lips as the pressure grew and grew, tightening my veins and locking them in place; my body freezing and going into an almost catatonic state as the orgasm gathered and grew from all of the energy around it.

It expanded... and multiplied, and in response my body tightened further and further...

And then the release.

With a gasping cry, the floodgates opened and I was overwhelmed to the point of drowning in this intense feeling. And with my eyes shut tight, my other senses painted their own pictures for me: Reaver's tongue eagerly lapping and collecting my cum, and his three fingers pushing themselves deep inside of me, so deep I felt his thumb press against my perineum. The mixture of all of these sensations left me almost delirious with pleasure. All I could do was keep my eyes closed and let the flood drown me alive, I would be its willing victim.

When the orgasm subsided and Reaver's tongue had collected the last bits of cum, I still found myself unable to move. I laid there, my mouth open and my chest heaving, and tried to collect myself after the intense climax.

Reaver laid down beside me and took me into his arms and kissed my wet cheek.

What about you though...? I wanted to ask what was wrong, but I couldn't.

I knew it was something though.

"I love you," I whispered to him through my heavy breathing, and I smiled when I felt his lips kiss my cheek again.

"I love you more," Reaver said back. I snorted when he pinched my nose playfully.

Well, at least he didn't seem upset... it would've been a lot worse if he was angry and frustrated. Maybe he was just tired?

There were a thousand explanations in my mind as to why our first time being intimate had gone the way it had, but none of them made sense when applied to Reaver. Reaver was complex and difficult to understand enough as it was, when applied to something like sex he was near impossible to read. I had realized that fact when I'd found out he was a chimera, because chimeras were sex-crazed for the most part, and thirsty for it... but my Reaver had always hated sex and intimacy, before me anyway.

I sighed and snuggled closer to him. If it happened again we would have a talk about it, but as of now... I think I'd pick my battles and, well, not borrow trouble.

I was here with him and safe, and that was good enough.

That night I found myself waking up. I opened my eyes to darkness but immediately I felt an icy snake slither down my spine and curl inside of my stomach. I realized, as I stared out into nothing, that something had woken me up. But what was it? If there was something outside or in the house, Reaver would've known long before I did.

My brow knitted and I slowed my breathing to try and catch what it was. I taxed my ears so hard static started to fill them.

Then I heard it... a groan.

No, not a groan – a strained cry.

I don't know which emotion hit me first: shock or fear. Because that sound was coming from Reaver.

Then another one, and the shifting of sheets. I squinted, and as my eyes adjusted to the night, I saw Reaver's pale face, his eyes shut tight, grabbing my pillow with a tight grip, and I watched him let out another cry through tightly-clenched teeth.

Oh, my god – Reaver... he was having a night terror, like I used to have.

But why?

In the muted silence I could feel my heart hammering against my chest, beating on my rib cage like it was trying to bust out to see what was wrong with the man it belonged to. And that cold snake slithering up and down my spine was multiplying, and those eggs of unease were hatching quickly. There was something about seeing my boyfriend in this vulnerable state that was absolutely horrifying. I had never seen my Reaver vulnerable like this, and I didn't understand why it was happening.

However, as I stared at him a new thought entered my head.

What if this was connected to what had happened with him earlier? Or more... what *hadn't* happened.

Reaver let out a grunt and twisted around, his face tight and scowling. When I was having night terrors my expression was that of pain and fear; his seemed like... naked anger for lack of a better word. He looked furious but also trapped. Even during what he'd see as a weak state, he didn't look weak... he just looked desperate and fearful.

What had happened to my baby when we had been separated?

The thought made my heart jump into my throat, and to my own surprise I didn't feel the tears come to my eyes, I didn't feel my heart break from empathy – I realized, and it was shocking to even feel it, that I was… I was angry.

My lower lip stiffened and so did my fists. As I stared down at my boyfriend, wave after wave of rage swept through me. We hadn't talked about what had happened to us while we were apart but I realized in that moment something had happened to my Reaver, and something bad.

I will kill whoever hurt him. I will murder whoever had damaged my boyfriend, immortal or not.

I lowered my hand and placed it on the side of Reaver's face. I stroked his cold, prickly skin and made soothing noises.

"G-get…"

I froze as Reaver attempted to speak. "Get…"

Slowly I retracted my hand but as I did Reaver's eyes snapped open.

"Fuck off, asshole!" Reaver screamed as he jerked his head away from me and started desperately trying to get away. He looked around, the whites of his eyes glowing in the darkness.

"Reaver. Baby… baby, it's me," I said to him quickly as he shifted away from me. But it was too late. Poor Reaver in his delirious state kicked himself backwards until he fell off of the bed right on his back. I saw him flip over and land on his stomach.

"Baby!" I cried. I jumped off of the bed as Reaver tried to scramble to his feet.

"Get the fuck away, Kiki. I'll fucking rip your fucking face open again!" Reaver snarled. He stumbled sideways, unable to keep his balance, and crashed into our dresser. He grabbed onto the side but ended up sliding down to the floor; his chest heaving and his eyes flickering around wildly.

Who was Kiki? The question burned in my mouth like fire but I swallowed it and kneeled down in front of Reaver. I put my hand on either side of his face and made him look at me.

"Reaver. It's Killian. Baby, it's okay. Wake up," I said to him gently. I was saying to him exactly what he would say to me when I was having a night terror. I couldn't believe I was the one doing this. "It's Killian. It's Killi Cat. See? Look at me."

Reaver's flickering black eyes finally focused on me. My heart broke when I saw intense relief on his face. Then he looked at his hands and held them up like he was searching for something.

"Killian?" Reaver said. He put his left hand to my face and felt it, like he was expecting me to be a hallucination. He felt my face for a moment, before he lightly put his hand against my heart.

"I'm right here," I said, letting him listen to my heartbeat. "Come back to bed."

I was so worried his senses would come to him and he'd get up and leave, making excuses that he had to go patrol or something, but... but he looked really out of it. I had never seen this happen to him before.

I stood up and Reaver let me help him stand. While I walked him back to the bed he looked around the room, half-asleep and in a daze, and his lower lip tightened. Then he got back into bed and I laid down beside him. Throwing caution to the wind, I put an arm around Reaver and drew him close to me.

I... I was the one holding him. Reaver was letting me hold him.

Another fresh wave of anxiety and dread claimed me as I kissed his forehead. Reaver's glassy and unfocused eyes were trying to take in the room, but I could tell he was falling back asleep. This was something so strange, so out of character; my hands started to tremble.

Something had happened to Reaver – something had rattled him and nothing rattles my baby.

I sniffed and shut my eyes tight, deciding in that moment I wouldn't cry over this, ever. Instead I searched myself and found the anger I had felt previously; I fostered it inside of my heart and fed it with my hatred for whoever had hurt this immortal god, the pillar of strength that was my boyfriend.

And as my mind wandered, it took me to my time with Perish; the last moments before he walked into that metal-plated room and closed the door as I cried.

Although it was a strange thing to think about now, I knew why my mind had taken me to that memory.

Because it wanted me to remember what Perish had told me; the strange instructions that he'd whispered in my ear.

I looked down at my boyfriend, his eyes closed and his face tense and stressed. My Reaper, my demigod, the strongest man I knew, who would move heaven and earth for me. Who had searched for me for hundreds of miles and had found me; who had taken care of me even though I was weak, and had never loved me less even though I didn't deserve a man like him.

Reaver had never judged me for being weak, and he had loved me all the same. And I would repay his patience and love by being the strong one when he was battling his own demons.

I wouldn't judge him for a second, and I wouldn't see him as less of a god for what he had shown me today. I would fight whatever demons he had and I would kill the person who had done this to him.

My teeth pressed together so hard inside of my mouth that they squeaked. And as I stared down at my sleeping boyfriend, I felt such an overwhelming amount of rage I had to remove my hand that was stroking his hair. I could only stare at him, my entire body shaking.

And I realized it wasn't really rage I was feeling – it was love. It was a love that was so intense I felt like setting the entire world on fire just to show everyone how much I loved this man. The realization I was feeling was jarring and frightening; I felt so protective of him I wanted to run out of here and kill the people who had hurt him.

Then I smiled.

Yes, I smiled.

I reached my hand down and once again petted Reaver's hair back, before giving it a gentle pat.

Because this vow, born from this intense and frighteningly powerful love I was feeling, would be one that I'd be able to keep. I would be able to kill the people who had done this to my Reaver, my Reaper, the black-eyed demon who held my heart.

Mortal or immortal.

'In about ten minutes it will all be over,' Perish's voice echoed inside of my head *'Now listen carefully, Killian... this is what you need to do after the light fades...'*

Because I held in my mind the knowledge that was mine and mine alone. A small but vital last instruction that Perish had whispered into my ear before the door of that chamber had closed on his tear-stained, yet smiling, face.

Yes.

I, Killian Massey...

... knew how to kill immortals.

CHAPTER 6

Sanguine

I SLOWLY STROKED BACK DRAKE'S BLOND CURLS AND beamed down at him when he gave me a sunny and cheerful grin. I always loved that boy's smile, and there wasn't a single chimera in our family that didn't feel a warmth come to their heart when Drake gave them a smile.

It was late afternoon, two days after I had sent Nero, Ceph, and Kiki off to the plaguelands. After coming upon the dilemma of how to get them there, I had been the one to fly them out into the radiation-flooded lands beyond our greywastes, and had returned in the early morning with everyone being none the wiser.

So here I was today, and though I was laying on the daybed of the sitting room with Drake's head on my lap, seemingly enjoying the warm sun beaming through the crystal clear windows, my mind was nothing but a thousand sores that kept bursting with every dark thought that entered my head. There was no clear window that I was looking through inside of my mind's eye, it was as grey as the greywastes and as infected as the plaguelands.

"Soon we'll be able to take the day bed out onto the patio," Drake said, his orange eyes shining and excited. "I love napping on the day bed outside."

"Mmhm," I said, wrapping a fragrant golden curl around my finger before giving his scalp a scratch. "We have many pictures of you sleeping on that bed outside. You look so adorable when you sleep, though not as adorable when you're dead." I tugged on the lock of hair I had been playing with. "You've been bad. You're almost sixty, why haven't you learned to eat slowly?"

Drake pouted at me and stuck out his lower lip. "I just wanted to show

Big Shot a good time. I really enjoy him, he has troubles with thinking like I do, and he doesn't get mad at me like the others sometime do." Drake shifted up until he was lying beside me and put an arm around my chest. "Like Master Silas, he's been so mean. When is he coming back though? I miss him. That's sad we weren't allowed to kill Reno, even after he said we might be able to, but I also like Reno. Reno has a nice dick."

I stifled down a laugh and let Drake snuggle into me. "Master Silas will be back soon…" My cheeks puffed as I let out a breath, and I stared out the window. Even the thought, the knowledge that I was going to have to get them soon, sent anxiety through my already sore stomach.

My sleep last night had been rough. Only when Drake had woken up and crawled into bed with me had I been able to go back to sleep, and only then because he had his arms around me and I didn't want to disturb him. It was too bad the cicaro wasn't able to keep my own mind from racing and travelling. There were so many little beehives inside of my mind, and the more I wandered around in my subconscious, the more of them I disturbed.

At least Nero and the other two were safe, and the concrete tomb of the mysterious man in place and his plucked out hair picked up. I had that going for me at least. I kept telling myself that over and over but it seemed like the equivalent to bailing out a single bucket of water on a ship rapidly sinking.

I sighed, and decided my own thoughts couldn't stay contained inside of my head. "I'm worried, Drake. Silas is going to be angry at me when he returns. I disobeyed him and I'm… in trouble."

Drake was quiet for a moment, when he spoke his voice was small. "I don't want him to punish you. I love you; I don't want you to go away."

His words pulled my heart but even still they further contaminated the open blisters in my brain. He brought a reality with his words that I think I had been trying to ignore – or at least remain in denial over.

"I don't want to go away either, lovely," I said to him. Then I sighed. "I might as well tell you since Silas will find out anyway. I freed Nero and I freed Ceph a couple nights ago. They're gone far away with Kiki and will stay far away until it's safe." I heard Drake gasp but I carried on. "I know it was wrong and I know Silas is going to torture me for it… but I couldn't leave him in there to rot. And it was time for Ceph to taste the outside air… it seems time for a lot of things actually."

"Y-you disobeyed King Silas?" Drake's voice suddenly rose. He pulled away from me and I looked to see pain in his eyes. "Why? You can't disobey him! He's..." Drake's face dissolved and he threw his arms back around me. "He's going to make you plead and cry, isn't he? He's going to hurt you and make you scream. I don't like hearing that. I don't like hearing that from you, just the others, but not you. You–" I shushed him and drew his head to my shoulder, the pull on my heart was now dragging me down it had become an anchor. I had to close my eyes for a moment to gather myself. I hated how much his fear triggered my own.

"I'm trying to think of something, little fox," I whispered to him. "Something to make him not hate me. If I could just... if he wasn't so miserable right now... this would be easier."

Drake sniffed; I could feel the wetness from his tears. Such a caring man our Drakey was. "What would make him happy?"

"Love," I whispered to him. I started tenderly stroking his hair again. "For him to find someone to love, like Nero found Ceph, like Elish found Jade, Garrett and Reno, Apollo and Jiro..."

"You and Jack?"

I ignored the jolt that his comment sent to my aching heart and nodded. "If I could find someone for him none of us would have to worry... and we could be happy. But unfortunately... I don't think he has anyone."

"Not even Reaver?"

I shook my head. "No, love. I don't believe Reaver will ever love Silas. Reaver has his own boy he loves and he will love him until the end of time. Reaver was looking for that boy when I saw him, and even if he doesn't find Killian I believe he will wait for him."

"Like Nero waited for Ceph?"

"That's right..." I said. "That's true love right there."

"I'll find someone for Silas to love," Drake said as he looked up from my neck. His face was red and his eyes were puffy from his tears. "I'll look all around Skyland and even Eros if I have to. I'll find someone who will love Silas and then he won't hurt you, and he won't hurt Nero."

Such a sweet little creature. I smiled at him and gently wiped the tears from his flushed cheeks. "I bet you will, little fox." Unfortunately it wasn't that easy. It would be grand if I could go out and find a cute boy for Silas to love, but the fact of the matter was that I was facing extreme consequences, for not only freeing Nero and Ceph... but that mysterious immortal as well.

I dearly wanted to know just who he was.

For a moment I was quiet, then an idea came to me. It may not help my predicament, but it could shed some light on that glaring mystery – and perhaps distract me from my maddening thoughts. "How would you like to invite Elliot over for a sleepover? And see if Luca and Juni want to come as well? Perhaps Lance and Todd too? You can have a fun night together while I do some work in Silas's bedroom." Or rather… Silas's laptop.

Drake's face lit up and radiated happiness and excitement. "Party with the sengils? I would love that! We can order food, dessert, and movies… we can have sex after. All of us! And I would be the leader, wouldn't I?" Drake grinned and started jumping up and down, and his hands began clapping together. "You're king… can I have drugs? Please!" Drake got down on his knees and clasped his hands together, begging me. Silly thing. "Please, please, please can I have some drugs!? Some ecstasy or some cocaine!? Oh please!"

I gave an annoyed grunt and shook my head, then I threw my hands up in the air in defeat. "Alright, as long as you promise not to disturb me when I'm in my room, or Silas's room. Promise? You can have all those things and all the sex you want but no matter how high you get or how great of an idea you think it is: you mustn't disturb me."

Drake nodded his head rapidly, and bounced himself into circles. "Promise! Okay, I'm going to go call them. I'll tell them the king demands they come over so then Artemis and Apollo can't say no! And since Master Elish is gone and Master Jack, Luca and Juni can definitely come too!" Then the cicaro ran off into the living room and picked up the phone that was resting on the wall.

I smiled thinly as I watched him go. It looked like I had a long night ahead of me then, and I would take advantage of this rare opportunity. Silas gaurded that laptop and he never let anyone on it. It held many secrets, and hopefully, it could provide me with some answers.

I wanted to know who we had freed, and perhaps just how much more trouble I was in.

The sounds outside of King Silas's bedroom were jovial and full of happiness. I could hear Drake's rapid voice and Todd's higher pitch tones, and every once in a while Elliot, Nero's sengil, butting in with a low quip followed by his unique laugh which sounded like a cross between a machine gun and a duck's honk.

All of the sengils were unique in their own way but every one of my brothers preferred a certain type. Elish's sengils were always blond, tall, and lanky which I suspected was because he wanted them to resemble Silas

– for obvious reasons. Nero's sengils were brute-like, slow but loyal like brute chimeras were; though the other two brutes: Ares and Siris, loved skinny sengils with high voices and those lisps they made gay men on movies and television shows have (which they mimicked because mimicking movies and TV shows was popular here). King Silas called them the *fabulous ones*.

I've only had one sengil, my beloved Valentine, though I had shared Juni with Jack before I became Silas's. Valen's ashes rested beside my oldest friend, a stuffed bear named Barry, on the dresser in my bedroom.

I looked back to King Silas's laptop and continued clicking around, the only light was Silas's ceramic lamp and the glow of the screen. I had been in this bedroom many times, and sometimes spent months sleeping beside Silas when he was in need of protective arms, though lately he had been sleeping alone in his stress and anger.

My heart kept jumping with every file that I looked through, every Excel grid I opened up and scrolled down. I had found a lot of interesting things but still nothing to allude to who was in those tombs.

Except Josu... I knew he was in there. Poor Josu had been in that concrete tomb for four years now. He was thirty years old, in the fifth generation, and a gifted scientist, beautiful as fuck too. He'd been placed in there after it had been found out that he'd made himself immortal without King Silas's permission. As we had seen with Ceph... that was an automatic condemnation to the concrete tomb. Only Silas got to decide who was worthy of receiving immortality and the scientists out of all of our chimera-types were the least likely to be made immortal because eventually they all pissed off Silas by not creating Sky's clone.

As far as I was aware of, I had no other brothers that I knew in those tombs. I had always wondered if Silas had made me forget since he had the remote control that controlled the implants to my brain but it looked like... that wasn't the case.

I sighed and kept searching. I wished I could invite one of Teaguae's sengils over, they were extremely tech-savvy and would be able to find anything I asked. Unfortunately they would go running back to Teag and Teag would undoubtedly sell me out to Silas. He could be quite the brown noser at times.

Finally after an hour of looking at chimera genetics, Excel grids, and even reading a few poems and short stories Silas had written when he was younger, I put his laptop away and went out to check on the boys.

Drake and the five sengils were sitting on the couch watching a movie. The lights above them were turned off but the electric fireplace was on and the TV, showing *Star Wars*, was glowing its light onto the walls. There was powder on the coffee table, open beers and many bowls of junk food around them. They were happy and joyous as they watched the television and did their drugs, it didn't look like any of them had a worry in the world.

… or I thought so. As I stepped into the living room I got smiles, all except for Juni, Jack's sengil and an old friend of mine. We had a lot of history between us, me and him. He had been a victim of a depraved, pedophile greywaster, the same man who had kept me prisoner for eleven years.

Juni was giving me a bitter look. And when everyone was saying their hellos, his was as crisp as a fall day and with an obvious edge.

"Where's Jack?" Juni suddenly asked, his voice a dark horse that was barreling right through what had seemed to be a content and relaxed evening.

"I said to be quiet about that," Drake said annoyed. "He asked not to be bugged."

Juni rose to his feet and I saw his dark eyes flash. Even though Juni was a sengil, and an adopted member of this family, he still had bite. Unfortunately for him though I bit back, and I definitely would not be taking shit from a sengil; even if I was one too.

"Can we talk privately," Juni said in a low tone.

I looked at him and then back to the others. Everyone was staring at us.

"Make it quick," I said with a short nod. Though this conversation wouldn't be happening in this apartment or any of our rooms. Silas had cameras everywhere and he moved them around regularly to keep the other chimeras from pinpointing where they are.

So I grabbed Juni's arm and took him out into the hallway. I dismissed the thiens guarding our doors and let them go for the rest of the evening. They wouldn't be needed here, not with me and Drake, no one would touch us.

Juni closed the door behind him, and I saw the concern and also unease that was on his face. "They went off to check out a radiation spike in the plaguelands and they haven't returned home in two days," Juni said in a hushed voice. "Why is this not a bigger issue? Why are you throwing parties right now and not looking for them? Where is he?" Juni looked to the closed door and then around the hallway, I could see the recessed lighting reflect in his dark eyes so filled with apprehension.

"Matters of chimeras are not matters of yours, Juni," I said to him casually. I crossed my arms over my chest and made a point to look down my nose at him. He was only several inches shorter than I was, he was one of the tallest sengils we had, though his thin body made him appear smaller than he was.

"Matters of my master are matters of mine," Juni said, his tone just dipping itself into what I would deem disrespectful and dangerous. "Jack wouldn't leave Black Tower for that long, and even more severe: Master Elish wouldn't leave Jade for this long. You know that as much as I do, and I suspect that isn't all that you know. So where is that Falconer and what are you hiding?"

He was challenging me.

How cute.

In a flash my hand grasped the collar of Juni's shirt. I twisted the fabric in my hand and watched his peachy skin go white as my grip constricted it. I narrowed my eyes and glared at this disrespectful little slave, and slowly shook my head back and forth.

Then I said to him in a gravelled whisper, "Matters of chimeras... are not the matters of slaves, little one." Juni stared back at me but I could see the nervous tremble on his lip. "You seem to have forgotten... so why don't we say it together: Matters of chimeras..."

Juni's trembling lip disappeared underneath the upper one. He stared back at me, the two of us so close together I could see my own reflection in his brown eyes.

"... matters of chimeras...?" I repeated. I smiled and saw the sengil become smaller under my squinting gaze.

"What did you do, Sanguine?" Juni whispered. "Where is Master Jack? Where is the king? Where—"

I gave the fabric in my hand a hard twist. Juni gasped and raised his hand up to grab mine, but I snatched it and held his wrist before he got the chance.

Then I started to raise him up off of the ground.

I tsked at him. "Matters of...?"

Juni grunted as he tried to catch breath, his eyes were starting to bulge.

"C-chimeras..." Juni gasped. "A-are not the matters of... of slaves."

I dropped him onto the ground. "There we go," I said. Juni stumbled back before crashing into an oak side table that held a vase of violets. The vase smashed beside him, surrounding the sengil in shards of porcelain, water, and the purple flowers. "Now clean that up and you can continue your evening."

"Sanguine…" Juni called back angrily. "Where the fuck are they? What the hell did you do!?"

I turned around, my hand on the door knob. "He will be home eventually, old friend." I turned it and walked inside, and was once again greeted with warm smiles.

And I returned the smile when I saw Drake giving me a sheepish grin, the reason why was explained in the movement below him. Todd, Artemis and Apollo's sengil, was giving him oral, the chestnut-haired sengil's pink tongue swirling around Drake's well-endowed penis and another hand was rubbing his testicles.

"Clean up after, Drakey," I said. "Not a drop on the couch you know how much Master Silas hates those stains."

"Can we go out later and find ourselves a prey?" Drake asked, his hand on Todd's head stroking back his hair. "We never get this free time from our masters. I want them to pretend they're chimeras for a night, just one night!"

A bunch of sengils hunting down a boy to rape? I sighed and rolled my eyes. "Luca cannot, Elish would murder me and he's already going to be cross enough as it is. Juni stays as well, but you can go out with Todd, Elliot, and Lance. Just do not get them killed, Drakonius, and I want I.D's checked and ages verified and no one that isn't coming out of one of the chimera bars." I had come a long way since my youth. I used to be horrified of things like this happening, especially after my own past. But I understood my family and it would make me happy to see the sengils go out and enjoy themselves.

Luca, to my amusement, looked relieved that I was making him stay behind. I think he himself feared what Elish would do to him if he found out he'd been out hunting with Drake. Anyway, I was suspecting that he and Juni's trysts were getting serious, and perhaps they wanted to remain as exclusive as two sengils could.

I turned around as Juni stalked inside of the apartment, his shoulders tense and his head hung low. He grabbed a handheld vacuum from the closet and shot me a poisoned glare as he stomped out to the hallway. When the sengils and Drake were gone I was going to fuck him until he bled, just to knock the snotty little shit down a few pegs. I wasn't liking this attitude of his at all.

I left the sengils and Drake to have their fun, and went to Silas's office which was several floors down. I had been in this office a thousand times and had memorized the locations to everything but not what was inside of the files in said locations.

Silas's office took up almost the entire floor, there was only a small waiting room in the front and a secretary's desk which was now empty. The office itself was impressive since the king needed to keep up appearances. Below me were polished marble floors of unique black with grey swirls, and around me, white columns that twisted to a ceiling that held designs of white and gold. The walls were wainscoting with the tops painted maroon, and the lower halves, black with golden patterns. There were paintings on the walls and statues that had been made beautiful again by Jack's unique touch, and also sculptures and whatever else that was unique and rare. It was quite the room, and indeed fit for a king.

I walked to Silas's wooden desk and ran a finger over the polish. I looked at the vast cityscape in front of me and smiled at my own reflection, then opened up the desk drawers and casually thumbed through several papers.

My eyes turned up when I heard a creak from one of the double doors. I slowly closed the desk drawer and walked to the middle of the room.

Standing in front of the door was…

I took a step closer.

Juni and Luca?

"Where are our masters, Sanguine," Juni said. The sengil looked angry and anger suited his dark features like a custom suit, even when he was small he could out-scowl the best of them.

I smiled at Juni and put my hands behind my back. I was partially amused to see Luca showing the same anger on his face. Luca never showed emotion, the meek little sengil was growing a pair of testicles, was he? Juni seemed to be a bad influence, I may have to speak to Elish about what I was seeing.

"Oh, Juni. Did you forget our little talk already?" I said in a singy voice. I smiled and started gliding towards the two of them. They were standing side by side like two puffed up kittens in front of a cougar. It was so amusing… and oh so cute.

Especially the moment the cougar takes their tender little bodies in between his teeth and rips them to adorable little shreds.

"I'm going to ask you one more time," Juni said darkly. "Where are they?"

I opened my mouth to give them one last singing warning, when Juni pulled a remote out from inside his black vest.

My remote.

I stopped in my tracks. And when Juni's dark eyes flickered up to meet mine, he smiled.

Juni smiled.

That fucking kid never smiled.

"Juni…" I said slowly; the song in my voice gone like the light atmosphere I'd been trying to cultivate during this tense interaction, all that remained was a tone thick with warning. "You do not know what will happen if you turn that on. He can't be controlled. He… he can't be–"

When I saw Juni's thumb raise to press the button on the remote, I screamed and lunged at him.

And in mid-air – he came.

Daisy, Daisy… give me your heart to do…

I shut my eyes tight and let out a heartbreaking scream. Still flying through the air, I grabbed my head and clenched my fingers around it, then fell to the floor with a heavy impact, one that shot bright lights and dizzying stars into my vision.

I heard Crow laugh, his dark and dry laugh getting into every fold, every tightly compressed crevice in my brain. It coated it like black oil, blocking out everything that made me Sanguine and instead forcing my submission to the man who had been my best friend since I'd met him as a bear-eared boy named Barry.

Another scream rang out and I heard it bounce around the room. My hands were still grabbing my hair and I could hear the high-pitched twang as I tore out the strands. I tried, oh fuck knows I tried, to push him away to re-take my mind, but with the implant inside of my brain now shut off I knew I was at his mercy – and the entire world was at his mercy too.

Oh, Sami, I heard Crow whisper into my ear. I growled and screamed at him to get the fuck away from me, but all that greeted me was a low and gravelly laugh.

You know it's pointless, he chuckled. And with an easy push, he shoved me away from my own mind and took control himself.

"Get away from him, he's waking up!" Juni yelled. I saw him push Luca out of the way, the boy had been kneeling over me, consoling me.

I jumped to my feet and observed the two sengils looking at me with twin wary looks. They both took two steps back. Luca had a gun in his hand, Elish's gun.

"Where in the plaguelands are they heading?" Juni said, glaring at me. He had a hand out to protect Luca, his eyes were blazing. He was such an adorable little thing, he thinks he's so tough but the only thing tough on him would be his meat.

I smirked and held out my hand. "Give me my remote," I said.

Juni paused before with a nod he put it in my hand.

"They're sixty miles east from Melchai," I said to them, tucking the remote into my own vest pocket. "Follow the white flames. Where they are now, I do not know, but that is where you'll start." I walked past them with a whistle on my lips. I had great plans for what I would be doing now. I had been dormant for far too long and there were so many fun things I'd been missing.

Then I heard a gunshot. The force of it knocked me forwards and I landed on my face. With a snarl I jumped up and quickly turned around.

Luca was looking at me with an expression of terror; the gun was in his hand and the smell of the gunpowder heavy in the air.

I ran towards him with a manic laugh and lunged at the little creature. I didn't even notice the shadow of black to my right before it was too late.

Juni knocked me over the head with something and once again I fell to the ground. I gasped and swore and held a hand to my head. I tried to force my body to get up but the impact had paralyzed me.

You little fucker… you little fucking bitch…

I squinted my eyes and tried to make my mouth move, but a dizzy heat swept me and I fell back onto the floor.

"You will pay for this little stunt, Juni," I snarled, finally able to find my words. I looked down and could see crimson raindrops making friends with the marble floor. "Count the days of freedom on your hand, little black bird."

"Sorry, Crow. I, above all of them, know how dangerous you can be. And I know Sanguine won't let us take the Falconer to find them."

I opened my mouth to say more when I felt a second impact on my head, this flooding my mind with flashes of images and audible hallucinations, before the finishing blow pushed me into the white flames.

CHAPTER 7

Elish

HOW DID I LET IT COME TO THIS? WHERE DID I GO wrong? I never used to error in so many ways.

Or perhaps I am viewing my past with rose-coloured glasses. For when I touch upon my past, before this, before Jade, before I realized I had created a born immortal – I see many errors and many things I should have done differently. But every time I made a mistake, I learned and grew from it, and never again did I make that same mistake.

So how do I grow and learn from this?

Elish tipped the bottle of dingy brown water as it was pressed to his lips and grimaced under the taste. He felt like vomiting every time he was forced to drink this water; not only was it irradiated, he also knew it was crawling with parasites. He would need blood tests when he came back to Skyfall to see if he had caught any diseases. Or maybe it would just be easier to kill himself and let the white flames take care of it.

The bottle lowered from his lips and he put it back into the knapsack he had in his hand, then slung the old green bag behind his back. If there was one silver lining to being so far northwest in the greywastes, it was that the scavenging was good. He had canned food and rice in his bag, and he had even lucked out and found a bottle of hot sauce and soy sauce. Though he had never asked Reaver, he was sure both of those condiments were worth their weight in gold in the greywastes. He could never eat rice without soy sauce and had even got Jade addicted to the stuff. The two of them went through a bottle of it a month and Luca knew to always keep some in stock. It was actually the family's love for the stuff that encouraged Apollo to create Dek'ko's own brand.

Elish looked to his side and carefully analyzed several houses that were off in the distance. This had once been a residential street, but almost all of the houses had been reduced to charred support beams from some fire long ago. They all looked like broken skeletons now, even more so with the intact houses in the distance. It was like the broken houses were lingering in limbo, forced to gaze upon their living comrades to be reminded of what they used to be.

And now they were nothing but useless ruins, though in all reality the houses with their intact roofs and four walls were just as doomed and just as dead; appearances were deceiving and never again would these buildings be brought to their former glory. Everything built before the Fallocaust was dead, the radiation just kept nature from consuming their corpses.

Much like King Silas, Elish said to himself darkly, but he sighed internally. *Now stop with your head in the clouds, you have things you must figure out. You have to have a plan when you come back to Skyfall. You must know what you're going to do once you're home. Your garden is in shambles, your strings in a snare, and your seeds dying... you must fix this.*

I will. I will.

Was it worth it? Reno's agonized voice rang inside of Elish's head.

And for a moment Elish closed his eyes and took in a deep inhale of warm greywaste air, then he opened them and continued walking towards Kessler's ground zero.

That night he made camp in a townhouse that was in a cluster of over thirty of them. They had been scavenged before but whoever had been here had left years ago. They had left behind an old barbeque grate leaning up against the exterior wall however, and a lighter, but the lighter's wheel was rusted. Elish didn't need lighters thanks to his own thermal abilities, but he pocketed it all the same. It still had fuel in it and he could make a poor man's stove if desperation called for it. Reaver had shown him how to make it with nothing but a soda can, a knife, and some tape.

That boy had taught me a lot, Elish said to himself. He was laying on a mattress he had covered with several musty blankets found in a closet, the cleanest one he had draped over himself. He had his green knapsack beside him and his handgun on top of it. Reaver had also taught him to break a window or light bulbs inside of a pillow case and then spread the shards on the stairs or in front of the window. It was a way to alert you if someone was trying to get the jump on you.

Elish closed his eyes and carefully went over everything the boy had taught him and filed it in its necessary locations inside of his mind. He had always thought of his own brain as being a large tower filled with rooms that held different files and he enjoyed going over each one when he had the spare time to refresh himself on the knowledge.

Though as quickly as he'd decided to touch upon his knowledge, he found himself recoiling from the memory of Reaver. It brought up an uncomfortable feeling in his stomach, so he decided to steer away from it in favour of other thoughts.

And as was his default comforting thought, he brought up the face of his cicaro, but the same feeling trailed behind him as well. Elish once again banished their faces from his mind, and refused to admit to himself it was rather his heart that was filling him with the discomfort.

Elish fell into a troubled sleep after that, his ears always open and his hand only inches away from his handgun.

"Tonight was nice," the boy whispered to me on a night almost a year ago. We were lying in bed together, naked and with the light grey top sheet a scrunched pile at our feet and the comforter on the floor forgotten. "This was the best birthday I've ever had."

I was laying on my side, my head propped up by my hand and my elbow resting on the pillow. The boy was staring at me with an expression that always made me stare back just a fraction longer than I would deem okay for myself. It was a look of devotion, of intense love and worship. This look on his face only intensified after I had made love to him. But only after making love, never after our intense marathons of sex, or our trysts of fervid and violent fucking. It was when I held that boy's quivering body against mine and drank in every moan, every shuddered gasp. It was when I let him hear my own vocalizations of pleasure; something I know he treasured.

The corner of my lips rose. I reached a hand out and brushed back a lock of his hair, as black as the depths of the universe, and tucked it behind his ears, small ears with a slight point to them, and three hooped earrings in each with different coloured gems.

One purple, one white, one black.

"Next you will be asking me to move your real birthday to this day," I said to him with a smirk. Since his actual birthday, when he had turned seventeen, had been quite the chaotic disaster, I had promised him a birthday to make up for it, any day he chose. Once our lives had calmed down, a month after Silas's game had come to an end and we had been married, he had requested for me to plan a day for him.

It had taken another month but I had decided my cicaro had been through enough and deserved a special day. So I had done what he would deem out of character, and I had cleared my schedule for him. I had taken the day off and had brought him to the Dead Islands to see Joaquin's brand-new leopard cubs and his other felines and exotic animals. Then we had gone for a pleasant walk on the beach which ended with a dinner laid out by Joaquin's partner, and Jade's friend, Jem. I had outdone myself, and had made Joaquin and Jem swear on their lives they would tell no one I had done this for Jade.

The boy had been worshipping me with his eyes the entire time, and never had I received so many kisses and smiles from him. On our way back to the plane he had slipped his hand into mine, and since this area of the island was deserted, I had let us walk hand in hand. However, once the animal sanctuary came into view and the thien guards could be seen, I had removed my hand from his and he was smart enough not to voice complaint.

When we got back to the apartment, Luca dismissed for the evening, we had both showered separately and I had come into my bedroom to him waiting for me on the bed. He was wearing nothing but a pair of leather briefs that hugged his hips tightly, and showed off the v-shaped curve that framed a faint trail of short black strands that ran from his navel down. I removed those from him quickly and made love to him for the next four hours.

And now the long day had ended with us here. The boy gazing up at me, and me gently tracing my fingers along his jawline, then slowly trailing to his lips which I caressed.

His yellow eyes stared into mine. "I love you."

Elish opened his eyes to the cold and empty bedroom of the townhouse. He looked around to see that everything was the tone of slate from the grey sun that rose up over the horizon. There was no colour here. The only colour in his existence now was from his cicaro's bright and mischievous eyes, and they were now faded as reality chased away his vivid daydream.

He sighed, and when he inhaled, the smell of musty blankets and sour wood greeted him.

No smell of mint and spice from my cicaro, or the hot muggy aroma of the shower if he had woken before me.

Just the smell of decades old death and a house slowly decaying.

Elish got up and tightly folded the blanket he had been using, then secured it with a telephone cord and tied it to the knapsack. Then he walked down the waning and bowing stairs, his boots crunching against the shards of window from an alarm system that, in the end, wasn't needed, then exited the townhouse.

He walked to the street, identical houses in almost identical states of decay all around him in what looked like a horseshoe shape, and started heading in the direction he knew would lead him to the highway. He passed a park with a playground several feet from a fallen chain-link fence, the green grass a memory but the yellow greywastes grass sprouting in random patches, then reached a long stretch of industrial buildings. But all on this particular road were collapsed and just heaping piles of debris and ash.

While he walked through this dull grey world, the eyes inside of his mind had him walking along his garden. A garden that had once been a sight of intense beauty, even if it was but an image drawn up from his own imagination.

It was a vast stretch of emerald green surrounded by a white fence that glistened with new paint. On top of this trimmed grass were raised beds made of untreated cedar, that held in their rectangular frames, black soil. Inside of this soil were little shoots of green and small flowers of various species, some extinct, some not.

Elish would walk along this garden during his quiet moments, or when he wished to bring calm and tranquility to a situation that caused him stress. And as he walked, he would think of each mental seed he had planted and dwell on them.

How old was Reaver now? How was his training going? When was Lycos supposed to call again? Once these questions were answered he would move onto his next seed and go over whatever list he had for that one. Every brother had his own raised bed and his own colour code, and on Elish's encrypted laptop, they had their own code names as well.

Before all of this happened, before I had found out that King Silas had been in Aras for the last few months, I had been working on bringing Grant to my side. Jade had read his aura and had confirmed what I had already known: that it was Theo, a younger brother he was obsessed with, who was the key to him aligning with me. Jade and I had been discussing using Sanguine to manipulate Theo, and how we could do it. I had found myself enjoying discussing this with Jade. Never had I had someone I trusted enough to disclose all of this information, let alone lay in bed at night and plot with him.

Elish's jaw locked as his mind brought up the last image he had of his cicaro conscious. The powerful creature standing crooked with blood running down his head, face, and neck. His yellow eyes turning black as he exercised a mental power that only he and Silas had. Then Kessler and his legionaries dropped to the ground, dead. Not only could Jade end their lives without touching them, he had the power to avoid killing his friends and husband.

Then he saw the boy lying in the white hospital bed, wires and tubes going in and out of him, all connected to beeping and humming machines that were all that was sustaining his life. He remembered when Lyle had told him that his brain activity was greatly diminished.

"Will he be able to walk? Talk?"

"Master Elish… we'll be lucky if he can even raise his head."

A jolt of pain ripped up Elish's mouth and he realized he had bitten a small chunk of his tongue. He spat the chunk on the ground, and with a deep breath, he went back to his garden. There would be no mental admission to the reality but his mind quickly re-checking what seeds remained was a window itself into what those memories had done to him.

I will check the hard drives, and I will comb through everything on there. Perish may have been a man of many odd quirks but he was obsessive when it came to logging and documenting all of his work, stemming from before I was even born. Those hard drives are the most valuable things in the world right now and, thankfully, I have them in my possession. None of this will be in vain, all will be fixed.

The day passed quickly with only the thoughts inside of Elish's head to keep him company. A lot of seeds were looked over and tended to in that time though his mind was always travelling back to the ruins of his previous plans. Reaver's seeds, Killian's seeds, the hope of finding out just how to kill an immortal. Which had been the only reason why he had sent Reaver and his small group into the greywastes.

The secret died with Perish. Elish wondered to himself just how long Perish had known. Or how long Sky had known rather. For all Elish knew he'd known in Kreig and all of this was just Sky's O.L.S telling Perish to go to the lab to kill himself.

Elish didn't know. Every person who would be able to fill him in on what happened... was dead or burning.

What now? How will I kill King Silas once and for all? Did Silas see Perish do it? Will he know when he wakes? If he does, it is foolish to think he will ever tell me? Most likely he himself will use it to kill the immortals who are alive against his will.

Elish reached into his pocket and pulled out a stale pack of cigarettes he had found. He lit one and absentmindedly found himself rubbing his upper left forearm. He had Jade's old collar wrapped around his arm and now his arm felt odd without the leather band.

And what of you, cicaro? What are my plans for you...?

You're only eighteen years old. You're my husband but still just a boy.

Suddenly Elish found himself turning around. He had heard a noise inside of one of the buildings he was passing. It sounded like something dropping, a clang of silverware on a kitchen floor, or perhaps dropped on a plate.

Elish's eyes scanned the building carefully. He was walking up a small hill, in the middle of a double-lane road with two faded yellow stripes splitting the lanes. On one side of him was a concrete barrier with a drooping chain-link fence, and to his left where the noise was, was a house and behind it a parking lot for several attached shops.

The noise was coming from that house... an attached single-storey house with a Remax sign in the front. It was a light grey with the wooden siding puffed out and swollen. Elish could see insulation inside of it too; a washed-out pink that was visible through the siding like cotton trying to escape from a torn jacket.

His eyes fixed on each of the broken windows, plastic hanging down in shreds which told him this place had been occupied at some point after the Fallocaust. It seemed to be empty, perhaps it was just a radrat.

Elish continued on, his ears now strained and on the alert for anyone else who may be occupying this road he was walking on. It looked like he was walking into a small highway-side town. The buildings were not close together though, so besides the increase in roads and black trees, this place was no different than the other areas he had been walking through.

Or was it…

Elish turned around again, his eyes narrowing. There was that noise again and this time there would be no ignoring it.

"I can hear you," Elish said in a casual manner and he continued to walk. "I would advise you to make yourself known or stop causing that racket. I am on a grueling schedule and have no time for greywaster games."

Then a great roar sounded from behind him, the sound of an engine motor being started and given too much throttle. Elish turned back around and saw a plume of ashy dust fly up from behind the Remax house he had passed, and the sound of sheet metal crashing to the ground. Another sound followed suit soon after, then a third. And in a matter of moments, Elish could see three dirt bikes coming barreling towards him in three different directions, kicking up clouds of ash in their wake. There was one behind him, one coming from the second noise he had heard, which was another stand-alone house, and the third half a block down.

When they approached and were close enough to be identified, Elish could see each dirt bike was carrying identically dressed riders. They wore greasy hats on their heads and biker goggles on their faces; they rode with open, grinning mouths and hooted and hollered so loudly the noise carried over the high octave motor.

Elish stood in the middle of the road as the three circled him on their bikes, laughing and making an annoying racket that grated against Elish's ears like nails scraping a chalkboard. There was no part of him that felt like humouring these three idiots or their obvious and pathetic attempts to strike fear into his heart.

So as they circled, kicking up an ungodly amount of grey ash that irritated his throat and eyes, Elish crossed his arms over his grey overcoat and watched, looking unimpressed and rather bored.

The three stopped, and revved their engines with fingerless gloves, their fingers so blackened and filthy the gloves were almost invisible. The smell as well was horrendous and made Elish's nose curl. And when their scabby lips peeled back to laugh and taunt through sneers, he could see their teeth matched the colour of their grimy hands; what few remained inside of their diseased mouths.

"What you doin' all alone, mah friend?" one of them shouted. He had a rusted assault rifle on his back and several nicked and tarnished knives on a belt of cracked leather. They were all wearing many layers of greasy clothing, all with holes to show what shade of brown or grey the next layer was.

"Hey, look," another one exclaimed. His eyes widened and Elish almost found himself mouthing what he knew he was going to say next.

He has purple eyes.

"He got funky eyes!"

Close enough.

Elish sighed and reached into his pocket. As he did there was the sound of shifting as the three struggled to get their own guns, but Elish was faster.

He took out the handgun and shot the first one right between the eyes, the filthy and pungent greywaster falling to the ground in a heap. Then he pointed the gun to the second just as he himself was raising his assault rifle, and pulled the trigger.

But as that one's head snapped back, and the sound of gunfire broke the cooled greywaste air, Elish himself felt a hard impact on his chest. He turned to shoot the third one, but as he made eye contact with the shocked and surprised man, he saw sparks and smoke erupt from the barrel of his assault rifle, followed by more hard blows to his chest and stomach. Elish didn't care though, bullet wounds healed quickly and the several hours he would waste resurrecting would be made up when he stole one of these fools' dirt bikes.

The third screamed and stumbled back as Elish shot him in the cheek, and again in the neck as he fell backwards. He still had his finger on the assault rifle as he lost his balance though, but besides feeling their sharp wind against his cheek, no more bullets hit him.

Annoyance quickly consumed any pain Elish was feeling in that moment. He looked down at the three dead greywasters but his attention was drawn to his blood-soaked shirt and overcoat. He had several bullet holes in his chest and stomach, and blood was trickling down each one and falling soundlessly onto the grey ground like rain.

Elish managed to put his handgun back into his overcoat pocket, and he turned around. His vision started to become blurry, but he focused his energy and stumbled towards a house with a partially ajar door. He would be dying inside of it.

"You fucking bastard!"

Elish turned around and saw two women running towards him, a younger one and an adult. The two sprinted with tears streaming down their faces, and further past, he saw another man and a small boy.

"That was my daddy!" the little girl screamed. Elish winced at the sound, little girls had the worst voices. "You bastard."

Elish gritted his teeth and leaned against the railing of the house. He reached into his pocket again and grabbed the handgun.

"Your foolish *daddy*... tried to kill me," Elish said through laboured gasps, though his mind was racing. He was going to die soon and he needed to die in peace. Greywasters let no meat go to waste and he stood to a real danger of being consumed. If that happened it could be half a year before his eaten body could fully have a chance to heal.

"What the fuck did you expect!" the little girl with brown hair in a ponytail pushed his side with small hands. "You came to our town! You shithead!" She let out a wail and smacked one of the bullet wounds on his side. "I'm glad you're dying."

"Chelsea, get away from him!" the woman screamed, obviously seeing the handgun. Elish managed to turn around, his vision getting distorted.

"Let me die in peace," Elish managed to gasp. He fell to his knees and spat out the blood that was collecting in his mouth. "Legion... are there legion here?"

"Why should I help you? You just killed my brother!" the woman shouted, holding the noisy brat far away from him.

"I am a prince from Skyfall." Elish turned around and pointed to his eyes. Her own widened. "If you can get me to a legionary – they will pay you for me. I will make you rich."

The gun slipped from his hand and landed with a *thunk* onto the ground; Elish clutched his chest and stifled a groan. "Get me a legionary."

"Fuck you!" the girl sobbed.

I really hate screaming little girls.

Elish could hear more voices around him. He looked up to see that the woman and the little girl were surrounded by more people. It seemed to be a family or a small community living together here. At least six of them, all greasy and dirty and with the same look to them. They were probably inbred, which would explain the moronic attitudes of the three he had just killed.

"He has purple eyes... he might be telling the truth," the woman said to another one. "The last time I was in Mantis there were legionaries over there."

Mantis... how far away is that? Elish felt a flicker of hope but the blood dripping from his wounds extinguished it.

"He just fucking killed Bobby!" an old man protested. "Why are we helping a man who just killed—"

"Because he could be more valuable to us than just food!" another voice said. Elish felt a hand on his shoulder and another one wrench him to his feet. "He's our prisoner now, and if he dies we have dinner for the next week. Come on... let's get him inside."

Elish wrenched his shoulder away as the man tried to pull him to standing. He steadied himself with two hands on the porch and took in a sharp but gurgling breath. He was dying and he knew it. The fact that he was about to die, surrounded by half-starved greywasters, was filling him with feelings he had been pushing down since Kiki abandoned them with the Falconer.

Anxiety, desperation... fear.

They were feelings that had once been banned from being felt by the cold chimera. A man who had tempered his emotions, and had smoothed out almost all the imperfections he had seen in himself. Elish Dekker was well-known for being cruel, for being emotionless and uncaring for the needs of others. He went through life like a god on a pedestal, peering down at his subjects with disinterest as he ordered them around with a mere wave of his hand.

Where did that man go? Who was this person with short blond hair, filthy clothing, and fatal wounds about to allow himself to be imprisoned by parasitic greywasters not worth soiling his gaze? How had he let this happen and why was he continuing to let it happen? He was a god; he was better than every man breathing in this world today.

Stop this weakness, Elish Dekker. Stop this desperation. You have already set fire to half of your garden stop setting fire to yourself.

"Come on, asshole. You're our fucking prisoner, if you want to live... get up and walk."

No.

I will not delay returning to Skyfall. I will not wait for these idiots to travel miles and miles to Mantis to find me a legionary who won't even have a remote phone. I will deal with no subhumans not worthy of gazing upon my face. I will do what must be done to ensure I am beside my husband as quickly as possible, and to hell with whoever stands in my way.

I may have taught the Reaper.

But the Reaper taught me as well.

Elish snatched the fallen handgun and whirled around. He pointed the silver gun to the little girl and shot her in the neck. She let out a sharp but short cry, before stumbling backwards onto the ground; a fountain of blood squirting up into the air and falling like crimson rain to the already red ground below.

As predicted, the others screamed and ran to her. Any other one Elish injured would call for guns and knives and attention towards killing him, but not the little girl. They would go to her.

Elish shot the man in the back of the head and threw the now empty gun at the woman kneeling over the dying girl. She cried out just as Elish raised a clenched fist and punched her with as much force as he could muster in the back of the head. The woman fell forward and Elish raised his boot and slammed it hard against her skull, twice.

He looked around and spotted the boy who had been standing underneath the awning of building. When they made eye contact he turned and ran into the house. Elish quickly scanned the area and focused his hearing, but all he could hear was the boy's little feet running up the stairs. He listened until he heard a bedroom door slam, followed by a closet. The young one was not running for help, he was hiding. It seemed like there was no one else in this small community.

Elish walked to the area where all of this had originally happened, where three dead male greywasters lay beside their dirt bikes. Elish analyzed each one and decided on a bike with chipped red paint. Then he put on one of the dead greywaster's assault rifles and harvested the clips and ammo from the other two… then went to find the boy.

He made no attempt to mask his movements as he walked up the stairs, and when he opened the bedroom door, he even tapped the barrel of the assault rifle against the ground.

"If you wish for me to let you live, you will come out of that room and tell me where the gas cans are being kept," Elish said curtly.

There was silence but the boy's heartbeat was racing and Elish could hear short gasps as he struggled to get breath into his tight chest.

"I don't suggest you dawdle," Elish said loudly. "I am pressed for time and have no patience for little greywaster boys. Come out now and show me where the fuel is being kept. If I had an intention of killing you,

I'd be littering the closet door with bullets."

Just as Elish's patience was wearing thin, he heard movement and the door open. A boy perhaps seven or eight pushed the door open and stepped out. He was huddled in on himself and trembling as he stared down at the ground.

"Where are the gas cans being kept?" Elish asked again. He stepped away from the door and motioned for the boy to go first. "Show me where they are."

The boy started walking towards the exit to the bedroom, and when he had to walk past Elish, his pace quickened. Elish followed him down the stairs and outside.

When the boy saw the massacre in full view in the middle of the street, his face twisted and he looked away. He let out a sob and started stumbling down the street towards what looked like a garage to a now crumbled home.

The boy pointed to it, and wiped his snotty nose with his sleeve. Elish walked past him and stood in front of the metal door. He looked it from top to bottom and grabbed onto a blue rope tied to a metal handle and, with an assaultingly loud sound of screeching rusted metal, he pulled the garage door up.

Elish let out a breath of relief when he saw a full jug of fuel. He wished for more but it would do. He had no way of carrying more than that anyway. So he went inside and grabbed the can and turned around to exit the garage.

And in his stealth the little boy had managed to grab a gun.

"Put that away," Elish said bitterly. "I have no time for–"

The boy fired it at Elish, the sound deafening inside of the garage. It missed Elish but by only inches.

Though what it ended up hitting was much worse.

The explosion knocked Elish off of his feet and for a moment his mind escaped him. He didn't know what the bullet had hit, all he knew was that it was combustible.

Elish's teeth clenched and he forced his senses back into him. He opened his eyes and saw that his overcoat was on fire, and there was liquid around him consumed in flames as well.

He got to his feet with the gas can and looked behind him. The entire north wall was on fire and everything that had been hung up on it, from coils of ropes, to tools, and oddly, a fishing net, was engulfed in yellow and orange flames. The fire was filling the garage with toxic smoke that made Elish's already swimming head pound, and his lungs burn like he was inhaling the flames themselves.

He ran out, took his smouldering overcoat off and discarded it, and as he sped down the street towards the dirt bike, he saw the boy running from him, gun in hand.

Elish put the can down and got out the assault rifle... then shot the boy in the back without hesitation. He then quickly topped off the dirt bike with gasoline and got on it, and put the gas can between his legs to steady it as well as he could.

With his eyes hard granite and his mouth pursed tight, he turned on the dirt bike and revved it. Then he turned it in the direction he'd been heading, and started driving back down the cracked double-lane road, not a glance spared for the boy he left behind in a pool of blood.

CHAPTER 8

Reaver

"YOUR HEART IS ABOUT TO BURST OUT OF YOUR chest like that thing from *Alien*," I said to him with a laugh. I squeezed Killian's hand firmly in my own and gave him a smile. A smile that I injected as much confidence into as I could.

Killian's eyes were huge, and his pupils a small black life raft being consumed by a blue ocean. He looked behind him to the unassuming garage where we'd parked the quad and I saw him bite down on his lip. He had a look on him that screamed terror and I understood why.

Melchai was approaching and I could now see each individual structure and the colours of their roofs. It was a large town and I remember Hopper saying that half of it was uninhabitable because it was ass-to-ass with the plaguelands and the radiation was too strong. Before the Fallocaust, Melchai was a huge town but now the parts of it actually occupied were clustered to the south area and the other unoccupied areas had been harvested for firewood or farmland.

And that was something else that was unique and interesting to Melchai. Hopper had told us all stories about the farmland and how portions of Melchai had been cleared from the radiation.

How they had done it was a mystery, but Elish had mentioned Sanguine having a connection to this place, so perhaps he'd brought Silas in to clear it off to be nice.

Fucked if I knew the reason, I just knew none of them would be here now and we could get ourselves some actual food. Perish's money was burning a hole in my pocket and there was a lot of shit I wanted to bring back to our place.

Yesterday we had spent all day clearing out what we'd decided would be our new house. It backed the river and was nice inside. The entire top floor was two bedrooms which we could easily tear down to make one big master bedroom, and there were two smaller main floor bedrooms for storage and Perish's stuff. In the excitement of it, I had gotten a kind-of-looking-forward-to-going-to-Melchai from Killian.

Okay, maybe not looking forward to it, but he didn't have an anxiety attack over it.

"I just…" Killian swallowed hard and shifted closer to me. He was wearing a grey beanie with a red stripe on his head to cover his almost entirely bald head, and I myself had a hat on as well. None of our eyes were a weird colour though, so I wasn't sweating it. We both just looked like greywasters. "I just don't want to be here… Hopper said they were crazy."

"We'll be fine," I reassured. "You're my immortal boy. Worst comes to worse, we die and come back. Isn't that a pretty good worst case scenario?"

Killian let out a slow breath. "The radiation was cleared from certain areas of this place and that had to be from King Silas."

"And it was done many years ago," I reminded him. "The only risky thing would be if we were slaves and we're not slaves. It's spring now, right? Shouldn't there be some fruit and stuff in season?"

Killian's mouth twisted to the side. "It's the beginning of June so, yeah, there will but… Hopper also commented that they had greenhouses." He frowned some more, but when I planted a kiss on his cheek. I felt the skin tense, and I saw I'd managed to kiss up a smile. To keep up the reassuring affection, I pinched his chin and kissed him again.

But that was it for the kisses. We were close enough to the town that I could see people standing around the shabby wall that surrounded it. So I went back into greywaster mode and slipped my hand out of Killian's. I stood up straight and Killian did too and we walked towards what I gathered was their east gate.

As I got closer to the gate though I noticed that the sentries standing guard were all wearing black robes with hoods over their heads – that was kind of weird.

And there was something else too… I was about to point it out to Killian when he elbowed me first.

"There are birds here, Reaver," Killian whispered. He pointed to the sky just as a black bird flew from one roof top to the other. "I think those are crows, or ravens."

"Hm…" I glanced at the bird, its black wings flapping as it landed on top of one of the bigger buildings, and when my eyes focused on that building, I realized there were more black birds perched on it… a lot of them. "Interesting."

"I have a really bad feeling about this place," Killian whispered, but I shushed him and he said nothing else. We were too close to the gate and these people were no doubt watching and listening to us.

The gate looked to originally be an iron rung gate, one of the ones you would see in front of fancy mansions, but it was covered in sheet metal, several pieces thick, which had been painted red. In specific places the bold red paint was faded, however; and when I saw a bird perched on top of the gate, right on one of the faded streaks, I put two and two together and assumed it was from them scraping off bird shit.

"Ah, blessed visitors!" Killian sprung up into the air like a frightened cat when that voice suddenly sounded from behind the gate. I put a hand on his shoulder as he took in a shocked breath and looked up to address whoever it was that was talking to us.

It was one of the people we had seen on the wall. He was dressed in a black robe with a hood drawn over his head, and he had stringy black hair that framed a ghostly white face.

But wait a fucking second…

The man had red eyes, but not the irises, the entire white of his eye was a washed-out red and the iris a weird purple colour.

I think… I fucking think this dude had put food colouring in his eye or something.

"You are early for our Festival of the Blood Crows, blessed visitors," the man said with a weird closed-mouth smile. "Or are you here to receive blessing? We welcome visitors as long as you are pure." The man bowed his head and spread his arms – there were… fucking feathers sewn into his arms.

"I want to go," Killian whimpered beside me, his voice low enough that the weirdo didn't hear him. Unfortunately I was a bit too fascinated with what I was seeing.

"We're here for supplies," I said to the weirdo. "We need to stock up and if you sell your fruits and vegetables, we'd like to buy some as well. Do you… accept regular visitors?"

The man's closed-mouth smile suddenly split into a grin. Killian gasped beside me when we both saw that his teeth had been chiselled into points. "Of course, of course." The weirdo nodded and clasped his hands together. "Yes, yes, we allow visitors as long as they will agree to be purified."

"Reaver…" Killian whispered, his voice high and full of terror.

"Shh," I said to him. "We need supplies. We were originally stopping here with Hopper anyway and he would've told us if they were going to murder us all, right?"

The expression of horror on Killian's face didn't diminish in the least. Yeah, sure, it was a pretty crappy bit of reasoning but something was stopping me from wanting to turn and leave. Call it morbid curiosity or call it wanting supplies, I didn't know.

I was kind of enjoying taking risks to be honest. For so long I had been having to be overly cautious to make sure Killian was safe. Before Killian I was running head first into any danger that I came upon, with no fear for my own safety. Reno and I had done so many stupid things during our adventures, and we didn't need to fucking justify it – we just did it because we wanted to fucking do it.

And I wanted to fucking do this. So fuck what Killian thinks, I… I…

I needed to get out of that plaguelands house… I needed to not be alone with my own thoughts.

My throat went dry as that realization entered my head.

That was it, wasn't it?

I pushed it down, far, far down into the colourless void. Far down where all my other thoughts were currently rotting on top of each other. At one point in time it was easy to throw those thoughts into that pit and forget about them. But now there were too many and they were decomposing into one big pile of rotten flesh, maggots, and a smell that would make even me want to cut off my nose.

Fucking little bitch can't even get hard to fuck your boyfriend. Too fucked up in the brain from being raped. Fucking coward, you're far away from Nero and safe but you're still being a bitch about it.

"No need for worrying, blessed one." The man's voice snatched me from my inner thoughts. I looked up and saw him hold his palms together as if he was praying, then he bowed his head. "Unless you have committed the most horrible of sin, you have nothing to worry about."

I raised an eyebrow. I hope he wasn't expecting us to be virgins or anything like that. "What is the most horrible of sin?" I asked. At least I was packing my M16, so if we had committed this sin, we could open fire and 'purify' all of them.

Two more men, one on each side, walked over and stood on the wall beside him. They bowed as well and I observed that they also had the red-dyed eyes and long black hair. It seemed to be their thing... which was strange.

"What are your names?" the weird one in the middle asked.

Obviously we wouldn't be using our real names. "I'm Chance," I said, and I put a hand on Killian's shoulder. "This is my partner, his name is Jeff."

All three of them nodded their heads in unison. "And Chance, have you ever raped a child."

Wha...?

Before I could stop it, my mouth dropped open. "What? No, of course not. What kind of fucked up question is that?"

The three exchanged nods before nodding at us as well. "And Jeff, have you ever raped a child?"

"No!" Killian exclaimed.

The nods continued, they looked like bobbing birds with how they did that.

And I believe from the black birds we saw flying around behind them, that's exactly what they wanted to look like.

They said nothing more to us. The three turned around and left the top of the wall and I heard them murmuring to one another as they climbed down to the ground.

"They're fucking crazy!" Killian hissed at me, but I raised a hand to shut him up. I heard his teeth grind together but he said nothing more, and a moment later, the sounds of rusted metal could be heard as they opened the iron gate.

I gave an impressed whistle when I saw the inside of Melchai.

Fucking everyone in front of me was dressed in a black cloak, and as these men looked at us curiously, I saw a sea of washed-out red eyes, their irises the colour of whatever their natural colour was mixed with red. They stood in the middle of a single-lane road that cut right through this town, with buildings on either side of them that were a mixture of residential and commercial houses. Every house was painted either black or red, and... there were stakes in front of a lot of these houses with dirty looking rats, the subhuman kind, tied to them – a couple arians as well but it was hard to tell if their skin was dark from the radiation, or just really filthy.

And to top off this strange town, there were those black birds everywhere. Fucking perched on streetlights, the awnings and roofs of houses, and… trees…

They had trees here!

But before I could check out the green leaves I could see poking out from behind these houses, the three cloaked figures walked into my line of sight. I could smell on them a strange aroma that reminded me of cherry gum.

"We already have several blessed ones here," one of them said kindly. "We are always happy to receive visitors and you are welcome to buy supplies and buy our produce. You will be coming to our worship this evening as well?"

Killian's heartbeat gave an enthusiastic jolt and I knew he'd skin me alive if I said yes. But from what they were saying before, I had a feeling that if we said no, we'd be out the gate and on our own. I wanted to buy supplies, no, I *needed* to buy supplies.

The rotten smell from that bottomless pit inside of me made my insides curl into themselves. It was a reminder that I needed a distraction from these thoughts currently driving me insane, from my mind that was hell-bent on ruining the peace and quiet that I had worked so hard to get for me and my boyfriend.

A boyfriend I couldn't even be intimate with anymore.

My face felt hot and that heat spread down and enveloped my body.

"Yeah, we will," I said, and the heart of my boyfriend began to thrash.

The man looked incredibly pleased with this, he did that squinting smile again, and the two others followed suit.

"Wonderful," the man said. "Our shops are clearly marked, please respect our community and stay on the main street, all others are off limits unless accompanied by a Blood Crow." He bowed again before reaching down and taking my hand into his, another one doing the same for Killian.

Then at once, all three of them said, "May Sanguine bless you."

Whoa, what?

Sanguine?

Killian and I exchanged shocked looks, before we both turned our heads back to the cloaked weirdoes who were clasping our hands with their cold, skinny talons.

It made sense. Fuck me, it made sense.

The red eyes, fucking pointed teeth – why hadn't I seen it before? Of course these dumbshits were imitating Sanguine. But how the hell did he become their, what, their god?

I found myself cocking an eyebrow. "Who's Sanguine and why do I want him to bless me?"

The cloaked man who had been talking to us the most, seemed pleased at this question. He clasped his hands together and a loving look appeared on his face. "Sanguine is our blessed saviour and the immortal god who cleared away our radiation after cleansing our community of the unworthy almost forty years ago. You will be hearing more about him tonight at our worship and a grand feast will follow."

I knew these people were obviously nuts, but... not *this* fucking out there.

But I had to fucking hear this shit.

So with Killian's heart threatening to rip out of his chest to beat me to death, I smirked and nodded. "We'd love to attend!"

This fucking made him happy. The man's pointed-tooth grin was a mile wide and he even bowed to us. "Another follower of Lord Sanguine will make Man on the Hill most happy. Come down for worship and dinner and we will tell you all about our community, and about our prophet Man on the Hill."

I put on a fake smile, and just to be a dick, I forced a great deal of mock enthusiasm into my voice. "That sounds great!" I exclaimed. Then I grabbed Killian's hand and we left the wing-nuts to do whatever wing-nuts did.

"Please be respectful of our crows as well," the man called. "Do not feed them. Our crows are on a strict diet."

"Okay," I called back. And because I'd always be a dick I debated finding a way to poison the crows, but I tried to refrain from tempting myself with something so hilarious.

But all amused thoughts were chased from my head when I felt how hard Killian's hands were trembling in mine. I looked at him and saw that he was staring, bug-eyes, at a staked rat. The dirty subhuman was chained to a stake in the front yard and when he saw us he started growling. Killi the weenie whimpered and clung to my arm as we passed him. I knew he was scared of everything and not just a dumb subhuman, but it was still kind of pathetic.

Unfortunately, me directing him away from the rat just reminded him of what I'd done. "What the hell are you thinking!?" His voice was so high-pitched I was expecting dogs to start to bark. "Reaver! They're insane, we need to leave!"

"Shh… we're fine," I hissed. I looked around the town to get a feel for it but my eyes kept travelling back to the trees I had originally seen. There was a big one I could see in someone's yard about half a block up. It was covered in what I guess were crows; they were perched on the branches and they reminded me again of the cloaked weirdoes.

"So I gotta assume that Sanguine had a thing for crows," I mumbled. "They might be weird but they have stores and places to stay. You can't expect every settlement to be full of normal greywasters, especially this far north." I opened my mouth to say more, but I saw a glimpse of the tree I had been eyeing in someone's back yard.

Killian gasped when I broke away from my protective hand-holding and tried to grab my arm, but I was already sprinting towards the first real, non-black tree, I'd ever seen.

I ran along the house it was behind and when I got to the person's backyard I stared in fascinated awe.

It was so beautiful!

It was a real tree surrounded by grass so green the contrast to the greys hurt my eyes. The tree had brown bark and emerald leaves in the shapes of the clubs on a deck of playing cards. It was just standing there, about twenty feet tall, with its thick branches splayed out and its leaves shining in the grey sun. I felt like I could like… I don't know, write a fucking song about this tree. It was just godly. Fuck Sanguine, I was going to worship this tree for the rest of my life.

I ran my hand along its bark and I turned to Killian with a wide smile. "It's so real!" I exclaimed.

And though Killian looked uneasy and terrified by this place, when he saw the happiness on my face he calmed down a bit, and even managed to smile at my discovery.

"But baby… we don't know if we're allowed," Killian said in a hushed voice. "We don't know their rules, and this is someone's backyard."

I knew he was right but… I had never seen a real life tree before. One that wasn't half-dead from the radiation and crappy sun. This might be a once in a life time opportunity, at least until I eventually travelled to Skyfall.

Then something else caught my eye. All along the backyard of the house were flowers, purple ones, blue, red, and yellow. They had three big petals and black in the center and a little bit of white so they looked like they had faces. Their colours were so bright it was incredible. I gravitated towards them.

Killian stopped me again but I couldn't help it. I walked to the flowers and kneeled down in front of them in awe. I gently ran my fingers over the delicate petals and leaned down to smell them.

Killian giggled behind me. I gave him a glare but said nothing. I didn't care if I looked like an idiot, this was blowing my mind. I wanted to dig up all of them and bring them to our house. I fucking wanted these everywhere; the blue ones were so blue they reminded me of Killian's eyes.

"Mama…"

I looked up when I heard a soft but high octave voice whisper. I was surprised to see a little boy with black hair and also dyed red eyes, look at us nervously in the back door's entrance. Strangely, he had a pair of what looked like the bear ears of a stuffed animal on his head, I guess on a headband or something.

When he saw me, he paled and ran away. I shrugged and went back to smelling the flowers, but Killian started pulling me away.

"Hello?" a female voice rang out, followed by the sounds of chains being dragged. I sighed, knowing my flower examining was over, and stood up.

Killian gasped when he saw her, but I only raised my eyebrows, though it looked like I could've done a lot more…

… since her eyes had been sewn shut.

Yeah.

The woman was being led to the back door by the boy. On top of having her eyes sewn shut, by thin black strings that left the puncture holes crusty and red, she had a slave collar around her neck with a long chain that led back inside of the house. Her limbs were skinny and her face gaunt, but she was heavily pregnant, and was wearing a faded green sundress and stockings that looked to be covering dime-sized sores. Kind of looked like radiation sores.

"Sorry, Ma'am," Killian said hastily. "My boyfriend has never seen flowers before. He… he was excited. We didn't mean to disturb you." The look on his face told me he was done with this place, flat out done, but unfortunately I wasn't. He needed to understand that not every community of people was like Aras. Aras was a block so it was controlled by Skyfall, and Skyfall would never allow shit like this to go on.

We were a long ways from Aras, and a longer ways from Skyfall. I wasn't going to not get us supplies just because some whackjobs lived differently than us. We weren't fucking super heroes and Killian had to accept that.

"Please… please leave my yard," the woman said, her face scrunching in fear. She put a hand on her stomach and took a step back. "I can't be seen speaking to you." The woman pulled the boy back and shut the door with a loud slam.

I heard a male voice yell from inside of the house, followed by desperate and fearful stammering.

Then a loud smack, and a scream… and then a thud.

Killian put a hand over his mouth, his eyes full of shock over what he'd just seen and heard.

I shrugged and picked one of the flowers, a blue one. "It matches your eyes. Look." I held it up to Killian's face, and as the boy stared at me in undiluted terror, I compared his blue eyes, as wide as they could go, with the pretty flower.

"Sometimes I hate you so much I picture myself clawing off your face with my bare hands," Killian said in a hushed whisper; his eyes blank and staring, suggesting that was exactly what he was doing.

I rolled my eyes and began walking back to the street, the sounds of female crying coming from the house. Killian kept looking over his shoulder, his face crumpling in sadness, but he didn't leave my side.

"Please, Reaver, we need to leave," he whimpered, and when he saw that I was ignoring him he gave out a small choking whine. "They worship a chimera. What if Sanguine is Man on the Hill?"

I *shh'd* him and gave him a warning look to keep his voice down. "I saw Sanguine, Killian." That made his eyes widen but I continued. "He's in Skyfall. Silas ordered him and Jack to go back to Skyfall before he left with me. Just tone it down, alright? Different settlements have different customs. These people have obviously never even heard of a chimera, they've been completely isolated. We can't judge people for living their lives weirdly; shit like this happens when you don't have teachers to teach you better."

"That woman... her eyes..."

I shrugged a shoulder. "I don't really care, to be honest. It's not like we're going to liberate all the women, rats, and kids." I looked to another staked rat, this one with matted and stringy hair and eyes unworldly white compared to his dark skin. He was growling at us, baring yellowed teeth as we walked by while holding what looked like a brown nut. I mock advanced on him; I hated when those retarded fucks tried to act tough. "We just need supplies."

"What about Man on the Hill?" Killian pressed.

"We'll be gone by tonight," I said. "And he can't be a chimera because Elish never told me there was one here. The only greywaster immortal I know of out here is Mantis and he isn't even a real chimera and Elish hasn't talked to him in forever."

Strangely Killian's heart jumped at this. I gave him a look and saw an uncomfortable expression come to his face.

"Perish... Perish mentioned Mantis a lot. Perish wanted me to shoot a flare into the air to signal him to come get me..." Killian said. He dropped his tone even lower; he was starting to be able to do the trick that only my brothers and I could do. The whisper that only chimera hearing could pick up on. "What... what did Elish tell you about Mantis?"

I looked around the double-lane street but there wasn't any cloaked weirdoes in earshot, just crows, and the concrete wall to our right looked thick. Still though, I spoke as quietly as I could. "Elish says he was an arian made immortal by the family but he took off for some reason," I said. Then, in that moment, I remembered Elish's parting words to me.

Our meeting point will be the town Mantis.

I'm sorry, my friend. You think Killian is dead and that I'm burning... and it has to stay that way.

I felt the pit of decay inside of me churn, exposing rot that had been buried underneath the more direct things that had been bothering me.

And this rot was my guilt over having Elish think I was burning and Killian dead. I'd had a fun time with Elish, even though the both of us had been stressed out and worried during our time together. In all respects, I considered Elish a part of my family now, and to a lesser extent the little ankle biter Jade too.

There was so many bad feelings inside of me it felt overwhelming. I... I think I had to rent a room and just do some drugs. Yeah, I needed drugs.

Did Jade know what happened to me with Nero?

Fuck. Silas knew. Silas knew so everyone will know.

Everyone will know what Nero did to you.

I took in a deep breath and was horrified when my chest gave a shaking shudder. I ended up choking, as if directly breathing in the putrid aroma of my own rotting feelings, and found myself grasping my chest when my breathing began to shorten.

I looked up and saw two cloaked men watching us, their eyes narrow slits. To further my humiliation I suddenly felt an overwhelming fear that they knew too.

Everyone knows you were Nero's screaming little bitch.

KILLIAN KNOWS TOO!

"Baby...?" Killian said lightly.

I jumped and immediately felt flustered. I knew that tone; I knew he'd noticed.

"Yeah?" I said quickly, and ran my hand down my face.

Fuck, I hated myself. I was a chimera, I was the Reaper... but right now I fucking felt like a wussy piece of shit. I couldn't even get hard to have sex with my fucking boyfriend. What the hell was wrong with me? What the fuck was wrong with my body?

It was a physical act, nothing different from the physical torture I'd endured with Kessler. So just... fucking stop it, stop feeling this way.

The heat travelled from my face, to my ears, and the back of my neck; they smouldered like there was a pool of lava under the surface. Inside I felt such an intense hatred it made me feel physically sick.

I had been feeling like this since I realized I couldn't perform for Killian. And when it was quiet, which it was a lot of the time since we had no electricity, the feelings came back. They were loud and echoing, and they just kept coming; flying in circles inside of my head like vultures.

Vultures circling this pit of rot.

"Don't think dark thoughts," I heard Killian say in a sweet and loving voice, but the tone did nothing but flood me with more humiliation. He knew I wasn't able to get hard, there had been no avoiding it. He'd just been nice enough to not mention it.

The embarrassment was unbearable, but I couldn't take off and go patrolling as was my usual escape. I couldn't leave him; he already didn't want to be in this town.

Killian took my hand and squeezed it, but then jumped again when there was a ferocious screaming growl coming from behind me. We both looked and saw a snarling rat, his chain tight, growling and snapping at us. This one was missing its legs however; he was clawing at the ground trying to drag himself towards us, a plastic dog bowl of water beside him with wooden bits in it, and a chewed-on femur bone resting in front. I wonder if it was his actual leg bone.

"Shut the hell up, retard!" I snapped. Then on the other side of the street another staked rat began to scream at us. This was another man, doing the same viscous snarling like they were dogs.

Like I had been placed into a small dark room, a wave of anxious claustrophobia suddenly grasped onto me. Even though I was out in the open, I felt the world closing in on all sides of me, the snarling racket of the rats becoming physical barriers that were pressing against me, seeping into my pores to inject anxiety right into my bloodstream.

"Shut up!" I screamed, a scream unlike my own. I walked over to one of the rats, the subhuman snarling and snapping and pulling on his chain, and I kicked him in the face.

He fell back with a shriek and a moan, blood trickling from his mouth like I'd turned on a faucet. And when I turned to shut the other one up, it cowered and backed away, its teeth bared but its eyes looking up at me in submission.

Behind him, I saw a woman with short brown hair. She was staring at us from the window of the house. She didn't have her eyes sewn shut but… it was hard to make out through the reflection but I think her mouth was sewn.

Killian took my hand and started pulling me away. "We need to get a room for you," he said anxiously. I gripped hard onto his hand, it was all I could do to keep myself from falling apart. My mind was racing, my breathing was getting short.

I heard cawing around me, the crows had started to make their racket. I saw a flicker of black from the corner of my eye and looked behind me to see the crows landing beside the rat I'd kicked. The subhuman himself was holding his jaw and moaning, and the birds were clustered around him like black insects – they were drinking his blood and one was even hopping up to pick at his face.

"Follow me, baby, it's okay," Killian said. "I…" He reached into his bag, his eyes looking around to see if we'd been noticed. "… I have some

Xanax in my bag."

No. I don't need to fucking be drugged. I was fine. There was nothing fucking wrong with me!

There was... there was...

... there was something wrong with me.

And here I was in the middle of a crazed fucking cult, slowly losing my mind and ignoring the obvious signs that we should get the fuck out of there, all because I needed a distraction from these feelings cannibalizing what should've been a golden time for me and Killian.

"I'm fine..." I whispered harshly, but I knew I wasn't. I let Killian lead me down the road, black and red houses on either side of us, almost all with staked rats, and we saw in the distance what looked like an old hotel. As soon as Killian saw it, he started walking faster, until he was practically running with me.

But when we got to the hotel we saw that it was beyond being inhabitable. The moss-covered roof had collapsed entirely on the left-hand side, and the weight from that had squashed several storeys below it. The hotel looked like it was squinting at us now from how the windows were crushed; a Quasimodo of a building with green and black slime stuck to the wooden siding on the front, and moss growing in thick clumps on the boards that had fallen to the ground. All of the windows looked to have been removed, and now shredded curtains hung sadly from the open frames, like tendons and flesh from gaping gashes.

The courtyard was beautiful though. It was like a real lawn you'd see on TV and movies, short green grass with dandelions both the yellow ones and the blowing-on puffy white ones. There was also a fountain in the middle of it, not in use and also slimy, but surrounded by painted rocks and, weirdly, garden gnomes. I wanted to admire everything, take a closer look at it, but I was too anxious. My head was stuffed to capacity and there was no room to appreciate what I was seeing.

"Are you looking for a place to spend the night?" Killian and I turned to see an ancient-looking old man standing with a younger guy, probably Reno's age. The two of them were dressed in the black cloak get-up, red eyes and black hair too, but the old man was sporting a long white beard.

"Yeah," Killian said. "We... we thought there were rooms here..." Killian gave the hotel another glance and didn't even bother to finish his sentence when the old man nodded.

"Since our Lord Sanguine and his angel cleared away the radiation, our buildings deteriorated quicker," the old man said, leaning heavily on a cane. He looked at the building and smiled at it, a glint of longing in his eyes. "But that is Sanguine's way, is it not? The building was putrid, and all that is putrid dies. Only those clean and pure deserve immortality." His smile widened at this. "Word of you coming to our town spread quickly. You will be spending the night then, after worship?"

"Uh…" Killian stammered. "We just need to rest before… the worship. We will be heading back in the evening."

But the man shook his head. "I'd advise against it. Ravers… ravers have been spotted, a new species of them." Jade's ravers were spreading it seemed. "I have a place for you two, you're welcome to stay." He turned around and waved for us to follow him. Killian looked hesitant, but with another glance in my direction, he nodded.

"Yeah," Killian said. "We heard the ravers were taking over towns."

"Yes," Old Man said. "Man on the Hill has guaranteed our protection. He and our Angel Adi will protect us."

And we still didn't know who he was. Killian's heart jumping at the mention of Mantis made me wonder if Perish had told him it was him. But if so, who was Angel Adi?

I didn't care. I really didn't care.

The Old Man led us down a street that branched off north from the main one we were on. About a quarter block down, past more red and black houses and chained rats, most of them missing limbs, he led us to a bunch of small houses that looked to have been built recently. The wood on these houses were covered in tar to preserve them, and I realized that the black I'd been seeing on some of the houses was most likely tar as well.

"How much?" Killian asked when he stopped us in front of one of the mini houses. He started to unzip his satchel but the man shook his head.

"Sanguine would not approve of charging people to stay for his worship," the man replied with a bow of his head. He opened his mouth to say more, when a sharp scream ripped through the air. We looked to our lefts where it had resonated from, Killian's eyes filling with fear; but all that was behind the small houses was the concrete barrier that I assumed held all of their plants and stuff.

"Just our tribute for tonight's ceremony," the younger one said, looking completely unfazed. "I suggest not eating tonight, we will provide you with a grand feast." He clasped his hands and bobbed his head like a bird before smiling at us. "I am Zachariah, and may Sanguine bless you."

I didn't even look around the room we'd been put in, as soon as the door closed I was digging out Dilaudid pills from my cargo pants and crushing them with the butt of my combat knife. Killian was smart enough to wait until I'd inhaled a good amount.

I got up and sat down on one of the two single beds and buried my face into my hands. I only looked up when Killian nudged my hand; he had a Xanax pill resting in his palm.

The anger that flared inside of me was unexpected, but it grabbed me with both hands and dug its claws into my brain. Before I could tell myself not to, I smacked the Xanax pill right out of Killian's hand.

The boy looked at me like I'd just smacked him across the face.

"I don't need to be fucking drugged!" I snapped and even when I was saying it I knew how ridiculous it was for me to say it. I'd just downed two Dilaudid pills and I was in this fucking room because I was losing control.

Killian stared at me, and I thought he was going to burst into tears but he didn't...

He got mad back.

"Then should we go and walk around with the fucking cultists outside some more?" he said coolly. "Or should we save our social interactions for tonight's worship of the sengil of the very man we're trying to remain dead to?" He picked up the Xanax pill, absolutely fuming. "I've humoured you enough with this shit, Reaver. I want to get the fuck out of here and you're not able to make intelligent decisions right now. We're leaving in an hour."

And like he was a lighter and I was a stack of dynamite, one with a thousand fuses sticking out of me, I exploded.

"Since when do you fucking tell me what I can and can't do?" I snarled. Killian's face paled and he took a step back from me. I wasn't having it though. I fucking stood up and spread out my arms, challenging him. "Who the fuck do you think you are? You're going to control me now? You're going to tell me what I can and can't do like you're my fucking master?"

Killian took another step back, the Xanax pill in his closed fist. "No," he said. "But you're crazy if you don't think that still remaining in this insane cult town is a smart idea."

"Who the fuck cares if it's a smart idea?" I yelled. I slammed my hand down on the side table by the bed. "You're fucking immortal, so am I. I finally don't have to worry about you fucking dying and maybe I don't want to run with my tail between my legs whenever we stumble upon something cool."

"Cool!?" Killian yelled back. Then he shook his head, his lips pursed in anger. "This isn't about you wanting a thrill because I can't die anymore. There's…" Just like that the anger faded and his eyes filled with worry. "There's something you're… trying to get away from, isn't there?"

His comment lit my brain on fire and made it into an oven; heat swept me, frying my face, my ears, the back of my neck. I stared at him, not knowing what to do, not knowing what to say… and terrified of what he was going to say next.

Because I knew what it would be.

"Maybe we should talk about… what happened by the river."

I got up off of the bed and beelined it to the door. Killian screamed at me to stop, sounding desperate, and he jumped in between me and my only path to escape.

"Lay down, please," Killian begged, there were tears in his eyes. "I won't mention it. Please, please, Reaver, I'm begging you… listen to me and just lay down. I won't say anything." Then he paused like he was thinking about something. "I'll go, okay? I'll go since I have the money; I have our shopping list. You lay down and I'll get our supplies."

My Reaver instinct told me to do the opposite of what he suggested but… the drugs were hitting me and I felt like utter shit. I wanted to go into zombieland for a while, and tune everything out.

Against all my reasoning… I nodded. "Just…" I turned around and pointed to my gun. "Take my M16 and if you feel even a little bit threatened… shoot him off and I'll be there. Don't, just don't go anywhere but the store."

I heard him sigh with relief. I didn't look at him and just laid down on one of the beds.

"I won't be long, baby, have a good sleep." I tensed when I felt him rub my shoulder. "We'll go to the worship tonight and we can gawk at the weirdoes." He kissed my cheek and I jerked my head away. The little idiot needed to stop touching me. "Be right back."

And he left, and I was alone.

Once again alone with my thoughts.

CHAPTER 9

Reaver

I YAWNED AND PINCHED MY FINGERS AGAINST THE
leather strap across my chest. I drew out the strap and tried to position it
where it would usually rest on my chest and shoulders but since Killian
had borrowed it, all of my grooves had been disturbed. Thankfully, the
stress of it always being buckled in one position had warped the leather,
but it was still uncomfortable.

Killian shrunk down when I gave him a haughty look. "Sorry," he
mumbled.

"Usually you just let it hang down loosely," I said, trying to adjust it
properly. It was like when someone borrows your quad and they fuck with
the rear view mirror. "You have shitty small shoulders."

"Sorry, baby," Killian said. He got behind me and laughed lightly.
"It's the collar of your jacket, dummy. It's scrunched underneath the strap
and that's raising it and making it feel funny." With a few quick
movements, him straightening out my collar I assumed, the holder was
adjusted and it rested as it should.

"There," Killian said, patting my back. "See? It wasn't me. I put
everything back how it was before I even woke you up." He began to walk
beside me again and there was a light laugh to my left. That would be
Zach, both Zachariah, and the older man Charles, were taking us to this
evening's worship.

Killian had woken me up a couple hours after he'd left to get our
supplies. I was surprised that I'd slept for so long; I didn't realize I was

this tired.

But I didn't believe it was physically tired… it was just mental exhaustion and what I think could've been the beginning of an anxiety attack – that I didn't like at all.

"How long have you two been together for?" Zach asked. His eyes had been freshly reddened, and from the spots of red on his fingers I did believe that it was from some sort of food colouring. They also had face powder on to make them appear more pale, and weirdly, they all had silver pock mark scars on their eyelids and mouth – I think at one point in time they'd all had their eyes and lips sewn shut.

"A year…?" Killian said. And he looked at me as if expecting me to know. "It's the beginning of June now and it was the summer when we first got together. Do… we have an anniversary?"

I snorted. "Anniversary? Who even has those anymore?" It was almost as ridiculous as me being forced to ask him to be my boyfriend last year. He was my partner, that's all that needed to be said. I wasn't fucking taking him to the ice cream social or the prom; I wasn't woo'ing him for his love.

But Killian seemed set on the idea. "Let's make our anniversary today!"

"Or…" I filled with mock enthusiasm. "I got an idea!"

Killian grinned with anticipation.

"Let's make it yesterday so we don't have to deal with stupid anniversaries!"

His face fell and I got a push for that. "Asshole."

Zach chuckled. "We have our own anniversaries. On August 2nd it will be forty years since our Lord Sanguine cleared Melchai of radiation. You have heard we will be holding a grand festival to celebrate it." Then he frowned. "Unfortunately we're low on sacrifices. Our slave caravan didn't arrive and we fear he never will." Ah, Hopper's caravan. Nope, they'll never be seen again, bud. "But we will make due. We always do."

"And these sacrifices are for Man on the Hill?" Killian asked, his voice only slightly inquisitive. I could tell he was trying to play it cool, but inside he was listening intently for any information he could get. Killian had calmed down about me wanting to stay in this town, even though they were obviously nuts; but in exchange for him not chewing my ear off about it, he was digging for information.

"Yes, our prophet." Like all of the other ones we'd talked to, Zach got this dreamy look in his eye, like he was talking about a celebrity. "When you come for our festival, you will get to look upon him. He speaks the words of Sanguine and he blesses us with new seeds to plant and he was the one who taught us about the ultimate purification."

"The ultimate purification?" I asked. We were walking along the concrete wall now and I could hear people inside, and see other 'Blood Crows' filing in from all directions. There were a lot of fucking great smelling things coming from inside of those walls now too.

"Yes," Zach said with a nod. "We use slaves a lot of the time, but twice a year we let Sanguine choose which of us is to receive this ultimate blessing. A way for us to ensure our harvest is bountiful."

The conversation was halted when we approached a wooden gate reinforced with metal. Zach and Charles got ahead of us, and when another Blood Crow gave us the stink eye, he politely told him that we were with them.

When I walked in, I was blown away. I'd had a camera feed inside of Perish's growing room, but what was inside of this concrete wall was like comparing Jupiter to Pluto. It was huge!

There were raised beds everywhere, the wood bright yellow and aromatic, and each bed was full of black dirt with flecks of white. Growing in that dirt were plants so green I found my eyes squinting, and fruits and vegetables of all colours that weighed down the plants they were attached to. They even had an irrigation system similar to the one I'd hooked up in Aras, black tubing with holes drilled into it, and I could see squirts of water shooting up into the air.

It was mesmerizing to look at and I kept blinking my eyes like an idiot as we walked into this enclosed area. The smell was something else too, the greywastes always smelled musty and dry but the smell was like... wet and rich.

But I had to keep my composure. I resisted the urge to shoot everyone just so I could pet and poke and dissect all of the plants without their judgement, and carried on. It didn't keep me from looking though; they even had more of the real trees in the distance. However, where we were going was off to the left, through a narrow concrete corridor that was more closed-in than I would've liked it to be.

"We're taking over this town," I hissed to Killian. Killian nudged me in the side but didn't say anything. I could tell he was nervous but hiding it.

Yeah, I knew a thousand things could go wrong here and if Killian was still mortal I would've never have stayed. But it was liberating to go out and explore shit without constantly having to keep Killian alive. So I wanted to have some fun, sue me.

The narrow concrete path took us to another section of raised beds and tall green trees busting with fruit, but this one was full of black-hooded men and alive with their murmuring.

They were everywhere, at least fifty of them, and not a woman or a child in sight. The Blood Crows were gathered around an empty raised bed talking in hushed voices, a floodlight shining on the bed which was only about seven feet away from the concrete wall. This wall appeared to be backing the no-go radiation zone that was the north area of Melchai, which was interesting.

And there were buildings still beyond this wall. I spotted one tall enough to peek over the rough concrete; it was dark, with a collapsed roof that was crushed against the structure like a god had put their palm on top of it and pressed down.

"Behind that wall… just radiation?" I asked.

Zach nodded. "Yes, everything beyond this wall is coated in lethal radiation."

We weaved through the crowd until we found a good spot and a good view. I was content beside a gnarled cherry tree that was covered in beautiful red cherries. It was funny though because my boot kept getting untied, so I kept on having to crouch down to tie it.

And weirdly, I was chewing every time I stood back up.

Killian elbowed me. "I got us a grocery bag full of cherries," he whispered. "And I rolled the quad in further into the garage, but I didn't see anyone when the guys that helped me load the generator onto the quad's trailer."

I reached down for another cherry and placed it into my mouth. Then, when I righted myself, I slid my arm around Killian's neck and kissed him. I pushed the cherry into his mouth and, thankfully, he got the idea as to what I was doing and didn't choke.

He chewed it and spit out the pit, then put it into a pocket in his satchel.

"You know we won't be able to grow anything in the plaguelands, right?" I whispered to him.

"Yeah," he said, but then he looked at me with hopeful eyes. "But I thought since you can make radiation, it means you can clear it too, right?"

I hadn't even given it any thought, but I guess he was right.

"I guess I can give it an attempt," I said. "I don't think I can do it on demand though but since Silas can… eventually I'll learn to do it better."

The gathering of the cloaked weirdoes suddenly fell quiet. Killian and I both looked up to see the black figures, packed tight and shoulder to shoulder, looking behind them towards another entrance in this concrete room.

We turned and watched as well. Everything was quiet, but I could hear a pulse in the far corners of my brain. It was their heartbeats, but they would remain just a faint noise unless I tuned my hearing to amplify it.

Then an old man with glasses emerged, he had to be the oldest person I'd ever seen. His face was just made up of wrinkles, and he was bald except for a strip of white that went from ear to ear. The old man was leaning heavily on a cane, and was being escorted by Zach and two other men about middle age. He must've slipped away after helping us find a perch.

Zach and the other two helped the old man to the front, and then with a bow, the three disappeared back into the dark corridor. The concrete path looked to be heading west but what was west was anyone's guess. How big this concrete wall was, and how much of Melchai it covered, I didn't know and it was hard to tell. Killian and I had stuck to the main street and had only branched off for the mini home. For all I knew this wall could have half of the town enclosed in it.

A scream suddenly ripped through the air. Killian's heart jumped but everyone else around us seemed completely unfazed. I sighed internally when Killian started giving the entrances to this place stricken looks, and when I didn't pay attention to his hinting, he started looking at me.

Another scream, this one pleading in a strangled, shrieking tone.

"These people are monsters," Killian whispered. I squeezed his hand but said nothing, and like I was saved by the bell, the old man began rapping his cane against the side of the wooden crate, and all attention was turned to him.

"Sanguine bless you all," the old man said, his voice rather loud for being so ancient.

"Sanguine bless you too," the Blood Crows all murmured back, and they were saying this as yet another scream broke the darkening night sky.

"It has been six months since Brother Jenkin required verbal purification," the old man said. He put both hands on his crow's head cane and looked ahead. "Brother Jenkin, come up here."

Verbal purification? I watched intently, curiosity creating many dead cats around me, and was fascinated when this Jenkin person made his way through the parting crowd to the front, where the old man was.

His lips were sewn shut, just like the pregnant chick's eyes. This made me look more closely at the other Blood Crows and, sure enough, I could see some of them had, not just their mouths shut, but their eyes, as well as some had coverings on their ears. I even saw a man who had his hands bound in barbwire.

So that was how purification was achieved? It made me wonder what the 'ultimate purification' was.

Jenkin bowed in front of the old man and everyone murmured their 'bless you' bullshit, and then he was ushered into a dark corner by a hunched over dude holding pliers. I couldn't see what was going on, the floodlight buggered my night vision, but I could guess he was getting the stitches removed.

"We have visitors today as well," the old man looked towards me and Killian, and so did everyone else. "Zachariah has been your chaperone. He tells me you've shown great interest in the Blood Crows and our Lord and saviour. During our tribute tonight and while this fortunate slave reaches our highest levels of purification... I shall tell you the origins of our blessed Sanguine." There was a sea of bobbing heads and while this was going on, the old man tapped his cane against the wooden box.

That must've been the signal because another scream broke up the quiet head nodding. This one was really close too. I looked to my right and saw a glow of a lamp becoming brighter and brighter in the corridor; and then Zach appeared, a chain in his hand.

At first I thought they were pulling a rat, but what was forcefully dragged into the clearing wasn't a rat at all, but an arian slave – and he was fucked up.

The man was naked, and his skin was this sickening off-green colour. He was on the extreme side of skinny but his stomach was bulging. The same kind of bulging I had seen last year when I'd pulled Killian from one of the fois ras pods.

The crowd parted as he was dragged through, a low and desperate moaning coming from lips that seemed... disfigured. It wasn't until he was brought to the light that I saw that his lips were split open on the corners, also not unlike Killian's, except this man's cuts were a good inch and a half on each side, and they hadn't been closed.

"Please..." the man rasped. Killian tensed beside me. "Please... arian... I'm a damn arian!" The splits on his mouth made him look like he was a Muppet, and inside of that mouth was a black teeth and tongue.

No, not just black... it looked like it was coated in fur.

"You are not an arian now, blessed one," the old man said calmly. The two men who were with Zach pulled the man's head back, allowing the old man to rest a hand on top of his head.

Everyone else bowed their heads too and began to mumble a prayer.

"No... no! Please..." The man looked around desperately and unfortunately made eye contact with the two people who weren't praying. "Please... fucking get me out of here. I'm not even a fucking slave, I was sold by my fucking ex-boyfriend." His eyes began to fill with tears. "Come on, dude, three months ago I was fucking just like you. My... my name's Matthew McCowell, I'm from a settlement near Mariano."

Killian's hand gripped mine and his jaw locked. That asshole just had to humanize himself, didn't he?

"No," I hissed to Killian.

"No, what?" he whispered back. "No saving them? Of course not, *you* don't save people because *you* have no soul."

I squeezed his hand hard, really hard, until Killian hissed and started to shrink down from the pain, and when I loosened my grip I heard him mumble. "I'm clawing off your face in my mind."

A shriek and a series of *No! No! No!* brought both of our attentions back to the front of the gathering. Killian took my hand again and scrunched close to me. Then we both saw a cloaked figure coming towards the slave with a long metal tube, but cut length wise so it was like a half pipe, and a plastic bucket full of something heavy.

"First off," the old man said, loudly over the man's screams, "let me tell you the story of Sanguine." One of the men holding the slave grabbed his jaw, and while the slave struggled and screamed he forced it open. The Blood Crow with the metal half-tube shoved it into his mouth, and another one took a blue scoop out of the bucket. The smell of shit, dirt, and chemical reached my nose.

"Come on..." My brow knitted when I heard this whisper come from Killian. "Come on," he said again.

I stared at him, but he refused to make eye contact.

"… and the townspeople, the unworthy as we called them, threw rocks at young Sami and chased him from our town. All because Sanguine was born with a special and unique gift of having eyes like blood and dangerously beautiful pointed teeth."

What the hell was Killian up to?

"Now I will tell you about The Putrid One," the old man wheezed on. The Blood Crow poured the blue scoop, containing a thick black liquid, down the cylinder and into the man's mouth. He immediately began to choke and gag; his body starting to shudder and shake from either fear or tremors.

And the other Blood Crows began to murmur.

"Bless him. Bless him."

"The Putrid One was a man who exchanged meth for little boys to rape and abuse. The townspeople knew this was happening but they turned a blind eye to it. Why? Because they wanted their drugs. They gave him these children knowing what fates awaited them." The old man shook his head in sadness, and right beside him the slave's screamings had become gurgling gags. The bright light on him was illuminating his bulbous stomach; his veins, snares of red and blue, some varicose, bulging out of his descended abdomen.

Bless him. Bless him.

"It so happened that when Sanguine was chased from this town The Putrid One followed him and imprisoned him in his basement. He spent eleven years raping and abusing him until Sanguine grew strong and killed the Putrid One with an inferno of fire he could make come out of his hands. Then Sanguine left but his heart was dark and soured from his time imprisoned."

They withdrew the metal half-cylinder from the slave's mouth, and the one holding him clamped it shut. A needle flashed in the floodlight, connected to a thick suture, and as the slave moaned, his eyes bugged out, absolutely terrified, they began to stitch his mouth shut. It didn't take long; they seemed like pros.

"Then… almost forty years ago, on August 2nd, 192 A.F, Sanguine came back to Melchai. Melchai was full of the unworthy. It was full of rapists, murderers, drug users; it was full of the worst people of the greywastes. And since it was so close to the plaguelands, their madness from the radiation only made it worse. Sanguine saw the evils that ran rampant in this town, and he started coming at night and sacrificing all who gave in to evil."

The slave was picked up, he wasn't thrashing that much anymore, and was laid down inside of the empty raised bed. It was then I realized just what they were doing... they were force-feeding the slaves fertilizer before they buried them in the raised beds. I guess to make the soil more nutritious for the plants.

Smart.

"Come on..." Killian whispered.

The old man raised his hands into the air and looked to the dark sky, the night clear and the moon shining down on us. "But then... Sanguine got caught!"

Bless our Lord Sanguine. Bless our Lord Sanguine.

"The townspeople paraded Sanguine around like a monster, crucified on boards like he had crucified them; all led by an evil man who had known Sanguine before. That man hung Sanguine up in front of the Holi Inn and everyone threw rocks at him, until he died."

Then the five who had been controlling the slave reached to their belts and pulled out knives.

Bless him. Bless him. The murmuring got louder, and their voices closer together, until it was a rhythmic beat. *Bless him. Bless him. Bless him.*

They didn't stab him like I thought they would, instead the men wearing their black cloaks, the hoods drawn over their heads, stood on four corners, and one on the front. They lowered their knives onto the slaver's skin, both arms, both legs, and his head, and slid the blades down, leaving a thin, but not fatal, laceration.

And that's when I heard the first crow. I looked up and, yep, the fucking cherry tree was full of them.

Dinner time? Not just fertilizer for the plants, but food for the crows.

They were on a special diet after all.

"Sanguine was dead on the crucifixion and they left him there to rot. The stories say crows from all around landed on him, crows with eyes as red as his." The old man looked above me, and I knew he saw them too. Right on cue. "They cawed and called his name and grieved for him, even when the people threw rocks at the crows they did not leave. And it was because the crows knew something that mere humans did not..." The old man smile came back and I knew what was coming. "... they knew Lord

Sanguine was no man at all, but a god. At twelve-thirty that night, Sanguine's eyes flew open and he woke… Sanguine rose from the dead. He pulled his arms free from the nails driven into his hands, and stepped down from the crucifixion to everyone's shock. He stood in front of the astonished crowd, his crimson eyes shining like hellfire, and demanded—"

Suddenly gunshots rang, sharp cracks but not from automatics, these ones were from a handgun.

And unlike the ignored screams, every single Blood Crow turned towards the noise and I saw the old man's face drop from shock.

A man burst through the concrete corridor. "The slaves are escaping!" he yelled frantically. "They got knives. One has a gun! They shot Brother Bertand." He looked behind him and gasped. Then there was a loud crack; the bottom of his jaw flew off of his face and he was thrown backwards from the force.

"How!" Zach demanded. His eyes scanned the black-hooded cultists before they fell on me and Killian. I swore in my head, thinking they were going to pin this shit on us, but instead of that he ran up to us, frantic.

"You have guns, we don't carry guns to our worship. Please, help us get them back. We need them for our festival we're already short slaves!" His tone was shrill and panicked, and even though it was night his pupils were tiny.

"We will," Killian said, a little too enthusiastic if you ask me; and before I even got a word in, Killian was pulling me down the corridor, flickers of fire flashing and shining on the concrete walls.

We ran out into a room inside of these concrete walls that had, what I'd assume, were slave pens: shanty houses coated in tar, dirty and smelling intensely like piss and shit. Blood Crows were fleeing down another maze-like corridor, and I heard one of them yelling to grab as many guns as they could.

"Follow me," Killian said hastily. He ran along the wall and down a northern corridor, opening up to yet another section of raised beds all in rows, and further on, trees, but the dirt in these beds smelled heavily of rot. I assumed other slaves had been buried here.

"There it is!" Killian sounded excited. I didn't know what the fuck he was talking about, or what the hell he'd been up to while I was sleeping, but he took me to a thick gnarled tree with limbs as big as my arm, and he started to climb.

"No!" Zach yelled at us. "There's lethal radiation! It'll kill you!"

"We won't be out in there long," Killian yelled back. "We'll get you those slaves!" He jumped onto the concrete wall and slid off and into the darkness below.

I got onto the wall and glared down at him. "What the hell are you up to?" I hissed.

My night vision adjusted itself and I saw a sheepish grin from him. "Balancing you out and being your voice or morality. Come on and jump, the quad isn't far."

I growled but jumped down onto the ground. I looked around but didn't see anything but a couple crumbled structures in the distance and the big building I'd spotted from the ceremony.

"What did you do?" I snatched his hand and began dragging him west, near where we'd entered Melchai. The concrete wall, a white glow against the darkness, looked to turn into the wall we'd seen covering Melchai. If I wasn't mistaken the quad wasn't far.

Killian seemed really proud of himself, but I was fuming that he hadn't tipped me off to what he'd been doing under my nose.

When he saw the anger on my face he looked away, but that didn't wipe the smirk from his face. "I just… Charles took me to the store and he accidently took a bag of our food. I was given a good excuse to follow him behind the wall and got lost…" The smirk turned into a grin, and even though I was glaring at him, oddly he hadn't burst into flames yet. "I stumbled upon the slave pens and I simply slipped a handgun and two butterfly knives I had in my bag… under a gap in the slave pen's walls… then I ran and found Charles."

I shook my head, my teeth still locked. "That was pretty fucking dangerous," I hissed. "What if they catch them and interrogate them?"

"They didn't see me," Killian replied simply.

"I don't give a shit. They could've fucking caught you. It's dangerous."

"Kind of like remaining in a town full of chimera worshipping cultists?" Killian said, his tone annoyingly cocky. "But hey, I'm immortal." He smiled at me. "It means we can take risks and have some fun right?"

I stared at him. "One day I'm going to start beating on you."

"One day, right to the moon?" he giggled.

"One day right in the face," I growled. I looked ahead, we were nearing the end of the wall. "Hurry up, we might as well fucking go home." This kid was getting a little too daring for his own good. He did all of this behind my back and had kept it hidden from me.

Then my mind flared and that hissing condescending voice popped up.

You were too unstable and a wreck, of course he wouldn't tell you.
Fucking pussy.

"Faster!" I snapped at him. The smile faded from Killian's face and instead his eyes began to fill. I didn't care; I yanked on his hand and we turned a corner on the wall, now back to the shabby wall of Melchai, and sprinted along the side of it. I caught glimpses of a parking lot in between the layers of sheet metal and house siding.

And to our right, I saw a dusty road heading up into the hills. I assumed that was where Man on the Hill was, tucked in those rocky crags somewhere.

Not my problem. I picked up the speed, not wanting any of the Blood Crows to see us sneaking back into the greywastes, and we both ran into the night.

We hugged the rocky hills pretty closely, until Melchai was hidden from us, then headed towards a belt of trees that surrounded several houses. In the middle house, the only one with an intact garage roof, would be our quad.

"You're pulling me too hard, Reaver," Killian whined behind me. "Slow down. I can't see like you can."

"I'll tell you if you're about to trip," I said icily.

And a fraction of a second later, Killian tripped. I turned around and tried to catch him, but he fell to the ground with a yelp.

I leaned down to help him up. "Come on, we're close to the quad."

Suddenly, a gunshot, so close to my ear it burst from pain and began to ring. I stood up and looked around – and my eyes fell on a half-naked slave sitting in a tree, looking terrified, and holding a fucking handgun.

He jumped down, the handgun still pointed at me but trembling in his hand. "Show me where the quad is," he stammered desperately. "Show me where it is… and I'll let you g-go."

A growl rumbled in my throat. I started to slowly walk towards him, the rage rising inside of me and filling my brain with hot blood. "Wrong move, my friend," I whispered.

The man began taking quick steps backwards, and he started to choke. "I need a quad. I just… I need to go home. I need to go home." His tongue was black, his teeth as well, and his stomach was bloated just like the other one. "Please…" His eyes filled with tears, and he lowered the gun, his head shaking back and forth. "I need to see my–"

I broke into a run and began speeding towards him. I heard a shrill scream from Killian but his voice was a thousand miles away –

– and in my sights, was my prey.

The slave bolted and began weaving in and out of the belt of trees that surrounded the houses. With my heart expediting the blood to my brain, and I could feel its pulsing behind my eyes, rapid beats like a techno song at a rave party, *thunk thunk thunk*, his desperate cries the background music that my own weaving body was dancing to.

And with quick turns and sudden stops, I closed the distance between me and him.

"No! No, I'm fucking sorry!" he screamed, and behind me Killian screamed too.

Then he made the grave mistake of looking behind him. When we made eye contact adrenaline shot through my body, and with a throated growl, I launched into a dead run.

I poured on the speed, my legs making long strides and my boots moving so quickly on the ground it didn't feel like I was hitting the ground. As I advanced and gained on the slave, I swore I had become the first chimera to fly.

Fuck, I felt alive. I gripped the combat knife in my hand and spotted a rusted car in a driveway. When the slave ran beside it, I jumped onto the hood, then the roof, and with my knife out and my face a wide, and most likely manic, grin, I jumped onto the slave and brought him to the ground…

… then drove my knife into his back and started stabbing him.

My knife went in and out of his skin like it was butter. I couldn't stop the dance. I couldn't stop the fluid movements. The knife went in and out, in and out, and while the blood poured from his back and coated my hands, my own breath became short and my head filled with a heat-filled pressure that pressed against my skull like a balloon inflating in a jar.

There was blood everywhere. He was already dead but I wanted more blood. I had to feel more blood. I automatically started sawing his head, opening up his neck wider with each methodical slice. I cut his windpipe. I cut the tendons. Then I wrenched his head back until the back of his head touched his shoulder blades and sliced to his spine.

My mouth flooding with saliva, and the next thing I knew I had my face buried into the stump of his neck, coating me with the warm blood and feeling the aromatic flesh press itself against my face.

The act reminded me of something and my consciousness was already diving so deep inside of my mind it took no time at all for me to realize just what that was.

I drank his blood and groaned into the shredded red and white that was his throat. It was reminding me of Tim... of when I had killed my little brother and had eaten the little fuck's heart.

That's what it was. This was no chimera blood, this held none of the cinnamony flavours that had made a tense heat gather inside of my groin, but it was hot blood and it had been a long time since I'd been able to exercise my chimera bloodlust.

I drank freely and deeply, loving the feeling of the sticky substance on my face. But my mind kept taking me back to Tim's body, and I decided I wouldn't fight my own vivid memories.

Too vivid of memories, but it was a memorable time. It was the first time I had tasted chimera blood.

And fuck that was the best shit I had ever tasted.

At the memory I found my eyes closing. And as I shut them my mind lit up like a television and graced me with the image of Timothy's brown and black eyes looking at me with pure terror, right before I bit into his heart. The taste of it was heavenly, pure unadulterated bliss at a time when I was losing and finding myself all at the same time.

Would I ever get a chance to taste chimera blood again? I took more of the slave's blood into my mouth and though the taste was entirely different I imagined it was Tim's. I imagined that I was back in Kreig on that cooled night with Jade beside me looking on, the heavy smell of Tim's blood seeping through the air. How I leaned down and took his still-beating heart into my mouth and bit through it, the red bliss gushing all around me, warm and steaming in the night air.

Then... yes, we stashed his body and I took his heart. I offered a chunk of it to Jade and wiped the blood from his mouth. Looking at him with full knowledge that if I was single, I would have bent him over a concrete median and fucked him right then and there.

"Reaver?" A light flashed over the body, a murder scene in the warmth of a summer's night. Killian had gotten out a flashlight.

I looked up from the body as Killian's shocked voice temporarily brought me to my senses. I looked at the slave's shredded neck in front of me, a mosaic of a thousand shades of red, and then slowly regained sensation in the rest of my body.

Holy fuck.

I was hard. Well, semi-hard, but fuck it was something.

I shot to my feet and turned around to see Killian looking at me perplexed and stunned. What was even more bizarre was that the quad was running a few feet away from him and yet I hadn't heard him get it. Killing the slave with my own hands, the blood, the carnage, and my own memories, had completely taken me away from reality.

But that didn't matter, none of this mattered, I'd figure it out some other damn time.

I started walking towards Killian, my cock burning in my boxer briefs. He stared at me and took a step away but all I had for him was a grin. I grabbed him and he let out a surprised cry, then I kissed him and started unbuttoning my pants.

"Reaver…" he gasped, but when he looked down at my pants being pulled down he took in a sharp breath. "Oh… killing and blood…" he said faintly; and I let out a rather dark chuckle.

"Take them off and bend over the quad," I growled to him.

Killian gave me a single stricken look that held apprehension, enough apprehension that if I wasn't deep into this bloodlust I would have stopped. But the memories of what I had done to Tim had taken over me, and my sex-starved mind was violently shoving away any care I had for Killian's reservations.

Killian and I both walked to the quad, Killian unbuttoning his pants. He put his hands on the leather seat of the quad, the flashlight beside him, and I pulled the black cargo pants down followed by his blue boxer briefs. I licked my lips as I admired his perky and tight ass, just perfectly formed and found myself leaning down and biting it.

Killian gasped and let out a cry, his cheeks tightening in my mouth as he tensed up. I licked my teeth imprints and the blood that had transferred from my face, and trailed my tongue down his crack. Then I stood up and found his neck.

"Fuck, Reaver… I missed you like this," Killian rasped before another cry sounded as I sunk my teeth into his neck. I grabbed his ass with both of my hands and squeezed it roughly; the bloodlust raging inside of me and burning like the center of my body was the sun's core.

I took a step back and grabbed my cock in my hand. I looked down at the stiff rod and stroked it up and down. I'd missed it thick and hard. I hadn't even had morning wood, nothing at all, it had been limp and useless... but not anymore.

To keep it hard and to keep my primal state, I drew up the feelings I'd had inside of me when I'd killed Tim. I imagined the blood gushing down my throat and the twitching, musculed organ in my mouth. Then, because I was horny and my mind was getting away from me, I drew up the lust I'd momentarily felt for Jade; and then when I'd gotten back to the library and had fucked Killian senseless.

At this thought I grabbed Killian's leg and urged him to bring his knee and place it onto the leather seat. His cheeks separated under this position and I spat on my hand and started prepping his hole. Killian groaned at this, and when I slipped a finger inside his ass rose as if greeting me. Fuck, I could tell he wanted it and wanted it badly. It had been weeks since he'd woken up and I had yet to take him, but his patience was about to pay off.

I would prove I wasn't damaged. I wasn't fucking damaged. Nero had...

No, don't fucking think of him, asshole!

My teeth locked together, and to distract myself from that toxic memory, I positioned my cock against Killian's hole and grabbed the side of his neck. I leaned down and kissed the nape and started easing myself into him.

It was tight and the only lube I had was spit, but I kept pushing. Killian cried out and raised his ass higher, his hand grabbing the handle of the quad and gripping it. I was determined though, I knew if I just got the right angle I would break through.

Killian sucked in a sharp breath and louder, more painful, cry sounded. I opened my eyes and looked over his shoulder and felt the head start to ease in.

Then something happened inside of my head. Something broke.

Fuck. No.

Something was happening to my body. Something was happening to my mind.

Something I couldn't control.

"You've had ressin before?" I heard Nero chuckle beside me. His cologne was thick in the air from his heated and sweaty body. It matched the semen, the lubricant, and the burnt smell of ciovi.

That was Nero's room; that's how it smelled.

I was on my knees gasping so hard I was bordering hyperventilating. I was looking down at my swollen dick, it had a tight black band around it which hugged the base. I'd never seen it so big but not in a good way, it was red, swollen, and aching from pressure. It was hot and sensitive but I couldn't touch it and I couldn't make it cum. He fucking wouldn't let me cum.

There was the sound of lips breaking a filter and a plume of smoke to my left. I could see Nero's leg, covered in a thin coating of black hair, and his own cock standing erect.

"Go on, just look at him for a second. You might change your mind," Nero said, his voice was slippery with amusement, just a ribbon of silk coated with gasoline. "Look at him."

I refused. So he grabbed my hair and wrenched my head up. I was forced to look ahead of me to where Kiki was; and when I tried to turn my head, he grabbed the metal collar around my neck and held it firm.

Kiki was on his hands and knees, his ass high in the air. His hole was shaved and just a tight glistening shadow between his round, pale cheeks. He was already lubed, already ready for penetration. His cock was hard between balls tucked up and small, and Nero had shaved all of his pubic hair off. He looked every inch a twink.

"Doesn't your mouth just salivate looking at that tight hole?" Nero purred into my ear. I jerked my head away as he licked my cheek. The cigar rose and I heard him take another drag, then he lowered his hand and started rubbing the head of my cock.

I tried to stifle the moan but I couldn't, nor could I resist pushing my hips towards his touch. The tension in my cock was killing me; it burned for release, it needed to cum. I'd never felt so desperate to cum in my life.

When Nero pulled his hand away I tried to raise my own to touch my cock, but the rattling of chains reminded me I was helpless. I was fucking helpless and completely under this monster's control.

"I'm going to fucking kill you one day," I gasped as Nero laughed. He lowered his head and swirled a tongue over the pulsing head. I felt like I was going to explode from the pleasure behind the warm tongue but the band on my cock stopped me. "I s-swear…"

"If you want to cum, puppy, then cum," Nero said as he raised his head. He reached over and pushed a finger into Kiki's hole. Kiki let out a moan of pleasure but then Nero withdrew the finger and gave his left cheek a hard smack. "Come on, peachy-keens. Just put it in and see how you feel. Just for a second."

No… fuck you… I closed my eyes and let out a snarl. I again tried to grab my cock with my hand and screamed my frustration when I was once again prevented.

Nero rubbed the base and pinched it, and I started grinding my hips against his hand. I hated myself, fuck, I hated myself. I needed to cum; the condensed fire in my cock was going to split the thin skin at any moment. I was going to burst; I needed to fucking release it.

Nero let me rub against his hand, but then he pulled it away and grabbed the leash holding my collar. "Come on, stud. I got you a bitch, mount him," he taunted and smacked my ass hard. Then he reached down and pulled off the ring around my dick, the one that was preventing me from cumming. "Mount him, stud." He smacked me again and roughly grabbed my ass. "Mount him, boy."

Fuck… oh, fuck. I looked at Kiki, moaning and waiting for me, then down at my cock standing fully erect with pre-cum dripping down the tip. The horror of what I was about to do was heavy and back-breaking but the painful burning, the lustful pressure from the ressin tearing apart my resolve, my self-control – was winning.

I had to cum. Fuck. I had to cum. I had to lance the pressure, feel the rush of relief and pleasure as I came inside of him.

Just… just for a second. I'll cum quickly and pull it out.

I'm sorry, Killi.

No, no don't think of him.

He'll understand – fuck, forgive me.

Nero let out an excited whoop as I crawled on my knees to Kiki. Nero held back my collar to prevent me from killing the twink, from slashing his face like I had already done, and managed to grab my cock from my already moving hips. He positioned it against Kiki's hole and I thrusted it roughly inside of him, making the orange-eyed cicaro let out a glass-shattering squeal.

Immediately, without pause, I started fucking him hard, fucking him to Nero's cheering taunting. He watched me with my leash in his hand and a cigar hanging out of his mouth as I fucked Kiki harder, faster, and with more force than I'd ever fucked someone before.

"Get him out!" Kiki shrieked. He tried to crawl away from me and a strangled sob sounding, but Nero grabbed the kid's collar with his free hand and stopped him. Kiki's cries filled me with excitement; I started moaning with my thrusts.

"Master!" Kiki sobbed. He collapsed with his legs splayed out and I fell on top of him, still thrusting and fucking him as he laid on the bed. His ear was right in front of me, and a row of inflamed stitches barely visible from the angle he was in. The kid was screaming and screaming, Nero was hollering and cheering. I – I was cumming.

Oh god, I was cumming.

"I will fucking kill you!" I suddenly screamed. I didn't know where I was but I knew I was stumbling backwards into the darkness. I felt my legs moving but they were caught on something. I fell on my ass on cold greywastes ground and started struggling backwards, trying to get away.

"I fucking swear, Nero. I will fucking kill you!" My voice broke from the intensity. I sucked in a shuddered and shaky gasp but my lungs and chest were too tight to give me the relief I needed. It was like trying to fill a cheap balloon, there was no give, the air escaped easily. I couldn't fill my lungs; I couldn't breathe.

I looked up and saw Nero running towards me, buttoning his pants but his belt was still undone. I screamed at him; I was scared of him. I screamed at him and continued to shift backwards until I turned around and tried to run. But my legs caught on something again. I think I was tied up. I ended up falling and I landed face first onto the ground.

"Reaver!" someone screamed. I recognized the voice but the television inside of my head had the volume turned up loud. Even though my eyes were open, and I knew I was staring at blood-speckled ground, I could see the back of Kiki's head.

The cicaro was screaming and crying and it was only later when I'd stopped cumming that he'd roll over with a giggle and a smile. Nero had told him to act like I was hurting him, knowing my chimera engineering would consume his pain. Fake fucking little cicaro. I'd fuck him one day until he screamed for real.

Hands grabbed my shoulder and I was rolled onto my back. I snarled like a rabid dog and tried to get away, but when I sat up, two hands framed my face.

"It's Killian. Reaver. It's Killian. You're not there anymore. You're here with me. Reaver, baby, look at me." The borders of my vision were shining and off-colour but in the center I started seeing his face, it was taking shape. Large blue eyes, eyebrows slightly darker than his blond hair had once been, pink lips, high cheek bones and the softest, whitest skin.

"Killian?" I croaked. The volume of the television playing against my will turned down and the image distorted. I could now make out his face and what he was saying was registering in my mind.

But I still found myself unable to take deep breaths, every time I inhaled my lungs rejected the air and pushed it back out. My brain was starting to panic and I realized I was trembling.

No, not just trembling – it felt like someone was grabbing my shoulders and shaking me.

"I'm here, you're safe with me," Killian said calmly. Even though my world was spinning like I was on a carnival ride, I felt surprise over how level his voice was, how – deep. He... he sounded like a man, not my little boy. "Reaver, listen to me, okay?" He framed my face again and made me look at him. And with my brain punishing me with anxiety for failing to fill my lungs with air, I looked back at him with desperation.

No... don't show Killian you're weak. You're the strong one.

I'm the strong one... not him... fucking not him.

But in this moment, I wasn't. I was standing on the tip of a knife, and I had been for months. I had been standing still with the razor-sharp edge underneath my boots, balancing my body carefully. I felt in that moment that Killian was grabbing me and steadying me, and setting my feet on solid ground.

"You're having an anxiety attack, Reaver," Killian said calmly, gently rubbing the sides of my face. "You're going to feel anxious and helpless and like you can't breathe but you can. I want you to close your eyes and concentrate on my voice." He unzipped his satchel and I watched him, until my eyes slowly closed.

"Everything will be okay, just try and take deep breaths." I winced as I felt him stick a needle into my arm. He was injecting me with heroin. "One after another. Try, even though I know it's hard, try to take in deep breaths."

To my surprise, I felt another needle get pushed into my skin. The heroin was already starting to take me, starting to coat me in warm, but he was looking for another vein. "Just calm down, it'll be over in a moment." I started to feel a darkness come to me, a black blanket as thick and weighted as lead, crushing me, and the red in my vision started to drip away.

"Shhh, there we go, baby, close your eyes."

Killian's voice started to fade.

I felt myself become limp, and then Killian catching me. I opened my eyes and saw everything around me start to dim, his voice getting farther and farther away.

And I realized… he'd overdosed me.

He was killing me.

"There we go…" Killian brushed my hair back, and as his face started to get consumed by the darkness I saw him smile. "Sleep well, *corvus*. I love you."

I died feeling his lips kiss the corner of my mouth.

When I shed myself of the white flames and took in my first conscious breath, I felt warmth around me, and comfort. I opened my eyes to see the green curtains of our bedroom drawn and the covers right up to my chin.

I was covered in a fleecy red blanket, and as I slowly sat up and squinted the crusty sleep from my eyes, I realized I was dressed in black cloth pants and a green t-shirt. It looked like he had made me as comfortable as I could possibly be, I was even wearing clean socks.

I rubbed my eyes and took in a deep breath. My lungs felt good as they expanded, like stretching after a drug-induced sleep.

And at that mention I did stretch, and as expected, an orchestra of bones popped and cracked.

"Hey, baby."

My head looked to the right and then down. Killian had been lying beside me, I hadn't even noticed that he was there. He was wearing identical black pants and a grey shirt with red stripes and he had a book in front of him.

But when he smiled at me all I could do was stare back feeling uneasy, and when the events of me winding up in this bedroom came to my mind, the embarrassment hit me like a cold smack in the face.

My heart dropped and I tried to get up. Killian put a hand on my arm but when I attempted to pull it away I found it was firm, almost forceful. "Stay," he said. And though his tones held a gentle ease, I heard sharp edges. He moved and I saw him with a glass of something red. It smelled like cherry Kool-Aid. "Drink and take a moment."

I yanked my arm away and refused the offer of the Kool-Aid. My mind was converting his attentiveness as taking care of me, which translated to my chimera mind as me being too weak to take care of myself. After what had just happened, I couldn't bear it. I couldn't continue to let him see me in this state. I'd already shown him so much weakness already. I'd already humiliated myself and erased years of establishing myself as the alpha male, the dominant beast who was shaken by nothing, and an unmoveable force. The fact that he was seeing me breakdown like this was too much to bear. Not him, not Killian. I was the one who supported and soothed him. I was his rock. Not the other way around – it just wasn't that kind of relationship.

Right?

I didn't think so but… I had never felt broken like this before. It never had to be tested.

"Drink," Killian said again. "I'm going to prepare you some heroin…"

"No," I said to him; my tone coming out with a thin layer of ice, one I hadn't even realized I'd put on it. "Stop taking care of me. I'm not a fucking kid."

I expected a hurt look and maybe even a glisten of a tear, but Killian remained stoic. He didn't look like Killian. He was collected and together; his eyes relaxed, his movements fluid and confident. He… he reminded me of…

… of someone else.

"I'm not treating you like a kid," Killian replied in a solid but gentle tone. "I'm taking care of you which is what partners do. Just relax and drink. I've been reading Perish's notes on immortal healing and the first thing your body needs is water. Drink."

Grudgingly I took it and downed the sweetened Kool-Aid in one long drink. I handed the glass back, and when I saw him pinch off a piece of the heroin brick I shook my head. "No. I don't want heroin. I don't want to be a sedated idiot; that's how *you* cope with shit, not me. And I'm not you and you're not me." I got up and walked out of the bedroom, and I heard Killian follow me to the living room.

He had yellow lines of powder laid out on the coffee table, half of them gone. A generator was on too, he must've set up the one we'd bought in Melchai.

I sat down in front of the coffee table, feeling pissed off with how well he'd set everything up here. We had lights now, a vacuumed floor – he'd done all of this shit in the small amount of time it took me to wake up from a heroin overdose.

My teeth gritted and I felt like throwing the coffee table across the room. I felt like taking the quad and going to Melchai and killing the entire city just to show Killian I was still the bloodthirsty beast he knew me as. I had to prove to him – the world – I was still the Reaper, not the mess I was now.

Not Nero's victim. Not Elish, Lycos, and Greyson's failed saviour. Not the sissy bitch who had an anxiety attack in front of his boyfriend.

"Some drugs will make you feel better," Killian said behind me, and he squeezed my shoulder.

I watched him walk to the living room. This... this weird calm way he was acting was making me uneasy.

Killian handed me the sniffer and went back into the kitchen.

I leaned down and took the remaining four lines of drugs. Then, unable to help myself, I threw the sniffer, and like that had flipped a switch, I picked up an ashtray in the middle of the coffee table and flung it. It flew across the room, hit one of the paintings we'd hung up, and went crashing to the ground behind a credenza. Running on the adrenaline that had filled me with, I picked up the lamp resting to my right and threw that too. Then, to top off my frustrated state, an angry scream bursting through my lips.

I had to get out of here. I turned around to grab my M16 to leave when I caught Killian's eye.

He was standing there, a neutral expression on his face. No tears, no fear. When shit like this happened it usually scared him to frantic crying, but he was... he was standing like nothing was happening.

"Sit down, love, and I'll get you some food," he said calmly.

For one frightening moment I wanted to put my hands on him. I wanted to take him and smack him across the face. I wanted to scare him. I wanted to make him scream and cry. All because my mind, my pride, commanded me to do anything possible to get back to our normal. A normal that was Killian crying and needing saving, and me being emotionally dead and strong as nails, saving him and comforting him.

Now everything was off-kilter, everything was different. I was the crazed one. I was the one losing control, and he was the one standing there calmly. What the fuck was going on? What the hell had happened to us?

"Why are you acting like this? BE NORMAL!" I suddenly screamed. The glaring reality that I was only showing him just how unstable I was, lost on me. I walked up to him and grabbed his shoulders and crushed them in my grip. "Stop acting so different!" I shouted right in his face.

My mind ignored the frightened look he now had, and I roughly shoved him against the wall and he hit it hard. "Stop it! Just act normal, act like everything is okay! EVERYTHING IS OKAY, THERE'S NO REASON TO ACT THIS WAY!" I grabbed him again and slammed him against the wall a second time; this time his neck snapped back and I heard his skull crack against the gyprock.

Killian cried out and tried to push me away. I slammed him again, my teeth clenched and bared through peeled back lips, and my face burning with the emotions running rampant inside of me. My crazed mind was telling me this was good, this was good. Killian's normal was scared. Killian's normal was scared. This was good. This was good.

"Reaver... Reaver, it's okay. Let me go. It's Killian!" Killian suddenly cried. He thought I was hallucinating again. But I wasn't. I wasn't.

Killian held the back of his head and I saw a tear run down his cheek as he started to cry.

"YES!" I screamed. My face felt like it was breaking out in a heat rash, my eyebrow was twitching. "Be scared. Be scared."

"I am scared," Killian whimpered, a trickle of blood ran down his nose and joined with the tears to make pink. "I'm scared, Reaver."

I dropped him and he fell to the floor with a cry. I nodded and turned from him. I walked to the edge of the living room and circled back. "And I'm not," I told him harshly. "I'm not scared. I am the clone of the man who ended the world. I am not scared; I am not a fucking coward. I am not a sissy. I don't care what the fuck he did to me. This isn't me, and what is happening to me isn't happening. Because it can't happen to me. Got it? So JUST – BE – NORMAL!" I screamed the last part; I screamed it so loudly my eyes were bulging out of their sockets.

Killian stared at me. He put a hand to his mouth and more tears rolled down his cheeks. I nodded my approval of this and sat down by the couch.

"We're going to play Mario now," I told him and I turned on the television and then a game system he must've bought in Melchai. He'd set everything up for me, good. "We'll do drugs, then have sex." When Killian didn't move I whirled around. "WE'RE PLAYING MARIO!" I screamed at him.

Killian quickly got up and ran over. He took the purple game controller with shaking hands and I nodded again. I kept nodding and watched the television as the game loaded.

The television's sound was low, so low I could hear Killian's frightened breathing and the rapid beats of his scared heart. I found myself staring blankly at the television screen with the controller in my hand. Time continued to tick on but it was continuing on without me, leaving me with my emotions scattered all around, and me so used to standing tall I hadn't been able to bend over to pick them up.

Killian had tried to pick them up for me, and tried to bear the heavy burden they put on his shoulders; shoulders trying so hard to carry everything, even though his back was breaking under his own.

I stared at the television screen and slowly closed my eyes. My hearing strengthened and I heard Killian's heartbeat even clearer… and my own. Mine was faster than his.

I inhaled a raspy breath that broke from the shaking in my chest.

"How did you handle being raped?" I asked in a quiet voice.

I slowly opened my eyes and stared down at the GameCube controller. I went over every button and its colour, the joystick, the curves and shapes. I had to tune out my hearing because the thumping of my heart was pounding against my ears, but the room was so quiet there was no escaping it.

Thunk. Thunk. Thunk. I could hear the squishing of my blood as my heart contracted around it, like squeezing the last of something out of a bottle.

"I had someone strong for me," he said after a long silence. "Someone who was kind and caring, patient and attentive. Someone who didn't judge me when I went crazy for a while."

I nodded and continued to stare at the controller, and then my hands.

"Kessler gave me back to Nero when I refused to tell him where Perish was, and when torturing me and Chally didn't work –" I began to say, my voice dead on my lips, "– Nero chained me to his bed in his bedroom in Cardinalhall. The first day he had me he fucked me; he laughed the entire time. As he came he bit my neck and killed me. He killed me many times." The words were coming from my mouth, from me, but I didn't recognize the person speaking. "He did things to me I don't think I can... can ever tell you. He had me there for weeks and he fucked me at least five times every day. Even if I was dead. If he was tired... he made me do things to his cicaro." My brow knitted and the controller slipped from my hands and landed on the floor with a loud clunk. "He..." I looked over at Killian, and saw a look of such unimaginable horror on his face it stole the words from my mouth. He was staring at me, his mouth slightly open, his eyes wide. He'd had looks of horror on his face before, but never one like this. I don't think this one had a name. "He drugged me with ressin and made me fuck his cicaro. I'm sorry. Forgive me."

Killian just stared. I turned from him and looked back down at my hands. "I had never felt such desperation, such... helplessness. I'd never been so beaten down, so broken. I thought I couldn't be broken. Eventually, I chewed my hand off... to escape from the cuffs. He found me, pinned me, fucked me... but... but Reno came, Caligula and Nico too; Elish was flying the plane. I went into rages once I was free from him, but when I was with Elish, he helped me through it." I pursed my lips tight and felt a flicker of pain. I missed Elish. "Elish and me... we bonded a lot. He... shared shit with me and I stopped going into those rage trances and... and being so worried about you helped distract it, but..." I looked around our house. "I think now that we're at peace and everything is calm... this shit is coming back. I thought I was okay but... but I'm not. I'm not okay."

I felt a hand rest on mine and I let him hold my hand in his. "No one can walk away from that unscathed, Reaver," Killian said to me. "No one."

"I know," I whispered back. I looked down at his hand and felt a jolt of unease. I tried to push it down but I started to feel uncomfortable. I had shared a lot with him and there was only so far I could go. I didn't think... I don't think I wanted to talk about this anymore. I had told him, that was enough.

I got up.

"Baby..." Killian whispered.

"I need to go patrolling," I said to him, my words coming out quickly and without pause. "Don't... don't mention this. You know what's going on but... that's enough, okay? Don't ever bring this up again." I grabbed my jacket and my M16, and before he could say anything back to me I opened the front door and walked out into the night.

CHAPTER 10

Elish

THE TERRAIN IN FRONT OF HIM WAS ROLLING, BUT
the roads were in good enough condition for the dirt bike to keep an
acceptable speed. In some places the ash had coated the road, and the
sparse rains had pounded it down so the wind would no longer blow it
away. But eventually there would be an overpass or a row of medians, one
in front of the other like slaves chained together, so he never lost the
highway.

Elish didn't stop, and because of that he had to eat sparingly. Every
time he passed a building or a gas station with its colourful sign broken
and stained, he kept on going down the road. The prospect of making
another mile before dark overshadowed the rumbling in his stomach, and
the fatigue that was continuously pouring sand onto his eyelids. There had
even been an incident the night before when three ravers had found him
and gave chase, but he kept on driving forward, the headlight off and only
his night vision giving shapes to the greywastes in front of him.
Eventually he lost them, and didn't stop until morning when the heat
gauge on the dirt bike started to walk amongst the red.

And even then he had slept only two hours in a fast food restaurant.
He slept amongst metal and plastic chairs and benches, and colourful balls
strewn amongst the rubble and dust; their old home a child's ball pit in a
separate area. For reasons unknown to him, he picked up a yellow ball and
carried it with him. Perhaps it reminded him of the cicaro's eyes, or
perhaps he was just sleep deprived and acting odd.

That afternoon, after pushing the dirt bike the entire morning, Elish noticed something that made him stop. He stopped the dirt bike and left it idling and jumped off to check it out.

There was no outward expression of relief, but inside a flicker of light flared. He was looking at disturbed greywaste ground beside a row of medians that separated the road from a steep incline. When he looked closer he saw brown blood stains, smears, and…

Elish looked closer. A bloody hand print.

Elish laid his hand on top of the hand print and stared at it. He knew with confidence that this was where Reaver had died. He had gotten onto a quad, and as Elish had told him… he'd ridden it until he had died. This was where he'd healed, before getting onto the quad and continuing.

Elish walked onto the road and though it was faint, he did see quad tracks. It was then, and only then, that he allowed himself a single sigh. Then he got onto his dirt bike and continued down the street, knowing for sure he would have Kessler's remote phone in his hand before darkness overtook the cloudy day.

As he rode down a flat stretch of road, Elish placed his hand onto his forearm, where Jade's old collar was belted. He rubbed it, as if for good luck, and let the boy's face dash the intense fatigue that was a heavy weight on already buckling shoulders.

Elish didn't know when he had started relying on that boy's memory for strength. It would be something he'd have to analyze when he was back home, and the events that had been making him a passenger and no longer a driver in his life. There would be a lot of thinking to be done once he came home, but that was for Elish of Skyfall, James the greywaster cared nothing for picking apart such things.

It had now been ten days since he'd gotten on that plane. Ten days since he'd left his cicaro in the care of Sanguine and the half-raver. He'd gone with Garrett and the others to check out a radiation spike, thinking he'd be home in no time at all.

And now… ten days.

So much can happen in ten days. What if Jade had taken a turn for the worse and I will go home to Lyle telling me he's dead? Sanguine was king right now, and Elish had a shaky hold on that man at best. The only comfort that he had was that Sanguine's love towards Jade was genuine – he'd never let anything happen to him.

But still… Sanguine was a mad man, and only a device as big as Elish's thumbnail was keeping him from being consumed by insanity.

Elish had promised him his freedom from Silas's remote control. What if Sanguine had decided to take matters into his own slippery talons?

That wasn't the only prospect to be worried over. Sanguine and Nero had an unbreakable bond. But if Sanguine freed Nero that was something that didn't concern him. At the very least it would keep Silas busy when he woke – woke full of despair from Sky's O.L.S being destroyed.

Yes, that was a plus. When Silas wakened he would be deep in grieving and that would give Elish the time needed to check those hard drives and recover the information Reaver and Killian died and burned for. They may be gone but their deaths do not have to be in vain.

And when Silas was gone... Elish could find a way to quench the white flames now burning in the plaguelands and he could bring Reaver back. He had two boys more similar to Killian than anyone else, and surely one of them would eventually worm their way into Reaver's heart.

Killian and those boys were cut from the same cloth. The same connection would happen – wouldn't it?

And if the white flames could not be quenched... or while I am researching a way...

The next time Mantis calls... I will be making the request from him he had been dreading for twenty years.

I will be demanding Adler's return to me.

Yes. See? Elish's jaw clenched firmly as these thoughts replayed in his head. They replayed again and again and soothed him like cold water on a fresh burn. Whenever the cold water stopped and the burn started to flare and throb, he would soothe it with these reassuring thoughts.

He had backups. He had backups. He hadn't just relied on one crop. He had another born immortal and he had another...

Elish swallowed, and oddly he found himself unable to say the secret, even if only in his head.

He had other Killians, two of then grown in different environments.

I have only seen Adler once since I handed him off, I have no idea what to expect. Will he be like Reaver? Worse? Better? Will he even need a Killian to calm him, or can I keep the other boys' origins a secret and not disrupt their life?

I do not know but I will find out.

Because I will fix this.

Was it worth it? Reno's echoing voice cut through his manufactured confidence.

Elish momentarily shut his eyes tight, then opened them and continued to drive the dirt bike. Now that he had the knowledge that he was on the right road, time seemed to go faster yet slower at the same time.

It was an hour before sundown when he saw the abandoned quads in the distance, but there was a quiver in his stomach when he saw movement as well. It wasn't much, just a shifting like a thrashing animal; a movement that would go unnoticed by the eye if it wasn't the only disruption for the eye to catch.

Elish touched the strap of the assault rifle he had on his back, as if to make sure it was there, then he continued to ride towards what he had started calling Kessler's Ground Zero.

As he approached the moving thing stopped, then a head poked up from a dark mound. Two large ears twitched towards him before pressing back, and the animal, a primitive version of Perish's beloved carracat, sprinted off with two kittens behind her.

She'll no doubt be back once I leave, Elish said to himself. He stopped the dirt bike and turned it off and dismounted. On feet taking him quicker than his usual gliding grace, he walked to the center of Ground Zero and observed the scene he had so quickly left behind.

The rot was one that crawled up your nose and clung to the fine hairs like oil. The flies had gotten to these corpses, as well as the carrion eaters. Limbs with shredded clothing still attached were strewn at all angles, and dried blood covered the grey with little white worms to break up the dismal tones. All corpses remained inside the circle of quads in a fashion that alluded to a cult's sacrifice more than scavenging animals

Elish stepped over a torso, green and grey and alive with insects who had embedded themselves in the scavengers' wound marks, and found Kessler's body. Grimacing at the smell, he leaned down and reached into Kessler's pocketed vest made out of thick canvas. He found the remote phone and pressed one of the buttons.

His heart sank when there was no illuminated screen to greet him. He clenched the remote phone firm in his hand and made the motion to toss it, when he stopped. Kessler had found them because of Reaver's sestic radiation outburst. He could've turned his phone off to avoid anyone knowing his whereabouts. All phones in chimera-possession had trackers, even if most brothers had easy access to blockers.

Elish didn't allow himself to feel the spark of hope, but his emotionless mind had stopped listening to him weeks ago. He pressed the power button and muttered a silent prayer.

The remote phone turned on, and as the relief flooded him Elish let out a loud *whoop!* and raised the phone in the air towards the heavens in triumph.

Then, with a cough and a glance around him, as if expecting one of his brothers to be there to judge him, Elish lowered his hand and searched the cell phone for Kessler's contact list. He decided to phone one of his brothers who would be in Cardinalhall; they would be quicker.

An audible sigh broke Elish's lips when he realized that wouldn't be wise. No doubt there were legionary looking for Kessler and the legionaries who never returned home. Since Tim had been killed months before, Tiberius would be manic over his husband and last remaining son becoming missing.

So Elish settled on one of the only chimeras he could trust with keeping where he was secret. The same one who most likely planned to strand them there in the first place. But Sanguine wanted to strand Silas in order to free Nero and possibly Ceph... he had no reason to strand Elish.

Elish found Sanguine's contact, and felt another trickle of relief when it connected and rang.

"Hello?"

Elish was puzzled for a moment before he recognized the voice. "Juni?" he replied. He could hear a hum in the background... he was in a plane. "Where's Sanguine?"

"I... uhh..." Juni's voice was fearful. Elish decided to backtrack. If the boy was in a Falconer and in possession of Sanguine's phone, there was no doubt in Elish's mind that he'd acquired both items in an underhanded way.

"You don't need to answer that," Elish replied. "Are you in a Falconer?" I need you to pick me up. We're stranded, as you already know. Where abouts are you?"

There was a rustling. Elish thought the boy was going to hang up the phone out of fear, but then he heard a familiar voice.

"Hello? Master?"

"Luca?" Elish closed his eyes with relief. That boy was about to earn himself another cat. "Where are you? I've been travelling northwest from the radiation pulse... do you–"

"I stole King Silas's cellphone tracker, Master. I – I know where you

are now," Luca replied. *"It just came on... we thought it was Kessler and we were going to ignore it. We're about an hour away. Hold on."*

The family may be forever intertwined in politics, but one can always rely on the loyalty of a sengil. Elish breathed out a sigh of relief and sat on one of the quads. "Is Jade okay?" he asked as quietly as he could.

"Yes. Big Shot is guarding him and Lyle is there. I just saw him before Juni picked me up," Luca replied. *"We've been looking for days. We got as close to the radiation and the fire as we could but our Geigerchips—"*

A steady tone cut off Luca and Elish pushed the end call button. He put the remote phone into his trouser pocket and wiped his hands down his face. Then, unable to stand the smell any longer, he found a median twenty feet away and sat down on it. Dark thoughts edged his mind but the fact that he would soon be back in Skyfall, and soon beside Jade, chased them away like light in a cold, damp basement.

Once he was home he could immerse himself in those hard drives and work. He was planning on doing his work from home as often as he could, and also move Jade's hospital bed and all of its equipment into his old room. Lyle was only a couple floors down, and he would have open access to Elish's apartment.

With this plan in mind, Elish brushed away all other toxic thoughts, and as if to prove to himself everything would be just fine... he raised his chin and stared forward.

Seeing the Falconer was one of the most welcome sights he'd experienced since he saw King Jade on his throne. Elish rose and watched the black spot in the distance come closer until it landed fifty feet away.

The door slid open and Luca jumped out. He ran up to Elish before stopping and bowing. "We were worried about you. Sanguine was acting like there was nothing wrong but we knew..." He started walking beside Elish to the plane. "I know we technically defied a king's orders but I justified it in... technically wouldn't Jade be king? He would've wanted us to look for you."

"Sanguine is going to have the scruff of his neck shaken when I see him," Elish answered back coolly. He nodded to Juni who was standing inside of the plane. "How's the fuel, Juni?"

The boy didn't look happy. "We were going to have to turn back soon..."

"Then you'll be dropping me back off to Skyfall and returning an hour before daylight. If fuel is low we won't have enough time to look to make it worthwhile," Elish said. He grabbed the sliding metal door and slid it shut, then turned and walked to the cockpit. He debated flying but it had been a gruelling ten days. He didn't trust his overtaxed body and the sengil was more than capable.

Juni sat down on the pilot's chair, his face troubled, but after a look from Elish he obediently took the Falconer's controls into his hands and the plane rose into the air.

"When we return I will be able to give you a map of the area," Elish told him. "I can mark off the road they are walking on. You'll find Jack quickly that way."

"Okay," Juni said, his voice was that of a put-out teenager. "His remote phone...?"

"All of our phones were destroyed from the heat of the flames," Elish responded. "It was just a lucky coincidence I found Kessler's."

"But... where is Kessler, Master?" Luca asked from behind him. Elish was amused when Luca handed him a steaming cup of tea. Leave it to the rough and barren greywastes to remind one's self how much a sengil did.

"His head has been removed. I can only assume whoever did it disabled Jack's death tracker. If Kessler even had his in," Elish replied. "I will answer no more questions on the subject. Any improvement from Jade?"

Luca was quiet behind him and Elish knew the answer to that. "No..." Luca said, his voice small. "He's still just sleeping."

He isn't sleeping... he's brain-dead. Elish's lip pulled but he hid it with a drink of tea. He nodded and soon heard the silent patting feet as Luca went to look out the cargo window.

The trip back to Skyfall was a long one and a quiet one. There weren't many words exchanged though in truth Elish would've liked a distraction, but the sengils were both quiet. It was their nature to be submissive and silent in the presence of chimeras, and Elish didn't feel like puzzling them by requesting conversation. So instead he sat quietly and in his own shroud of stoicism, and not even a relieved sigh broke through his lips when he saw the city of Skyfall in the distance.

The plane landed and Elish opened the sliding door. He stepped foot onto the roof of Olympus and closed his eyes for a brief moment. Then he walked to the door which was, ever since Jade's kidnapping, guarded by a thien.

161

Elish nodded at him, and to the thien's credit, he showed no surprise at Elish's rugged state. He had a beard, a blood-splattered body, and clothing in desperate need for a wash. Cleaning could wait though, he had to make sure Jade was okay with his own eyes.

Juni and Luca immediately took off towards the army base to refuel the Falconer, leaving Elish by himself. He sped down the flight of stairs to the elevator and felt a jump in his heart when the elevator gave a lurch.

He didn't want to admit it, even to himself, but he felt old feelings come back, and perhaps that was why he was anxious. Jade being kidnapped by the Crimstones was still fresh in his mind. It seemed he almost had slight PTSD regarding the incident; his heart was racing over anticipating the doors opening to a blood-soaked carpet.

But there was nothing. The doors opened to a clean hallway and the hum of a television inside the infirmary.

Elish walked into the hallway and immediately purged himself of the racing pulse and cold sweat. He made a mental note to be harder on himself over these needless fears and feelings, and walked into the room where his cicaro laid.

Elish stopped in his tracks.

Leaning over Jade was a young man he had never seen before. The man had short black hair with a frock of white on the left-hand side. He looked to be in his twenties and was horribly skinny, the small t-shirt and cloth pants only accentuating his state.

And he wasn't only leaning over Jade's hospital bed, he had his hands clasped on both sides of Jade's head.

"What the hell do you think you're doing?" Elish barked. The young man jumped high up in the air and looked at Elish with wide eyes.

They were mismatched, one was dark blue and the other black. He had heterochromia and they were looking at Elish like a deer who had spotted the hunter.

Elish stalked towards the boy, but no sooner had he taken two steps, the boy ducked under Jade's hospital bed and skidded to the other side. Elish charged at him and tried to grab him but the boy dodged his grasp and sprinted out the door. With his teeth clenched and a rage boiling inside of him he gave chase.

Then he heard choking behind him. Elish turned around and saw Jade heaving, his mouth opening and closing over the tube going down his throat, and his yellow eyes open and staring.

"Jade?" Elish said breathlessly. He turned around and ran to Jade's bedside and gently started extracting the tube.

When it was out, Jade started gasping for air. Elish put his hand on Jade's chin, the other on his chest. "Calm down. There is no need to be frantic, you're making yourself choke," Elish said. An energy filled him like he had swallowed the power of the sun. He took in a sharp breath, almost not wanting to ask it. "Do you know who I am? Can you speak?"

Jade took in several rasping breaths before his breathing started to normalize. The boy, still in a daze, looked around, his eyes going in all directions. He didn't look like he was registering anything.

Elish patted his cheek, feeling his heart sink to the floor. "Maritus?" he whispered. The sadness washed over him and he felt his throat tighten. "M-maritus? Come on… say something to me. Jade? It's… Elish."

Jade's amber eyes squinted and they stopped moving around. Then slowly they focused on Elish and squinted again.

Just say my name…

Jade stared at him, and Elish took his hand into his own. "If you recognize me… squeeze my hand."

Elish scanned Jade's eyes for any signs that he was registering what he was hearing, or registering anything at all.

Then Elish felt Jade's hand squeeze his.

In spite of himself Elish took in a shuddering breath and nodded. "It's… it's something, isn't it?" Then he looked behind him and scowled at the open door, the last place he had seen that strange man. Someone he had never seen before.

Was he a chimera?

No, that was impossible and an outlandish thought. No chimera had heterochromia, Silas had never requested it. And no chimera had white frocks in their hair either.

Elish felt his hand squeeze again. He looked back to Jade and smiled.

"You noticed my mind wandering, did you?" Elish said. He caressed Jade's cheek and brushed back his hair. "Do you… do you remember seeing someone strange in here?"

Jade stared at him.

Elish's head turned when he heard rustling. He squeezed Jade's hand then slid his own hand free, and walked towards the noise.

Laying slumped in his favourite chair with a text book splayed out on the ground was Lyle, and several feet away was Big Shot. Both of them were just starting to come to, but from what?

Elish turned and looked back to the doorway. He could feel his mind start to gather all the clues he had about this strange scene he had walked in on, and compare them to the knowledge he already had of his family's chimeras. But as he thought about it, one possibility kept sneaking into his mind. At first he banished it as folly, an impossibility, but with the half-raver and his retired sengil seemingly put to sleep and this strange boy found hovering over Jade.

It was as if… he had the same abilities King Silas himself wielded.

Impossible.

Elish shook his head and walked up to Lyle, and promptly smacked him upside the head. "Wake up, you imbecile. Big Shot, why the hell aren't there thiens…" Elish turned around to where a row of beds were and saw two pairs of boots beginning to move. He walked over to them and his own questions were answered. Two thiens were laying in a heap, their arms just starting to shift and writhe as whatever had taken them off of their feet wore off.

"Master Elish?" Lyle mumbled. Elish turned around and saw his sengil sitting with a hand on his head. "What the hell…?"

"Do you remember anything?" Elish already knew the answer to this but he wanted to make sure. He kicked the thiens in their boots before walking over and lightly kicking the half-raver in the side.

"N-no…" Lyle said. Then his eyes widened. "Jade? Is… he?"

"He's fine… better than fine," Elish muttered. He walked back to the boy and gently put a hand on the side of his head. "I want him moved to my apartment."

"Master Elish… he's too ill. He…" Suddenly Lyle swore and there was a scraping of a chair as he jumped to his feet. "His breathing tube! He needs his…" Elish raised a hand and Lyle skidded to a stop. His eyes swept the room to make sure the three other sets of ears were too lethargic to listen, and dropped his voice. "He's breathing on his own and he knows who I am." Then he hesitated but decided to tell Lyle what he had seen.

When Elish was done, Lyle looked nothing less than flabbergasted. He went to the EEG, a machine that measures brain activity, and his mouth dropped open. Elish hid the hope this brought and watched the doctor press several buttons on the touch screen.

"He's not at normal, nowhere near normal brain activity…" Lyle said with a shake of his head. "But where there was nothing there is now something. He's breathing on his own, obviously." The doctor leaned over Jade and tapped the edge of his eye.

Jade's eye shut and squinted.

"I asked if he knew who I was, he squeezed my hand," Elish said. "His mind must be back… it's just his body."

A look of doubt crossed Lyle's face. Elish's lips pursed at this, he almost wanted to punish the doctor for disagreeing with him, but he knew enough to keep his mouth shut. Elish had studied medicine, but over the last several years Lyle had made it his mission to become an expert on Jade, inside and out.

"Jade," Lyle said loudly. He grabbed a pen and wrote out a math problem: 6 x 8.

"He wouldn't even know that if he was well. Make it easier," Elish said irritably. He snatched the piece of paper from Lyle and quickly wrote out another one.

2 + 2.

"Squeeze the answer," Elish said, his voice one again dropping to calm. "Take as much time as you want."

Jade stared at him.

"Look at the paper." Elish held the paper in front of his face. "What is it?"

Jade kept staring.

Elish sighed and lowered the paper from his face. "I suppose you always had to disappoint me, hm?" he said with a sad smile. Then he glanced up at Lyle. "I want him moved to my apartment like I said. You'll have free access, you and Nels, and you can come and go as you please. I don't want him far from me and I will be running Skyfall from my apartment."

"Not… Silas?"

"Silas is resurrecting at the moment," Elish said with a bitter edge to his voice. "And when he wakes up I doubt he'll be capable of doing anything but screaming and crying."

Elish could tell that Lyle wanted to enquire, but he knew his place enough to only nod. There were no more questions after that, or comments.

Soon Big Shot was awake, and when the two thiens woke they were dismissed with a firm warning not to mention to anyone what had happened to them. Then Elish picked up Jade and returned to his apartment.

For a moment he found himself hesitating when he opened the doors to what had been his home for decades. He didn't know why and stood in the archway to contemplate his hesitation.

With an angry hiss between locked teeth, he realized it was once again his own paranoia. The feeling went hand in hand with the same PTSD-type flashback that had struck him when the elevator doors opened to Lyle's infirmary floor.

Elish forced down this unease and mentally berated himself for letting these emotions crop up inside of him. No, he had to be strong now, stronger than ever. He had to fix this and that meant purging his emotions and feelings over the events that had transpired. If Reaver saw him feeling unease at elevator doors opening and entering apartments, the boy would laugh at him until tears formed in his eyes.

And with that, Elish tightened his hold on Jade and walked confidently into his apartment. He was greeted by a content Biff who weaved in and out of his legs, the cat's tabby tail high in the air and with a slight curl at the end.

Elish set Jade down on the couch and propped his head up with a pillow. He'd requested a recliner for the boy so he could sit up, but that wouldn't get delivered until later.

"I'll be taking a shower now, as you may have noticed I was delayed in the greywastes," Elish said to Jade. He took the remote and turned on the television and found Jade's own personal channel, but when he saw that *Jeopardy* was on, a favourite for the two to watch and match wits (Elish always won), he decided against it and found a cartoon for him to watch. He didn't want Jade to feel badly for not knowing any of the answers.

"I'll be right back." Elish patted Jade's head and walked towards their shared bedroom.

But when he was unbuttoning his blood and dirt-stained shirt he paused, then walked over to the doors to the outside hallway and locked them. Lyle had a key now anyway, if he wanted in before Elish came back, he could use that.

Then Elish stripped down and took a much needed shower. When he emerged he shaved and evened out his eyebrows, and slowly but surely, felt himself become Elish again. To solidify his transformation back to the leader and king he now was, he dressed in his silver robes with the blue trim, and wore underneath, a new white button-down and black trousers.

He looked into the mirror as he straightened out his robes. "You're a chimera," he said to himself in a low voice. "Act like it." He nodded at himself and adjusted his collar, then walked out into the living room.

Lyle was there with young Nels, the two of them were plugging Jade's machines into a power bar. Jade himself was now moved to a beige recliner thanks to Elliot, Nero's burly sengil, and seemed to be watching *Fairly Odd Parents* on the television.

"I'd like for him to be kept on the heart monitor, Elish," Lyle said as he attached the wires to the pads on Jade's bare chest. "If his heartbeat drops it'll send an alarm so you'll know. I wheeled in a defibrillator as well just because I know you'd want me to. He can't eat on his own... do you want me to walk through how to feed him through the tube?"

Elish shook his head. "No. I've had to do tube feeding before, just make sure there is enough milk and powder for the next week. Luca can get more once he returns."

Lyle nodded. "I can send Nels down a few times a day to check on him and change the bags. And I've been sponge bathing..."

"I plan on doing everything," Elish replied. "Nels will not be needed, only you for whatever medical needs he'll have."

A look of pure shock came to Lyle's face. "Everything...? Medication, cleaning? He... he can't do anything on his own, Master Elish."

Elish gave Lyle a cold look and the doctor visibly shrunk down. Though now in his forties and physically older than Elish, he looked like the young sengil he'd once been when living with Elish.

"Are you implying I am incapable of taking care of my cicaro's needs?" Elish asked, not hiding the razor's edge in voice.

Lyle shook his head rapidly and raised his hands. "You know me and you know I'm not. My apologies, Master. Can I write out his instructions at least?"

Elish gave him a stiff nod. "You may and write them neatly. Your handwriting has gotten dismal since you've become a doctor." When Elish turned around and walked to Jade, Lyle could be seen letting out a tense breath through wide, rather surprised, eyes. But Lyle quickly hid it before Elish could see, and followed behind him.

"Nels?" Lyle called, but his apprentice was already there with a pen and paper. Lyle sat down on the couch and started writing out everything that Jade would need.

"Where is Luca?" Lyle looked around with a furrowed brow. "I told him you'd come back when you were ready, but I swear he birthed fifteen kittens in the time you were gone to your return."

Elish ignored Lyle's light pry for information and made himself a cup of tea. "Luca will return tonight," he said simply. "Your job is finding a way for my cicaro to get the rest of his mind back, not sticking your nose where it doesn't belong."

"I was merely curious," Lyle said with a sigh. "You bring me half-ravers, mute greywaster boys, and Jade in critical condition, and then you wring my neck when I ask a question."

"I don't need an excuse to wring your neck, Lyle. Continue to write out my cicaro's instructions. You'll need silence for it."

The corner of Lyle's lip rose, but he said nothing after that.

Two hours later found Elish alone in his apartment with Jade on him. After cleaning him and dressing him in warm pajamas, Elish wrapped him in a blanket and laid with him on the couch. Jade was lying on top of him, his favourite position to sleep, and all was silent in the apartment save for the hum of the electronics that the chimera ear seemed to pick up when there was nothing to distract it.

"*The cart was too heavy to push into the wet woods and they nooned in the middle of the road and fixed hot tea and ate the last of the canned ham with crackers and with mustard and applesauce,*" Elish read. He turned the page with a smirk, holding the book over Jade's raven-coloured hair as his cicaro's head lay on his chest. "The world has ended and they still have tea. One of the reasons I always enjoyed this book. This man has good sense." Elish stifled a yawn and managed to reach his bookmark to slip in between the pages. "Did you fall asleep?" He couldn't see Jade's face from the angle he was at, but, feeling clever for thinking of the idea, he took out his reflective metal bookmark and tried to catch Jade's reflection.

Yes, fast asleep... good. Elish turned off the light, then reached over and tilted Jade's heart monitor away from his face to increase the darkness around him.

Elish rested a hand on Jade's head, and was content to hear the boy's heartbeat thump against his chest. No one would believe this man, with a countenance carved from the clearest of ice, was at ease in this moment, but he was. After almost ten days out of Skyfall, stranded in the greywastes and having to resort to shooting little girls to steal a dirt bike, he never felt the tightened binds that had been constricting him, loosen so.

The darkness was forever a cloud above his head, and now more than ever did he know the twisted and difficult path ahead of him… but somehow having Jade with him banished those caustic thoughts… if only temporarily.

When did I come to rely on him for comfort? Elish's brow furrowed at this, even though his eyes were closed. He disliked the thought of relying on the boy for anything, but his feelings in the greywastes couldn't be ignored. When Jade was with him he had found himself feeling stronger, because he had to be that immovable rock for his cicaro. Jade expected it and relied on it himself. The two of them fed off of each other, each giving the other what the other one needed. Jade though, had no idea just what he gave Elish, or how much Elish had come to need it.

Which of course… would continue. There was no need for the boy to know, he was still young enough to use it against his master.

Elish relaxed his body and listened to Jade's heart, and though his failures in the plaguelands eventually extended its tentacles and wrapped themselves around Elish's calm state, he managed to push them away by counting the boy's heartbeats. It was a temporary distraction, but one he would take.

Was It Worth It? Reno's voice echoed in his head, just as strangled, just as full of pain as the day he had heard it, and like Elish had been doing with all the other dark thoughts, he pushed it down and purged it from his system.

Killian's death, Reaver's fate… will not be in vain.

He will fix this.

I will fix this.

"Well… looks like we have some déjà vu. I swear I've seen this scene before."

Elish opened his eyes and saw the blurring image of Garrett slowly start to come into focus, further on was Luca and beside him, Jack.

"It would happen less if I took your key away," Elish muttered. He steadied Jade and shifted himself until he was sitting up. "Help me put him in the recliner. When did you get back?"

"About five hours ago," Garrett said. He smelled like soap, and the dusting of facial hair he had been growing in the greywastes had been shaved off, save for the pencil moustache he had been sporting for the past three decades. "I went to the infirmary, I suspected you to be there. Lyle says Jade's improved?" Garrett picked up Jade with a grunt and walked the boy over to the black recliner. He laid him down before sweeping the boy with his gaze, then snapped his fingers in front of Jade's face.

"Stop that," Elish said annoyed. "He knows who I am and he's breathing on his own. Besides that... he's still rather unresponsive."

Garrett nodded and took a steaming cup of coffee. He brought the cup to his lips and followed Elish with his eyes as he walked to the bathroom.

"Silas will be waking up soon," Garrett said when Elish returned. "His heart started beating an hour before Luca, Juni, and Saul found us. Jack is giving him a day."

Elish was surprised at this, a surprise that quickly soured his stomach. "He had such severe burns, I was sure it would be a month."

Jack took a cup of coffee too and swirled the contents with his finger. "That's immunity to sestic radiation for you. Most of his burns were surface burns; he would've been back sooner if his arm wasn't so charred. I do hope you have a plan as to what you're going to do when he wakes up."

"Keep him from ending the world," Elish muttered and he sat down on the couch. "I'll be doing all of my work from my apartment. I'm not leaving Jade. I'm assuming Silas will be insane with grief, and I'll be too busy to deal with him. He can be Sanguine and Drake's problem for the time being."

Elish's eyes shot to Jack when he noticed his younger brother's mouth pulling to a frown. He stared at him until Jack noticed, and saw the uncomfortable look on his face deepen. "When I was close enough to Skyfall for my trigger watch to go off... I got quite a few notifications," Jack said. "Drake I resolved, he resurrected on his own but... Sanguine died and the homing signal as to where I am to find his body isn't working. Kessler's went off as well and it's the same issue. Those homing signals can be destroyed, of course, but... it means they both must've died from a lot of head trauma. Kessler's in the northern greywastes too."

Which means Reaver was either smart enough to dig out anything he found in his brain or he threw him into a deep enough pit it broke itself... either way, that at least is good.

But Sanguine...

Elish looked at Luca and saw his sengils posture stiff and his eyes staring forward. There was no mistaking the boy had the answer.

"Sanguine will show up," Elish said in a casual manner, then, since he was in possession of his phone and the cellphone tracker would soon be back in Silas's possession, he added: "I stumbled upon Kessler's body. It seems he was met with unfortunate circumstances while in the greywastes. I found several abandoned quads, many dead legionary, and Kessler's rotting body. I'm guessing he found Reaver and our dark brother beat him quite successfully."

Jack's eyes widened. "He had a legion quad when Sanguine, Silas, and I found him. You're right... I'll tell Tiberius to re-trace Reaver's steps, and Caligula and Theo can scan the zones with dangerous radiation levels." He nodded at Elish and Garrett. "Excuse me. I might as well take care of this now. I've been dreaming of a nap out on the patio with my daybed since Kiki flipped me off."

"Wait... has anyone checked to see if Nero and Ceph...?"

Jack turned around and Elish observed both he and Garrett adopt mutual expressions of unrest. It wasn't a surprise, Elish himself had no plans to check on the twenty-fourth floor. No one wanted to be the one to discover what Sanguine and Kincade had most likely done.

"No," Jack and Garrett both said in unison, then Garrett cleared his throat and spoke for the both of them. "We're... um, Silas will be awake soon."

"Silas is already going to be manic. It shouldn't be him discovering what Sanguine and Kiki did," Elish said. "Confirm the reasons Kiki abandoned his brothers in the greywastes and confirm that Sanguine is gone. I'm assuming Sanguine left with Nero."

Luca made a funny noise in his throat, then visibly shrunk when three sets of eyes shot to him.

"He..." Luca shifted his weight. "He didn't go with them, Master Elish."

"Say nothing more," Elish replied, then he motioned to the door with his jaw. "Jack, you may take your leave."

"Gladly," Jack muttered under his breath. "Tell Sanguine I want to see him when he comes back and if you find his body I'll collect him immediately." He bowed to everyone in Elish's apartment before he glided out of the doorway and into the outside hall.

"Close the door behind him, Luca." Elish's eyes shot to Garrett. "I assume I still have your trust? Or did your greywaster fiancé poison your mind to me?"

"Elish…" Garrett's voice dropped. He sat down on the white chair beside the couch and cupped his coffee cup with both hands. "I would never go against you or betray you… but Jack and I have been talking and… we're all going to have a sit down soon about this and talk. We think with what happened to Sky's O.L.S and all of his brain matter being gone, and what happened to Reaver… Elish, love, I think Silas has suffered enough. Don't you?"

Elish's already bitter expression became even more distinguished. "Yes. I have a grand way to end his suffering, Garrett."

Garrett sighed, and out of the corner of his eye Elish saw him rest his face into his left hand. "Reaver is as good as dead, the clone who was mostly Sky. Kessler is missing, so is Sanguine; who knows when Nero will return with Ceph and Kiki. Timothy is dead. Silas is going to be inconsolable with grief and our little Jade kitten…" Garrett looked over to Jade. The boy was on the recliner, his eyes unfocused and his mouth slacked. He was drowning inside of the white comforter Elish had bundled him in. A hollow, pale face with eyelids a deep lavender, and underneath those lids, two slabs of gold that peeked out like ore in black soil.

As Elish looked at Jade, Garrett spoke, his tone thin but that seemed to only amplify the emotions spilling from his words. "Elish… the family needs to band together and be a family right now. We need to find ourselves again and be Dekker's instead of players on you and Silas's chessboard. We have all suffered grave losses and, brother, we need to put these games on hold for now."

But, true to his nature, Elish shook his head, Garrett's words bouncing off of him like he had been flinging crumpled up paper instead of words. "No, if anything this is the time to strike." Elish rose at this and with his coffee cup in hand he walked to the window. "Silas is weak and I know I have the information on how to kill him on those hard drives. Sky's O.L.S may be gone but Perish had it implanted in his head for months. It's fully possible, no, *expected*, that he would put the information on there about how to kill immortals. I just need to find it and now that I'm home I will." Elish turned around, a flood of disdain rising inside of him when he saw the intense look of sadness and pain on Garrett's face.

Elish pushed past the expression. "From what I know… they had to have had some sort of contraption or machine to amplify their radiation. If

I can find out exactly what was in the plaguelands lab... I can see if there's another one. I can put a stop to this quickly and once I do... I will quell the white flames and find Reaver's remains."

Garrett stared at him, his lower lip so tight his chin held several dimples. "You're relying on a lot on Perish's hard drives... for all you know nothing is on them."

"No!" Elish snapped; Garrett's words grating his theories like sandpaper on a burn wound. Though as Garrett's depression deepened, Elish realized with vexation that if his theories weren't so fallible, Garrett's words wouldn't have had such an impact.

"There is," Elish spat. "Perish wouldn't let the secret die with him. He hated Silas!"

"No, he didn't," Garrett whispered and Elish heard a sniff. "Perish loved him with his entire heart, which is why he let the secret die with him."

The coffee cup crushed in Elish's grip, spilling its hot contents all over his hand. The liquid seared Elish's skin and filled his body with pain, but there was no registration of it on his face. Garrett noticed this and his morose state held the first flicker of a deeper worry.

"The secret did not *die with him*." A lethal toxin seemed to lace every word that fell from Elish's mouth. But Garrett drank the poison with nothing more than a shake of his head.

"Look at me, Garrett," Elish commanded. And when his brother gazed up at him with eyes that had swallowed the sadness of the dead world, Elish's own looked back.

And those deep violet eyes held no sadness, no despair, or even doubt; they were two burning asteroids breaking the sound barriers from the speed to which they were crashing towards the earth.

"The secret did not die with him," Elish repeated; his coffee-covered hand steaming and the skin now swelling with redness. "I will find out how to kill him and I *will* kill him. Then I will quell those white flames and bring back Reaver. I will give Reaver another Killian and he will rule the greywastes beside me as I rule Skyfall. The family will be content; the world will be content. This *is* what will happen. You can either be a part of it, or you can watch your own white flames quench like any other immortal who decides to choose Silas's side."

"You never threatened me like this before," Garrett whispered, his voice heavy with sadness. "Or the ones we love. I don't see how you think this attitude is better than Silas's. If anything you're the one becoming–"

Elish whirled around and backhanded Garrett right across the face. Garrett's own coffee dropped from his hand and splashed onto the ground, a yelp sounding from his lips.

"If you ever compare me to that monster…"

"What monster!" Garrett suddenly screamed. He shot to his feet, his face red with anger and his body trembling under his own emotion. "I don't see a monster!" he cried. "I see a man who now has to finally accept that Sky is gone, and that Perish is now also dead. I see a heartbroken, two hundred and fifty-five year old man who has endured a hard life and now has his heir, his golden boy, plotting his death in his darkest hour! I see my best friend, my brother, threatening to kill me and my fiancé if we don't align with him as he slithers around like a fucking snake desperately trying to manipulate his family to go against our master. I see no monster in the man who sobbed in your arms after the white flames roasted him alive. The only monster I see is the one who continues to plan his destruction after you sentenced an innocent boy to death, a born immortal to twenty years of pain, and your fucking husband to brain-dead retardation, all because SILAS REFUSED TO MARRY Y-"

Another strike, this one a direct punch to Garrett's jaw. Garrett flew backwards and landed on the couch, a stream of blood running down his face like a turned on faucet. Behind the couch, Luca stared, his eyes wide and terrified, before the sengil turned and bolted to his bedroom.

"Don't you dig up that carcass and display it at my feet like it's some sort of fetid weapon to be used against me," Elish snarled. "That was years ago and–"

"And ever since he laughed at your proposal, your heart has hardened towards him!" Garrett screamed, his hand now cupping a pool of blood, and in the center, three teeth. "Don't take me for a fucking idiot. This isn't because of him killing our lovers and being a tyrant at times, it never was. It's because he humiliated you, it's because you opened your heart to him and he pissed in it. This began as a jilted lover needing revenge, and your fucking delusional mind has done the mental gymnastics necessary for you to believe it's to protect the family." Garrett stood up and though Elish was staring him down with an energy that was as powerful as the opal flames, Garrett, for once, did not cower.

Instead he pointed to Jade. "You have a husband now, Elish. You have a boy so devoted to you it makes Silas seethe with jealousy, and most of the family as well. You have your partner, you need to forgive Silas for what he did and move on. The family will never turn their backs to Silas, and you must look past your own pride and put an end to this before it's too late. End this, before you lose the respect of your brothers and sister, and you lose Jade as well."

"Jade's empath abilities are because of Silas. I stand to lose Jade because of Silas's plan to control me by creating a terminally ill chimera for me," Elish snapped. He tried to ignore the feeling that he was scrambling to find the words to match Garrett's own. That was something unheard of to him, Garrett never won arguments... Elish always knew what to say; he always had the words to verbally massacre his brothers.

It was, it must be... it must be that he was just fatigued from the journey.

"Jade's brain-dead because you pushed him to use those empath abilities," Garrett said back. "Because you forced him to develop them before his brain matured. Valen lived to twenty-four before he passed; your fucking *End Game* shortened Jade's life by six years. Do you realize that? Do you realize this is your doing? And let's not even mention the fact that you're too fucking stubborn to make the boy immortal because you insist on having the boy age. You readily put us all at risk, including your precious *parvulus maritus*, all so you can have every-fucking-single-thing you want. You put Jade in danger of dying just because every last detail must be to Elish Sebastian Dekker's specifications. You're a fucking idiot, Elish. A complete fucking idiot and your house of cards is falling down."

"My reasons for delaying Jade's immortality are my own." Elish's tone dropped. "You know nothing and you prove it by the shit spewing from your mouth. When Silas kills Reno, and his blood soaks your hands, you will remember this conversation and weep for your insolence."

"And when Jade dies... what will you weep for?"

Elish slowly turned around and faced his brother; he stared at him before, with a narrowing of his eyes, he smirked.

"I will weep for you," Elish said coldly, "and all who oppose me. For when my husband awakens from his first resurrection... there will be nothing stopping me from culling those who do not deserve to live in my new world."

Garrett wiped his mouth, blood streaking his face, and slowly he shook his head. "You really are his heir," he said in a tone heavy with sadness. "I see no king promising us our lovers and a life of peace. I see King Silas in all his glory before Sky died and his soul slowly succumbed to madness. I see how our master was in his prime. Do you want to know my predictions, brother?"

"No. I believe it is time for you to leave," Elish responded.

"I think Jade is going to die," Garrett said, "and I think you'll finally understand Silas when he does. I think you have never known true pain, brother... and... and I'm scared that you're about to. Because there is no one in the world less prepared to deal with the gut-wrenching, life destroying agony and guilt of losing someone you love, and having their blood be on your hands."

Elish fell to silence, before in a voice that seemed woven by Satan himself, he replied back: "We can't all have the practise that you've had dealing with such things, *brother*."

Elish expected another outburst, he expected objects flung and shrill, pain-filled voices, but what he didn't expect was what happened next.

"I love you," Garrett's small voice could be heard, followed by a sniff. "And... I'm so scared for you. Please... please stop this campaign against Silas, and make Jade immortal now, before you lose everything."

"Goodbye, Garrett."

Elish heard a sniff and a hand pat his shoulder. "Goodbye, Elish." And a few moments later, the door gently shut.

CHAPTER 11

Jack

JACK WALKED DOWN THE HALLWAY OF KING SILAS'S office apartment and eyed the blood splatter on the bottom half of the wall. Then his eyes travelled down and he observed several large pools of dried blood; their dark stain camouflaged almost perfectly with the colours of the carpet runner.

"The blood soaked through it…" Jack observed in a subdued tone. He heard Ares and Siris snicker behind him, but they had instructions to stay in front of the elevator and they had obeyed. "You went into the storage room and threw a new carpet runner over it, didn't you? Why did you not just clean it?"

Juni, who had his hands behind his back and a tight expression on his dark features, seemed to wince at Jack's words. "I… I was in a hurry, Master Jack. I wanted to find you immediately."

"Indeed…" Jack mumbled, and the two of them walked over the dark stain and into Silas's office. After closing the door behind him, Jack carefully went over every inch of the open concept space, and when no signs of Sanguine could be seen, he felt a twinge of worry inside of his heart. "And you left Sanguine here to die?"

"I left *Crow* here to die," the sengil replied simply. "The same Crow who was lunging at Luca with intent to kill him. I didn't have a choice. I–" Jack silenced him with a cold glare and Juni became quiet. His heartbeat, however, was racing, and he kept swallowing nervously.

"You had a choice, Juni," Jack replied darkly. "You tampered with a chimera and now he is a mad man missing from our family. You might've been adopted by this family but you are very much a greywaster made into an immortal by Silas's pity and my begging. What were you thinking using Sanguine's remote against him? Do you know what Silas will do to you if he finds out?"

"He was refusing to tell me where you were," Juni replied, his voice defensive but his posture slouched. "You'd been gone for over a week. What was I to do? What am I supposed to do when I know a chimera is actively betraying his brothers; one of those brothers is my master whom I love? What was I supposed to do, Master Jack? Let Sanguine keep the family, including the king, stranded in the greywastes?"

"Yes."

Juni stared at him, looking taken aback by the answer. Jack walked over to Silas's office desk and quickly looked for any signs that Sanguine could be around. "When you get caught up in our family's politics you better have the strength and authority to endure the repercussions, and you, Juni Dekker, do not. You did a dangerous thing, and now I'll have to pay the price for it."

"I'll take—"

There was a beeping coming from Jack's watch. He looked down at it before motioning towards the door. "The king is breathing on his own. Continue searching with Ares and Siris, I must be by his side when he wakes." Jack sprinted ahead of Juni and past the twins who were observing Jack's sudden switch in demeanour with cocked eyebrows.

"Keep looking for him," Jack replied as he pressed the button for the twenty-seventh floor rapidly. "He has to be near here. Especially if he's still Crow. That mad man will not stray far."

"Yes, Master," Juni replied in a small voice, before shooting a concerned glance at Ares and Siris; both twins were gazing at the boy like he was a fresh slab of meat. As the elevator rose to Silas's floor, Jack almost wished for the twins to jump Juni's bones, if only to punish him for the trouble Jack could very well be in.

The king is going to have a lot of things to react to when he wakes...

Jack took in several deep breaths as his feet carried him to Silas's apartment, but when he entered all air got sucked out of his lungs.

Silas was standing in his bedroom doorway, his green eyes staring into nothing like the steady flow of time had forgotten about his existence. There was nothing on his face; it was the most dead and lifeless thing to be seen on this immortal being. How could such a powerful person look so vacant?

"My king," Jack said and walked to him. "I'm sorry for not being here when you woke... I was looking for someone."

Not a single shift in expression could be seen on Silas's face, not one flinch. The king continued his oddly fixed look, and at this, Jack felt a low tremor of apprehension inside.

What barriers Elish had tried to put up in front of Jack and the king dissolved as Jack stood in front of Silas. The unease he was feeling igniting an intense well of devotion – but riding the same wave was also empathy and an urge to help.

"Silas...?" Jack dropped his voice. He gently laid a hand on the side of Silas's face and tilted the king's head towards him. He opened his mouth to speak more, but when Silas's eyes locked with his own, his gaze stole the words on his lips.

The depth of agony that Jack saw inside of Silas's eyes physically stung his heart. How could a single look hold so much pain inside of it? Jack found himself transfixed in this heartbreaking gaze, and soon the corners of his eyes burned.

Their relationship had never been as such, to treat Silas has a partner was something Sanguine did, or Elish, but in that moment Jack felt such a pull to comfort Silas he couldn't stop himself. He gently stroked Silas's cheek, his eyes blurring.

"Lovely?" Jack's voice broke. "S-Silas... are you okay? Speak to me."

Silas's lower lip tightened before quivering. "Elish..." he managed to say, his voice thick with agony. "I need Elish."

Elish...? Jack shook his head and gently stroked Silas's cheek. *No, Silas... you don't want him. Silas, he's trying to de-throne you. Don't you see? You can't show weakness in front of him.*

Jack felt a tear roll down his cheek. "Love. Elish... Elish can't be the one to help you. I can get Garrett? Want to see–"

"I NEED ELISH!" Silas cried, and he collapsed onto his knees before Jack could catch him.

There was no part of Jack that wanted to get Elish for him, but what could he do? Jack took in a shuddering breath and picked up the remote phone that was resting on his coffee table. He dialed Elish's number and shut his eyes as he heard Silas start to hyperventilate behind him.

"Silas...?" Elish's voice sounded on the other end.

"No, it's Jack but he needs you, now," Jack said, making no attempts to hide the disdain in his voice.

There was a pause. "I'll be there in five minutes. If there is a mortal with you, tell them to evacuate." And Elish hung up. Jack put the phone down and turned back to Silas.

The king was on the floor with his hands clasped behind his neck; his eyes were wide and his heartbeat sounded like it was single-handedly massacring his chest. He reminded Jack of Sanguine in that moment, when he'd first come to Skyfall, and Jack wondered then if the king he had once known was gone for good.

Jack kneeled in front of Silas and put a hand on his shoulder. Then, sensing someone else in the room, he looked around and spotted Drake looming in the doorway of his room.

"Go into your room and close the door, Drake. Don't come out," Jack told him. "Put on your headphones and listen to some loud music. That's an order."

Drake looked at Jack and then to Silas, the cicaro looked scared of the state his master was in, and for good reason; Drake had never seen Silas lose control and the mentally stunted chimera wouldn't know how to handle it.

"Maybe it would make him happy to see my new pet?" Drake asked in a small voice.

"Do as I said, Drakonius," Jack said sharply, and at that Drake disappeared into his room and the door slammed behind him.

Not too long after, the door behind Jack opened and Elish was there. Jack gave him a look as his oldest brother swept past him, but Elish had nothing to offer him in return. The golden boy was his frozen self, the mask of the emotionless chimera firmly on his face. What fears Elish had regarding his cicaro, or the plans unravelling between his fingers, had either been left behind or locked up tight where no one could access it. Jack both admired and hated him in that moment.

He calls Silas the mental shapeshifter but look at him, Jack said to himself as, with a heartbroken wail, Silas opened his arms for Elish to hold him. *He plots his death and fills our minds with malice, but here he holds our king and becomes his rock. All with a devious and cold smirk on his face when the king isn't looking.*

I'm glad we ended our relationship when we did. Or else I would have become just as bad as he. I may have shot every emotion I had when

Sanguine left me, for my own self-preservation, but at least I'm not underhanded and devious to those who depend on me for strength.

"Tell me we have more of him somewhere!"

Jack's attention turned back to Silas when he heard his king cry out. "Please, Elish... tell me there's something. This can't be the end. This can't be the end."

Elish rubbed Silas's back in small circles and made shushing noises. Jack's stomach turned at the display.

"I'm sorry, love, but I'm afraid this is the end. Our only solution would be to quell the flames in the plaguelands and retrieve Reaver," Elish said gently. "Do you want us to try that?"

"No."

Jack saw Elish's eyes narrow at this. Jack's fists clenched when he saw it.

"Fuck Reaver," Silas said, his voice a strangled cry. "Fuck him. Even if there was a way... fuck him. When the flames cool I want his bones encased in concrete. He's the one that let that little blond shit destroy Sky's O.L.S. He's the one who held me back. I will never have him as my partner. I will revel in his pain when he wakes and Killian is long dead. Fuck him. Fuck Sky!" Silas let out an agonizing cry and his grip on Elish's robes tightened. "FUCK SKY!" he suddenly screamed. He pushed himself away from Elish, his chest heaving. He tried to stand but stumbled back and only fell to the ground.

Silas tried to get up again but fell back down to his knees. He looked around like he was lost, like he didn't know where he was. But as the king's face dissolved and his eyes closed... Jack realized Silas was looking for comfort from someone who no longer existed.

Someone who had been dead for well over a century.

Jack held a hand to his mouth, and when Silas let out an agonizing cry, tears sprung to his eyes. Unable to hold back he ran to Silas and threw his arms around him, and when he made eye contact with Elish's burning, bordering on threatening gaze...

... Jack glared right back.

Jack tightened his arms around Silas as the king sobbed in his shirt, and secured him in his hold.

"Get the hell out of here," Jack said to Elish, frost forming on every word he said. "And don't you dare touch him again with your bloodstained hands."

Elish slowly rose, and to Jack he had never looked taller, or more threatening. He was the god of ice this one, and though a fifteen-year-old cicaro had managed to thaw that frozen heart; it was clear now that the boy's impact had, perhaps, only maddened him further.

Elish before Jade was an intimidating sight of strength and pride.

Elish after Jade… was a terrifying tyrant, who would stop at nothing to keep his husband safe no matter whose soul he crushed underneath his boots.

And this fact was only proven when Elish smiled down at Jack. A smile that held behind it such a sinister and evil presence, Jack's bravery shot right out of him, and it took all of him to not show it on his face.

"Ares and Siris…" Elish suddenly called. "You may bring him in now."

Jack looked at him suspiciously before his eyes turned to the door.

If there was any bravery left inside of Jack, it vanished the moment Ares and Siris walked in… dragging a thrashing and snarling Sanguine behind them.

"No!" Jack cried. As Silas pulled away from him, Jack jumped to his feet. But as he ran towards Sanguine, he felt Elish grab the collar of his shirt, and after a short struggle, Elish successfully pinned Jack's arms behind his back, crushing them into Elish's torso so he was unable to move.

Jack screamed at Ares and Siris to let him go, and that scream only got shriller when Sanguine looked up, blood covering his face and dripping down his hairline.

No, no, it wasn't Sanguine… it was Crow. It was fucking Crow!

"Let go of me, you asshole. Or I'll tell him everything!" Jack snarled. He whirled around to bite Elish's arm but he wasn't even close; his teeth only clipped together, and with that, another scream broke his throat.

"You won't, because you're a pathetic little coward," Elish hissed in his ear. "You won't because you know if you do… Sanguine falls right along with me, and you, and Garrett; Juni as well. And that's if he believes you which he never will. But I regress… call my bluff, Anubis, sing your song for the king."

Another cry sounded from Jack, until it dissolved into a sob and he felt himself collapse, only Elish was holding him up now.

"What is wrong with him?" Silas's dead voice asked. Jack looked over to see Silas, once again standing, looking at Sanguine with nothing behind his eyes but the ghosts of a thousand long dead emotions.

"He's the one behind trapping us in the greywastes," Elish replied, and as Jack screamed at him to stop, he felt a hand over his mouth. "We were stranded for ten days while Sanguine freed Nero and Ceph. Those two, plus Kiki, who he put up to stealing our Falconer while we were in the plaguelands, are now gone. Juni and Luca activated Crow to learn where we were, and rescued all of us. Something seems to be wrong with your little *crucio* though... he seems to be stuck in his madness. How unfortunate."

Suddenly a low and horrifically insane laugh sounded. All eyes shot to Crow as the madman looked up from under his brow to Silas, Elish, and Jack.

"Oh, that's not all he did, familia mea," Crow chuckled. He smiled his closed mouth smile and his eyes squinted in the dim lighting. "I'm afraid I must apologize for them, my king. For Nero and Sanguine freed someone else. He is quite the mystery though. Who was that odd-eyed man?"

Jack was struck when he felt Elish's heart give a leap, but before Elish could give any audible reaction, Silas's own expression drew everyone's gaze.

Silas was frozen again, but instead of a look of heartbreaking sadness, it was like someone had walked up to him and slapped him.

"W-what...?" Silas said in a dropped tone. The change was so drastic Jack felt Elish let go of him, but Jack made no motion to run to Sanguine, or even move. Everyone in the room, including Ares and Siris, had their eyes on Silas.

The complete turn in attitude had everyone suddenly standing on cracking glass.

"He..." Silas took a step backwards and his head shook back and forth. "You..." Silas looked past Sanguine, and without another word, he ran out of the room.

With their malice temporarily forgotten, everyone in the room, save Crow, exchanged fleeting looks before Jack, Elish, Ares, and Siris all followed behind Silas. The king led them to the stairs and Jack knew with a vice on his heart just where Silas was leading them, to the twenty-fourth floor.

What the hell just happened...?

Elish was ahead of them, no one dared push themselves in front, not even Jack. Jack was only a half-step behind him though, and that was the reason why he slammed into Elish's back when his oldest brother stopped in his tracks; and with a grunt of pain Ares, and then Siris, slammed into him too.

Jack squeezed himself out from between Elish's back and Ares's front, and tried to walk into the room, but Elish held out a hand to stop him. When Jack looked into the room he knew why.

It was like the greywastes had been brought to Alegria, there was crumbling concrete all around the room and the heavy smell of dust and dirt.

But as Jack counted, he could only see that two concrete slabs had been removed.

Elish entered the room and walked to the concrete coffin in the corner, Silas right beside him. The king had his back turned to Jack but he saw him raise a hand and touch the concrete tomb that Jack, the entire family actually, had always thought was empty or only holding remains.

Silas's hand pulled away from the tomb like touching it had become painful, and that hand then was held to his mouth.

Silas turned and looked down, his green eyes sweeping the concrete on the ground before he bent down and picked up a small chunk.

Silas moved the chunk around in his hand and Jack saw what he was observing. One side of the piece had a shiny surface to it, like it had been coated in a thin metal.

There was silence in the room, all but the scraping and crunching of the disturbed concrete, and it was because of that silence that everyone observed Silas's lips purse and his expression suddenly turn dark.

As Silas's fist closed around the egg-sized brick of concrete, there was a crunching sound. Then Silas raised his hand and let the crushed concrete, now just sand, fall to the floor.

Jack stared and took step backs, until his own back hit one of the twins' bodies.

"You didn't answer me, King Siley-pie," Crow's voice suddenly sang behind them. Jack felt nauseas as Crow strolled down the hallway with a smile on his face. "Just who is this odd-eyed man?"

Silas's eyes flashed when he saw Crow. A look of pure hatred came to his face, and to Jack's horror, he saw his king step back into the same maddened state he had seen him in earlier.

Though this wasn't one drawn up by inconsolable sadness, this was anger.

The man who ended the world… was angry.

Jack spun around grabbed Crow by his black vest. He tried to shove him away, a desperate cry sounding from him. "Run. RUN! RUN!!" he suddenly shrieked as he kept pushing him. "BABY, RUN!"

"GRAB HIM!" Silas screamed. "GRAB HIM!"

Siris grabbed Crow, and as Jack held onto Crow's vest with an iron grip, Ares roughly pulled him away. The strength of the pull ripped two of Jack's fingernails from his fingers, but successfully tore his hold from the man in Sanguine's body.

Jack shook his head back and forth. "No, no, no," he whimpered as Siris marched Crow to the king; and when Crow was in front of him, Siris kicked the back of his legs until he fell to his knees.

"Yes?" Crow said in a cheerful voice, unfazed by the emotion that was ripping through the air like lightning. "What can I help you with, love?"

Silas glared down at him; his body trembling with anger and his eyes cradling flames.

"I should have never, ever taken you out of that house," Silas said in a whispered and deadly tone. "I should have let you continue to be Jasper's whore, you damaged, worthless creature."

"NO!" Jack screamed. "NO!"

Silas didn't acknowledge Jack's cries or even blink. His gaze burned Crow as the mad man kneeled before him, the insane chimera himself not moving under the king's scathing words.

Then Jack heard a chuckle, a dry raspy laugh. "You damaged him, lovely. You do not like what you created?"

Silas slowly shook his head. "I am not above making mistakes, crucio, and I am one to admit when I have made them." His eyes flickered to Siris. "Take him back where we found him. Chain him and make sure he cannot be freed from Jasper's basement. If he insists on writhing in his own madness he can do it where the madness began. Go."

"NO!" Jack had never screamed so loudly in his life. A panic set into him that made him thrash and desperately try to pull himself away from Ares. "SILAS! PLEASE!" Jack sobbed. "I'm begging you, not that, not that! Not–"

"You… you can't put us back in there."

Jack looked at Crow who was being dragged behind Silas by Siris. He cried out and put a hand over his mouth when he saw something unbelievable to him…

Crow scared.

"You can't put us back – back in there…" Crow stammered, his red eyes wide.

Then they shot to Jack. "Stop him… you know what it'll do to Sanguine. Why are you just standing there? STOP HIM!"

"SILAS!" Jack pleaded. He broke down sobbing, unable to control himself. "Don't do this to him. He didn't mean it! PLEASE!"

But Silas was gone, disappeared down the hallway with Crow stammering and pleading.

And then… and then Crow started screaming.

"SILAS? MASTER!" Crow's cries echoed in the stairwell. "Please… not this. Not this. Not this."

Not this.

Not this.

Jack dropped to his knees, and to his surprise, he heard a sniff behind him and a forehead rest against his shoulder. Ares… Ares was crying into him.

"I'm sorry, puka," Jack heard Ares whisper. "I had to follow orders." The brute chimera squeezed Jack to him but all the Grim could do was stare at the last place he'd seen Sanguine.

Not this.

Then a cold chuckle. Jack looked up to see Elish walk out of the room, until he was standing in front of Jack.

The cold chimera crossed his arms, and his mouth rose in a taunting smile so frozen Jack could practically see the ice on his lips.

"Quid nunc, Anubis?" Elish said through his smile. "I hope we learned our lesson." Then, with a sweep of his robes, he disappeared down the hallway.

What now, Anubis?

Jack stared at the hall, at the dusted footprints now broken up by the streaks of Sanguine's dragged body.

What now, Anubis?

Jack's gaze dropped to his hands and he saw blood dripping from his ripped off fingernails onto the grey floor; the red contrasting the grey, it looked… it looked beautiful.

"What now?" Jack said faintly. He rose and took a stumbling step into the hall. He turned around to where Ares was, an expression of devastation on his tear-streaked face.

Quid nunc, Anubis?

Jack made it one last step, before his legs gave out from under him and he fell to the floor. He looked down as the dizziness swept him, and as he stared at his hands, his mind cleared.

"What now?" Jack whispered. His gaze rose to the ceiling and he closed his eyes. He saw Crow's own eyes slaying him with their unsuppressed fear. He saw Sanguine's mournful, psychosis-filled howls when he woke up back at Jasper's.

He saw Sanguine as the scared and timid teenager he'd first seen in class, then the mentally ill man he'd watched him become as Elish and Silas crippled his wings one after the other.

So what now, brother?

Now, Elish, I think it is time… that you are stopped.

Drake

Drake sat on the top of the steps licking a popsicle and occasionally checking out his tongue in a handheld mirror he'd stolen from Ellis. He snorted a laugh when he saw that his lips had now turned blue, along with his blue-stained tongue.

He had just come back from milling around the sengils' kitchens to snitch some extra food. He had to give two blowjobs for the sack full of snacks, but he didn't mind. He'd wanted to experiment and see if their dicks would turn blue and, sure enough, they did. He even got some pretty enthusiastic squeals when he put his cold mouth over their heads. It was always fun getting the sengils to make those noises, his brothers rarely made those noises unless they were teenagers or cicaros. The older they got, the more stiff they got.

Except me. I'll never be too concerned about that bullshit. Drake bit the end of the popsicle and crunched it, before he reached over and grabbed a marshmallow cookie. Then, as if remembering why he'd gotten the snacks in the first place, he rose to his feet.

But the moment he turned around he heard a faint scream. Drake's eyebrows knitted together and he craned his head to listen.

Another scream, this one closer. Drake leaned over the railing to look down the stairs and heard a door slam and the screaming continue. It was coming closer and closer and…

Oh no. It was Sanguine. Drake frowned and leaned against the metal door that led to Silas's hallway and apartment. He got out of the way when he saw Siris pulling a screaming and thrashing Sanguine.

Oh… nope. It's Crow. Crow's bad. Drake tilted his head to the side. "Come back soon, Sanguine. I love you," he called and waved his hand, then he blew him a kiss. *I hope he gets well soon and comes back. I miss him already.*

Drake put the popsicle back into his mouth and sucked on it some more. Then he saw Elish stalking up the stairs and took it out.

"Hey, do you want to see my new pet?" Drake asked excitedly.

"No one wants to see your fucking pet!" Elish said sharply. "Get back into the apartment and stay there."

Drake cowered down and sighed. With a shrug of his shoulders he grabbed his bag from the kitchen sengils and opened the metal door back into Silas's apartment.

None of the stupid family ever spent time with him, like personal good time, except Sanguine and now he was gone.

Drake roughly plunged his hand into the box of cookies, pulled two out, and angrily crunched on them.

No wonder he had to get a new pet. He was lonely. His master had been deading in his bed ever since he came back, and the moment he wakes up he doesn't even fucking say hello. They just scream at him to go away, and then they scream at each other, then drag someone away screaming, and no one even says hello to Drake.

Fucking assholes, all of them. Why did Crow have to come and be taken away? I want Sanguine, he's my best brother. Sanguine would've seen my new pet and probably liked him too.

Drake slammed the door shut behind him, walked across the apartment and down the apartment hallway, and then to the left where his room was.

"Elish didn't want to see you either," Drake said. He threw the bag onto the bed and fished out the box of cookies he'd already opened, then half an apple pie, six filled donuts, two one litre bottles of ChiCola Root Beer and a bottle of rum. "I can't think of anyone else but Sanguine, and he just went all crazy and he might not be back for a while."

Drake cradled the food in his arms and turned towards the closet door.

He juggled a few things and opened the wooden door, then walked inside.

The walk-in closet was a good size and he was able to make it super dark. His new pet got spooked in the daylight, he wasn't used to seeing the sun. Drake surmised that he must be nocturnal. At least he was now used to the dim forty volt light bulb that Drake had above him. So Drake put the food down and turned on the light.

"Come on out, I have good food and good drink." Drake sat down beside his food and brought out another cookie. He made a kissing noise like he was coaxing out a cat and giggled to himself. "Sanguine told me so many stories about how he was like this when he was ill. But… you were in a much smaller cage, huh?"

There was movement behind several black garbage bags of clothes, then, slowly but surely, a blue blanket was drawn down and thin legs could be seen. Those legs moved to kneeling and a man with black hair, and a white frock to the left side of his head, looked over at Drake, his mismatched eyes staring with fear and his movements slow and cautious.

"You didn't tell Silas?" the man asked. He sat down in front of Drake and gently took one of the marshmallow cookies. Drake smiled as his pet bit down on it politely and ate it. He was so different than what Drake remembered Sanguine being, but like he had said, they came from different places.

"No. I would have to if he asked but I don't have to say willingly… Sanguine calls that a *loop hole*," Drake said. He opened up the root beer bottle and set it down in front of the man. "I've asked two people if they want to see you so far and both gave me the same typical answer which sums up to: Fuck off, Drake. Story of my life."

The young man finished his cookie and wiped a hand down his face. "I need to leave soon. If Silas is awake… I can't stay here."

Drake thought for a second. "Want to go back to Olympus?"

The young man shook his head. "You said Sanguine is gone. There isn't a point."

Drake stopped chewing before swallowing his food. "What do you mean? What do those two things have in common?"

The young man's expression changed to worry. "He was the one who broke me out. I hurt him when I was scared and when I described him to you… you said he was in the hospital bed."

Drake looked at him puzzled, before the pieces connected themselves together. "Oh, shit. That's Jade. He's my other brother but he has a lot of

Sanguine in him. He's really really sick." Drake looked at his friend and his face turned to worry too. "I love Jade. He's such a good brother, even if I like it when he gets punished."

"Jade?" the man said back to himself. "I could sense how sick he is. He's sicker than you. I wanted to help him. I don't like seeing him sick."

Drake laughed at this as if the man was making a joke, even though his expression was grave. "Oh, you can't help that!" Drake grinned at this. "We're all mad here. I'm mad. You're mad."

"I'm not mad," the man said back.

"You must be!" Drake said back animatedly. "Or you wouldn't have come here!"

The man raised a single eyebrow and Drake burst out laughing, though he stopped when he saw the man wasn't laughing with him. "That's from Alice in Wonderland. What I said, it's from a book I love. You did it perfect. Good job." Drake put a hand over his heart. "I once had a tattoo of the Cheshire cat for ten years but it got burned off. I'll get a new one, one day."

The man shook his head and took a long drink of pop. "I may hide in Olympus again... where Jade is. I can't let Silas see me." He looked around the dimly lit closet, his one blue eye shining under the light. "I need time still to just be in darkness. This is still really overwhelming."

"You did seem really scared when you came back from Elish's," Drake said and he started eating a donut. "You get really weird when you're scared."

"I get weird whenever I reach any intense emotion," the man said quietly. "I think that's why I was locked away."

"You don't remember why?"

The man shook his head. "I just... remember walking around the dead world until I saw Skyfall. I remember I died a lot to get here but besides that... he locked me up soon after I met him."

"That sucks," Drake said. "But I'll take care of you, Napoleon."

The look the man gave him was flat and almost pained. "I told you that's not my name."

"You have two different colour eyes and different colour hair."

Slowly the man closed those mismatch eyes and he let out a long, tense breath. "You're thinking of Neapolitan. Neapolitan ice cream is vanilla, chocolate, and strawberry..."

"It still reminds me of different colour things. I've never had a human pet before. Come on, let me name you. Anyway… you need to be in hiding and he'll recognize your name if I say it, *Gage*."

"Very well, Drake. You can call me Napoleon. I guess it could be worse." The man looked up as Drake rose to his feet and watched him stretch.

"I'm going to take a nap on the porch. I'll visit you tonight and just be quiet if you hear Silas," Drake said with a smile.

The man named Gage nodded slowly. "Thank you, Drake. For calming me down when you found me, and helping me stay hidden. I appreciate it… I know you don't know me from a hole in the wall."

Drake grinned. "You're my pet, I need to keep you safe. And don't worry… you won't believe the crazy stuff that we have happen. Because remember…" Drake let out a shrill and crazed laugh as he walked out of the closet, before he poked his head back in. "… we're all mad here!"

The closet door shut.

CHAPTER 12

Killian

"I CAN'T BELIEVE IT," I SAID WHILE WAVING THE DUST motes away from my face. I stepped through the window that Reaver had broken and took a moment to just take all of it in.

It was a Wal-Mart and it was completely untouched. A spread of darkness was in front of me, only a spot of light from the flashlight I was holding lit my way, and even that was swallowed easily by the darkness. I envied Reaver for his night vision and wished Perish had given me those enhancements.

My flashlight shone on a display of diapers and below that I saw dust-covered fluff and chewed on boxes. Those were just radrat or scavers who were collecting things for their nests, or the plaguelands' equivalent; it looked like this place hadn't been stepped into since the Fallocaust.

I could hear Reaver's boots crunching on rubble and dust ahead of me. He had gone in first to inspect it to make sure it was safe for me. I didn't see a point since I could no longer permanently die, but in his words 'hauling your ass back and waiting for you to resurrect is a pain in the ass' so I respected his wishes and let him do his thing.

I walked past the diapers to a display of soda pop, long since flat, and let out a squeal when I saw stacks and stacks of potato chips, and beside it, Oreo and Christie cookies.

"We're going to get so fat!" I exclaimed with an excited hiss. I heard Reaver chuckle and shone my light to where I heard him. He squinted under the light and made a face, so I turned the beam back to the dusty floor, now holding his boot prints. "I'm so happy I made a list."

"Yes, Mother Massey, your list is in my pocket," Reaver said with a smirk before he coughed into his hand. It was really dusty here. "Why don't you get a shopping cart and start loading things up? I'll be hauling the electronics to the trailer and any video games we want."

"Don't forget Pokémon!" I said as I grabbed a bag of chips and opened them. I tried one and handed the bag to Reaver. They were stale but not too stale. I could bring them up to snuff with the deep fryer that Reaver had fixed for us, that was crisping everything up great.

We were going to get fat here.

There might be some downsides to living in the plaguelands, but there weren't many when you were immune to radiation. We had enough food to last us forever, enough entertainment to keep us from getting bored at night, and we had a river and water piping into our house too. It was perfect... I'd never been happier.

"Jade got you hooked on that shit too, eh?" Reaver took the bag and disappeared into the darkness with a shake of his head. "Okay, no more talking so I can keep listening. Big Shot told me there are some fucked up things here and I want to hear them before they hear us. Do you have your wimpy whistle?"

I looked at him, or his back anyway, rather flatly, then picked up the whistle he'd put over my neck before he went into the Wal-Mart. "Yes, I do. Do we have to call it that?" I'd blown on it as a test and Reaver couldn't stop laughing at how pathetic and half-dead it sounded. I'd suggested an air horn just to be an ass. I could only imagine how much that would kill his chimera hearing.

"Killi whistle? We'll call it the Killi whistle. Don't take off your Killi whistle now, Killi Cat," his voice faded as he got further and further away, but his chuckling seemed to echo around the Wal-Mart.

I smiled and shook my head before turning a left to where the store's food was. I liked him being playful like this, any sign that he was back to normal was a welcome one.

It wasn't like he wasn't being normal... for about eighty percent of the time he was my Reaver. It was just at night with his night terrors and... and whenever we started to get frisky. The frisky times had been few and far between and when they happened it was all about me and he didn't even take his pants off. Once he'd made me cum we were done and that was it.

I hadn't said anything, of course, but still... I wondered how long this would go on for, and I also wondered if the sun had risen and set on us having sex. It had almost been six months since we'd done it back in Mariano. I missed it.

I really fucking missed it.

But I also understood it wasn't something he could... *do* right now.

Reaver had been hunting, a lot. Killing things distracted him from what was going on in his head. He had to keep himself busy or else I knew the dark thoughts creeped up on him. I hadn't minded, the house needed a lot of dusting and cleaning and he was getting parts for our new Dyson vacuum cleaner with hopes it would be fixed soon. He went out and hunted, and I stayed home and cooked and cleaned.

I scowled. I should offer to go hunting more; I hated feeling like a housewife.

And as I looked around a dusty aisle, boxes of grey with only faint wisps of their former colours peeking out under the ash, and underneath my feet, crumbling rubble and the occasional shard of thin plastic from broken ceiling lights, I realized where I was. I was in the food aisle with a list in my hand, as my boyfriend got parts to fix electronics.

Mental note: Do more manly things. You're an immortal being now, Killian.

I found an abandoned shopping cart, and after clearing out some papers and an old purse, I tipped it up right and tested the wheels. They were good enough, so I started wiping off boxes and collecting us our food. Cereal was a big thing, and powdered milk, as much canned meat and vegetables as we could carry and Chef Boyardee and canned chili, things like that. I also wanted spaghetti sauce and noodles, rice and Rice-A-Roni...

I scanned my list and decided I really had to get to work. Reaver only wanted us to make trips in the quad once a month to conserve the fuel. It would be a long walk here and a longer wall back hauling this stuff on our backs.

I pushed the shopping cart to another aisle and was amazed to see both rows of shelves had been undisturbed. The packages had been left where they'd been stocked and the only disturbed part was where a ceiling light had come down, taking what looked like cookies and cracker boxes with it. I fished through and found a few uncrushed boxes and threw them in the cart, then continued on with only my flashlight to light my way. It was amazing how dark this place was, usually in the greywastes you had streams of light coming in from where the roof had collapsed but nope... not here.

I pushed the cart down to the next aisle which looked like canned things. I dusted off a can and was delighted to see a *Del Monte* label. That meant canned fruit which was Reaver's favourite, even though he always stole my cherries if it was fruit cocktail. The cherries had no taste at all, he just liked them because they were red.

Whatever makes him happy, he was such a dolt. I threw five cans into the cart and kept pushing it down the aisle.

I passed something curious though... another purse. I kicked it with my boot and coughed from the dust. I shrugged and carried on, but in the next aisle when I was loading up on Chef Boyardee, I found another purse and a diaper bag and then two pairs of glasses.

That was weird. I picked up the purse and peeked inside. There was a wallet in it and some perfume, makeup, pens, and old receipts. It had been left here.

Then I realized with a scowl that there weren't any bodies here. From what Perish, or Sky, had told me, the Fallocaust was sudden. Anyone this close to ground zero would've died instantly which I guess explained the purses and things being left behind... but it didn't quite explain why there weren't any bodies.

Actually we hadn't been seeing much in the ways of bodies in any of the stores. Inside the houses we occasionally found one. They looked like dried up pieces of jerky, no moisture at all just brown hardened skin and meat stretched over bone. The radiation had screwed with the bacteria and preserved them until they dried up; there had been no predators to eat them the radanimals hadn't evolved for probably decades after.

Odd. I continued on filling up my cart, and after kicking what had looked like bundles of ash, I found more purses, knapsacks, and a few grocery carts filled with food. I'd have to tell Reaver and see if he noticed.

The creaking of the squeaky wheels was all I could hear inside this vast building. I bet it would be a sensory deprivation nightmare if I didn't have this flashlight and the noisy cart.

At this mention I started shining the flashlight all around me. I shone it on the meat section, full of pink Styrofoam plastic with blackened saran wrap over it. The black, dried blood and meat, had travelled up the coolers and it now looked like it was coated in mould. I looked down and even saw some of the mould on the...

My inner monologue stopped when I thought I'd seen something move in the open cooler. My brow furrowed at it and I focused on the flashlight beam. The more I stared at it though the more I became uncomfortable with the fact that I could only see my surroundings via a small beam of light. For all I knew there were predators all around me and I just hadn't shone the light on them.

I whirled around and shone the flashlight behind me. But all I could see were rows of grey shelves and dusty boxes to my left and the rest of the open meat coolers, and further on, the produce section. The only thing disturbed here were my own boot prints and the wheels of the cart; they were trailing behind me and so crisp it was like I was walking on the moon.

This place was starting to freak me out and I only had my own imagination to blame. I sighed and shook my head, feeling like an idiot, and decided to be the man I knew I was, the immortal man, and not let my dumb imagination scare me.

Then I turned around and shone the flashlight beam back onto the open cooler... and I screamed.

In between the pink Styrofoam and the blackened but shining plastic was... what looked like an eel, or a... long worm. Its tip was thin and pointed and it was...

I took a slow step back as its tip, or head, rose into the air. I looked down, trying to gauge how long it was but... I couldn't, it seemed to be growing as it slithered into the air.

My flashlight rose the higher it got. I didn't know what it was going to do; it was strange but I wasn't scared of it. Why would I be scared of a... of a...

I blinked as its black pointed tip started waving around in the dead and musty air, then its raised body bowed down until it was making an ark. It twisted around almost entirely until its head tip was pointing at me.

I stared at it and tilted my head, trying to figure out why it had stopped turning.

I think... I think it was looking at me.

Then suddenly it shot towards me like it was being rocket propelled. I gasped and took a step back as it wrapped its whip-like body over my neck and plunged down my shirt. I picked up its body and pulled it out, its body hard but at the same time extremely flexible, it was like I was pulling a cross between a strip of leather and an elastic band.

I screamed when I felt a stabbing pain in my neck. I dropped the flashlight and grabbed onto its body then yanked it as hard as I could. I felt something rip out of me, and when I managed to fling the eel-creature, I saw a sheen of blood on its pointed tip. It had fucking... I think it had fucking bit me.

I turned around, put the whistle in my mouth and launched into a dead, but blind, run.

My lips closed around the whistle and I blew it as hard as I could. I think I was screaming into it as I dashed down the dirty aisles, I kept stumbling and tripping but every time I did I got up and continued running.

But I was losing my barring. I looked around the pitch black, darkness consuming me and eating me alive. I felt disoriented, confused. I couldn't see anything, and the terror scrambling my senses was telling me there was no objects blocking my path, no displays of chips or metal crates full of DVDs. I ran into them and when I fell, I got up and kept running.

When I slammed into something soft, I screamed from fear. I pulled away from it but it grabbed me and ripped the whistle out of my mouth.

"It's me, Killian, it's me. Quickly, tell me what it was? What scared you?" Reaver said rapidly. He started pulling me towards what I assumed was the entrance. I let out a terrified cry and pulled away, him pulling me roughly into the darkness was terrifying in that moment.

"Killian? You need to tell me now. I need to know what to do. What was it?" Reaver said more harshly. His head was snapping in all directions, I could see the outline of it as I strained my eyes to see any sort of shape or movement.

"It was a giant worm!" I cried. "It was a big worm, eel thing."

Reaver stopped and I think he was looking at me. "A... worm?"

I nodded and held a hand to my neck, it was sticky with blood. "It was over ten feet long I think. It fucking bit me."

Reaver continued staring at me–

–and he started to laugh. "A worm? You were making that racket over a fucking overgrown worm? Jesus Christ, Killian."

Anger replaced my fear so quickly I could hear the sonic boom behind my ears. I held up my hand which I knew was covered in blood and showed him. "It bit me!" I screeched. "It attacked me, you fucking asshole! We have to get out of here. It was after me; it was chasing me!" I was so angry and so terrified, and so fucking pissed off he was laughing right at my fear, that I roughly pushed him.

"Was it at least thick like an anaconda or something? Did it at least have giant shark teeth? Or spikes?" Reaver put a hand on my shoulder and checked out my wound. More rage swept me when he chuckled. "It's a tiny little hole. I've put bigger holes in you in bed. It's as big as a pencil dot."

"It's still after me!" I screamed, and Reaver finally put a hand over my mouth.

"Then stop screaming, dummy," Reaver said and removed his hand. "I'll walk you out and go get your cart. I can see the light of the flashlight. I'll go and see if the worm is still there while you wait outside."

I whimpered but tried to swallow my fear. He'd understand when he saw it, it was fucking acting like a predator.

Reaver put an arm around me and gently steered me away from the items stacked in the middle of the aisle, and wherever there was something I could trip over. We didn't talk the entire time, not until I stepped into the bright grey plaguelands. It temporarily blinded me, it was hard to believe there was such thing as daylight when the inside of that store was so dark.

Reaver gently tilted my neck back and shook his head. "I'll go and check it out." He put his hand to my belt and pulled out my Magnum. He gave it to me and licked his bloodied fingers. "I'll be right back. If you see another inch worm just sound the Killi whistle."

I scowled at him and he flashed me a grin and pecked my lips. Then, with a playful but rather demeaning pat to my cheek, he ducked back inside the Wal-Mart.

I was starting to hope that eel ate him, just so I could be right once he resurrected. I'd shove it in his face at every opportunity, and I'd never let him live it down that I was right about it.

At this thought I stood up a bit straighter and crossed my arms over my chest. That fucking eel had been after me. It was smart enough to know I was there and brave enough to attack and bite me.

My body shuddered when I remembered its odd leathery elastic skin; it was hard and the more its body stretched out the tougher the whip-like skin seemed to get. Maybe it was some kind of leech and that's why it had bit me? I didn't know... I just wanted Reaver to come back with the grocery cart so we could go home. I had almost everything I needed and he must too.

Suddenly I heard a scream inside the Wal-Mart. My chest turned to ice and I immediately looked towards the broken window.

Reaver was screaming.

It had gotten him. It had gotten him.

I screamed too and brought out my Magnum as I heard the screaming come closer. He was trying to run outside; I could hear him, he was running fast.

Reaver jumped out of the window; he had something black over his neck. I shrieked, forgetting the gun in my hand, all I could do in my terror was stand there and scream my head off.

Then Reaver stopped dead in his tracks. He turned around and I saw the biggest shiteater grin on his face.

He threw the black thing around his neck at me. I screamed and jumped back, and looked at him in horror as he started laughing at me.

I looked down and saw it was a frayed electrical wire.

"I fucking hate you!" I screamed through tears. Reaver started howling with laughter, and as I stalked up to him, he fell to his knees with tears streaming down his face. He was laughing so hard he had to take in gasping breaths.

"I hope you fucking choke and die!" I wailed. I couldn't believe he would betray me like that. He knew very well how scared I was, and he thought it would be funny to scare the shit out of me?

Reaver flopped over onto his back, his hand up to his face as he struggled to laugh and breathe at the same time. I was so angry at him, I walked up to him and kicked him in the ribs.

"I should've shot you in the face, you're such an asshole!" I cried. "I was terrified. You... fuck you, it's not that funny!"

I turned away and started stalking back to the quad.

"Killi..." Reaver called after me in between laughs. "Come on. I couldn't help it! Come back here. I'm sorry." He laughed while saying he was sorry. He wasn't sorry for shit.

"Killibee... come on, you have to be my best friend and my partner now. I don't have Reno to abuse, you're my only entertainment," he said through chuckles. I heard his footsteps, and when I felt a hand on my shoulder, the rage seething and boiling inside of me blew.

"Ede faecam!" I whirled around and yelled. Then I pushed him back and walked to the quad. I sniffed and wiped my nose and got in the back with the boxes he'd carried back. I waited there and he came with the shopping cart, and I stayed sitting as he surrounded me with boxes and cans. I think he knew I wasn't going to be riding up front with him.

At least he'd stopped laughing.

When he was done I felt the quad shift and the sound of gasoline sloshing in the tank when he leaned against it. I heard a flick of a lighter and then a blue-embered cigarette entered my vision.

I took it and started heavily smoking it. It was an opium one, I blew out silver smoke.

"Can you… forgive me for just a second and answer a question for me?"

I looked up when I noticed Reaver's tone was more serious than I expected. That brought with it a sense of apprehension, but I still answered him back with a short snip. "Yeah."

"I want you to answer me honestly and if you don't know, say it."

"… okay."

"Tell me what *ede faecam* means."

I paused. It had just slipped out. I had been learning some Latin before when we had spent all those weeks in Elish's secret apartment in the greyrifts. I assumed it was that. But I didn't know what it meant.

"I don't know," I admitted bitterly. "Oh tell me wise Latin-implanted chimera, what dumb gibberish did I say to you?"

Reaver was silent, and I realized he might be upset I was using his family's other language on him.

Then I swallowed, and it had all started with Asher's pet names for us. He called me *cicaro* which made sense; he called Reaver *bona mea*, his property, and other love words.

"You… told me to eat shit. You said it the exact way I can see it in my head. That's just… weird. You've said Latin a few times when I was… you know, doing things to you, and… can you… not?"

His words made a burning come to the back of my neck. I nodded stiffly, feeling embarrassed and guilty. I hadn't really realized that I'd been doing it. I had been around a lot of chimeras this past year, so I guess that justified it.

"Yeah," I said simply.

"Thanks…" Reaver's voice trailed, before he added. "You can go back to being pissed now."

"So happy you gave me permission, fuckhead," I said.

Reaver laughed. "I love you too, Killi Cat." I heard the flick of a lighter again and a whiff of a quil cigarette, and he got onto the quad.

Then all fell quiet. I leaned back against some pillows Reaver had brought out for us and waited for him to start the quad.

"Stop moving," Reaver suddenly hissed in a dropped voice. "I think I hear something. Quickly get off of the quad and put your hand over your chest I can't hear anything with your heartbeat."

I scrambled off of the quad and did as he asked. I started scanning the horizon and the abandoned parking lot around us. There were tall buildings, in almost all directions except west where there were only black trees and mountains.

Reaver got off the quad and looked behind him, right as he turned back and motioned for me to follow him back to the quad, I saw what he'd heard... a plane in the distance.

"The white apartment buildings." Reaver pointed as he jumped back onto the quad. I got behind him "It's southeast but it's a Fisherking. They have heat sensors and we need to be inside and hidden before nightfall." He revved the motor and turned the quad towards the white buildings, they were standing on the other side of the street but there was still an entire Wal-Mart parking lot between us.

"They can't see us, we're too far away," Reaver reassured over the rumbling engine. He started driving down the parking lot, dodging rusted cars and trucks. I thought he was going to take us to the apartment buildings but he turned a hard left. I realized he was bringing us to the back where a bunch of semi-trucks were, some of them still upright but several had fallen down. Their trailers were blue with streaks of rust dripped down like tears, and there were dissolved boxes with their contents peeking out like disturbed coffins. But why was he taking us towards them? I didn't know what Reaver was doing until he turned the quad towards the back of one of the tipped over trailers and drove the quad and our little trailer in.

Reaver killed the engine and hopped off. He grabbed my hand and quietly we ran out of the metal container, past another askew semi, and towards the white apartment building.

My chest was burning when we got to the front. Reaver eyed the plane and swore to himself then kicked the bottom half of one of the two glass doors entrances of the apartment building. Without him telling me to I went first, knowing that's what he wanted, and he ducked in after me.

Reaver let out a breath and the string of expletives continued to flow out of his mouth. I turned and saw that we were in a simple lobby, furnished with a radrat-chewed couch and tipped over vases, some broken and lying in piles of faded dirt. Further on was an elevator and beside it a red metal door with a forever dead EXIT sign above it, and a simpler sign, almost completely covered in dust, saying *Stairwell*.

Reaver took my hand again and led me towards the stairwell. He opened it and we both started walking up the creaking but solid stairs.

"Third floor." The shock of hearing Reaver's voice after so much silence made me jump, but I nodded and followed him to the third floor hallway; the gyprock ceiling completely collapsed and raining down insulation like pink cotton snow. It was in bad condition, this must've been low income housing, but it would add a benefit – we'd be able to hear things coming.

Unless that worm found us.

I shuddered and the anxiety inside of me resurrected with vengeance. The last thing I wanted to do was spend the night here. I hope Reaver wasn't going to say we were–

"We're spending the night here."

It took everything to hide the panic on my face, but I did. I followed Reaver into the farthest apartment from the stairwell, and watched with a lump in my throat as he tried the door. It was open so he peeked inside and motioned me to follow him.

Well it looked like we got two for the price of one. This apartment must've been built by a one-handed carpenter because the floor of the living room was sunken in and in the center it had completely collapsed, giving us a view of the room below us. I wanted to ask Reaver why, but before I could he pointed up, and I saw there was a leak in the ceiling. It had a hole in it the size of a dinner plate and there were shreds of insulation, and wires spilling down like it had been disembowelled.

"Are we going to try somewhere else?" I asked, eyeing that hole in the ceiling with mistrust. My mouth even opened to tell Reaver that the eel-worm could get in through there, but then I remembered how he almost killed himself from laughing too hard so I decided against it.

Reaver shook his head as he tried out the floor around us. I could see his boot sinking in and in a couple places the wood whined and creaked. "No. This just means we have a lot of escape routes," he said. "If we have to, I can jump down and catch you when you jumped."

"Three-storeys?" I said nervously.

Reaver shrugged at this and smirked. "The broken leg you might get will take like a day to heal. You keep forgetting you have nothing to worry about, ever. We'll be fine here tonight, the biggest threat we have is the chimera in that plane finding us."

My throat made a nervous noise but I nodded. "It's still quite a few hours until night... can't we just go home after it's been clear for a few hours?" Reaver walked into a bedroom and I followed him.

"I'd rather not," Reaver said back.

I cringed when I saw two dried up bodies in the bed, but then my heart gave a flicker of empathy when I saw these two people were holding each other. That was so sweet.

I walked over as Reaver rummaged through their things and looked down at the dead couple. The blanket covering them had been flattened against their bodies from the dust and powdered gyprock, but I could still see patterns on it. I brushed it away with my hand and let out a long breath. They had entered this bedroom thinking today would just be another day and then... and then Sky and Silas happened.

Or maybe they went to bed wondering if more bombs would be dropped on them. Or if they were going to get drafted to fight this Cold War that no one wanted. A part of me wished I had asked Sky more questions when he'd been inside of Perish, but I just hadn't been mentally able to do that.

And now he was gone, just like these people and everyone else was gone. The billions of people in this world had been reduced to the population of Skyfall and the greywastes. All because of two men who had convinced themselves the radiation they both harnessed could stop the missiles.

Silas hadn't ended the world to show it his hurt – he'd thought he was saving it.

I shook my head and dismissed the empathy those words had left behind. Even if Silas had originally thought he'd been doing good, he still was a tyrant. He was fixed on getting Sky back to the point where he went insane.

I'd wanted Silas to think it was Sky's O.L.S, when it had really been Perish's empty one, but I ended up dropping it somewhere during the escape. I'd never tell Reaver that. I'm sure he thought more highly of me knowing that I had destroyed the last part of Sky in front of Silas; with his twin brother dead behind him and only the born immortal Reaver to carry on any strains of his DNA.

I turned and watched Reaver as he picked up an old pack of gum and smelled it. He shrugged and put it in his pocket. When he spotted me looking at him his eyes narrowed. "What?"

"Nothing," I said with a half-smile. "I'll find us some food to eat and some books to entertain you."

"Comics," Reaver called after me when I walked into the hallway. He always had to have his superhero comics. I wonder if he ever imagined himself as a superhero... but this being Reaver I suspected he was the villain.

Actually since the Legion called him the Raven, maybe in his head he was the hero? He was my hero, even if he was a tad nuts.

I found him some comics, and though it was slim pickings since we didn't have water or anything like that, I did find us a can of corn and a can of mixed vegetables.

Reaver looked at the cans and sniffed. "I'm not eating this crap when we have an entire case of ravioli on the quad's trailer. I'm going to run back there and get us some food."

"This was a bounty in the greywastes; you're such a picky ass nowadays," I said with a roll of my eyes.

"Could be worse. Just imagine how spoiled Man on the Hill and that Angel Adi must be with their real food," Reaver said as he sat down on a chair he'd positioned in front of a window in the living room. His sentry station of course. "Fuck. Remember how much fruit those Blood Crow nuts had? I'm so pissed you made us miss out on the feast after." He groaned and stretched. "You know their sacrifice festival party is coming up." He raised his watch which also had a small section for the date. "We could still go to it."

He chuckled at the expression on my face, then shrugged. "It might be nice to see a Blood Crow get sacrificed. Remember they said two of them get chosen a year? I'd like to see it. I kind of miss..." He paused then shrugged a second time. I saw a pull on his lips. I thought he was going to say more but he only turned back to the view in front of us.

I walked to him until I was standing behind the chair he was sitting on. The Wal-Mart was in front of us, its flat grey roof empty except for air vents and what looked like a cooling system. Around it was the parking lot, full of rusty cars and semis, and the staple of all store parking lots: shopping carts. They were thrown everywhere, some of them with objects that were just piles of mush from being rained on and then dried out again and again.

And past that parking lot there was a street with telephone poles, streetlights, and traffic lights, and the usual grey buildings standing empty and desolate with their black windows looking right back at me. Unlike in the greywastes, almost everything was solid and still standing; it was the closest we would ever get to seeing the world how it was. Even Skyfall looked different than these places; it had its own culture now, its own architecture.

"Here, baby," I said handing him a comic.

He took it and blew the ash off of the cover. "Oh, Conan. Awesome. Did you know he used to have a late night talk show?"

I looked over at the muscular black-haired guy in the middle of killing some weird beast. He was surrounded by scantily-clothed women. "That was Conan O'Brien, love. He was a skinny red-haired guy."

Reaver scoffed. "Skyfallers are so stupid." I put a hand on his head and shook it before turning back to the kitchen to open up the corn. He might be going out later to get us better food but we would be needing liquid and the corn had juice inside. We had passed some rivers on our way to the Wal-Mart but they were too far away for us to risk it, plus it would be dark soon and if the chimera planes had heat sensors there would be no hiding from them. And one problem with us being in the plaguelands was that any human in here automatically meant chimera, or well... a sane human, I think ravers, or a type of raver at least, could survive here.

"They can," Reaver said when I asked him, "but even ravers weren't dumb enough to stay. Big Shot said the ravers stay out of this place due to what's here." He glanced up, a dirty rag in hand; he was cleaning his gun. "I don't know what he's talking about. The biggest thing I've seen is the irradiated deer."

The giant worm-eel was at least six feet long... I kept my mouth shut though. I had tolerated his harassment just because I wanted him to keep making jokes and being happy. He'd scared me with how he'd been acting, and even if he was picking on me more than ever, I didn't want to discourage that.

The one sure sign that Reaver was bored was when he started harassing me.

Well, that made me frown... I didn't want him to be bored out here. I know I was his only source of human contact but for fuck sakes he was a complete shut in in Aras. But I guess even the shut in went to Leo and Greyson's, had a full time job as sentry, a best friend, and exciting scavenging trips.

He seemed happy though... but I couldn't help but worry that I was seeing a caged tiger right now. But what could we do about it? We were fugitives. No one in the entire world knew that I was alive and that Reaver wasn't trapped inside of Sky's old lab burning.

And we had to keep it that way.

Reaver went out just as dusk was descending on this small town. He set me up with his M16 and let me pretend to be a sniper. It was fun, but I knew he was doing it just to make me feel like I was doing something useful. Like giving a kid an unplugged Nintendo controller so he'd stop bugging you to play.

He came out of the tipped over blue trailer with a bag of chips, some cookies and canned goods and I greeted him when he came back.

"I got fruit cocktail and canned coconut milk for water," Reaver said when he dumped his loot onto the kitchen table I'd half cleared of debris. "I'll be staying up all night so you can go to sleep whenever you want." He reached into his pocket and pulled out his baggy of drugs and sat down at the kitchen table to crush them. "How's your war wound?"

I rubbed my neck, it had clotted completely now but it still ached. "It's fine..." I turned to the darkening store in front of us and shuddered. It seemed spooky now. I just wanted to get back home. I always found it interesting how much light can slay the anxiety that darkness brings. Light is in all respects artificial, the world's natural state is complete darkness.

Fuck, why did I have to think such terrifying things?

"It's fine," I said, and pulled up a chair to get my share of the opiates. "I wish you'd take me more seriously about it. It was intelligent. It attacked and chased me."

Reaver snorted. He picked up an old credit card belonging to one of the occupants of the house, Rose Wentworth was her name, and started cutting his lines. "Killi... what would it have done once it caught you? I think you just got scared and panicked. The worm was probably a dangling cable, I saw a few of them where I found the flashlight."

Now he thinks I was seeing things? "I didn't imagine it. I..." I stopped when I realized hallucinating things was nothing new to me, but still I had the bite to prove it.

"You fell down quite a few times. You were thrashing around like a scaver caught in a trap." Reaver pointed out after I'd made that comment.

I scowled, and when he snorted two lines he passed me the rolled up piece of unregulated Canadian currency and did my share too. "I wasn't hallucinating. I bet if you went back in there tonight you'd see it."

"Yeah, I'm not leaving you alone, ever," Reaver said. "I don't need you trying to liberate the slave worms or whatever noble thing you decide to do when I'm not around to tell you no." He rubbed his nose and got up, then took his place back in front of the window. I pulled up a chair too and sat beside him.

"I am immortal now... you can start leaving me sometimes," I said. "You leave me alone in the house, don't you?"

"That's different. That's our house and you have guns and knives and I almost fixed you a Taser. All you have outside is your Killi whistle, a knife you can't use, and a Magnum you can barely shoot."

I really didn't want that name for the whistle to stick...

I let out a long huff. When he was having those night terrors, and when he'd had that incident outside of Melchai with the slave, it had been me comforting him. I was his rock in those fifteen minutes before the Xanax kicked in and he fell back asleep, and I had been the one to put him in the back of the quad and take him home. Could I point that out though? Nope... he'd be so humiliated he'd probably start sleeping in a locked room so I couldn't see him like that. He'd gotten angry enough when I had calmly handled his meltdown right before he told me about Nero.

He wanted to keep me as the Killian in Aras who was scared and mentally fragile. Who depended on him for everything and stayed at home to cook and clean. He wanted this, and I understood him needing to make things as normal as possible but... I was now eighteen. I was immortal, and I had been through a lot with Perish and Sky; and even before that, keeping Perish and Jade from killing us, and the slavers from killing us too.

"I want to be your partner," I suddenly found myself saying.

Reaver looked at me. I could see him out of the corner of my eye but I was still staring at the blue semi trailers in the loading lot of the Wal-Mart.

"Did you just have a stroke? We are partners," Reaver said, sounding perplexed.

"No, I mean... I don't want to be stuck at home like a housewife while you go do man's work... then tucked into bed while you sentry. Or only given a Magnum to defend myself with. Or not going out into the plaguelands alone without you... I want to... start being treated like an adult, like a man. Nothing bad can happen to me anymore, and you understand this since you took risks in Melchai with the cultists. I don't want an eternity of being sheltered and protected."

Reaver fell to silence, then he let out a dry laugh. My lips pursed at what I knew would be a complete dismissal of my feelings.

"It's just how I see you," Reaver said with a partial shoulder shrug. "You're Killibee. Who hates dark houses and being out at night. Who makes great food and neurotically cleans. Who loves too much and forgives too easily. Who falls to little manic pieces sometimes but recovers quicker than anyone else I've seen. You... I love you because you're not like anyone else I've ever met." Then I saw him frown. "Why would I ever want you to become like everyone else?"

His words flattered me and I drew them to my chest and memorized every one. I did love how much he knew me, even when it seemed like he was lost in his own world. Reaver knew me inside and out and loved me for it, but...

"There has to be a happy medium," I said to him in a subdued voice. "Could you at least try to look at me a bit more like someone you can depend on? Someone you don't always have to think you need to save?"

I was surprised at my own words, and the pull of Reaver's brow told me he had the same reaction. I didn't realize it until I said it but that was a lot of what I wanted... I wanted him to be able to depend on me.

Like he could depend on Asher.

Like he could depend on Elish.

Elish... the way he talked about him. The smile on his face when he told me stories of their time together.

What if Jade dies and Elish comes after Reaver?

My eyes widened at this.

"I can try but..." Reaver paused for a second. "... it's kind of a bad time right now considering we just saw a plane. We both are going to need to lay low and I'm going to be boarding up our windows so any plane flying overhead won't see our lights. And I'll be strengthening the Styrofoam around the generator shed... we need to be careful, Killian. If that plane sees humans they're going to know chimeras are out here."

"Yeah... I guess," I said, still frowning at the thought of Elish and Reaver together. Now that was a weird, weird thought. Reaver noticed and pulled me close to him.

"I don't want you to change," Reaver said again. "I just want everything to be normal... like it was in Aras."

But we're not in Aras... so much has changed. You've changed, and I've changed. I want you... to see me like you saw Asher and Elish. I want you to turn to me to help you when the raver is about to chew your face off... not look to see if I'm in danger.

Then I thought of what Reaver had personally been through, and the problems he was still struggling with. There were demons all around him, ones so thick and real I was sure Jade would be able to see them with his aura reading. They stalked him and attacked him when he let his guard down, and never did they let his idle mind stay at peace for long.

Reaver had fought many battles, but he was now fighting one he didn't know how to arm himself against. Unlike me who had been having to compartmentalize my trauma since I'd seen Cholt the mercenary, the one who'd helped take me and my parents to Aras, eaten alive.

I don't think normal is what he needed... I think he needed to see me as a real partner. If he could rely on me, he could share things with me and trust me with his vulnerability. I could be strong and help him, and even offer advice that had helped me when... Silas had assaulted me, and Sky inside of Perish.

I wanted that so badly my throat tightened. I wanted him to see me as someone he could talk to, confide in.

But he didn't...

At least not yet, but I knew I could prove it to him. I could be better than Asher and better than Elish. I was the partner of Reaver, the strongest chimera and born immortal in the world, and I had to stand just as tall as he did.

And I would.

CHAPTER 13

Reaver

I DASHED SOME OF THE DILAUDID POWDER INTO THE center of my fist, in between my thumb and my index finger, and quickly snorted it. I was loading up on it tonight but my tolerance was rising and I was trying to get off the needle. It was relaxing at least, and I still had five more hours until daylight. We were going to go home at first light; I wanted all the windows boarded up and the generator ultra sound proof before night time again.

There was no such thing as overkill right now, and I'd made the decision that if we saw another plane we'd be abandoning our house and going deeper into the plaguelands. We wouldn't be able to go to Melchai often, maybe only once every six months, and we'd have to live without fuel and electronics. But I'd sacrifice all of that just to make sure my family continued to think that we were both gone.

I looked down to see Killian sleeping soundly. He'd beaten the dust out of the couch cushions and had laid them down by my feet. He was now wrapped up in a blue blanket snoring lightly.

He looked so innocent, and yet he seemed adamant on making me see him as a… I don't even know the word for it. He wanted me to see him as more of an adult, but I didn't want to. It weirded me out when he started acting all calm and controlled when I had been flipping out over Nero. That just wasn't Killian.

And his outbursts of Latin… it was like he was trying to become a chimera, but he wasn't one. He was the least chimera-type I'd ever seen. Fuck, Reno would be a chimera before he was and Reno was no chimera.

I just wanted him to stay Killian... I liked rescuing him and watching over him. That had been my job for over a year now.

Everything in my life had changed... why did he want to change too?

I hadn't changed... had I?

The thought soured my stomach because I knew I had. I fucking hated it, with every ounce of stamina and fire inside of me, I hated it. I was disgusted and disappointed in myself because I knew Nero had gotten to me. When I was out with Elish chasing our partners, it'd been ignorable and I'd thought it would fade into the backgrounds of my mind. But I'd stitched tight an infected wound and now the pus was leaking out and getting everywhere. Not only that... now fucking Killian knew.

And I knew that was the catalyst, that was why Killian was now trying to take steps into dominant land. It was because of me; it was because I was acting like a fucking bitch about this.

But why, for fuck sakes why, couldn't I get what had happened while I was in Nero's custody out of my head? Why was it sending me into such a tailspin? Not only destroying twenty years of proving I was top dog but also fucking me up mentally, so much I couldn't even fuck my boyfriend. I was a limp-dicked, mentally unstable, sissy bitch.

I did more drugs and stared out the window. The Wal-Mart was tinted blue now, as were all the objects around it. I had seen nothing out here, and had heard little but the occasional fly and the squawking of a bird-type species I'd seen before. The plaguelands were silent, but that silence only amplified my self-derisive thoughts.

Another thing I hated was that staying here in the plaguelands with only Killian, with food being easy to catch and scavenge and water in spitting distance... it felt like I was in limbo, or some fucked up Groundhog Day. Every day was the same and I couldn't break myself from this cycle. There was nothing to challenge me, it was just too easy to live.

I'd spent months chasing Killian and imagining him in my arms, and not for a moment did I take this peace for granted but... but I was a fucking hunter, a predator... I wish I could kill more, torture more, snipe legionary, or set the deacons on merchants we didn't like. Killian might be whining about being a househusband but I didn't even have a big role to fulfil now.

Oh well. I just had to suck it up. There was nothing I could do about it but let time kill it. Killian had told me he was able to swallow what Asher and Perish-Sky had done to him with my support, and he may not realize it, but he was being there for me just by being there. There was no reason for him to try to become a chimera... he wasn't one. He was just my immortal boy.

The drugs hit me nicely and I found myself momentarily closing my eyes to enjoy a brief moment of zombieland. Dilaudids numbed your emotions, and that's why they had been my best friend since coming here.

My other best friend thought I was gone for the next two decades.

Jeez, Reaver... you're really holding yourself a pity party tonight. Another way you've changed, limp dick.

Bah. I shook my head of it, and while I enjoyed the warmth sweeping me, I decided to think about the time I'd tortured Bridley. That was a fun thing to remember, and it let me be with Reno in a way. Damn, I missed that man. I hoped he was okay and that Garrett was treating him right. If he thought Killian was dead, and I was as good as dead, he'd need him. The only way I'd ever see Reno again was in twenty years and he'd be forty-four if Garrett didn't make him immortal. How fucked up would that be to see him age and me and Killi still be twenty-four and eighteen? That stupid fuck better make him immortal. If there was one person who should never grow old it was Reno Nevada.

I wish I could just let him know I was okay, and Killian was too... Reno deserved that.

My thoughts travelled and went in all directions, and to my disdain these thoughts brought emotions I had rarely experienced: guilt was a big one, fear of being found out by my family, and even worry over the way Killian had been acting.

And then, because I was Reaver and even to myself I was an asshole, my mind took me to Nero. The disdain and betrayal I felt over my own mind defaulting to that would make Jade's self-loathing problem seem egotistical in comparison.

Elish told me to channel my feelings over Nero into killing and expending energy, and just being the dark chimera I was. But how could I when the biggest thrill I'd had recently was burying my face into the lacerated throat of a dead slave?

Suddenly I jumped. I opened my eyes and yet another wave of self-hatred came over me when I realized I was beginning to fall asleep. I sighed and shook my head rapidly, and looked out the window. It was almost a full moon tonight and it was now hovering in the east. It was brightening my night vision and making the shiny metal of the semi-trucks reflect and glow.

I yawned and decided to go outside with my chair. I wanted a smoke and some fresh air, maybe that would shake my mind from all these girly emotions. This is what happens when people don't have the constant threat of death, or starvation, or trideath; they become all brooding. No wonder people were all on antidepressants and shit back before the Fallocaust. No wonder Killian was all emotional and Jade all nuts; that's what happened when you didn't have enough threats in your life.

I lit a smoke and closed the sliding glass door behind me. I pulled my chair up and kicked a rickety piece of railing down to the ground so I could have a good view. It landed and echoed, but with a glance behind my shoulder I saw that Killian was still fast asleep so I hadn't woken him.

This was nice at least, being outside. Fuck, this place was boring though. Dead, boring plaguelands. Big Shot was nuts when he said there was scary shit out here, probably radiation poisoning.

I was halfway through my cigarette when I saw movement on the street, or well, beside the curb before the sidewalk. I watched it intently then brought my M16 scope up to my eye to find out what it was. It was probably a rat, a regular rodent one not the subhumans, it was too small to be a…

Well, I'll be fucking damned.

It was slithering… it was a worm, just like Killian had seen. I watched as it branched off from hugging the curb and slid into the street, exactly like the snakes I'd seen a few times in the greywastes and on nature shows. It was weaving and seemed to glide gracefully on the pavement.

And weirdly, as Killian had described… it seemed to be able to bunch itself up, then make itself long. As it slithered past me, its body coiled into itself until it was as fat as my arm, and then it would start moving again and become so thin I swear it was the width of a string Twizzler. What an amazingly fucked up little worm-thing.

I shook my head and debated shooting it. But it was just cruising along without a fuck to give about anything, and I didn't want to shoot my gun for no good reason, even if I was tempted to get a better look at it.

Ah, whatever, it was just a stupid worm.

I made the motion to get up, but stopped when I saw another shifting of movement. I sat back down and raised my eyebrows when I saw two more cruising down the street. They were side by side just slithering along…

When I saw three more behind those two, I started to feel more uneasy than fascinated. I decided to remain perfectly still as they glided down the street, remembering what Killian had said about the one he'd seen. What had been a hilarious example of Killian's overactive imagination was now turning into a rather unsettling reality.

I craned my neck towards the north to see if there were any more to look out for – and it was then that my jaw hit the floor.

Immediately, as quietly but as fucking quickly as I could, I dropped to the rough patio floor and flattened myself against it.

I didn't know what the fuck it was but it was huge and it was making its way down the street.

This is what I get for calling this place boring, isn't it?

More of the worm-snakes slithered down the street; the amount of them making their way past me in the dozens now, and thickening by the minute.

Then I saw a bigger object, not the massive thing but still huge. I focused all of my senses to my eyesight and saw the figure start to get the blue sheen of my night vision.

It was one of the raddeer, the same type of deer I'd been hunting but something was wrong with it. It was walking crooked and its movements were jagged and uneven. It was like someone had it on puppet strings and was making it walk. There was no fluid movement with it; it was just roughly walking down the street with the black worms slithering around it and in between its feet.

And then another one… this wasn't a deer though, this was… what the fuck was it?

It looked like a raver but it was bigger. Holy fuck was it ever bigger. It had brown skin and long, disproportionately long, limbs. It was at least ten feet tall and it had its mouth open in a permanent yawn.

Its features were human but it had no hair, its eyes were black and lifeless, and like the raddeer, it was roughly raising its five-feet-long legs high in the air before taking leaping steps… like you'd expect a fucking spider or an insect to walk. This creature was walking not five feet from the deer, both abominations paying no attention to one another.

My heart was racing, the blood was pooling in my brain and making my ears succumb to a low roar. There was something extremely fucked up happening, and I had no fucking idea what it was.

But it was only going to get worse... the giant mass, the one two-storeys high, was coming closer. It had no shape to it from what I could see, it just seemed like a blob. It was the biggest living thing I had ever seen, and not only was it tall but its mass took up both lanes of the street.

I swallowed hard and was thankful Killian was sleeping through this, because he would be terrified.

My body flattened further, and I attempted to slow my breathing. I glanced down and saw another jaggedly walking animal, a centipod from the looks of it, then my eyes deflected to the left where the first portion of the massive creature entered my vision.

Words escaped me when I started to get a good look at it, because nothing could explain or rationalize what was in front of me. My mind only allowed me to stare with a blanked expression on my face as the thing slowly moved, just forty feet in front of me, down the street.

It wasn't just one animal.

It was a collective mass of hundreds. Hundreds of animals pressed into each other by some weird force. Every one of them dead and preserved from the radiation and squished up against other dead animals. An assortment of multiple shades of fur, jutting out limbs, and the occasional dead, staring eye. It smelled too; fuck did it ever smell... like rotting mouldy leather and pungent decay.

I tried to make out any shapes I could, and recognized a deacon, an extremely irradiated version of one anyway. It looked like one of the freshest ones; it still had blood dripping down its nose. It was stuck and pressed against a leathery carcass of a large cat, possibly a plaguelands version of a carracat, and another humanoid-type thing with its white skull shining under the moonlight.

It was hard to pick out where one animal ended and another began, it was just a moving mass of death.

But something inside of it had to be alive...

I looked down to see if I could see feet or something, but it just lumbered on; a few of the bottom carcasses showing road rash and wear, but that was it.

This was the most bizarre fucking thing... what were they?

My attention turned when I heard a shriek; it was one of the irradiated deer. I looked to where I'd heard it, the Wal-Mart parking lot, and watched in absolute perplexity as I saw the deer dash out from behind one of the blue cargo containers. It sprinted across the parking lot, and in direct pursuit were dozens of the worms.

The deer didn't have a chance. Like what Killian had said, the worms chased after it, their bodies long and whip-like and moving faster than I'd ever expected. They pursued this deer like a pack of wolves, chasing it towards a row of rusted shopping carts to my far right.

Behind those shopping carts were more worms. Jesus fucking fuck, they were smart enough to lure it towards the awaiting worms.

And those worms didn't miss the opportunity. Five of them shot to the deer like leeches, and I watched in morbid fascination as they wrapped themselves around its body.

How were they going to kill it? And eat it? Like a snake, or what? I found myself enthralled and curious as I watched this all go down.

The deer screamed and thrashed. It tried to jump away, but with a strangled bellow, it fell to the ground, whips of black snapping in the moonlit air as they consumed it. And because of that very moon, I could see the most fucked up shadow I'd ever witnessed: it looked like the deer had become Medusa with how the worms bodies wiggled around.

But they weren't eating it... I looked curiously and narrowed my eyes, wondering just what I was seeing. The deer was now dead, I think, and the worms were just thrashing and shifting and...

No they weren't. They were wiggling *into* its body.

The worms were getting inside of it.

Then it hit me.

They weren't worms – they were fucking parasites.

This fact was confirmed when I saw the dead deer's body give a hard jerk. Its stick-thin legs kicked and its head snapped back and forth. I could see a reflection against its eyes as it moved, it wasn't dead like I had thought, or not yet anyway.

The deer rose on unsteady legs, no more worms could be seen, all five of them were inside of the deer now, with only shining blots of blood to show that they were ever there.

And as the deer gave a jerking walk in the direction that the other worms had been heading, it was confirmed with an eerie terror that the parasites were now controlling it.

The long-limbed leather-skinned humanoid, the centipod, even the giant moving carcass... I think I understood what I was seeing. These parasites buried themselves into their hosts and controlled them, even after the host died... I guess they could still make their bodies move, or they added them to the mass of what I now suspected was being entirely controlled by these worms.

Okay, Big Shot, you win. This place is fucking insane. I didn't want to be here anymore. Fuck this. Fuck all of this.

I glanced around and saw that the trail of snakes was getting thinner. There were only a few of them now, and the giant one was lumbering ahead somewhere. I waited until fifteen minutes went by without me seeing one, then I slid off of the patio and braced my legs and body as I dropped three-storeys onto the ground. I landed easily but loudly, my boots smacking against the pavement and echoing throughout the buildings. Without wasting a second, I ran to the Wal-Mart semi, my eyes never leaving the street and hyper focused to pick up any movement. There was none though, and soon I found myself inside the blue semi.

I wasn't fucking around with this. I unhooked the trailer, thankful now more than ever that I had backed in for an easy escape if needed be, and turned on the engine. I was hoping Killian would hear the motor and go and see what I was doing, or take the hint that we had to fuck off. If I was lucky he would be…

When I exited the cargo trailer and looked to the white apartment building, a jolt of horror went through me; six black snakes were testing out the walls of the house. I revved the engine and sped towards the building, now seeing motion in front of it.

The big one was just a shadow in the darkness, too far away to hear what was going on, but it had left its friends behind – and they could smell us.

"KILLIAN!" I yelled loudly. I couldn't stop swearing inside of my head. They must be able to sense heat or life or something. Fuck, I didn't know, all I knew was that kid better know how to fly.

"KILLIAN!" I screamed. I rode over a raised concrete bed, and for a moment the quad became airborne. It slammed onto the ground and almost bounced me out of my seat, but I held on.

The parasites knew he was in there. As I crossed onto the sidewalk and jumped over the parking lot barriers, I could see them raising their pointed heads and wave themselves around in the air; their bodies getting thinner and thinner. When they got to the size of a narrow whip they started crawling up the apartment, one even testing the edges of the patio's railing.

Killian opened the sliding glass door, his satchel under his arms and my own bag in his other one. He ran to the edge of the patio, and I stopped the bike and jumped off.

"Jump! JUMP!" I yelled. "NOW"

Killian stared at me in horror and confusion but he was smart enough to trust me. I took a deep breath and prepared myself for broken bones and looked up to catch him.

We both fell to the ground, Killian right on top of me. Killian jumped off and I shot up, but as I stepped back to the quad my foot buckled and I fell.

I looked down and saw blood, and I saw white. My leg was broken.

Then I felt a stinging pain in my neck and Killian's shrill scream. The boy lunged at what I knew was a parasite and pulled it back, only to have it wrap around his arm and sink the tip of its head into his neck. I jumped up, leaning on my not broken leg, and ripped the parasite out of his neck; then, with all my strength, I tore it in half and tossed it.

I pushed Killian onto the bike, blood running down his neck, and we both got on.

Killian yelled again, and I felt the strange hardened leather of the parasite on my back. I put my trust in him and gunned the quad. I felt Killian start to rip and claw at my back, and then him shouting that there were two more.

But there would be more and more if I didn't get us the fuck out of here, so I rode towards the Wal-Mart parking lot, hoping I could circle and cut the giant parasite off since it had been heading south, the same direction we would be going back in.

I swore and grabbed my neck when I felt a sharp sting. I barked at Killian to pull it out but a second one was trying to burrow itself into my side.

There was a ripping sound that seemed to resonate inside of my head, followed by a great amount of pain in my neck. I tried to steady the quad while I attempted to pull the parasite from my side, but the roaring behind my eyes was scrambling my thoughts.

But I was with it enough to know that I had to turn the headlight off. The headlight would only give me a partial view of my world but my night vision would illuminate everything. I knew Killian hated the dark, especially plaguelands dark with dead animals infected with parasites, but he'd just have to fucking hold...

"Reaver..." Killian's calm voice said in my ear. My eyes widened at his tone, he didn't sound scared at all. "Pull over, right now."

What...?

"I'm not fucking pulling over," I said back to him. "There's a really fucking big one. I'll explain it when we get home. We need to ride until we get home. We need to get back home."

We had to get home as quickly as possible – and I think we needed to find the bigger parasite as well.

"Reaver... please listen to me," Killian said again; the eerie level tone was making my stomach turn with unease. "Pull over."

A chill went up my spine and centered in my heart... I think one of them had gotten Killian. Was this what happened when one of them got into a human? How would it even know what to do? No humans came here.

I would be pulling over, but it wouldn't be to get infected by more parasites...

... it would be to kill Killian.

I had to kill Killian. I had to kill Killian; he was infected.

I stopped the quad and stared forward. I saw Killian's glowing blue hand turn on the headlights and, just like that, my night vision disappeared; only the light-bathed road and the floating dust specks could be seen.

Then, with a deep breath, I grabbed my knife, turned and lunged at him.

To my shock he wasn't where I'd last seen him. He was quick, the parasite was quick.

I had to kill Killian and find the host.

My body whirled around and I saw Killian now in the headlights. I clenched my teeth, my knife in hand, and ran towards him.

The kid had moves, I'd give him that. Killian jumped out of my way again and into the darkness where I couldn't see him. That sneaky bastard was using my night vision against me; it was smart and it already knew what I could do.

Turn the headlights off.

I nodded and turned around. I reached out to turn the small metal switch, when I heard a scrape of a boot and a stabbing pain in the back of my neck. I bellowed with rage and started to thrash, trying to get him away from my neck. Then I felt another stab.

"Stay still!" Killian yelled. "Stay still, I almost have it."

Have what? HAVE WHAT!?

KILL KILLIAN
FIND HOST

I snarled and threw myself onto the ground, pinning him underneath me, but when I tried to rise I realized something was keeping me down. That odd sensation was followed by a sickening pulling, not just in the back of my neck but… it fucking felt like it was inside of my brain.

Then lights started flashing in my vision, followed by rapidly talking voices, or a buzzing, clicking almost, all sorts of fucked up colours, sounds, smells flooded me and fried my senses.

But as quickly as they came, they went. I heard a cry and Killian's body beside me. I looked over to my side and saw a long black thing, sheening with blood, in his hand, then a combat knife rise and slice it in half.

Killian looked right at me as my mind swam and twisted around itself. His blue eyes were bright and wide, and his forehead glistening with sweat. He got up and grabbed my arm, then started pulling me towards where the light was and all the noise.

'Up! Reaver… get up! UP!' I struggled to my feet and I saw the outline of the quad. Somehow in my confusion and jumbled thoughts I got onto the quad and Killian got in front of me. He said something, and in response I wrapped my arms around his waist, and he started speeding away.

Everything inside of my brain seemed shattered. It was a window that had a brick thrown through it. My thoughts were fractured, mixed up and separated, nothing was where it was supposed to be. I just felt grabbed by the brain stem and shaken.

My eyes closed but a shoulder shrug by Killian kept me conscious. *'Stay awake. Stay awake. Twenty more miles.'*

'Ten more miles, Reaver. Stay awake. Five more miles, I think. I remember that sign.'

'Reaver… stay awake.'

'Reaver, we're home. Okay… you can die, baby. Go ahead.'

'It's okay. I got us home.'

When I woke up, my mind was back… but everything was different. I woke to complete darkness and realized we were inside of the basement of our house.

I looked around and saw Killian sleeping by the door to the upstairs. He had my M16 in his arms and a turned off flashlight beside his satchel. I crawled over to him.

"Killian?" I said. The boy jumped and scrambled for the flashlight. He turned it on and it shone right in my face. I squinted and he deflected the light, and gave out a relieved breath. He lunged into my arms and hugged me.

"I've been living down here since I got home… I didn't want to be somewhere so open in case they followed us," Killian whimpered.

I squeezed him to me and kissed his cheek. "So you haven't seen any near here?"

"I don't know," he said back. "I parked the quad, and after I dragged you down I barred us inside with food and water. I haven't been up to the surface since. You've been out for almost a full day. You broke your leg really bad, and I had to gouge a huge hole in your neck, but I sewed you up as well as I could. "

I stood up and Killian handed me my M16 and then my combat knife. I opened the door and looked up the flight of stairs. It was dark and if I'd been out for a full day that meant it would be around one in the morning, or later depending on how long it took Killian to get us home. Either way, not a good time. But I wasn't sure if the parasites were nocturnal, so every time could be a bad time.

I walked up the stairs cautiously. The house was warm and dark; it was brighter outside than inside with the moon full. It was a clear night too, so everything was coated in a silver glow.

I looked out the window, then walked to the door. I opened it and stepped outside, as the warm night air hit me I heard a squeak of the stairs behind me, and I knew Killian was going to be my backup.

My eyes swept our backyard and the houses across the street. I couldn't see anything but it had only been a day. The giant one would be slow and even the normal ones must have their limit and eventually need rest.

Which made me uneasy. I knew nothing of these creatures. All I knew was that they were smart enough to lure and ambush that raddeer, and even more fucked up… I'd had one in my own fucking brain without even realizing it. The urge to kill Killian, thinking he was the one infected, had been overpowering, and I wasn't going to fuck with that.

"We're going to Melchai," I turned around and told him as I walked into the house. "Bring our personal things, enough for a few weeks. They could be coming towards us, and if they do…" I couldn't help the shudder as I realized something.

I looked up at Killian and made eye contact with him. "If we get infected…"

"… that's it for us," Killian said in a hushed whisper. "We're immortal… we'd just come back to them still in us." There was no argument from Killian. He turned and ran into the living room and started packing our important belongings. I went to the bedroom and did the same.

We met in the living room a quarter hour later. We both left the house, and as I boarded up the door, he fuelled up the quad and tied down our stuff.

There were no words exchanged but a quick kiss that I knew he needed. The fact that we had just made a home here, and now had to leave it behind, left a bitter taste in my mouth. But this wouldn't be the end to our life in the plaguelands… we just had to leave until we knew the parasites wouldn't be coming to get us. I could come back and check on the house in a few weeks, and if everything was the way it was… we'd be okay.

Just… no more deep plagueland visits, I guess. I wasn't going to fuck with a mind controlling parasite; because that could mean me and Killian spending the next five hundred years wandering around the dead world without anyone in the greywastes, or Skyfall, knowing.

What the fuck, plaguelands? If I found out this was Perish's invention I was going to piss on those white flames.

There was a bright side to this at least. These things couldn't survive out of the plaguelands or they would be all over the greywastes. Maybe they needed radiation to survive? Hell, I wasn't sure. Who else knew about these things? Elish never mentioned them.

I could feel Killian shifting around behind me, then I felt his face bury itself into my back and shoulder. He couldn't see anyway and I knew he was freaked out. It looked like brave Killian came in spurts; he was terrified right now.

For a moment I took my hand off of the quad and moved it behind my back. Killian put his hand in mine and I squeezed it. We were on the highway now, and besides having to occasionally steer the quad around cars or fallen light poles, I was able to steer it with one hand on the handlebar, and the other one in his.

Suddenly I slammed on the breaks; there was something in the middle of the road. Killian gasped and his head knocked into mine just as the thing thrashed and twisted around.

I saw a paw... and I saw a foot. Not another paw. A foot. But the noises it was making sounded like two deacons going at each other, but this thing wasn't a deacon...

I swore loudly and backed up the quad. I knew what that was. Yep, I knew what that was.

And I was right, as the quad backed up I saw two reflective eyes shining at me, eyes that slowly rose as the beast got up on two legs. It was eight feet tall, covered in hair, with a snout, and opposable thumbs...

... and had once ripped a cage full of prisoners to bloodied shreds.

You've been travelling, Gianni. Or is this your wife? Hell, for how long it's been it could've been one of his kids.

The whipwolf's lips peeled back and my chest shook as it growled. Killian, blind in the darkness, gave out a whimper, and when I turned on the headlights to try and blind it, Killian screamed.

The whipwolf squinted before opening up its mouth and letting out an ear-splitting roar. And as its long and burly arms lunged forward so he could run towards us on four legs... I saw five snake-like tails flail on his back. He was infected; he'd been running from the fucking worms.

I gave the quad the throttle and gunned it. It shot forward and I sped off of the road and onto the plagueland ash. I heard Killian get his Magnum before he let out a panicked and desperate scream. I knew his different screams though, this was his scared-but-I-don't-see-anything scream, not his I'm-about-to-die scream. I turned the quad and got back on the road and brought the four-wheeler to full speed. I wasn't going to stop for anything. I didn't care if Leo waved me down that fucker would be on his own.

"Can you see him?" I yelled to Killian, the wind catching my words and making specks of hard dust fly into my mouth. My eyes were already stinging but I had to push through it.

"No," Killian yelled back. "But I can barely fucking see. I can only see with the moonlight, just... just keep driving. If he's infected the worms can't survive out of the radiation, I think."

He'd come to the same conclusion I had. I nodded and turned back to the winding road, dodging cars and askew medians like the most fucked up obstacle course in existence. If we got a flat tire right about now we were both fucked.

When I started seeing the yellow *Keep out by order of Skytech* signs I gave out a loud sigh of relief. "I see the signs, Killian. We'll be in Melchai in just a few…" I looked ahead and another sigh came to my lips. I could see lights. I pointed them out to Killian and squeezed his hand.

"It's over… they can't get us now," I said, and I felt two arms wrap around my waist and a muffled sob. As Killian cried softly into my jacket, I drove us towards the gates of Melchai.

I killed the quad and got off of it, the engine popped and clicked behind me and in record time, guns cocked as well. I looked up and saw two dark figures, their pale faces shining silver underneath the moon's glow.

"I'm Chance and I'm with Jeff. We were here last month," I said. "And–"

"Chance and Jeff?!" one of them exclaimed, or as much as you can exclaim when you're trying to talk quietly. "The slave rescuers? But… but you… you survived the radiation?"

Oh right… that. "Ah, yeah," I said. I wracked my brains to try and come up with an excuse. "Where we're from, we have a better immunity. So–" My voice trailed when the two Blood Crows turned their backs to us and started talking in quiet whispers. Unfortunately they were up too high for me to hear it.

Killian and I stood in front of the gate as the two conversed, but then they disappeared altogether. I was about to give up and find shelter in the garage we'd originally parked the quad in, when the gates opened.

Like ten of them were there, all of them standing side by side… staring at us.

"I… we don't really feel like talking," I said. The last thing I needed was to explain our ordeal to these whackjobs, or explain why we took off after we jumped over the wall. I fucking had to get Killian inside and decompress from almost becoming worm slaves. "Can we just talk about this shit in the morning?"

One of them stepped out of the shadows, it was Zachariah and he was smiling at us. He looked mighty thrilled to see us; he was fucking grinning like a shark-toothed jack o'lantern.

"You're here for our festival, aren't you?" Zach said. He reached out and clasped my hand, his hand clammy and gross. I resisted the incredible urge to pull it away, however, but it was hard.

"Ah, yeah, I guess," I said. "We want to... pay our respects to Sanguine too." I just wanted to fucking lay down, you fucking whackjobs.

Zach nodded, looking excited. "Excellent. Yes, yes. Okay, I will escort you to the residents you stayed in before. Yes, yes, you're wounded. Will you be in need of medical help?"

I sighed internally with relief, and shook my head. "No, it's not that bad," I said. "Nothing Jeff can't take care of. We're just... really fucking tired."

Their heads bobbed up and down as they all nodded. "Yes, Chance and Jeff. It does seem like you've endured quite the ordeal. Come with me, I will escort you to your home."

The mini home had never been more welcome. I shook off Zach and left him with his creepy cultists and locked the door behind us.

And as soon as the door was locked, Killian lunged into my arms and started sobbing hysterically.

I squeezed him to me and shushed him as best as I could. I rubbed his back in small circles and just waited it out as he completely broke down.

He had a reason to though. Killian had had to fight and outsmart me to get that parasite out of me, then he'd been the one to drive us twenty miles back to the house and get me into the basement, and there he waited for a day until I resurrected. Not to mention our eventful ride out of the plaguelands and into the greywastes.

A faint smile spread across my lips and I gently pulled him away from me. Killian, a complete messy wreck with tears and snot all down his face, looked up at me as he shook like a half-drowned kitten.

"I'm so fucking proud of you," I whispered as I cupped his chin. "You are growing up, eh? You keep acting like this you can have my back anytime, Killer Bee."

Killian stared at me before he threw his arms around me again and continued to cry. Eventually I got him onto the bed, and I held him against me as his tears started to dissipate to whimpers and hiccups.

"I'm scared," Killian whimpered into my tear-soaked shirt.

"You don't need to be, baby," I said to him and I patted his back. "The parasites can't survive out here."

But Killian shook his head. "We can't go back into the plaguelands. They know where we are now and if they don't... we'll never be able to relax knowing they're out there, or scavenge, or anything. We're going to have to stay here, and they're going to fucking find us; eventually they'll find us."

He was right... but I couldn't let him know that. "If I think it's safe, we'll stay here for a few weeks and then I, or both of us, can go and grab Perish's laptop and his research records. I don't know if he created them, but since there are whipwolves with fur in the radiation zone it means Perish has either dropped animals off here, or it could've even been Sky since he had his lab out there. We can look up information on them and... who knows, if they're isolated to this area we can go to the East or something. Far away from where they would be."

"We don't know how far they've spread," Killian whimpered. "For all we know they're not Perish's and the entire rest of the world is infested with them. Or they are Perish's, and have spread everywhere."

"Or they're Perish's and are localized to a small area," I said back. "We don't know, but what we do know... is that we made it out and we're safe. Our next move will be planned and calculated. I'll think of something, you know I will."

Killian nodded wiped his eyes with the side of his hand. "I knew it was too good to be true, being safe and happy. I knew it wouldn't last."

If I believed in superstition like these crazy Sanguine-worshipping whackjobs I'd say I jinxed it, but I knew better than that. I still wouldn't tell Killian about my internal comments of feeling like I was stuck in Groundhog Day, and calling the plaguelands boring.

My thoughts took me to the twenty-foot-high mass of dead animals shifting back and forth with the parasites' movements, and the tall and long-limbed humanoid walking with its jerking spider walk – Yeah, the plaguelands were anything but boring.

"It never does," I said back, hiding the bitterness in my voice, "but we'll be safe here for now."

"What about Man on the Hill? And Angel Adi?" Killian said. "I think it could be Mantis..."

I shrugged. "Even if it is, he doesn't know what we look like, right? Elish hasn't talked to him in a long time he said. And even if he does know about us from Elish's mentions, there is no way for him to know what we look like. And we don't have purple eyes or anything to make us look chimera-like. We'll be fine, and the plane we saw wasn't anywhere near Melchai either, so they weren't being dropped off there." I kissed his nose. I knew when I had to spread the reassurance on thick. "And if Man on the Hill is Mantis, he's hiding from Silas anyway, possibly with a chimera, that Angel Adi. So if we are going to encounter family members, they might as well be ones hiding from Silas too, right? They could even help us, or possibly explain the–" I didn't even bother finishing my sentence because Killian pulled away from me and gave me a look of horror.

"Alright, we won't ask them to help us," I said with a thin smile.

Killian look of horror didn't dissipate, and in my head I mentally counted down to the breakdown I knew was coming.

Three...

Two...

"I think I want to know who they are too."

Wha...? I looked at Killian and he looked at me back. I was surprised to see a hardness come to his eyes; it was an alien expression on him, and one that didn't suit the terror I was so used to seeing.

"Just a look at first to see if we recognize them," Killian said slowly, and I had a feeling it was more to himself than me. He was looking at the full picture, not just immediate threats, and I think he was seeing what I had been seeing... that we had to know who was around us.

"Perish didn't recognize you, even though you're Silas's clone with a lot of Sky in your DNA," Killian said, his brow wrinkling from thought. "Elish didn't brief you on chimeras still out there?"

I shook my head. "No, just the immortal greywaster Mantis, but... from what I remember, Elish never said where he was. Unfortunately anything else Elish told me about him I don't remember. Perish didn't say anything helpful?"

Killian thought for a moment. "Perish said Mantis helped him a lot. He's the one that got him water and made sure the power worked and... whatever else. He might've even told me in a note he left, but all of his belongings are back at the house. I... I wish I looked but it hurts to think about him." Killian sniffed again and I saw his eyes brim. "If it is Mantis... he wouldn't recognize us, I don't think. But... I don't know. Elish mentioned him, Perish knew him... maybe we shouldn't."

My mind was decided though. I wanted to know who those two were, and Killian's brief agreeance to my plan only solidified it. We were going to that festival, and we were going to find out just who Man on the Hill and Angel Adi were.

They wouldn't recognize us and on the off-chance they did... well, one thing was obvious, these two immortals were hiding from Silas just like us, and I wasn't above using that to my advantage.

If I was going to be spending a few weeks here with Killian, I had to know who those two were. For Killian's safety and mine. I wanted to know if I had to take Killian back into the greywastes away from this town, before it was too late.

At least I had some time to snoop around these Blood Crows and ask questions, maybe pretend I'm interested in their cult. So when the festival did come, I was prepared. I knew how to be quiet and how to move around without being noticed. Though I did suspect most of my time would be spent in this room with Killian. Out of sight, and hopefully out of mind.

I missed Groundhog Day already.

CHAPTER 14

Elish

"WHAT A STUPID GAME. HOW COULD YOU EVEN stand playing this?" Elish muttered. "If that stupid cow is going to use rollout on me I'm never going to get enough hits in before she kills me. Really, you beat this game, how did you manage to get past that bitch?"

Jade didn't answer, but Elish never expected him to answer, and it really wasn't the point. He was half-lying on the couch with Jade lying on him as well; the boy's back on Elish's front and Elish's arms wrapped around him so he could see the Gameboy Advance he'd been playing for the last hour.

Elish reached over and picked up the Pokémon Gold and Silver guide that Jade kept in his drawer, and flipped over to the Pokémon in question.

"Weak against… fighting," he mumbled to himself. "Well, I have your Gold game already completed and you have that machop." Jade had named him Nero. "We might as well level him up since Jade the charizard is useless, much like you." Elish rubbed Jade's head and reset the game. He'd been resetting every time he lost against the cursed miltank Pokémon, if he didn't he'd go broke and that was unacceptable.

But then Elish glanced at the clock. "It looks like beating that cow will have to wait. I need to get some work done." Elish gently slid Jade off of him and brought him to the recliner. Then he took the remote and found a television show for him to watch.

His life for the past four days had been taking care of Jade and running Skyfall from his apartment. His feet hadn't touched terra firma since he'd come back from Alegria, where he'd witnessing Sanguine, or

Crow rather, be shoved into the Falconer screaming and shrieking like the damn demon animal he was.

Silas had been silent since then, and Elish had no idea what he was doing or who was tending to him with Sanguine gone. Elish assumed it was Garrett, or Jack since he seemed to have weakened under Silas's snivelling breakdown.

Jack was the kind of chimera to retreat into darkness, however; so he could very well be in Black Tower with that gothic-looking sengil of his. Elish decided he would have to ask Luca, who had been sneaking in visits to Juni for the past several months. Elish had been turning a blind eye to their secret love but eventually it would have to be squashed. There would be no Romeo and Julian in Skyland, but for now he allowed it – he wanted spiders in Jack's tower. That Grim Reaper was in emotional agony without Sanguine, and he could end up doing something Elish would make him regret.

When Elish was in the middle of feeding Jade, Luca came home; and the expression on his face told Elish that perhaps his spider had just been scooped up in a plastic cup and tossed outside.

Luca wiped his nose and picked up his vest. "Would you like me to finish feeding him, Master Elish?" he said as he buttoned the black vest. Classic to the sengil, he was refusing to show emotion on his face, but it was obvious he was upset.

"No. I'm almost done," Elish replied. It wasn't that difficult to feed Jade. He had a tube sticking out of his stomach and all he required was a supplement mixed in with milk. "Do you have any useful information for me?"

Luca put his hands behind his back and fixed his green eyes to the window; a habit he fell into when he was about to deliver news. "Jack hasn't left Black Tower, or the couch actually. Juni confided with me that he was like this after Sanguine left him for Silas. Jack doesn't look like he's going to be doing anything but being catatonic and depressed, Master. But..." Luca's chin rose. "But Juni ended our relationship and he says I will no longer be welcome in Black Tower."

"I figured as much," Elish mumbled as he handed Luca the now empty feeding syringe. "You did well, Luca. You may see Chally tomorrow and move onto the next phase of our plan."

Luca bowed and gave Elish a slight smile. Elish looked back questioningly.

The sengil's smile widened just slightly, almost looking coy. "I just like being a part of your plans. That's all."

"You just like the perks of having relations with whoever I sic you on," Elish said casually. "You can start your cleaning now. I have work to do. Skyfall still needs to run even with half the family sulking like beaten dogs."

"Is there anything specific you'd like me to find out about Garrett and Reno, Master Elish?" Luca asked. He walked into the kitchen and Elish could hear rummaging as he got out his cleaning supplies.

"I want to know if I need to keep a better eye on the two. Their wedding is next month. If Garrett isn't talking about it and draping his entire apartment in colour swatches and bolts of fabric, that means he has other things on his mind. If he is, it means he's fine and most likely not trying to turn the others against me," Elish said. "Reno is unable to hide his emotions. Bring me up randomly and gauge his reaction."

"What do you recommend I do with Chally?" Luca asked.

"You know what Chally likes, people who don't treat him like he's an idiot. Get him alone in his room and have your fun, but I want him locked to your hip by Sunday. Understand me?" Elish said. His gaze was fixed on his sengil, and Luca both straightened up and got smaller under the purple flames.

"I won't let you down, Master," Luca said firmly.

"No, you won't," Elish said with a single nod. "I need to count on you, alright? You need to be my eyes and ears, Luca. I am counting on you."

Luca stood in Elish's shadow, forever looking up at his master, but under Elish's smouldering gaze Luca found himself receiving his master's energy and using it to strengthen his faith in himself. Never in the history of Elish's sengils had one been treated as more than a devoted servant, and here Luca was spying for his master. It was enough to make him want to jump up and down once or twice.

"Yes, Master. You can count on me," Luca said. "I have become quite talented over the years. I've had good instructors."

Elish gave him an apathetic look. "I do hope you mean in the art of stealth, and not what I think you're implying."

Luca bowed, completely straight-faced. "Of course not, Master." And the sengil was off after that.

Elish sat down on the couch nearest to Jade and got out his laptop. He then reached to the side table where a stack of black portable hard drives were, and beside them, a desktop hard drive and a laptop hard drive. Elish grabbed the top black portable one and plugged it in. There was a lot of information to sift through still, and he hadn't had much luck locating any of Perish and Lycos's files on Reaver.

And what he did find was after the child had been created: birth weight, length, and progress pictures. Elish watched the little baby grow a frock of black hair, then get bigger and longer, finally there was a photo of him with his large insect-like eyes, the white pupils barely seen until he was one and a half. Lycos loved him though, that was seen with how many pictures Elish saw of the two of them together.

Forgetting what he was supposed to be looking for, Elish continued clicking on the photos. This looked to be Lycos's personal hard drives, so it came from the bunker near Aras. All of Lycos's personal photos and videos were on here.

Elish clicked on a video file. The file loaded a video of a skinny little baby with black eyes, stumbling towards the camera before he fell, to everyone's cheering. "This is baby Chance walking! He started walking today." Lycos's voice was cheerful and bubbly.

Elish scrolled down and clicked on another one. This video recording was waving back and forth until it centered on a teenage Reno Nevada. Then it lowered and Elish realized Reno had his boot on a legionary's neck. The legionary was gasping, blood running down his nose and puffs of grey ash flying in the air from his breathing.

A smirk came to Elish's lips when he heard Reaver call Reno over, then the camera exchanged hands. Reaver was fourteen with short black hair and a smile that belonged in a horror movie. The boy looked positively nuts in that moment, but as alive as Elish had seen him when they were killing the merchant and bodyguards back in the greywastes.

Elish scrolled the video ahead, and watched in fast motion Reaver stabbing the legionary rapidly in the neck; then eventually sawing his head off and holding it up to the camera with a laughing grin. This video was obviously not supposed to have gotten into Lycos's hands, but well, parents will be parents and Lycos was always sticking his nose in people's personal business. He probably poked through Reaver's room daily.

I hate how much I miss that boy.

I hate how much I enjoyed my time with him.

Elish closed the window and unplugged the hard drive quickly.

"Luca," Elish said and rose to his feet. "We'll be expanding my plan. I want you to manipulate Chally but I'm also going to start you on Drake. Drake will be difficult, do you think you can do it?"

Luca walked into the archway separating the kitchen from the living room. He looked nervous as he wiped his hands on a towel. "D-Drake too? Even with King Silas... and Sanguine? Master, you know Drake follows King Silas's moods. He's so violent when upset."

Elish shook his head rapidly, garnering a confused look from Luca. He stopped wiping his hands and watched his master pace the room, something that Luca had never seen him do. Elish looked unsettled and was far away from the graceful god Luca was so used to seeing. The sengil watched, perplexed but mute, as Elish walked to the window and nodded his head again.

"If you think we can sway Chally... we will. If my brothers will betray me I will take their servants' loyalty out from under them, the cicaros too," Elish said firmly, his eyes narrowing to small slits.

Luca swallowed a tightness in his throat. "Master Elish... the sengils and cicaros love their masters. They–"

"I can offer them better," Elish said darkly. "I can offer them freedom..."

"But... we don't want freedom, Master–"

Luca's words faded to silence when Elish gave him a scathing and searing look. "Do not doubt my abilities to manipulate those I have use for, Luca," he said coldly. "Can I rely on you or not, sengil?"

Luca shifted nervously on his feet and nodded. "Of course."

Elish nodded stiffly and turned around.

Then his eyes flickered down to Jade.

Jade's face was white and his lips blue, his yellow eyes staring blankly off into the distance. Elish swore and grabbed Jade by his shoulders and shook him. The boy's muscles were spasming and his left arm twitching.

"He's not breathing, run ahead and open the door," Elish barked. He picked up Jade and ran to the door. "Call Lyle." Then flew down the hallway, to the elevator, and pushed Lyle's floor. He put Jade into the ground, blew air into his lungs, and started pumping his chest.

The elevator ride crawled even though it was only several floors down. When the two doors opened Lyle was waiting. Elish ran past him and put Jade onto his hospital bed then stepped back as Lyle and Nels worked.

Elish stared at the chaotic scene in front of him, his eyes pools of anxious energy. If he wasn't so fixed on Lyle pushing on the boy's chest, he would've realized that he was forgetting to breathe.

Then Jade's chest heaved and his eyes opened wide. He looked around the room like a lighthouse searching for a ship, until his gaze found Elish's. They locked on Elish's own purple eyes and seemed to plead with him to help him.

The boy was Elish's responsibility and yet here he was helpless. He had picked up a bird chained around the neck in the slums of Moros, and had proceeded to make him fly into dangerous situation after dangerous situation, and allowing him to continue to fly free even though he kept returning with broken wings.

And now this little black and yellow bird was crippled and no longer able to fly, and Elish had no one to blame but himself. Because the boy had done everything Elish had wanted him to do, and Elish had given nothing back but pain.

Elish stared at Jade, and the boy stared back. What Jade could see, Elish didn't know, but he was seeing enough for the both of them.

Jade's eyes deflected to Lyle, who was pushing a small needle into his arm, and Elish saw his chest slowly rising and falling. He was breathing again.

And that's all I need. I just need him to breath. He will survive the surgery. He's strong.

"Elish…" Lyle began after Jade's brain had been hooked back up to the EEG. "He's still breathing on his own but… it looks like the increase in brainwaves we saw is dissipating."

Elish tried to steel himself against this information. But as he tried to dismiss Lyle's words, they instead became all the more concentrated and condensed inside.

Lyle's eyes were still on him, the hesitation on the doctor was apparent and Elish did nothing to encourage him to say what was on his mind, on the contrary, his own gaze turned cold.

"Master Elish… may I speak freely," the doctor said; his words stifled as if they had trouble penetrating the tension between the two.

"You may make the attempt," Elish said coolly.

Lyle looked at Jade. The boy's eyes were distant and dazed, but he was breathing and he was alive.

"It's time, Elish. It's time for you to speak to Silas about making Jade immortal," Lyle said. He had a way of nudging his controversial words towards Elish like a child shyly handing a parent a bad report card. "If this happened at night…"

"I would've woken," Elish said, his tone hovering on dangerous.

"Even so, it doesn't change his state. What progress we saw is disappearing. Elish, please… it's time. It's past time," Lyle pleaded. "I was first your sengil and now I consider you not only a boss, but a friend… Elish, it's time. I know you wish the boy to be older but I fear he won't survive to nineteen, let alone twenty."

Elish looked to Jade and felt his limbs stiffen.

"Master Elish… I don't understand why you're so set on him being older. I don't understand how you can continue this suffering over… over a small detail in your bigger plan. I think you need to let this one go and just… do what's right for the boy." Then Lyle paused, though his words lingered like an overpowering smell.

Then finally, he let out a breath. "Why is this so important to you?"

"You're not permitted to ask such questions," Elish said. He turned and started walking towards the exit. Then he paused, and as he looked into the hallway his eyes widened as if something had occurred to him.

Elish nodded to himself as if confirming whatever thought had entered his mind. "Once he is stable you'll be moving him back to my apartment. His breathing machine will go with him. The only reason he wasn't hooked up to the alarm was because I'd just finished feeding him. He'll be fine."

"Elish…"

Elish whirled around. "No questions, Lyle!" he snapped.

Lyle didn't flinch, or even bat an eye under Elish's anger. He only nodded stiffly. "Yes, Master Elish."

Elish walked to the elevator but he didn't press the button for his apartment, instead he rode it down to the lobby. When he exited, he made a beeline for the two thiens guarding Olympus.

They opened the door for him and bowed, then gave Elish equally surprised looks when he stopped to address them.

"You will be taking leave tonight," Elish said to them. Then he turned around and looked to the view in front of Olympus's entrance. There was a grassy lawn with a large granite walkway leading to the polished clean stairs, and further on the sidewalk, and the road. Past the road was a building that doubled as a parking lot for chimera storage for everything from old musical instruments to cars. There were shrubs in front of the building and trees, but little else.

"Yes, Master Elish. We'll call our replacements," one of the men said, but Elish shook his head.

"No replacements. I want my doors sparsely guarded tonight. You–" Elish looked at the second thien, a young burly man with a short blond beard. "–will be the only man guarding Olympus's entrance tonight." Elish dropped his voice as the guard looked at him perplexed. "You will be doing the entire round of the grounds. I only want you to pass the entrance every half an hour on the dot. Am I understood?"

The thien's puzzled look deepened, but he knew not to question so he nodded. "Yes, Master Elish."

Elish snapped his finger at the other thien and pointed to the stairs. Then, with a single blink, the thien bowed, and walked off to wherever off-duty thiens went.

Elish turned back to the blond guard. "If you see a man lurking with black and white hair, and two different coloured eyes, I want you to ignore him and let him enter Olympus."

The blond-haired thien nodded and saluted Elish. "I will, Master Elish."

Elish had to give the man credit for that. His instructions were bizarre but necessary. It was that man, the same man that King Silas had sent Sanguine away for freeing, that had healed Jade before he had interrupted him. He wasn't sure if Jade's decline was because of the seizure, or if the odd-eyed man's influence was temporary, but in the end, it didn't matter. There was hope that if Elish had scared him away… perhaps he'd return to finish the healing.

If Silas wasn't sulking about that damned O.L.S being destroyed Elish would've been able to ask him just who that man was, but there was no part of him that thought it wise to engage the king right now. Silas was on a rampage, and if he would send his beloved *Crucio*, his Sanguine, to rot in the birthplace of his madness, there was no telling what he would do if Elish became his next target. No doubt Jade would suffer and Elish had done enough to Jade already.

Elish didn't like it but he had no choice. Jade wouldn't die, and right now there was a man on the loose who seemed to want to help the boy. If born immortals were attracted to one another, perhaps empaths were too, and it was obvious that strange man had some talent inside of him.

It was also obvious that Elish wouldn't be able to find out on his own just who that man was. Silas's laptop was locked up tight, even if Elish could get his hands on it, which he couldn't. If Silas had been successfully keeping the odd-eyed man from the family... it was folly to believe Elish could find out who he was now. He wasn't created after the first generation, that much was for sure. So who was he?

Perhaps a born immortal that Silas created, but I saw no similarities to any of my brothers' features, Elish said to himself as he made his way back to his apartment. *He looked like a completely separate genetic entity. I saw no Sky and Perish in him, and no Silas.* The chimera gene pool was diverse now, but the first generation were pretty much arians with chimera enhancements. They came from Silas's stock with slight infusions here or there to genetically diversify them. Then technology changed and Silas got more mad in the head, he started creating stealths, intelligence, brutes, and science-types.

So was this perhaps... the first chimera? Or did Silas have an even bigger secret kept tucked under his cloak. Another born immortal?

Elish dwelled on this for the rest of the evening while he distracted himself with work. It wasn't until nine that Lyle came down with Siris behind him. Siris was holding Jade in his arms, the boy wrapped in a fleece blanket.

"I gottsa little rabbit," Siris said in a jovial voice. "Where do you want him, Master E?"

"On the recliner," Elish said as he motioned towards it. "Lyle, hook him up and you may have your leave."

Lyle did as he was told with a scowl on his face. Elish ignored him and continued working on his Skyfall work without being bothered.

"Aw, it's so sad seeing him like this," Siris said. Elish glanced up to see the brute chimera leaning over Jade and staring right into his eyes. "He was so full of piss and vinegar before this Aras-Reaver shit. He got real hurt there, eh?"

Elish nodded. To the rest of the family, save a few, Jade had gotten hurt in Aras and his mind had been failing ever since. "Unfortunately yes, but he'll be fine in time."

"I hope so," Siris mumbled. "It's weird seeing you without him now. It's like you're literally missing your shadow." Siris chuckled at this and pinched Jade's nose and shook it. "Wake up soon, bunny beans." Then, with a gentle slap on the cheek, he followed Lyle out.

The rest of the evening was spent in silence. Luca had been shoo'd out by Drake since apparently the odd boy was busy with things, and was at home sewing a new outfit for the cat. The poor cat in question was sporting a black vest with a green bowtie, which had been altered more than once to make him not lose any of his mobility and to make it comfortable. Elish had been planning for quite a while to forbid Luca from putting clothes on the cat, but it kept the sengil busy, and he needed the distraction since Jade was no longer something he could nurture.

After Luca went to bed, Elish stayed up until Jade fell asleep in the recliner. Then Elish prepared himself a bed on the couch and left the apartment door unlocked. It was a long shot but right now that was all Elish had.

But tonight was not his night, he woke up to Jade staring blankly at him, giving his master the same forlorn and sad look.

It was foolish to think the odd-eyed man would come back here… but wouldn't it have been just as foolish to believe he'd come in the first place?

Inside Elish burned with frustration. He was used to getting whatever he wanted with nothing but a cooled look. Now he felt stripped down to the bone with reality nothing but ice on raw skin. If there was one thing that he hated feeling it was helpless, especially when Jade was involved. It was enraging, and an emotion that Elish had not missed feeling.

"I need to find that man… but for all I know he's fled to keep himself out of the clutches of Silas," Elish mumbled to himself. He nodded to Luca as the sengil, dressed to the nines and smelling like flowers, went off to manipulate Drake; today he was using the tuxedo-fitted cat as bait (he was planning on giving Drake sewing lessons and needed a wingman).

Once the door was closed Elish knelt down in front of Jade.

"Even if you saw him, you can't say a word," Elish said in a low tone. He gently rested his hand on Jade's prickly cheek and smiled thinly. "What I would do to have you call me an emotionless bastard, a psychopathic tyrant… what I would give for you to call me… Elish." Elish sighed and continued to stroke his cicaro's cheek. "Come on, maritus. Breakout of this, get up and yell at me, throw things at me, threaten to run back to the ravers." He felt a tightness to his throat and, unable to suppress it any longer, a pull to his lips. "Maritus… I found you and I brought you home… only for you to run to the only place I cannot get you."

Jade stared back at him; the grave sadness on his face never looking more prominent, and never more... did Jade look old. The boy who had once been a hard-nosed brat in Moros, seemed older than Elish as he looked at him. Jade looked tired, burnt out. He looked like he'd seen the lifespan of the human race a thousand times, and had swallowed its history of violence, of sadness, of loss.

Elish deflected his gaze. "I know you're wondering why I am letting you suffer like this, when I could ask Silas to make you immortal. I wish I could tell you... but I once told another man why and he laughed in my face." The corner of Elish's mouth rose, though the smirk that suited his face so well was weighted with sadness. "You're a young, impulsive idiot, maritus... and I know if you ever did the same..." Elish leaned in and kissed his forehead. "I would strangle you until the light left your eyes."

Then Elish's landline rang, the phone that they used to communicate with the sengils in the building and the other workers. He quickly walked over to it and picked it up.

"Yes?"

"Master Elish..." an unfamiliar male voice said on the other end. "I just saw the person you described; he's hanging around the grounds and he's looking sneaky. I thought you should know."

Elish's eyes widened. He looked over at Jade. "Go home for the day." He hung up the phone and sprinted over to Jade. He unplugged him from his EEG and took the IV out of his arm, then picked up Jade and headed down to the lobby.

He got a strange look from his receptionist but she didn't say a word. Elish walked down the hallway with Jade wearing only pajama pants and a t-shirt, and headed towards the door. He opened it with his foot and kept it open with his shoulder, and slipped out with Jade in his arms.

Elish walked down the steps with a determined look on his face, and started walking along the side of the skyscraper. There was a small parking lot that wrapped around the rest of the building, and further on, greenery and trees until the twelve foot wall that surrounded the back section of the building.

Elish looked around but spotted nothing but several butterflies, and a relaxed stray cat sleeping in the sun.

Should I start shouting for him? Elish thought to himself, but dismissed the idea. If Silas had been keeping this strange mysterious man in concrete no doubt he wouldn't trust any direct contact. *But what then?*

Elish sighed and looked down at Jade, then an absurd idea popped into his head. He leaned Jade up against the side of Olympus's brick wall, under a tree and in the shade, and walked away from him to the other side of the green space. When he got to the wooden fence, about thirty feet away from Jade, Elish sat down, out of sight, and waited.

Never more did he feel like an idiot – but the hope of this working far outweighed his own dignity and pride in that moment.

Time ticked on but Elish was patient. He sat beside the tree, making himself as invisible as possible, and kept his eyes on the near comatose boy. Jade wasn't moving, just lying in a heap where Elish had left him; and even though he held no expression, Elish knew the boy was judging him.

I bet he thinks I've lost my mind. If he remembers this when he wakes I won't be happy.

About a half an hour later, Elish saw someone walking towards them, though he was coming from the sidewalk to the left. Elish looked over and recognized him as Saul, Garrett's bodyguard. His son was taking extra shifts in Olympus training guards, and he was no doubt visiting him.

Saul continued to walk as he ate a sandwich. Then his head turned to Jade and he paused for a moment as if trying to figure out this mystery. He then looked to his left and made eye contact with Elish.

Elish stared back. Saul took a bite of his sandwich, looked at Elish for several more seconds… and then kept on walking without second glance.

It was another hour when Elish spotted a second figure. He looked to his right, and his eyes focused on a partially-hidden person loitering around the corner of Olympus. Elish crept back slowly and watched the person intently.

But when Elish saw who it was, rage swept him. The person he was seeing sneak up to Jade triggered such a furor in Elish, he felt a thousand old emotions, ones he and Jade had both buried, rush to the surface.

And when that man kneeled down in front of Jade, Elish exploded.

"What the fuck do you think you're doing?" Elish roared as he jumped to his feet.

Kerres convulsed from the surprise and his eyes shot to Elish. The man, himself looking older, wearier, retracted his hand from Jade's neck.

But then his face twisted from shock to an accusatory look. "What did you do to him!" Kerres cried, tears springing to his eyes. "He looks fucking dead. What did you do to him, you fucking monster!"

"I'm trying to save him, you delusional lunatic!" Elish snarled back. "You have five seconds to remove yourself from my gaze, or else Jade will witness what I have been meaning to do for years."

Kerres stepped away from him, but when he looked back at Jade his brown eyes filled with agony. "He's not safe with you," he screamed. "Why haven't you made him immortal? If he's so sick… why the fuck are you letting this happen to him!?"

Elish advanced on Kerres, his fist clenched and ready to deliver a fatal blow to the man's skull, but Kerres, like the cockroach he was, skittered off and quickly disappeared through a hole in the fence.

Elish's teeth ground together, and with acid in his heart, he picked up Jade and brought him back inside Olympus.

Once he was home he set Jade back down in the recliner and hooked him up to the machines. After that, Elish fixed himself a cup of tea and sat down on the couch. He sipped his tea in silence and gathered up the juggling balls that had scattered around him.

Kerres, now there was a flea that Elish had been wanting to squash. The only reason that boy was alive was because Silas knew how much it bothered him. Kerres was no insect with the skills to slip and skitter around unnoticed in between the chimeras' feet, Silas had told the thiens to allow him to skulk around in Skyland. For all Elish knew, Silas had given him a residence. The Crimstones were always a welcome distraction in Silas's eyes, and at one point, before it became personal, Elish agreed as well. The Crimstones could be used to sway popularity when opinions were down on the royal family. Or if there was some war in the greywastes or a famine going on, they could be used to fill in news coverage.

Manipulating the free media was easy, especially since it was free in name only. The Dekker's controlled the media, both the SNN, the Skyfall News Network, and the UFM, the Underground Free Media. Hell, Silas had even sent out Sanguine to continue his murder spree when the Crimstones were dormant and not able to be used to draw away the glaring public eye.

Silas controlled everyone, even his enemies.

Everyone except me, and what scattered seeds I still have, Elish said to himself. *So many have blown away, and so many have been set aflame.*

But I will not let the spiders overrun my garden – there is only room for one.

The rest of the evening was spent doing work, and he did more work in that day than he had the previous two weeks. Funds were given out, budgets approved, and mayors of each district conference called and counselled. He even held several meetings inside of his home while Jade slept. Artemis and Apollo got their time and even Joaquin came over and proceeded to throw himself into an anxiety attack over the state of the family. Jem had to calm him, the boy was good at that and it was obvious that Jade had matched the two well.

When Jade was bathed and put into his pajamas, Elish hooked up all of his monitors and made him comfortable. Then he read to him, something that Elish had been doing often, and turned off the light after he'd fallen asleep.

Like the previous night, Elish made himself a bed on the couch and left the door unlocked. Then, with the help of an opiate cigarette, he lulled himself into a troubled sleep.

CHAPTER 15

Jack

"HE NEEDS TO BE STOPPED," JACK SAID QUIETLY. HE looked down at his bloodwine, but when he saw a flicker of his own reflection he looked away, and instead continued to gaze at a framed painting hanging up above his fireplace. "As much as I know it hurts you to admit it... you know it's true."

Jack slowly turned around and his eyes found Garrett. The man was staring forward with a look of someone who was witnessing a horror movie play out in front of him; though the tremble in his hand clutching the wine glass suggested he was still watching it.

"He knows," Reno rasped. He was a husk of the man he'd once been. He'd lost a great amount of weight and the silver that had been in his hair had been cut away in a fashion that suggested it was in a fit of rage. He was sitting on the couch, staring at Jack's stone coffee table. Or perhaps he was looking at the black marble vase that held red flowers. Juni had picked them, red to match the red-eyed crow in the painting Jack had been staring at.

"Elish is g-going through a lot right n-now," Garrett said, his voice skipping like he was a scratched CD. He set his glass of wine down and sat on Jack's leather chair. "Jade... you know how he is when Jade's in danger."

"And if Silas gets sent away and it's just Elish... we're still going to be one Jade crisis away from another family meltdown," Jack said coldly. He took a drink of his wine and turned back to the painting. He'd drawn it for Sanguine when they were still together, a crow perched on one of the radiation signs with its wings stretched out. "Elish isn't our new leader. Perhaps he was before Jade, but the boy has weakened him."

"Jade will be made immortal soon enough... Elish will come to his senses about Jade, I know it."

Jack spun around and his black eyes narrowed dangerously. "Making that boy immortal will be the worst decision our family makes. I've seen Jade in action and Sanguine has too. The worst thing for the state of the world is to have an empath chimera be made immortal."

"I remember that argument," Garrett's quiet voice said. "I remember you said the same thing to Silas when Sanguine begged him to make Valen immortal. The king agreed with you."

"He won't be agreeing with anyone now," Jack said darkly. "Silas is in his own turmoil, and with Sky's O.L.S destroyed he won't be granting any new lover immortality."

"Which is why I must stick with Elish," Garrett said. Jack turned around to see Garrett reach out and rest a hand on Reno's leg.

"If you make me immortal I will dissolve you in acid," Reno said, and jerked his leg from Garrett's touch. "And I told you if you stick with Elish I'm gone. It's about fucking time you stand up for yourself and stop picking sides. Make your own fucking side, Garrett, because both Silas and Elish are wrecks right now."

"Elish will be fine once Jade is made im-"

"Elish is responsible for killing Killian and trapping Reaver!" Reno suddenly cried. "For his dumb fucking plan! Silas is responsible for all of this shit to begin with. Why are you being so moronic and trading one tyrant for another? Fuck both of them and fuck both of you too." Reno turned to Garrett, his face was twisted in agony. "You can't keep letting this happen! Stop being so fucking weak. Stop being their bitch! You're a chimera for fuck sakes."

"I know very well who I am seeing in Elish, and I told Elish this. Once he's scared enough for Jade he'll make him immortal, and then Elish will be fine. We just need Jade well!" Garrett said with a bit more force behind his words. It was as if he'd scanned his brain and had accepted the least hostile thing to say back, with still being able to keep what shreds of pride his family had left him with.

"Or dead."

Garrett and Reno both turned to Jack at the same time, and Jack did nothing but smile back at them.

"I'm not listening to this," Garrett said as he rose to his feet. "I'm done with politics. I need to concentrate on my fiancé and running Skyfall. You're insulting yourself if you're convinced this malice towards Elish is from his lack of being able to function at a hundred percent, and not because of his help in getting Sanguine in trouble."

"He pointed a gun at Reno with every intention of killing him," Jack said, the ice still lingering in his words. "And you fled from Olympus with tears in your eyes, and confided in me that Elish is becoming a monster and that he's refusing to make Jade immortal until he's twenty. You're the one that came to me, Garrett, and I'm telling you... it's time we take down Elish. And we need to take him down while he's at his weakest."

"I won't hurt Jade," Garrett said faintly. "I love that boy. This isn't his fault, and I'd never hurt Elish so."

"Elish wouldn't blink at killing Reno," Jack said. "And Jade is a danger to everyone. An immortal empath can control all of our minds, and Jade's shown he has that potential. He knocked Sanguine and me out when we threatened that red-haired boy after the Crimstones got him, and Sanguine slipped hints about him being able to do even more. Let's cull our monsters while they're weak, even if it means sacrificing a few innocents."

"And then we can go get Sanguine, right?" Garrett mumbled. He started walking towards the door. "All of you think you're doing what's best for the family, and yet weaved in your hostile and self-assured words is the need to save your partners. You want Sang-"

"Sanguine is not my partner," Jack said sharply. For a brief moment his visage changed, but he quickly deflected it with a smile. "All I want is for Elish and Silas to stop their madness."

"You want them to pay with blood for the people they've hurt."

"What's wrong with that?" Reno spoke up, still looking at the coffee table blankly. "Elish and Silas... what's their kill list at now? Leo and Greyson, Killian, countless cicaros and sengils, a bunch of chimeras in concrete. Reaver for the next twenty years. Jade crippled. Sanguine locked in the place where he was raped as a child. Why do we gotta be boy scouts and say... nah, we can't pay them back in the same way they hurt us. This is the dead world, and I lived in the greywastes... we pay blood back with blood."

Garrett seemed to choke on Reno's words, but Reno only shook his head and rose too. He looked at Jack. "I want Elish to feel the agony I've been feeling for the past two months. I'm a greywaster, and I really don't have any fucking morals."

Then Garrett grabbed Reno's arm. "Reaver was his friend and Jade was both Killian and Reaver's friend," he snapped. He turned and started pulling Reno towards the door. Reno went with him, but with a look behind his shoulder they made eye contact.

"Get him back," Reno said simply. And then the boy left.

After night had fallen Jack got into his favourite black sports car and drove over to Alegria. Juni was left at home but the painful tightening inside of Jack's chest came with him; that familiar, irreverent burning that felt like someone was putting cigarettes out on your heart.

It may be dangerous... but Jack and Jack alone knew the repercussions of Sanguine being back at Jasper's. Silas had had almost a week to calm down, maybe he could be swayed to let Jack go to the northern greywastes to retrieve him. Jack had to try, paying Elish back for the hurt he'd caused was one thing, but Elish's agony wouldn't get Sanguine back.

Sanguine had burned Jack many times, until a thick layer of skin had formed around Jack's heart, and all his emotions. But deep down inside, past the scar tissue... his heart still pulled towards that red-eyed mad man.

Jack got out of his vehicle and handed the keys to Juano. The chauffeur gave him a giddy grin back, a grin of anticipation to park one of the last Lamborghinis still running. The Grim glided up the stairs, and as he made his way to the top floor of Alegria, he cauterized and welded off every frayed emotion that still lingered inside of his heart.

He would do what he was best at: compartmentalizing everything he was feeling and pushing it down and out of sight. He needed to be calm when addressing Silas, and if there was one thing that Jack was, it was calm in dire situations.

Though every family member had their kryptonite, and unfortunately Jack was coming to realize his was, and would most likely always be, Sanguine.

He had to get Sanguine back, and he had to stop Elish's frighteningly steady climb to power.

When Jack was in the elevator, however, he paused for a moment and closed his eyes. It was then he realized that his family had indeed pulled him into their game. He'd been enjoying a peaceful life with Juni and his cat, no one bothered him or forced him to take sides. Jack was merely the Grim who collected the dead, bathed them, made them pretty, and then sent them back out into the world. That was all he had ever wanted.

Never more than during the ride to the top floor of Alegria, did Jack wish to press the emergency stop on the elevator and just go home... but Crow's frightened eyes and his desperate pleas had permeated his thick skin and had stained it black and red.

I am around creatures of madness, and here I am as the only sane, level-headed one in the family. Maybe luck will be on my shoulders and I can walk out of here with our family's issues resolved and us at peace.

This used to be Elish's job... we always depended on him when Silas was at his most manic. He was Silas's rock. How sad that under that cold countenance was a man with a thirst for power and an obsession with vengeance.

Hell hath no fury like Elish Dekker scorned.

The elevator doors opened and Jack stepped out into the hallway. He wasn't sure what he was expecting but it wasn't the peaceful atmosphere that had greeted him. Everything was silent, all but the hiss of the elevator doors closing behind him.

Jack gently knocked on the door and waited. There was no answer, but Jack was half-expecting that. Sanguine was gone and Drake was probably off entertaining himself somewhere.

Jack debated his options but decided to throw caution to the wind. He tried the handle, and when it opened, he walked inside.

Still quiet... still oddly quiet. Jack looked around the large apartment, and though messy, it was lived-in mess, not the mess of someone trashing things out of anger or agony.

"Silas?" Jack called lightly. He walked through the living room and saw a generous amount of drugs on the coffee table. There were even a few needles and burnt spoons – Well, that made sense if Silas was on a bender but it could've been Drake too. That boy loved drugs, sex, and eating, and when no one was watching him he usually did them all until he died.

Jack pattered to the hallway and turned to Silas's door. It was open just a crack but dark inside.

Well, since he'd already swallowed the poison by just being here, he might as well give himself a second dose.

Jack opened the door and closed it behind him.

When his night vision clicked on, Jack's heart broke. Lying on the bed, staring into nothing, and with his arms wrapped around a stuffed leopard... was King Silas.

"Silas?" Jack walked to him and kneeled in front of his bed. The king was just as bad as he was when he'd first woken, if not worse. Even though Jack hated to shed any other light but a negative one on what Silas had done to Sanguine... the king at least been alive in that moment. It may have been fleeting but the fire had come back to him.

Now it seemed that fire had died.

"What do you need, love?" Silas asked in a dead voice, his eyes not even focusing on Jack.

Jack gave him a faint smile and stroked his hair back. It was greasy and unkempt, he hadn't even been able to bathe.

"I wanted to come and spend time with you," Jack said lightly. He knew how Silas felt, because he'd been the same with Sanguine – both times.

Jack managed to keep his smile, even though his heart hardened over Silas sending Sanguine to Jasper's basement. Especially since no one seemed to know just who Sanguine and Nero had freed, and why Silas was so angry about it. No one knew still who it was, and the family was completely buzzing with gossipy rumours. Everyone had their own conspiracy theory, but Jack had been too upset and comatose from Sanguine's punishment to give it much thought.

"With me?" Silas said faintly. His brow knitted like he couldn't understand. "I didn't call on you... did I?" Silas sat up and pressed his golden hair back with his hand, then he wiped his nose and stared down at his legs. "No, I called for... for Elish but no one is around to fetch him for me."

Jack's jaw clenched at this; he found himself biting the inside of his cheek. He watched Silas look around before his grip tightened on the leopard. "I need Elish, lovely. I need to speak with him."

Jack's pointed molars dug in further to his cheek. *Elish? You blind man, you fucking blind man. He doesn't want to see you, or have anything to do with you. You have dozens of men who love you unconditionally and this is the one that you call for? This is the man that you lean against? Silas... Silas, you foolish king.*

"Elish... is busy tending to Jade," Jack said slowly. He watched as Silas made the leopard stuffed animal look back at him. Jack tried to keep his smile and sound encouraging, but his teeth were clenching too hard. "Why do you want to speak with him?"

Silas made the leopards head turn back and forth with his fingers. Then, oddly, he reached inside of it with his thumb and index finger. Jack watched as Silas pulled something shiny out, and he realized it was a ring. It had a silver band and three stones embedded in it: one green, one white, and one blue. The king turned it around in his fingers before a deep sadness washed over his face.

"Because Sky is gone, love," Silas said; his voice a wisp, a breath of cold air easily consumed. It was like the Ghost was finally evaporating into the darkness. "And I think... I think I'm ready to accept it. The last of my Sky hates me with such a fiery rage that even the white flames that char his bones would stand no chance. And once he realizes Killian is dead..." Silas brought the ring up to his lips and kissed it. Jack saw tears well in the corners of his eyes.

"I have tortured my family for years because of my own misery," Silas choked. He closed his hand around the ring and rested his chin on top of it. "I have mistreated my babies and I'm sorry." Jack's mouth dropped open, but he couldn't move, or even speak. "I turned away a man that loved me because he wasn't exactly what I wanted. Because he wasn't Sky. I turned him away and shamed him, and he's slowly grown to hate me ever since. Don't think I don't see the veiled disdain in his eyes every time he looks at me."

Oh... fuck... no.

"I... I have a device, something that Perish made, and if I can find his backed up hard drives I can perfect it. It'll make Jade still age until its removal. I'm going to make Jade immortal; I will make him into a cicaro again...

... and then I'm going to marry Elish."

"What?" Jack's tone hit the floor and continued to fall into the abyss. "You... you want to marry... Elish? Why... why not..." Jack wracked his brains trying to think of someone but ended up blurting. "... anyone else?"

"Because he's the one that I need to repair things with the most," Silas replied dully. He slipped the ring onto his finger, and Jack realized he'd been wearing the ring's twin.

And Jack would bet anything that the other ring belonged to Sky.

"I need to fix our relationship... I need to make him happy," Silas said. "He's been so loyal to me, so helpful. I've spit on it, and I wish for him to look at me with the same love as he used to. If I make Jade immortal with the spiderwire to have him still age… I can achieve that."

So Elish gets everything he could ever want? He would jump at the chance to marry Silas, I know it! He would be king. He would get Skyfall and the greywastes used to only seeing his face. And he will grow stronger with his immortal cicaro he can age to whatever number he wants.

Elish gets everything. Ever since I was a child I have witnessed that fucking bastard get everything. I have seen him cripple people emotionally and physically. I've seen him destroy people for denying him the slightest of things…

… I have been a witness to his plans of destroying Silas. He wants to send him away – No, Elish would never just send him away; Elish would encase him or worse. And when Reaver woke, the very born immortal Sanguine told me he was helping…

Reaver… who was found in Aras with Lycos.

Jack's eyes widened as a realization came to him. *Did perhaps… he hide the born immortal Silas yearned for, to begin with? It wasn't solely L-Lycos taking the boy and fleeing…?*

That is exactly what Elish would do. He would manipulate us into believing Silas was an insane tyrant with one hand, and drive Silas to be that insane tyrant with the other.

That fucking bastard.

"You can't marry him!" Jack blurted. He put a hand to his mouth and shook his head. "You can't… you can't give him that much power. You can't give him control over you like that. He'll destroy you."

Silas stared at him, before chuckling dryly. "I'm centuries old, love. Elish is no match for me, you know this. I am not as helpless as I look in this bed."

Yes, you are! You can't even see what's right in front of you. How long Elish has been playing you!

Silas's eyes narrowed at Jack's expression. "Don't look at me like I'm an idiot, Jack. I'm smarter than you, and I know your brothers more than you. Now, why are you here?"

Jack flinched at Silas's change in tone. Once again Silas's personality had come through; from being sullen and depressed to staring at him with flashing eyes and an accusatory glare. This was the king through and through.

"I was here to check to see if you're okay…"

Silas rose and shook his head. "I know when you're lying, lovely Grim. You're here to beg for Sanguine's release and I will tell you right now: no."

Jack surprised himself with the injection of rage that seemed to have been stabbed into his heart by a hypodermic needle. Anger was a foreign emotion to him, he never got upset, least of all towards his king that he loved. But as Silas stalked away, seemingly leaving the husked shell of his sadness behind in the bed, Jack's brimming glass spilled over.

"You just fucking said you would stop torturing us!" Jack snarled; his lips peeled back and his stance like a man ready for a fight.

Silas turned around, the corner of his mouth raised in a half-smile. "I always wanted to ask if you yourself had an imaginary friend. You get so different when you enter that little state of mania," he said in a taunting voice. "Admit to me you were only here to ask about Sanguine. Admit it."

"Why wouldn't I be?" Jack yelled. "You locked him in the place of his nightmares. The cruellest thing you've ever done! You're going to erase over fifty years of his healing! And for what? No one knows what he did, who he let out, because you keep secrets from us! You lied to us."

"Lied?" Silas spat. He took several dangerous steps towards Jack but Jack stood firm in his stance. "I lied? I've been in the living world longer than you've been alive, and the dead world for two hundred and thirty-two years. My first generation is ninety-one. I had been in the Fallocaust without chimeras for a hundred and forty-one years. Do you think during that time I sat around with my thumb up my ass with nothing happening? Do you think life for me just suddenly got dramatic and interesting once you became old enough to see it? You moronic fuck, I've lived a century and a half in the dead world and believe me... I have secrets that would make your hair turn white."

Jack stood stunned where his king's verbal lashing had left him. Silas turned around with a shake of his head. "You think my life only began when records started being kept?" Silas walked to his laptop, picked it up and shook it at Jack. "I am the only one in possession of records dating back before my first chimeras were born and I intend to keep it that way."

"Why...?" Jack whispered.

"Because I've done a lot of bad things to a lot of people," Silas replied. His face darkened. "I made mistakes... and I wish for that one mistake to stay swept under the rug."

Jack took a step towards him and tried to find his eyes, but Silas was staring blankly at the window in front of him. "He was… a mistake?" Jack asked slowly. "You made a… he had to be a born immortal, you didn't perfect immortal-making until the first generation was thirty-three."

Silas shook his head and picked up an empty syringe; he tossed it away and the lines on his face deepened.

"He's a born immortal but not of my creation. Perish told me he remembered him but his childhood memories were taken from him by me as well. Another mistake."

"Perish knew him?"

"Yes," Silas said to him. "His name is Gage Kohler, a living bomb of radiation. Not only that, he has mental techniques that trump mine tenfold, and suffers no ill effects from using them. He was sent by the military scientists who created us to…" Silas's voice trailed off and there was no indication that it would pick up again.

Jack gaped at him. "No ill effects from using his mental powers?" He looked over his shoulder in alarm, and his heart jumped to his throat as a new reality hit him. "He's loose in Skyfall?"

He didn't understand when Silas just looked at the floor. Why wasn't he tearing Skyfall apart looking for this man? He could cause a lot of problems for the family; he had to be stopped. "He'll be angry at you for locking him up, angry at the family. We need to find him before he hurts one of the mortals."

"I don't believe he's a danger, not yet anyway. He came to Skyfall years ago. He was filthy and skinny, but… friendly," Silas said. His brows touched as he scowled. "I had seen him before the Fallocaust and he was entirely different. He was tough, confident and arrogant, ruthless and without mercy. Everything you'd expect from an…" Silas once again paused, and Jack knew then he was leaving something out, something important. "The man had the most bluest eyes too. But when I saw him again, he had one blue eye and one black eye. He was also polite yet unstable. His personality was entirely different, and he remembered nothing of who he was before. But… I couldn't risk it, he was too powerful. I put him in concrete."

"And he's been in concrete ever since?" Jack whispered. The world was spinning around him. He desperately needed to sit down and take in all of this information.

Silas nodded. "I made a special one for him… coated the inside in Mag-strips so he couldn't use his radiation to make the concrete explode.

It would only kill him. There was nothing else I could do with him... even if he seemed to have a different personality now – he's too dangerous to be let free."

"Do you have anyone looking for him?"

Silas shook his head. "He doesn't know who he was before the Fallocaust, or the terrible things he did to my previous family." Silas laid down on the couch. "If he wants to destroy me... he can."

Jack was quiet for a moment. "If... if I find him, my king. Will you bring back Sanguine?"

The silence shifted over to Silas and there it remained for a solid minute.

"You dare bargain with me? Like my punishments are given so flippantly that you can buy their removal?"

Jack's jaw locked again. "I love him," he hissed through his teeth. "You cannot expect me to act rationally when Sanguine is currently being tortured with his own psychosis."

"You may leave now, Jack," Silas said dully. "Go to Olympus and fetch me Elish. I need him tonight."

"NO!" Jack suddenly screamed. He clenched his fists and snarled as Silas rose to his feet.

Jack glared at him from under his brow, his black eyes glistening spheres of darkness. The stress of hearing about this mysterious Gage, coupled with Sanguine's agony, was boiling him alive. "You will release my boyfriend. You will release him to me."

Silas chuckled and crossed his arms. "What bite you have, Jack Anubis. Or would you prefer just Anubis? Elish's little nickname for you. Please tell me this anger is perhaps because... you love Elish?"

Jack exploded at this. "Nothing could be farther from the truth!" he raged. "You blind, insane, self-deprecating little insect! I have been naught but loyal to you, and you're dumb enough to marry the one man trying to bring you down? You stupid mania-" Silas lunged at him, and when Jack fell to the ground Silas raised his fist and brought it down onto Jack's face. He struck him several times, each time his fist connecting and crunching against bone.

Silas jumped off of him, his chest rapidly heaving and his fists, now spotted with blood, clenched. "Get out and bring me Elish like I told you." Silas then spat on him. "And for my own pleasure... you can call him King Elish from now on, just to amuse me."

Jack staggered to his feet, his left eye bloodshot and a trickle of red running down his nose. "So Elish gets what he always wants then? And I get what? I get what for my loyalty and love for you?"

"You get to walk out of here without me encasing you," Silas said and turned his back to him. "Get out before I change my mind."

Jack stalked out with his sleeve to his nose. Leaving a trail of blood behind him, he walked to the elevator and pressed the button for the lobby.

He'd never felt so much rage inside of him, and the throbbing in his face where Silas had struck him only made it worse. Never before had his anger burned him like this, it was a blistering wound that was already festering and boiling. Every thought Jack had infected it further, until he found himself shaking with an unholy rage as he walked outside of Alegria and directly towards Olympus. There were people walking on the sidewalk, but every one of them jumped out of the way when Jack stalked by. He didn't even hear Juano when he asked Jack if he wanted his car.

There would be no need. Olympus wasn't far. Jack kept his pace steady and quick, his eyes fixed and never leaving the skyscraper he could see coming closer and closer.

The lights in Elish's apartment were turned off. Elish was sleeping. Good. Jack was glad he was because it would have to be quick. It would have to be silent.

No, Jack... you can't do this, don't do this. Jade is innocent. Jade is practically Sanguine. You cannot use him to hurt Elish.

But this is the only way I can pay him back.

For hating Silas.

For Silas, in his deepest of depressions, still loyally trusting him.

For letting Sanguine get taken back to Jasper's.

For manipulating Sanguine in the first place.

For being about to be handed all of his dreams, and more, on a silver platter.

It was for everything. Everything. For every smug look, for every toy he broke, for every time he battered his cicaro and tormented him, only to have that STUPID BOY LOVE HIM MORE!

Jack looked down as he heard a low toned beep. He checked his watch, and when he saw Sanguine's name pop up, with the longitude and latitude of the place where he died being where Jack knew Jasper's house was, Jack let out a hackle-raising, terrible scream of both madness and pain – and the Grim broke off into a run towards Olympus.

When he sped down the greenery of Olympus, towards the emergency exit he knew the code to, he found himself stopping in his tracks. Another flare of rage searing him when he saw two familiar people standing front of the door.

"What the hell are you doing here?" Jack snarled. It was an odd sight that made little sense, and it suggested that Jack was walking in on something. It was Drake and he was sitting on the concrete steps with Luca.

"Pet's inside doing pet things," Drake said casually, a marshmallow candy stick half-finished in his hand. "We're guarding the door 'cause Jade's ex-boyfriend keeps trying to get in and Silas says we can't kill him, which I think–" Drake jumped to his feet with his eyes wide as Jack let out a snarl of rage and started running towards the stairs to the metal door.

Then something caught him. Jack whirled around and took a swing at Drake who was holding him back.

"Why are you crazy? Why are you Crowing? Why are you mad?" Drake asked hastily, his words said so rapidly and squished together they were almost indiscernible.

"Because I'm going to rip out the throat of that little yellow-eyed piece of shit in front of Elish," Jack roared. He pushed Drake and he fell backwards down the stairs. The boy landed on his shoulder and did a flip, before slamming down onto the grass.

"What?" Luca cried from behind Jack. Jack turned around just in time for Luca to punch him in the face.

Jack barely flinched, and when Luca saw what little impact his hit had on the Grim, his face fell.

But the sengil was determined. He lunged at Jack but this time Jack was waiting. He grabbed Luca by the hair and pushed him over the railing of the landing the metal door was on, and jumped over the side on top of him.

Jack raised his fist and punched Luca in the face, then rapidly delivered him several more blows and, to top off the insane state he was in, he bit the sengil on the neck and gave him one last vicious hit right in his eye socket.

When Jack rose from his assault on Luca, the sengil wasn't moving.

Jack fixed his eyes on the exit door, and without a lucid thought inside of him, only blinding rage, he walked up the concrete steps and into Olympus.

Unbeknownst to him, someone else was following him inside.

CHAPTER 16

Elish

Earlier That Evening

ELISH SQUEEZED THE SPONGE OVER JADE'S HEAD AND watched as the water ran over the boy's eyes. He was no longer blinking or reacting to the water, that had stopped yesterday.

Even though he was done bathing Jade, he picked up a handful of water and flicked it onto Jade's face to try and get a reaction... but there was none.

The boy had almost fully regressed. The only thing he could still do was breathe and even Elish was waiting for that ability to be taken from him too. He had his breathing machine and the tube ready for when that day came at least.

Elish picked up Jade and dried him off, then put him into clean pajamas. Elish's mouth downturned when he saw the skinny frail frame laying on the bed. Jade was losing more weight but Lyle had said it was just his muscles wasting away. Supposedly the boy was getting all the nutrition needed, but Elish had his doubts.

He was having doubts about a lot of things. From the odd-eyed man never returning, to if Jade could make it to next month, let alone two years.

The constant thought in his head had been that two years would mean a lifetime. That those two years would disappear and be forgotten, but the rewards would stay forever. Elish had told himself this over and over until he could recite it like gospel.

But in truth, the cold chimera was also having second thoughts about that. Perhaps it was because Jade had been confined to a hospital bed, and when he had come home he was better. Now Elish was seeing him regress back into a completely vegetative state, and since he was now Jade's caretaker, he himself saw what Lyle saw.

Jade was dying.

And it was his doing. Garrett had been right, as much as it filled Elish with bitterness to admit – Garrett had been right. It was he who weakened the boy and it seemed that Jade forever eighteen would have to be the penance.

Maybe it won't be that bad?

Not for the boy, because nothing would change between us… ever. He'd be my cicaro and I would be his master.

Elish laid Jade onto the recliner, read to him for an hour, and then turned off all of the lights. He wasn't tired yet but he had found himself in a state of contemplation… and had decided that perhaps it was time to think things over.

Time to… let go of this futile hope that that strange man was in Skyland, or even Skyfall. Time to fix what he could already fix, so he can move on to collecting his seeds. Jade would be an asset in swaying the cicaros and sengils; he'd be no doubt wanting in on whatever plans Elish had.

Though as Elish drew up a thousand reasons pertaining to his own personal seeds or vendettas, he knew deep down he was only drawing them up to mask the real reason he wanted Jade back.

Because I so dearly missed that boy. I missed having someone I can trust completely.

Elish rose and turned on the light. Jade's eyes were still open, still blankly staring.

"I think… I will be speaking to Silas tomorrow," Elish said to him. He brushed back Jade's bangs and nodded as if confirming it to himself. "Whatever he requires, I will do it. I think it is time I pick my battles." Elish leaned in and kissed Jade's forehead. "If we're lucky he'll not delay. Maybe I will have you back in a matter of days. Then we can get to more important matters, like picking up these shattered pieces. You're a nuisance, Cicaro, and I'm growing tired of being your sengil."

He turned off the light soon after and laid back down on the couch. Out of habit, he lit and smoked an opiate cigarette, and soon after that he felt himself fall into sleep. One not so troubled.

Sometime later Elish opened his eyes, his ears picking up on a familiar sound... the apartment door opening. He stayed silent and listened, picking up the quickened breathing and anxious heartbeat of someone creeping into his apartment.

The mysterious person stepped slowly and carefully, and Elish realized just from the way he was moving... that he didn't have the night vision that every chimera and Silas had. This sparked a curiosity inside of him. He watched without fear of being seen, and waited for the man to make his appearance.

The electric fireplace was on in the sitting room, but it had been turned towards two chairs so only a faint glow was on Jade. Elish had done this deliberately to give the odd-eyed man easy access to his cicaro, and it looked like it was about to pay off.

And it did. Elish became a statue as the man he'd seen over Jade's hospital bed slipped into his vision like a forgotten shadow. He looked surprisingly good, his hair was cut and groomed, his white frock now styled into a wave which made bangs over the left side of his forehead, and he was clean and looking like any normal man.

Not only that...

He was wearing... Jade's black Iron Maiden shirt? *No, no, I had made Jade give that to Drake. He was wearing Drake's clothes.*

Elish slowly locked his teeth together as the realization came to him.

Hey, do you want to see my new pet? That damn mental case had been keeping him the entire time.

The strange man looked around the living room before his eyes found Elish's feet and then travelled up to his face. He looked at him for several moments, then affirmed to himself that Elish was asleep, and turned to Jade.

Elish watched him intently, waiting to spring into action if he did anything to hurt his cicaro, but the man did exactly what Elish thought he would do... he rested his hands on both sides of Jade's head... and his single blue eye turned black to match the other.

The same thing that happened to Silas. Yes, this boy was definitely something.

When Silas had healed Jade it had taken several minutes, if he correctly recalled. But Silas's abilities were full of bugs and glitches, he couldn't do much without it killing himself, so he used his powers sparingly. He'd even told Elish that Jade was beyond his own repair and

Elish knew he wasn't lying.

This boy, however, didn't seem to suffer from the same debilitating repercussions of empathic abilities like the others did.

What an interesting specimen. His release from his concrete tomb could prove to be beneficial to my campaign. If I have this boy at my side, and Jade healed and back in his prime... there's no telling what I could achieve.

Then suddenly something strange happened. The subtle noises in the house, the hum of the cable box, the whir of Elish's laptop, and the lights in the apartment, went out. Everything around Elish died and fell to an eerie calm.

The power had gone out. Elish turned to the boy to see if it had been something that he'd done, only to see the odd-eyed man jump up in shock, look around in a panic, and dash towards the door.

Elish scrambled to his feet, and as the low-toned emergency alert beeped around him, he ran after the odd-eyed man.

"E-Elish?" Jade's weak voice sounded.

Elish hesitated, and made a choice in the moment to keep pursuing the man who was dashing to the stairs. He opened the door and disappeared into the stairwell, now bathed in a red glow from the emergency lights.

Elish turned and ran to the elevator. He stopped in front of it and rapidly pushed the button. If he could get to the bottom, he could shut off all of the exits and the boy would be trapped in Olympus. It might take a week to scour every floor, but they'd find him.

Elish looked at the elevator, wondering why he wasn't hearing anything – and hated himself. The elevator wasn't going to work, the fucking power was out!

With a frustrated growl he ran to the stairs, but as he dashed down the first flight he heard the oddest of noises. It sounded like an angry scream, a snarl from the lips of some beast. It was coming from... Elish walked to the metal door leading to the floor he was on, and opened it.

Another scream. Elish felt perplexed when he realized it was someone trapped in the elevator, and whoever the man was, he wasn't happy about it. Elish exited the door and kept running down the stairwell, pausing to listen for any noise the boy could be making.

His ears filled with static, and the alarm that kept beeping its protest to Olympus's power outage. There was nothing; where was that damn man?

"I'm not going to harm you," Elish called down the stairwell. He got to another landing, the eighteenth storey and stopped to listen again.

He heard a squeak and a whine of a door opening, followed by a soft click. "Wait!" Elish shouted. He ran down the steps, wishing in that moment that he was a stealth chimera and about ten years younger.

The low beeping around him, and the distance, made Elish unsure of which floor the strange man had disappeared to, but it had to be one of three. Elish made a guess on the sixteenth floor and opened the door.

It was an empty floor full of storage, just his luck.

"I'm not going to harm you," Elish said again. "I'm the husband of the young man you've been healing. I just want you to go and finish it. All I want is for you to heal him, and I will have never seen you."

Elish opened the double doors and looked inside. All around him was furniture and musical instruments covered in plastic and sheets. There were boxes stacked high to the ceiling in scattered rows, and shoes and spilled contents on the ground. The windows' curtains were thin as well, but the city lights in front of him did little to light the area. It was a maze of boxes with barely enough room to navigate, like a child's greatest dream for hide and seek but right now it couldn't have been a worse room.

"I just want you to finish what you started," Elish said again. "I don't know who you are and my life is quite complicated enough as it is. Heal him, and I'll give you all the money you need. I'll give you a place to live far from Silas…" He paused, then reached into his sleeve for the last and most powerful ace he had. "… and if it is your desire – I will help you kill him."

Elish swiftly turned around as he heard a crunch of papers. He crept past a stack of five blue totes and peeked into a small alcove that had been made in the clutter.

It was only a radrat sitting on a nest of pink babies. Elish growled and, purely out of frustration, tipped the totes right on top of the little family. He stalked out of the apartment, down the hallway, and made his way to the fifteenth floor; the red lights above him stunting his night vision and making everything look like a low budget horror movie.

And to this boy I might as well be the monster chasing him through the haunted skyscraper. But this monster will be nothing compared to the one I'll turn into if he slips from my grasp once again.

Elish opened the door to the fifteenth floor and saw that this was a sengils' residence. He looked down the plain green hallway and noticed that the door was slightly open.

Then Elish smelled something… it was cologne, Drake's cologne. No doubt the dumb idiot had been grooming his pet, and right now the boy's path was as visible as a glowing trail.

Elish quietly walked into the room and closed the door behind him. After the *click*, and with the alarm in the stairwell becoming muffled, he listened.

His head snapped to the left when he saw a flicker of shadow in the sitting room. There were two bookshelves arranged to closing in the area, two chairs in the middle, and behind that, a large window. It was the same floor design as Elish's own apartment and it looked like the sengils living here had borrowed how his sitting room was arranged. Another plus, he would be able to charge in there and grab the boy before he wiggled out of his grasp. If he had to kill him to keep him from escaping, he would.

Elish remained as shrouded in shadow as he could. He crept to the wall, then to the bookshelf, and when his ears picked up a thrashing heartbeat, Elish knew he had found him.

Elish took in a deep breath and decided to try and settle this the easy way. "I know you're in here," he said loudly. He heard a startled gasp before it was muffled by the boy's hand; the boy was terrified, this was good. "My name is Elish. I'm Jade's husband. I just want you to finish healing him and I will never mention you being here."

The silence was a physical weight on Elish's shoulders, each moment passed by at a desperate crawl, prolonging the anticipation that felt like burning venom in his veins.

"Please," Elish said through his teeth. "I don't know who you are and I don't care. Just heal my husband. He's all I–"

The boy suddenly made a run for it. He tried to dash out of the sitting room and towards the double doors, but Elish whirled around and grabbed him. The odd-eyed man screamed and tried to rip himself away.

Then Elish felt a strange feeling in his skin, an odd prickling sensation that was getting more and more concentrated as the milliseconds went on. Elish looked down and realized it was sinking into his muscle, his bones…

The cold chimera looked at the odd-eyed man, and his heart dropped.

"NO!" Elish bellowed. He grabbed the man and let out a desperate yell when he saw the back of the man's skull start to glow white; the bright light lighting up his veins and his skull like a well-carved jack o'lantern. It was a horrific and terrible sight. The white light made the orbs of his eyes turn black, and the fillings he had inside of his mouth darken as well. He was a glowing skull that quickly became a skeleton as the light ripped through his veins and bones.

Elish lunged at the man, but the moment he touched him, he exploded. Elish was flung backwards and towards the window. It shattered upon impact and Elish was thrown out of the fifteenth storey of the apartment; the bright light following him like an aftershock, and in its rippling, air-disrupting waves, Elish could see shards of glass.

Elish looked up as he fell, and for a moment, time slowed and he was able to see the beautiful picture above him. A light that held shades of white Elish had never seen, and colours he had never known existed. They shone like opal ribbons of aurora borealis above him, with the sparkling shards of glass acting like their twinkling stars. Elish wanted to reach up to touch them... as if he knew that this iridescence would be the last beautiful thing he'd ever see.

Then the twisting and weaving streamers of white faded, and the glass falling around him stung and stuck to his face. The wind screaming in his ears became unbearably loud, and darkness covered all but the white flames he was seeing engulf his tower.

Elish's eyes widened as he saw the fire burst through the windows, but as he opened his mouth to scream... he hit the grassy ground below and he succumbed to the darkness.

The next thing he knew he was being shaken awake. His mind encouraged him to ignore it, but just when he was about to fall back into unconsciousness, reality hit him and his eyes snapped open.

And it seemed during his time unconscious, the bowels of hell had opened and spilled their fiery contents onto the dead world. He could smell smoke, and see the flashes of emergency lights.

Elish looked around and saw Big Shot shaking him, his Geigerchip reading so much radiation it was like an angry wasp was inside of the half-raver's chest. "Jade! They not let me in. They not let me in. Jade's inside. King Jade inside!"

"Jade?" Panic flared inside of Elish. He jumped to his feet but fell to the ground when his back and hip gave a horrible pang. He got up again and tried to take a step, but though he managed a limping walk, he could hear bones grinding together.

Elish walked to the front of Olympus and saw Garrett there, Artemis, and Ellis. They were standing in front of the door and Garrett was on a radio. Just as Elish stepped onto the concrete walkway, he saw a fireman run out with a sengil, half-conscious, in his arms.

"Jade?" Elish asked. He tried to stand up as straight as he could, but he knew a lot of things were broken. "Where's... Jade?"

The look that the three of them gave Elish made a fresh injection of panic shoot into him. Without another word, he ran to the doors of Olympus and pushed them open.

"Elish!" Garrett ran after him, his voice breaking. "Everything above floor fourteen has collapsed. The entire eight floors are smashed and melting together... Elish... Elish, tell me he's not–" Elish turned and ran full speed towards the stairwell, a cry bubbling inside of his throat.

This cannot be my reality. No. I refuse to believe this is my reality.

Elish took in a sharp breath, his lungs filling with toxic smoke, and he began to climb up the flights of stairs. He passed crying sengils and their partners; some holding cats and dogs, others rabbits, and two people even birds. They looked at Elish but not one of them spoke to him, only their eyes stared back wide and unblinking; they seemed to glow in the ever thickening smoke.

By the twelfth floor Elish had his nightshirt over his mouth, attempting to breathe through it. It was hard to get breath in this smoke and heat, and his head was pounding from the chemicals. A thick smoke and a burning heat was enveloping him like he had been submerged into lava, and as soon as he turned to the last row of stairs leading to the thirteen floor landing, it became a toxic black wall.

Then Elish's foot hit something. He looked down and saw a body beside his boot. Elish's heart lurched; he bent down and turned the corpse onto his back.

For a moment Elish's eyes closed tight and his fists clenched. He put a hand on Lyle's dusty shoulder but all he could do for his loyal former sengil was pat it gently. Then he rose and continued to the shrouded stairs. Four steps up he saw the body of Nels, and a slick of blood; that blood stuck to Elish's boots as he climbed the stairs higher and higher, and soon he was crunching gravel.

Elish choked and coughed, his eyes watering and burning from the toxic smoke. But he kept walking; he kept putting one foot in front of the other, as he climbed to where his husband was.

"Jade?" Elish's words were lost in the smoke and he realized he was sweating heavily. Each breath was like inhaling chemicals through a blanket and it was doing nothing to appease his screaming lungs.

When he reached the thirteen floor landing, he collapsed onto the ground. Elish choked and felt the darkness press against his skull like he was stuck inside of a twisting vice. He gathered up as much strength as he could and pushed through it, and took another step.

Then his head hit something. Elish put his hands in front of him and felt concrete and a twist of rebar. Elish shook his head, the panic now claiming him, and let out a cry. He raised his hand and hit the concrete, then felt around him for any opening in the stairwell. But there was nothing, the rest of the floors had collapsed like Garrett had said.

There was no way to get Jade.

"Jade!" Elish screamed. He clawed and ripped at the concrete, pulling on the rebar until its rough metal shredded his palms. A desperate bellow sounded from his lungs and he found his sanity slipping away. "JADE!" Elish pounded and pounded, his fists leaving smudges of blood like an ancient cave painting. He didn't know how long he was screaming Jade's name for, but eventually he felt hands pull him away.

"Leave me!" Elish screamed.

"I got him," Ares choked, his voice wobbling. Elish heard a sniff and a hand clench his shoulder.

"You... you..." Elish turned around and faced Ares, behind him was a similar shadow which would be Siris. "Move the... the concrete. Move the concrete we need to get Jade. We need to get Jade." Elish grabbed Ares, a desperation etched into his face, and turned back to the concrete filling the stairwell.

"I'm sorry, bro," Ares sniffed. "We need to leave. It's all on fire. It's all gone..."

"The fire truck," Elish said hastily, his eyes widened at the thought. "The ladder extends to the top of Alegria, it can extend to Jade..." He turned and started running down the stairs, the speed he was going and the injuries he sustained from the fall making him stumble and trip, but every time he fell down he jumped to his feet and kept running. There was no pain inside of him, he felt nothing, every receptor in his brain was focused on reaching Jade.

He was on the top floor... if the roof didn't collapse on him, he'd be okay. He'd be okay. I can reach him.

I have to reach him.

Elish kept running down flight after flight. Once he got to the bottom he had lights flashing in front of his eyes, and a consuming heat kept descending in the form of conscious-bending darkness. He ended up staggering outside of Olympus's entrance, and before he could fall to the ground, he grabbed onto the railing by the stairs.

Garrett and Ellis ran to him and helped him stand. Elish looked past the two and saw Reno with his face blank and stunned, and behind him, Knight was holding back a screaming Big Shot. There were other family members too, all of them standing still like sculptures in a garden.

"Jade?" Elish said, his voice now strained and sore from both the yelling and the smoke. He began to stumble down the stairs. "You need to get a fire truck's ladder up there... it'll reach. It'll..."

"Elish..." Garrett's voice was choked, throttled from his emotions. He watched as Elish staggered to the bottom of Olympus's stairs and onto the grass. "He's gone."

"No..." Elish shook his head. The bottom of his boots now melted and sticking to the grass. "He's immune to radiation. He–" Garrett gave out an anguished cry. He grabbed Elish by the shoulders and spun him around so he could see the skyscraper he'd just ran out of.

The entire top of it was consumed in flames, the flames so bright it had burned the sky above them a burnt orange. There was no telling where his apartment floor was now, or the one below it, or anything above the thirteenth floor. There was nothing left; it was incinerated.

Everything was destroyed.

Everything...?

"Jade?" Elish whimpered. He took a step towards the skyscraper, his eyes still fixed on the rippling white flames. "Maritus?" He heard Garrett let out a muffled cry of despair, but he ignored it.

There would be no surviving this.

This is it.

Jade is dead.

I was... I was too late.

"The... truck's ladder," Elish stammered. He turned around and took a step towards the flashing red and white lights of the fire truck, but sunk to his knees. With his head shaking back and forth he tried to stand, only to collapse again. "The truck ladder can... it can reach him. It can reach him."

"Eli..." Garrett choked and took in a shuddering breath. "I'm so sorry."

"It's not too late; it's not too late." Elish rose again and took another step. His head was still shaking back and forth like his brain had taken this new information and had directly denied it. "It's not too late... it's not too late."

Elish paused, unable to take another step. He stared at the ground and saw a red glowing ember fall onto the green grass and smoulder, then he felt a hand on his shoulder.

"It's..." Elish choked on his next words. He outstretched a hand and leaned against an oak tree in front of him. "It's too late." He closed his eyes tight. "It's too late."

Jade is dead.

My husband is dead.

I had held his fragile weakening spirit in my hand and I had let him slip between my fingers. I had taken so many risks with him... I had rolled the dice for him countless times and now... and now... snake eyes.

Because of my own stubbornness, because of my own need for perfection. Because of my unwillingness to give up yet another dream as every one of my gardens was razed in front of me. My seeds burnt to ashes, my plans, decades in the making, destroyed.

My brothers turning their backs to me, one after the other.

And because I wanted this wish for Jade and this one last wish for me. If I could at least have this, then perhaps I could settle for a life under Silas, if Jade was by my side...

If he was...

Elish slid his hand down the rough bark of the oak, and sensed Garrett behind him. His eyes shut as he heard the hurried and panicked voices amplify; one he recognized as Silas but he was far away.

With his eyes shut, Elish took in this chaos; he took and drew in every sound, every inhale of toxic, chemically smoke, and every stinging burn on his skin. This would be a moment he knew he'd relive forever, and he might as well give his nightmares the vivid memories they deserved.

He never wanted to forget this time in this life, for this was the last night that Jade Shadow Dekker lived.

"You wanted to know why I didn't make him immortal?" Elish suddenly spoke, his voice an odd tone. "You wanted to know... why I took the risk with someone I loved so much?"

There was silence, before Garrett sucked in a shaking breath. "Yes."

Elish looked down at his bloodied hands, raw and bleeding from pulling on the rebar. "I... I didn't want to keep him as a cicaro," he said, and his hand slowly closed into a fist. "Because whenever I looked at him, I saw this teenager. I saw a cicaro who acted as a cicaro, and would until he grew out of it." Elish shook his head and turned to Garrett, his purple eyes overwhelmed with sadness; they looked lost. "I didn't want him as a cicaro forever, Garrett. I... I wanted him to grow to be my husband. My partner."

Elish walked past Garrett, and looked up when he saw Reno staring at him. The young man had no expression of smugness on his face; he looked to be in a state of shock and despair as the white flames burned above him.

"YOU'RE GOING TO LOSE EVERYTHING!"

"You're going to fucking lose everything and all you'll have to blame is yourself. You disgusting fucking monster! Just stop! JUST STOP THIS!"

My husband, my Jade, is dead.

"WAS IT WORTH IT?"

Reaver burns. Killian is dead.

"WAS IT WORTH IT?"

Lycos dead. Lyle dead.

So many different shades of red drip from my hands. I am coated in their blood, and their faces will now haunt my dreams. I will hear their desperate cries and demands for an explanation. Why did I let them die? Where did I go wrong?

Or was I ever right in the first place?

Elish paused and stared at the ember-covered ground. It was strange to feel so numb, and yet, holes were being ripped into every single wall he'd ever erected inside of his mind. What places that had once felt emotions had become dormant, but on the same hand, feelings he'd never experienced, doubts that had been buried like toxic waste, had been dug up to contaminate everything that it came in contact with. All at once, it came crashing down on him, with the only spectator to Elish's revelation, his own self.

"It wasn't worth it."

Reno turned as Elish said this. And when he looked at Elish, Elish looked back and shook his head.

"It wasn't worth it."

Elish walked past Reno and onto the sidewalk. He staggered past shadows of people whose faces no longer mattered, and carried on far away from the flames that devoured what had once been his home.

"Elish..." Garrett cried. His footsteps became louder as he ran to him. "Where are you going...? Elish, please come home with me. I'm scared for you."

Elish kept walking, one foot in front of the other, his hands and face bleeding onto the grey, chalky sidewalk. There was so much light around him, and yet the world had never seemed darker. A light had gone out inside of him, one he hadn't realized had been illuminating everything.

"I'm going for a walk," Elish said. He paused and heard Garrett sniff.

Slowly Elish turned around and saw Garrett and Reno staring back at him. Both of their eyes were red and puffy, and their faces flushed from their grief.

"Where... when, when will you be back?" Garrett asked, his voice cracking.

Elish's eyes turned up to the pyre burning above them, now a tower suited for the King of Hell himself. A testament, a beacon that defied the very darkness that surrounded it; one that charred away the stars in the sky to replace them with crimson embers, and heat so hot it seemed to distort reality around it.

"I don't think I will be coming back, Garrett," Elish said simply, his eyes reflecting the crystal inferno. "I think... I think I must take my leave."

Then, with a single nod towards the two of them, he carried on his way.

And soon disappeared into the darkness.

CHAPTER 17

Killian

SOMETIMES I WISH I WAS AN EMPATH. OR MAYBE I wish I could just take a hammer to his head and spill his brains onto the floor so I can see everything that he's thinking. I wanted to know what thoughts went through his head when he was staring out the window. I wanted to know what wounds he'd grazed over when I saw that tug below his bottom lip. If it was a penny per thought for Reaver Merrik I would've made him a millionaire long ago.

But he was closed up tighter than Fort Knox. I rarely got a chance to peek in, and whenever I did, it was only what he allowed me to see. As our relationship continued to cling to time's coattails I had been seeing more and more.

And even though those fleeting glances into his subconscious were a double-edged sword, the older I got and the more I got to know him... the more I found myself rising to the challenge to calm the Reaper. I wanted to help him, love him, and perhaps one day... have him lean on me when he couldn't stand on his own.

Even if I knew he'd never let me.

I put my book down. I was just too distracted to read. I looked over at Reaver who was reading a comic book at the table, and wondered if he too was having trouble registering the words that were appearing on the page... or, I guess, the drawings.

My theory was confirmed when Reaver let out a sigh. He eyed the drugs he'd laid out on the table and set the comic down in favour of topping himself up. That didn't sound like a bad idea so I did the same.

This time when a scream rang out from outside, we didn't even look up. There was no mystery behind it now, we knew what the Blood Crows were doing with their slaves. It didn't make me happy, I still felt a queasy gurgle in my stomach, but what could I do?

"And in goes the tube," Reaver mumbled after taking in two lines. "And then the fertilizer…" He paused and craned his head, then smirked triumphantly when the second scream, this one noticeably muffled, sounded. "Yummy. Yummy." He reached over and grabbed one of the cherries we had in a bowl and popped it into his mouth. "The suffering gives it so much more flavour."

Occasionally I wondered if I was making Reaver more complex than he really was.

There was a knock at the door. I looked at Reaver's wrist watch and saw that it was six in the evening. "I didn't think we were going to get fed today considering the festival," I mumbled. "Well, we'll eat sparingly."

And eating sparingly wasn't something that we were used to doing. Since coming here several days ago they had been stuffing us with fruits and vegetables. Zach or Charles had been bringing us food three times a day, and while we ate he told us about Lord Sanguine and all he has to offer us. It was obvious that we were being recruited, but while they tried to get us to adopt their insane religion… we were getting treated pretty well.

Which was good considering I hadn't stepped foot outside since we had gotten here. Reaver had, but only because he was driving me, and himself, crazy being cooped up all day. Reaver had been going for long walks around the outskirts of Melchai and where the Blood Crows had said it was okay for him to go. Though because Reaver was Reaver, I suspected he was poking his nose into places that it didn't belong, but he was smart enough not to tell me when he did.

We'd been learning a lot about these Blood Crows, and what Reaver hadn't discovered, Zach and Charles had been more than happy to tell us. Even the most grisly of rituals, the most fucked up, disgusting tradition – they told it to us like they were telling their favourite story. I was taken aback with just how desensitized they were to human suffering. It was like once they had their prophet and their 'god' telling them it was okay, it gave them the moral freedom to do even the most depraved of things to their fellow man.

Reaver got up and opened the door. I saw his eyebrows raise and he blinked. "Well, hello," he said slowly. He looked over at me. "We have... lots of company."

I got up and opened the door all the way.

In front of the mini house were about a dozen of them. Every one of them with their hoods drawn over their heads and their hands clasped to their fronts. They were looking at the ground except for the one at the front – the one I recognized as the ancient old man who had done the ritual.

The leader...

"Blessed Chance and blessed Jeff," the old man said with a smile. He bowed his head and while it was bowed all of the others echoed their blessings. "I would like to come in and speak with you, if you will allow me."

If we would allow him? I exchanged puzzled looks with Reaver and I saw Reaver's eyes flicker towards the dining room table, where his M16 was, but I put a hand on his shoulder.

"Of course you can," I said. Reaver would waste the old man if he became threatening, and it was the day of the festival so it wasn't out of the realm of possibility that they would be acting different.

The crows bobbed up and down and exchanged pleased smiles. My hackles rose at this, they looked a little too happy right now, but... it looked like we were going to go with it.

The old man took a bag from one of the Crows and walked in. Reaver closed the door behind him. However, when I walked past the window, I could see that they were still standing there, staring forward with their washed-out red eyes glinting in the August sun. I wondered if they got hot in those robes. We had a fan in here and without it I'd be roasting.

I pulled up a chair for the old man and he sat down. He tented his hands and looked at the both of us as we sat down.

"I am here personally to give you important news," the old man said. He reached down and picked up the bag, and placed it on our table.

He opened it up, and inside were two black robes. "You will become Blood Crows tonight," he said simply. And as me and Reaver exchanged surprised glances, the leader pulled out another bag, this one contained a small red bottle of food colouring and a plastic container full of white powder.

"We have a ceremony of indoctrination," the old man continued. "But with the festival tonight, it will be done during our next worship. We ask you to please dress appropriately for the occasion, Man on the Hill will be there with his Angel Adi and it would be frowned upon for our new Crows to not look the part." He rested a hand on mine, and his other hand on Reaver's. "The festival will be starting in a few hours." He began to rise to his feet, I couldn't stop looking at the robes and the food colouring. "Once the horn sounds, make your way to the parking lot north of the north entrance." Then he bowed. "Sanguine bless you."

Automatically, since it had been said to us for the past several days, Reaver and I said it back. The old man then left us with the robes and the makeup, and he was gone.

"So I take it we're leaving really soon?" I asked. I unfolded the black robes, they smelled like cherry gum just like the Blood Crows seemed to.

Reaver reached behind me and picked up the red food colouring. "Nope," he said. "We're going."

I turned around and gave him a horrified look. I guess he thought it was rather amusing because he started to laugh.

"You said you want to figure out who Man on the Hill and Angel Adi are, right?" He picked up the white face paint and opened up the little container. "This is the perfect way of doing it. We're going to be dressed up in our Sanguine Halloween costume, it'll be perfect."

"We don't know anything about what's going to happen at this festival..." I stammered. Then I felt a spark of anger. "You're taking more needless risks, that's what you're doing. If we join this fucking cult, there's no coming back to Melchai once we leave."

"So what?" Reaver shrugged. "You want to hang out all the time with the Blood Nuts? I thought you didn't want to stick around here."

"It's still not good to alienate ourselves from a town, and you said yourself Jade's ravers have been attacking the other towns..." I felt a weight start to drag down my chest, this whole situation made me nauseas.

"And they're not going to let us stay here unless we become a part of their cult," Reaver pointed out. He put on one of the black robes, looking like someone from Harry Potter. "Do you see people visiting here? No? Neither do I. Because there are only slaves and Blood Crows here. You wanna be a slave?"

"No," I said. I buried my face into my hands.

"Then become a Blood Crow, Killi Cat." He threw the robe onto my lap. "Put it on and help me with the food colouring. I want us out of here so I can scout out where this festival is taking place."

I looked down at the robe; I felt like throwing up.

Reaver suddenly laughed, and I was pissed to hear it was rather mocking. "Such a coward," he chuckled.

My head jerked up from looking at the robes. I glared at Reaver, and surprisingly quick, all of the apprehension turned into anger.

"I'm a fucking coward?" I raged. I got to my feet and started putting the robes on. "I'm the one who saved us from the fucking worms in the plaguelands. I'm the fucking one who dragged your fucking ass back home after that incident with—"

"Watch your fucking mouth!" Reaver suddenly spun around and snapped.

I stared in shock, his anger snatching the words right out of my mouth. Reaver glared at me, his black eyes now flames, and he continued to stare me down until I looked away.

I busied myself whitening my face, and I could hear Reaver opening up the bottle of food colouring. Quietly and awkwardly, we both turned ourselves into Blood Crows, no words exchanged and nothing said.

And it continued to be quiet between the two of us for the next couple of hours. We both made ourselves look like Blood Crows, and in between that time, we read, watched TV, and did anything and everything we could to avoid each other.

Then, finally, it was time to go; but before we did, Reaver brought out the bathroom mirror.

Boy, did we look like fucking something else.

My hair was still really short, but it was hidden behind the hood drawn up over my head. My eyes were now bright red, the irises purple from mixing with the blue, and my face was snowy white. I didn't even recognize myself, which... I guess was exactly what we wanted.

And Reaver, well, with the red dye mixing in with his black eyes... he just looked demonic. There was no other way of saying it, he looked like the Anti-Sanguine.

"Let's go," Reaver said flatly. "I'm bringing the M16 and your satchel. We'll put them in one of the abandoned buildings in case shit goes south." I grabbed my bag with a single nod, and we carried on outside.

I hated it when there was tension between the two of us, but lately it had been happening a lot. Reaver had been tense and easily agitated, and if he believed that I was going to bring up the weird states he had been falling in, or his inability to be intimate with me, he verbally tore into me until he was satisfied that I'd gotten the hint.

It had led to a lot of tension-filled silences between the two of us. I didn't like it but... there was nothing I could do.

I wanted to help him but... I didn't know how. All I could do was be the strong one in the shadows, since he'd knock me down if I ever showed that side of me in the light.

But there was something wrong with my boyfriend. I knew this and he knew this. The state he'd fallen into when he'd woken up from killing that slave... I'd never seen that happen before, and it was terrifying.

I wanted my Reaver to just be happy...

Then my teeth clenched, because I wanted to pay Nero back just as much as I wanted Reaver to be okay.

Reaver lit a cigarette and handed it to me, then lit one for himself. We stepped onto the main street and I was happy when he took my hand. It was so I wouldn't wander away from him but I took it as a sign that he wasn't pissed off at me anymore.

I squeezed his hand and we followed the crowd of Blood Crows towards the parking lot that the old man had directed us to.

"Blessed Jeff and blessed Chance!" We both looked as we heard Zach. He bowed at us and we both bowed back. "You look wonderful. I am looking at Sanguine right now!" he said happily. "I will be calling you Brother Jeff and Brother Chance soon. Won't I? We have a wonderful night ahead of us." I noticed that Zach was holding a plastic jar in his hands full of slips of paper, but before I could ask him what was inside, he walked away from us.

"I guess we better hope our names don't get drawn," Reaver commented under his breath. "Remember they sacrifice a Blood Crow for the harvest. I bet our names are in that jar."

This made a chill go up my spine. We might be immortal but that didn't mean I was too keen on getting fertilizer shoved down my throat and buried alive. I still had nightmares about my time at the Typhus Canyon Factory.

But if that happened, we would get out of it.

Not just Reaver, *we* would. Even if Reaver was hell-bent on keeping me weak and useless, the proof was in my actions – and I think I had been doing a good job when he was in his compromised state.

It didn't make my Reaper any less powerful, it just proved that we really were right for each other.

I looked over at him as we continued to walk towards the parking lot. He had a neutral expression on his face but his resting face was always one woven from darkness. Even when he didn't mean to look it he looked threatening, ready to devour you whole and spit your bones out between inhales of red-embered cigarettes.

We stayed behind the hooded crowd after Reaver stashed his M16 and my satchel. There was about fifty of them and I could see more in the parking lot ahead of us. Everyone was bathed in blue from the creeping darkness, and from the orange glow I could see in the distance, it looked like torches were lit.

I glanced around, and as we walked I found myself feeling a new spark of discomfort. There were a lot of Blood Crows around, seemingly more than the ones at the worship. And, yeah, wow, I could see the women and the children as well.

I shuddered though when I saw that all of the women had something sewed. I recognized the pregnant one that we'd scared, her eyes still tightly sewn shut; and another pregnant woman with the same.

Actually, all of the pregnant women had their eyes sewn shut and the ones who weren't pregnant had their lips done. I... wondered why, but it was obvious that there was a reason behind it.

And I noticed something else as well. The women were walking with men that didn't seem to be Blood Crows, they were dressed normally.

I spotted Zach with his jar and dragged Reaver over to him.

"Zach," I asked him. "Who are those men?"

Zach glanced over, the jar held tight in his hand. "Those are our breeding slaves," he said cheerfully. The Blood Crows in listening distance nodded with him. "We are unable to reproduce and we believe sex with females is sinful. Those slaves fill in the necessary role of reproduction."

I could practically hear Reaver cheering on this belief.

"And their lips and eyes? What's up with that?" I asked. Reaver crushed my hand under his grip but I didn't care. We were becoming Blood Crows to these guys; we had a right to ask questions.

"We believe that during gestation a women should be in a completely pure environment. She shouldn't be exposed to any sin, even visual sin," Zach explained. "A child's life is precious and we give our future Blood Crows the best upbringing and the childhood that we dearly wish our Lord

Sanguine had." He looked past me with that creepy smile. I turned around to see who he was looking at and saw the little boy we'd seen. He still had those weird bear ears on his head.

I decided not to ask about that.

Zach wandered off after we'd finished asking questions. I continued on with Reaver but not one minute later, Reaver was pulling me closer to him. "Just so you know, last night…" he began to say, his voice quiet. "I moved our quad back to the garage. If anything bad happens, you can run fast with me, right?"

I nodded. "If we get busted by chimeras I'll be running faster than you," I said to him and he tightened his grip on my hand. "We'll be fine… they don't know who we are. Hell, I barely recognize us."

Reaver said nothing back and I understood why… we were catching up with the mob and clear in front of us, brightly lit with torches and spotlights… was the parking lot.

The crowd had formed a circle around nailed wooden planks, crucifixes I guess, and there were five torches that were standing beside each nailed-together board. The torches' flames cast an ominous X-shaped shadow against the chattering crowd, as if condemning them ahead of time for what transgressions were about to happen.

And there were crows perched on these makeshift crucifixes, lots of them. Those birds seemed to know that they were about to get fed.

I stepped onto the pavement of the parking lot, and as we walked closer, I saw that the crowd was split in the middle, a five foot gap was separating them like an invisible wall was keeping them back. There was no rope or anything stopping that strip of darkness from being consumed by the excited people, the Blood Crows just knew not to step there.

I looked past the crowd and realized that behind them, way back and in the darkness, was the dirt road that Reaver and I had seen. The invisible pathway to the front of the crucifixes was probably made for Man on the Hill and Angel Adi.

I kept having to tell myself that we were under disguise and that whoever Man on the Hill and Angel Adi were, they wouldn't recognize us. Even if it was Mantis, it wasn't like Perish could've sent him a picture of me, right?

My eyes scanned the crowd of Blood Crows, the sea of hooded men with their shining black hair framing such pale faces; the glow of the torches flickering against their long robes. These people made me uneasy and I hated the fact that they killed slaves like they were slaughtering bosen. But at least once we got a good look at Man on the Hill and the Angel, we could lay low until we decided it was safe to return to the plaguelands.

Then we could go back and get Perish's things, find out, ideally, what the worms were, and where we had to go to avoid them.

For a brief moment my heart stung as I thought about Perish. I had been doing everything I could to not think of him. Think about what he'd done to me, both good and bad. It was hard, because I missed him – dearly.

But I still… hated him.

For leaving me.

"Wow, look, Kill- Jeff." I looked to where Reaver was pointing and saw what looked like wire dog cages. Reaver pushed his way to the front of the crowd and whistled.

They were the slaves, bound, gagged, and blind-folded, visible through the blinding torchlight that bathed their bodies. It was hard to see from the angle but they didn't look like they'd been force-fed the fertilizer – they actually looked all cleaned up and groomed.

Those were the slaves for Man on the Hill…

Then the horn blew, a sound between a trumpet and a car horn, oddly enough. Reaver and I both looked towards the dirt road, where the sound was coming from, and my hand slipped into his.

The crowd became hushed around us, even the several children who had been running around scampered back to their parents. All eyes were on the five crucifixes, and soon the three shadows that slowly approached.

It was Zach, the old leader, and Charles. They walked side by side, their heads lowered and their hands clasped together.

As soon as the crowd of Blood Crows saw them, they lowered their heads as well. Me and Reaver did too, but when everyone began muttering *Bless them bless them bless them*, we remained silent. I guess Reaver could only be pushed so far.

The three stopped in front of the crucifixes and bowed to all of us, then they turned towards each other and bowed to each other as well. Then Zach and Charles stepped back and started picking up torches.

"Fucking whackjobs," I heard Reaver mumble. "This is what happens when you don't teach your kids logic and common sense. Didn't this happen like a billion times before the Fallocaust? Didn't they worship narcissistic idiots with god complexes too?"

I nodded. "Yes," I whispered as quietly as I could, "and it never really ended well. It all usually ends in blood and violence."

"I think they need a new god," Reaver mumbled and lit another cigarette. "What do you say we both get ourselves nailed to those crosses and we pretend we're Satans?"

I shuddered and watched as Zach and Charles stood behind the old man, torches in hand. "I don't think I want to be a god to these people."

"If it wasn't for the creeps on the hill I might, just to have some fun," Reaver said with a mischievous smirk. "Think of the shit we could make them do. We could bring Stadium here and teach them to hate what I hate."

I glared at him. I glared at him until eventually he felt the searing heat on his neck and looked back.

"What?" Reaver said exasperated.

"Nothing, King Silas," I said icily.

Reaver rolled his eyes and continued smoking.

"Sanguine bless you!" Zach suddenly cried. I looked over and saw him beside the crosses. He had a white bucket that looked incredibly heavy; he was dragging it towards the crowd. "Sanguine has given us a beautiful evening for our anniversary."

"Sanguine bless you too," the crowd murmured.

"Because the festival is about celebration and being thankful, we will be letting our newest Blood Crows pick the first stones," Zach said as he looked at us with a beaming smile. He walked over to us and set the bucket down... and proceeded to hand me and Reaver small rocks the size of a golf ball, if not a bit smaller.

Reaver threw his up into the air and smiled at it. "I have a good feeling about this," he said happily. I didn't feel the same however, but I wasn't a psychopath like my boyfriend.

While two men I didn't recognize handed rocks to the other guests, Zach continued speaking. "For those who are new, this is our reenactment of Sanguine's banishment from Melchai when he was but a child. Brother Charles... release Fledgling Daniel."

Fledgling Daniel? My heart jolted at this.

Charles walked into the torchlight and I was horrified to see a little boy with black hair, and the same bear ears that the other kids had on top of his head. He had a blindfold on and his hands were bound as well.

I checked his lips and was relieved to see that they weren't sewn but... but what were they going to do with him?

Reaver grabbed my shoulder and squeezed it. I knew he was mentally warning me not to do anything, but if they were going to kill the kid... I just might have to. I don't care how mad Reaver would be; if it was a cat instead of a little boy, he'd be planning on doing the same.

"He'll be fine," Reaver hissed into my ear. "He's a Blood Crow. This is probably like a fucking honour to the little shit. Don't forget these people are insane, this kid will grow up insane too."

... and that boy would end up cheering the next kid on. This information sat inside of my throat like a jagged pill but I swallowed it anyway. I killed the empathy inside of me and stood up straighter. It was a good thing I steeled myself too, because when they took off Daniel's blindfold, I saw eyes full of terror. The poor kid looked like he didn't know where he was; he was giving the cloaked men that surrounded him terrified looks.

Zach put a hand on the kid's head and spoke to him. Daniel looked up and nodded and I saw him sniff and stand up straighter.

Then Zach looked past the boy, and his eyes widened.

"Man on the Hill and Angel Adi are coming!" Zach gasped, and a collective gasp swept the crowd as well. All at once a spark of electricity ripped through the air, and the passive watchers began squirming in their spots.

I looked towards the dirt road and so did Reaver. I tried to hide my shock as I saw two flickering lights now appearing on the darkened mountain side, but I couldn't hide the palpitations inside of my chest.

And when they got closer I realized... there weren't just two of them, but four, and they were dressed up just like the rest of us. But instead of white powdered faces and food colouring in their eyes, these four men were wearing white masks with their black robes.

These masks looked... strange. The middle of the mask was elongated and pointed, like they were supposed to be beaks, and the eyes were just big black glaring pits. In the darkness they looked like pale floating heads, but the closer they got, the more I could see. They were wearing black robes like we were, and the torchlight was reflecting against silver buttons that went up their fronts.

The crowd remained silent, deafeningly silent, and in that silence I could hear their boots scraping against the ground. There was no noise besides that, no sniffing, coughing, shifting, the only other sound reaching my ears was the snapping and cracking of the burning torches. I had never seen anything like this in my life.

These four people… could be Reaver's family. They could be chimeras, or at the very least someone who was made immortal by Silas.

And this fact wasn't lost on my boyfriend. Reaver's face had fallen to the depths of darkness. He was glaring at the four like it was King Silas himself who had strolled down the mountain. It made me wonder if he was having second thoughts about this, especially with the knowledge that there were four of them down here, not just two.

What if one of the two knew us?

My stomach filled with nervous butterflies.

"Whackjobs…"

Reaver's mumbling was like a cold sip of water. I was happy that he wasn't feeling this anxiety, one that was shredding my stomach like I had swallowed the blades of a blender. He seemed to be okay, but maybe he was being strong for me?

There was no time to ask him and I was too caught in watching these four figures to squeeze his hand for reassurance. My focus remained fixed on the four, now walking down the invisible barrier like Noah after he had parted the sea.

They stepped into the circle and bowed their heads. In front were two that were tall and lanky, and behind them, burlier ones, with arms that looked like they could snap me like a toothpick.

"Sanguine bless you," the one in the front said. His voice was gravelly; I didn't recognize it.

"Sanguine bless you too," the crowd murmured back; every syllable matching so perfectly, it was as if this cult had become one single person.

The old man walked to them and shakily got down on his knees. He bowed, and when he rose his nose had dirt on it from touching the ground. Behind him Zach and several other more official-looking Blood Crows did as well, and like a rock thrown into a pool of still water, the crowd followed suit and did the same.

And though I knew he didn't want to, Reaver bowed and so did I.

The four masked men walked to the X-shaped planks and it appears that they were looking them over. While this was happening, Zach and the others quickly walked behind the makeshift crucifixes and I saw four heavy-looking wooden chairs, complete with a padded seat, get hauled out.

The seats were placed in front of the entrance to the lot where the four had just come from. When they were positioned, the four sat down in silence, not a single word exchanged or a sound made, even though it felt like an earthquake was going off in my head.

When the four were settled in, Zach walked into the middle of the circle and clasped his hands together. I realized as he smiled that he had a black headset on his head.

"Our festival will officially start now! Sanguine bless you," Zach said. And, sure enough, when he spoke it was amplified. I followed Reaver's gaze and found the speakers positioned in front of the crowd; they were painted grey to look like chunks of concrete.

"Welcome," the crowd mumbled back. "Sanguine bless you."

Zach nodded and inclined his head, then he drew down his black hood. "Over sixty years ago, the old residents of Melchai brought shame upon themselves," he said as he walked around the crowd that encircled him. "A young boy came to this town with money and good manners. He came and requested a place to stay, a place to buy supplies."

Zach then drew his hood back over his head and retreated into the shadows. Daniel stepped into the torchlight, now dressed in a patched little suit with a red bowtie, and put his hands behind his back.

"My name is Sami. I'm all alone with no parents," Daniel said loudly. He shouted it like a child performing in a school play. "Can I please buy some tact and some water? I haven't eaten in days."

Three shadows appeared behind him, and attached to those shadows were Zach and the two other Blood Crows I'd been seeing him with. They walked back to the center of what I could only call their stage, fully cloaked and with their heads bowed.

At the same time they raised their right hands and pointed at Daniel.

"His eyes are red!" Zach called.

"He has pointed teeth!" another yelled.

"He is a mutant! A demon child!" the third one roared. "Cast yourself from our home, demon, and never come back!" He raised his left hand and I saw a rock. I gasped and made a nervous noise as the man raised the rock and threw it at the boy.

It hit him in the shoulder. Daniel grabbed his arm and cried out, then with wide eyes he looked at the crowd and let out a scared whimper. I saw a rock from the crowd soar through the air and land beside the boy with an echoing crack before it bounced out of sight, soon the other rocks followed.

Seeing, and not missing, his cue, Reaver flung the rock without a moment's hesitation. His aim was disgustingly accurate, and it hit Daniel right on the side of the head. The kid was thrown off of his feet and he landed with a cry onto the ground.

Reaver snorted back a laugh and tried to take my rock from me so he could throw it too.

Instead I grabbed Reaver's arm and dug my fingers into it as hard as I could. I stared forward with my lips pursed, unable to move as more rocks got thrown at the kid now struggling to his feet. Blood was running down his face and I could see a gash below his ear, but quickly he stood, and as soon as he did, he started running towards the opening in the crowd, past Man on the Hill and the three others.

"Throw it!" Reaver hissed to me. I dragged my dug-in fingernails down his forearm, feeling wetness follow and threw the rock as sloppily as I could. It bounced two feet away from the running boy, but it didn't make me feel any better... blotches and spots of blood were trailing behind him and I could hear him choking and crying.

My heart broke and I had to look away. Why the fuck were we watching this? Why did these fucked up maniacs allow this shit to happen to a child? Even if he was cut from the same cloth as the Blood Crows it didn't make it right. Sanguine wasn't a fucking god; he was a crazy demon chimera and probably an asshole.

Reaver jerked his now bloody arm from my hand. "You need to get yourself together. I can't comfort you right now," he hissed. "You say you want me to treat you like a man, you need to act like one right now and understand when there is nothing you can do."

I took in a shaking breath and nodded. I let go of Reaver's arm and looked back to the center of the stage. One of the Blood Crows, I didn't know his name, was now standing cloaked and shrouded.

"The boy fled and never returned," the man said. There was a hostility to his tone, a flamed edge that burned the ears of everyone listening. "But he did not flee alone..." Behind him I saw someone else get pushed into the circle. His bloated stomach and sickly appearance immediately telling me who he was: another slave.

But it looked like this one had a role much greater than just being used as fertilizer.

I swallowed hard. If he was going to be playing the role I thought he was… he was going to be dead soon.

I fucking hated this place.

The man looked around, his eyes looking scared and desperate. Deep down I wanted him to make a break for it, or to pull out a knife or a gun, but instead he lowered his head and quickly walked towards the gap in the crowd where the boy had fled to.

"The Putrid One followed him and kidnapped him. He brought Sami to his house and raped and tortured this boy of only eight." I felt cold as he said this. We had heard this story at the worship but I think I had to convince myself it wasn't real. The thought of anyone going through that, even if he was a chimera, was soul destroying. "He knew of Sami, because he exchanged meth for information. People willingly told him that the boy was an orphan, and willingly told him which direction he'd fled in. Our god's soul was sold for meth and his innocence was taken from him. It was our fault. We betrayed our god."

As the man continued to tell the story, basically condemning Melchai and making everyone feel guilty. I saw Daniel out of the corner of my eye. He was now in his mother's arms, blood running down his head and a horrible tear on his lip. The mother herself didn't look good; her mouth was tightly sewn.

My attention was turned when I saw the slave come back. He was hunched over and looked terrified and dazed. I could see the other slaves behind him as well, bound and silenced, their metal cages reflecting the torch's flames.

Zach took the slave and quickly shackled the frightened man, then he walked him over to a concrete barrier that had an embedded metal link. He chained the man to the barrier and vanished once again into the shadows that continued to press themselves against the firelit stage.

Something was going to happen to that man, and the terrified look in his eye, and the other slaves around him, told me that he knew too.

The nervousness inside of me became too prominent to ignore, I found myself pulling on Reaver's hand, sticky from his own blood. "I want to get out of here," I whispered to him. "I don't like that there's four of them here… I think we should duck out and get the quad."

My heart fell when Reaver shook his head. He was absolutely transfixed right now; he didn't even look at me as he told me no. This was… this was his thing, this was what Reaver liked. He loved carnage and gore but… I suddenly had an overpowering urge to leave this place.

"Then after eleven years of being raped and tortured, split in half by The Putrid One. Sami found his strength and rose from the blood and dirt to become strong, to become… Sanguine." I watched as the Blood Crow turned to the shadowed area behind the crucifixes.

Another person stepped into the light. It was a young man with badly dyed black hair. He was a slave too but was wearing a suit and bowtie, much like I had seen Sanguine wear in the photos Elish had shown us last year.

This man… unlike 'The Putrid One' didn't come empty-handed though.

My mouth dropped open and I heard Reaver snicker when I realized he had a tank strapped to his back… and resting in his hand was a metal hose.

Fucking hell… it was a flamethrower. They were giving a slave a fucking flamethrower?

There was no mistaking why he was. The story had said… he had risen and killed The Putrid One… risen like a phoenix from the ashes.

And that was what happened. When the Blood Crow was done telling the story he disappeared with several quick steps. The slave who was playing Sanguine looked down at the metal hose he was holding and then to the man shackled to the concrete barrier.

I wondered why he wasn't screaming… until I took a closer look at him and saw that underneath that slave collar was a horrific red scar. He'd had his throat cut, he wasn't able to make any sounds at all, least of all screaming.

The man who was playing Sanguine hesitated and looked into the shadows. He shook his head and everyone then heard Zach's angry voice. "You are commanded to finish the task that was set out for you. This is tradition. Fulfil your role!"

The slave's chest rose, and to my and everyone's shock, he took off the flamethrower's tank and dropped the weapon onto the concrete. "Fuck all of this, you crazy fucks," he said loud and clear. "I'm a resident of Greendale and I was kidnapped to pay my brother's fucking debt. There is no god named Sanguine and your fucking crops have nothing to–" The man was tackled to the ground by two Blood Crows. He landed hard and tried to punch and thrash his way out of the dog pile on top of him but he was easily overpowered. The stage was filled with the sound of swearing, scuffling, and scraping concrete but… that was it. The residents weren't jeering, weren't talking or hooting, or hollering. Unlike when Reaver was in Aras, this crowd was completely calmed and in control. They only watched, and the crows on top of the crucifixes watched as well.

Reaver's body tensed with anticipation but mine only withered when Zach appeared with a rock in his hand.

"Our town tolerates no disrespect to our festival or our god," Zach announced, his voice was like a sharpened knife. He seemed enraged at this small disruption in this morbid play that the town was putting on. "Sanguine asks little of us as does our prophet and his angels." Zach kicked the man and his loud groan broke the silence around us. "Prophet, Angels… what do you want us to do with this filth? This impure one."

The four masked men were still, their narrow eyes seemingly fixed on the bleeding man in the center of this fire-lit circle. Time dragged on as everyone watched them for any reaction, any raised hand or nod of their head, but they didn't move.

"Make him scream one last time," a male voice finally said. It was the same raspy voice I had heard before. "Then cut out his tongue and sew his lips, let him choke on the very blood that has given him life."

I stood there petrified, and the fear that was seizing my heart was tripled when I heard the faintest groan come from Reaver's lips. My attention shot to him as the man's screaming cut the previously muted air; there was a look of pure bliss on his face,

"Oh, fuck yeah," Reaver moaned.

Then I saw the blade flash in the torchlight, and a gurgled scream. The slave recoiled back, his hands clasping his mouth as blood spilled through his fingers; and when Zach turned around, he was holding up his tongue.

Reaver looked like he was in paradise. That was all it took for my Reaper to be happy and at ease with this crazy shit that was going on around us. No matter that there could very well be chimeras that know us in our presence, Reaver fucking Merrik was seeing people die and that was good enough for him.

"Well, it looks like we will need another man to act as our Sanguine…" one of the Blood Crows said. The tongueless man was being dragged into the darkness behind the crucifixes, his screaming muffled but shrill. "Who–"

"I will!" Reaver suddenly called out.

My jaw hit the floor, and as Reaver took a step into the circle, I acted fast and snatched him back.

"What are you thinking?" I hissed. My face started to burn when I saw all of these eyes on me. "Are you fucking insane?"

In the clearing, Zach chuckled. "It doesn't look like your husband will let you, Chance." And the other Blood Crows chuckled lightly.

The look Reaver gave me as they laughed at him, was so hostile and threatening, I thought he was going to backhand me. "Shut the fuck up," he said, and it was loud enough for everyone to hear.

I was too shocked by his words to do anything but stare. I think I would've rather him hit me then talk to me in such a hateful tone. I didn't know what to do, they were all fucking staring at me, so I stepped back from him.

"Tell me how to work this thing," I heard Reaver say. I looked at the ground and at my boots, feeling humiliated and heart broken.

"I'll help him." I didn't even look up when I heard a deep voice speak, even when I knew just from where the voice was coming from that it was one of the masked ones. I didn't care, fuck all of this.

I sniffed and wiped my eyes. How could Reaver talk to me like that? How did trying to stop him from exposing himself to those four men, who we knew were somehow connected to his family, justify talking to me like I was some submissive housewife in an abusive marriage.

There was talking, one of the voices was Reaver, and a few minutes later... an ear-piercing shriek sounded, followed by a roar of concentrated fire.

I looked to the stage area and saw the outline of someone completely engulfed in brilliant orange and yellow flames. The slave was crumpling in on himself like an insect hit with a can of Raid, the flames burning his skin and his clothes, creating heavy black smoke that dissipated into the dark summer sky.

And there was my Reaper holding the flamethrower. My boyfriend, shrouded in oily smoke, looked like the devil himself as he pointed the nozzle towards the living fireball.

He looked alive too. There was no mistaking that expression on his face. He may be battling demons inside of him, but this chimera was a demon himself. His black eyes seemed to glow, stealing the embers of the flames, and his lips were peeled back in the most satisfied of grins.

My boyfriend was in his element, literally. I could see as plain as day why Greyson and Leo feared for his future, and as I watched Reaver mercilessly burn the slave to carbon char, I feared for him as well.

And it was with that realization that the fear and hurt disappeared, and in its place… I felt anger.

He was the one constantly telling *me* I was changing. He was the one mistaking me wanting to be treated as an adult as some great offense on his manliness, but fucking look at him right now.

Reaver wasn't capable of making smart decisions, that was in front of me, plain as day.

Zach and the other two appeared with two more slaves. Zach left the slaves, these ones with grey skin and bulging stomachs, with the two and faced the crowd.

"Our next re-telling is of the blessed day that our prophet and our angel blessed us," Zach called out. "However we were ignorant; we didn't see it as a blessing at first." He then turned around and smiled at the slaves.

Both of the slaves looked to be in a daze. They were dressed in rags and hunched over, looking at all of us with hopeless looks. My heart hurt for them.

"Twenty years ago," Zach began. "A mysterious man started living in the mansion with a ten-year-old boy. I personally remember the day he came. I was only eight at the time but it has imprinted itself on my memories." Blood Crows grabbed the two slaves. They both gave out animal-like cries and struggled, but they were too weak. "At first our leaders were outraged that someone would show such a lack of respect for our saviour, and the man who had cleared away our radiation. We all grabbed torches–"

It always has to be torches, what's with mobs and torches? I shook my head and watched five Blood Crows surround the slaves with torches in hand, the fire illuminating their scared faces.

"–and walked up the winding hill and path to the mansion, ready to grab them and sacrifice them to our lord. Then the man and the boy came out and told us he was a prophet for Lord Sanguine." Zach's face became dark, and I saw all of the Blood Crows and the breeders lower their heads in shame. "We didn't listen…"

Zach nodded to the Blood Crows with the slaves. I got another queasy feeling in my gut, and it only amplified when they picked up the screaming slaves and began bringing them up to the crucifix.

But they were fighting. The two bigger masked men got up and helped… and though I saw a flicker of worry in Reaver's eyes when they did, it went away quickly… and he fucking began to help.

He knew he was going to get another chance with the flamethrower.

I hated my chimera boyfriend sometimes.

The slaves screamed as they drove nails into their hands, five of them in each palm and wrist, when they were secure, Zach nodded his approval and turned back to the crowd.

Reaver looked quite excited as he held the flamethrower's nozzle.

"We didn't listen, and we're sorry," Zach said, and he bowed to Man on the Hill, Angel Adi, and the two others. "And because we saw it fitting, we nailed them to boards like what had been done to Lord Sanguine, and we burned the man and the boy… alive."

Wait…

He burned them alive?

But…

I looked at Reaver and saw a brief moment of shock before he hid it.

And, sure enough, Zach smiled and said. "And just like with Lord Sanguine, the man and the boy both woke up; they came back from the dead."

The… fucking boy did too?

The fucking boy is immortal?

A born immortal?

My pulse started to race. What did that mean? Who was he?

I heard the flamethrower's now familiar roar, followed by screaming, but I couldn't concentrate. I just stared at my shoes, my mind racing.

And then I heard laughing, from not just Reaver, but the masked one who had been helping him.

Anger quickly followed, again.

I loved Reaver. Fuck knows I love Reaver.

But in this moment I wanted to gut him like a scaver.

"Wow, you fucking charred him good!" the masked one said happily. I looked up, my teeth now clenched hard, and saw a satisfied smile on Reaver's face. He was standing beside the charred crucifix, the two bodies now slumped forward, their skin blackened, but with the occasional fissure of red from where the skin had split. There was liquid dripping off of them too, enough to create a small pool underneath them. That was their own fat, what little they had, mixed in with their blood.

I shook my head, the smell of burned meat and fuel was heavy in the air, and resisted the urge to run at him with a knife.

Reaver took off the flamethrower and handed it to the masked man. The man seemed happy at this, and he showed it by pressing the nozzle a few times to burn the crucified corpses some more. There wasn't much left of them to burn though, but two grown men had flamethrowers so that wasn't important.

"Bless Sanguine!" I heard the crowd start to murmur in tandem, a twisted chant that was said in a steady rhythm. Its pace reminded me of a slowed heartbeat. *"Bless Sanguine. Bless Sanguine."*

Reaver walked back towards me, smoke coming off of his clothes. He looked happy but when he saw the expression on my face, the smile faded.

He stood beside me without saying a thing, but when I felt his hand grab my shoulder I yanked it away. And when he grabbed me a second time, this one rougher, I whirled around and pushed him as hard as I could.

Reaver took a single step back and I saw a face so cold even the flames behind me would've frozen to ice.

I turned back to the center of the crowd, completely ignoring Reaver, and my attention turned to the man still holding the flamethrower.

Two Blood Crows came and relieved him of the weapon, and once he was free, he clapped his hands together a few times and shook his head.

Then he pulled his mask up and over a frock of red hair. At first my heart froze, anticipating recognizing him, but I quickly realized I didn't.

The man wiped his forehead, two dark green eyes flashing with an impish glee. He turned around with his smile and looked towards the three who were still sitting.

"See, I told you I'd make a good Sanguine, Nuuky," he laughed.

No, there was something I recognized... but it wasn't his face, or the name he'd called one of the other ones. I recognized his physique, I recognized parts of his facial features...

That was a brute chimera.

I thought my reaction was going to be fear, but I surprised myself when anger bubbled up inside of me again – anger towards the dumbshit who made himself stand out. Whose desire to use a flamethrower on three unfortunate slaves outweighed our safety.

And not only that... it was obvious that one was a brute chimera, and that one was immortal, and another was a fucking *born immortal*!

"You fucking idiot," I said through clenched teeth. I watched the green-eyed man, his face shining with laughter, try to beckon another one up to join him. To his left, the Blood Crows were bringing in slaves, not the fertilizer slaves but the ones that looked cleaned up and primped.

"Excuse me?" Reaver said, his voice low and dangerous. "What the fuck did you just call me?"

The bubbling rage rose from my stomach and began pooling in the back of my skull, boiling my brains and filling my head with pressure.

There had once been a time in my life when I trusted Reaver completely, and trusted that he would never put us in harm's way. But it looked like that time had passed.

"*Tu sturdus?*" I turned to him and snapped. "What the fuck—"

Reaver suddenly grabbed my jacket. I gave a yelp, and when he whirled me around, he pushed his face right into mine. "I told you not to fucking use those fucking words on me," he snapped. "Now shut the fuck up. You're drawing attention to us. Fucking idiot."

"What!" I suddenly screamed. "You just went and fucking introduced yourself to them and now I'm the one that's drawing att-" In a flash Reaver had his hand over my mouth, his other arm wrapping around me as I started to struggle.

I saw red. I fucking saw red. I was so infuriated with him I did the only thing I could think of.

I fucking bit him.

Reaver swore, loudly. He ripped his hand away, copper filling my mouth from the force of my bite, and then he smacked me in the back of the head.

So I turned around and slapped him right across the face.

Reaver's head snapped back. I froze, surprised at my own response. I thought he was going to start beating on me and I wouldn't be surprised if he did. We were both two sticks of dynamite with a fuse on one end and a lighter on the other. The two of us in this moment were dangerous catalysts and it wasn't a question of *if* this would get explosive it was *when*.

"We're leaving," Reaver said. "Smarten the fuck—" I walked to him and shoved him hard.

As always, he didn't move an inch, but he did grab my wrists with both of his hands and roughly pushed me backwards. I fell onto the ground, right beside two of the Blood Crows.

I got up and turned my back to him, fully prepared to ignore him and watch what was going on. But when I looked back to the torch-lit area, I realized everything had gone silent, and even worse... Zach and the brute were staring right at us. The red-haired one looking quite entertained with what was going on.

"You seem to not care that your shouting is disrupting this holiest time of year." Zach's voice was a shard of ice with a sharpened end. The calm and collected Blood Crow nowhere to be found. "Is there an issue, blessed Jeff?" He was standing beside the brute, and to his left were five male slaves, the cleaned ones, huddled together blind-folded and bound.

"Aw, lover's quarrel," the red-haired one laughed. I froze when he looked directly at us. I kept expecting him to yell our names or something, but he didn't seem fazed. "What's the fight about?" Then he looked towards the other three. My throat felt dry when I realized they were all standing.

Reaver was radiating anger. He pushed past me to the front of the group. "Little guy just wanted to use the flamethrower. You know how kids are."

I could hear my teeth grinding together.

The red-haired brute laughed again and started walking towards us. I started swearing inside of my head. I couldn't believe this was the situation Reaver had put us in.

The brute smiled a sunny smile at the two of us, then his eyes focused on Reaver. "What's your name, peaches?" he purred.

To my shock, Reaver's face paled and he went stiff. I couldn't understand why, obviously he didn't recognize him, or we would've been out of there.

"Chance," Reaver said. He was standing rigid, a complete change in the countenance he'd had previously.

The brute winked at him. "My name's Ceph." He reached out his hand and pinched one of the black buttons on Reaver's robes. Reaver licked his lips and pursed them. He was stressed, I knew that look and I knew those movements. "You wanna have some fun with us tonight, puppy?"

Reaver choked. No, it was like a dry heave. And he shook his head. "Ah, I'm with him. I'm... I'm good."

Ceph smiled and glanced behind him. "Hey, Prophet, check out these two. I kinda like this dangerous-looking one." He made a clicking noise with his tongue, and I saw he was still holding the button of Reaver's robe.

Behind Ceph the one I knew now was Man on the Hill approached, and as he did, he took off his mask.

I felt was a flood of relief, I didn't recognize him either and I knew just from his features that he wasn't a chimera. He looked to be at least as old as Elish, with short dark brown hair combed to the side, short stubble, and a clean, almost primped, appearance.

His charcoal grey eyes looked Reaver up and down, a thin, almost invisible smile, on his face. There was definitely something about him that reminded me of the Dekker family, however; he had an air of narcissistic smugness.

And when those dark grey eyes fell on me and we made eye contact, that observation was all but confirmed. He was looking at me with pink lips that rose in a smirk and dripped self-assurance. Like he was a sophisticated aristocrat walking amongst the homeless on skid row giving them nothing but polite yet patronizing smiles, before he hopped back into his limousine.

I think I was looking at Mantis. That's the only one it could be.

So who were the other two? And who was the born immortal?

"Yes, good choice, Ceph," Mantis said as he picked me apart with his eyes. "This one especially… are you a virgin, boy?"

His comment completely took me off-guard, and I found myself stammering. "No… I'm… with him." I looked at Reaver who still seemed frozen under Ceph's touch. I realized grimly that Reaver hadn't moved since Ceph asked him his name. I didn't get why.

"Too bad," Mantis said with a cluck. He took my collar into his hand and started pulling me into the middle of the crowd. I looked behind me and saw Ceph leading Reaver into the center as well. "One of my angels enjoys taking virgins. You could've had your consciousness for a little longer." He turned and nodded towards the two other figures, both wearing their masks.

"Nero, come hold him still and make sure they stay put. I wish to look at our other offerings."

CHAPTER 18

Reaver

NERO?

Nero was here?

How could he be here? In what realm of existence could Nero be here?

This didn't make any sense, and the longer I stared at the mountainous figure the more I was sure I'd suffered some sort of stroke. It couldn't be possible for many reasons, and it wasn't just because of the laughably horrendous odds, it was because Silas had told me he was encased in concrete. Silas had told me he wouldn't see the light of day until I told him Nero could.

But Nero was here, and he was reaching up and pulling the mask off of his face.

I looked at him, refusing to deflect my gaze. I was fully expecting him to ask for Killian personally. He might've mistaken Chally for Killian but he would know who he was now, and it would be Nero's personality for him to take Killian right from under my nose, or fuck him in front of me while these cultist assholes held me back.

What the fuck had I done? What was wrong with me?

I was making so many mistakes tonight, and I didn't even know why. I couldn't fucking control myself anymore around carnage and death. My need to see those slaves burn alive had trumped everything else.

And Killian knew it, and I'd almost hit him for it.

I was a fucking idiot and I was losing myself – I was fucking losing myself and now Nero was here. Not to mention the two fucking immortals that had made themselves known through Zach's story.

But to my absolute perplexity, when I made eye contact with Nero, he only stared back with a bored and rather disinterested look. He walked towards us, Killian whimpering beside me, and there wasn't a hint of recognition on his face.

He wasn't even fucking acknowledging us.

This was weird.

And it was only going to get weirder. When Nero stopped in front of me and looked down... I saw that he now had two different coloured eyes. The left one was still a mixture of purple and blue, but the right one was... black. Behind those eyes I didn't see Nero either. I didn't see the sadistic brightness I'd been forced to observe for an entire month; that cocksure smile that you could see as clear as day. Those mismatched eyes held a window to a different person, and that person standing in front of me was not Nero Dekker.

This person didn't recognize me.

But no... no, I fucking didn't care. We had to get out of here, and we had to get out of here right now.

My fucking gun was still stashed in the building behind us. I didn't have anything useful on me...

It didn't matter. We were done here.

Now.

And when Nero grabbed me and wrapped his arms around my torso, my brain kicked back into chimera mode, and like a switch had gotten flicked on, all of a sudden I felt myself come back.

Where the fuck had I been?

My eyes snapped open and I pressed my teeth together hard. I gathered up all of my strength and I raised my legs up off of the ground, making Nero have to bend himself backwards to keep himself from falling over.

Then, using the momentum gathered from my raised legs, I slammed my boots onto the dirt, braced my legs, and lifted Nero up off of the ground.

With a bellowed yell, my muscles screaming and burning from the weight of the brute chimera, I tilted Nero forwards. When he was on my back and I could see his head over my shoulder, I thrust my back upwards to flip his body over mine.

Nero landed hard. I reached into my cargo pants pocket and took out my pistol. I shot Nero in the head while I jumped over him, and as the Blood Crows cried out in shock, I grabbed Killian.

We made it two steps before something snatched me. I felt myself get lifted into the air and I heard Killian scream. I was tossed like a ragdoll and landed right on one of the torches. I saw embers spill onto the pavement like a dropped jar of glowing red beads and felt a searing pain in my side.

Killian let out a holler of rage. I turned around to see him with something metal in his hand. He was stabbing Ceph in the neck with a pocket knife; the blade sliding in and out of the brute's neck and chest like he was stabbing soft butter.

I ran to him, ignoring the screams of the Blood Crows behind us, but I was too slow. Ceph raised a fist and crushed it against the side of Killian's head, throwing him backwards into one of the crucifixes; blood erupting from his nose and spraying onto the pavement.

I ran past the brute but he grabbed me by the arm. He yanked my arm backwards with so much raw force it felt like he was ripping my muscles in half with his hands. I bit through it and tried to free myself, only to have a direct punch land in the back of my head, one that was so hard I temporarily saw black.

"Burn them both," I heard Man on the Hill's faint voice. My eyes went back into focus and I saw Killian. He was leaning up against the crucifix, blood pouring from his ear which was hanging lower than it should. The part that connected it to his head had been partially severed.

"You don't want them for the proxies?" a male voice, an unfamiliar one, asked back. The last cloaked chimera, Angel Adi.

"They're too injured; they'll be of no use to me now; and no flamethrower, I want them to suffer."

I slowly rose to my feet, taking in deep breaths to try and force energy back into me. My mind was too shot to even react when I felt stinging coldness get splashed onto my body, or smelled the intense aroma of gasoline. The only renewed sense I got was that of pain when the fuel soaked into the injuries on my body, especially the raw burn from the torch I'd landed on.

"N-no…" I rasped. I took a step towards Killian. My voice was weak and without power but I tried to say it as loud as I could. "I'm – I'm Elish's… I'm Elish's… Reav-" I choked and fell to my knees in front of Killian, and witnessed a splash of fuel get thrown onto his face. Killian's eyes squinted and he let out a cry.

I put a hand on his shoulder and buried my face into his neck. "S-sorry, Killi." I coughed and tried to hold him to me, hoping the flames would burn me and not him. If I covered him, perhaps I could have him first die of smoke inhalation.

Killian tried to answer back but he was too dazed. His words were slurred but desperate, and my heart broke for what I knew he was going to endure – pain worse than when he'd been burned in Sky's lab... followed by what could possibly be half a year in the white flames.

Suddenly behind us there was a bright light and a loud explosion. I turned around just in time to see dozens of Blood Crows flying up into the air, with a cloud of smoke and fire around them. I watched, stunned and confused, as they flew higher, their bodies mixed in with debris.

They all met the ground with loud thuds.

Then I saw a small black object fly past my head and land right where a mob of fleeing Blood Crow were running to. It bounced twice before landing unseen by everyone... and a moment later there was another ground shaking explosion that brought, not only residents, but chunks of concrete and median, up into the starry sky.

Man on the Hill, who I was now sure was Mantis, and all of the others, turned towards the explosions. I saw Ceph running ahead and grabbing Nero as the debris rained down on all of us.

A severed arm landed beside me, but I was so puzzled at what I was seeing I only stared at it; and when there was another low thud of a second body part falling from the heavens, I didn't even turn to look at it. The chaos was coming quickly and suddenly, the screaming and running around to my right were overloading my chimera senses and rendering me, for the moment, struck dumb. It was like someone had turned a stereo on to full volume after spending a day inside of sensory-deprived darkness.

Then I heard a scraping and heavy breathing to my left. I looked over and saw a figure wearing an executioner's hood over his face and dark sunglasses. He was dressed in a black leather jacket and black jeans and...

... and he had my M16 on his back and Killian's satchel.

"Get up! Get up!" I recognized the voice but couldn't place it. It was enough to at least give me the mental shove to push this stunned haze out of my mind.

I jumped up, running on pure adrenaline, and picked up Killian. I took a look behind my shoulder and thanked the universe that everyone was distracted by what I now knew were thrown grenades, and nodded to this mysterious person. "You have my gun. Do you–"

"I have your quad. I've been following you," he said hastily, and he started to run. Killian kicked himself out of my arms and I realized with relief that he wasn't as badly injured as I thought.

"The gate was open when I went to get it," our saviour called as we both sped towards the main road. "Hurry."

I took Killian's hand, both of ours sticky with drying blood, and we ran with him. I had no idea who he was, but I knew when he took off the mask I'd recognize him. The voice was familiar, very familiar.

The relief I felt when I heard the quad rumbling in the distance was enough to banish the throbbing pain that had rooted itself into several different areas of my body. Whoever this chimera was, he would be my best fucking friend. He just saved me and Killian from at least five months of resurrecting, and god knows what sort of situation we'd wake up to. If there was one thing I could say about my family – we had fucking good timing.

I went to jump onto the quad but the man stopped me. "I have a house I've been living in; it's ten miles from here," he said. "It's solid and it has a garage for the quad. They won't be able to find us. Let me drive."

He might've been saving our ass but I immediately didn't like his suggestion. For all I knew he would be leading us to Silas, or Kessler's husband. But it was dark and we had no place to go; no way we'd be returning to the plaguelands at night, not with those worms still out there and an infected whipwolf on the loose.

So I made another split-second decision to trust this ally. I put Killian half on my lap, so we would all fit, and sat behind this man who had just saved us. And although I knew he was a chimera, just from the fact that I recognized his voice, it was confirmed when the headlight of the quad turned off, and my, and I knew his, night vision took over.

We sped, full speed, down the road, and I was pleased when the man pointed to Killian's satchel, tied to the side of the quad, and yelled over the motor. "I filled it with grenades. If anyone follows us... you know what to do."

I nodded and slipped a grenade into Killian's pocket and one into my own. The other one I held onto in case anyone was dumb enough to try and follow us.

Poor Killian was shivering in my arms. I tightened my embrace and kissed his cheek. "I'm sorry, baby. I won't be that stupid again," I said to him. Killian didn't answer back but he craned his neck to try and look at me, or at least I thought he was until his lips twitched and I realized he was trying to give me a kiss.

I couldn't reach his lips but I kissed his cheek and squeezed him tight. He was injured and in a great deal of pain, and so was I, but we were safe and about to get our asses far away from this crazy town and those fucked up immortals and chimeras. I had no idea what Mantis had done to Nero but it wasn't my problem. Fuck him, he can be a zombie forever. This experience had only driven in the reality that we had to be careful. It was only dumb luck that Nero had had shit done to him and that Mantis didn't know who we were. We'd come dangerously close to being found out and it was my fault for letting my bloodthirst get a hold of me.

That just doesn't happen to me... I don't lose control like that.

Another way that Nero and what he'd done to me was fucking me up.

What was happening to me? I had been secure in my authority, and as confident as they came, but now I felt like a teenager taking stupid risks because he wanted to prove that he was okay. I fucking had nothing to prove; I had earned my stripes... but Nero had taken from me what I hadn't thought was possible. What I didn't even know someone could take. Now I was such a weak piece of shit I had to bully my boyfriend to try and force him to believe I was okay. I was desperately picking him apart and plucking out every strand of bravery I found in him, and it was leading to a knotted string of bad decisions. It just made me sick.

And not only sick...

... it worried me. It made me not trust myself and that was a scary reality. My entire life I had felt like I could only rely on myself, and the prospect of me not even trusting my own judgement was a lead weight in my stomach.

I had to figure out how to fix this. No matter what it took. I had to fix this at all costs.

Fuck. This was worse than I thought – and I think tonight that harsh reality that had been chasing me, had finally lunged and sunk its teeth into my neck.

"How long?" I asked the kid, half an hour into our journey. I kept checking behind me. The lights of Melchai had disappeared and there was only blue-tinged darkness around us, and the faint shine of the moon and stars; but my eyes were always peeled for the glint of headlights on the horizon.

"Ten minutes," he called back. Then he pointed ahead.

We were on a double-lane road with thick black trees and shrubs on both sides of us. There were houses in the distance and ahead which was good. If we were heading into an abandoned town they'd be more likely to look for us there. But a dime-a-dozen house in an area broken up by smaller side roads, black trees, and shrubs, it would be harder for them to find us, especially if we could hide the quad in the garage.

The house was just what I had hoped for: a small rancher tucked in the middle of a thick forest, well thick for the greywastes. There was a steep slope behind it too, with large rocks below that must've fallen off of the cliff sometime in the past.

From what I could see of the area, the top of that slope would give me a view of the main road we had travelled down, before detouring to the smaller suburban streets. I would be able to see anyone coming towards us, and the slope behind the house guaranteed no one would ambush us from the back.

Whoever this kid was, he had chosen the right place to hide out.

Attached to the rancher was a single car garage. It was made out of worn but sturdy-looking red brick with a white metal door that was now discoloured, dented, and scratched from the fine bits of greywaste ash that blew around during the rare winds we had here.

The kid stopped the quad and hopped off of it. He grabbed onto a blue rope that was tied to the door's handle and pulled it the rest of the way up as I drove inside. I killed the engine and jumped off to gauge my surroundings.

The garage was cleaned and freshly swept. It had metal work tables up against the left wall with a warped corkboard that had once been there to keep the tools organized. The corkboard had become too brittle from age though, and all of the tools had fallen down, leaving gouges in the brown wood that were clustered and close together like honeycomb.

To the right was a blue tarp that was covering old boxes. I could see brittle papers and a red figurine sticking out of a brown tote, and behind that, a rusted freezer, a pile of bicycles, and what looked like a lawnmower.

The kid appeared with a blue lamp, the cold glow reflecting off of his sunglasses, making him look like some masked marauder. He caught me looking at him and, interesting enough, he shrunk down.

He motioned towards the open garage door with his chin. "Do you want to close it?" the kid asked. "I… I don't want you thinking this is a trap. So just tell me how you want to go about this." Before I could ask he took off my M16 and handed it to me, then his hands went behind his back and he stared at his shoes.

This… this reaction was interesting to me. My mind had been focused on getting out of Melchai, not so much this kid's identity.

"You're not capable of taking me," I said to him. I scrutinized his body but he was covered from head to toe in black. Where his leather jacket ended, there were black leather gloves, and even the rolled up cuffs of his jeans held laced up black army boots. In a way he reminded me of how Jade dressed, except with more clothes, and I knew he wasn't Jade. I'd recognize that little knucklehead in an instant, and he'd never hide from me.

The kid took in a deep breath. I gave him another analytical look and helped Killian off of the quad. I noticed right away that Killian was breathing in short and rapid puffs, and I wanted to get him inside.

When I looked behind me, I saw an open metal door and a white wall above a grey carpet. I didn't want to bring Killian inside without first figuring out who this kid was, but this situation I had found myself in was one I had control over. I saw no tracks coming to or from this house, and I didn't smell anyone else inside of here. If this kid was the bait for an ambush I'd salute the asshole who had managed to pull it off, because it truly did seem like we were alone.

I picked up Killian and motioned to the door. "You first. Do you have power?"

The kid nodded. "I have some charged Ieons, but no generators or anything like that. I have a SolarSky that's attached to the roof, and that gives me enough power on sunnier days to recharge the Ieons, but… it's not much. Enough to use a hotplate, my laptop, and some small electronics." He walked inside and I followed with Killian secure in my hold.

The house was clean, really clean. All of the trash had been cleared out and it even looked like he'd been able to vacuum. I walked down a hallway and saw a shining and bleach-smelling bathroom, then to my left, what was now the chimera kid's bedroom: a stack of three mattresses on a sleigh bed made out of black wood, and blue totes of things in a corner beside a wooden dresser. The window was still intact too, and it had been cleaned so well that, if I was a bird, I'd have broken my neck trying to fly through it.

Then the main part of the house, a good size living room with a picture window that was framed with washed blue curtains; it was dark but once day came it would light up this room well. For now, the kid's bluelamp shone onto painted blue walls, grey carpet, and matching blue furniture: a couch and a love seat, with a wooden coffee table in between, and several credenza-type things.

I put Killian down on the couch and checked out the kitchen as well. It was amazing how different houses looked when they were cleaned, especially once they were vacuumed of the ash that blew in and the shit that fell from the ceilings as gravity and time drew them down to earth. I had never been in Skyfall, but it had blown my mind when I had been in Elish's hidden base. If I lived in a house pre-Fallocaust with electricity and television and computers, I'd have never left my house.

There were no traps, nothing to suggest this kid had something up his sleeve. I walked around the interior and checked all the rooms and the finished basement that was downstairs.

The kid was still masked with sunglasses hiding his eyes, and when I walked in I saw him handing Killian a glass of water and a box of crackers.

I crossed my arms and stared at him. "Who are you?" I said, getting straight to the point. I hadn't even had the time to mentally go over my chimera checklist. Elish had drilled into me all of my brothers and even my sister and her kids, but instead of checking each one off of the list, I cut to the quick.

Interestingly enough, the kid's heartbeat picked up and he rubbed his nose before staring at the ground.

"I was hoping that you knew already," he said, his tone dropping. "Please... please don't kill me. I'm all alone here and... and I have no one, Reaver."

Killian put the glass of water down. "We won't hurt you. You saved us," he said. He could speak at least, but his ear was bowed and angled funny. He'd have to be dispatched tonight, and me too. "As long as you're not hiding anyone else..." Killian looked at me. "You won't hurt him, right?"

I shook my head, but my curiosity was piquing at the kid's anxiety over me knowing his identity. Why would he be scared of…

Then it hit me. I knew who he was. At first I felt an overwhelming feeling of rage, a boiling anger that slammed me down like someone had dumped a semi-trailer full of asphalt onto my head; but while my fists clenched and my jaw locked, my mind was rapidly telling me to calm down and keep still.

Keep still, even with the fury seizing and vibrating every muscle I have, I had to keep calm.

I had to keep calm.

Even though Kiki Dekker was standing right in front of me.

"Take off your hood," I managed to say, my tone plunging to bottomless chasms. Killian's head shot to me and his expression turned to fear. "Take it off." A twinge of pain burst from my jaw; I was speaking through teeth, not just clenched, but pressing together so hard I was waiting for the crunch of my molars breaking. It was taking everything, oh fuck it was taking all of me, not to lunge and kill him.

Kiki reached up and took his sunglasses off, revealing eyes so unworldly orange they stood out more than Killian's dark blue oceanic pools. Then he slid off his hood, making his hair, longer now, tumble past his ears.

The cicaro pursed his lips, a soft but rosy shade of pink, and deflected his gaze. When he looked to the side I saw a jagged red scar. It started at his ear and ended an inch from the lower corner of his lip. There was also a scar on his neck… the exact shape of my mouth.

"No, you look at me," I said to him. Killian's expression was one of confusion. He had no idea who Kiki was, or what things I'd been forced to do to him and with him, or what he'd done to me. He'd only heard my brief confession to being forced to have sex with him in passing, and it had never been brought up again. "Look at me."

Kiki's orange eyes slowly lifted up from under his plucked and perfectly arched eyebrows. He was clean shaven too and his clothes freshly washed; although now speckled with ash and dirt. Even in the dirty environment that was the greywastes, he'd kept up appearances like any cicaro would.

I looked back at him, injecting as much disdain into his willowy frame as I possibly could, and I saw the kid slump down further from the weight of it.

"I'm sorry," Kiki said to me. His eyes were large and his bottom lip tight. I hated, positively hated, the honesty coming from him. And I hated even more that he next looked at my boyfriend.

"Why are you sorry? You had the fucking time of your life," I spat at him. "What the hell are you sorry for?"

Kiki shifted his weight. Killian was still giving the both of us dumbfounded looks.

"You're right, I did. Because I didn't know you from any of the other men. You weren't any different, so why would I care? But I'm still sorry. Okay?"

Then suddenly I heard a piercing scream. The noise took me to Killian, thinking something was killing him, only to see a blur of blond run past me and towards Kiki. Before I could react, he had grabbed Nero's cicaro by the jacket collar, and as I ran to stop him, he raised his blood-soaked fist and punched Kiki in the face.

It looked like Killian had clued in as to who our rescuer was.

"Killian!" I barked. Killian raised his fist to punch Kiki again but I grabbed him and pulled him away. Kiki stumbled back when he was released, and slammed into a desk by the TV stand. The rickety desk sent the cicaro crashing to the ground, taking with him a dusty lamp and a radio. But in a flash he was jumping back to his feet.

"No! Let me go!" Killian shrieked, his voice rising to a level of mania. He tried to rip himself free from my grip but I managed to hold onto him.

"Let me fucking go!" Killian screamed. I expected a sob, any sort of sad emotion, but I realized to my own shock that he was angry. Not just Killian angry, like a little kitten hissing with its fur all puffed up, but a furious rage that told me he would kill Kiki if I let go of him.

Killian let out a snarling scream. "Fucking let me go!"

Kiki, with his hand cupping his nose and blood spilling through his fingers, stared at Killian in terror, and when I looked into the reflection of the living room window I knew why. Killian looked like something I had never seen before; his face was twisted in rage, his blue eyes wide and fully insane. He was swiping at the air, clawing at it more like it, his teeth bared and his lips peeled back in an inhuman snarl. This was new, completely fucking new, and it was weirding me out to see this side of him.

"Killian!" I said sharply. "Calm down." I had my own feelings of hatred towards Kiki, and the last thing I wanted to do was bury them, but I felt that if I showed any more disdain towards the cicaro that Killian would never snap out of his manic rage. "I'm calm, see? If I'm calm, you gotta fucking be calm because this shit happened to me, not—"

"Mark my fucking words," Killian suddenly growled, the tone of his voice taking me completely off-guard. It was low, lower than his usual high-toned natural voice, and it was smooth, like a silky liquid that contained a deadly poison.

I had heard that tone before, but not from him.

I found myself making eye contact with Kiki, and our gazes locked as Killian spoke.

"Mark my fucking words," Killian said again. "I will pay you back for what you and your master did to him. It may take a day, or it may take the next twenty years, but I swear on the white flames, I et conteram."

I et conteram.

I will destroy you.

Kiki and I stared at each other, and for a moment, a brief moment, the two of us shed off what toxic histories we had and shared a look of complete bewilderment. It was like the cicaro knew that Killian didn't act like this, and he knew it was baffling me as well.

But with a hard jerk of Killian's body to try and free himself from me, I broke eye contact with Kiki. "Killian, calm the fuck down," I said to him harshly. "If I'm fucking calm you have to be too. Come on, *voice of reason*, if anyone has the right to kill him it's fucking me, and I'm not going to hurt him. Nero isn't here and he's the one you want, not his little chew toy." I jerked Killian back, and when he temporarily stopped fighting me, I twisted him around and forced him into my arms.

Killian's eyes were open and staring off like a mental patient who had just been put in a straitjacket. I kept waiting for the tears to come like they always did, but he just glared at the wall like he was telepathically trying to set it on fire. His head was shaking too, almost like he was having a light seizure.

"Killian?" I whispered. I glanced at Kiki to make sure he was going to stay put, and moved a hand to Killian's head. I tried to stroke it. I was angry, fuck knows I was angry, but Killian was starting to disturb me. This was like that odd calmed state he'd assumed when I'd flip out in the plaguelands house, but this had another air to it... a psychotic air. I was seeing many new sides to my boyfriend, a boy who had once been a meek, polite young man with his nose in a book.

I pulled him away from me and put my hands on both sides of his face.

"What's happening to you?" I whispered to him.

As soon as those words left my lips Killian's crazed eyes softened just slightly, but the intense stare into the abyss didn't waver. Even when I gently wiped his flushed cheeks with my thumb he wouldn't look at me.

"Killi Cat?" I said. "I'm okay. There's no need to get all worked up. Kiki didn't personally do anything malicious. He only did what Nero told him to do. He–" The words stung my tongue like droplets of acid. I looked up to Kiki. "Go to your room, you're not hearing this shit."

Kiki lowered his head, walked past us, and left the room. I heard the floorboards of the hallway squeak, then the click of a door closing.

I let out a long breath and continued stroking Killian's cheeks with my thumbs. "We want Nero, Killian, not Kiki. Kiki's his twinky cicaro and, like I said, he never hurt me. I was the one that hurt him. Did you see that scar on the right side of his face? And the bite scar on his neck?" Killian didn't answer me so I continued. "I did that. I got a hold of him and ripped his face open and tried to rip out his throat. I hurt him more than he hurt me."

Killian kept staring forward – then his eyes narrowed.

"So you don't hate him?" he said; his voice once again plummeting and picking up that odd poisoned satin. "You have Nero's cicaro in your possession and you're letting him live?" Killian pulled away from me, his glaring eyes flashing dangerously. "Why is he still alive, *Reaper*? You have Nero's treasured little cicaro in your hands. Why aren't we torturing him right now?"

I stared at him, absolutely fucking dumbfounded. Killian brushed away my shocked stare and continued to glare me down. "We have someone that Nero loves right here. What the fuck is wrong with you?"

My temper flared, like a volcano breaking through a thick sheet of ice. That kid had a deadly way of being able to draw up my anger and sear it to blistering red with his words. Killian was playing a dangerous game with my tolerance and patience for him; he was playing with fire and I knew he was going to eventually get burned.

And he was stupid, he was an amateur. I realized I had no intentions of hurting Kiki right now, and as the question of why presented itself in my mind, my dark thoughts rose up and answered. The answer was as clear as day, and was ringing through my clouded, sadistic mind like church bells on a Sunday.

Why? Because as I retreated into my own mind I saw a much more beautiful video playing in the background. I saw an opportunity in front of me, wrapped up in an orange bow. I had just been dealt a solid hand of cards, and if I played them right, I could hit the jackpot.

I could finally get my revenge, and oh did I have the most sweetest of revenges planned. And to have this become a reality, I'd need to keep my boyfriend from jumping up on the table and kicking around our chips.

This stupid boy had no poker face. He was a teething lion right now, testing his adult fangs on everything he could get his mouth on; but he risked ruining my game with these manic emotions clinging to his sleeve. I had to control him, because if I could pull this off…

I found myself actually closing my eyes at the prospect, and when my eyes closed I heard Nero's desperate pleading, the rattling of chains – and Kiki rhythmically crying out.

Ah – Ah – Ah – Ah.

Then Killian's accusing voice pierced the bubble of pleasure inside of my head. "You got all riled up using that flamethrower, and you got hard killing that fucking runaway slave. We fucking have Kiki right here!" he said to me harshly. "So what's so fucking special about him? Huh? Why don't you want to fucking kill him too?" He was a distant narrator to the wrong movie though. Because through my closed eyelids I was seeing something that drew up such an excitement in me, I felt it pluck the invisible strings of my most darkest desires. I was seeing something new, something I'd never fantasized about before, and like a pre-teen discovering porn for the first time I found myself feeling like I'd stumbled upon the most forbidden, the most taboo of thoughts.

In my head I was seeing Nero's desperate face. He was stricken with anguish as I pinned down Kiki; the cicaro's tight little ass in the air and my hand pulling his right cheek to the side to expose his tight hole. Killian was behind him, fuck he was naked and rock hard, pre-cum on the tip of his cock. My own cock was engorged from desire and my body pulsing with hunger. We were both naked in front of the pet, side by side with this screaming victim splayed out like he was on a butchering block.

This new prospect flashed through my vision unexpectedly, and the fever it brought in it exploded like it was a barrel of gasoline getting dumped on a bonfire.

Then a second image, and this one nearly brought me to my knees with want. I saw not only Kiki being dominated... but I saw Nero. And like an upgrade to first class, all other thoughts were dismissed and my mind focused on that one. I brushed the fringes with Kiki, but I think I knew what my innermost desire was.

I could dominate Nero. That would cure me of these problems.

Would that cure me?

For a brief moment my mouth pulled down in a frown, because all I wanted in my life right now... was to just be cured, to just be okay and stop... stop feeling so fucked up. I wanted the flashbacks gone; I wanted to have sex with Killian again, not just fuck him but make love to him.

Jesus fucking Christ, I just wanted to be normal and not feel so broken inside.

"– So what the fuck?" Killian raged on. He'd never stopped spitting his venom at me, though my mind had been everywhere else but with him. The fleeting moment that was my silent plea for normalcy was gone with the wind and I almost felt the thud as he grounded me back to my reality.

"We have him right here, *Reaper*," he snarled; his voice had now reached a level that was condescending and insulting. "Let's do it! Fucking come on and show me–"

I opened my eyes and saw Killian's eyes flaring. Blue eyes in pools of washed out red that threatened to reduce me to cinders. A fire that I knew I would extinguish and stomp on, because this little shit had gotten too big for his boots and I was all about taking him down a few pegs.

In a flash, and without any warning, I grabbed Killian by the back of the head and drew him in for a forced kiss. He immediately tried to pull away, but when he did I roughly seized his jacket and yanked him towards me until we were face-to-face; so close our noses were touching.

"That kiss wasn't a fucking suggestion," I growled to him. The mask of flames on his face weakened at my sudden aggression. I pulled him back into the kiss and opened my mouth. His lips trembled and my tongue slipped between them to find his stiff tongue, tucked back towards his throat like a scared dog. I caressed it with my own, my mouth opening and taking him in deeper.

Then I slid my hand down the back of his jeans and grabbed his bare ass. I squeezed it so hard he cried out, then, as I broke our lips, I dug my fingernails into the back of his head and I forced him into a constricting embrace. "You think I'm fucking weak now?" I growled into his ear.

"Using your fancy Latin words like you're some sort of fucking chimera?" He tried to pull away but I dug my nails into his scalp harder, forcing his head to remain over my shoulder. "You think I have something to prove to you? You could always make me laugh," I hissed. I could feel wetness coming from both of my hands, and shreds of skin getting pushed into my fingernails. "Since when do you call the shots, Killi Cat? Since when did you start thinking I've gone soft?"

"I– I didn't…"

"No, you listen! You want to play with the big boys you'll be fucking treated like one," I snapped, and scraped my dug-in fingernails up his ass. Killian cried out and more skin got pushed into them. "Now you listen to me, you brazen little shit." I dropped my voice. "What satisfaction would we get from killing him now, huh? No one cares. We'd kill him and that would be it. Not to fucking mention Jack would be here within hours, or did you not think of that? You don't think ahead, do you? You want to throw your insulting, condescending words at me when you have no idea what you're talking about. If we killed him now, we'd be throwing away a diamond that has landed in our hands. Do you want Nero to suffer?"

"Y-yes…" Killian stammered.

I closed my eyes and squeezed Killian's ass. I could smell the blood from my fingernails breaking the skin. I drew up my previous fantasy and felt the heat start to pump to my groin. The rage I felt from Killian challenging me was turning into lust.

I think it was time to educate my little boyfriend.

I squeezed a wound I could feel and collected blood onto my middle finger. I burrowed it in between his cheeks and found his hole. I felt it tighten, and at the same time Killian gasped from surprise. He lifted a leg up and onto the coffee table, and I roughly pushed my middle finger into him. I felt the tight band clench around the digit before I thrusted deep inside of his warm flesh.

"Think ahead," I hissed into his ear, pressing down on his head hard. I could feel his throat against my shoulder blade, it was tightening and flexing as he tried to swallow. "Kiki is here because Mantis has done something to Nero. Kiki is going to want us to help, that's why he saved us. Make sense?"

Killian let out a shuddering gasp as I dug the finger in; it was now up to the knuckle. "Yes," he gasped, his breathing becoming heavier.

"Why would we kill him now, when we have the prospect of having

Nero and Kiki both as our prisoner? Both of them chained and bound and under our control. We can torture Kiki in front of him, and believe me, Killian, Nero is in love with that little bitch. He was scared when I attacked him. If we're patient, we can have them both." Then I craned my head to the left and slowly licked Killian's neck. Then, quickly, I pushed a second finger in and wrenched them up, stretching his hole. Killian let out a cry, and started standing on his tip-toes. "And you know what I want you to do when we have Kiki and Nero both?" Lust braided down my spine and pooled into my groin. My hard cock was pressed into his jeans, and I felt his own greeting mine like two lovers on both sides of a brick wall. The erotic heat from my own imagination was filling me and making my vision blur. The lewd fantasies were feeding on my sexual deprivation and the fire that was being fuelled was one I felt unable to control. I was losing myself in this, and I fully realized that.

"What do… you want me to…do?" Killian gasped.

I smirked and sucked on his neck. The vivid fantasy I'd had in my head was drawn up but I allowed myself to go further this time.

Killian and I in front of a naked Kiki, who was face down on the bed with his ass in the air, and beside him was Nero in the same position. I knew both of their bodies perfectly, and I could even smell the desperation seeping off of them. And on the heels of that wonderful smell, was the aroma of sweat and sex.

In my head I looked at Killian, and I saw that anger that I'd been seeing change to an intense desire. We were going to do something together that would either heal me, or, if we weren't as secure as we both thought in our love for one another, permanently break us apart.

Because there was something I wanted to do, and there was something I wanted to see him do.

"I want you to fuck Kiki in front of me," I whispered into his ear. "And you're going to watch me fuck Nero until he dies underneath me."

My words electrified the air like static and hung in the room long past when I had spoken them. Killian at first said nothing back, but I heard his breathing quicken and his hips press his hard cock into my own.

"You… you want me to fuck… Kiki?" Killian said. His voice was lustful but I heard the unsure tones. He was horny, and horny minds went to the most depraved of places, but even with the desire boiling in him he sounded nervous. "Are you… serious?"

My two fingers started pushing in and out of his ass, and even with his nervous tones his hips started grinding into me. "Oh, is that too far for you?" I taunted. "All full of talk but that's too much for the Killer Bee?" I snorted, and in a fluid motion, I ripped my fingers out of his ass and pushed him away from me. "All talk and no action." I smirked. I could tell from the way he was looking at me that he wanted to, a large part of him wanted to at least, but his conscience was fighting him. "Or is it me you want to fuck?" I took a step towards him and he took a step back. "That's it, isn't it? Because I'm too fucked up to fuck you – now you're putting on the dominant shoes, eh?"

Killian's eyes widened and he shook his head. "That's not it at all, and don't ever fucking think that again. I'd never and you know that," he said angrily, and another step was taken backwards. "I... I just don't think that's a good... idea. I don't want my first time being rape. I just–"

"You just want to kill him?" My eyes narrowed to slits. "Kill him and that's it? You're boring. You buzz around like a bee caught in a jar but you have no substance behind your words, no real thirst for revenge. You just want the easy, lazy way out." I shook my head dismissively. "You challenge me like you actually have balls, but let me tell you, boy, you're a fucking amateur. And you standing there like a pussy shocked at the prospect of me bringing you into a real, solid plan to get me back to normal, and–"

"You think that will get you back?" Killian cut me off, the uncertainty and the lust drained from him. I saw a solemn desperation in his eyes, the same one I had in the fleeting moment when I myself brushed on the prospect. He looked at me, his blue eyes big; they were practically begging me for reassurance.

"I think torturing Nero might help," I said. And I found myself closing my eyes, wanting to bring back that image. "The thought of it excites me, and the idea of you being beside me while I do it. You're so desperate to be a man... maybe I might like watching you become one on that squealing little–"

I didn't even hear Killian approach me, but I did feel his lips suddenly greet mine. I opened my eyes and saw his were closed, and I glanced down just in time to see him unbutton my pants.

And moments later, my pants and boxer briefs were on the floor. With our lips locked, he directed me to the couch and pushed on my shoulder until I sat down.

Apprehension started to rise to my surface, anticipating more flashbacks, but I hoped with everything that had happened, maybe I could do it.

Killian reached into one of the left pockets in my cargo pants, and pulled out the small travel size bottle of lube. His pants were quickly lost, followed by his underwear, and I watched him pour some of the lubricant onto his blood-covered fingers.

A groan escaped my lips. I hadn't felt his touch in such a long time. My body relaxed under it, letting more blood flow into my expanding veins. I wanted to close my eyes to maximize the feeling, but I couldn't stop watching his talented fingers rub the lube, and the now re-liquefying blood, into my swollen crown. There was intense pressure in my cock, to the point of being uncomfortably enlarged, but that told me at least that I wouldn't go soft like the previous times. I might just be able to finally fuck him, it might not be making love, but this wasn't the time nor the situation for it.

Killian straddled me and drew my chin up so our lips met. When we broke apart, he leaned down so his face was by my ear. "Do you really want to see me fuck him?" His breath against my ear sent a shiver up my spine, and his words did too.

I went to grab my cock but Killian beat me to it. He took the hard and twitching rod and I felt his hole, burning hot, against the head. I didn't answer him in that moment. I had to focus on what was happening or I was afraid my mind would escape me and the flashbacks would return.

My hips thrusted up. I looked past his spread apart legs, past his blood-streaked dick with the foreskin gathered up behind his crown, and watched my cock disappear between his cheeks. I felt a puff of air from Killian exhaling, and as he sucked in a long breath, I grabbed his thigh and pushed myself up. With a satisfied cry from him and a grunt from me, I broke into him.

I froze and stared forward, my heart racing from the anticipation of my mind breaking like it had done after I'd killed that slave. But there was nothing rushing through my brain but the fantasy of having Nero and Kiki under my control.

I think I was okay. I began to relax my body and Killian felt it. The boy let out a moan and started to ride me.

The pleasure was overwhelmingly good, but I wasn't going to cum within five pushes like I'd feared. My restraint I'd had to learn from our previous healthy sex life was still there; so I further relaxed myself, and almost like picking up a bicycle after a year of not riding it, I settled into my role and started rhythmically fucking him.

Not making love, fucking him. This wasn't the time or the place. And to let him know this, I engaged his previous question.

"Do you want to fuck him?" I whispered back.

Killian let out a long moan and started jerking his hips up. I put a hand on his hip and enjoyed the visual of my cock gliding in and out of him; his own stiff dick bouncing up and down until I grabbed it and started rubbing the slit. I wanted my eyes open, just to keep my consciousness in this reality, but it felt too good and the satiation of my sex-deprived body was making my eyes close in ecstasy.

So, only half-realizing I was doing it, I closed my eyes. I felt like all of the tension I had been feeling for the past several months was slowly getting pushed out of my body; with every slam of Killian's frame, and every penetration my cock made into his tight ass, more stress left me. It was a powerful feeling. I'd forgotten just how much I needed sex with Killian to center me, to relax me. I'd never been a sexual person before him, but I still jerked off to release myself; this had been the longest stretch of not being able to cum I'd ever experienced in my adult life.

I realized I was moaning in tandem with him. I could feel his hot breath against my neck and his own groans and heavy breathing in my ear. What a beautiful thing to hear, and it made me want to hear him cum. I knew he'd be driven wild hearing me cum inside of him.

My hips started to jolt up and down faster. Killian rested his hands on my shoulders and used them as leverage to pick up his own speed. I put my hand on his cock again and started to jerk him off, my eyes still closed and my mind wandering around my thoughts like I was walking through a museum.

"I didn't think I did..." Killian suddenly gasped. "I can't believe I'm saying this but–" I felt his lips and my mouth opened, our tongues met briefly before he nipped my chin. "–I want to see you fuck Nero. I want to do it at the same time. I'll kill him as you cum."

"Slit his throat," I groaned. I took his bottom lip into my mouth and bit down on the soft flesh.

My memories took me to when I'd held down that legionary for Reno, how I cut his throat and let the blood spray on me as Reno came. "His body... it'll spasm when he dies, tense up and contract. Think of how it'll feel–" I let out a hard breath and picked up my speed. "–on your cock."

"Fuck," Killian said, and he stopped talking. My mind didn't halt my fantasy, however; even though Killian had gone quiet, my imagination was still alive.

And then my mind betrayed me.

I should've known.

I opened my eyes and saw Kiki on my cock. He was crying, and the black eyeliner he had worn a few times in the bedroom was streaked down his face. He was shuddering and gasping, with Killian behind him holding a knife; he was jabbing the kid in the ass every time he slowed down. Blood was pouring down the little nicks in his backside, I could smell it. I'd lick it off of that smooth white ass and force Nero to eat my cum out of it.

Then, suddenly, my lust-filled fantasy got ripped out of my mind like something had literally grabbed it and yanked it away. And in quick succession, a new one replaced it. The switch came so rapidly, and with such a physical force, I felt like I was being slapped.

All of a sudden anxiety replaced the lust, and it swarmed in my stomach like I'd swallowed wasps.

"Go on… get on top of him."

No, no. Fuck. I was doing good. I was fucking doing good!

I jolted and took in a shuddering gasp.

Then I realized everything had been a dream. I'd never escaped Nero's room in Cardinalhall. All of this had been a delusion, a fantasy that I had conjured up out of pure desperation. If I opened my eyes Nero would be beside me, naked and pleasuring himself to Kiki riding me. He'd have a cigar in his mouth which he'd extinguish on my balls, or the head of my cock so Kiki could lick the ash from the blistering wound.

Killian being immortal, us being assumed dead and burning, it had all been a manifestation of my deepest desires. Killian was gone. I was never going to get him back. Killian was gone.

I heard a high octave moan, and felt the pleasure multiplying in my groin. An intense hatred planted its flag inside of me and claimed my body as its own; and, unable to resist its hold on me, I let it fester for this ditzy little cicaro riding my cock.

"Ever have another ass squeeze your cock, Reaver? Or just your little Killi?" I heard Nero ask beside me. I felt his minty breath on my cheek and he kissed me, but when he tried to kiss my lips I pulled away, a hiss escaping from between my teeth. "When I get a hold of that little twink,

I'll fuck him until he shudders and dies."

He's already dead. Killian's already gone.

Nero tried to kiss me again but I once again jerked my head away. I was about to push Kiki off of me but then I remembered what my plan was all along. The plan I had inside of my head to kill him.

And it wasn't going to be long until I implemented it; Kiki's moans were getting louder. My entire body was shaking from him bouncing up and down on my cock, and I could feel from his breathing that he was jerking himself off. Not only that, his hole was tightening, taking my cock in deeper and pulling it inside of him as if craving more.

Then, sensing I was close, he licked my neck before nipping it. His face was near mine.

His face was near – I let out a scream as the pleasure multiplied, a bellowed, angry cry – *his face was near mine. Get him, get him, punish him for making you fuck him. You're Killian's, your cock belongs to... to* –

My eyes snapped open as Kiki quickly got off of my cock; he must've read my mind and knew something was wrong. Quickly, before he could get away I lunged at him and we both tumbled to the floor. Kiki let out a scream and I saw his soft, porcelain neck shudder... right before I leaned down and savagely bit it.

I felt his windpipe crush underneath the power of my jaws, and heard shrill and desperate pleading; someone was shrieking my name over and over. I put all of my strength behind my bite, and when I felt warm blood from my teeth puncturing the satiny thin skin, I whipped my head to the side.

I swallowed the chunk of skin and sunk my teeth back into the gaping crimson hole in his throat. Then I started biting through it, searching with my teeth for the artery as my hand grabbed my cock and I furiously started stroking it.

Then I found the sweet spot. My tongue located the pulsing vein and immediately my teeth clipped it. A spray of blood shot onto my face and I eagerly wrapped my mouth around the flow. I ignored the boy's wheezing gasps, and his hand clawing my neck, and drank from the squirting fountain of blood.

I opened my eyes only once to see the blood gushing from his wound, pooling in the center to make it almost appear black, and running down a neck no longer alabaster white. I moaned from it, and just when I thought I couldn't feel any more pleasure, my breathing started to get short and my hand sped up its rhythm. I looked down at my cock, sprinkled with blood, then buried my face back into the pulsing wound.

Then the tension reached its critical point and overwhelmed me. I locked my lips around the gouge, now only able to breathe through my nose, and felt my entire body tense and tighten as the orgasm started.

I gasped and grunted from the pleasure, but as the toe-curling climax rolled through me I was confused as to why Nero wasn't beating on me. Why he hadn't taken Kiki and called for Sid. I had killed Kiki, but where was... where was...

As the orgasm subsided, this odd reality started to come to me, and I realized with confusion and dread that the puzzle pieces just didn't match up. Something was wrong, and now that I had cum and the madness was subsiding with it, I was coming to the realization that I'd just returned from a manic episode.

But... but what was reality and what wasn't?

I removed my mouth from the gaping wound, now only weakly pulsing blood. I looked down at the hole in the kid's neck, a lake of red like a cup of wine that had overflowed, and I waited for it to disappear. I waited for all of this to vanish into the delirium, and for me to wake up to wherever it was that I had been previous.

I glanced down and saw my soft cock, a thread of cum hanging off of it like a spider's string and a pool of liquidy clear and opaque semen on the bare leg of my victim. I reached down and touched the kid, and my heart jumped when I realized with a mind-freezing rush of dread... that he was real.

And then I recognized the leg.

With a coldness in my chest, I slowly looked up, and put a hand to my mouth when I saw Killian's half-open eyes staring off into nothing, blood covering his face and the two inches of blond hair he'd grown since it had been burned off.

I stared in horror, and a whimper fell unabashed from my lips as I touched his cheek. His cheek was still warm, but as I listened for his heartbeat I heard nothing. Flooded with shock, I rose to my feet and looked down at his naked body, absolutely coated in red like it had been falling from the sky like rain, the blood most concentrated on his throat, the one I had ripped out, and pooling underneath his head. He looked beautiful in a morbid way, where the blood didn't touch was the most flawless of skin, pure white like it had been painted by an angel.

I had tried… I had tried to fool myself into thinking I would be okay enough to have sex with him, but I was wrong – I wasn't okay. And if he was still mortal, this would've been the day that I killed him.

"Oh my god…"

I turned around and my eyes locked with Kiki's. The kid's expression was pure terror. He put both of his hands to his mouth and keeled over as if unable to handle this horrific scene.

And it was a horrific scene. I was standing naked over top of my dead boyfriend, blood around my mouth and dripping down my chin, to my neck and chest. All of this happening after he'd, most definitely, heard us have sex. What that kid was thinking in that moment was beyond me, but the shock on his face suggested he himself had walked into a nightmare.

Then, before I could tell him that Killian was immortal, the kid took a single step backwards, before the grisly scene in front of him proved too much to handle. Kiki fainted.

CHAPTER 19

Jade

"JADE?"

That voice – he was here? Had he broken through the thick yet transparent wall that was blocking me from reaching him? Was he so powerful that not even my own deteriorating mind could prevent him from saving me?

He must've done something because I could hear him... before I had been nothing but a wraith without a body, floating in something that had no colour, texture, or form. I could only call it limbo but if this was where one went when they died, it was proof that there was no afterlife, only a shapeless hell.

It had felt like I'd spent a lifetime in here, but in the same breath, time had no meaning. How could I know time enough to count it, when there was nothing around me to gauge its passage? Not even an inner monologue of my own thoughts to help remind me that I was still an organic, living, breathing being. There was nothing of that where I was, and as I held onto his voice I felt terror at the prospect of going back to that void of nonexistence.

But the feeling of terror was, in itself, a relief, because it meant I could feel emotions again.

I was no longer nothing, that voice which came to me in the forms of opal ribbons, came and gently wrapped themselves around me, and lifted me higher and higher until my body broke the surface and I took my first breath of air.

I felt contact on my chin. Awareness came to my eyes but I had no control over them. They rolled in their sockets and looked around the bright room, taking in shapes, sounds, and smells. The physical objects placed around me felt foreign, and inside of me they drew up alarm. I was no longer used to seeing this world that had been my world since before my birth. My life was that of a meaningless entity, floating in the plains of nihility, and it was there that I had forgotten where it was I had once belonged.

"Calm down. There is no need to be frantic, you're making yourself choke," he said. I could see him out of the corner of my eye, and because he had brought attention to it, I realized I was gasping for air. My brain was commanding me to breathe hard, like it was waiting for a hand to grab my foot to pull me back down into the darkness, so I had to fill my lungs with as much air as I could.

But his voice calmed those desperate impulses like a warm blanket wrapped around a cold and shivering body. It soothed me, and when I realized his hand was touching my bare chest, his cooled skin against my own, the tense strings that were wrapped so tightly around my body started to loosen.

Beside me, I heard him take in a sharp inhale. "Do you know who I am? Can you speak?" He said it as if it were a plea, a tone that was a stranger to both of us.

I filled and stretched out my sore lungs with one last deep breath, and my brain was satiated enough to allow my own breathing to normalize. However, it wasn't enough for my eyes to stay in one place. I kept looking from one object to the other, trying to figure out and recognize each one, but before my mind was able to register it and accept its existence in my new reality, I was already looking at the next thing. I knew he was talking to me and I wanted to look back, but my frantic cognizance was doing everything but, and my paralyzed body offered me no further help in letting him know I could hear him. He was like a voice on the wind, easily carried off and away from my consciousness, and there was nothing I could do about it. All of my thoughts were shattered into tiny pieces, and it was taking all of my strength to just breathe properly, and to not panic over the shock of being out of the terrifying limbo that had been my eternity.

A hand patted my cheek. Already I was feeling like I was going underwater again, but I tried, I tried to keep my head above the void. His touch was helping. I wish I could tell him that.

"Maritus?"

"M-maritus? Come on… say something to me. Jade? It's… Elish."

Elish… yes. I knew who he was, but I knew him as a feeling only. I knew him as a pillar of strength. I knew him as an embodiment of a love so strong it could extend through realms, through worlds. I knew him as… as my husband.

My husband.

In that moment I missed him so much my heart physically hurt, and when I heard the tightness in his voice, the tones of desperation, these emotions, ones that my cold-as-ice master never felt, never let himself feel, my soul broke. He had reached his hand through worlds and had taken me and brought me back to reality, where he was fated to spend eternity, and yet I wasn't strong enough to tell him how much I loved him. How much I missed him.

I drew up all of the strength I had in me, and pushed through the darkness that was continuously trying to drag me back down – and I managed to stop my eyes from jutting around. I then squinted them hard, and looked at him.

My husband.

He looked so different but I knew him; I felt his presence inside of my mind and outside of it. He had his hair cut shorter now, just several inches past his ears, but his bangs remained to fall over his eyes. He looked tired, but still a man that had refined dignity and grace to make it his own. Even sitting beside me in this room, he radiated elegance and tranquility. Had he been able to snatch me from this darkness because he was really a god?

I felt his hand slip into mine, a hand that was no longer soft but rough. I knew why. I knew it was because of where we'd been, but the colourless haze, it was creeping along the corners of my vision like a rising tide lapping against a jagged rock, slowly rising, consuming…

"If you recognize me… squeeze my hand."

I looked at him and inside I felt those purple eyes draw me to him like we were magnetized. We stared at each other and through the strength I found in his loving, yet worried gaze, I squeezed his hand.

"They collected some old boxes and built a fire in the floor and he found some tools and emptied out the cart and sat working on the wheel," he read to me, his voice soft; the electric fireplace was bathing him in an orange glow. This scene was familiar to me, but I had forgotten where I

had experienced it before. My mind told me in its weak voice that perhaps I was stuck in a loop, that my life would just replay scenes over again forever, and the only knowledge I'd have of this happening would be faint feelings of déjà vu. *"He pulled the bolt and bored out the collet with a hand drill and resleeved it with a section of pipe he'd cut to length with a hacksaw. Then he bolted it all back together and stood the cart upright and wheeled it around the floor. It ran fairly true. The boy sat watching everything."* The page turned, the book, dog-eared and worn from being read so many times, in his hand. He had read this book to me continuously each night, but he never finished it. He would get to the point where I'd see only several pages remaining and then he would stop.

This had happened again, just last night.

The little boy was with his sick papa.

"But who will find him if he's lost? Who will find the little boy?" he would read. *"Goodness will find the little boy. It always has. It will again."* Then the book would close, and his silver bookmark would slip between the pages. He would set the book down.

The next night…

"When he woke in the woods in the dark and the cold of the night he'd reach out to touch the child sleeping beside him…"

It was back to the beginning. I wanted to ask him why. I wanted to ask him how it ended and why he wouldn't finish those last pages, but the tendrils of the void had been gradually taking me and now it took all I could to even breathe, and to remember just where I was, who I was, and what was happening to me.

My entire world was his voice and his caring touch. I lived for him to be beside me, and when he was beside me, I lived. I breathed better, my thoughts were more focused, and sometimes, even if just briefly… I felt emotion again.

But it was brief.

The limbo that held no time, no sensations, the abyss that came from having no activity in my brain, was taking me, which is why when I did feel emotion, it was unrelenting horror and panic, an inhuman desperation to plead with Elish to not have it take me again. I was terrified of it, and it was because of that terror that I fought as hard as I could to stave off its inevitable claim on my brain.

If people knew how terrifying it was to be dead, to feel nothing, to see nothing, to be stuck inside of a vast place with no boundaries but yet you felt like the entire universe was closing in on you, pressing up against the last shreds of your consciousness… they'd stop at nothing to become immortal.

His voice glided along the words he read like an eagle soaring on thermal air, his tones varied just slightly to a softer side when he spoke for the boy, and harder, more confident when he spoke as the man. I soaked up the hour that he'd spend with me every evening reading that book, a brief respite from the battle I fought every day to stay alive.

Tonight I wasn't feeling well, so when he closed the book I stared at him, wishing he understood that I needed him to keep reading tonight. But my gaze never left him whenever he was in my vision. And if he didn't position me in the recliner towards the television, or if I was able to move my head to the side where he was on the couch, I'd have never stopped looking at his face.

I wanted to tell him… that I didn't think I'd be able to fight for much longer. That I needed him to help me because… because I was getting tired and each morning I woke up, it was proving to be more difficult to even remember who he was. My moments of lucidity were getting farther apart, but he didn't know this. All he knew was my gaze and that didn't falter, even though there were times when I was mentally alert.

Elish… I think I might die soon. Please, don't let me die. I'm afraid of death, it's where you can't find me.

He put a blanket over me and kissed my forehead, then the lights went out. The sparking synapses in my mind were functioning enough for me to feel emotion, and like most of them this one was not good. It was desperation, a sad plea that was so intense inside of me I felt like I would scream just out of sheer frustration. *Elish, Elish, I'm going to die. Help me, please.*

Sometime later, the lamp on the table between the recliner and the couch turned on. I saw Elish sitting up in bed, and on his face was an expression of sadness that tore my heart.

His eyes searched me, and I wondered if he would find what he was looking for. He must be looking for something because it was like he was taking in every detail of my face. Was he committing me to memory so he'd remember me when I died?

Then he rose, walked to me, and knelt down beside the recliner I slept on.

"I think… I will be speaking to Silas tomorrow," he said to me, his voice was as sad as his face, but I also heard another tone, it was defeat.

Yes. That is what I saw, not sadness… my master looked defeated.

Elish rested a hand on my forehead and brushed back my hair, and I saw him nod. "Whatever he requires, I will do it. I think it is time I pick my battles." He leaned in and I felt his lips press against my forehead. I couldn't move, or react, but his words were enough for me to mentally push away the abyss slowly taking me.

"If we're lucky he'll not delay. Maybe I will have you back in a matter of days. Then we can get to more important matters like picking up these shattered pieces. You're a nuisance, Cicaro, and I'm growing tired of being your sengil." He patted my cheek and gave me a smile, then he rose. I watched him turn off the light and I closed my eyes.

And I felt an emotion I never thought I would feel again.

Happiness.

Then everything inside of my brain went haywire.

There was nothing I remembered before, the first thing I became aware of was the feeling of my head being electrocuted, but at the same time, heated. It was like an uncomfortably thick blanket was being tightly wrapped around my brain, not my mind, but my physical organic brain. And when it was wound so tight I thought the pressure was going to make my head cave in on itself, a sudden and powerful surge of electricity shot into me and electrified every fibre of the blanket.

My body was frozen. I was unable to scream from the unbelievable pain, but inside my mind felt like it was being violently shaken; the electrical current rattling me and plunging what remained of my consciousness into a blinding light.

And that light was emanating from the coating on my brain, and the electricity, so vibrant and powerful I was sure it was alive, dove deep inside the grey matter, inside every wrinkled fold, and shot light where there had once been dark, and breathed life into what had once been beyond medicine. Like a billion switches were being turned on, one after the other with blinding speed, I felt my brain come back to life.

Then as quickly as it came… a hand seemed to reach out and stop the light. I took in a sharp breath and my body twitched and spasmed, the half-on switches, mixed in with the ones turned on and the others still dormant, absolutely scrambled me. I opened my eyes and saw darkness everywhere but I couldn't stop twitching. My body was off-kilter. I felt like a knot of frayed live wires, some tied to the wrong partner, others dangling and shooting off sparks. I felt almost worse than before because I now had the capacity to feel just how much I was damaged. I was a fly with only one wing torn off, buzzing in circles, and circles, unable to fly, unable to stay on the ground, just manically spinning, too damaged to do anything else.

My lips pursed and I closed my eyes, but then, realizing that I could now move my lips, I opened my mouth and whimpered out the one thing I'd been wanting to say for months. The name that I sometimes remembered, sometimes forgot, but always, always I knew his presence and his gentle touch.

"E-Elish?"

But there was nothing. He had left me, as if chasing the blinding hot light that had disappeared as quickly as it had come. His absence had been noticed, however; I could hear a low and long drawn-out beeping. It was an alarm, but an alarm for what?

Dizziness descended on me and nausea soon followed. I rested my head onto the recliner and whimpered. I closed my eyes as the unpleasant feelings rolled through me like they were making up for the time I had spent feeling nothing, and then, with a heave, I turned my head and threw up white liquid and bile.

The acidic bile burned my throat and made it raw. I wiped my mouth with a weak hand, but as quickly as I raised it, it flopped down onto the ground. I was too weak to lift it.

More haze claimed me and I started feeling even worse. I tucked myself up into the fetal position and groaned, the room spinning around me, tilting up and down and around and around, taking me on a ride I didn't want to go on. The alarm didn't help, my head pounded under its continuous beeping, each sound a hammer blow attempting to crack my skull in two.

I felt my hold on reality slip again, but not back into the void that had felt like death. It slipped into a muddled black fog, like the smoke left over from the white fire in my brain was collecting and choking up these senses I had only just now gotten back.

I wished there was light in this apartment. Why was everything so black? Usually a light was on, at least the electric fireplace or the light on the stove that was usually kept dimmed. There was nothing, and when I glanced around, vomit dripping down my mouth, I saw that the lights of his laptop, and the numbers that were supposed to be on the cable box... were off too.

The power went out. That was why the alarm was going off. But why? What was happening?

My mind was overloaded with questions but I had no answers; even if the answer was right in front of me there was too much distortion in my mind to see it. I found myself only able to stay as still as possible to attempt to keep myself from throwing up again.

Then a light stung my closed eyelids. I opened them and my heart thumped when I saw a shadow holding a flashlight. My first thought was that it was Elish but he'd have no reason to have flashlight with him. Could it be Luca?

The person with the light lowered it, and when I saw who it was I thought I was hallucinating. There was just no possible way he could be in front of me. He was the last person I'd ever expect to see here again.

"Jade?" My ex-boyfriend choked on my name. He ran and knelt down beside me. He placed a hand on my cheek and stroked it, tears running down his face. "Jade, baby?"

Kerres was breathing heavily and the light of the flashlight made the sweat on his forehead sparkle. He looked exhausted, and not just from what I guessed was him running up over twenty flights of stairs, but there was a weariness in him that had sunken his once handsome facial features, drawing out the lavender in his eyelids and highlighting his cheekbones to give him a gaunt, sick appearance. Kerres was tired, but he looked at me as if I had promised him a second life, a rebirth. There was so much love in his eyes, and relief – why did he look so relieved?

"I have to get you out of here," Kerres said. He rubbed my cheek and kissed my nose. I furrowed my brow at him and looked past him into the darkness, wondering when Elish was going to come to chase him away. He wasn't allowed here, and yet my mind cautioned me against dismissing him. However, my body felt so heavy, my tongue as well, I didn't know how much I would be able to say. I wasn't even a hundred percent convinced that this was real. Everything had this odd tilt to it; my world was a snow globe that had been picked up and shaken violently. The furnace that had seared my mind had done wonders but I had this sinking feeling that it had been interrupted. And now, like a laptop being unplugged during an update, I think my brain had been bricked.

Kerres looked behind his shoulder and back at me. "One of the chimeras... Jack. He says he's going to kill you. I turned off power to the skyscraper to trap him in the elevator, but we have to get out of here before he escapes." My eyes widened at this. Kerres grabbed my arm and started pulling me up off of the recliner. I let him, and decided to try and see if I could stand upright.

As soon as my bare feet hit the ground, they trembled and started bowing. Kerres put his arm around my back and steadied me.

"Elish?" I whimpered and looked around, then my legs gave out and I fell to my knees. The dizziness was overwhelming and I felt myself get drawn back into unconsciousness, but Kerres kept shaking me, kept pleading at me to get up.

I threw up, unaware of what was going on. My world was once again swirling around like I was on a spin cycle, and the events that kept transpiring even though my focus was frozen and my awareness reduced, was lost on me.

There was the sound of shuffling and scraping, and I heard the door open to the stairwell of the skyscraper. My awareness came back to me in weak waves, allowing me to register what was in the frame of my vision for only a fleeting moment before it was taken from me; time would then jump forward, and I'd find myself experiencing an entirely new set of sensations.

First I was walking down the stairs, Kerres's voice was encouraging in my ear but also tight with fear. He was telling me in a low tone when to step, the flashlight lighting up the set of stairs and casting long shadows of the railing onto the grey ceilings. It wasn't our only light anymore though, there were red lights now, emergency lights.

There was also angry screaming. No, anger wasn't the right word, it sounded downright hysterical and insane. The screaming was echoing as well, filling the stairwell with its disturbing sound. The man, he was yelling threats, vows and oaths that were sworn on immortal brothers and the dead world we all walked on.

I looked up at the red light above us and squinted my eyes, but even the act of glancing up threw off my equilibrium, I stumbled and started to fall backwards.

Kerres snatched me but his hands grabbing and pulling me ended up further jarring my balance. I let out a gasp as I was yanked forward, and I heard Kerres scream and jerk my arm back as I fell.

My feet left the ground and I was in the air. I saw Kerres's face and the expression of pure fear, his hand gripping my forearm. Everything was in slow motion but I was aware of the fact that he was getting further away from me, and that his fingernails, white from clenching my forearm, were leaving behind trails of pink with shreds of skin.

Kerres got smaller and smaller, and for just a fraction of a second I was confused as to why… then I felt a heavy impact; so hard it threw my mind from my body and paralyzed me from both the shock and the unbelievable amount of pain.

The pain gathered up inside of me, before it was distributed throughout my body. My back throbbed, my arm felt like the two bones in my forearm were being wrenched apart, and my head, my head… my head was being assaulted without mercy, hammered on and pummelled. The pain was too much; I tried to cry out but my lungs refused to allow the air to be used for anything else but attempting to keep me alive. So instead I gasped and heaved, trying to stop my rattled brain from failing me once again.

But it didn't work – I heard Kerres scream as I was thrown into a seizure.

Then I heard an explosion above us and the ground shake underneath my body. There was nothing after that, but the colourless void.

Kerres

A cry of desperation sounded from Kerres's lips as he threw himself over Jade's body. The world was ending around him, there was no other explanation for it. The entire skyscraper was shaking and his Geigerchip was vibrating with anger underneath his skin. He had been taught about the Fallocaust when he was in Edgeview Orphanage, and he knew this was what he was experiencing.

Then the rumbling stopped. Kerres looked around the red-bathed stairwell, shocked that he was still alive, and grabbed the flashlight that was lighting up the floor and the corner of the rubber-coated stair to his left. He gripped it hard, and shone it towards the metal door that led to the apartments on that floor.

He was on floor twelve. They had made it a good distance… he could make it, couldn't he?

Kerres let out another cry through teeth clenched with fear, and dropped the flashlight. Then he stood up and looked down at Jade.

He tried to push down the panic when he saw his boyfriend. Jade was twitching, his mouth open like a fish that had just been pulled out of the water and bludgeoned. There was blood inside of his mouth, coating his teeth and pooling in their crevices, and his chest kept heaving, kept jerking up like he was suffering aftershocks from the seizure. It was a terrifying thing for Kerres to see, but there was no time to comfort his boyfriend. Something had exploded above them and he had to get Jade out of here.

Kerres picked up Jade and held him in his arms. He started walking down the stairs, carefully but as quickly as he could. Jade was light but it was still difficult, and he found himself having to adjust him often. He tried to push through it, tried to bite through the exhaustion, but it was slow going down the seemingly endless flights of stairs illuminated by red. By the eighth floor he was panting and heaving, and had no choice but to put Jade down and take a break.

But as soon as he lay Jade down on the stairs, he felt a fresh wave of horror. He could smell something burning, the intense aroma of toxic chemicals that immediately made his head throb. He looked down at Jade and took his shirt off of his back, and gently tied it around Jade's mouth to filter out the noxious chemicals. Kerres then coughed into his hand, the powerful smell taking away his breath, and picked Jade back up.

Then he saw the smoke starting to creep down the stairs like a phantom slowly stalking its victim. It rolled down each step and coated it in a thick black cloak, a wall of charcoal black only several feet behind it.

Kerres saw it and his heart dropped. He turned and took a step towards the set of stairs of the eighth floor, and when his legs wobbled from fatigue, he let out a frustrated and desperate cry and fell to his knees. It took all he could to keep Jade from slipping out of his arms. He was so weak and exhausted; he could barely hold him, let alone walk eight more flights.

Kerres's mind raced but the panic that was ripping through him allowed him no other thoughts than doing whatever he could to get Jade and himself out of this burning skyscraper. There was only one thing he could think of doing, and though it filled his heart with agony he didn't have a choice.

Kerres clung onto Jade and held him, tears running down his face and snot, not just from his own agony but from the toxic black smoke that was now consuming him.

"Elish!" Kerres screamed. He closed his eyes tight and kissed Jade's forehead, he let out a mournful cry and started to slowly walk down the stairs, every step jarring the young man in his arms and threatening to drop him down the stairs. "ELISH! HELP!" he cried as loudly as he could. He knew what the consequences would be. He knew that Elish would, at the very least, take Jade from him and once again rip his boyfriend from his arms, but he couldn't have him die in this stairwell.

The black wall of smoke was all around him and it had now covered the red light that had been lighting his way. Kerres coughed and hacked, spit running down his mouth and his eyes stinging so badly he could barely see. The alarm was still beeping above him as well, and his Geigerchip was angrier than ever.

I'm not going to make it... Kerres thought to himself, even the voice inside of his head was desperate.

Then he heard panicked voices below him, but the sounds of them running down the stairs soon followed. Kerres called for them but there was nothing, whether they ignored his pleas or were too far down the stairwell to hear him, Kerres didn't know.

Finally he reached the seventh floor. Dizziness took him and Kerres stumbled forward; he crashed into the wall with Jade and dropped to his knees. He gasped and coughed, his head throbbing like it never had before, and looked around desperately for any other person evacuating, to help him.

But all of the voices he heard were below him. There was no one.

"Elish?" Kerres choked. "Help... him." He could see nothing in front of him but black, even Jade's half-covered face was almost entirely shrouded in black.

Kerres tried to get to his feet but collapsed. The realization hit him that this was where they were going to die. He had nothing left in him to make it down the last seven flights of stairs.

Kerres leaned down and buried his face into the crook of Jade's neck and inhaled a shuddering breath. "I'm sorry, J," he said weakly. "I tried." He kissed Jade's cheek, then slowly, knowing it would be the last time he did it, shifted his lips to Jade's and kissed them gently. The feeling of his boyfriend, no... his former boyfriend's lips on his drew out an agony inside of Kerres that overwhelmed him, and he gave out one last disheartened, mournful cry, one that rang out and echoed in the stairwell before it was also enveloped by the noxious smoke.

"H-hello?"

Kerres looked up and rubbed his stinging eyes. For a moment he was sure he'd imagined the voice but it was too close, too strong to be a hallucination.

"Help," Kerres choked. "Please help."

Kerres was astonished to see the smoke start to thin and then a figure take shape. A man filled that shape and stared at Kerres in bewilderment.

Behind him the smoke was thinner, and Kerres saw that he had his hand raised. The smoke seemed to be repelling from that hand like dish soap dropped into an oil slick, it seemed impossible but yet... but yet it was happening right in front of him. The man was able to clear the smoke away, and though it was still gathering behind him it was noticeably thinner.

"You have Jade?" the man said breathlessly and his face fell in relief. He picked up Jade and held the limp man in his arms. "Come, walk... you must walk. I have to get out of here before they find me. The doctor's... they're behind me, and others too. They know him; they can't see me."

Kerres's brain snapped back into action; the man who had seemed to have manifested just from Kerres's own desperate pleas breathing new life into him. He was still weak, his legs shaking and his headache practically blinding him; but he managed to walk behind the man, hearing indeed the sounds of doors opening above him and rapid voices.

And another odd thing... Kerres realized that his Geigerchip had stopped buzzing as loudly. It was as if this man was able to dissipate the radiation. He must be a chimera but Kerres had never seen him before.

Kerres struggled to keep up but he did, watching in fascination the black smoke repel from the man's body. None of the smoke touched him, but in the same vein, the radiation that had been making Kerres's Geigerchip hum seemed to be sucking into his body like he was a vacuum.

Finally they reached the emergency exit. Kerres stepped out into the fresh air and gasped. He leaned against the railing but the man who had Jade was pausing for nothing. He looked around with an expression of fear on his face, and ran down the steps.

"W-wait!" Kerres gasped. He ran after him and they crossed the grassy open area to a grove of trees. The man constantly watching where the front of the building was and Kerres saw why. He was able to witness the first fire truck pull up in front of Olympus, and could hear shouting and in the distance, sirens.

The man, with black and white hair now falling over his brow, pressed his back against the fence that surrounded all of Olympus. His eyes were wide and his chest heaving. He looked at Kerres and Kerres saw that his eyes were two different colours, one blue and one black.

"Do you have a place?" the man asked through his gasps. "I can't let them find me. Please, please take me some place safe."

Kerres wiped his mouth and nodded. He didn't know who this person was, but he had saved him and Jade. With what he could do with the smoke and radiation, he had to be a chimera, or a born immortal like Silas.

But that was irrelevant in that moment. Kerres turned and started walking along the fence, so close to it that his shoulder was rubbing against it, and brought the man to the hole that he had made over the last several months. It was originally made so he could be as close to Jade as he could, and with Silas ordering the thiens to look the other way with his loitering, he'd been able to spend many days and nights in these sparse trees of Olympus. Something that had given him comfort after he'd left the Crimstones.

Since killing Meirko, and leaving Reno and the cicaro Trig, he had wandered Skyfall seeking a purpose to his life, but in the end his feet always took him to Olympus where Jade was. Admittedly, he was happy when he'd seen Reno on the television with Garrett, and his heart had hurt when he'd learned from lurking in bars that Trig had died. The anger that had been so strong for the Dekker's, and especially Elish, had fizzled to intense sadness and depression. He no longer felt like he wanted to live, but until loneliness killed him he'd stay in front of Olympus and watch the top floor. Seeing glimpses of Jade gave him a brief moment of happiness, though when his shadow would disappear, or when he'd see the tall silhouette of Elish beside him, the depression came back worse than before and his own damaged brain would throw him into manic rages.

Kerres grabbed the wooden board that he knew was loose and pulled it up and to the right. He stepped through, and held a hand to the back of Jade's head to protect him from the boards as the man slipped through with him. A parking lot and a one-level building was in front of them, then an empty street and further on, more abandoned buildings that stretched out until you reached a small pocket of active area that surrounded Artemis and Apollo's shared skyscraper.

"It's five blocks up," Kerres said, but when he glanced down at Jade, another twinge of pain and sadness swept him. "I'll take him now... I have to get him to a hospital. He's... I can't keep him this time."

"This time?" the man asked curiously. He didn't let Kerres take Jade, he walked across the parking lot and glanced back only once. Kerres looked back too and was taken aback with what he saw.

The top of Olympus was on fire, flames shooting from the windows of one of the upper floors and sending the noxious, poisonous smoke up into the sky. The tall and looming building that had been an ominous shadow in his mind now looked like a lit flare, a glow of red and orange showing in the floors below the inferno, and quickly travelling up as well.

"He is..." Kerres paused to cough violently into his hand. "He's my boyfriend. I've known him since he was just a kid."

The man gave him a puzzled look, the same one that everyone did when Kerres said that, and he knew what was coming next so he shook his head. "Elish stole him from me. He... he abused him and tortured him. He brainwashed him until he forced Jade to fall in love with him."

Kerres saw the man's eyes widen. "Really?" He picked up his pace, and the two of them ran across the road. Kerres's lungs were screaming with pain and his brain felt like it was trying to push itself out of his skull, but he kept up his pace. "We – we have him now," the man said. "Elish won't get him back. I can fix him. I have... things I can do. I will help with the radiation you've absorbed too."

Kerres almost cried out with relief, but instead he used the man's reassurance to push himself to run faster.

There was silence between the two of them as they made their way to Kerres's small house. Every time Kerres looked behind him he felt a churn in his stomach at how quickly the fire was consuming the upper floors of Olympus. In this moment Elish was either dead, trying to escape, or on the ground looking at the same flames Kerres was.

Kerres felt a faint feeling of satisfaction at this. Elish Dekker was getting what he deserved, and he was also getting what he deserved: Jade back.

And then suddenly Kerres stopped, his mouth opened and his heart gave a hard thump against his sore rib cage.

Elish was going to think that Jade was dead.

Kerres looked ahead, the man still sprinting with Jade. His boyfriend was limp in his arms but his eyes were half-open and his chest still rising and falling. He was sick, but the man said he could make him better. Could it be true?

Could this be... my second chance?

The thought was like a lighthouse in the middle of a raging storm. Kerres ran to catch up with the man, and for the first time in years, his heart held a flicker of hope.

CHAPTER 20

Jade

THE INFERNO WAS BACK, AND BECAUSE THE GREY matter and the synapses in my brain had now been activated through the intense heat, I could now feel the pain and pressure from his touch.

I closed my eyes tight and bit down hard on the book that had been put in between my jaws and squeezed the hand that was holding mine. I tried not to scream but the pain was like a trash compactor squeezing both sides of my skull, pressing the bone into the soft sponge and constricting it so tight I was sure I could feel my own brain leaking out of my ears.

But in that pressurized oven I also continued to feel the light switches get turned on, and it was because of that intangible awareness, I held on and endured the pain. The pain might've been consuming and blinding, but through it I could feel my life rush back into me. Emotions I had forgotten, sensations, knowledge, and memories.

My memories.

Elish.

The hand in mine shook from how hard I was squeezing it, and I could feel my metal incisors bite through the hardcover book and touch the paper inside. And like his hand was a trigger, the pain and pressure suddenly multiplied to the point where a scream did finally break my lips.

But then I felt it dissipate, before it faded completely and left my closed eyes, not seeing white, but darkness.

Beautiful darkness the colour of black… I had missed you.

Yes. My thoughts were back. My thoughts were finally back, and when I dove deeper into those thoughts I found my memories. I found my past, I found my time in the greywastes, my adventures with Reaver, Killian, and Perish, and… and…

My master.

My heart pulled to him and filled with a profound love. The memories of what had happened after my brain had failed me were scrambled, wisps of recollections on a ribbon wrapping around me so quickly, I couldn't focus on one thought for long. But the feelings I drew from them were there, and those feelings held inside of them a love I hadn't thought I was capable of feeling. I had loved Elish for years now, but sometime in the last several months of him taking care of me that feeling had grown all the more vibrant and intense.

Then to my embarrassment, the emotions overwhelmed me. I opened my eyes, everything blurry in front of me and the room spinning, and I felt my face crumple and my heart give a painful surge. I wanted Elish. I needed Elish.

I started to whimper, and heard a familiar voice cry out and throw his arms around me. I was confused as to who it was, my mind was still reeling, still recovering from this onslaught, but everything was so overwhelming, I needed a hug. So I hugged the person back. I was desperately seeking comfort in this confusion I'd woken up to. It felt like a lifetime of memories, emotions, feelings, a lifetime of living, was getting poured into a single empty glass.

"His mind is overwhelming him. His brain… it was completely dead," I heard someone say. "It's a lot for him to take in right now, and it's all rushing back. Give him some time to get himself straight." This person was speaking aloud exactly what I was feeling. Who was he? How did he know what I was going through?

"But he's okay?"

My eyes opened wide and they started to focus. I pulled back from the person holding me and stared at him, not believing that he was right in front of me. How was that possible?

"Kerres?" my voice was hoarse and raspy. It felt like I had swallowed a hot iron bar, I could barely speak.

Kerres choked, tears running down his face. He looked awful, like he'd taken ill, and the relief mixed in with agony on his face didn't make him look any better. But he managed a nod and hugged me to him again.

"My J. I have you," Kerres's voice was just as scratchy as my own, but the intensity of his emotions made it several octaves higher than mine.

"I missed you. Fuck. I missed you."

I swallowed hard and felt a lump form and press against my Adam's apple. Kerres being here offered me none of the relief and joy that I could feel radiating off of him, it only drew up a feeling of queasiness. I had resolved my feelings for my boyfriend long ago, and I had continued to hope that he would as well. That fool's hope had been dashed many times, including just last year when he'd kidnapped Reno Nevada and some cicaros to try and get Elish and, in turn, me, but I had still hoped that… that he'd get over me.

Or at least that King Silas would grow tired of letting him live just to stick it to Elish… and he'd just one day disappear.

My eyes closed and I let out a long breath. At least it didn't seem like I was a prisoner, but how I was going to get back to Olympus without destroying Kerres's heart… I didn't know.

"Hey, K," I whispered to him. I pulled away from him a second time but he immediately framed my face. He stared at me, his chocolate brown eyes full of love, yet looking so weary and unhealthy. He hadn't been taking care of himself at all, he looked just awful.

Then Kerres smiled and rubbed my cheeks with his fingers, my stomach twisted at this, my body confirming what my mind already knew, that no lingering feelings for this man remained… and that my heart belonged to my master… my husband.

"I think he is back," Kerres said to the man kneeling beside me. I realized that I was in a bed, and the bed smelled heavily of Kerres; the unkempt room that surrounded me did as well. "He's finally… finally not brainwashed. You cured him, Gage. You brought me back my J." Kerres removed his hands from my face and hugged the man beside my bed.

But when I made eye contact with the man named Gage, I realized he wasn't a complete stranger. I had seen him before, but briefly. I remembered his odd-coloured eyes, and the tuft of white that erupted from his black hair like a glacier in the dead of night. He had loomed over my bedside before; I had completely forgotten.

The man put a hand over Kerres's back and patted it, and without breaking his gaze he said to Kerres. "Yes. He's back," he said slowly, and his lips pressed as if wanting to say more but knowing he shouldn't. "He's back, Kerres."

I was going to have to play this carefully. Kerres's brain had been altered and damaged and I knew he wouldn't be able to make rational or logical decisions. The Crimstones had done a number on him, and not just physically drilling into his brain like they had me, but also brainwashing him constantly to hate chimeras.

And I was a chimera, as much as Kerres didn't want to admit it to himself. He hadn't spent time with me in years; he didn't know just how much I had grown to love my family – and love my master.

"Jade, this is Gage," Kerres said when he pulled away from the man. "Olympus was on fire and one of the chimeras wanted to kill you. I overheard them and–" Kerres smiled. "I saved you." Then he put a hand on Gage's shoulder. "Gage healed you. He's special like King Silas, but more powerful than even he is."

One of my brothers wanted to kill me, which one? I filed that in my folder of questions for later, right now I wanted to know how this man named Gage had healed me. "What do you mean? I've never seen you before. Who are you?"

Gage dropped his gaze and shrugged one shoulder. I could already tell that he was shy and reserved just from his body language. "I had been locked away for quite a while. I was freed by one of the chimeras, a man named Sanguine." My eyebrows raised at this but I let him continue. "I hurt him, and I hurt the two men he was with. I hid inside of the skyscraper and was found by another man… Drake."

"Drake?" I repeated. "Really?"

Gage nodded. "I wanted to heal Sanguine, repent for the damage I've caused, but my description of him matched you, and Drake got confused… Drake helped me sneak into Olympus and I healed you, or tried, but the blond-haired man, Elish, he caught me. I found out you were not Sanguine but you were so ill… I don't like seeing people sick. I attempted again, but while I was healing you, the power shut off." Gage looked to Kerres who was gazing at me with eyes full of love and devotion. The gaze alone made me feel nervous. I felt like I was rock star and he was my biggest fan, only if I tried to leave he'd break my legs.

And I had a feeling that was what was going to happen when I left to be reunited with Elish.

"Elish was chasing me," Gage went on to explain. "And when he cornered me…" Gage ran a nervous hand over his hair, the white tuft getting slicked back before it bounced forward and fell over his odd-coloured eyes. "… you see I have this problem with sestic radiation."

"S-sestic radiation?" I said loudly. Gage slunk down at this and stared at his knees. I quickly got up but Kerres grabbed my arm, and the only reason why I didn't stumble forward and fall on my face from my buckling legs was because he had my arm. Kerres pulled me back and I fell back on the bed, now in the sitting position. "No, Kerres, I–" I was about to tell him I had to go back to Olympus, but I caught myself just in time and said instead: "I need to see what's going on."

"They've stopped the flames," Kerres said hastily, his grip not weakening on my arm. "They just did a few days ago. SNN says Silas drew in the radiation surrounding Olympus and with the help of the fire trucks the flames were extinguished. The twelfth floor and up is destroyed but it's out now."

The twelfth floor and up? My home was destroyed, the home I shared with my master, with Luca, and Biff. All of our things, all of my belongings…

I couldn't hold back the sadness overwhelming me. I put a hand over my mouth, knowing that if I spoke I wouldn't be able to keep the tears at bay. I had to get back to Elish. I had to let him know I was okay. Oh fuck. Oh fuck if ten floors were gone… did he think I was in there?

"It's okay, baby," Kerres choked. I felt him sit down beside me on the bed and pull me to his side.

And then he said what I had dreaded could be the truth.

"Silas announced your death on SNN during the meeting. You – baby, do you understand what this means? You're free," Kerres said through a tight and breaking voice. His head leaned against mine. "You're finally free of them."

The pain was overwhelming. Each word that fell from Kerres's mouth felt like its own thousand pound weight, and they were being stacked one on top of each other on my back, making me physically bow over. My entire world had been destroyed in the course of fifteen minutes and now I was standing amongst the ashes all alone, with only the ghost of my past beside me. In my mind I fell to my knees under the back-breaking emotions, and looked to the grey scorched sky for my opal ribbons and my crystal cold light; but there was no master to pick me up and help me stand, and the ghost was too weak, and I was too broken.

No… I wasn't broken anymore. I was fixed. I was repaired.

I stared at the stained light blue carpet and looked to Gage. The man with the two-toned hair and eyes was also downcast, and I took that opportunity to draw up his aura.

Unlike my experiences drawing up the aura of born immortals this one didn't make me recoil in fear, or charge at me like I had opened the door to where the murderer was hiding. But that being said, whereas the born immortal's auras held that black hole that consumed all light and colours and fed on them, this one's aura was faded and monotone, with a texture to it that reminded me of crumbling concrete, worn from wind and rain until it was rough underneath my touch. There were hints of colour in it, blue and green, but they were only faint memories. Like there was a film covering it.

Yes, there was something covering it... that was what was making it look so faded. I realized as I stared at this aura that there was something wrong with it...

Suddenly I touched upon something that made me jump, something I didn't understand. It was a corner of his subconscious that seemed teeming with life. It was like I had been walking through a monotone mansion and I'd just opened a sound proof door to a packed-full party. One with music blaring and dozens of people inside.

I recoiled away, confused.

What the hell was that? Maybe – maybe it was just his mental abilities making his aura that way? I'd never felt this from Silas but, then again, his had been a void, I wouldn't have been able to see anything.

"Why don't you get Jade some food?" Gage's voice brought me back to my reality. I squinted my eyes and rubbed them, still confused over what I had seen. "Do you have something liquidy for him?"

Kerres nodded and rubbed my back before getting up. "I have some ramen and vitamin supplements. Once you feel better, J, we can talk about our plans." He turned around, the lines on his grey face vivid in the indoor lighting. Never more did I see how tired he was, and never more did I feel such a sense of guilt. This would not end well for him, but what could I do? I had to get back to my master. If he had me, his home, and his sengil destroyed... I had no idea how he would be but I knew it wouldn't be good.

But how would Elish be? My chimera was a figure of frozen dignity, a flawless demigod that, on the outside, held no emotions but a practised art of cruelty and indifference. He was a statue carved from the ice flows of the Arctic and there he stood on a pedestal on high that he had earned.

At least that is who he was to everyone else... but me.

To me, he was my husband. To me, he was the man who I now

remember reading to me every night, who played Pokémon with the handheld game in front of me so I could watch; who bathed me, dressed me, and to my humiliation now, even cleaned me. Elish had stepped out of his position of my lord and master, and had become my caretaker – all because of his love for me.

The Elish outside of Olympus, the one that everyone else saw, may appear as fine, but the one I knew inside those closed doors… I couldn't imagine what he was going through.

Kerres was moving around in the kitchen, and I continued to sit on the bed with Gage in a chair beside me. The man with the frock of white hair that covered the front left-hand side of his face, stared at his shoes. New shoes designed for a chimera, they must be Drake's.

I looked to the kitchen and dropped my voice. "How was he?" I asked, my voice pleading. "How was Elish?"

To my surprise, when Gage raised his head to look at me, his expression was puzzled. He reached a hand to my head, and when I felt a burning heat from his fingers, I jerked it away.

"I… completely cured you," Gage said under his breath, his thick eyebrows drawing close together. "You still feel affection towards that blond man?"

I gave him my own puzzled look before the pieces started to click together. Gage had been with Kerres, and it was foolhardy to think that Kerres hadn't told him his belief that Elish had brainwashed me.

"Kerres is… he's really sick," I said to him. Even with his strange aura, there was something that pulled me towards trusting him. I didn't see him as having any allegiance to Kerres, it looked like he had just been in the right place at the right time. "He's my ex-boyfriend and he's… never gotten over me. Elish did, sort of, kidnap me but chimeras can take anyone they want as cicaros. We've been through a lot, but I love him and–" I looked down to show him my wedding ring, but my chest turned cold when I saw it was gone. "–and we're married. I'm not brainwashed; Kerres is the one who's sick, not me."

"He is sick and I cannot help him like I helped you…" Gage said gravely, and looked towards the kitchen. "He's weak too, but… they're saying they have use for him." The man looked back down to his sneakers. "They're telling me they have use for everyone I've come in contact with."

They're telling him? Did he have voices in his head? Or maybe his time in the concrete had made him develop split personalities like Sanguine. I didn't want to offend him, so I just took it as a unique way that he spoke.

"Were you… one of the concrete prisoners?" I asked. "Are you a chimera?"

"I don't know what I am," Gage replied simply. "I only remember wandering around the dead world until I saw Skyfall in the distance. I remember other things I wish not to share, but in the end I was put in concrete and it was there I stayed." Gage then touched the back of his neck. "Being in concrete did help us, however." Then his brow furrowed. "Our memories are still divided. I… we're not used to this. We're still getting used to this."

I stared at him. Yeah, maybe the weird corner in Gage's mind, where I saw all that activity… maybe he had split his personalities. Poor fucking guy.

Our attention was diverted when we heard the tinkling of silverware, Kerres would be returning soon. "I need to talk to you in private, without Kerres," I said to him quickly. "I… I can't stay here with him. I need to go back to my master. He'll help you too, I promise; he'll do anything you want for healing me." Then Kerres appeared, and the conversation was forced to be dropped.

After I had eaten the chicken-flavoured ramen, and had swallowed down more than my share of vitamin supplements, I sat on the couch so I could try and watch SNN, the Skyfall News Network. I was desperate for information about the fire in Olympus, and even more desperate to see Elish. I kept telling myself I would see him soon; I just had to wait for Kerres to fall asleep and I would be out of this house and running to his arms.

"Why don't we watch some *Friends*? Just like we used to," Kerres said when I turned on the television. He took the remote out of my hand before I could even get the second number pressed, and turned it to TTG *The Teaguae Channel* where *Friends* was on often, almost every chimera had their own custom channel. I did too now. "It's eight and there are always ones on in the evening."

"Ker…" I said, and shot a glance to Gage. Gage was sitting right beside me. I would've thought that since he didn't know me he'd sit on the easy chair beside the couch, but he was kind of like a love-starved dog in that sense.

Gage offered me no help, he just looked at the coffee table and remained silent. I sighed and tried to take the remote. "K, I want to see what's going on on the outside. I want to see what happened to my home... to..."

"... Elish?" Kerres whispered. And like Elish's name was just as cold as the man himself, the temperature in the room seemed to drop. "... why? Why would you ever want to see him?"

This was one of those times where it would be best that I lied, but I wanted to take him by his collar and shake him, shake him and scream in his face that I loved Elish. That Elish was my world and that Kerres should appreciate that I was waiting until he fell asleep to run to him.

"I want to see if Luca survived," I said. My words held a shred of honestly, because I was worried about him. He wasn't just our sengil – Luca was my friend.

"Silas didn't mention that he died," Kerres replied simply, but in his tone I could see the spines start to slowly come out. "Olympus is burned to the twelfth floor and I haven't seen Elish. That's all you need to know."

"Kerres... I just want to–"

"There isn't a need to!" Kerres suddenly cried. He gripped the remote and I saw his knuckles turn white from the strength of it. "You're free. Look." He got up and walked to the other side of the living room, where I saw dust-covered knapsacks and duffle bags. There were a lot of them, but everywhere inside of this house were bags and boxes of things, so they hadn't stood out.

Kerres grabbed a map, but my eyes weren't on him, in that knapsack I saw the butt of what I knew was an assault rifle, and boxes of ammunition. I had a feeling that stash was Crimstone weaponry.

This gave me apprehension, and I was starting to become aware that perhaps I was in more danger than I previously thought. If Gage couldn't help Kerres it meant my ex-boyfriend was still suffering from mental issues stemming from his time with the Crimstones. They had done surgery on him, I remember seeing the scar on the back of his head. I wasn't dealing with normal Kerres, this was insane Kerres.

Kerres sat down beside me and unrolled what I realized was a map. "We're going to be moving here as soon as you can make the journey," he said, his voice quick like he was already running there in his mind. "This is–"

I recognized it, and the apprehension grew. "Irontowers."

Kerres nodded. "Almost all of the Crimstones are dead. Silas apprehended and executed almost everyone after Reno and the others, it's just me. There is a base there and in that base is enough weapons and ammo to destroy Skyfall, and supplies that will last us years. We even have the Falconer that we used when we saved you."

Saved me...? They'd kidnapped me and I'd almost died thanks to Milos, the former leader of the Crimstones. I tore Kerres's ear off; Milos had pulled out my teeth. They'd all beaten on me... Milos had tried to kill all of us in the end by being a suicide bomber.

"We can stay there and if they find out you're alive... we can bring them down. Isn't it perfect?" Kerres's eyes started to well. "It's going to be just like before. Just like before Elish kidnapped you." He sniffed and put an arm around my waist to draw me to him, but all I could do was stare at that map. "Just think of what we can do to get your revenge on Elish. Olympus burning will be nothing compared to what we'll do to him, and the rest of that abomination of a family."

"I'm a part of that family, Kerres," I said before I could stop myself.

Kerres gave me a sharp look. "No, you're not," he said back. He shook his head rapidly back and forth. He... he reminded me of my mom in that moment, or the woman who had raised me in Moros. "Jade. That's just residue from your time with them. You're different than them. Look." He pointed to the map, a drawn map but it was impressively detailed. Kerres was pointing to a building that was labelled as being an old bank.

"We have our ammo and weapons in there, and the Falconer is here." He pointed to a mechanic's shop. "We don't need to attack right away. We're too weak just the three of us." Three? I heard Gage's heartbeat pick up, and I knew he was just as in on this as I was. "But Moros will join us. I know they will. And there are settlements not too far from the factory towns with greywasters and refugees that Silas had denied entry to Skyfall. Starving people, bitter people, we can resurrect the Crimstones, J. And we can wipe out the chimeras once and for all." He smiled again, and I saw hope in his eyes... crazed hope. "We're the leaders of an organization that's almost a hundred years old. With your abilities, and my knowledge of weapons and the inner workings of the Crimstones... we can do what Milos and Meirko died trying to do... we can put a human back in power and... we can save our race."

"Kerres..." I said. I put my hand on his and slowly took the map away from him. "We're not going to do that, baby. I've fought enough battles."

Reaver and Killian's faces appeared in my mind, and more questions followed their images. I had to get home. I had to know what had happened while I was gone. Was Big Shot still alive? Deekoi? Did Elish find out how to kill Silas? My life wasn't here with Kerres, and I felt like I was wasting precious time. I couldn't stay here idle when the world had gone on without me. I'd left this planet for the plains of nothingness at the wrong time. "I just want peace now."

"We can until you're strong enough," Kerres said, and he took the map back from me. He got up and put it back into the duffle bag. "Once you've had time to get your head back."

I took the remote and turned it to the Skyfall News Network. I ignored Kerres, even though I had seen him pause while he was putting the map away. I didn't want to hear his shit, and I wasn't interested in it. As much of an asshole as it made me seem... I didn't love him enough to humour his delusions. I had to get back to Elish and find out what was going on and how my friends and family were. I couldn't let Elish continue to think I was dead, and every second I was here was a second that I was without him.

I appreciated Kerres saving me, and if he'd asked for anything as thanks I would've made Elish give it to him, but I didn't owe him my life for what he'd done. I'm sure it makes me into a bad person, but it was what it was.

Kerres's hand reached towards me to grab the remote but I pulled it away. "I'm watching SNN," I said with an edge to my voice. Then my attention turned when the SNN chime sounded and the digital logo flashed around the screen.

Kerres froze, but whatever expression was on his face I didn't see or care to see. I watched the television intently, and when I saw the remains of Olympus I couldn't hold back the gasp.

My home... my home was... it was just incinerated. Olympus was half the height it used to be, and the new top floor was nothing but the compacted remains of the apartments that used to sit above it, with smoke that stained what was below like black paint dripping down the handle of a paintbrush. The new top floor wasn't burned, but it would never be habitable again, there were layers and layers of black and grey, with pieces of framing twisting out at all angles like the legs of a squashed insect.

And the floors below had in no way been saved from the fire. Almost all of the windows had been blown out, and what ones that had been spared were forever blinded by the black smoke that stained everything. The remaining floors now stood in complete darkness, their empty frames staring out into the rest of Skyland. They had no faces but to me they looked empty and sad, for they were now doomed to gaze upon the repaired structures around them. Whereas in the greywastes everything was dead, Olympus, once the second most impressive skyscraper in the world, now had to stand amongst the living. This was my home and yet it was like I was staring at the skyscrapers of the greywastes. I couldn't help in that moment but think that we had brought the greywastes home with us, in more ways than Elish and I could've ever imagined.

I sniffed and shook my head as the camera zoomed out. I witnessed a piece of concrete fall from the top floor and land onto the ground below. I was dismayed to see that around the remains of Olympus were heaping piles of melted debris, blackened glass and concrete, the grass that had been so lush and green now destroyed from not only the falling material, but the tire tracks of what I had guessed were the fire trucks. Even the stairs had a huge gouge taken out of them, with the culprit, a slab of concrete with the siding still attached, laying several feet away; the dust of the steps it had destroyed still showing on its surface.

"Recovery operations resumed today, the upper floors now finally accessible to rescue crews," the voice over said. "Ten bodies have been recovered but, as King Silas has confirmed, the remains of anyone in the upper floors would have been incinerated in the heat, including that of Prince Jade Shadow Dekker, husband to Prince Elish Dekker." I glanced as white text appeared on screen. *Chimera Jade Dekker Dead at 18.*

And the next text to appear after made my heart plummet. *King Silas Announces Elish Taking Extended Leave of Absence.*

Then Olympus disappeared and I saw Garrett on screen with Reno beside him. Both of them were dressed in suits and fully done-up to look as official and in control as they could. I could see past the suit and tie and the good hair though, I saw the sadness in their eyes, especially in Garrett's. He was doing his best to hide his emotions but I knew him.

Then the remote got snatched out of my hand, just as Garrett opened his mouth to speak and Kerres pointed it at the TV and shut it off.

And I lost it.

"Turn it the fuck back on!" I suddenly yelled. And as Kerres looked at me stunned, I took the remote back and gave him a hard push. "You're not my master, and you don't fucking tell me what I can and can't watch. That's my fucking family!" I turned the TV back on, my entire body trembling with rage. The emotions were rushing through me, and I felt myself unable to control it. I had to get to him and get to Elish. If I had to kill Kerres, fuck, fuck I swear I would. I just had to get to my master, I couldn't let him go through this.

I started walking towards the door, when a voice made me stop in my tracks.

"Yes. I'm afraid Elish is no longer in Skyfall," I heard Garrett say.

I turned back to the TV, my mouth open and a cry forming in my throat.

"We are unsure when he will return, but Skyfall will run as normal until that time. King Silas will be ruling Skyfall behind the scenes, and until further notice, it will be me and my fiancé doing all public appearances and running the council," Garrett continued, and I saw Reno nod beside him. *"As I have previously stated, it was an accidental release of sestic radiation by King Silas after he fell into illness and he has since recovered. No other comments on the incident will be made."*

Elish... he wasn't in Skyfall anymore?

"Jade's funeral will be held tomorrow as Apollo stated. Is Elish expected to attend?" a woman's voice asked.

I saw a pull on Garrett's lip, and, ignoring Kerres's whimpering tears, I leaned towards the television, hoping beyond hope he would say he was.

"No. Elish left immediately after the incident with Olympus, and he is not expected to return for some time. Even for Jade's funeral, I'm afraid."

Oh, Elish...

I did everything I could to fight back the tears, but they were spilling from my eyes and running down my face. My heart had never hurt this bad before, there had never been so much despair inside of me, and empathy for my master. Knowing that he left Skyfall the night of the accident shone a heartwrenching window into his mental state.

Then a flare of anger took me unexpectedly, and I shot an accusatory look towards Gage. "Why couldn't you control it?" I found myself yelling. Gage winced like I had just struck him, and shrunk down. "Why did you let that happen?" I inhaled sharply as my sobs took away my breath, and started crying into my hands. "You took everything from us. How could you?"

Gage stared at me but his gaze deflected. "I'm sorry... I've... I've been having trouble regulating my emotions. I can't… we couldn't, we couldn't stop it."

"Then that's why fucking Silas locked you up!" I screamed before doubling over in hysterical sobs. I put my hands over my head and let out a mournful cry. My world was crumbling all around me, and I couldn't hold back the devastation I was feeling. It was consuming me and eating me alive. I felt frantic and desperate, and my breathing was coming in short and rapid puffs. I couldn't be here. I had to find him; I had to find my master. Our life was in ruins but we still had each other, and I knew we could get through anything together.

I got up. "I need to go," I said, my chest shaking from my grief. I felt like a battering ram was hammering against my rib cage, and with every hit it was knocking my breath out of my lungs. "I have to–"

Suddenly I heard a loud bang, like someone had lit a firework and thrown it into the living room. I jumped up into the air and turned around quickly; my eyes wide and my already taxed heart in the process of being destroyed from anxiety.

And it was only going to get worse. Because in the corner, by the packs and the duffle bag, was Kerres… and he was holding the assault rifle I'd just seen, in his hands.

"He's not cured!" Kerres suddenly shrieked. His face contorted right in front of me to that of a monster maddened with rage. His brown eyes were wide and boiling in their sockets and his entire body was trembling with instability.

His burning eyes shot to Gage who was shrunken in on himself. "You told me he was fucking cured! HE STILL LOVES HIM!"

"I'M NOT BRAINWASHED!" I screamed at Kerres. I saw a flash out of the corner of my eye and saw Gage run to the door to outside.

Without a glance back, he then opened it and disappeared.

I was too angry to chase after him, instead I walked up to Kerres but as I did he kept taking steps back, the assault rifle raised and pointing right at me. "I love him! Don't you understand?" I said as loudly and as clearly as I could. "I love him!"

I pushed Kerres into the kitchen table and slammed my fist down on it. "I am in love with him and I have been for years. I'm not brainwashed, Kerres!" I slammed my fist down again, with so much force this time a stack of boxes fell to the floor and spilled their contents onto the ground.

"I'm sorry, okay? I'm sorry but you need to get over me. You need to move on, Ker." I held up my hands and clenched them, pleading with him. "It's been over three years now. You need to find someone else and stop this. I'm a Dekker now; I'm Elish's husband, and if you saw how well he treats me, you'd understand. He doesn't hurt me anymore. He loves–"

I ducked as Kerres raised the assault rifle and tried to move out of his way, but I was still too weak from my recovery, and still too slow. Kerres struck me on the head with the butt of the gun and I spilled onto the ground.

"If I have to brainwash you into loving me... I will," Kerres's broken voice said, a weak whimper but one of crazed determination. "If I have to do what Elish did to make you love me. I will. You're mine, J – and no one else's."

And as the world spun around me, and red dripped down my vision, pooling underneath my eyes. I heard the rattling of chains, and saw my ex-boyfriend with the thick chain of a dog's leash in his hands.

CHAPTER 21

Elish

ELISH SLOWLY WOKE UP TO THE SOUND OF A FLY buzzing around him. It was faint at first but it became louder as he faded in and out of consciousness, and soon it was flying in circles around his body.

Then the buzzing stopped. Elish opened his eyes and saw the botfly on his folded up jacket, cleaning its wings and its antenna and skittering around the grey overcoat Elish had been using as a pillow. It flew back up into the air when Elish moved, and once again, the buzzing continued, sounding like a little race car driving in circles.

Elish squinted and sat up. He looked around the covered wagon he had fallen asleep in, until he spotted his bottle of wine, half-empty, but the rattling to his left reassured him that he had another crate waiting for him. Not only that, beside it was a smaller wooden crate with bottles of rum, painted black to conceal its contents from any curious greywaster.

Elish reached past it to the crate and grabbed a fresh bottle of vodka, then got up and jumped off of the cart.

"Good lord, James, vodka isn't breakfast," Robyn said, sounding exasperated. "Are you serious?"

Elish unscrewed the cap and brought the bottle to his lips, and at this, the leader of Broken Road Caravans chuckled. She reached a hand out as Elish swallowed down the burning liquid, and when he was finished, he handed the bottle to her.

Elish looked out at the road in front of him. He could see two mercenaries taking the lead, all of them with automatic rifles on their backs, ammo belts across their chests, and weapons tucked into holders on their waists. Behind them would be two more mercenaries, and Robyn's son who hung around anyone who would tolerate his presence.

Elish retrieved his vodka and took another drink, before lightly tossing the bottle back into the bosen-pulled cart. He then grabbed himself a bottle of wine, tucked it underneath one arm, then lit himself a cigarette.

Ignoring Robyn shaking her head at him, he walked to the front of the caravan to see what lay ahead.

Though he wasn't expecting to see anything new. The greywastes rarely changed, and the only thing interesting that broke up the many different shades of grey were the occasional crucified corpse, green and bloated, or spray-painted buildings which would mean a hard turn in the opposite direction to sneak past the cluster of ravers living inside.

Sometimes he hoped for the ravers to find them, just so he could see if any of them were Jade's, but he didn't wish for the caravan to be overrun and destroyed. Travelling with the caravan meant he could get drunk and high and still make good time. If he was travelling alone, by three o'clock he would be stumbling around, and after that he'd be lucky to make two miles before he passed out on the side of the road.

He was in the North now, taking the same road that he and Reaver had taken on their way to Mantis.

How he'd gotten this far north was not something he was proud of. He had wanted to get as far away from Skyfall as he possibly could without anyone knowing where he was. He was left with the puzzle of how he was supposed to achieve that without stealing a Falconer which he didn't want to do. So he ended up enlisting a thien that Caligula had previously complained about giving him trouble, then offered him a silver flask of vodka as a thanks with instruction to go back to Cardinalhall. The flask of vodka was poisoned and within ten hours the thien would be dead.

So no one knew that Elish was in the North, which was exactly what he wanted. No one here knew he was a chimera and no one would know. He was James the greywaster, however with how he was acting he was more like James the drunk. At least this drunk had a lot of money at his disposal, carried with him in a locked metal box he kept inside of his backpack. He had already cautioned everyone around him that if they dared touch his things that they would not live to see the sunrise, and so far that threat had been respected.

Everything he owned now was in that backpack: several pairs of boxer briefs he stole from Kessler's room in Cardinalhall, along with wool socks, a blue button-down, several books he'd also stolen from Cardinalhall, a toothbrush and toothpaste, a razor and a bar of soap, a drug stash Reaver would be proud of, and also… a Cilo guitar.

There was nothing else to his name, everything had been destroyed in the fire, and what things might've been saved in the lower levels were unimportant, just items in storage that held no personal value. All things that had meant something to Elish had been cremated.

Fire has always been my enemy, and now it has taken everything from me.

Everything.

Elish looked down at the bottle of wine and noticed his knuckles had paled from gripping the bottle so hard. He looked ahead at the grey landscape, scattered black trees with their long branches reaching out in all directions around him, and put his hand over his left upper arm. He felt Jade's collar, still securely wrapped around his arm, and felt a painful lump in his throat, one that spread to the back of his eyes and filled them with a stinging burn. Elish closed them tightly and raised his head to the grey sky, as if trying to enlist the help of gravity to contain them.

My husband burned alive, unable to move.

"E-Elish?" Jade's voice echoed inside of his head.

But conscious enough to call for me.

He called for me, and I left him.

My Jade…

Elish opened the bottle and took a long drink, then wiped his mouth before the pain inside of him made him take a second. He lowered the bottle and stared into the clear glass spout and let the alcohol do its work. As he walked he felt it warm his ears, and like a tide coming in to rocky shores, it gradually travelled down his neck, to his chest, and fully coated his body. He topped off the falsely soothing feeling with an opiate cigarette, and tried to ignore the additional sting when the blue ember flared up below his butane lighter.

"Share the wealth, James?" Robyn's son said behind him. There was scraping of boots on dirty pavement and a shadow to Elish's right. He handed the boy the wine bottle and continued to smoke the opiate cigarette.

The sound of lips breaking a seal were heard. Max was fifteen years old, but like most greywasters he looked older, nineteen or twenty. He was tall with respectable muscles and a short trimmed beard and a buzz cut. Fair on the eyes but the boy got bored easily, and when he was bored he pestered people. If Elish was half the man he used to be he would've got it across early that he was not one to be bothered, but unfortunately he had too many thoughts plaguing his mind to intimidate the boy.

"It looks like you found the perfect caravan to tag along on, huh?" Max said. And after taking another drink of Elish's wine, he handed the bottle back. "The one carrying all the liquor." He chuckled and squinted his eyes as he looked to the east. From where the sun was, it appeared to be late in the morning. Elish had never been a fan of sleep, but now it was all he did. "I'm hoping Vince snags us some meat tonight. It's summer, and a baby deer will be big enough to make a good meal."

Elish said nothing, he only exhaled the silver smoke from his lips, not bothering to take the cigarette from his mouth. Max continued to scan the east, already used to Elish's silence. "I was thinking of scouting in some of those buildings once we stop to rest the bosen. You want to join me? Change of scenery?"

Elish slowly sucked in another lungful of smoke. He looked at the highway in front of them. Before the Fallocaust the four-lane highway was separated with medians, and in this area those medians had stayed in place. They were placed one after the other in rows, previously put there to keep wandering traffic from going into the opposite lane. Now they did nothing but make it more difficult to lead the bosen if there was a large vehicle in their path, but since this road was well-travelled by merchants and caravans, every road block was accompanied by a way around, usually a median pulled out of place by a bosen so the carts could pass by safely.

Elish's mind was on this particular stretch of road because he remembered walking down it with Reaver. And he remembered what Reaver had said off-hand when they passed the very buildings Max was pointing to.

"They've already been scavenged many times over," Elish said, echoing Reaver's words. However Reaver had been complaining because he hadn't come across any good scavenging and he was seeing it as a personal failure. The boy had been sensitive to failure at that specific time. "There would be no use. It could be used as shelter for the night, but that's about it. You'll find nothing there."

Max made a disappointed noise and Elish looked to see him kick the ground with a sigh. "We don't usually go on this route," he said when he saw that Elish was watching him. "It's usually just going back and forth from the five brothers." The five brothers, large towns in the northwest with a dedicated trade route; one so popular the roads were monitored by the Legion to make sure they were safe. "This is supposed to be my adventure, man." He stuffed his hands into his pockets and let out a huff. "Mom won't even let me go hunting with Vince."

Elish tried to ignore the boy and took another drink of wine. He wouldn't admit it but he didn't want anything to do with fifteen-year-old boys. That was the age Jade had been when Elish had claimed him as his own. A boy as green as the emerald grass in Skyland, with an attitude that reflected his slumrat upbringing. He was a foul mouthed, hot-headed brat who was impulsive and over-emotional, and when Jade did find himself at his emotional peak, he'd go to any length, even if it meant hurting himself, to be heard.

Many times he injured himself to get Elish to listen to him, and in the beginning Elish only saw it as the boy being manipulative. But as he got to know Jade, and started to question his own dismissive nature of the boy… he had learned that that was Jade's last resort when he desperately needed Elish to take his emotions seriously.

I jerked a gun out of his hands milliseconds before it fired; it had been pointed at his head. I grabbed his arm and yanked him as he leapt off of my balcony. I even looked down at the greywastes in horror when he jumped from the Falconer after I told him I'd be leaving him in the greywastes with Reaver. How I hated in the beginning that that boy would go to such extremes for me to listen to him, until I realized it was me who needed to be taught different methods.

I had always prided myself in knowing my own mind inside and out. It was because of this knowledge that I was able to become the person I used to be. When I know what I react to, I can then proceed to cauterize and shut off those catalysts and steel myself to them. Over the years I took everything that had drawn out those negative or vulnerable feelings and I destroyed them. It was a golden age for me. Oh, was I ever at my prime.

Then Jade came and I hated him for how he made me feel. I hated him the moment he asked me to read to him aloud… because my heart, for a brief moment, softened at the request. I had found it endearing.

And I despised him for that, because I was Elish Dekker, I was a prince and he was nothing but a pile of dog shit deposited in my study. How could such a disgusting little flea make me feel endearment? And then worse... worse, the moment I smelled his blood my mind flared like I'd inhaled fireworks. All of a sudden I had to have his body, and though I had many fit and attractive chimera men, even ones his age, at my disposal, I felt myself lusting over this gangly, injured wretch. He had Ares and Siris's cum visibly dried down his inner thigh, and he was staring at me like I had just betrayed him in the most horrible of ways, but I fed on it, and with my own groin throbbing, I stripped him of his brash and snarling attitude and made him dissolve into my hands.

He collapsed into my arms, his body heaving and his hips thrusting as he climaxed. He moaned in my ear and it was tantalizing music. Then when I got home, I called Sanguine, and in his words, 'gave him the most roughest, wildest night he'd had in years'. I fucked him in the darkness and in my head I was fucking that hard-nosed brat.

I thought it would be over after that, but it wasn't.

I couldn't stop watching him. I enlisted Sanguine to gather all the information I could and I poured over it, and when I got that Mp3 player in his possession it became an unhealthy obsession.

And I hated him for making me feel this frenzied, just as much as I hated myself.

I was foolish and blind for not seeing he was a chimera, but it was what it was.

Elish lowered the bottle and tried to hide the despair on his face, the memories of Jade leaving another painful laceration on his heart. He wanted to stop himself from thinking of the boy, but yet he treasured every memory he had of him.

Perhaps it was he who was the masochist now.

"So do you?"

"Hm?"

Max snorted in amusement. "I thought you were off in lala land. You didn't hear a word I was saying."

"You obviously weren't saying anything important," Elish responded dryly, and at this, the amused snort from Max turned into a laugh. It was a common occurrence for people to mistake Elish's bluntness for sarcasm.

"I was asking if you wanted an energy bar. Try and soak up all that liquor you're having for breakfast, or lunch, I guess," Max said, and he offered him a Dek'ko Speedbar. Elish took it. He wasn't hungry, he no longer had an appetite, but he received it anyway and took a bite. It was apple and cinnamon... Elish washed it down with more wine.

That evening they made camp in what had once been a mechanic's shop. Elish sat away from the group with his own fire. There were two things that he had requested when he'd paid Robyn to take him to their destination. One: The amount he was paying would mean he was free to do whatever he wanted without anyone bothering him to contribute, even if it was nothing but sleeping and drinking. And two: No one would harass him into being social. So far it had worked out well, it was the evenings that seemed to be the hardest, even when he was drunk.

Elish watched the flames burn the boards they had stripped from a house nearby. A metal rack with a half-eaten deer steak was beside him, cut up to pieces for him to slowly pick at. He also had the Cilo guitar near, but he hadn't been playing anything on it.

But if there was one positive thing about alcohol, it was that it stripped one of their inhibitions, and that coupled with the fact that Elish no longer cared about anything, found him watching the flames, and debating drawing a mournful song out of what had been the guitar he had given Killian; found by Caligula and Nico a month before. Elish had told them about the resort town and the massacre he and Reaver had found. While out searching for Kessler they'd scavenged it, and had returned several items that had belonged to the two.

Caligula had handed it to him with his own look of sadness on his face. Sadness for a father who was still missing, and a second father who was driving himself into neurotic insanity with worry. Elish, of course, hadn't told Caligula that Reaver had taken Kessler's head with him.

If it wasn't for Kessler, Jade would've never suffered such mental damage from his empath abilities, and further physical damage from the bullet that scorched his skull. Elish hoped he was burning with Reaver. If he could be without that bull-headed man for twenty years he would be just fine with that. Caligula as well. He loved his father but there were no getting away from the benefits of his absence. Caligula was practically running the Legion with his boyfriend Nico.

"Where's Jade, Uncle?" Caligula had asked him, looking confused.

He knew Elish wouldn't go anywhere without Jade, not after his time being stranded in the greywastes.

"Jade's dead," Elish replied simply, his words dying before they even left his lips. He then walked past Caligula, Sid, and Theo who had come to the hangar to greet him, and went directly into Kessler's room to gather what he would need for his departure.

"Jade… died?" Caligula said behind him. He sounded shocked. "I'm… I'm sorry, Uncle Elish."

Not as sorry as I.

Elish's mind continued to swirl inside of his head, and his world did as well every time he broke his gaze from the flames. He had been drinking all day and all evening, and it was only nipping pieces of Intoxone that was keeping him from becoming a slobbering mess. The greywasters he was travelling with were in awe of how much he could drink and still remain standing, and how he never suffered from a hangover the next morning. Skytech was good for many things, and one of those things was inventing the cure for the hangover.

He heard footsteps behind him and ignored them; even when they came closer and the person they belonged to sat down beside him, he continued to stare at the flames with his bottle of wine in his hands.

"I gotta say… I've never seen someone as sad as you," a voice he recognized as Max said. He sounded tipsy but not drunk. "What's your story, man?"

Elish reached down and grabbed a piece of siding and laid it on top of the fire. "I paid your mother a lot of money to not have to answer such questions."

Max made an amused noise. "Yeah, I know." There was a sound of rustling and a paper bag full of assorted candies was put on his lap. "Something from our stash. I have a huge sweet tooth, and I always crave sugary stuff when I'm drinking too."

Elish looked down at the candies and shook his head, but found himself picking out a gummy green mint in the shape of a leaf and biting it in half.

"Yeah, those are my favourite too. Mint survives really good in the Fallocaust," Max said, further attempting to push conversation. "Mom says we'll be in Mariano by tomorrow early evening. Are you sticking with us all the way until Mantis?"

"I am," Elish responded and ate the last piece of candy.

"What's for you there?"

Elish was silent and Max's words faded into the darkness, but the night had its own noise: the snapping and crackling of the fire, the hoppers chirping in the yellow grass that surrounded them, and once his chimera hearing automatically tuned itself thanks to the quiet, he could hear Max's heartbeat as well. The strong heartbeat of a young man just entering adulthood, one that beat blood into muscles just twitching to show their strength, and a brain that seemed overly eager to make every mistake imaginable.

"More bad memories," Elish finally responded, his tone barely above a whisper. He took out another opiate cigarette and lit it with his lighter. Then, for reasons he didn't know, he offered one to the boy, and handed him the lighter as well.

"If you're running from something… why are you running back to the bad memories?" Max asked. Elish felt a twinge of surprise at his words; they were more sage-like than he would peg on a boy his age.

"Because right now memories are all I have," Elish found himself saying back. "The good and the bad. I find myself wanting to be in the places I last felt happy, and this is one of the only ones that were not incinerated." He took a long drag of his cigarette and heard a flick of the lighter, followed by a blue ember flaring like a one-eyed beast staring at him in the darkness.

After more silence, Elish took the cigarette out of his mouth and drank another mouthful of wine. He hadn't had any Intoxone since they had made camp, and the warmth that was making his head swim was lubricating his tongue. The only comfort he had was that at least these greywasters had no idea who he was. James the greywaster may have been Elish with a panama hat on for many years, but it looked like he was developing a personality outside of Elish's own.

Or who Elish had once been.

"You… you're wearing a wedding ring." Elish's jaw tightened as those words hit his ears. "Did you lose her… him?" A probing question that grazed on so many raw wounds if Elish was half the man he used to be he would've backhanded the idiot greywaster across the garage.

But tonight, he felt an odd need to speak of the boy. Jade had been a constant presence inside of his head and yet unknown to everyone around him. It felt like he'd only ever existed inside of Elish's own mind. It seemed a shame that the rest of the world didn't know just what a diamond he had uncovered. Every living person should be weeping for the loss of that boy; it was an injustice that they didn't know him, didn't miss him.

"Him," Elish responded. "His name was Jade. He died last week."

Max lowered his cigarette and Elish saw smoke blow out of his mouth. "Shit," Max mumbled. "I'm sorry."

"Me too," Elish said. "I'm sorry for a lot of things."

"Well... you should be careful with all the drinking you're doing," Max said. "My mom lost my dad when I was ten and she drank and almost died. You shouldn't die, cause..." Max let out a dry laugh. "I don't know you so I can't give you any reasons. You have cool eyes, so there's that."

"Yes. Wouldn't that just be the cruellest of jokes?" Elish murmured to himself and he took another drink. "I lose everything because I was so determined to kill a man who scorned me, and the story ends with me being the one to wish death." Elish ran a hand down his face and shook his head. "These memories I go over... things I thought I would be able to blame on others, my brothers, my master, my husband, or my dark assassin and his lover, even the scientist. I see that shining string attached to it, and when I follow the strand of silk... it leads me to my own spider web."

Elish inhaled from his cigarette and paused, before slowly blowing it out of his mouth. "Every seed I had planted in this garden, I connected them together through little silk threads of silver. I grew my seeds, my plans, some extending decades, and as they grew I connected each seed to strengthen my final product. I united Sanguine and Jack, and connected Jack to me to secure both of them. Then Nero and Ceph, Grant and Theo. And when I was able to, I wrapped my thread around seeds not even planted: I gave Lycos to Greyson to grow Reaver. An empty shell to Jeff and Kristin to grow his lover, and during all of this, I planted more seeds, wrapped around their shoots more strings, and I was the spider looming over them, content in my web, forever weaving and planting... weaving and planting." Elish looked down at the burning ember of his cigarette. "I looked down on my subjects and tended to them. I manipulated their growth and made sure they grew in the direction I wanted, with the strength I wanted... and I watched the green break the black soil and reach to the heavens... and I waited for my garden to bloom, so I could not only kill the other spider, but live my life in the paradise I constructed.

"Then... I met Jade." Elish closed his eyes, seeing the red of the fire through his eyelids. "And because I was in my web above them, they were able to witness me fall from grace, onto the ground below, and every time I tried to climb back to my web that boy called me to him and I could not help but walk into his cupped palm." Elish opened his eyes and the flames lit the violet rubies inside. "I stayed with him and tried to tend to both. I tried to be with him and continue to nurture a decades old hate, an obsession, and I tried until I unknowingly set my own garden on fire with him too broken to save himself. And now I am here, and in those ashes I have only a dead husband and a garden reduced to nothing but smoke and ash, and an infestation of new spiders, wanting what remains of my garden for themselves.

"And since I was the one pulling the silver strings... I was the one who built and grew this tinderbox in the first place... I only have myself to blame, just like the greywaster said. In the end, I am the architect of my own destruction, and all I have now... is a garden of spiders."

"Wow," Max said after there had been silence between the two of them. "I have no idea what you just said, but you should seriously write poetry, or a book, or something."

Elish stared into his bottle and took a drink. "I was never one to speak aloud my feelings, let alone put them on something tangible for people to read and judge me on."

Max shrugged and reached over to take a handful of candy. "I guess, but it helps to get it all out, doesn't it? I write songs but I can't play music; maybe on the road we can make music for my songs. That might be fun."

"I guarantee you that will never happen," Elish said coolly. "The guitar belonged to... a boy I once knew."

"Your husband?"

Elish shook his head. "No. He was someone I created for someone else. Both of them are dead now, also my fault."

Max whistled. "Sorry, man, but it really sounds like you fucked up."

Elish was quiet, but he took another drink. The world around him continued to get blurry with the more alcohol he consumed, but it helped with the boy's prying voice. He wondered to himself just why he hadn't told him to piss off yet, but at least it could be blamed on the alcohol.

"You shouldn't come out here to die though," Max continued. "And it looks like that's what you're trying to do. You know... it's really fucking dangerous here, up north. We're near the plaguelands, and not only that, the ravers are starting to learn guns after they got taught to put in Geigerchips. I'd like to meet the asshole who taught them that."

Elish didn't show it on his face, but inside he smiled just slightly.

"I couldn't die even if I wanted to, Max," Elish said, and he handed him another cigarette. "I'm the immortal prince of the dead world, who fled my home and my position of power to wander the greywastes in my own self-made misery."

Max laughed, and to Elish's distaste, the boy patted his knee in a friendly manner. "See. You need to write a book, or travel from town to town to tell stories. You're an interesting guy to listen to, James. I bet you have a lot of stories."

"You have no idea," Elish mumbled. Then he handed the candy back and took back his lighter. "I'm going to sleep now. Go bother someone else."

The next afternoon found Elish sitting in the bosen-pulled cart. It was a hot day outside, and a second thick canvas had been draped over the first one in an effort to provide some shade. It was sweltering however and Elish found himself sitting up against the back of the cart wearing nothing but a pair of airy cloth pants he'd bought off of Robyn's stock of clothing she was selling, and a pair of Adidas sandals. He'd even paid the woman a dollar to cut his hair even shorter than it had been previously, and with an electric razor she used on her son's hair she had been able to do just that. Elish's new haircut resembled Reaver's now which he was okay with. The back of it was cut short but he'd left his bangs long, long enough for him to tuck them behind his ears when they got annoying. His hair had never been this short, at least not since he was pulled from his steel mother.

He no longer recognized the ghost staring back at him when Robyn had given him a mirror to check out his haircut. He looked tired and defeated, his face holding many lines and his lids lavender like they'd been bruised. The only thing that was himself were his purple eyes, and the most he did for cleanliness now was brushing his teeth. Water was rare in the summer, and he had been too drunk and low to bathe when they did come across the occasional river.

Elish ran his hand over the back of his head; it was a weird feeling to have the air on his neck. If Jade saw him now his jaw would've hit the floor. Hell, if anyone saw him now their jaws would hit the floor.

Elish sighed and looked towards his bottle of vodka. He had taken some Intoxone an hour ago after he had started to lose his mobility, but after revealing too much to the greywaster boy the previous night he was feeling a new low. The boy had been by to visit him several times in the morning and afternoon, and now seemed to think they were friends. Elish wanted to be left alone and the boy's smiling face only made him feel worse. Even though he looked nothing like Jade, his face was round, his eyebrows ungroomed and thick, and his short hair showed off a lumpy skull, he was still a young man, and right now that was enough to make Elish fall deeper into the chasms of darkness.

So on this note, Elish did something he debated every morning but always ended up grabbing the liquor bottle instead. Since he had the haircut to go with it, he decided to channel more of the boy who was now burning for twenty years, and unlocked his metal box to reveal, not only bundles of one hundred dollar bills wrapped in blue elastics, but Ziploc bags bulging with drugs, and even syringes and heroin. The latter had surprised Elish, and on shifting feet Caligula had revealed Kessler's secret relapse on heroin after losing Timothy.

His life was already a mess, and the opiates had always taken the edge off of things. Elish crushed up some yellow Dilaudid pills with the help of the vodka bottle and the top of the metal box, and used a hundred dollar bill to inhale them. He then made himself comfortable, and hoped that they would, at least temporarily, take the edge off of what was now his life.

Right now I would be feeding Jade. Mixing up the powdered meal supplement with milk and putting it into a large plastic cylinder to be pushed directly into his stomach.

And if it was before I found out that King Silas was in Aras, we would be sitting down for lunch at the table. If he got to decide the food, which I let him if I was busy with work, he'd usually choose hamburgers and potato fries. If it was me, I'd order soup and a sandwich, and if I was busy, a wrap I could eat while I worked.

At dinner I was more apt to force him to try something new, something his Morosian nature would make him cock his head to the side at. I had turned him onto coconut curry, and chicken alfredo, or white spaghetti as he called it.

Elish felt a sad smile come to his lips. *I remember the first time he tried sushi. He ate one bite of it and his eyes lit up; he declared it the best* thing he'd ever tasted. Even for a chimera it was a treat, since fish were rare and the seaweed paper needed to be scavenged. But every time I came home with it he danced around me like a cat when you shook the bag of treats.

Seeing Jade discover just how good it could be to be a chimera had been an unexpected joy in Elish life. Elish had been raised a prince and had enjoyed the benefits of being one his entire life. Jade stepping into his own as a chimera, and as Elish's cicaro had given him a new appreciation for a world and a life he had grown accustom to.

But then Elish's thoughts took a dark turn. The smiling face of Jade started to fade and like a cruel inner voice reminding him of the real realities of his life with Jade, he saw the look of despair on the boy's face whenever Elish had been cruel to him, and the fear in his eyes when Elish became violent.

I used to hit that boy and feel gratification when I did it. I loved knocking him to the floor whenever he had the audacity to challenge me, and when he'd come crawling to my feet on his hands and knees, begging me for forgiveness after, it filled me with sadistic joy. I enjoyed it immensely as I enjoyed seeing everyone around me submit to me. I drank in the boy's terror and loved every tear he shed from my hand. I licked his blood and fed on his fear and misery, and I tempered and trained him until he himself became steel.

There were times when the boy deserved a sound beating, all my brothers did at times, and yet there were other incidences when the only reason I beat him mercilessly was because I hated how he was making me feel. I so despised that boy for making me love him.

And I hated him for giving Silas a tool to use against me, when I had systematically eliminated all weapons the Ghost could use on my body and mind. From not having a partner of my own, to growing my hair long as a decoy. Jade was my Achilles' heel and that parasite of a king knew it, as did my entire family.

Elish closed his eyes, but he was unable to shake the image of Jade on the floor, his chest heaving and his mouth open and gasping. There was blood running down his nose and mouth, staining the carpet. It was a scene that had played out many times before, Jade had been disobedient and like a dog he'd been disciplined for it.

And my chest would shake with adrenaline over his fearful pleas spilling quickly from his lips. His tone would be high with real fear, and his yellow eyes wide and terrified. I'd leave him bleeding on the floor and I would go back to my laptop, or go into my room, deliberately ignoring his crying... then he'd crawl to me with his tail tucked between his legs, making cautious movements and shrinking down if I myself moved.

I beat him, but because I had destroyed everything he'd ever had, and I had isolated him from the rest of the world to make myself the sole person he could go to... he'd crawl to his abuser for comfort.

I'm a terrible person.

And I did not deserve that boy.

This sudden conclusion filled Elish's mouth with bitterness. He swallowed down the constriction that was tightening his throat and crushed more pills. He inhaled them and closed his eyes, but all he saw was that boy bleeding on the carpet.

Suddenly Elish let out a scream of anger. He picked up a crate of empty wine bottles and threw them down onto the caravan's wooden floor, smashing the crate like a thrown egg, and shattering the glass bottles inside.

Broken glass went everywhere and he felt shifting as the bosen became anxious. Elish clenched his teeth and let out another cry, then he raised his fists and started punching the broken glass bottles. With every hit they sliced his hands, but he cared not, blood sprayed all around him and shards of glass flew through the air, but still he rained blow after blow down; mournful and agony-filled cries coming forth from his lips until he let out one last sob and folded his hands behind his neck. He pressed his hands against the back of his head, his mouth open and his face twisted in remorse, then he closed his eyes, feeling blood running down his neck and chest.

When he opened his eyes he saw Jade sitting in front of him, the boy's image blurred from his own tears. He looked as he did in his prime, during the several months they spent together in happiness after their game had concluded. His hair was longer and curling in the back, his pale face healthy and his thin lips the most beautiful shade of pink.

Elish choked and raised a lacerated and bleeding hand to touch the boy's face. To run his fingers down his warm cheek, to feel Jade's head tilt towards his hand, one last time.

But the boy only smiled, before he disappeared from Elish's vision, only the shocked eyes of the greywasters peering into the caravan remaining.

CHAPTER 22

Elish

ELISH ROLLED OVER ON THE DOUBLE BED; THE SMELL of old blankets washed in bar soap and a room cleaned with Pinesol and bleach filling his nostrils. The aroma sat there stagnant, making a home inside of his nose with no intents of departing.

He hated that smell. The dreams he'd have of Jade, of holding him in his arms and taking in his scent, no matter how vivid, were uncovered as fake as soon as his senses became sharp enough for him to smell that room. There was no escaping reality it seemed, not even while he slept.

Slowly Elish opened his eyes after one particularly heartwrenching dream, one that had him holding the boy in his arms. It was the last time he held the boy while he still had his mind; the last night before Kessler came.

And even though Elish knew that he would eventually see headlights on the horizon, and the sounds of the legion vehicles, he cherished that dream anyway.

Every moment.

Elish squinted his eyes and his metal lock box came into his focusing vision. He stared, with more awareness than he felt comfortable with, and wondered if he could continue the dream where he left off.

Or perhaps if I close my eyes now, I can control the dream... I can change the past and kill Kessler as soon as he steps off of that plane.

If only it could be so.

If only.

Elish got up, the room dark around him thanks to a blanket he'd hung up over the paper thin curtain, and relieved himself. He looked over his now healed hands but saw that in several places there were raised bumps from where his resurrection hadn't pushed out the glass. He sat down at a small table, only big enough to fit a chair on either side, and sniffed ground up Dilaudids through his rolled up money. After he picked out the glass with a pocket knife, he went back to bed with a bottle of vodka and closed his eyes. The drugs would be kicking in soon at least.

The false comfort started behind his eyes, and leaked to the back of his head like someone was pouring liquid warm onto his face. It pooled like water flowing into a dam, and once it overflowed and spilled over the edges, it sunk into his veins, joined his blood, and spread to the rest of his body. The center of the drug-induced warmth was his head, however; and he let the intense high cradle him and wrap him tightly in its blanket. He found the drugs to be the only arms he felt like he could crawl into without judgement, so he did, with his eyes shut tight and his knees drawn up to his chest.

But no drugs could silence the boy's voice, and inside he debated his own masochism when he found himself replaying every word Jade had ever said to him, good and bad. He found himself now treasuring every acidic nip, every shouted insult. But instead of remembering the flares of anger that accompanied the boy's disrespect, or the cold satisfaction and the smirk that followed when Elish knew he'd gotten to him, in Elish's memories he only threw his arms around Jade and held him tight to his body.

The boy's voice seemed so clear and ringing, but Elish was saddened to realize that every day that went by, the voice was changing. Like he was replaying a video cassette so often it was wearing and distorting, but instead of becoming something different, Jade's voice was becoming Elish's.

He'd replayed Jade's memories so many times it was now his voice he was remembering.

And for that, a new sadness rooted itself in Elish's chest, and its vines wrapped around his bones and embedded their roots.

The fear that he was going to forget Jade was all too real. He was immortal and he knew the realities of that. Once feelings he had felt so strong would become faded and washed out, and with every day he woke up, the short few years where Jade was a part of his life would get farther away.

Elish swallowed a lump in his throat and blinked away the stinging that had appeared behind his eyes. He closed his eyes and drew up Jade's face, and as if his mind had decided to take advantage of his own inner fear, it cruelly made Jade's image faded and full of inconsistencies and holes.

All of the pictures he had of the boy had burned up in the fire. The only records he would have would be the ones Silas was in possession of. Cruel videos he kept out of pure sadistic enjoyment: Jade and Sanguine having sex, the wedding which Nero had filmed happily, and other ones he most likely wasn't aware of. The photos perhaps he would have more luck on... but even those would be old ones. Jade had been away from the family for quite a while.

His memory will fade, as it did with the other men who once claimed my heart. Early in my years, when I still had a heart to claim.

Elish got up, unable to stand the thoughts so cruelly infecting his mind. He did more of the drugs on the small table and sniffed them up his nose, in a desperate effort to make them hit faster.

The drugs were a saving grace now; however, they were a double-edged sword. Every time Elish inhaled them, or swallowed down the pills, he was rolling the dice.

Sometimes the drugs would throw him into an agony-induced rage. The despair would claim him and slay him, reaching down his throat and grabbing his heart before ripping it out through his mouth. The pain was so profound, he would most often fall to his knees and lay on the floor until he could slip himself a suicide pill to quell the anguish eating him alive.

Elish opened his eyes, the pills doing their work and rendering him almost too out of it to move. He stared at the turned off television, and rested his hand on the collar wrapped around his upper arm. He stroked it slowly and swallowed with a trembling throat.

I could have had him immortal months ago, but, once again, I had to double down and gamble with the last chip I held in my hands. After losing everything else, I offered up the last thing I had... and I had lost.

Now I am nothing. Nothing but a drunk and a drug addict, passing the days in a dark apartment waiting for death. However death will never find me. It has claimed Killian, and it has claimed Jade, and yet it passes me by each time.

Reno was right, they deserved life and I do not.

There was a knock on his door sometime later. What time it was he didn't know, he never paid attention to whether it was day or night; but there was a thin strip of sunlight on the wall behind the television, so it must be sometime during the day.

Elish got up, his bones cracking and popping; he slipped on a pair of leather gloves, and opened the door.

Max was standing there, holding a bag in one hand and a book in the other. When he saw Elish his face grew concerned. "I thought I told you not to try dying..."

"I thought I told everyone to leave me alone," Elish said dryly, but for some reason he stepped away from the door and let the boy walk in. "Is it time to leave?" The timeline was hazy now, but he remembered coming into Mariano. He had lost a lot of blood from cutting his hands on the glass but had refused all offers of medical help in favour of retreating to a room at the inn.

"No, we're still waiting for the big caravan to come in," Max responded. He put the brown bag, which smelled like pub food, down onto the small table, but kept the book. "Once we buy the supplies from them we'll be going first thing to Mantis. You're lucking out again. It's more wine." Max chuckled at this. "Well, wine plus some other shit." Then he looked at Elish and the concerned look re-appeared on his face. "How are your hands?"

Elish sat down on one of the two chairs in front of the table. "Fine," he said flatly.

"You really scared Mom, and the mercenaries wanted to leave you behind... I know you'll probably hate me, but I told Mom, just Mom, that your husband died. So she's kind of understanding now."

Elish's mouth pulled at this but he said nothing. He'd be rid of all of them once he arrived in Mantis.

But what was the point in going to Mantis? To drink and get too stoned to feel anything in a different apartment? Elish had no answer to that, but it was where he felt compelled to go, so it was where he would go. What happened after that he did not know, nor did he care.

For once in his life he had no future plans.

"So... um." Max sat down and put the book he'd been carrying on the table. He looked at Elish and indicated with his eyes for Elish to take it. "I saw this in the shop and bought it for you."

Elish picked it up. Its front was soft worn leather, a chestnut brown, and when he opened up the book he realized the single line pages were empty. "I kind of... I like writing songs like I said, and once I had a friend who bought me a book and I taught myself how to write. I don't know if you know how to write, but if you do I thought it might help for you to... you know, write stuff since you seem so sad." Max scratched the back of his head, his cheeks reddened. "If you don't know how to write, I'm sorry. But you could learn, or maybe draw pictures or something."

For a moment, Elish just stared blankly, trying to wade through the thick haze to gauge how he felt about the boy's offering. Max continued to stumble over his words as he did this, tripping and falling like he was tumbling down a dictionary rather than a flight of stairs.

"Why do you care?" Elish found himself saying in a low tone. Then his purple eyes lifted from the blank book to Max's flushed face.

The boy's eyes, green, shifted from Elish's and he shrugged his left shoulder. "Every time I go near you I just feel this overwhelming sense of sad. I'm not a monster or anything... I feel bad and I just wanted to help. Maybe one day when I'm at the lowest point in my life, someone might help me, right? Today you, tomorrow me for all I know."

Elish set the book down. Then he saw a rough hand set a rollerball pen on top of the soft leather cover.

"You're rather thoughtful for a greywaster," Elish replied. "Most of the ones I've met, they're hardened already. They don't trust anyone, let alone feel empathy towards them."

Max seemed amused by this. "I shot a merc in the back of the head when he hit my mom just last year, man. I stalked a merchant who ripped us off and cut his throat. We ate well for a week. Don't take this as me being soft. I just... I don't know... for some reason you stand out to me."

Elish's brow furrowed at this. He reached to his belt and pulled out a small pocket knife. Max gave a questioning look as Elish unfolded it, and that look only intensified when Elish made a 'come here' motion towards Max's hand.

"What are you doing?" Max asked cautiously, but trustingly he gave Elish his hand.

"Not making the same mistake twice," Elish said, and he took the boy's hand firmly in his. "I am going to draw blood. You're a greywaster, you're tough enough to deal with it. If you don't ask me further questions and close your eyes... I will give you fifty dollars."

Max blinked, then he closed his eyes. "You can get a hell of a lot more out of me for fifty bucks," he said, but his tone was nervous.

Elish didn't answer back. He pressed the tip of the knife to the inner area of the boy's middle finger and cut it. Max sucked in a breath and grunted as Elish squeezed the wound to extract the blood; then Elish put his lips to the wound quickly and ran his tongue over it.

"Holy..." Max opened his eyes and pulled his finger away. He looked down at it and his chest shuddered, his heartbeat spiked as well.

Elish ran the blood along his mouth and shook his head with a sigh. "You're a greywaster. I thought as much but I've been fooled before. I–"

Suddenly Max grabbed the collar of Elish's jacket and pulled him forward. Max pushed his lips against Elish's and kissed him.

Elish immediately broke the kiss, and like a rapid strike, he grabbed the boy's chin.

"No," Elish said, in a tone that held such a dangerous warning it was as if, for the moment at least, he'd become the chimera he'd once been. "If you ever do that again, I will kill you." Elish's violet eyes seared the boy's own, reducing whatever fleeting feelings he'd had to cinders. Max melted underneath the glaring threat and stayed a puddle of embarrassment right where Elish had left him.

"You're going to hate me now..." Max said, and slowly wiped a hand down his face, a streak of blood was left behind from where Elish had cut him. "I just thought... why did you...?" Then he seemed to remember the rules for receiving his money, so he paused and instead continued his self-loathing. "I just fucked it up, didn't I?"

"There was nothing to fuck up," Elish said. He rose and sat back down on his bed and picked up his bottle of vodka. "You can leave."

"Can I stay...? Please?"

"No."

"But I'm lonely. Come on. Please... I'm... I feel sad too."

Elish was quiet. His mind taking him back to the campfire the night before Kessler came. How he held his cicaro as he slept, and the last kiss that they had shared. The boy had looked so much older with his beard, and rugged with his eyebrows ungroomed and his hands rough and callused.

He remembered the last time they'd been intimate, and Elish was drawn further into sadness when he realized that, in a few short months, it would be a year. He'd last taken his husband in the greyrifts apartment, before they had left on that worthless mission.

I will never feel that boy's soft naked body against my own. I will never feel like one piece of a two piece instrument, making the most beautiful music as we played each other perfectly. How can I ever be intimate with anyone when it would be nothing compared to what it was like sharing a bed with him.

I had grown to dislike sex, thanks to Silas's constant use of it to dominate me, and it was Jade who lit that fire inside of my soul. Before Jade, sex was something I scheduled like a meeting. To call Drake to my office or house to perform on me orally, have one or two orgasms and send him away. Or if I was frustrated about something, or angry, to fuck one of my brothers until I made them bleed. It was only done because testosterone commanded the release and I'd grow, as my brothers would say, all the more insufferable if I didn't get rid of that tension.

Then I met Jade, and I discovered my passion for it again, to the point where it was like composing a symphony making love to him. Our bodies and our minds became one living and breathing entity, and I no longer knew where I ended and he began.

And when we fucked it felt like I was becoming a god inside of him. I took that sadistic joy I felt making him suffer, and the frustration my feelings for him had filled me with, then I turned it around to transform it into the best sex I had ever had. I ravaged that body again and again, unable to quench my thirst even when he was pleading at me to stop, and each thrust I made drew more droplets of blood onto our sheets. The smell of his blood parched my throat and his screaming pleas were like oil to my hips. I had to draw out every bit of him until he was nothing but a crumpled heap of tender flesh, blood, and my own semen.

Elish's teeth clenched, and he threw the vodka bottle across the room. It shattered against the cold fireplace and sprayed the apartment with shattered glass.

Max got up, his eyes wide and terrified, and he ran towards the door.

"No, stay," Elish barked, his chest heaving and his heart racing. He clenched his hands to fists, and when he felt a stinging pain rip up his jaw he realized he was clenching that as well. "Do you know how to prepare heroin?"

He could feel the boy's eyes staring at him.

"Y-yeah."

"Then do it."

And it was in the heroin that Elish finally found himself plunging so deep inside of the rabbit hole that he no longer knew what time was, let alone how many days had passed. His life now revolved around Max sticking him with needles and bringing small bits of food for him to eat. Then sometime in the black shroud that covered all of his memories like a thick film, Robyn came as well. He remembered little of when she first arrived, only her talking angrily to her son before she tried to rouse Elish off of the bed that he rarely left.

When he got up off of it, he saw that it was covered in orange caps; the caps that you broke off of the disposable needle and usually discarded. They had built up and surrounded his sour unwashed body like flowers being tossed over a gravestone. He remembered hearing the pitter-patter as several fell onto the wooden floor.

Half of the payment now, half when we get to Mantis, Elish had told her, and he knew it was for that reason that Robyn and Vince the mercenary were helping him down the stairs. He was almost too weak to even make it to the caravan, but he was with it enough to clutch his knapsack, which still held the metal box of his money and drugs safely inside.

When Elish was laying in the back of the bosen cart, he closed his eyes and called for Max to prepare himself more heroin, but the boy wouldn't come. So instead he let the drugs already in his system take him away on their path of warmth and numbness. The drugs themselves felt like a coating of wax on his heart and his brain, a thick layer that repelled all the haunting thoughts that wished to pick at him.

But, in turn, he was so disconnected from the world around him that nothing mattered anymore. He didn't eat or drink unless it was to get Robyn or the boy to stop bothering him and let him slip back into his half-conscious stupor; and it took all of his efforts to get off of the cart to relieve himself. No longer did he brush his teeth, or even change his clothes, he lay in the back of the cart with nothing but the haunting image of Jade to keep him company, and the accusing voices of those who had died because of his stubborn dream.

Sometimes the old Elish would come out, slamming his fists against his mind and roaring at him to get up and do something about the situation. The old him would fix his violet eyes on him and glare with a face thick with disdain and hatred. He would tell Elish that there was still hope.

There's still Adler! he'd shout, a snarl rimming his lips. *There is still one more!*

Go with the original plan, before Mantis took him. Find Adler now, train him and correct his thinking. Send him to Silas with renewed hatred and get Silas into your hands. And while Adler is distracting Silas, find a way to quell the flames that Reaver burns inside of – and take Reaver for yourself. Temper his agony and rage over losing Killian, use it to your advantage and make him love you. You two will be unstoppable.

"Just stop it," Elish said out loud, and inside the voice of his former self bellowed with an inhuman and frustrated rage, calling him weak, calling him a quitter, calling him worthless.

"You already lost everything," Elish told him, and he picked up a needle full of brown liquid and tied off his arm with a telephone cord. "It's over."

It doesn't have to be! You can still win this. You've planted so many seeds, you have backups for your backups. You have another born immortal, and you have two other Killians!

"None of this matters without Jade," Elish whispered.

Then he dropped his hand from his arm and let out a slow breath. He shut his eyes tight, feeling the sadness inside of him start to break through the coating the drugs had covered him in. The haze was thinning, and there was only one cure for that.

Elish opened his eyes and picked up the needle, then looked down at his arm. All up his forearm were small red pocks, some of them swollen, and one even an open sore which Robyn had been treating for him. Only this arm had been cleaned, the rest of him was tanned now, grey and brown from the dirt and ash covering his skin. He hadn't seen what he looked like, but he knew not even his brothers would recognize him now.

"Stop doing this to yourself…"

Elish froze, the needle sticking into his arm. He stared at it, his mouth closing tight over the sound of his voice. Sometimes he thought he'd forgotten it already, but when his husband spoke to him all of the memories came rushing back, and Jade's young voice, that softened just for his master, came back to Elish with such clarity it was like listening to an old treasured song and realizing you still remembered the lyrics.

"Master… please stop."

Elish felt his eyes burn, and this time he didn't close them. He let them sting and sear his eyelids until a tear slipped down his cheek. Slowly he looked up and saw Jade looking back at him, sitting only a foot away with his legs crossed, an expression of intense sadness on his face.

"I can't," Elish whispered, his voice broke.

"But you can do anything," Jade said back to him. "You're my master, you're unbreakable. You're the strongest man I know, a figure of strength and power... what happened, Master?"

Elish blinked away another tear, and smiled at Jade sadly.

"You happened, maritus."

Then the image of Jade, the one that looked so crystal clear inside of Elish's mind, would disappear, and in his wake the pain would hit Elish like he'd slammed into a wall at full speed. And after looking into the boy's eyes, and seeing that haunting look on his face, there wasn't enough heroin, opiate pills, or alcohol in the world to dull the despair so organic inside of him.

"I think he wants to die, Mom..." Max whimpered. Elish felt a cold cloth on his head. He could hear a river rushing in the distance and the cart was tilted forward. The bosen must be unhitched to drink from the river and rest themselves.

How long until they reached Mantis? Not like it mattered. He was only exchanging one bed for the other, just this time he wouldn't have Max to make him his heroin.

"There are many people in the greywastes wanting to live, hunny," Robyn's voice said. "And the world has no patience for those not willing to fight for their right to do so. You can't help him if he's done. All we can do is just get him to Mantis, so the two of us can keep surviving."

Elish felt another hand on his head. "He's lucky he came to me instead of some of the others. They'd eat him and break open that lock box he has. I hope he appreciates my honesty, your father never did. Jesus... you could fry an egg on that forehead." He heard shifting around, and as his eyes drew themselves away from a memory soon lost in the black veiled haze, he could see Robyn kneeling over him, and Max beside her. "I wish your father loved me as much as he loved his husband. I wonder what he was before he lost him? I heard from a merchant once they have mutants in Skyfall, but I'd never think one would wind up here. Or be so... normal."

Normal? I was never normal...

"I think he's an angel, Mom."

Robyn laughed lightly. "There aren't any angels in this world, Maxi. Mutants maybe, not no angels; I taught you better than that. Don't give him any more of the heroin. James..." Robyn raised her voice. "James. I have some meat in a container for you."

"Okay," Elish answered. To their surprise, he shifted himself to the sitting position and saw a green container holding pieces of cooked meat with a sprinkling of salt. "How long until we arrive in Mantis?"

"Just one more day. I hope you didn't blow my other half of the payment on all those drugs," Robyn said as she crawled out of the cart. Behind her Elish could see thick yellow grass, a sloping hill, then a river that cut through the road. The road picked up again, but chunks had been taken out and deposited into the river bed, making artificial rocks that he could see several of the mercenaries perching on as they scrubbed their clothes. The smell of water was a break from his own rancid stink, but not enough for him to leave what had become his enclosed comfort.

"No," Elish responded. "I was in possession of them before I departed."

Max put a hand on his shoulder. "Come outside to the fire," he said and shook it. "Please?"

Elish could see a look of sadness on the boy's face, and when Elish shook his head, Max's deep frown was added to it.

"I wrote a new song... I thought maybe we could try and put music to it," Max said in a low voice. "I'll make you a fire away from everyone else..."

Elish shook his head again. "No."

Max gave a disenchanted sigh, he crawled backwards until he was out of the cart. "If you change your mind..." He let that hang in the air before he turned around and disappeared out of sight.

Elish didn't feel like he wanted to, but his mouth was parched and his lips raw and peeling from lack of water and the dry heat they'd been experiencing. So after an hour of nodding off from the drugs, he finally left the oasis in the back of the cart, to the surprise of everyone and the smiling delight of Max. As Elish wordlessly walked past the camp to the river, he saw the boy get up and start gathering firewood.

He drank deeply from the river and washed his face and limbs. He unwound the bandage that was now on his arm and took a bottle of antiseptic from Robyn to douse it. It hadn't gotten any better, but also it was no worse. It looked like a small pink crater halfway between his wrist and his elbow, with the edges white from the gathering pus and a ring of blood from when he'd disturbed it.

There was no want in him to bathe himself, he felt almost comforted by the dirt he was covered in, almost as if it was a protective barrier like the intangible one the drugs provided. So once his arms and face were washed, and his teeth brushed, he walked to his fire which had been made beside a shabby shed, and sat down on a liquor crate in front of the boy.

Max looked at him, but then he blushed and looked away. He was holding a spiral-bound notebook that was well-worn and there was a bottle of beer and his bag of candies on either side of him.

Max offered him the bag, a coy smile on his face. Elish gave him a questionable look, wishing in many ways he hadn't decided to leave the back of the caravan.

"What is that look for?" Elish asked, and took a drink of water from a plastic bottle he'd filled.

"I don't want you to think I'm stupid," Max said. He busied himself thumbing through pages in what Elish realized was his music book. "I always get embarrassed when I show people my songs. Hey, I always wondered… if a song doesn't have music, does that make it a poem?"

Elish shook his head no. "Music usually has a chorus, poems can but it is not necessary."

"Oh, alright. Do songs have to have music?"

"No, but they should be sung."

"Oh, alright," Max said again. He folded the book in half and Elish could see the tips of his ears, ones that stuck out a lot over his buzz cut, redden.

"I don't care enough to laugh at you," Elish stated dully, and he decided to pull out a regular tobacco cigarette from inside of his jacket. It was wrinkled and bent to one side; he didn't smoke these ones as often. "You might as well just do what you wanted to do so I can go back to the caravan." He brought his lighter out and flicked it, but the butane had run out. Instead he leaned over and lit it on the flames before taking an inhale.

Max's dirty sneaks, with grey laces knotted in several places, scraped the dirt as he shifted them. "Okay… just go back to the caravan if you don't like it. Don't get mad at me or anything…" The boy's nose scrunched in nervousness and he looked behind Elish as if to make sure no one else was listening.

"Max...?"

Elish looked behind him and saw that all four mercenaries and Robyn were standing up in front of the fire. And as soon as he saw that they were on alert, he heard the sounds of a motor. He turned and walked to the front of the shed, and saw headlights on the road they'd been travelling on, and the silhouette of a vehicle.

As if he had been unceremoniously awakened from a deep slumber, the black fog that had surrounded him for what could've possibly been weeks, dissolved into the air like it had been nothing but a manifested phantom; and in its place an intense feeling of dread took him. He didn't know if it were the reminders of the recollection of how Kessler and his legionaries had ambushed him, or just that he was no longer used to feeling dread or other anxious emotions, but he found himself acutely aware of his reality.

"Get the boy to safety," Elish commanded. And all heads turned to him, looks of surprise on their faces like when he'd first stepped off of the caravan.

"The boy is fifteen, he's not a child," Vince said irritably. He walked to Max and handed him an assault rifle. "Cover my ass, alright?"

Elish's teeth gritted when Max nodded. He glanced to Elish and the corners of his mouth rose.

"I told you, James. I'm not as nice as I look." He walked past Elish, his notebook still in his hand, but Elish grabbed his shoulder.

"Hide, that's an–" Elish stopped himself; the realization that he was no second-in-command, no prince of Skyfall, sat in his mouth like a bitter pill. "–do this for me."

"Max!" Robyn called. "I need everyone here to make an impression on them. Everyone get your guns out and get to your places."

Max winked at Elish and sprinted towards the campfire. He tossed his notebook into the back of the caravan as he did, and then he stood behind Vince. Elish watched him puff out his chest and hold the assault rifle to it, the sounds of the vehicle's engine getting louder.

And behind the vehicle were two other single headlights – Elish realized with grimness that they were legion vehicles.

Did I not just have this scene play out? Elish debated his options, but felt like he was between a rock and a hard place. He didn't want to hide like a coward, but everyone in the Legion would recognize him just by his purple eyes.

Then he almost gave out a cry of relief, but instead stifled it to a tense breath. He walked to the caravan, the vehicles approaching now changing tone as they went from the cracked and dirty pavement to the bumpy greywastes, and got a pair of sunglasses out from his backpack. He put them on, slipped a pistol into his pants and buttoned up the first three buttons on his jacket.

When he took his place beside Max, the headlights were now bathing all seven of them, and the engines were slaying the humid air and filling it with a tenseness that made Elish's blood rise in temperature.

The lights turned off, all but one, and that brought another uncomfortable recollection to Elish. He found himself shifting his weight, then crossing his arms. Subtle signs of anxiousness that anyone who knew him would pick up on. If Silas were here to witness these movements, he would've eaten them up with his eyes before pouncing like a lion would after picking out the sickest wildebeest in the heard.

But there was no one around him with such an ability to read physical signs of stress, and even if there were, all eyes had become fixed on the jeep that had stopped in front of them, and the four-wheelers idling on each side.

"Good evening," a deep voice called. A man stepped out, dark skinned with a uniform that suggested he was a middle-ranking officer. Elish didn't recognize him, but he had the authoritative air on him that made it obvious he had worked for his role. "I'm Senior Officer George Lowell of the Legion." He smiled thinly before nodding to their weapons. "Please put away your weapons and gather all those in your group so we can address everyone."

Elish had to restrain himself from automatically demanding the officer to tell them why he was here, why he was in the northern greywastes. Legionaries were rarely seen this far north, and the greywasters clustered to these northern towns for just that reason. Men and women hiding from legion recruitment, deserters, or wanting to dodge the census; there were many reasons to migrate towards settlements far out of the Legion's hands. The monarchy had laid down laws for the greywastes, no slaving for one, but unless you were in a block or had a mayor who believed the same, it was only the Legion who upheld that law and killed those who broke it. That was why slaving was quite accepted here, and other things not allowed in any place that there was a legion presence.

"What's this about?" Robyn asked.

Then the jeep's engine cut out, and everything fell to an uncomfortable and heavy silence. The kind of unsettling silence that one heard when in the dark, but yet knew they were in a room teeming with people.

And when the senior officer spoke, it broke the muted air with such an unexpected ferocity that Elish jolted, his heart following suit. He had to shut his eyes, and when Elish wiped his head he realized he was sweating.

This scene was too familiar – and to Elish's own self-derision and inner hatred for the emotional weakness he continued to drown in, he realized that he was unsure if he could stand here and watch what was going on. Over the past weeks, he had found himself having internal reactions to things around him, usually igniting an anger or plunging him into fresh despair… but never had he had an uncontrollable physical reaction. He was sweating, his breathing was shortening, and his hands were twitching with his legs, as if urging him to flee this scene.

He kept his eyes shut, and thanks to the sunglasses, no one noticed.

However, the senior officer's voice found the part of Elish's brain still able to take in real stimulus, not just the ones his quickly deteriorating mind was replaying, so Elish listened to him.

"We've already found the location of his body but the head had been removed," George said. Elish felt a percussion rip through him; his heart felt like it was being pulled to his throat by a thin piece of twine. "It has been several months so he would still be dead. Have any of you seen something that could resemble him?"

Elish kept his eyes closed. His heartbeat was a steady knocking against his ears, like it was commanding for it to enter his brain to further contaminate what was really happening around him.

"We've also learned that several cities have been taken over by ravers. The Legion has been commanded under Kessler's son General Caligula to exterminate this new raver problem. The Legion is committed to keeping peace in the greywastes, and the greywastes includes the northern–

–"You're in no position to threaten me."

The senior officer's tone suddenly glitched like a scratched CD skipping. Elish found his inner ear itching and the discomfort spread rapidly, until his brain felt like it was covered in mould.

"You got ten seconds, Elish. Let me take the clone or I'm shooting your husband on the spot."

Elish's eyes flew open. His body became paralyzed; his boots welded to the floor.

And when Elish looked through his tinted sunglasses, he saw Kessler standing there – and right in front of Kessler, was none other than Elish himself.

Elish stumbled back and stared, trying, but failing, to comprehend what he was seeing and why.

Elish, the other Elish, the one who still stood tall with grace and confidence, looked behind him.

He looked to… he looked to…

"Jade?" Elish choked. He could see the boy standing behind him with an assault rifle in his hand. Why wasn't he behind the rock where Elish had put him? Why wasn't he hiding?

Then, like he had broken a cardinal rule that anyone seeing into the past had to follow, all attention turned to him.

Kessler glared him down with eyes that dripped poison; the old Elish himself stared with a cold glint of annoyance, and Jade… Jade just looked puzzled.

Elish took his sunglasses off, and held them so firmly in his trembling hand that they snapped. "Run," Elish croaked. Everyone stepped back as he stumbled towards Jade, his knees buckling with every step. "Run far away from here."

Jade started taking steps backwards. Kessler called to Elish out of sight, but Elish ignored him.

"Don't disobey me!" Elish shouted when the boy still only stared at him confused. "I said get the fuck out of here before he kills you!"

Elish gave a frustrated yell when the boy refused to run from this scene. The scene that would leave him half-dead, with a bullet that had almost embedded itself into his brain, and a mind that had finally succumbed to his abilities when he'd been forced to use them to save his friends and master.

Then Elish felt a hand on his shoulder; and when that hand dared try and pull him away, Elish felt his loose grasp on reality finally slip –

– and he whirled around and struck the person in the face.

Without pausing he ran towards Jade and grabbed him by his jacket. "Run!" Elish screamed. The boy hollered with fright and dropped his rifle, and behind him Elish heard hurried voices and guns being grabbed. "RUN!" Tears were stinging his eyes, running down the creases of a face twisted in desperation. His mind was in overdrive, like an engine stuck in acceleration. It was screaming to him one thing, and that thing was that this was his chance, this was his only chance to change the past, and have Jade still be alive.

Then he heard what he thought were fireworks going off around him, and Jade screamed. Elish gathered every ounce of his strength and pulled the boy into the darkness, down the incline towards a river he could hear behind him.

Then more fireworks, before shadows burst out of the shade and ripped the boy from his grasp.

"NO!" Elish cried. He lunged towards Jade but the black shadows dragged him off into the darkness. "JADE! NO!" he screamed, and broke down into choked sobs. "Don't leave…" His eyes dropped to the ground, blurring from his tears, a tremble rocking his chest and stealing his breath. He looked up one last time and saw Jade's face fade off into obscurity, and then four shadows stood in front of him, blocking Elish from seeing anything more.

Another pop of a firecracker going off, but this one strangely made Elish's chest jerk backwards like someone had punched him in the gut. He fell onto his back, and with one last pull of adrenaline, sprung to his feet.

Then he looked down.

The shadows watched him wordlessly as he put a hand to his chest and withdrew it. It was shining with blood; and when he looked down at his body he saw more blood soaking through his jacket, and falling like tears into the darkness.

Death… will you remember me this time? Will you take me to him?

Elish turned his back to the shadows and limped away from the scene. He looked to the greywastes sky and saw the moon shining over him with its mask of ashes.

When he took his next step, he felt wetness in his boots. He glanced down to see the moon again, though now it was rippling and waving in the reflection of the river.

The silence was broken by one last crack, and Elish's back heaved forward. Then, in an instant, his legs disappeared out from under him, and the frozen water of the river greeted him and consumed him like a hungry beast.

Take me to him... Elish said to himself, and even as the cold water filled his lungs, his voice remained calm, as did his mind. *Take me to him.*

The white flames claimed him soon after.

CHAPTER 23

Reaver

KIKI WAS STARING AT THE LIVING ROOM CARPET; HE was scrunched in on himself with his knees tucked up to his chest and his arm wrapped around them. He was never this submissive little mouse when Nero had me chained to the bed, but now he was in my world and under my control, and the timid cicaro knew it.

The room was quiet, all except for Killian in the kitchen seeing if our ramen was done. It was a tense time. I'd just been able to coax the terrified black kitten out from the attic, and there he sat, as far away from me as he could get, staring at a stain on the carpet. Or the opposite of a stain; it had been a stain scrubbed so hard, it was now lighter than the rest of the carpet.

Kiki had downright fainted when he'd walked in on what couldn't have been a worse moment, and when he woke up he'd bolted. I'd let him go, knowing it would only scare him more if I chased after him. I'd thought he was going to lock himself in his bedroom, only to hear him pull on a string attached to the ceiling, which folded out a rickety set of stairs. When I realized what he was doing, I did persued him, but he'd already vanished into the darkness.

I had climbed the stairs, and had poked my head up so I was eye level with the floor, and like I'd let a feral kitten into my house, I saw two white orbs peering at me from behind a steamer trunk.

I'd told him Killian was immortal and he'd come back, and I'd, angrily I might add, told him this was because of what Nero had done to me. All I'd heard back from an apology I felt pissed that I had to make, was the teenage chimera's rapid, hyperventilating breaths and nothing more. After that I'd left him to his shadows, I had to take care of Killian anyway, and I needed to dispatch myself also to get rid of my own personal injuries. Not trusting the kid in the house with us dead, I tossed him a two litre of water and a stack of energy bars I'd seen in the kitchen, and had locked him up there.

Two days later found us sitting on the couch. My eyes pinning him down and his own eyes wide and so orange they seemed like they were coloured in with felt marker. The terrified expression on his face and his pale, stricken complexion, only made them all the more brighter. This kid was a testament to just how unnatural me and my family were.

Killian came back with two bowls of steaming ramen noodles, and my mouth salivated as he handed it to me. This shit was a special kind of ramen, it came in a bowl and was called Nong Shim, some Korean stuff that was spicy and made my nose run. We'd found stacks of it in the kitchen, all of it with *Melchai* written on the side. I assumed Nero had stocked up, which made me think that they had been living here before Mantis had gotten him. Or had at least used it as a storage house. Anyway, the shit was fucking divine, and Killian and I had already eaten two bowls each today.

I took mine and inhaled the spicy hot smell. Killian handed his to Kiki, who stared at him before taking it in such a cautiously gentle way it reminded me of Deek taking a treat from me after I'd yelled at him for snatching it from my hand.

Interestingly enough, I caught an exchange of gazes between Killian and Kiki. I wouldn't have noticed it if I didn't see a wince from Kiki like he'd been physically struck, automatically I looked at Killian and saw an expression of pure unadulterated hate.

But like he was slipping a new mask onto his face, as soon as he turned away from the cicaro the expression vanished like it hadn't even been there, and a more neutral one, bordering on timid himself, took its place.

I stared at him, and hid my surprise at this brief display I was never meant to see. It was obvious now that I couldn't leave these two alone together. Yes, I had promised Killian revenge on Kiki but honestly… I'd expected that desire from him to disappear after the sex was done. Killian and I loved our dirty talk while we were having sex, but it rarely manifested itself into reality.

Kiki sniffed and put his bowl down on the coffee table. He peeled back the lid before his eyes flickered to mine and he pushed the bowl towards me. "Will you please take the first bite?"

I gave him a questioning look. My fork already twirling noodles around it. I shrugged and dropped my own noodles and dug into his.

"We're not going to hurt you," Killian said, and once again I was thrown for a loop hearing his calmed and even tone. Like it was out of this world for Kiki to think that we'd hurt him. I saw the fucking look Killian had given him... that damn kid was playing me for a fool.

In a way it was intriguing to see Killian put on this show, but in another way... it pissed me off. This darker side of Killian was becoming more and more apparent. What had first only revealed itself when we were in intense situations of danger, was starting to blend itself into everyday Killian. This didn't sit well with me and I was finding myself increasingly bothered by it.

I decided against eating the forkful of noodles and instead switched bowls with him. The entire time I did it I monitored Killian's heartbeat in case he did contaminate the food, but besides looking annoyed, he was quiet. This was enough for the cicaro though, he said a meek *thanks* that sounded like a baby bird's chirp and started politely twirling his noodles around his fork.

"So... what I know already is that something is wrong with Nero," I said in between bites of food. "What happened to him, and why the hell are you guys even in the North? Silas told me he'd put Nero in concrete." I had a lot more questions but all of them could be answered with one request. "Start from the beginning, and I want honesty or I'll sick the tom cat on you." I motioned to Killian with my fork.

"I... I stranded Silas's rescue party in the plaguelands, and Silas too. Well, I heard Silas screaming, but I didn't see him," Kiki began quietly. My eyebrows raised at this and Killian and I exchanged glances. So Silas had made it out of the lab, that was unfortunate. "I did it to break out Nero. Sanguine and I both planned it together. We love... love Nero." Kiki poked his noodles with his fork and sniffed again. "We also freed Nero's husband Ceph."

What...? The red-haired guy was Nero's husband? "Someone was dumb enough to marry that psychopathic meathead?" I said with a twitch at the corner of my mouth. "He must be as big of a moron as you."

Kiki shook his head slowly. "Sanguine says Master Nero wasn't always this way. Well, he was… but not as extreme. He got worse when Ceph was encased in concrete. He… he was so much happier with Ceph here." The orange-eyed cicaro looked around the living room and his shoulders slumped. "Ceph was normalizing after being in concrete for so long… but then we found Mantis."

To me, Ceph was just another tool I could use to torture Nero, and if Ceph was mentally fragile from being encased for fuck knows how many years – all the better. Killian put a hand on my knee to tell me he shared the same thoughts as I, and we let Kiki continue.

"We were in Melchai getting supplies and we heard what you probably did as well… that they worship Sanguine there. Nero wanted to see who Man on the Hill was, and we walked up to the mansion when it was dark enough for the Blood Crows not to see… and we banged on the door." Not the smartest thing. "I was against it, terrified even." I guess at least that kid was smart. "But when he discovered it was Mantis, he was happy… he said he knew Mantis before Mantis left. And… and that was when things got strange."

I swallowed my food and found myself getting invested in this story. When Kiki paused to take a mouthful of noodles I was tempted to take back the bowl just to force him to tell it quicker.

Kiki politely swallowed his food. He had the impeccable manners of Jade and Killian. I never understood it. In the greywastes you ate quickly so you could start stealing food from everyone else dumb enough not to eat quickly too. Reno and I both had our share of fork mark scars on our hands from us defending our meals from each other, a couple bite marks as well when candy was involved.

"Mantis was polite with us but we saw another man just fleeting, and then he disappeared and we didn't see him anymore. Several days in, Nero questioned Mantis about him and Mantis said that he was a servant and came and went… Nero started speaking to the both of us about it and we concluded it must've been Angel Adi. Nero expressed…" Kiki sighed. "… wanting to be Sherlock Holmes and decided to start searching for who he was with Ceph – or Watson as he called him after he bought that Sherlock hat in town."

Nero was such an idiot in so many ways.

"I was left behind since I am still mortal, and Nero has always been protective of me. And one night he came back with Ceph, excited. He said that behind the mansion was what he described as a paradise. There was grass, bushes, trees that held acorns and fruits, gardens… and surrounding this place that he said looked like it was from the old world, were little cabins. He commented that there were animals too, mutated animals, but normal ones also. Ones he said Perish had been trying to perfect." I leaned in further, fascinated as all fuck, and Killian did as well. "He says he saw the man we had seen before but that wasn't what he was excited about… he kept saying 'I have to tell Silas. I have to tell Silas he's here'. But he told me I wouldn't understand, and after we were intimate and I fell asleep." Kiki's face fell and he scratched his chin, now with a thick covering of black stubble. "When I woke up in the morning… he was gone and it was just me and Ceph. Ceph left to go looking for him and… and then the two of them came back for me."

Kiki took in an uneasy breath. "They were side by side in the doorway and it was… so odd, Reaver. They walked normally but I could tell something was off. Nero had sunglasses on too which was so strange. Obediently, I went with them as requested but I got scared when they led me to a metal door at the end of a hallway, one that had always been closed and locked. When it opened and I saw how thick the door was, and the touchpad…" Kiki's voice dropped, as if expecting Mantis to be in this room with us. "… I think there's a laboratory under the mansion."

My eyes widened. "So you're smarter than Nero and Ceph apparently."

Kiki nodded and rubbed his nose. Jade had once told me that all chimeras rubbed their nose when they were stressed, and it was amazing how correct he was. "I hesitated and started backing away. I knew something wasn't right with them. Nero kept urging me to follow him. Then I saw something strange, I saw he had an injury on the back of his neck. I knew–"

"The worms!" Killian suddenly exclaimed. All hostilities towards Kiki were forgotten, at least for a moment. Killian looked at me with shock, and I myself felt the blood drain from my face when Kiki nodded rapidly.

"You know about them?" Kiki said hastily. He looked at the two of us, stunned. "We saw them when we were dropped off in the plaguelands, which is how we ended up here. We didn't know what they–"

"Finish the story first," I said. I wanted to know how it ended.

Kiki nodded again, more energy behind his words now. "As soon as I saw the wound I knew what had happened, and it was because Mantis didn't think I knew of them that I believe he didn't just grab me. I turned and fled, and got several feet up the rocky trail behind the mansion before Nero caught me. His sunglasses fell off... and you saw it, didn't you, Reaver? Some of the worms change the colour of your left eye, always the left eye, or well, our left, the victim's right. They change it black. It didn't on Ceph but it did on Nero. I panicked and I injured my master and I ran. I lost them in the hills behind the house and I had been living there, coming back here for supplies and food, ever since." Then his orange eyes looked at me. I saw hope in them, the hope that only a delusional cicaro could have. "I saw you and Killian come, and I started following you around. Please, Reaver... I know you hate Nero and you have every right to. But please understand that... Nero hurt you, not because you're Reaver, but because Silas encased Ceph because of him being upset about Sky that day, about a clone of Sky dying. Ceph was punished for being found out that he was immortal at the wrong time. Nero hates Sky, the entire family hates Sky for what he did to Silas, and because Silas mistreats us from his anguish over Sky dying. Nero had nothing but good things to say about you ever since you escaped. He thinks you're awesome. He respects you, and he loves you as a big brother should. It was nothing personal; he was just getting back at the closest thing to Sky he had. Nero loves–"

"If you say he loves Reaver one more time... I will make it so you never speak again," Killian suddenly said, his tone bringing a frost into the room.

Kiki shrunk down. "I just... I just wanted Reaver to know..." Kiki looked at me for help, but my stomach was churning over his words.

"I'm sorry for what he did, Reaver," Kiki's voice broke, and I saw his eyes well. "Please give him a second chance."

"A second chance?" Killian said haughtily. "You're fucking acting like Nero stole Reaver's fucking bike. Are you so used to Nero torturing and raping men that the reality and consequences of what he did is lost to you? Are you that fucking–"

"Killian... you're not helping," I said. A deep chasm of nausea was being created inside of me, and it quickly bred dizziness. I looked down at my now empty bowl of soup just in time for Killian to take it from me and put a hand on my shoulder.

"I'm sorry, baby," Killian whispered. Then his voice got sharp. "Go to your room."

"No. He can stay," I mumbled.

But then I shot to my feet. I ran outside and made it out just in time to throw up noodles onto the greywaste ground. I closed my eyes, my breathing laboured, and once again tried to purge myself of the contaminated feeling that still remained months after Nero had raped me. Why was that asshole's presence still buried inside my core? Why was this happening to me? I had once been able to control everything but now I felt like I was in the middle of the ocean, at the mercy of the tide in a shitty little life raft. The weakness that felt like it was embedded in my bones was maddening.

I slammed my hand against a support beam of the porch, and turned and stalked inside, wiping my face of the vomit stuck to my facial hair.

Killian was a blur. He sat perfectly still as if expecting me not to notice he'd moved. Feeling frustration and vexation I shot him a glaring look which he cowered down from.

"I'm in charge," I said, my tone so low it made my throat vibrate. I looked to Kiki as well. "I'm leading this. I will help you get back Nero, but in doing so, you're going to let me pay him back... understand me, Kincade?"

I saw Killian do a double take, and I realized he must not know Kiki's real name.

Kiki nodded. "Yes, sir."

"Good," I said, and then I turned to Killian. "I need to trust that you won't hurt him. Can I trust you, Killian?"

Killian met my gaze for a fleeting second, but still cowering under the look I was giving him, he nodded, showing me submission and obedience which calmed the maddened beast that stirred inside of me. "Yes, Reaver."

I nodded at the both of them. "We all have things to gain with this and we have the element of surprise, and Kiki... you know what the inside of the mansion looks like, right?"

"Yes."

"You're going to draw us a map. Killian, while he does this, you're going to brainstorm with me a plan to get Nero back. You were the one to pull the worm out of me, you know how it's done. All we have to do is come up with a plan on how to either get inside, or lure them out."

Killian stood up straight and gave me a smile. A smile of confidence and lightness, one I now rarely saw on his face. "We can do it. I know we can." Then he glanced at Kiki and I heard his heartbeat spike, then a flash of both sadism and lust replaced that sweet smile I'd once come to depend on during the darkest times of my life.

Then as quickly as it came, as if catching himself, it vanished.

"We can get Nero and Ceph back," Killian said in a deceptively sweet voice I found unnerving. Kiki looked up and gave him a shy smile, and Killian matched it with a smile of his own. "... and then we can all get what we want."

I woke up and saw that Killian had his arm over my chest. He was sleeping face down, his boxers pulled halfway off of his ass and his head tilted towards me. His mouth was half-open and he was snoring lightly, a damp patch visible on my arm from either the heat of his breath or drool, I wasn't sure which.

He looked so innocent while he slept... and yet he was so different when he was awake. What had once made up the millions of little pieces that stitched together to make Killian, had changed, the fabric of him had changed, and seemed to be shaping into something completely different. Now in front of me, on full display like he had willingly stripped himself naked, was someone I didn't recognize.

No, I did recognize him... I was seeing him take my own essence and weave it into a new cloak, a new mask. I was seeing parts of me starting to combine with parts of him, making this whole new person step forward from the remains of who had been my Killi Cat. It had started out with him taking charge when I had admitted my issues stemming from Nero, and now with every step I made into instability, I was seeing him take several more into... I didn't even know what to call it.

It was a toxic combination. It was a boy who had been abused, raped, tortured, and mentally destroyed finally tasting power, and now not fearing death. And the active ingredient, the catalyst I was now seeing... was that I didn't have the power over him to keep his ass in check. He'd never admit it, but he was taking advantage of my weakness.

And here I thought I could count on him to help me through this...

I had to fix myself... not only for me, but for Killian.

And not only for Killian – but for our relationship.

Because it was changing, and with it...

I hated to admit it. I hated myself for feeling it... but I truly was starting to hate who he was becoming. It was my responsibility to fix this, I had broken it in the first place. And right now was a vital time because we were establishing the foundation for a relationship that was going to last forever. No matter what I had to do.

No matter what I had to do.

I would fix myself, and fix Killian… and fix Reaver and Killian.

"Wake up, sleepy boy," I whispered, my heart heavy over my own internal thoughts. I took in a deep breath and nudged him.

Killian's eyes squinted, the sun from outside probably stinging his beautiful blue eyes. Even though my heart was steeling over this person I was seeing, never for a second did I think of leaving him. It just motivated me to repair what mess we had made.

This boy would one day be my husband, and I was going to marry him as Killi Cat… not whoever he was now.

No matter what.

I kept repeating that, and maybe I knew why I was, because I think it was a harbinger to what things were to come.

"Morning'," Killian said, the corners of his mouth rising. "You slept all through the night." He puckered his lips and I pecked them with my own.

"You did too," I said with a yawn. I laid my head on the pillow and looked at him, going over every part of his face. He'd shaved just yesterday and he looked beautiful. His hair was a bit over two inches long now, and he no longer looked like how cancer patients did on TV.

I realized he was looking at me too, his blue eyes full of love. I was relieved to see that.

Our eyes locked, and he reached a hand up to brush my face. "You look troubled," he said quietly. I felt his thumb stroke my cheek. "You know I'm immortal. We'll be fine."

He could always read me. I never thought of myself as wearing expressions on my sleeve, but Killian always seemed to know what I was thinking and feeling. That boy knew me inside and out, but yet he didn't know the storm that was gathering inside of me, or the thoughts in my head.

Thoughts that seemed outlandish to think when we were lying in bed together, calm and content.

"It's not that," I said, and I sighed before I could stop it.

Killian paused. "What's wrong?" His voice rose, as did his heartbeat.

"I just…" I tried to think of a way to say this. I wasn't going to tell him everything, but maybe planting the seed inside of his head would help him at least be more aware of it. "… I've noticed you're changing a lot," I began. I saw his mouth fall into a frown, and his eyes became troubled as well. "And… I don't like it."

Killian removed his hand from my face, and I caught a fleeting flicker of apprehension. "I said before… I just want to be treated more like an adult, instead of some weak damsel."

His eyes downcasted as he said this, but they lifted when he saw me shake my head. "It's not just that, Killi. It's how you acted at the festival, how we almost came to blows; it's this roughness towards me when you'd usually be… I don't know, submissive? You're challenging me, and you're stepping above just wanting to be treated like a man, you're acting like a little prick when the mood takes you." Killian's mouth dropped as I said this but I pushed on. "And I've seen you hiding your treatment of Kiki from me, and it's gotta stop. Killi… I don't want to argue, I just want you to promise me something, okay?"

Killian's mouth snapped shut and his lips disappeared into it. He deflected his gaze and said, over a sheet of ice: "Okay."

"Promise me you'll pay more attention to yourself… okay? And you'll tell me if you start seeing what I'm seeing. 'Cause I'm seeing you become more like me and… and I don't want to be partners with me, Killian."

Killian's face fell and his eyes widened. He started pulling away from me but I was confused as to what had triggered that reaction. I'd said a lot of things that could potentially cause this but this was rather sudden.

"What…?" I sat up as he ripped off his boxers and grabbed a clean pair of briefs. He turned around with the clean pair in his hands, and I saw his eyes become two blue flames.

"You're implying you're going to break up with me if I don't become that weak pathetic bitch I was before?" Killian said, his voice raising.

What? I rewound my mind to go over the words I had said, before I found the culprit. Saying I didn't want to be partners with myself.

I sighed at the stupidity of him. "I'd never leave you, Killian. I'm just using my fucking words and talking to you about what's bothering me, just like you've always dreamed. Don't shove it back in my face by throwing me a paper tiger." He'd taught me that saying by accusing me of doing it. I bet he regretted it now.

Killian pulled up his briefs. He opened his mouth to unleash hell, but as I rose off of the bed, I saw the anger disappear… and a look of anxiousness take its place.

"I don't want to be weak anymore," Killian said in a subdued tone. "I want to be a partner beside you."

I walked up to him and took him into my arms with a cluck of my tongue. "But it doesn't mean you have to go all psychotic, Killer Bee," I said lightly. "You're kinda going a bit overboard with this 'trying to be a man' campaign, and now you're starting to act like a little shit. Can't you see that?"

Killian put his arms around me too and rested his head on my shoulder. "Maybe…" he mumbled.

I smiled and kissed his ear. "I know you want us to be partners, and we are. We always have been… if you have to make the effort to be a little shithead, then that's not naturally you, right?"

His heart was beating rapidly against his chest, and it was meeting my own. Together they pushed against our ribs like they were knocking on one door, waiting for the other to answer.

"What if… I'm not trying," Killian suddenly said. "What if… I'm starting to have to try not to be like that…?" My brow knitted at this. "I've found myself getting angry a lot and I find myself… getting angry at you. When you talk to me and order me around – for some reason my brain no longer lets me take it and accept it. I keep feeling like I have to challenge you and… I don't like it." Killian pulled away; he looked concerned. "Reaver… I've been thinking." He put a hand to the back of his head and touched where his scar had been. "I think after we do what we need to do with Nero and Kiki… we should go back to the plaguelands house and look at the notes Perish left me."

I pulled back, surprised and taken aback by his words. "W-what? Why?" I asked confused.

"Because before he knocked me out for surgery he held up his own O.L.S, and something else," Killian explained. His expression was strained and I got the distinct feeling he was treading lightly over Perish's mention. Not for my benefit, but because I think he missed the crazy idiot.

But wait… it took a moment before my brain clicked. "Something else?" I said out loud. My eyes widened. "You think he put something in your head to make you into an asshole?"

Killian's stricken gaze turned flat. "I was going to phrase it better, but… I just want to rule it out. It was an interesting looking thing." He rubbed his short blond hair. "A small piece of metal but coming off of it was at least a dozen thin wires with silver balls on the end."

"You don't think… he put his O.L.S in you…?" As I said that I realized that couldn't be true. He'd eaten one O.L.S, the other was still in my pocket.

Killian shook his head, but then hesitated. "I… I actually ate Perish's O.L.S and it was empty. He used the brain matter inside to make me immortal, and no remnants of who made you immortal remains after. I tricked Silas but…" He sighed. "I dropped Sky's O.L.S." As I reached into my pocket Killian made an angry noise, directed at himself. "If we had it, we would have Silas eating out of… oh my fucking god!" I pulled the O.L.S out of my pocket and grinned at him.

I could almost hear Killian's mind explode as he took the O.L.S from me and examined it. "How!" he gasped. I had never seen that much awe on his face. It was like I had just told him that Santa Claus was real. "Where did you find it?"

The grin didn't leave my face, and in truth, it wasn't because of the O.L.S. It was over the prospect that what was happening to Killian was organic, something Perish might've implanted in him. If that was the case, it meant it could be taken out… and I'd have one less thing to worry about. It made me want to say fuck Nero and run to the plaguelands now.

"You had it clutched in your hand when you were resurrecting," I explained. I almost felt giddy and my jovial aura was being matched by his own. The entire room seemed lighter now. I never realized how much I missed Killian until the prospect that it could all be a device was presented to me. "We could fucking destroy Silas if we ever wanted to." But then my grin turned into a smirk. "It'll be a gambling chip for all of eternity, but we're not doing shit now." I took back the O.L.S and kissed his cheek. "Right now we're going to pay back Nero, then go to the plaguelands and find out what Perish did to you. Then we can take it out and make you normal again."

Killian kept his smile but I saw unease in his eyes. "It… it might not be that though, hun. I just wanted to make sure… you know?"

I shook my head, my mind concreting it as fact automatically. "No, it is. It explains your attitude perfectly. It was something Perish did to you. I know that for sure now. That's why you've been acting so unlike yourself, that's why I don't recognize you sometimes." I kissed his cheek before my lips shifted to his own.

But when I tried to kiss them, he pulled away.

"You... don't recognize me?"

"It doesn't matter... it was Perish. You'll be back to normal soon," I said reassuringly, joy ripped through my heart. I started to change into my clothes. "We have our plan there is no need to wait. Let's get that asshole back so we can go back to the plaguelands house; and when we find out what that device is..." I put a hand on Killian's head and shook it playfully, refusing to have his crestfallen look kill the happiness and pure relief I was feeling. "... we can take it out and I'll have my Killi Cat back. Just think, Killian... after you're fixed everything can go back to the way it was. I can go back, and you can go back." I took in a deep breath and sighed.

Then I saw Killian's eyes well. "What...? This is good, Killian... it means you're–" Killian pushed past me, and with a shuddered sniff, he walked out of our bedroom.

CHAPTER 24

Reaver

IT FELT GOOD TO HAVE THE WIND IN MY FACE, AND the goggles that Kiki had given me were a godsend. There were no more annoying little specks of greywaste ash getting into my eyes, even though I always thought I looked like a tool with riding goggles.

Killian was behind me and he had his arms wrapped around my stomach. He'd been sulking ever since I'd expressed my joy over getting that implant out of his head, but now that we were on the road and heading towards Melchai, all of this had been pushed aside and the mood around the three of us had taken a more serious turn. Before anything happened with the potential implant in Killian's head, we had to break out Nero and Ceph.

And Killian knew how to do it… he'd pulled the same worm out of my neck. Killian had reassured me that he could do it and quickly, and as soon as we had one brute with his mind back he'd be able to break Mantis's fucking neck. I'd seen that guy, we could take him, and Angel Adi if he was there. All we needed was just one brute chimera.

As the greywastes flew past me, a quiver of adrenaline ignited. It made my lips curl into a smile, but to say that it was happiness I was feeling was a gross understatement. There was nothing positive taking place underneath my skin, only the dark satisfaction that tonight I would finally have my revenge. I would have Nero underneath my muddy boot and he would be the one strung up like a puppet and dismantled.

No, maybe there was happiness in that, but it was a sadistic happiness that could only be drawn up and nurtured by me. One that would have made any normal person cringe and turn away like they were gazing upon an abomination of the world, because no one in their right mind would be happy about the sick things I had planned for Nero, and his husband.

And this time – Killian would be right beside me, right beside me and hopefully adding onto the sick, disgusting ideas that I would come up with during my time with Nero. My mind was a creative playground that only I was allowed to play in, sometimes Reno, but this time I was going to bring this formerly submissive and polite little blond kid to my dark side.

That would be his only taste of sadism, because after that I would be removing that implant and bringing him back to the Killian I had fallen in love with. He'd get one opportunity to show me just how sick he could be, but just one.

This thought did make me smile. I had never felt happier. I felt so happy I knew if I let go of the handles of the quad I would float away. I don't think I had ever felt this much euphoria, or maybe it was just my own bloodlust taking on a different form.

Oh, I was going to fuck Nero until his intestines came out of his ass, and then maybe I would make Ceph suck out the rest of them.

Yes. That would be fun to see.

Everything was indeed coming up Reaver.

I nudged Killian and he shifted to the left so I could check over my shoulder. Being pulled in an old metal trailer behind the quad, was Kiki. He was leaning against the painted black frame looking into the northern greywastes to make sure we were alone. None of us were expecting to see anyone but I felt better having another pair of eyes on the lookout. Kiki had Killian's Killi whistle around his neck in case he saw something; he wouldn't have to blow it hard to alert me.

Kiki had a brave expression on his face. I had to give that kid credit, he was a twink and a bit of a ditz, but there was no mistaking he was a chimera. It was kind of the same transformation I had seen in Jade. They acted one way when they were safely with their masters, being pampered and fucked into a coma every night, but when they were thrown out into the greywastes and forced to act like adults, they did step up to the plate. Kiki was a brave kid; hell, he was mortal but he still threw those grenades into the middle of the festival and saved Killian and I from being burned alive. Plus Mantis would've most likely found out we were immortals before we woke up, and we'd have one of those worms inside of us.

In truth, I really held little animosity towards Kiki. Everything the kid had done was under Nero's orders, and as much as it filled my mouth with brine to admit, that Kiki didn't know me from any other asshole greywaster. Like Kiki had said, it hadn't been personal. I would let Killian fuck him, and if Killian would let me, I'd have a go at him, just to hear him squeal, but after I'd let him be.

He would never go back to Skyfall though. I wouldn't risk him alerting the others. Killian will fucking murder me, but Kiki was mine now; and once I found one in Melchai, I'd be putting a collar around his neck.

I was getting ahead of myself though. We weren't going into this with a real solid plan, but everything was so up in the air I didn't know how much of this I honestly could plan. The mansion, from the drawing that Kiki had made, was huge and with two floors, an attic and a basement which Kiki was positive was an underground laboratory. Behind the mansion was a trail that led through the mountain, not unlike the trails we took to Reno's house, or the ones in the red canyons north of Aras, but this led to an enclosed valley. One that apparently was full of abominations, trees, greenery and… at least one more chimera, which I assumed was the born immortal.

Our plan was to follow the path Kiki had taken to escape from the mansion. It would take us up the steep rise and then we'd supposedly see the house below. We were going to make some noise and lure one of them out. If it was Nero or Ceph, we'd jump them, if it was someone else… we'd take him and hold him as ransom to get Nero and Ceph. All this time we were going to be wearing face masks which Killian had made in a haste. They were basically a pair of socks cut and stitched big enough to be put over our heads, with eye holes and ear holes.

So we looked like hobo bank robbers but it was what it was.

Killian's grip around my waist tightened when Melchai came into view. I turned off of the road right before we hit a stretch of bumper to bumper vehicles forever stuck in traffic, and started towards the modest rocky hill that, according to Kiki and from where the cloaked chimeras had descended for the festival, held the mansion somewhere inside.

This feeling inside of me was acting like a potent drug. Not only was I riding on the adrenaline of knowing that all of my problems were soon going to be resolved, it was also a nice feeling not to have to worry about getting Killian killed. There were a lot of bad things that could happen during this screwed up rescue mission, but Killian dying wasn't one of them. I wouldn't say that this was a little less planned because of that fact, but when your worst case scenario is no longer losing the boy you love... you tend to jump into things a little easier than you would before.

And Killian had been demanding for the last few months for me to treat him like an adult and not a damsel, and he had been taking charge when he had to, so... maybe I was starting to realize I could rely on him for certain things.

When I parked the quad underneath a deposit of grey rocks, all clustered together like giant dinosaur eggs, I shared this with him.

In return I got a beaming smile which quickly turned shy. "You don't know how much it means to me for you to say that," he said. And because Kiki was there I didn't get a kiss for it, only a squeezed hand and a bright look.

"But if I'm giving you orders and you disobey me..." I said in a warning tone. I didn't want him to get cocky. He was even more pre-disposed to that since his campaign of being a haughty little back talking shit. "I will stop looking at you as someone I can depend on if things get heated. You have to fucking listen to me, okay?"

Killian nodded all too seriously. "You can trust me. You know you can."

I hoped I could.

We all loaded ourselves up with weapons. I had my M16 on my back, a pistol and my combat knife on my hip, and explosives in my pocket. I also had a knife belted to my leg as well and had strapped one to Killian's leg too. It was Nero's according to Kiki, but it was Killian's now.

The cicaro kid was also armed to the teeth, and he had a bullet proof vest on him, done up tight. He was wearing it underneath a black button-down, and over top of that was a black leather jacket with chains hanging down off of the pockets. His pants were tight against his body too. Kid had nice legs.

I turned around from devouring the kid with my gaze, to see Killian giving me a look that would've burned a weaker man to cinders.

"Like you wouldn't look twice at that," I said as I motioned behind me. I glanced over my shoulder and saw Kiki glance up from buttoning up his cuffs. He saw the two of us and flushed. Killian was still murdering me with his eyes so I thought I'd play nice. When Kiki's back was turned I slapped Killian's backside and pinched it. I got a giggle for that and a swat.

"You seem pretty relaxed for what we're doing," Killian said as he tested out the beginning of the rocky hill in front of us with his boot. It wasn't as rocky close up as it seemed to be from the road we'd been driving on. For the most part, it was made up of compacted dirt and brittle brush and grass, with grey-brown rocks erupting from random places like the hill had papilloma. It wasn't the best for being discreet, I could see the discolouration in the dirt from Kiki's descent, but it was better than going in head-on.

I looked at the sky darkening all around us. "We need to get to the top before dark, or blindy here is going to fall," I said to Kiki with a hand on Killian's shoulder. "It's too bad we couldn't make nice with Mantis. He might be able to give you night vision." I secured the leather strap holding my M16 and motioned for the boys to follow me. "Hey, Kicky. Silas can do that right? Give you guys the enhancements after the fact?"

"So he has his own nickname now too?" I heard a crisp voice snip beside me. I didn't turn around and watched as Kiki nodded, now zipping up his leather jacket and starting on the hill.

"Yeah. It isn't rare for one of our enhancements not to develop during our time in our steel mothers," Kiki said as we all started to climb. The moon was behind us, just starting to make itself visible over a string of mountains off to the east. I could see trees on the hills in front of it, jagged black rises full of prickles, like a giant arching cat. "A chimera who's our doctor and really intelligent, Sidonius, or Sid, can perform them. He's Nero's friend. I know Nero will be sore–"

"You know what? Why don't I give you a nickname?" Killian suddenly said in a pissed voice.

"–sore towards you after what you probably have planned. But Nero forgives easily–"

"I think I'm just going to call you fucking douche–" In a flash, I put Killian in a headlock and stuffed my black sock-mask inside his mouth. He started struggling and trying to wiggle away but I pushed my fingers into his mouth and, as such, the mask as well. I grinned at Kiki and the kid blushed and bit on his lower lip to hide a smile.

"Go on," I said.

Kiki muffled a giggle as Killian started biting my hand through the mask, digging in his feet and flailing his arms to try and get any piece of my flesh he could. "–he forgives easily and I think he would give Killian all the enhancements just as a thanks for saving him and Ceph and not hurting me. Sid doesn't know Killian. So he could just do it as a secret favour for Nero, and Silas wouldn't even have to know."

I let go of Killian, who gasped and started grabbing his throat once he was free. He looked up at me with a hand still on his neck and I saw Satan himself in those blazing blue eyes. Eyes that were about ready to grab the assault rifle on his back and riddle me with holes.

I grinned back and stuck out my tongue; I blew a raspberry at him.

Killian's lips pursed to hide his own smile, then he gave me a hard push. "I'm going to pay you back for that, douche bag. But I'm going to be the mature one and just be happy that you're in a good mood."

And just to show how good I was feeling, and to give him the reassurance I knew he needed, I roughly slapped my hands onto both sides of his face and gave him a long drawn-out kiss. Not just a PG one either. I opened up his lips, locked them with mine, and found his tongue. I ran my tongue over it and his greeted me back, a small and subdued moan tickling his throat which was followed by a sharp increase in his breathing.

When our lips broke, Killian's cheeks were red and warm, and his pulse quickening. I glanced at Kiki, who was biting his lip again, before I put my arms around Killian and whispered in his ear. "After this is done, and they're all tied up... before we have our fun, I'm going to make the sweetest love to you. Just some personal stuff that we've been missing... before I make you into a man on that little twink's body."

Killian shuddered and swallowed through what I was sure was a dried throat. "You...think you can?"

"When I have that piece of shit firmly under my boot... I'll be able to do a lot more than that, Killi Cat." I kissed his neck and motioned to Kiki. "Okay, no more talking, no more fucking around. We're going into stealth mode."

The boys nodded, Killian now looking just a bit more flustered, and they followed me while we climbed up the steep rise. This rise was one of many around this barren land, but none of them made mountains like the Coquihalla Highway. Everything was folded, with only slight lumps and bumps in the terrain before falling flat again. The mountains were just faint grey shrouds in the distance, surrounding us like we were inside of a giant bowl centered in the middle of it.

It made for better travel at least. Around Aras, north was the canyons and east was rough and rocky terrain that stretched from the canyons to the towns that eventually led us to Donnely. This place might border the plaguelands, and be so out of touch with what little society we had that they believed a chimera was a god, but at least you could get around quicker than where my old home was.

I caught Killian as his boot skidded on a dry stone, and braced my arm while he steadied himself. The higher up we got, the more rocks were jutting out of the ground, until soon we were climbing over them and weaving around the bigger ones. It was good cover, but Killian and Kiki were both making more noise than I was comfortable with. At least in the silence I could confirm that there were no cameras watching us. It seemed the rocky hills were a satisfactory enough cover for Mantis and Angel Adi.

And whoever else he had in there.

"Kicky," I hissed. He was a blue shadow, his orange eyes balls of silver light now that the steely darkness was covering everything around us. "Was it just Mantis and the other one in there?"

Kiki nodded and spoke quietly. "But Nero commented that there was at least one other man living in the valley. He didn't get a good look at him at all though."

But not living in the mansion? Good.

I jumped up onto a sleek rock and helped Killian up. Kiki, however, needed no help. Showing the stealth that I'd seen in Jade, he grabbed onto a ridge and climbed up it like he was half cat. Kiki stood on the rise but immediately he shrunk down. I took his lead and didn't stand upright when I'd finished helping Killian up. I stayed crouched and quietly turned around.

Below us I saw the mansion, well, more like a large house, not at all like the mansions I'd seen on television. It was an impressive size though, and tucked into a quarry much like Reno's house was.

It looked deceptively welcoming. There were LED lights in two of the many windows and one on the balcony. The lights on the balcony were illuminating closed blue curtains and the other two were downstairs: one in a picture window and the other in a kitchen. I could see inside of both. The two lit up windows had planters in front with flowers and greenery, and below, where the light hit, I could see a sea of green. It took me a moment to realize that it was grass, they actually had a lawn here.

There were trees as well, and hanging between two of them was a hammock. This place was like a suburban home in a Martha Steward magazine.

Yep, it definitely was… as my eyes carefully scanned the outline of the house I saw a concrete patio-area with outside furniture and even a fucking BBQ pit made out of polished stone.

Funny enough, I found myself feeling jealous at this setup. Here me and Killian were living in squalor without even a safe home to call our own since the plagueland worms came; and now, right in front of us, is this asshole living in radiation-free luxury. He was hidden from Silas and had a pretty sweet deal with the Blood Crow idiots giving them pretty slaves in exchange for seeds if they were good. Why the fuck couldn't me and Killian have something like that?

I paused, and my eyes narrowed.

Why the fuck *couldn't* we have something like that? What the hell was stopping me? This was the greywastes and I now had Killian and my new cicaro to watch out for.

What had been a passing jealousy only seconds ago, was rapidly turning into an honest question. These idiots had electricity, a beautiful home protected from the family, with no one knowing where they were, and a valley of animals and fruit trees just down the road. We could wear the masks and keep fooling the Blood Crows into thinking we were the prophet and Angel Adi or, fuck it, put on a show and convince them we were the new prophets.

Or just fucking kill them.

The idea burned in my head, and the more I gazed down at the mansion, and the warm and welcoming lights that shone around it, the more I realized I wanted to live there.

I was a fucking born immortal chimera. I was Reaver Merrik, son of Greyson and Leo Merrik. I took what I wanted and did what I fucking wanted too.

A rather evil smile came to my lips. I looked at Killian. "Do you want it?" I said as I motioned to the mansion.

Killian looked at me and I saw confusion. "What do you mean?" His eyes narrowed and I knew he didn't trust the smile on my face.

"I mean this is a paradise that Silas doesn't know about. Why take Nero and Ceph out and to our plaguelands home and risk getting taken over by those worms… when we can stay right here. Mantis is one man and I can take Adi… do you want this place? I'll give it to you and it can be ours."

Kiki swore, he was kneeling to my left. I looked over at him. "You'll be staying with us. I don't trust you to go back to Skyfall."

"… what about Nero and Ceph after you – you get your revenge?" his small voice squeaked.

He thinks I'll let them go, but I won't. If I have to put a slave collar instead of a leather one on Kiki to keep him from escaping I would, but right now I needed him to think eventually I'll let Nero go. "After I've tortured him for a month, you three assholes can stay in one of the houses in *my* new valley," I said, which was a complete lie. "You three aren't going back to Skyfall from the sounds of it anyway. You help us take it over… you stay safe."

"We stay and…" Kiki's voice trailed before his smile came to greet my own.

"We become gods," I said and I turned to Killian. "What do you say, Killi? You want to become a god with me?"

Killian broke our eye contact and looked down at the mansion below us. There were a lot of unknowns down there, and we could very well be walking into something bigger than we might be able to handle.

But I didn't fucking care. I wanted this and I was sick and fucking tired of not getting what I wanted.

"Let's do it," Killian said, and I saw his face darken. Instead of getting pissed at his menacing look, I found myself turned on. This side of him could be sexy when this roughness wasn't directed at me. "We were almost burned at the stake because of that asshole, and I was almost tossed to his little born immortal pet for him to lose his virginity on. Let's show them just what we can do, and show them you don't fuck with chimeras."

And at this, I slid down off of the rock and my boots slammed down onto the compacted dirt and yellow grass. Kiki jumped down to my left, and Killian to my right. All three of us started walking down the ridge; Killian's hand in mine to help him see in the darkness, and Kiki's shoulder brushing against my own.

I felt like howling to the moon. I felt like running in there with my gun in hand and shooting everything that moved. Claiming this place as my own and sticking my flag into the green grass that I could now smell sweet on the air. I was the clone of King Silas and Sky Fallon, the men who destroyed the world, one of them now ruling it. If I was no longer going to take Silas's throne, I could at least stake my claim on a small oasis in this dead world. The greywastes should be happy this was all I was asking, because if fate had turned out differently I would be demanding much more than this.

"Kiki," I said to him. "You stay–"

"No," Kiki cut me off, his voice low. "I'm a chimera. Nero never lets me do anything; he's too overprotective. If I'm going to live here with you, I want to have a hand in taking this place. I owe Mantis for what he did to my master and Ceph. Let me come."

I could respect that. "Get your gun out, shoot whoever you see. If they matter, they're immortal anyway. Understand?"

Kiki nodded, and when I looked at Killian, he nodded back with a serious yet excited look on his face. Fuck, did he ever look beautiful under the glow of my night vision. If I could just channel his new attitude into shit like this... I'd love this new side of him.

The three of us skidded down the rest of the hill and landed on the grass with three muffled *thunks*. We all got behind a large tree and started digging through my pockets.

But Kiki held up a hand to stop me.

"If you will..." Kiki said quietly. "Mantis shares a similar affection for a certain animal. I know how to lure him, or any chimera in there, outside." I gave him a puzzled look but Kiki only smirked back. He swallowed before, to my amusement...

He meowed like a frightened cat. A long, mournful howl like Greyson and Leo's old siamese cat made when she forgot which room we were in. I shook my head at the kid, despising myself for quickly growing fond of the little shit, and drew my M16. Killian followed suit and so did Kiki, and all of our focus was on those sliding glass doors.

Kiki meowed again, and his howl hung in the air before it was swallowed up by the silence. I realized then that I couldn't hear a generator, not even the muffled hum of one in a noise-proof shed like mine and Reno's in Aras. This made me even more excited to take this place over. If it was energy self-sufficient we'd rarely need to go into Melchai, and by the time we needed to, we'd have convinced those losers that we were their new gods.

Two hearts on either side of me jumped when we saw Mantis look out the window. His face was creased with confusion and his hands were at his hips. He looked like a suburban dad in that moment, he was even wearing a purple robe that was done up at the waist.

Mantis disappeared for a second before he came back with a tin. He opened the sliding glass door and stepped outside, slippers on his feet, and started shaking it. It rattled, undoubtedly full of cat treats.

"Kit-kit-kit-kit kitty!" Mantis sang. I rolled my eyes, and if we didn't have to be so quiet I knew there'd be several snickers coming from us. We stayed quiet though, frozen like statues and just shadows behind this large tree. Admittedly, we could've been hidden better, but I knew the lights from inside would blind Mantis, his night vision wouldn't be working and his normal vision would render the backyard nothing but black.

"Tommy!" Mantis called. Oddly, he looked up at the trees and shook the tin again.

My heart spasmed when I heard a snap above us followed by the heavy sound of beating wings. My eyes shot to Mantis to gauge his reaction and saw a smile on his face before he took a step back.

A black creature flew down. A giant bat, I think? It dropped from the tree its wings spread out, then it landed in front of Mantis. It folded its leathery black wings behind its body and stepped into the light.

It was a fucking cat... a cat with wings.

Holy shit. I had completely forgotten. Killian had mentioned these little fuckers, last year before we went to Donnely. He'd read that book to me and commented that Skyfall had them, but their wings were more bat-like than the fluffy wings they had in the book.

Sure enough, Killian nudged me gently. I nodded, watching this cat's tail stick straight up in the air as Mantis opened a silver tin of treats. My ears were so in tune to the activity around us, I picked up a low purr as the excited cat waited patiently for its treat.

I almost forgot why the fuck I was there.

As Mantis turned around, the cat on his heels, I raised my M16, got Mantis into my scope... and I pulled the trigger.

A sharp bang echoed off of the ridges surrounding us, and though I braced myself for the recoil, my back still hit the rock behind me. I watched as the bat-cat jumped a mile high, and as Mantis was thrown off of his feet, the top of his head getting blown off and brains and blood shooting out of him like a cherry bomb had detonated inside of his head, the cat skidded into the house.

Mantis fell hard, the tin crashing to the floor with him. I hissed with success, but when Kiki motioned for us to run into the house, I held up my hand and waited to see if anyone else was around.

My eyes were fixed on the light behind the blue curtain, and I watched it to see if I saw any movement. There was none however. Mantis lay still, blood pooling behind his head, and with the spilled tin of cat treats all around him.

We waited and watched, and during that time the flying cat came back, with three other winged friends, and I watched with amusement as all four of them, ignoring their dead master, polished off every single treat that surrounded him. A big grey one, a tom cat considering he had nuts the size of marbles, even took several licks of Mantis's blood before trotting back inside the house, nonchalant as fuck.

I analyzed the scene, and tried to tune out the boys' breathing to hear if anyone was approaching, but it seemed like Mantis was alone.

After watching the body for several minutes, I decided to slowly approach it with my blade drawn and my ears focused on what was around me. I knew chimeras could be quick though, and who knows what kind of enhancements the born immortal had.

Unfortunately my hearing wouldn't pick up what was inside the house, only the outside, so I kept a firm hold on the blade and trusted that the boys would be two more sets of eyes.

I stood over Mantis, and tapped the remains of the piece skull that had blown off, and picked up a chunk of his brain.

I popped it into my mouth and ate it. I heard Killian hiss at me but I waved him off and picked up a bigger piece. I hadn't had fresh arian in forever, and it was a huge no-no to eat brains because of kuru. Now I was immortal and didn't have to worry about prion diseases, so I started eating the bigger piece without care and started sizing up the rest of his body. That would be one way to make sure he resurrected slowly. If Mantis had cold storage, which he undoubtedly did, we could hang him up, age him a bit, and eat good until fall. If we found Angel Adi, all the more fresh arian.

This was shaping up to be a good–

"Reaver!" Killian suddenly shrieked. At that precise moment I felt a back-breaking impact on the back of my head. I fell to my knees, the lights getting knocked out of me, and flattened myself against Mantis's body knowing what was coming next.

And I was right, a second later gunshots rang through the air. I heard a bellow behind me and I lizard crawled out onto the patio and stood up when I was out of the boys' range. I looked to see what had gotten me and saw the red-haired one, Ceph, on the ground.

Killian and Kiki ran towards the sliding glass door, but I barked at them to stay put. I sprinted over and picked up my dropped combat knife and watched Ceph intently.

I watched and waited, and sure enough, the worm I knew was inside of Ceph tried to escape. At first it was just a flicker of shadow in one of his nostrils, then it slithered out and began flapping back and forth as if trying to free itself from inside of Ceph's body.

I pulled it out and sliced it in two, then I rolled Ceph onto his stomach and motioned the boys over to me. As they approached, I stabbed Ceph in the back of the neck and made a good gouge, and whistled when I saw strings of black pulsing from the wound I'd made.

"An important note apparently," I said, glancing up at Killian. I started slicing the worms and pulling them out; feeling their coiled bodies retracting as I did, like I was grabbing a snake. "They either breed inside of them, or others come and infest them too." I handed the pieces of still wiggling worms to Killian so he could give them a few more slices. "It doesn't look like Mantis was infected, but we know for sure Nero is." I looked over my shoulder. The dimly lit living room looked like something out of a museum, one of those classical houses that sophisticated serial killers live in, and there were bookshelves everywhere, telescopes and electronics too. "We know Nero's in here, but that's it. Watch out for each other. I was infected by one of those things and I can tell you... you won't even know it's in you. Come on."

"Do you think the cats are infected?" Killian asked. His face was a strange mixture of brave and terrified.

"No. Unless they're immortal cats. I don't think it takes long for the animals to die from the parasite... and then it seems like they use their own bodies to control the person, like a puppet." I looked down at Ceph. "He was walking normally, but maybe they're there to control immortals after they die."

"So if we get infected... we'll awaken still under their control," Killian said grimly.

"Yep."

We walked from the living room to the open kitchen which had two lit hallways branching off of it. The first one just had more closed doors, but the second looked like it led to an open area.

I was right. At the end of that hallway, adorned with a red rug and black recessed lighting, was the main entrance to the house. Right in front of us was an oak staircase twisting up to the second level, and to the left, double doors which were reinforced with metal and had the same cardkey activation that Perish's laboratory had.

I paused when I walked into the heavily decorated room. Every part of this mansion that I had seen before was ritzier than the last, and it was obvious that someone with art sense had gotten a hold of this place.

The entrance room I had walked into was painted coffee brown, with panelling that started halfway down the wall and the red rug I'd seen previous was covered in swirling little designs. As I looked around to take everything in, I saw intricate paintings hung up on all four corners, the ones that looked to have been made in the old-old times, and statues pressed against the walls. One of them was almost as tall as me. It was a statue of a curly-haired man, made of white granite or another type of rock, and below it a taxidermy of a grey wolf with its lips peeled back in a snarl.

Then I saw something near the staircase reflecting in the dim lighting, and decided to walk to it. I was fascinated to see that the table had a glass top, and inside were rocks with crystals growing out of them, or clustered inside. Some of them were white, others purple, and all of them were sprouting from the rocks like beautiful little tumors. They were also laying on purple cloth that looked good enough to eat; it was all purply and velvet.

These things were all just unwanted distractions though. I told myself I would have all the time in the world to look at these things and motioned towards the stairs with my head. "I'm going up there," I said. I knew there was someone up there from the light I had seen. "Killian. I want you to have my back. Stay and guard the stairs." When Killian nodded, a dead serious look on his face, I turned to Kiki. "Where's the lab you said you saw the guys emerge from?"

Kiki turned around and walked to the wooden door beside the stairwell. I drew my gun and pointed it over the cicaro's shoulder as he pushed the door open, in case there was someone on the other side, but it was empty.

Which door led to the lab was obvious. Exactly like the doors in Donnely, and the ones I had seen in Sky's lab. It was metal and without windows, and there was a keycard slot with a red light beside it.

"The other two doors, one is an office, one is a bedroom," Kiki said, and he pushed the door all the way open so it would stay. "Be careful, Master Reaver." The cicaro inclined his head to me; I ignored the twitch I saw in Killian's eye.

I squeezed Killian's shoulder before I turned from the two and started slowly walking up the flight of stairs. My other senses strengthened with every step, but the one I was most focused on was my hearing. If there was someone upstairs they would've heard my M16 go off. Silencer or not that fucking thing was loud, and the steep ridges that surrounded this mansion would have the sound bouncing off of them like a pinball.

My eyes were fixed on the top of the stairs, but I saw nothing. Unfortunately the light on the second level was buggering my night vision, but I could make out the gold frame of a painting that was hanging over top of a wooden table full of flowers and books. That was it, no brother holding a big gun or a parasite whipping around in search for a living host for it to penetrate.

I reached the top of the stairs and looked in both directions. I saw the faint glow of light from underneath one of the doors, and channelling all of my knowledge on being quiet and stealthy, I walked towards the door. My ears were filling with static at this point, the only other noise was my own heartbeat which I was trying, unsuccessfully, to block from my chimera hearing. I kept on straining to hear something, anything, to tell me if there was someone in that room.

Perhaps this was Mantis's bedroom, and he had the light on before bed? I should've asked Kiki where Mantis's room was.

Suddenly an ear-shattering noise ripped through the tense air; the deafening sound a thousand times more loud and painful with my hearing fully tuned. Unable to help myself I yelped and jumped, and quickly slammed my M16 down on the table so I could cover my ears. I gritted my teeth, the pain temporarily disabling me, and when I'd retracted my enhanced hearing I realized someone had turned a music player on in the bedroom. I swore under my breath and picked up my gun again.

Then I heard a surprised yelp from downstairs. I whirled around and started running towards the stairwell – but something grabbed my arm and whipped me backwards.

I saw a bare, muscular arm locked against my own for a fleeting second before I was yanked towards him, then past him, and thrown against the wall. My M16 dropped from my grasp on impact and landed onto the floor with a *thunk*, and my face met the painting. Stars burst into my vision and I stumbled back, my balance lost in the confusion.

But before I could fall, my mind snapped into action. I purged myself of all senses of confusion and pain, and I went into survival mode. In what seemed to last minutes but in reality was only seconds, I regained myself and whirled around to face the person who had grabbed me.

It was Nero. In front of me was Nero.

He was smiling at me with a manic grin that split his face like a deep throat wound, and his mismatched eyes were sparkling and vivid gems in the recessed lighting above us.

For a moment, just one small – fucking – moment, I was frozen, my feet rooted to the ground. There was something inside of me, an automatic conditioning, which rendered me incapacitated when I was finally faced with him. Something was stopping me from doing anything but being that trapped dog tied to the bed; that victim awaiting the next brutal assault on his body.

But my nature made me proud. That survival mode snap, the same one I'd experienced moments ago, rushed to me and pushed that conditioning out of the way, then screamed at me to prove I was in control and that I had no weaknesses.

And I was in control. I reached to my belt, drew my combat knife, and started backing away from him.

Nero kept grinning, his eyes brightening and an obvious window into his thoughts. I could practically see the movie playing in his mind. I knew he was seeing me naked and bloody underneath him. I knew he was reliving the times he successfully broke me, the times he made me scream in pain. Or the times he forced me to cum. I knew Nero, and I knew him well, worm infested or not, at his core he was still the same asshole.

But I was no longer chained and bound, and though I still had hairline cracks all throughout me I was actively finding ways to repair them. I might have my issues, but I was the fucking Reaper. I was the killer of immortals.

And he was in my fucking world now.

"Hello, Nero," I said, keeping my voice as steeled, as level, as I could. I felt a smile break my own lips, through a jaw locked tight, and I forced it into a grin. "You're far from Skyfall." I took another step back, not wanting to make it obvious I was backing away from him, and kept my eyes locked on his. There was a hope inside of me that our fixed gaze would dissuade him from realizing what I was doing.

But it backfired. Nero mock advanced on me, and to my own inner resentment, I flinched. Nero let out a barking snarl at this and his head lowered.

When he lowered his head, however, I saw it. A brown scab at the nape of his neck, one that blended in almost perfectly with the slight curls of his, now longer, black hair. It was about the size of a Dek'ko token and in the middle of healing. It was almost in the exact same area that my own had been when I'd been temporarily infected.

That was my target.

My back hit the wall at the far end of the hall. I looked to both sides and saw the open door of the bedroom I'd seen from outside and another closed one. The bedroom I could dash into to jump out of the window, but I wasn't going to run from him. I needed to get him to turn around and give me access to his neck.

But how would I do that without him breaking my damn arms? I had to think quickly.

"I need to talk to Mantis," I said as I stared into the bedroom; that was the first thing that jumped to the front of my mind. "Take me to him."

My eyes temporarily shot to his and I saw that his grin had become a crooked half-smile, and as if the smile was weighing down the side of his head, he tilted it. He looked at me with false affection and winked, then took a step closer.

And then, to my surprise, he spoke.

Or… the worm spoke?

"I'll take you to Mantis, but first you need to do something for me," Nero said sweetly. His expression, even when holding a smile, looked menacing. He had an oval-shaped face, eyebrows trimmed to have arches, and a strong chin and jawline speckled with black stubble. That face had such a resounding effect on me now, I felt my mind stop and go like someone was pressing fast forward and pause at the same time. The psychological effects of my time with him was fighting with my pride, a fight to the death in front of my eyes but the only physical sign I let show was a hard swallow.

"What do you want me to do?" I managed to say, and my eyes deflected to the grey carpet in the bedroom to my right.

Nero chuckled, and this time when he took another step I saw brown loafers. He was close enough to me that I could see his feet.

"Why can't you look me in the eye, Reaver? How can I tell you if you won't look at me?"

My eyes widened. I realized then that he was right. I was doing everything to avoid looking him in the eye, and when I did I found any excuse to look away, just like the weak piece of shit I had become in his bedroom. Seconds after being face-to-face with Nero, not even real Nero, parasite Nero, I was plunging back into being that caged animal.

So with a clench of my teeth I looked up at Nero, and looked him dead in the eye. Fireworks exploded throughout my vision as I stared at him and he stared back. Looking him in the eyes filled me with such a rage I felt my body shake, unable to contain the physical feelings he was drawing out of me.

Sensing my state, a cold laugh rolled from his lips and he tilted his head again. This time when he did, I saw the shadows of the scab behind his neck again. My hands twitched at this, the knife was on my belt, I just had to get to it.

Nero closed the last foot of space and looked down at me with a lurid grin. "Kiss me," he growled. He flicked his tongue in a perverted, lewd fashion and bit down on it before he wiggled his eyebrows at me and continued to devour my body with his eyes.

But I kept my cool, I let him have his dominance. I calmed the beast screaming and throwing itself against my rib cage, and though I felt like I was floating on air from the sheer anger it was filling me with, I nodded.

I fucking nodded and motioned him towards me. "Come here." My words didn't sound like my own, solely because they were never words I thought I'd say, but they spilled from my mouth regardless.

And to further hammer in my compliance, I put a hand on his waist and drew myself to him.

Nero grinned at me and put a burly arm behind my back, slid it down to my ass and grabbed it roughly.

Red filled my pulsing skull to the point of bursting, and my body continued to shake from rage. I was surprised the fabric of the universe hadn't torn itself to shreds from this crime against nature I was about to perform, but the world kept on turning.

And, as such, I kept performing. With the red now translating to an intense pressure that tried to push my brain out from behind my eyes, I did it. I let Nero wrap both of his arms around me, pulling me to him in a firm embrace, and before I closed my own eyes I saw his close, and those thin lips surrounded by stubble, inch towards mine.

Our lips met and his immediately encouraged mine to open up more. I hesitated to give him a challenge, and let him start to suck on my mouth and lips. In an oddly and confusingly gentle way, he softly pushed his lips against mine, nudging them open like he was lightly knocking on my bedroom door.

I had him, excellent. Discreetly so I wouldn't alert him, I grabbed the combat knife and pretended like I was hooking his upper arm. I opened one eye to get the angle right, then, with as much precision as I could, I drove the tip of the knife into the back of Nero's neck, right into the scab.

Nero bellowed and pulled away, but to my shock and confusion, when he jerked his head back… I saw what looked like a black cord between his lips–

–and it was leading into my own fucking mouth.

I inhaled sharply and dropped the knife, right as Nero stumbled backwards and lost his balance. The cord that went from his mouth to mine stretched, and I could feel it tugging behind my throat as it became taut; then, with a sharp spasm of pain and the sensation like a cactus was getting pulled from my mouth, the cord shot out from between my lips and landed on the fallen Nero like a severed rope.

Without thinking, I snatched my combat knife, and while Nero rolled on his back, gasping and groaning with his hand clutching his bloody neck, I grabbed the worm thrashing and writhing in Nero's mouth and cut off its head. I then wrenched it like I was pulling the cord of a lawnmower, and as Nero bellowed, trying to grab hold of the worm as well, I drew out the parasite.

It was long, fuck was it ever long. By the time the tip of it was withdrawn it was in ten pieces. There was no time to waste though. I grabbed Nero's shoulder and rolled him onto his stomach like I had Ceph. Nero swore at me and tried to get up but with a sound kick in the head he groaned and, for the moment, lay stunned.

Then I heard a shout from Killian downstairs and gunfire. I looked down the hall, horror rushing through me, but my attention was diverted when I saw a churn of movement inside the bloody gouge I'd made in Nero's neck. My eyes took me towards it, and though my mind screamed at me to run towards the gunfire, my attention was only on the contorting snare of black rope that was currently spilling out of Nero's wound.

Like Ceph, there were a lot of them, all of them seemingly braided into each other. I wasted no time, I punched Nero in the head to keep him down, and I started grabbing the strings like I was yanking out spaghetti, and started cutting and pulling, fucking cutting and pulling.

More gunfire downstairs and I heard Kiki yell something. "Killian, come upstairs!" I hollered. I wrenched out a long braided cord and slashed it with my knife; my hands quickly becoming covered in the brown-red liquid that was the worms' blood. I gritted my teeth and threw the cut up cords into the corner of the hallway and continued my extraction. "Killian?" I shouted, yanking more strings out of Nero. At least it seemed that all of the worms ended at his brain, so when I got the last of them, that should be the last. There wouldn't be any hidden ones in his fucking legs or anything.

"Killi?" I bellowed. I growled and snatched out another braid before slashing it, my knife cutting the red rug underneath us as I did. I looked inside the wound and opened it with my fingers to look for more but all I could see was blood and twitching muscle and tendons.

"You... I think you got 'em all," Nero suddenly croaked. He started to shift and somehow I trusted that it was him enough to jump off of his back. I looked towards the hallway, the hair on the nape of my neck prickling at the deceptive calm downstairs. There was no more gunfire, no more yelling, everything had become dead quiet.

Nero stood up. I turned to him, not knowing what to say, and as I stared at him I saw that his left eye was now missing, just a bloody hole with a loose eyelid. He seemed to have his mind still intact as well; mine had been scrambled after the parasite got into me but maybe he didn't have that much of a brain to begin with.

"We can talk about this shit after, pup," Nero said when we made eye contact. He must've seen the disdain in my eyes. "We gotta get our boys first. Truce?"

My mind screamed at his comment. A fucking truce? I didn't want a truce! I wanted to lunge at him and drive my knife up his ass. I wanted to fucking torture him and give him the nightmares for the rest of his immortal life. I wanted to turn *him* into a fucking flashback-suffering, weak fucking bitch he'd made me! A truce? Fuck you!

But as my inner voice shrieked this, and called me every derogatory name in the book, my head only nodded before my body turned and ran down the hallway. I heard thumping behind me as Nero quickly followed, that and metal clicking against metal.

When I got to the top of the stairs, I saw my M16 creep into my vision. I looked and realized Nero was holding it out to me, a sober expression on his flushed and blood-covered face. Without a word I took it, and ran down the stairs.

I stopped at the bottom of the stairs. "Killian?" I called, forcing down the anxiety that was clawing its way up from this overflowing pool of bad emotions currently holding me hostage. I looked around and swallowed hard when I saw nothing but an empty entrance and empty hallways. "Kiki?"

"You… you have Kiki?" Nero said behind me.

I nodded as I glanced over to the hallway where the laboratory door was, but before I could answer my body froze over what it saw.

The carpet runner was bunched up like there had been a lot of activity in the hallway. I sprinted to the hall, my eyes fixed on the ground, and when I saw blood splatters I let out a loud FUCK!

They can't kill him.

Keep calm. They can't kill him.

It wasn't much blood but it was there, a steady trail of it like Hansel and Gretel's bread crumbs. I followed it, and my eyes travelled to the closed laboratory door. Even though I knew it would do nothing, I tried the handle but it was locked.

Then I looked down, feeling something sticky on the handle, and realized my hand was coated in blood. It was all over the door knob.

I started pounding on the door. "Open the fuck up!" I yelled. I kept slamming my fists against it and once again pulling on the door knob. "Open the fucking door!" I swallowed down a scream of frustration and decided to try and keep my cool in front of Nero.

That lasted for about five seconds; I shoved the metal door with both hands. "Killian?" I pressed my ear up against it but I heard nothing, only Nero behind me also swearing colourfully. "Killian?" I shouted as loud as I could, but finally I shook my head and gave up. "There's no getting into that fucking door." Then something occurred to me, something my mind didn't want to even flirt with being a reality. "By the living room," I said. "I killed Ceph and Mantis…"

I turned around and saw Nero for a fraction of a second, before he disappeared back towards the entrance. "Cephy?" I heard him call. "Kiki?" I let him yell, knowing they weren't anywhere near us anymore, and re-traced the mysterious blood splatters. They took me to the kitchen, then into the living room, and then…

The foreboding I'd felt was correct.

"The bodies are gone," I said grimly. I looked around the living room and realized a struggle had taken place here. A side table had been overturned and broken, and a lamp was shattered beside the couch. The worms I'd cut out of Ceph were still there, lying dead, and the empty cat tin too... but that was all that remained from our initial assassination. Someone either came and managed to overpower the boys and get the bodies, or else... did I miss a parasite in Ceph and it had reanimated him?

Nero sprinted back. "Kiki?" His voice echoed throughout the mansion. "Come out, pickles. It's okay, it's me."

"He wouldn't hide from me. Killian wouldn't either." I shook my head at him and walked towards a puddle of blood, now with many smears and streaks, and kneeled over it. The puzzle pieces continued putting themselves together and I knew exactly what happened.

"I shot Mantis and the boys shot Ceph. I pulled the worms out of him. Maybe I missed one?" I said to Nero. I put my fingers in the blood and tasted it. I wasn't Elish though, or a blood-fiend, I couldn't taste the difference between chimera and greywaster blood, not yet anyway. "I'm guessing a worm reanimated Ceph and he overpowered the boys. There's a lab here, right?"

When I stood up I saw Nero, looking stressed and still bleeding heavily from the neck, nod and wipe a hand down his sweaty, flushed face. He wasn't the brute monster I'd seen in that bedroom. It was strange and unsettling to see him as a person and not that cackling, cocksure piece of shit I'd been imprisoned by. "Adler and Spike were in Adler's bedroom when you came," Nero said.

"Adler and Spike?" I asked. I didn't want to know, I didn't need another two people to worry about but I knew I didn't have a choice. Know your enemy; that was why I wanted to snoop around this place in the beginning. I wanted to know who Mantis was and...

Angel Adi... Adler. Well, that answers that.

Nero nodded. "Adler's a born immortal like you. Ceph was encased in concrete when Silas thought he'd failed the born immortal test, but it looks like you were the second Sky baby to get smuggled into the greywastes. He's a nice kid, I think, from how Mantis spoke of the servant I asked about, but unfortunately that isn't going to matter since technically... we're the bad guys in this."

"And who's Spike?"

"Spike... Spike's a part of your generation. Like Jade, he was supposed to die after Silas had his mental breakdown but like Jade... that didn't happen and he was sent away to live in the greywastes. He's a stealth and either science mixed in, or intelligence, I'm not sure which but he's a genius. Both he and Adler have been Mantis's lab rats. They heard what was going on out here and I'm guessing once the kittens were left alone they pounced. It couldn't have been Ceph if you gutted him. There needs to be multiple proxy worms to control a dead body; they work together and are all in your insides. If you took them out of Ceph, he wouldn't be able to come back."

Great. Elish had a nice little faction here apparently. This was dangerous. There were more chimeras here than I originally thought. Not just a scientist and a born immortal, but developed ones who knew how to fight and defend their home.

But this mansion was mine now. I couldn't just abandon the plan halfway through. I had to imprison the immortals, kill the mortals, and take this place over. Both because I wanted to get back at Mantis for what he did, and to keep my secret a secret.

"Is there an exit to this underground lab?" I asked. "Any way for us to rush it while Mantis and Ceph are dead?"

I saw Nero's teeth clench together then he shook his head. "No. I was down there, this is the only escape. They're locked down there until they surface and we'll be here waiting." He turned with a shake of his head and motioned for me to follow him. I did, and traced his steps into the kitchen, one with black cabinets and a stone island with stools lined up on the outer side. I leaned against the kitchen island and tried to steady my heart. It was in the process of trying to escape from my chest, just continuous thrashing beats that were sending jolts of adrenaline to my brain. A brain that kept telling me that Killian was going to die, and I had to burn the world to save him. It was wringing me like a damp washcloth, and no matter how many times I told and reassured myself that Killian wouldn't die, the voice was persistent.

Even if he was immortal though, I didn't want the kid far from me. At least, even if I hated it, he was getting stronger. Killian would be okay, maybe he'd be the one opening the door and coming out covered in blood, with a grin on his face and a story to tell me.

Fuck. It was hard not to worry about Killian dying. That had been my life since I'd started following him around. My existence had been keeping Killian alive, but now I just wanted to make sure he was safe and not... full of parasites.

I looked up when I heard a fridge door open, followed by the tinkling of bottles. Nero turned around with two bottles in-hand, and before he closed the door, I saw fruit, vegetables, and containers of food mixed in with the other bottles of beer.

As Nero approached me, I felt my body automatically stiffen, and when he offered me the beer I was frozen on the spot and unable to take it. I stared at it, the bottle already open and with vapour coming off of the spout like mist.

"It'll help. It's good stuff," I heard Nero say. I wanted to look up at him, stare directly into his eyes and glare him down but it was like I'd been thrown into suspended animation. "I got a shit ton of drugs too. We can do some and figure out just how the fuck we're going to get the kittens back."

When I didn't take the beer, he put it beside me and I heard his lips close around his own, then break away. "Thanks for not killing him."

My body stiffened like it had become stone. I'd rather face a roomful of parasites coming at me than be in this room with him. So badly did my mind scream at me to get away from him, but here I was, welded to the spot and useless.

"You... you are so about to fucking kill me though," Nero chuckled dryly. I saw a hand enter my vision and he picked up the bottle and tried to get me to take it. "Look, bro. It wasn't personal, alright? You just were the closest thing to a dude I really hate, and it got me off to finally get my hands on him. And, honestly, you fought too, which kind of drove me wild."

I looked up at him and saw him tipping the bottle of beer from side to side.

"Silas?" I asked, trying to talk through the knot in my throat.

Nero shook his head and took another drink. "Nah," he said when he lowered the bottle. "Sky. I hate that dude. Never met him but the entire family fucking despises him for what he did to Silas." His eyes, or his remaining eye anyway, looked at me, and I refused to look away this time.

But focusing on his face accelerated this growing storm inside of me. It was like staring at the sun, my eyes fucking burned, the temperature of my body was shooting to the sky. It infuriated me to feel these emotions, ones that I had used to never feel, be thrust upon my body without my say.

Why the fuck was I such a weak bitch now? Look at him, Reaver. LOOK AT HIM!

I kept staring, forcing myself to grow used to his presence. Like taking small sips of arsenic, I needed to build up an immunity to him. I couldn't fucking act like a pussy now. I couldn't show him that what he'd done had any permanent effect on me. If I did he'd look down on me and I'd rather die than have that son of a bitch think less of me.

I swallowed hard, my eyes laser focused on his. Nero stared back with the same expression of mild concern and fatigue, a look that was drawn out from his concern over Kiki. It had nothing to do with me and I couldn't show him that my own expression had anything to do with him.

LOOK AT HIM!

"Calm down, Ducky," Nero said and he pointed to the beer beside me with his own. "Have a drink before you start another fucking Fallocaust. I'm not going to hurt you."

Not going to hurt me? Not going to *fucking hurt me*?

Without even realizing I was nearing the edge of what my mind could handle... I exploded.

"Hurt me?" I snapped back. I pushed myself off of the kitchen island and grabbed the bottle of beer. I stalked up to Nero, who put his own bottle down with a *clunk*. "You think you have the fucking capacity to hurt me now? Do I fucking look tied up to you?"

Nero's eyebrows raised and I pushed myself into his space and put my face near his. Anger stole my breath and there was a pounding in my head like someone was beating a slab of sheet metal with a sledgehammer. "No, you mustn't know me well, Nero. Because the only fucking reason you were able to do that shit to me was because you had me chained like a fucking animal," I snarled. My body was trembling with the earthquakes of rage rumbling through it, percussion after percussion rocking me from my head to my toes. I didn't like this; I wasn't in control – but I couldn't stop. "You think you can fucking best me now? You fucking want to try and dance with me now, you cowardly fuck?"

Nero kept his stance, no sparkling lust inside of his eyes like what I'd seen when he'd been infected. He looked at me before waving his hand like he was swatting a fly. "Get out of my face, Duck. Stop puffing out your chest. I don't want shit from you."

"Want shit from me?" I bellowed. I pushed his chest, the spout of the bottle dangling between my fingers. "Want fucking shit from me?" The more I got worked up, the more I felt myself losing control. The darkness would soon descend over my vision, and take my sanity with it. But there would be no Elish to restrain me and talk me down. The only man who was able to keep me from plunging over the edge was long gone.

"Well, I fucking have shit for you, *bro*!" I hissed, dropping my voice; the words were flowing out of my mouth like I'd taken a hit of coke. I wanted to smash, kill. I wanted to expel this energy that was electrocuting me alive. "I have a fucking lifetime of shit for you. You fucking think it's bad with Silas? Just wait until I take over Skyfall, *puppy*. I will make you fucking sing like a canary." I pushed him again.

And when he did nothing but stare down at me with dismissive, cold regard, I cracked.

I clenched the bottle of beer and swung it as hard as I could over the side of his head.

It shattered on impact and Nero recoiled. He dropped his own bottle onto the floor, which broke against the hardwood, and stumbled backwards. I watched as he tried to steady himself as his legs wobbled underneath him.

"What the fucking–" Nero was abruptly cut off when, unable to stop, I grabbed him by the t-shirt he was wearing and pulled him away from the counter.

I shoved him towards the island. Nero slammed against it with a grunt and a curse, sending a toaster and an empty water glass sailing to the floor with a loud crash that reverberated throughout the mansion.

Nero grabbed his head, blood pouring out of the wound I could now see glistening in his black hair. He looked up at me angrily, but when his mouth opened to say shit I didn't fucking care about hearing, I dealt him a hard blow to the face; one that snapped his head to the left and sent him off-balance and struggling to keep himself from falling over.

"This is only the fucking beginning," I growled. I grabbed his ear and wrenched his head up, trying to force him to look at me. "You're going to wish you stayed encased in concrete, my friend."

Nero's remaining purple-blue eye drifted up to mine, streams of blood running down his face, travelling in the creases and collecting on his facial hair. He stared at me, and slowly removed his hand from his bleeding neck.

Then, to my own overwhelming fury, he laughed. "I really fucked you up, eh? Holy shit. I like... permanently damaged you, didn't I? You were so laughy and taunting with Kess and now look at you. You're broken. Where's your confident swagger?" He chuckled, my blood fucking boiled at that laugh. I found myself too stunned and infuriated at his words to speak. "If I knew you would get this damaged from being raped, I would've gone easy on you. I thought you could handle–" I suddenly heard a scream. Not a normal scream, but one drawn from the bowels of hell. A scream that could only be made by someone who had been through the worst kinds of torture, and was still being actively tortured. It had so many different octaves of pain, it was as if it had been handcrafted from the souls of the dead world.

And it was coming from me.

With the darkness enveloping my mind like a swarm of bees, distorting my vision and controlling me like a willing puppet, I grabbed Nero again. But he was ready for me this time. In slow motion, I raised the shattered glass bottle but Nero reached up and locked his hand over my wrist and dealt me a punch to my face. I didn't feel it, or acknowledge it, instead I raised my free hand, made it into a claw, and drove it towards his last remaining eye.

But before I could gouge out his eye, I felt a hard impact on my stomach. The force of it made me stumble back, and when Nero grabbed his bottle of beer and pommelled me across the face with it, I flew, and landed on the floor.

I coughed, the wind getting knocked out of me, and saw little white shards spray onto the floor. In my dazed state I stared at them dumbly, before realizing they were my teeth.

My mouth was gushing blood. I ran my tongue along my teeth and realized the entire bottom row were shattered, and the top row was almost entirely shards. I spat and inhaled, then started violently hacking blood and bits of tooth.

I saw brown loafers. I tried to rise but collapsed, my stomach throbbing with a dull ache and my feet slipping out from under me whenever I attempted to get up.

Then I saw the brown loafers themselves slip, the feet they were attached to wobbling. I looked up just in time for Nero to drop to his knees, red pouring from a scalp wound so deep I saw a flash of white skull.

Nero keeled over with a wheeze and glanced over at me, or at my stomach. I saw blood coming out of his ears and I knew he was as done as me.

But what was he looking at? I looked down and saw my shirt was ripped. This was my favourite red shirt and he fucking ripped...

No. I wasn't wearing a red shirt.

I put my hand over the rip in the fabric and blood squirted through my fingers. He'd stabbed me. Sometime during this he'd stabbed me.

There was a *thunk* and the floor shook. My body was getting weak and my head was starting to swim in its own juices, but I managed to look over at Nero. He was lying on the floor now, and what white skin I could see in this world of blood was ashen and grey.

"We need to find a way to – to get along, D-Duckling," Nero rasped, a bubble of blood appeared between his lips as he spoke before it burst. He took in a sharp breath; his lungs gurgling and popping like he was burning dry kindling. "Kill each other after..."

"... after the boys are safe," I finished, my own breathing getting increasingly difficult with every inhale. It looked like a serial killer had gotten into the house; the two of us were bleeding out together, side by side, in the kitchen.

Nero nodded. "You got big issues now 'cause of me, don't you? Bet that's really fucking you up, eh?"

I stared at him but I was dying. I had no biting words for him or oaths to make over the organs shutting down inside of me. A glare was all that was allotted in this time, that and a shred of honesty I could utter before the white flames took me.

"Yeah. It's been fucking me up," I admitted to him bitterly. My chest jolted from panic as my brain realized I couldn't get enough air. My survival instincts still didn't know I would come back; they still filled me with the primal thirst to survive. "And I'll destroy you for it, and I'll destroy your fucking husband too."

Nero looked at me, a serious expression showing through the blood. "I can help you, brosy. If you let me... I can help you. I can help you make all your weaknesses your strength. I can do that for sorrys, since we're both fugitives now."

"I'll be fine once you're back in concrete and your little cicaro is fucked to death by me and my boyfriend," I growled, my eyelids slowly drooping before I caught myself and my head jerked back up to try and keep me conscious. "I keep promises, Nero. I told you in Cardinalhall, you'll be the f-first... to – to die."

My eyes closed and I could see the white flames burning the corners of my vision like the smouldering rays of the sun. But before the inferno of immortality took me I heard Nero chuckle, and a hand sloppily pat my knee. "I know, baby. I know you'll kill us all."

That was the last thing I heard.

CHAPTER 25

Reno

"YOU LOOK LIKE A PRINCE, LOVE," HE SAID TO ME. I saw his smile in the reflection of the mirror, but when he made eye contact with himself there was a pull on his lip. Even he didn't believe his own smile anymore.

"I'm not one," I said. My voice was a husk now, something hollow and full of holes. Whatever love or light I'd let in would quickly spill through those holes, and it would then be carried away like so many of the good things in my life.

"You will be soon," he replied. He put a hand on my shoulder and squeezed me to him, his large green eyes brimming and filled and that fake smile that only had itself to fool now.

I had stopped believing his words long ago. It hadn't taken me long to realize most of the things he was saying were things he himself didn't believe.

I remember when I first met this man, I held every syllable from him close to my heart.

Now my heart was just… shut down, closed for business, stripped down to the studs.

"Yeah, I know…" My eyes swept the reflection of my body. Garrett says I look like a prince, but the only reason I'm in front of this mirror is because I once again couldn't fit my own clothes. They were falling off of me now, the belt had run out of notches, the button-down shirts hung off of me like liquid. Nothing fit so… it was another trip to the sengils for re-suiting.

Garrett turned me to him and straightened my collar, gently folding it over the black blazer before he adjusted my tie. He put his hands on my arms and rubbed them, still that fake smile... still that fake... fake smile.

Why don't you give up like the rest of us?

"Well... let us go see the king then," Garrett said with a pat on my arms. He took my hand and we walked from the apartment that we shared to the elevator. "My prince seeing our king. My Prince Reno."

Second-in-command Garrett Sebastian Dekker... but he'd been making a note to call me a prince. Thinking, what? That it would make me feel happy?

Prince Reno. What would the residents in Aras say to that, or my family for that matter?

They wouldn't recognize me, and I'd tell them with a sad smile that I no longer recognized myself. So they can make me whoever they want me to be. I would be clay in their hands. I honestly no longer cared; I had died with Reaver and Killian.

Yeah, I wasn't crazy; I knew Reaver would come back in twenty years when the flames cooled. But I knew the man who would eventually open his eyes to whatever was the greywastes and Skyfall, wouldn't be Reaver. When he found out that Killian had been dead for two decades, he wouldn't be my friend.

So in my mind... Reaver was dead.

"Oh, thank you, Chally," Garrett said hurriedly when we were almost out the door. Chally was handing him a lit cigarette, and he had one in between his fingers for me. Garrett liked having a smoke while he was being driven to his destination, and Chally knew this. The former slave had become the perfect sengil, and his gratefulness towards Garrett and me for adopting him and letting him live in luxury, showed through his dedication to making our lives as easy as possible. Chally apparently had been a houseboy in the greywastes as well to some rich asshole who owned a gas refinery. He'd been constantly abused, and used as a sex toy at a disgustingly young age. Ten, I think. Once he'd turned twenty, he'd been replaced by a younger model and sold to a slaver named Hopper. The same man who'd taken in Reaver, Jade, Killian, and Perish as mercenaries and cooks.

What I would've given to be beside my friends during this time. I belonged with Reaver. My place had been beside him.

Chally caught my gaze. He reached over and grabbed my hands and squeezed them; then he let go and signed *smile* to me, basically running his hands along his lips and smiling.

I tried to smile but my lower lip quivered, so I had to purse my mouth to hide it. Chally clucked and gave me a hug.

"Oh, muffin," Garrett whispered when Chally pulled away. He took my hand and held it tight. "You can have some leave for the evening, Chally. Perhaps you would like to check on Luca?"

Chally nodded and signed *I would like that. Thank you.*

Ten minutes later we were in the car being driven to Alegria. There was no feeling left inside of me to be worried about what Silas wanted for us, or why I had to come along. In the dead of night when I couldn't sleep, I felt worried for myself. I used to be so full of feeling. They used to say I had twice the emotions to make up for Reaver's lack of them, mostly in the sense of morality and empathy.

Now I just felt nothing. My love, happiness, and humour had died with Reaver and Killian, and my empathy had burned brightly before fizzling when I saw the crushing look of despair on Elish's face. The chimera I had hated so passionately, for decades of mistakes leading up to that night, for putting his pride and his stupid plans ahead of the safety of my friends and his husband, had such an expression of anguish it had destroyed the venomous contempt that had been burning inside of me.

And with those emotions pulled up from the root and killed, I now was void of both positive emotions, and negative. I was just a walking dead man, waiting for my body to get the drift that I was done with living.

This inner barrenness was shown when I heard Garrett sniffing and didn't even look at him. I kept staring out the window, watching Skyland go by. All of these people in their summer clothing, bright colours which were in fashion right now, going about their business. Some smiling with friends, others walking with briefcases and stern expressions, no doubt going over what they needed to do before returning to their nice apartments and their family. None of them had any idea just how in shambles the Dekker family was. The SNN was reporting Jade's death and Olympus's destruction, and they knew Elish was gone, but that was just the tip of an iceberg that went down for miles. They had no idea that all of the strong members of the family were wraiths, shadows of the men they once were.

If the Crimstones were alive somewhere, they'd have used this opportunity to attack, but I think they were all dead.

Garrett's hand rested on top of mine and he tried to hold it. I let him but there was no strength in my grip. He clenched it anyway, and eventually brought out a kerchief to dab his eyes.

He was King Garrett right now, I guess. He was leading Skyfall since Silas was in no state and Elish was gone. So one day I'd be a king?

All I ever wanted to be was Reaver's sidekick. Once I wanted to be his boyfriend, and all of Aras was waiting for it to happen too, but that ship had sailed; and then the island I had watched it depart from, had sunk.

We were in the hallway now, the double oak doors closed. Garrett was directing me with his hand in mine, towards the door.

He knocked, and we waited, and when no one answered Garrett opened the door and peeked in. Since we had an invitation I guess it gave him leave to walk in without someone answering the door. Drake was gone; Sanguine somewhere being tortured by his own madness from what Garrett had tearfully told me, so no one was here to let us in but Silas.

I didn't care about Sanguine. He shouldn't have arranged our abandonment in the greywastes.

I followed Garrett inside of Silas's apartment which was frigid compared to the blistering heat outside. Good ol' skyscraper integrated air conditioning. A part of me was expecting the apartment to be trashed, or covered in dirty dishes and garbage from him not having a sengil to clean everything; but it looked like the living room and his sitting room to the right had been left untouched. Not completely clean, however; there was an obvious bloodstain on the carpet behind the couch.

"Silas. Lovely?" Garrett called. He led us to the hallway and towards Silas's bedroom, the door half-closed and showing a dark room. "I'm here with Reno."

We both paused when we heard shifting in Silas's bedroom, the sound of blankets being moved around. Then the door opened, and I had to hide the surprise on my face when I saw Silas.

Silas's face was hollow, ghostly grey, and with circles so black the king looked like he'd been punched in both of his eyes. His blond hair was messed up and greasy, and his clothing, just a grey sleeveless undershirt and matching baggy drawstring pants, were stained. I had lost a lot of weight, but I was healthy compared to him; his ribs were showing below his collarbone, and his cheekbones jutted out.

"Oh... lovely," Garrett sobbed. "Why are you doing this to yourself?

Reno, love, get him some food. How long has it been since you've eaten?"

The expression on Silas's face was of a man who was lost. That look of hopelessness, of fatigue. Maybe it wasn't lost, I think it was a look of a man who was searching for something that no longer existed... and he'd finally realized he'd never find it. There was so much distance in his eyes, and pain. And when his eyes travelled up to ours, I saw a disconnect that made me wonder if he was fully aware that we were actually present.

I turned away from him. I was glad Garrett had given me a request, so I didn't have to see that haunted look. I walked into the living room and opened the fridge, but I closed it with a grimace when I was assaulted with the smell of rotting food and plastic containers that had held in them a cornucopia of different colours of mould.

So I closed it, and rooted through the cupboards until I found some Dek'ko fruit rollups and sandwich cookies, basically Oreos. I knew there were no health benefits in the flavoured wax or chemical cookies, so I used the dial-a-sengil phone and asked them to go to the restaurant and get us some pasta.

I put the phone down and turned to go back to the hallway, but then I saw Garrett leaving the bedroom with a pained look on his face.

"He... wants me to leave," Garrett said slowly.

I shrugged and started walking towards the exit.

"No, Reno... he requested you stay with him." Garrett's left cheek sunk in and I knew he was chewing on it. "If you..." He glanced behind him and grabbed my hand. "Let's go," he whispered.

I pulled my hand away and shook my head. "No," I said blandly. "If he wants to talk to me that's fine. I don't care either way."

Garrett looked at me like I'd just broken off our engagement, but then the horror turned to intense worry, and finally, acceptance. "You're sure?" He glanced to the coffee table and I did too. I saw Silas's remote phone resting beside drug residue and an empty glass pipe. "If you need me just call. I'm going to visit Elliot, Nero's sengil. He's living several floors down. I'll... I'll come running, okay?"

I nodded, a part of me wanting Silas to just kill me and end it. "Okay, Gare."

Garrett kissed my cheek and hugged me tightly. "I'll be close. I love you."

"I love you too," I said, my tone hollow. "Talk to you soon."

The door closed behind him and I stood in the living room wondering what to do next. Eventually I cracked open one of the fruit rollups and walked to Silas's door.

"Hey… so here I am," I said. I didn't know what else to say. I took a bite from the flavoured candy and poked my head in.

Silas was curled up on the bed with… aww, man, he had Perish's stuffed Pokémon in his arms, the charmander. He was laying on his side with the orange thing clutched to him, that haunted look on his face.

All I got was a blink. I continued to eat, leaning against the frame of the door and just standing there like an idiot. I don't know if it was awkward for him, but it was to me. I didn't want to be here. I still remember the anger twisting his burnt face when he told me, in the cruellest fashion, that Reaver and Killian were dead, that if Reaver did have a moment of consciousness before he suffocated or burned, he'd see Killian's scorched bones.

Because Silas had made the lab explode.

You would think that even these memories would draw up some despair, but I just swallowed the sugary goop and fished out a Dek'ko Oreo out of the bag.

Then I heard the faintest, feathery knock on the door, no doubt our pasta. I turned without a word and left.

"Don't leave me," a weak voice whimpered behind me.

I paused, and realized a lump was forming in my throat. I shook my head and pushed it down, remembering just who this monster was, and walked back to the doorway. "I ordered us some food," I said to him awkwardly. "I'll be right back."

"Okay," the little mouse holding the charmander said. I nodded and greeted the sengil, one who I'm guessing pulled the shortest straw from the terrified look on his face, and grabbed us some forks and poured us two glasses of ChiCola. I put it all on a serving tray and walked into his bedroom.

"Can I turn a light on?" I asked. He not only had the blinds drawn but two large canvases were covering the floor to ceiling window on the right, and the regular, but still big, window on the left.

"Okay," Silas said. He closed his eyes from the glare of the light, so I threw a dirty t-shirt over it to reduce the brightness.

I walked to a white fabric chair and dragged it over to the bed, but when I motioned to sit on it Silas raised his head. "Sit on the bed?" he said. Not in a demanding way, he said *bed* in a higher tone, like he was asking if I could.

I had already taken off my shoes on entry so I sat on the bed, smelling heavily of stale sweat and holding a few darkened patches which I suspected were blood stains. I crossed my legs and was surprised when Silas started moving. He sat up, put the charmander beside a stuffed leopard and a stuffed grey cat and slumped over, his elbows resting on his knees.

This was just bizarre, but I think it might've been less bizarre for me than it would've been for someone else, even some of his family. I'd woken up next to this man several times when he was living in Aras. I'd made him oatmeal for breakfast, but he called it mush, saying it was just what his family called it. I'd even started saying *mush* after he left.

I handed him a fork and opened up the container of spaghetti. There were two but I'd only brought one into the room. I wasn't expecting Silas to eat, and if we finished it we'd break open the other one. There were also two pieces of garlic toast. I'm guessing they must've known it was for the king, because it was loaded with garlic and dripping with butter. There was an overabundance of ground bosen in the sauce too, and it was covered in parmesan cheese so thick it was like we'd just had our first snowfall.

Silas stared at the food as I began to eat. I didn't have an appetite; I only ate when Garrett was with me and that was because if I didn't his eyes would start to well. I didn't want to spread my misery, so I'd eat for him.

Now... now I was eating in hopes of encouraging this living, breathing monster to eat as well. The man who released the sestic radiation that killed Killian, and sentenced Reaver to a fate just as bad. Not to mention the terror he'd been spreading amongst the family for fuck knows how long.

I should be smug and enjoying seeing the king fall from grace. He had caused so much misery to the family who loved and worshipped him. Who still protected him and took care of him, even after he'd murdered their partners, and tortured them at times. Just like I should've been happy to see Elish lose the love of his life through his own selfishness, his own inability to just let things go, and to stop this plan of his that was deteriorating in his hands. It was because of him, and his obsession with figuring out how to kill immortals, that sent Reaver and Killian on that mission to Krieg and eventually Falkvalley.

But that just wasn't me. Unlike Reaver and so many other chimeras, I didn't take joy in other's misery. I just felt sad all around. I knew Silas was a monster but I didn't have it in me to feel satisfaction over their pain.

So maybe that was why I twirled noodles and sauce on my fork and handed it to him. "If I have to eat, you gotta," I said simply. "I'm not hungry either, and I'm making an effort."

Silas, surprisingly, took the fork of food and put it into his mouth. He even chewed sadly, gazing at the food with green eyes full of melancholy, and swallowed.

"You've lost a lot of weight," Silas said, his voice still a fragile shadow. He picked up his fork and slowly speared a chunk of ground bosen with cheese on it. He stared at it in a way that made it seem like he was being asked to run a marathon in ten seconds, not take a bite of food.

"Yeah, you have too," I said. I started to make a spaghetti sandwich out of the garlic bread. "I've kind of lost the will to live, to be honest."

Silas only nodded at this and forced himself to take another bite. The conversation died after that, and the room returned to its original silence. It wasn't one of awkwardness though, not like it had been before. It seemed like a natural state for the two of us. We were each drowning in our own misery, a slow drowning that had spanned months, and we had just floated past each other and had decided to drown together for the evening.

I had once hated silences. Reaver had loved sitting in silence with me but it would drive me nuts. I always felt like I had to entertain him, make him laugh since that had originally been the only reason he'd hung out with me as a toddler. I could make him laugh and I felt special because Leo said I was the only one. So when he wasn't laughing it felt like I wasn't doing my job, and there was no reason for me to be there.

Now I think I was understanding the power of silence, because in this heavy blanket of muted misery I was able to feel... I don't know a way to say it... more present with him? That I was seeing Silas in a more organic form, not just someone actively shapeshifting from one larger than life personality to the next.

When I had eaten as much as I could convince myself to eat, and Silas had finished pecking at the food, I put the lid on the container and decided it was cold enough in this room to just put the food and the forks onto his dresser. Then I sat back down on the bed and wondered just what was supposed to happen next.

Silas picked up the charmander, held it to his chest, and stared at the blue comforter of the bed. I just watched him. There was nothing else to do. The television in the corner of the room was off, and the only thing that changed in this dark, sweat-smelling room was the burl clock on the wall.

When I had been there for a solid hour, Silas's eyes started to droop, but every time his head nodded he jolted himself awake and opened his eyes wide like he was trying to prevent sleep from taking him.

I wasn't sure why he wasn't just letting himself sleep. But then I became aware again of the black circles under his eyes, and the dead look, and decided to ask him. "Hey, how long have you been up for?"

Silas didn't react to my voice, even though it shattered the dome of silence we'd both been sitting in for quite a long time now.

"Off and on," Silas replied quietly. "Nightmares... you know... I see them."

I nodded. I could relate to that. I found my reply was more honest than I wanted it to be, but it was what it was. "I wake up and for a moment I forget, and I feel okay... then..."

"... then you remember," Silas whispered.

I nodded again, the lump coming back. "And I just fucking... cry." I swallowed the lump to try and prevent it from rising up. "Or I used to. I think I'm broken now... I don't cry anymore."

Silas looked up and made direct eye contact with me, and at this, the rock in my throat got bigger and it started to hurt. I didn't like looking into his eyes, it was making me feel things I no longer thought I could feel. He was just radiating despair, a kind of anguish I don't think a normal man could project. Like his immortality had given him this new level of emotion that us mortals, or even young immortals, didn't know were possible to feel.

I had to look away, it was too much for me to handle. How was it humanly possible for someone to be this sad? How had the fabric of the universe not collapsed from this intensity? He ended the world because of his sadness, and now I was worried that he was going to end the universe.

"I cried in the beginning," Silas said to me. "Now, like you, I don't. I find myself... scared, Reno. I'm terrified."

Caught off-guard, I glanced at him again; this time trying to look more at his lips and short beard than his eyes. "Scared? Why?"

A small exhale sounded, and he hugged the Pokémon to him.

"Because I have no escape. I can't kill myself like any man feeling this hopelessness would do. I'm forced to live this life I no longer wish to live. I realized, Reno... I want to die, and I can't. I'm stuck in this deep sepulchre of loneliness, of isolation. There is no way out."

His words struck me, the silence and ambience of the room making each syllable amplify and sink into me more than they ever would during normal conversation. Not only did I hear them, I felt them, and the despair that chased the tones like wild dogs.

And when they had permeated me, saturated my skin to my heart, I felt an overwhelming swell of sadness. I... felt something.

But this new influx of feelings was nothing to celebrate. I wanted to continue my walking death; I had swallowed enough anguish. I only wanted to feel nothing.

This new wave of empathy had me thinking of a solution for this broken king. "Can't you just get them to cut off your head or something?" I asked. "Make it so you're dead for a long time?"

Silas shook his head. "That's worse. The white flames are no sanctuary. I have died enough times that it is like being in a dream. It would be worse... it would be the nightmares I already experience but I'd be unable to escape them. I wish for... nothing, for a reprieve of this miserable existence."

"Wow," I whispered. I made a move and put a hand on his crossed pant leg, and when he didn't shift it away, I rubbed it. "Doesn't that mean you just need to do everything you can to make your life better?"

Silas looked down at my hand. "There's no point. All who I have loved are dead, or will emerge decades from now with a blackness in his heart that I will never be able to extinguish. Sky is dead; Sky isn't coming back." His face twisted and his eyes shut tight. "His clone did not come and save me like I had created him for... he came and took what shreds of Sky I had left. He... he... destroyed me one last time." My jaw locked; the lump in my throat tightened and burned, and travelled up in the form of throbbing heat. I tried to swallow. I tried to force it down, but I found myself on the verge of begging him not to mention Reaver and Killian. I couldn't hear it; I didn't want to feel more pain.

Silas opened his eyes and looked at me. "You're in anguish," he whispered.

I held a hand over my mouth and choked. "Don't talk about him," I begged, my voice several octaves higher than normal from my own grief.

"Please don't do this to me. I… I know you hate him, but I can't hear it. Please, Silas."

Silas's green eyes, like a patch of grass in the middle of a coal bed, looked not just at me, but into me, deep into my heart and soul. I could feel him probing, seeking and sifting, slowly stripping off what little armour remained to render me emotionally naked. An intense feeling of vulnerability hit me, and a single tear rolled down my face.

"I must tell you," Silas whispered, his tone dead, absolutely dead. He raised a hand, and with those intense eyes still drinking me in, snatching me from the caves that I'd used to hide myself, he rested it on the side of my head, and cradled it. "When we entered the lab, he went to Killian, I went to Perish. I was overwhelmed with grief when I saw him. And when Reaver walked in and kneeled down and saw he was dead, I crawled into Reaver's arms, and begged him to hold me. And he did." I didn't hide the surprise at this but I didn't speak, there was nothing in me to form the words. "I noticed Sky's O.L.S was gone and I panicked; I was terrified. That O.L.S was my key to implanting the clone with Sky's personality." He was telling me these things in such an empty tone. You would think this recollection would draw out some sort of emotion, but it was like he'd completely separated himself from the person and people he was talking about. "I looked up and I saw Killian, beaten and bruised, hair missing from the plaguelands' radiation, he was holding the O.L.S."

Another pause.

"He ate it in front of me, Reno, and when I lunged at him… Reaver held me back, whispering taunts in my ear as he kissed my neck, and he made me watch Killian destroy it."

Was he… telling the truth?

When I looked back into Silas's eyes, I knew he was. Because as he stripped me down to nothing, I realized he was doing the same to himself. He was taking off the metal coating that had covered him like a reinforced fort, and baring himself to me without strings, without alternate motives.

I was… I think I was seeing Silas.

The real Silas. Why was he showing me this side of him? Why me?

"I was in such grief, Reno," Silas continued. "I just remember screaming and screaming, and I realized when it was too late that I was releasing radiation. The next thing I knew there was an explosion, from the concentrated radiation. It didn't affect me, but when the building started to burn with orange flames, they seared my skin like anyone else's." His hand dropped, and his distant, lost gaze appeared again. "Please believe me… I didn't mean to do it. I never meant to kill them. It was an accident. I was mad from grief… as you saw when I found you and my family. I… I didn't want them to die." Silas's lower lip stiffened for a brief moment before, like he was physically exhausted, he slowly laid down and stared blankly at the wall. He said nothing else, but I still felt this thick connection between us, like he'd planted tendrils inside of my mind and they had rooted into the grey matter of my brain. I could mentally feel him inside of me, and with that, the continuous rush of despair.

But what he had said… when I had replayed that interaction with Silas in the plaguelands, it had driven hatred into my heart; one that doused all other feelings in gasoline, including my rage towards Elish. I had honestly thought he'd done it on purpose. I'd even flirted with the idea that he had trapped them inside.

As I looked at this fallen king, his sad state overshadowed all the wrong that he'd done, all the pain he'd caused; and if only for a fleeting moment, I wondered if everything that he'd ever done, was drawn from this same inner pain that he couldn't escape. That no one in this world was perfect; as Elish had shown me from the anguish I'd seen on him from losing a teenage cicaro he'd only known for several years. This man openly judged and despised a king who'd been dealing with the loss of a boyfriend he'd been bound to for decades and decades; a man he'd experienced the end of the world with, and had rebuilt it with too.

Yeah. Silas had done terrible things. But once you stripped away every piece of armour he'd nailed to himself, and saw the naked huddled mass with that haunted stare… you realized that deep down inside, he was just a profoundly sad man.

"Silas?" I whispered. I swallowed to try and push down the tightness in my throat, but the burning behind my eyes was making them sting.

"Yeah?" Silas whispered back.

I sniffed. "You wanna cry with me for a while?"

Silas looked at me and I saw those green emeralds start to drown in their pools.

"Yeah," he said weakly back.

I laid down beside him and Silas immediately shifted into my arms. I held him tight, and as I thought of Reaver, thought of Killian, his cheerful smile and innocent nature now never to be seen again, I started to cry, and

I heard Silas start to cry too. He wrapped his arms around me and clutched me tightly to him, his wraith-like frame shaking underneath my hold.

We stayed in each other's arms, for a long long time, unleashing all of the feelings inside of us that we'd both thought were dead, soaking each other in tears and snot from running noses. When our crying eventually turned into shuddered gasps for air, and trembled aftershocks, we kept our embrace.

I felt his body relax in mine, and with my eyes closed, I gently stroked his hair. I didn't realize I had been waiting for him to sleep until I heard his steady, shallow breathing, and once I knew he was, at least for the moment, free of his anguish, I fell asleep too.

I woke up to someone caressing my hair. I opened my eyes and saw Garrett put a finger to his lips. He was sitting behind me where there was still some space left.

Silas was still in my arms, his head on my chest and one arm was around me, the other tucked up near his chin. He wasn't snoring, just breathing heavier; he was completely winked out.

"When I didn't hear from you I became worried," Garrett said, and to prove just how loving and not possessive he was, he smiled. "He looks so at peace. What happened?"

"I…" I paused, trying to find a way to word it. "I saw Silas… the real Silas." When Garrett's already large eyes widened at my admission, I sighed and looked down at the sleeping king, his face smushed against my chest. "We talked and I didn't feel like I was talking to the Ghost. I talked to him and we both… connected. I think I might've helped him."

Garrett stroked my hair back and rubbed my cheek caringly. "I think he might've helped you too, love. You sound better."

"I do?" I said surprised. I wasn't expecting that.

Garrett nodded. "You're talking to me," he laughed lightly. "Are you okay here? I'd hate to wake him. I don't believe he's been sleeping well." A flicker appeared in his eye. "Was he violent with you at all? Lovely, would you think he'd like it if…?"

"I stayed with him?" I said. I searched my heart, and though I'd just woken up, I didn't feel like that was a bad suggestion. Truthfully, I felt flattered that he'd been comfortable enough to fall asleep with me. "I don't feel threatened at all with him. He's so depressed, Gare. He's just given up. A part of me feels shitty for feeling it, but… I don't hate him.

He explained what happened and it was all an accident. He didn't purposely…" I hated mentioning them. I still couldn't handle it. "… purposely kill… *them*." I took in a deep breath, held it, and exhaled.

"I think I might understand him. I feel awful for him," I continued. "He's fucking two hundred and fifty-five years old and it's taken a toll on him. I think he's just done."

Garrett stopped moving his hand, which was making small circles on my cheek. His calmed face fell to the depths. "He said that?"

I nodded. "It was like watching someone actively getting torn in two in front of me." I shook my head. "I know I should hate him… but… fuck. I think I want to help him be happy again. I think that if it's me, and not one of those chimera assholes who'll only manipulate him, or take him out killing as a way to make him happy. If it's me… Garrett, I think I can steer him in a better direction. I think I can help him repair the family with positive things, not threats and fire and brimstone. If it's me… I can do what's right."

Garrett took in a sharp breath. He looked at Silas. "You… love, you really think so?"

"I do," I whispered. "He opens up to me, and I bet you'll tell me that he hasn't spoken to practically anyone about what happened since he came back."

"No… he hasn't," Garrett admitted. The hand that had been hovering over my face, so close I could feel the heat from it, trailed to Silas's and he gently ran his fingers through Silas's greasy, but still wavy, golden hair. "It's been exceptionally worse since he banished Sanguine, and the last straw was Jade dying and Elish leaving. Silas would never admit it, but he did love Jade." Garrett's eyes welled at the thought of the yellow-eyed cicaro. Mine didn't, but I did miss Biter. "It was just another tragedy to further fracture the family. Otter, love, if you think you can help him… please, please do all you can. I'll help in any way."

"You wouldn't mind me staying here?" I asked. I was happy he wasn't upset, but honestly sometimes I wish he was a bit more possessive of me when it came to his family. If it was someone who wasn't a chimera, like poor Jesse Saint James in Tintown, he was a maniac but I bet I could flirt with any of his brothers and he'd just sit there with his proud smile.

Garrett thought for a moment. "Why don't I temporarily move into one of the old apartments downstairs? Ares and Siris have been bored silly since they returned from the Dead Islands, and I can put them to work moving our things. This way we can see each other all the time." He leaned down and kissed the corner of my lips. "This actually would be splendid, love. It'll give me more time to devote to Skyfall. I was wanting to organize a holiday before fall hits, something to bring the city together and show our people that we are still a united force. Think of a name for it, sweet Otter, perhaps Silas will be well-enough to give us some input."

I saw such a look of hope in his eyes, it made the black ice that had encapsulated my heart start to crack away, revealing the damaged, but still beating, organ inside. My heart beat hope into my bloodstream, and longing, longing for some shred of happiness, for something to make this pain go away.

Maybe doing this would be my first step on the path of repairing what I had previously believed was permanently broken. Maybe helping Silas would help me too, and fixing this fractured family would give my lost and depressing life some purpose.

I raised my free arm, Silas still breathing rhythmically with his face against my chest, and I drew Garrett down to my lips. I closed my eyes and we kissed, the taste of his mouth and the warmth it brought to me adding more determination to this weak heart.

It wasn't without its conflict though. A part of me wanted to turn my back on this life and Skyfall, and go back to Aras to live in misery. I'd love to say to myself that Reaver wouldn't want me to be sad in Aras, but he was Reaver and not a cliché. For all I know he'll hate me for further sewing myself into this tapestry that was the Dekker family, but maybe Killian had changed him enough in his last few months for Reaver to want me to try, at least try, to be happy.

And I was the most happy when I was helping other people be happy; whether it was making them laugh, or just being the goofy guy I was. I had proven that from bouncing back after my time with the Crimstones. I was resilient; I was made out of tougher stuff than I thought I was.

It looks like I was about to take on my biggest challenge yet. I was going to bring Silas back from the darkness he was lost in… and in turn, I was going to repair his family.

"I know I can do this," I said to Garrett when our lips temporarily parted. "I think it'll help me to feel… useful again. Like I have a purpose. My life's purpose had always been–"

Garrett kissed me again, more passionately this time. I knew why he was doing it. He didn't want the consequences of me mentioning Reaver's name. He knew it always made me sad.

When Garrett pulled away, he rested his forehead in the crook of my neck. I rubbed his back and looked down at the sleeping king.

I had a purpose in life again.

CHAPTER 26

Jade

"THE FACT THAT YOU ACTUALLY THINK SOMETHING like this will work, just shows how insane you are," I said. My voice was scratchy and raw from screaming and flinging every curse at him that I could think of. Every time I swallowed it felt like I was trying to push down little fish bones; everything hurt.

I braced myself when I felt the tinkling of chains, and gasped when the collar around my neck tightened, digging prongs into my bleeding neck. The blood was dried to my bare chest like I had been dipped into a vat of it and hung by my neck to dry. I must look like a pretty piece of art right now. Though who was here to see me?

"I didn't tell you you could speak," Kerres said in a cold tone that did nothing to emulate my master's.

Kerres, you've gone crazy.

"I didn't tell you I fucking cared," I snapped, baring my teeth in the direction I had heard his voice. I was blindfolded, chained to the bed with my hands tied behind my back and my legs out in front of me. I was completely naked, and the smell of Kerres's bedroom was now thick with the heavy aroma of blood.

And it was about to be joined by more. A hard slap to my face rewarded me for my attitude, and in return I spat blood in his face.

Or I tried to anyway.

My molars ground in frustration and spectrums of colour flashed in front of my eyes as if my own aura reading was illuminating my own frustration. I didn't know how he knew to do it, or if he even realized what he had done – but being blindfolded had rendered my newly blossoming 'I will kill your fucking mind' empath abilities useless.

Because if I could see him, and I could use the trick I now knew how to harness… I would kill him. Without a fucking doubt, or a shred of sadness, I would melt his mind and stomp on his head until his eyes popped out. I would twist his head off of his body and piss down the fucking hole in his throat.

All in all – I was going to fucking kill Kerres. My master was missing, he was fuck knows where thinking I was dead; and here I was chained to Kerres's bed unable to kill him with one of the only useful advantages to having this brain destroying ability.

The frustration multiplied and I let out a yell. Kerres hit me again, and I felt the snap of his whip against my chest. My lips peeled back into a vicious snarl, like a cat spitting, and I started pulling and struggling to try and get myself out of these chains; or at least get this blindfold off of my head.

Kerres laughed when my zapped energy left me panting and wheezing. I took in sharp and deep inhales and felt panic burn inside of my chest when I started breathing in my own recycled air. That, and the fact that my burning throat was further preventing me from taking a deep breath, was filling my head with an anxious heat.

"I can't fucking breathe! Let me breathe!" I gasped. My head was throbbing, the blood its own pulse behind my eyes. I was desperate to take a deep breath of cold air; my brain demanded it in order to relieve the anxiety that anyone slowly being suffocated felt.

"Ask me nicely and I might."

I am going to fuck your fucking skull.

"Please, *Master*, take this fucking thing off of my head!" I yelled, trying to grab my throat but my chains only tensed, recoiling my hand back. There was a thin razor's edge between keeping my sanity, and going completely off the rails, and I was walking on it barefoot.

"I didn't hear you."

"Take this fucking thing…" I inhaled my own stale breath, my lungs screaming in response. I started hyperventilating, and it was then that I felt Kerres roll up the black cover he had over my head.

I gasped, and started filling my painful lungs with the smell of copper and dirty clothes, but it was a welcome breath compared to the covering over my head.

"See… you worked yourself up into a rage and you punished yourself for it," Kerres said; his tone was just dripping satisfaction. I could see Elish doing this to me in the beginning, but Kerres was nothing like him. No one could match the control Elish had over me, even in the beginning. When my hatred for him was at its worst I still shuddered under his touch; I still ached for his praise.

Each word that spilled from Kerres's lips lit my brain on fire. I could feel the grey matter melting into a pool of bubbling lava inside of my head. It was dissolving so it could be reconstructed, built up into something stronger, something impenetrable.

Kerres only knew me as being weak. He didn't know what I had gone through in the greywastes. He didn't know that I had survived when everything was thrown against me. I had survived Perish, I had survived ravers, and not only that, I was their king. I had survived my mind overloading to the point of being brain-dead. I had been marked for death inside of a burning skyscraper and even that I – fucking – survived.

I kept inhaling, every breath I took strengthening me, curing the coating I had inside. I was patient, I would wait for my moment and then I would strike.

I was a chimera – and I'd act like it.

"Thank you, Master," I said through gasps. My mind was taking me back to when I had to pretend I was under the control of scopa. When Perish was trying to get those passwords from me. If there was one thing I fucking knew how to do… it was to fake it until I made it.

"That's better," Kerres said. I tried to hide the grimace when I felt his hand touch the side of my face, and it took all of me not to recoil when I felt his lips press against mine. I wanted to bite him, rip his lips off of his face, but if I did that I'd never get this hood off of my head.

"Kerres, this is insane," I said when he separated our lips. "Did you really save my life just so you could torture me in your bedroom? Come on, you have to see how crazy this is."

His heart rate didn't even change from my direct call out of what he was doing. I knew he was batshit insane before, from the Crimstones, but I was starting to get insight on just how bad he'd gotten. Silas had commented in a singing voice how Kerres was camped outside of Olympus watching me. I'd be lying if I said it hadn't made me feel pity for him, sadness that he couldn't move on. I hid those feelings from Elish to avoid his scornful and patronizing looks, but it was what it was. I'd felt bad for him… and… maybe kind of flattered?

But now… now I realized he wasn't following me like a disabled, injured puppy… he'd been downright stalking me. If only I'd have been smart enough to recognize how unstable he was before I opened my big mouth and started screaming at him about how much I loved Elish.

If only Gage hadn't beat it out of there as soon as he saw things get loaded between me and Kerres. He was a god amongst the empaths, surely he could've killed him with one look? Or maybe he didn't want to see his new friend in this state. It seemed like those two had become pals.

"Kerres?" I called again when he hadn't answered me. "Come on. Unchain me, this isn't good for you, and it isn't helping me. Unchain me so we can just talk about it. Remember all the times you fucking wanted us to talk? Here's your chance." This is why I loved Elish. Both of us would down a shot of arsenic before we sat down and talked about our feelings. It only happened when he'd pushed me to my limits, or I had pushed him to his, and then we just yelled our feelings as we tried to beat each other to a pulp. I hated feelings.

"You've already said enough," was my response from Kerres.

"Yeah, well…" My mind scrambled for a fish to throw him. He was a starved animal right now and a crazy one as well. I could do this. "You pissed me off, okay? I said some things I maybe didn't mean. Hitting me and trying to be Elish, which I assure you, you're not, isn't going to fix this. If you want to work on this relationship…"

"Don't bullshit me, Jade!" I felt a smack across my face and I fell to my side on the bed; the chains rattling behind me as they rubbed up against the metal frame. I had hoped it was wood but while Kerres had been sleeping last night I tongued it, and nope, fucking metal.

I swallowed the growl and tried to force the hood over my eyes. If only I could just see him… if I could see him I just know the rage would trigger the empath death stare, or whatever the fuck Silas called it.

"What the fuck do you want from me then?" I shouted. Once again, Kerres was crushing my every last nerve. There was only so much I could take, and this crazy whackjob had already brought me to the end of my rope, and was now stepping on the fingers that clutched to the shredded fibers. "Tell me what you want? Do you even know what you want?"

The room settled around us until all I could hear was his heartbeat, and the stale aromatic smell of unwashed clothes and drying blood. I knew he didn't know, and I didn't know either. Kerres had been clinging to the rotting remains of our relationship like those chimps on nature shows who carried their dried-out babies around after they died.

"Ker." I hoped his silence meant vulnerability, but I wasn't sure. I held out my arms as if welcoming him into them. "What if I got you help?"

There was no shifting towards me, but I did hear a jump in his pulse. "Gage says he can't help me. It's physical alterations to my brain, whereas yours was… different, I guess."

So… he was admitting something was wrong with him? I wasn't sure if that was new; I just didn't know shit about what was going on in his head. He was a jar of shaken liquid right now, too cloudy and full of bubbles and whirlpools for me to see anything.

"Yeah, but… we have real smart doctors. Sid, one of the chimeras, he can do some really neat shit. He was genetically engineered to be a doctor, I think," I said slowly. I knew I was once again treading on dangerous ground. "Look, K. There is no end game to this… end game is you killing me through suffocation, or something like that. But if you just fucking unchain me… I can help you."

"Yeah, and then what? I get to be a fugitive in Moros being lorded over by you mutant pieces of shit, while you get to continue being Elish's little sex doll? Fuck you, Jade."

And like he'd stepped onto the pressure plate of a landmine, I exploded.

"THEN WHAT THE FUCK DO YOU WANT!" I screamed.

I felt like crying. I was so fucking frustrated, and my heart was physically hurting for my master. I couldn't let him believe I was dead. I knew his dignity would never allow him to show that it had affected him, but he loved me and I knew he'd be sad.

I didn't want Elish to be sad, every time I'd seen him sad it was when I was hurt. Elish was fucking perfect. He was a god and I was a shadow; a serpent that was lucky enough to be allowed to curl up under his feet. I wasn't worthy of making him feel that emotion… fucking no one was.

I bowed my head and felt a tear run down my cheek. I squeezed my eyes tight and quietly cried to myself. There were so many emotions pulling my guts out. Not only was I feeling empathy for what Elish was going through… but I also think I was sad knowing that he wasn't going to bust through this door to save me.

No one was.

Everyone thinks I'm dead but Kerres and the guy who took off so quick I'd barely gotten a chance to say hello. He just... healed me and bolted.

"You know what I want?" Kerres shouted back to me. "You know what I fucking want, asshole?" I ducked, knowing what was coming, and sure enough, I was right. Kerres's fist hit my jaw and then the side of my head. I didn't know if he composed himself enough to open the fist, or if he was just wanting to hit me differently, but the next several blows were open palm but just as forceful, smack upon smack on my head until I felt something spasm inside of my brain.

The seizure came swiftly. It was as if someone was grabbing onto my brain stem and yanking me backwards into that dark limbo. It forced me into darkness, and in that void I felt a million little electric prongs shock my body, making my muscles spasm and twitch.

Then the pain came, and I screamed. I expected to hear Kerres's panicked voice, and his arms on me to try and take the seizure away, but I suffered alone and in darkness until it eventually subsided.

After the last spasm left my body I was a crumpled heap of nothing. I opened my mouth as wide as I could and gasped like a dying man, filling my compressed and aching lungs with as much air as I could get.

"Maybe this is what I want...?" I heard Kerres say faintly. "Maybe I want to see you suffer as much as you've made me suffer these last few years." His hand grabbed my chin and tilted it up. "Payback's a bitch, isn't it... chimera scum." He shook my chin, but I was too exhausted and out of it to say anything back, even though inside I was blazing. "Maybe I'll keep you in here, and let you burn alive when I bomb Skyland. I have the weapons to do it; they're in Irontowers and I know where."

I know where they are too, asshole. I groaned and tried to roll onto my side to breathe better.

"At least you're finally being honest with yourself," I rasped. "Still loving me was just a mask, isn't it? You want to torture me." Torture me for falling in love with a man he could never compare to. "I might be chimera scum... but you're just as bad, Crimstone."

I got a punch in the eye for that. Pain shot through me and filled my head with a throbbing buzzing sound. "You're worse than chimera scum, you're a chimera's whore," Kerres snarled. "You were kidnapped, Jade, fucking *kidnapped* by Elish. He physically abused you, he mentally destroyed you, he raped you, and when you told him you loved him... he abandoned you in Moros." My lips pursed as old wounds got ripped open, wounds I had healed long ago. "And yet you fucking follow him around on the leash he still has you tied to."

"And what's my alternative?" I snapped. "Get beaten some more by you? What are my fucking options, Kerres? You let the Crimstones make you into a bad-tempered, insane loose cannon."

"I saved your fucking life!"

I spat a mouthful of blood. "Thanks," I said angrily. "Thanks for saving me, just so you can tie me to your bed and beat the shit out of a chained chimera. Call me a fucking whore–"

"YOU ARE A WHORE!" Kerres screamed this so hard in my face I felt his spit on my lip. "How many of your fucking brothers have fucked you, whore? Huh!?

"I'd rather let Silas fuck me than have your slimy, fucking–" This time when Kerres hit me I felt myself get wrenched further away from my conscious. I would've been comfortable there, or anywhere besides this fucked up madness I had woken up in, but then I felt his hand press up against my groin.

This was enough to shoot my mind back into my body, and like a boulder being thrown into a cold lake, I felt myself coated head to toe in frigid water.

"Y-you've got – got to be kidding me," I rasped. I pulled away from him but my boxers stayed where they were, firmly in his grip. "You've seriously... got to be kidding me, Kerres."

I heard the cloth crumple under his fist, then the sound of him smelling my fucking boxers. More cold washed through me, freezing my blood and locking every muscle in place.

No, I don't care how fucked up he was in his brain... he wouldn't do this to me. Kerres was in there somewhere, I had seen glimpses of him before.

"I hate you," Kerres whispered, his voice was cracking as if it was being roasted over the flames inside of him. I could smell the smoke on his breath, the anger, the three years of pining, stalking, pursuing; the three years of convincing himself that I was Elish's prisoner, that I was a chimera's slave that he had to save. He'd joined the Crimstones to try and free me, he'd climbed up twenty-two flights of stairs to rescue me from the brother who had vowed to kill me.

Then he carried me through the smoke and flames to save me.

No…

Not save me.

I clenched my teeth and screamed through them when I felt Kerres's penis push against me. I thrashed my arms up in a useless attempt to hit him, to get his heavy breathing away from my ear.

Never to save me.

Only to pay me back personally – for everything I had done to him.

"Kerres!" I screamed. A rip of desperation went through me when he grabbed my left leg and pushed it back. I tried to rear my right leg to hit him, but as soon as it recoiled he punched me again in the face.

And as I laid there, stunned, he pushed himself into me, drawing a bellowed scream that tore my throat and filled it with blood.

"I fucking… hate you," Kerres cried. His voice switching from one born from hell, to one of agony. He thrusted his hips and broke me further, and a second scream rang from me, this time doubling me over in hacking coughs as I choked on my own blood.

Kerres didn't care, and if he did, the brain damage that I knew was controlling him wouldn't let him feel it. He was gone; Kerres was gone – but I knew that, didn't I?

The pain was unimaginable. Each thrust he made was like he was wrapped in sandpaper. I could hear my own flesh rip, and I could feel the wet blood fill me as he tore me apart from the inside out.

"I took your hand when you were ten years old." He said those words through teeth locked tight, through lips trying to form the words his mouth wouldn't allow. "I fucking did everything for you. I waited for you; I tried to help you." His voice started to rise, and with that his thrusts became harder. I cried out and tried to kick him a second time, but he only punched me again; this time filling my nose with more blood. I could feel it pooling in the back of my throat.

"Kerres, this isn't you!" I cried, before attempting to breathe through the blood slowly choking me. "K. K? It's J… it's J," I stammered. The flickers of anxiety were starting to burn inside of my chest again, and like previously, they quickly multiplied. "K, baby? Baby K? It's me." While I pleaded with him, I tried to push down the panic and remain calm.

Calm? I was choking to death. I was being raped. How can I be calm?

"KERRES!" I sobbed. "Stop! STOP!" But he wasn't stopping; he was only speeding up.

I closed my eyes, my dark world now nothing but the sounds of his wet penis fucking me, and the panicked, desperate gasps that were searing my lungs. I started sobbing hysterically after that, and as I did, I realized I could feel his cock pulsing and twitching as he came inside of me.

I let out a pitiful whine and turned my head to the side. I tried to muffle my tears, solely to save myself the embarrassment of him seeing me cry because of this.

"J?" a faint voice whimpered. I heard him let out a confused cry and he pulled himself out of me. "Jade? JADE!" he suddenly screamed hysterically. "I'm sorry. Baby, I'm sorry. Oh my god…" I felt his hand on my backside and a horrified gasp. "No, no, no… no…" The hand removed itself from what I knew was a massacre down there, and I felt tears dripping down onto my chest. "I didn't mean to… Jade, oh fuck. Jade, baby, I'm sorry."

Then a hand was placed on my head… and the hood was pulled off.

I squinted and saw Kerres looking down at me, his brown eyes wide and framed by the whitest eyeballs I had ever seen. His hysterical look seemed to make him glow; I'd never seen anyone look so horrified.

Kerres's expression dissolved when he saw me. I saw a mop of red hair, and then his face buried itself into the crook of my neck. He started to cry.

I stared up at the ceiling, brown rings from water stains looking like the rings my master's coffee cup left behind on the marble coffee table. My eyes remained fixed on them as Kerres lost himself on top of me.

Kerres pulled away, and with trembling hands he reached down, past my line of vision, and I heard a jingle of keys. I watched as he pinched a small silver key, and with sobs breaking his lips, he crawled to the side of the bed and I heard him start to unlatch my cuffs.

The rattling sound of chains being drawn over metal could be heard, and then a pressure was released from both of my cuffs. I moved my hands until they were in front of me, and looked down at the bloodstained palms. There was a vicious ring of red now circling my wrists like a bracelet, dripping down my pale skin to join the rest of its friends.

"J?" Kerres put a hand on my shoulder. "C-come on, baby. Say something."

Say something?

My eyes narrowed, and out of the corner of my eye I saw Kerres suddenly go rigid.

"Say something?" I said through my raw and tortured throat, my voice sounded like coarse gravel. I barely recognized it. "You… want me to… say something?" I heard Kerres choke, but I didn't look at him, not even when I saw a hand fly up to his head. I kept my own eyes fixed on my bleeding hands, and I watched them make a fist.

"I'm free, Kerres," I said, and I slowly swung one foot over the bed, and then the other. Only when I stood did I turn around and see Kerres now on his knees with his face tensed. Both hands were on his head, clenching his fiery red hair from the physical pain I knew he was in.

I liked what I saw.

"You made the grave… grave mistake…" I took a step towards him, and found a smile come to my lips.

Kerres narrowed in my vision as my eyes squinted contently. I smiled wider, just to make sure he could see the metal canines I had implanted, and all the other metal teeth I'd gotten from when the Crimstones had tortured me.

"A grave mistake, love." I tightened my fists, and with my movements, Kerres shrieked. He looked up at me, and his mouth fell open at what he saw. I saw his pupils narrow, and when I was close enough to see it, I saw my own ebony black eyes stare back.

I put a hand out and touched Kerres's cheek. "I hate you, Kerres. And this isn't the madness talking; I fucking hate you. I was with you for six years and I felt more for Elish than I'd ever felt for you after five days with him. You're nothing but a gutter rat, a terrorist, an insane, pathetic excuse for life, and I'm quite tired of you popping up in my life like a fucking COCKROACH!"

I dug my fingernails into my own palms and pushed this invisible mental force into Kerres. The entire time I did this, I watched him, and because I was watching so intently I saw the first gush of blood spray from his ears; a sickening, low squishing sound, one only chimera hearing could pick up, immediately following.

Kerres cupped his ears and let out a horrific scream. I watched his bulging eyes burrow into my own, tracing my face for any signs of mercy. Then he drew down his hands, looked at them, and let out a low moan when he saw all of the blood.

"J?" Kerres whimpered. His lower lip began to tremble, and soon the rest of his body followed suit. The tremor swept him like a shockwave following an explosion, and after several seconds of shaking, he slumped down onto his side.

Pathetic.

I turned my back to him and immediately found what I was looking for, a nice size knife. I knew it wouldn't be far; this house was just so full of weapons. My family would be happy to have them back.

"J?" Kerres said again, his voice a weak cry.

I smirked at this.

"I'm not J," I said, my tone dropping. I pushed the blade into my index finger and started twisting it around. "I am many things, Kerres, but I am not J."

I turned around. "I am Jade. I am slumrat. I am the Shadow Killer." I loomed over him as he lay there trembling, his own terror surrounding him like he'd pissed it himself. "I am Biter. I am brother. I am Catullus..." I gripped the knife in my hands, and as the anger ripped through me like an intense orgasm, I stabbed him in the chest.

"I am Cicaro."

Kerres gave out one last wailing Swan Song, his hand flying up to try and pull out the knife. He struggled with it, like he was the wrong man in front of Excalibur, and as he tried to pull the handle with bloody fingers that kept slipping, I grabbed his neck with both of my hands and started squeezing.

"I am Maritus."

I started strangling him, a part of me urging me to look away as his brown eyes bulged out of his head, but I realized as I kept my gaze fixed on him, that I wanted nothing more than to see the light finally fade from his eyes.

"I am a fucking chimera," I said to him with a smile. His mouth opened in a soundless scream and his blood-soaked hands grabbed my wrists and desperately tried to pull me off of him. "And I was merely waiting for you to give me the opportunity to show you how much I can act like it." I leaned down and kissed his bottom lip, tense and thin from his muted cries, before I leaned down and drew my tongue around the blood that had collected on the knife.

"You taste like shit," I growled as I licked my lips.

Kerres's eyes started filling with blood; they were bulging now like angry boils on diseased skin. He clenched his teeth, and I saw that he'd forgotten to tuck in his tongue. As he desperately clawed my hands with less and less strength, I saw his teeth sever the tip, fresh blood immediately running down his lips.

I leaned down and took the tongue tip into my mouth, and as Kerres's hands dropped and his blood-filled eyes rolled into the back of his head, I began to chew.

I stood up and looked down at Kerres's still body. I felt only one thing as I stared at him.

Fucking satisfaction.

"Time to go find my husband," I said to him, and I began to turn around. "Goodbye, Kerres. I won't–"

The words flew out of my throat and I stopped in my tracks.

There were two people in the doorway, both I recognized. One of them was Gage… and the other one was my older brother, and fellow stealth chimera… Theo.

Gage was giving me a look of pure horror, his mouth open and his mismatched eyes filled with shock. Theo on the other hand, was looking at me like he'd just discovered his new god.

"We're here to save you," Theo said with a brightness to his voice. He grinned, showing off his homemade pointed teeth, before he elbowed Gage in the side. "That's a stealth thing. Don't worry too much about it."

"W-why…? Why did you do that?" Gage stammered. His hands were cupping his mouth in a way that made me think he was about to throw up.

"Isn't it obvious?" Theo said with a cocked eyebrow. "I can smell rape from a mile away." He strolled up to me, the same swaggered walk that Sanguine had perfected, and craned his neck back with his hands on his hips. "You broke free, obviously." Then he picked up my free hand and made a smacking sound with his lips. "Bound and chained. Good job, dead boy. Ready to depart then?"

"He raped you…?" Gage's strained voice asked. He walked to Kerres and put a hand on his head, then his eyes widened. "He's… he's almost dead."

Theo chuckled. "I've known him for like two hours and I can already tell he's going to be interesting company." He clapped me on the back and started opening Kerres's drawers.

"What are…" I paused when Theo turned around and handed me a pair of blue jeans from Kerres's drawers, and a red t-shirt.

He helped me unfold them. "I have a jacket you can use… wow, slumrat clothes suck. We need to get you something more pretty, even if it'll all get covered in dust. I was dressed in worse but I managed some clothes in Black Tower. The sengils are out… long story."

Then my mind snapped back into action. I looked down at the jeans, then met Theo's eyes; they were glowing like crystals from the faint light coming in through the curtains.

"Depart?"

Theo smiled wide, and I had to shake my head at the horrible things he'd done to his once normal teeth. I'd only seen Theo three times and we'd never been alone together, Elish made sure of that. What I knew was that he was a stealth chimera like Sanguine, Jack, me, and the little chimera Hunter, and that he worshipped Sanguine and Jack.

Theo followed behind me as I walked to the bathroom. I had to get this blood off of me, and Kerres out of me.

"Silas has Sanguine locked away in the greywastes," he said, his voice echoing in the bathroom. "In a place of his nightmares. After that, I must take him back to Skyfall and hide him from Silas. Silas will do nothing and look nowhere; I have never seen him so depressed."

I turned around and looked at Theo, puzzled. "A lot of shit happened while I was out… didn't it?"

Theo shook his head, the corner of his mouth rising like it was attached to a string. This one had a disturbed look to him, Sanguine's eyes seeped his dark nature but Theo? He unsettled me, and his aura, if I remembered correctly, was no better. "Oh, dead boy, you have no idea." We both heard Gage retching in the kitchen; Theo chuckled dryly. "Any idea where your master is? You do realize everyone thinks you're dead, right?"

"You guys… don't know where Elish is?" I said, my voice catching.

Theo shook his head a second time. "Not at all. He got Klein to fly him somewhere and Klein started bleeding from the ears by chow that night, and stone dead by dessert. Elish didn't want anyone to know where he went." Theo shrugged and motioned to the shower. "Get cleaned up, that smell on you is making me twitch." He gave me a lurid wink before trying to get a glance at my backside.

I snapped my finger in his face and he looked up at me. "I am seriously not in the mood. I just fucking killed my ex-boyfriend," I said darkly. "Go get Gage some fresh air while I get cleaned."

The copper-eyed chimera blew a sigh, the strands of his black hair flying up before falling back over his arched eyebrows. "I suppose you technically are still Elish's husband, dead boy. Alright." He left after that.

This is why Elish hated stealth chimeras, and that knowledge was most likely why Silas decided to make me one. We were more susceptible to… weird quirks.

To put it lightly.

I locked the door and turned on the shower. While the water was warming up I started exploring the damage that Kerres had done to me.

I grimaced as I probed down there, and winced as a jolt of pain punished me for it. I could feel a tear, and when I raised my hand I saw the tips of my fingers coated in glistening red mixed in with streaks of opaque… his semen.

I wiped it on a face cloth, jumped into the shower, and started washing the rest of his presence off of me. Inside and out, no matter how much the hot water burned me down there, and fuck did it ever. The hotter the water was, the more I felt like I was getting clean – cleansing my body with fire I suppose.

Proud of me, Master? When I see you in the greywastes I'll get to tell you Kerres is finally dead and would never darken our lives with his presence again. No more being given a pass by King Silas, Kerres was dead.

This drew a smile to my face. I washed my hair twice and scrubbed myself to raw. At least I wasn't that filthy besides the blood… Elish had been bathing me regularly, I think it was just to distract himself from his troubles.

I turned the water off and got out. I opened the cabinet underneath the sink and got out a brown towel, threadbare and matted, old like the ones we had used in Moros. I was used to fluffy towels that felt like angels rubbing against you, but even this would be a step up from the rags we'd be given in the greywastes.

When I was dried and dressed, I walked into the now cooled, but still incredibly rank, bedroom.

Though I scowled when I saw that the rest of Kerres's body had been moved. He was now slumped over the bed on his knees, and with a sheet draped over him. There was also a strange buzzing I could just barely hear. It was coming from something covered because it was muffled and barely audible.

I shrugged it off, my mind already too crowded to play detective. I walked into the living room and saw Theo standing in the entrance to the house; the warm and welcoming outside behind him.

"Why's Kerres moved?" I asked him. I grabbed a canvas bag and started filling it with weapons. Kerres's house was full of them.

Theo looked back at me, a cigarette in his hand. "Gage wanted to say goodbye. He'd spent time with him," he responded casually. "Kicked me out for it too. He's odd."

"Can we leave here now? Is Jade okay?" I heard Gage's weak voice croak. I saw his black jacket sleeve; it looked like he was leaning up against the side of the house.

I walked out with the bag and gave Gage a look. "Thanks, man. How did you manage to find that whackjob?"

Gage wiped his mouth, there were splatters of grey, pungent vomit on a gnarled bush behind him. He looked horrible, and from the sweaty and glassy expression on his face, it didn't seem to be over.

"I… need to go back inside for a second. Don't follow." A spurt of thick grey vomit erupted from his mouth and Gage quickly dashed inside. I swung the backpack over my back and looked to where Theo was standing. He was all dressed in black leather from head to toe, sticking to his skin and accenting every inch of his body. They certainly did love to dress us in these types of outfits.

"He found me. I've been taking over for Jack being Skyfall's Grim Reaper," Theo laughed. "He literally thinks every stealth chimera is Sanguine and he thought I was him. That boy has trouble recognizing us. Supposedly we all look the same? Anyway, he owes Sanguine for helping him, so we shall be rescuing Sanguine. Who else is going to find him with Jack charred and burnt?"

"Charred and burnt?" I followed Theo as he started walking towards a red sports car parked in front of Kerres's house, and when I glanced over my shoulder I saw Gage emerge from inside, still wiping his mouth.

"Yes, dead boy. He was the one trying to kill you." Theo looked over his shoulder and beamed at me. "No one is really sure why. Perhaps he finally snapped? Master Jack has always been such a calm man, but oh when you see that mask get ripped off, it's nothing but flames and demons." Theo got into the car and I folded the seat back for Gage.

Jack, or the Grim as a lot of us called him, was a tranquil man that had an aura I'd imagine a Buddhist would have. He walked around with a grace and peacefulness to him that told us he'd reached enlightenment, and only wished for you to keep your drama away from him. He was just something else, and I always felt myself calmer when I was around him, almost transfixed with his presence.

On the other hand, however, I didn't dispute Theo's words. The more you were around stealth chimeras, or any chimera in general, the more you learned that under *every single one* was a thousand layers, each one peeling back to reveal a darker colour, until you eventually reached black. Some chimeras had more layers peeled back than others, and some had nothing left on them but darkness. I saw Jack's aura, one that told you he had all layers on him still, but when I started to learn how to read chimeras... I realized the closer I looked, the more I could see that every layer had been glued back on with such haste and panic, you could still see the bloodied fingerprints.

He was, in all respects, an emotional fraud, except he believed himself so much he was his own victim. That's how Jack could emit such a level of calm, because he mentally had given himself no other choice.

Interesting man, but...

... why was he trying to kill me?

I thought about this as the car started speeding towards Black Tower, Jack's skyscraper. If Sanguine was banished, and not soon after Jack went crazy... I would bank on my master being a part of Jack's rage. I was constantly in the crosshairs and they knew I had become Elish's one and only weakness.

"Are you okay back there, Gage?" Theo called. I saw him look at the guy through the rear-view mirror. "This is the only car of this type still in existence, so tell me if you're going to puke on my leather seats, okay?"

"Y-yeah," Gage said wearily. "I'll be okay."

"So agreeable and polite. This guy was encased in concrete for decades?" Theo said as he pulled out a remote phone resting in an empty cup holder. Then, with a cackle, he pressed down on the gas and we lurched forward, closer to the tower that loomed in the darkened corners of the city. "I need to make a call. Tell me if someone fat is crossing the street, the skinny ones will be merely speed bumps."

I shook my head and sighed internally; the noise of the revving motor drowning out all other sounds. I found myself staring out the window as Skyfall flew past me, and if only for a moment, being shocked at where I was.

I was healed, thanks to this strange odd-eyed man behind me who I knew nothing about. I'd gone from being brain-dead, a vegetable who couldn't even breathe on his own, back to who I had remembered I'd been. I'd been brought back to life, and my soul had been breathed back into this shell.

When we got out in front of Black Tower, I trailed behind Theo and walked with Gage.

"Thanks… for healing me," I said to him. He still looked sick over what he had seen. This was strange to me, but I remembered the heaviness I'd seen in his aura, and I realized that I was perhaps being unfair. I was so used to being around my family, and my family danced in blood, they didn't throw up at the sight of it.

But even though he looked so fragile, like he was made out of paper, he had already shown an incredible amount of endurance and an impressive amount of power. He might be the most powerful person in the world. He'd demonstrated healing powers that would have killed Silas within a minute if the king had tried to do the same. There was no doubt in my mind that this man could be a great ally to my master's campaign.

My master's campaign.

A light bulb went off inside of my head. I think… I think I knew where to find him.

The last thing I remembered was us being in the northern greywastes. He told me if Reaver showed signs of releasing radiation and exploding, I was to run to a town called Mantis… and demand to know where Dr. Mantis was.

Holy shit. I knew where Elish was. He was going to the northern greywastes to wherever Reaver and Killian were. Of course he would go back and try to find them.

Gage gave me a thin smile; his eyes were heavy. "I just feel this great pull to help him… they're telling me to find him and whenever I find the wrong one, they're not pleased," he said to me in a timid whisper.

He was speaking about *them* again, but who *they* were I didn't know. I wasn't going to ask. I only wanted to find my master, and once Gage was on our side, maybe Elish could help him with his head stuff.

But until we found Elish, I would make a point to be this kid's best friend. Not only because he saved me, but because I think Elish would want me to. I was Elish's social skills when he needed to get in with someone without intimidating and dominating them. This kid wouldn't respond to it, but he'd respond to me. Another one of my many uses.

Gage's eyes dropped to the ground, and he took in a shuddering breath. "That poor man…" he whispered. "He was so broken."

My mouth twisted to the side. "You do know… Kerres was suffering, right?" I asked him.

Gage was quiet for a moment, but when I held the door open for him to walk into Black Tower, he gave me a slight nod. "We all get what we deserve. I gave him what he deserved. You... I don't understand why you were so brutal to him. Why it was so... gruesome?"

"Does it matter in the end?" I asked honestly. "Dead is dead."

"You could have just let your mind kill him... it would've been faster."

I did a double take. "You... know about that?"

Gage nodded and we walked into the elevator.

"Do you know that since I'm mortal using it kills me? That's how my brain got fried."

It was Gage's turn to do a double take. He looked confused at this, but then I saw his scowling face soften, like he had took in the information and had accepted it. "I never thought of it like that, but it would be deadly. You'll not live long then." Gage said this rather matter-of-factly.

"My master will make me immortal soon," I replied back. "I think he's going to do it as soon as he realizes I'm alive. If he... doesn't kill me for being dead that is." Elish's face filled my mind, and I felt my heart skip. I wanted to find him with such intensity I felt like I could transport myself to his location, that my will alone would bring me to him.

How was he?

"Theo..." I said as we all stood in the elevator. "Where's Sanguine?"

Theo watched the illuminated numbers above the elevator's doors slowly climb up. "Northern greywastes. Silas locked him back inside the basement where they found him." Theo's face darkened just as my eyes widened. "It's a horrible place. I... know I stand the chance to be punished for it, but I am hoping that Silas's depression will have him handing the reins permanently to Garrett; and once he does, Garrett will be fetching Sanguine anyway. Jack will be resurrecting for weeks with his injuries, and it is up to me to save Sanguine and Crow from their psychosis."

Northern greywastes? Fuck... perfect, fucking perfect. I just needed to locate where Mantis was and I would find Elish, Reaver, and Killian. I knew it.

"Locked him inside of a basement? Why?" I heard Gage ask, his voice strained and upset.

Theo walked through the elevator doors, in front of us was a simple concrete hallway and a beige door that would lead us to the rooftop.

"Because he freed you, my friend," Theo replied. "Silas was livid."

Gage's confused facial expression turned to shock. He had a really animated face that reminded me of Reno in a way. But Reno's animation was usually to make him more goofy and funny, Gage just kept showing me new ways of looking terrified. "We have to find him. I have to heal him. They need him to be strong. The… the others aren't strong enough."

The others aren't strong enough?

Weird.

"That's why you're coming, pretty boy," Theo said and pushed the door open. "But first, Jade. I have something for you. This is a special gift from me and Gage to you, dead boy. We couldn't leave without them seeing you. They will, of course, keep your secret."

Theo walked into Jack's rooftop garden and I followed. I could see, beyond the marble statues and greenery, the Falconer and… and something else…

My walk slowed down when I saw two men sitting side by side on a bench, facing away from me.

One of them had raven black hair with scars visible on his scalp, the other… was wearing a pair of black cat ears on a headband. They were both tense and unmoving, as if they themselves were expecting something bad to happen to them. It made me want to draw up their auras, and I saw, weaved into their colourful hues, a heavy sense of despair. Yes. I could see the black flecks hidden in the dimming colours. My friends were deep in grieving.

"You two look like your best friend's died," I spoke, my mouth twitching to a smile.

Like a bee had stung both of them, Big Shot and Luca jumped to their feet and turned around. Big Shot's expressive eyes widened and his mouth dropped open, just as all of the colour drained from Luca's face; the poor sengil was looking at me like he was seeing a ghost.

"KING JADE!" Big Shot yelled happily. "JADE!" He ran towards me and roughly slammed his hand on my head. "KAH!" he cried, every tooth visible as he grinned widely. Oh, were those green eyes ever bright. I'd never seen my half-raver friend so animated and full of life.

Big Shot threw his arms over me and hugged me, squeezing my body to his and constricting me so tightly my ribs creaked. I hugged him back and laughed. "I missed you, Big Shot." I looked past him and saw that

Luca still hadn't moved, nor had his dumbstruck expression changed; I don't even think the poor guy had blinked.

I patted Big Shot, and after giving him one more squeeze, I gently pulled him away and turned to Luca. I walked up to him, and was surprised when the first movement Luca made was to take a step back. I don't think he was able to believe I was still alive.

"It's me," I said to him through my smile. "I managed to escape with Gage's help."

Luca's brow furrowed. He reached up and touched my face gently, and when he saw I was solid and not a manifestation, his lower lip tensed.

Then poor Luca let out an emotional wail and jumped into my arms. The sengil, one who took pride in not showing his emotions, in being a wallflower, out of the way, obedient, and never distracting his masters with whatever negative emotion he might be feeling, sobbed openly as he clung to me.

"Shhh, it's okay, Luca. You don't need to cry."

"Jade... Jade... I'm so relieved. I'm so happy!" Luca cried. "You have no idea what this means. Oh, Master Jade. I can't believe it's really you."

My smile was so wide my cheeks hurt. "I'm here, Luca. I'm healed too and I'm going to go find our master."

"You need to find him!" Luca sobbed. "Jade... he left Skyfall. He left as soon as he realized you had died. I've never seen him like this before. You have to find our master."

My heart lurched and filled with despair, and that despair translated to tears in my own eyes. "I will, Luca. I'll bring him home, I promise."

Luca sniffed and I felt him nod. He pulled away and wiped his eyes with the sleeve of his white shirt. "He changed so much when you were ill," Luca said. "He loves you, Master Jade. You must find him. I can only imagine how sad he is to have left Skyfall. Please bring him home."

"I will," I whispered. And I put one arm around Big Shot, who was still grinning so wide the world could see, and one arm around Luca, and hugged them both. "You two take care of each other while I'm gone. Promise me, Big Shot?"

When I pulled away Big Shot nodded, and Luca did as well.

"I protect family," Big Shot said gravely. "Luca is family, this is my truth. You find husband, I'll look after little slave." He rested a hand on Luca's head and patted it lightly.

I gave them both one more hug and a goodbye for now, before turning to Theo. He was standing beside the plane with several figs in his hand, looking rather proud of himself. Gage was beside him. My new friend looked somewhat happier than he had been previous, but his eyes still held a lot of heaviness.

We all boarded the plane and I saw Theo hand Gage a fig and me one as well.

"Promise we will find Sanguine first? He's locked up because of me," Gage said as he gently took the fruit Theo was offering him. He turned it around in his hand like he didn't know what to do with it. "I've already caused a lot of trouble."

I decided to throw the kid a bit of love, reaffirm my commitment to get him on our side.

"I promise, we'll find Sanguine. And it's not your fault," I said to him. I took his fig and split it in half and handed it back. "Look. You seem pretty bewildered with what you've been thrown into, but... it'll get quieter after this. Our lives will all calm down." I glanced as I heard the sliding metal door of the Falconer close, then Theo disappear into the cockpit.

I directed him to the back area of the Falconer with a hand on his shoulder, and dropped my voice. "I'm going to be leaving on my own after, to find my master. Elish has caused some friction here, and I don't want Theo knowing where he is." I motioned to the cockpit; I could hear Theo whistling as he set everything up. "I want you to come with me. I'll protect you, these nuts won't. Want to come with me? You'll be like eight hundred miles from Silas, and you'll be safe."

Gage considered this. "I eventually need to return to Skyfall..."

I nodded. "Elish and I will have to come back eventually too. My master will make sure you're safe. He won't let anything happen to you after what you did to help me."

Gage fell silent as he thought this over. It made me wonder if he was communicating with the voices I was suspecting were inside of his head. "As long as I can have some time alone with Sanguine, to speak with him. Yes... I believe that will work. Sanguine... he'll be safe in Skyfall?"

"Yeah," I said. "He has a lot of people that will protect him, and Theo's saying that Silas is all depressed." As I said this, I realized I didn't even know why.

I walked to the front of the Falconer. I peeked my head into the cockpit, just as Theo was turning on the engine.

"Hey, why's Silas depressed?" I asked. I'd ask if it was because I was dead, but I didn't want Theo to die of laughter before he took me to the greywastes. "Is it because he still hasn't found Reaver?"

I saw Theo's head shake as he began pulling on the Falconer's wheel. "No, dead boy," he said, his tongue poking out of the side of his mouth as he concentrated on the plane's ascending. "There was an explosion in the plaguelands, in an old laboratory. Reaver will be burning in white flames for the next two decades, and his pretty little boyfriend is dead. I'm sorry to have to tell you this as well, love, but Perish killed himself too. Silas is an absolute wreck about it. The blond boyfriend destroyed Sky's O.L.S before he died."

What?

Reaver?

And Killian?

The bottom fell out from under me. I stood there in the door frame of the cockpit and just stared, before I turned around with a nod, and closed the metal door; the last rational thing I could think to do before the pieces of my hastily constructed world fell back apart.

I made it two steps towards one of the metal benches that lined both sides of the Falconer before my wobbling legs brought me to the ground. I cupped a hand over my mouth, and stared at the ribbed metal floor as the shock dropped on me like gravity had lost its force.

"Jade?" I heard Gage say. I felt a hand on my shoulder. "Were they your... friends?"

I tried to open my mouth to answer back but all I could manage was a nod. Shock and despair were two circling monsters in my head, each chasing the other to grab dominance over these thoughts taking over me. One wanted me to remain in a state of animation, staring at the floor like someone who had just bore witness to a terrifying nightmare; the other wanted to scream and cry and tear out my hair.

My friends were dead? I had travelled with Killian, protected that little fucker from Perish. I had helped Reaver escape by destroying my own mind so he could find Killian. Those two were my friends, Reaver was my brother. He'd been determined to find Killian. I had seen the resolution burn in his eyes; he'd do anything to find that boy.

Did he at least get to say goodbye? The thought that Reaver found Killian, only to have the lab go up in flames, devastated me. I was sure they would be all right.

What had happened in that lab?

That question was answered quite easily. From the pieces of memory that my torn and shredded brain could solder together, it had been Silas who had caused the sestic radiation outburst. That would make sense, even in his madness I knew Perish would have never hurt Killian.

It was Sky and Sky's O.L.S – which was now destroyed.

Then, because my mind was a machine constantly working against me, another bombshell was dropped onto what was already a smoking crater, this one making me have to close my eyes from the dizziness.

Elish.

My master had lost everything, hadn't he? Not just me, but the boy he had been hiding for twenty years. His carefully crafted plan had been destroyed with an apocalyptic swiftness that reflected the devastation that was the Fallocaust.

But then...

Was he even in the northern greywastes? If he wasn't in the greywastes to find Reaver and Killian, where was he?

I sniffed and blinked away the tears, barely feeling Gage's supportive hand on my back. I tried not to cry, but the lump in my throat was physically painful. I didn't trust myself to talk, or do anything but keep swallowing and keep blinking until I felt some shred of control.

I had to find Elish. I had to let him know that at least I was still here. We could come up with a new plan. He was smart... he always knew what to do.

The next thing I knew, I was in Gage's arms. This weird, way too innocent kid holding me while my body shook from grief. It helped, but the comfort of being in someone's arms again drew out their own feelings of longing and loneliness.

I just hoped soon these arms would be my master's, because I knew now, more than ever, I had to find him.

I had to find my husband.

CHAPTER 27

Elish

ELISH'S EYES SLOWLY OPENED. FOR A BRIEF MOMENT he was confused as to where he was. Should he not be in Jack's skyscraper wrapped in silk and resting in the library on a day bed? Why was he hearing the gentle soothing sounds of a river behind him, and feeling the sun heating the back of his neck? Stranger still, his clothes were stiff and had the unappealing aroma of clothing that had sat too long in the washing machine.

Elish wiped the sleep from his eyes and sat up. He put a hand to his head and looked around to take in this strange scene. He was laying two feet away from a river, with a rocky ledge behind him, and in the distance, grey mountains dotted with black trees and the shadowed outlines of structures and power poles that still remained standing.

Elish stared off into that distance, looking through the haze that the summer's heat had drawn up. He stared blankly before, with a low sigh, it came back to him; the series of events that had led him to waking up beside this very river.

In a fit of drug and despair-induced hallucinations he had lost himself, and in the end, it had gotten him shot – multiple times.

So how long had he been resurrecting for? And what distance has this river brought him before washing him up on shore? Elish rose and tested his legs. He was relieved that they worked easily, meaning that he couldn't have been out for more than two weeks. If it was only gunshots it should've only been several days, but who knows if he was prevented from resurrecting due to being submerged in water.

Well, he was here now, and they hadn't consumed him at least; he must've been swept away from them too quickly. There was little doubt in Elish's mind that if the greywasters had gotten a hold of him they would've made a fine meal of his body.

And from the amount of drugs he'd consumed, they'd probably get high as well.

Elish started walking up the steep ledge behind him. It was at a sharp incline and the gravelly ground was loose, with every step Elish disturbed rocks and chunks of pavement which rained down the hill before rolling into the river. Elish climbed to the top to see what lay beyond, but found himself nose-to-nose with the front of a previously burned house. Elish shrugged and went inside; he scanned the garbage-strewn kitchen and found a metal chair to sit in. Without hesitation, he reached into his pockets and brought out a metal tin trimmed with rubber, and held shut with elastic bands.

He opened it, and was relieved to see it had remained waterproof. He rested a cigarette on his knee and crushed a yellow Dilaudid pill between his fingers and deposited the dust into his palm. After inhaling the drugs, he pursed the cigarette between his lips and lit it with a pinch of his fingers; a trick he hadn't been able to do in front of the greywasters.

Elish smoked the cigarette and stared at the dirty floor. He was completely sober now and not surprised to feel himself more depressed than ever. Without the drugs, the descending and crippling dark cloud was above him, and the physical weight on his shoulders even more taxing than usual. At one point during his binge drinking and chain drug use, he'd wondered if once he became sober he'd kick himself in the ass to take back his life and be the man, the prince, the chimera, he'd once been before Jade died... but now that he was face-to-face with what had transpired he wanted nothing more than to get high again and numb the sharpened memories that sliced him every time he grazed them.

At least through his resurrection his tolerance to the opiates was nothing. One pill was enough to get him to his feet, but he inhaled another one before standing, for no other reason than just wanting to. There was nothing else for him, he didn't even have that annoying greywaster boy to keep him company.

Elish brushed the dirt and sand off of himself. He must've been resurrecting out of the water for quite some time if he was completely dry. It was a plus at least, he didn't feel like stopping to dry his clothes or make a fire. He needed to get to a town and buy more drugs.

Then Elish paused and swore under his breath. His backpack was with the caravan that had shot him, all of his money was in there. This made Elish grit his teeth in anger, and swear revenge on those idiots for shooting him in the first place. Though it was obvious just from his own behaviour that he'd deserved it. If any man had come near Jade with such madness, he would've broke his neck before the man's hand had touched Jade's jacket.

Elish walked out of the house, and after drinking from the river he climbed the ledge again and walked along the large house to find a road, a road that would hopefully lead him…

There was a town in the distance.

Elish's eyes widened. In front of him, not but five miles away… was the new town Mantis. He recognized it from when he and Reaver had visited. A small town still under construction, and even now as he started walking towards it he could see that a wall was currently being built. Robyn had mentioned the booze and material they were bringing were to pay the workers hired to help build this wall. A project now on rush to help keep out the ravers currently taking over towns west of here.

It was luck – great luck, and the thought of getting what little possessions he owned back made Elish walk faster towards civilization. He needed his money back for his drug habit and drinking habit… and he didn't want to lose Killian's guitar either.

A prince with millions of dollars worth of possessions and now the only thing I want is a small guitar back. Elish shook himself of the degrading thought and kept going, wishing he had a bottle in his hand and a gun on his hip. He should get both returned to him soon enough.

The road in front of him was almost non-existent. It was segmented like someone had taken a hammer to glass and it sloped down to an abandoned town surrounded by trees. The trees were large and embedded in between bushy shrubs and yellow grass. The excess of life was thanks to the river Elish had just come from. It looked like the river wound around the abandoned town like a slithering snake before it disappeared into Mantis, and where it started again Elish didn't know.

But as Elish walked towards the abandoned town, red flags were immediately raised. There were bright colours breaking the monotone slate greys and rusty browns. Not just the normal reds or blues from plastic bins or shop signs, but neon paint and small collections of brightly coloured garbage made into nests like it was the home of some beast.

Then a foul stench reached Elish's nose. He wrinkled it but didn't stop his pace. He knew from where he'd found Jade that this was the home of ravers. This realization did nothing to him; he only carried on down the fractured road, wondering if perhaps they were smart enough to make their own alcohol yet.

His air-dried boots echoed as he entered this ghost town. Elish followed a particularly rancid stench and observed several heads on stakes; their skin falling off of their faces and sliding down their brown skulls as if they themselves could no longer stand the smell. Below the spiked heads were circles of brown. They gave off the false appearance of being the heads' shadows but were only the dried fluids that now stained the ground directly below the skewers. And not just that, on closer inspection, maggots could be seen writhing, and as soon as Elish adjusted his hearing he realized there were flies all around as well.

No ravers though. Elish glanced into the dark windows surrounding him and inside the doors left wide open. There were signs of activity everywhere: dismembered body parts rotting off of their greasy bones, piles of shit heaped in corners, buildings saturated with urine, and radrats too. There were even several stray irradiated dogs skittering around with their fur patched and their skin scabby and leaving behind white dandruff flakes that could be seen whenever they scratched themselves

Elish's eyes turned to a shotgun leaning against a house that was half-enclosed with a rusty chain-link fence. He grabbed it, ignoring the putrid smell on the handle, and checked to see if it was loaded. It had no strap, however; so he carried it with the barrel against his shoulders and moved on.

Yes, these were Jade's Ravers. The realization was heavy inside of Elish, and he had to force down the despair that followed his cicaro's name like a relentless ghost. Jade was the reason these ravers could now use weapons, could now take over towns. His boy had gathered a following of loyal worshippers whereas a normal greywaster, or even a chimera, would've been consumed on the spot. All of this with a horrendous head wound, scarce supplies, and in the dead of winter as well.

There was a flicker of pride inside of Elish's heart, before the sadness soaked through and extinguished it. He continued to smoke the last of his cigarette, ignoring a scrawny puppy who was wagging his tail at him with his head down, no doubt wishing for a pat since there seemed to be food everywhere for him to eat.

While Elish walked through this town, one that had their structures close together and framed with still standing electricity poles, street lamps, and street lights, he noticed the sun had set over the mountains in the west. A coldness started to mix in with the nose hair burning stench of death and rot, but that seemed to only awaken his nose from its suicide. This could perhaps be the reason for the ravers being gone, out hunting perhaps.

But was there a need for hunting? There were bodies heaped everywhere, bloated corpses pressed up against curbs and leaning beside buildings, with shreds of clothing waving in the faint breeze, and chunks taken out of them like a shark had grown feet and had made its rounds. Down an alley, Elish saw bodies reduced to their component parts: stacks of arms, legs with the thigh and ass cheek attached, and torsos looking like discarded mannequins.

Interesting. Elish walked to this alleyway and observed ripped up office chairs in a row behind a metal desk. He walked around the desk, and was made further curious when he saw a metal box full of childrens' toys, all of them brilliant colours and cleaned to shining. Besides that, a box of batteries, also cleaned off, and a bin of Walkmans.

This was… a store.

Elish scanned the alleyway and a shadow of a smirk appeared. The ravers were developing a civilization, all thanks to his cicaro. How fascinating.

Elish left the aromatic shop and carried on to the other end of the alleyway. It opened up to a single-lane road with rusted cars parked nose to rear and townhouses stuck together, each supporting the other, with some so deteriorated it was only their comrades holding their shoulders to keep them from falling into further ruin.

They weren't high enough to prove much use for scouting, but he spotted an apartment building in the distance framed by two gnarled maples. With the skinny grey puppy following behind him, still determined for that pet, he walked down the corpse-strewn road to the apartment building and crossed a parking lot. There were bright neon paintings that looked to glow in the dark all around the building, and with another curious shake of his head, Elish saw actual designs on the apartment; not just the usual splattered scrawls of mad men wanting to see bright colours. There was an obvious painting of a raver, done in bright pink with black eyes that dripped from the spray can being held too close, and further on, severed heads with red paint for the blood, also dripping from an eager raver's spray can; however, the red that seeped from the stumps was more fitting in that particular image.

Another wall of stink. Elish could right away spot five dead bodies, most consumed down to the bones, with the meat that still remained green and shifting with maggots and other insects. Clothing, all of it faded and stained, clung to their bones, bits chewed and taken out in typical raver fashion. It looked like the subhumans still had no patience when there was fresh meat on the menu.

He kicked a pile of papers out of the way and started walking up the stairs, only turning around once to try and tap the puppy away with his foot, but all he did was look up at Elish with pathetic eyes almost crusted shut. He debated booting it down the stairs, but he'd already started walking up the stairs by the time he'd decided on that action.

Each floor was more deteriorated than the next: collapsed ceilings with their gyprock innards now on the floor to mix in with the dust; loose papers and insulation; wires hanging like nooses just waiting to snag you; and bones in all states of rot stacked like kindling.

Then, finally, Elish reached the top floor and entered into an open apartment door that would give him a window pointing towards Mantis. He looked past the chewed on and destroyed furniture, the chairs with twisted legs, and broken TV set, and saw a balcony with a shattered sliding glass door. He walked onto the wooden balcony, his boots crunching glass, and stepped out onto the swollen boards that replaced the stench of rot with one of soured wood.

It was more than obvious where the ravers were when he gazed out over the town of Mantis. Elish could see a string of orange, like a long whip set ablaze, probably a mile from the town, four miles from where he was. Further on, he could see the beginnings of buildings being set ablaze, just several of them, but their black smoke was already starting to darken the horizon.

Then, just faintly, he heard the popping of automatic gunfire.

Well, hopefully the caravan was still in the town. The ravers would have no use for a guitar and money was not their currency. As long as Jade hadn't taught them how to do drugs perhaps a town taken over by ravers would be a blessing. No one to bother him, and if he got there quick enough perhaps he could secure a house for himself, free of their filthy lifestyle.

Elish found a chair and watched the sun set over the battle going on just several miles from him. The wave of fire quickly closed in on the large gap where the wall hadn't been built. There was more popping and a series of faint screams, then an explosion that Elish could feel in his feet. He saw a plume of black rise up with flares of fire tucked into the thick billows. Then, as the building that was on fire burned more, flames started to appear.

A rush of adrenaline went through Elish, and he found himself wishing he was down there in that town. Jade had told him his adventure taking over that town with the ravers; how he burned them alive in the hall and shot the ones trying to flee. Oh, how the boy's eyes had lit up like flares when he spoke of it, it was enough to make Elish wish he'd been right beside Jade. He'd never gotten the chance to kill with Jade, and now he wished they'd been able to do that together.

Then Elish's thoughts drifted to the adventures he'd had with Reaver. The two of them killing that merchant and the bodyguards had been a highlight in an otherwise stressful excursion. He remembered vividly twisting off the man's head – and also what happened afterwards.

Chimera engineering for you, Elish told himself. He shook his head and observed, as the darkness of night turned on his night vision, the insects below scurry and scramble. It was like invading army ants attacking a peaceful nest, black, fast moving specks beelining towards slower ones, mobbing them, filling the night with screams, before leaving them splattered like a finger had come down from the heavens to crush them. Then they would move to the next, mob, consume, mob consume, with the gun-wielding ones behind them taking down snipers on the roofs, and hidden gunmen sheltering in buildings and alleyways.

Another pill was crushed and inhaled, followed by a cigarette, and somehow during that time the puppy had braved the glass and had curled up between Elish's boots for a place of warmth.

When the entire front of the town was glowing with fire, and the stars had been blocked out by smoke, Elish rose and exited the apartment. He walked out and into the night air, his last cigarette from the waterproof tin in his mouth, and headed in the direction of Mantis. He had the shotgun leaning against his chest, and his air-dried jacket closed from the night's chill. He wasn't sure what to expect, but he knew what to do when the ravers spotted him.

The closer he got to Mantis, the more he could smell the remnants of the battle. The aroma of charred bodies were now on the air, the smell laced with the sounds of arians dying and wood crackling and burning. His surroundings felt weighted, like they were heavy from the souls of the departed and the agony they'd experienced as they died. If he believed in ghosts, surely this place would become haunted.

Elish saw a dark figure walking against one of the shabby-built walls; then it turned and looked at him before its mouth opened with a hiss.

"Where's your leader?" Elish asked casually. "I am King Jade's husband. Take me to the raver that leads you."

The raver didn't miss a beat. He immediately charged towards Elish, and as he rapidly approached Elish could see the rotted state the subhuman was in. His scalp was completely peeled back, the piece of skin flapping in the wind with his stringy dark hair the streamers. As he stretched his arms towards Elish in anticipation of eating him, Elish could see calcified fingers and a chest that had bare ribs sticking out like claws protruding through grey soil.

This one was not chipped. Elish pursed his lips and whistled, and like the raver had hit an invisible barrier, he stopped, dirt skidding up underneath his sneakered feet.

As the raver's hands flew up to his ears, Elish raised the shotgun and shot the mad raver in the head. Like he'd shot a watermelon, the top half of the raver's skull exploded, then, with a *thunk*, the creature fell dead onto the ground.

Behind him he could hear small, energetic barks. Elish looked down to see the skinny puppy in a state, barking with vigour behind the protection of Elish's leg. This got the puppy nothing but an eye roll, and Elish continued on.

He walked underneath the shrouded awning of the building, and then to a single-lane street that held tree-covered greywastes on both sides, a park at one time Elish wagered. Elish scanned the trees, picking up sounds of growling and snapping in the distance, and saw a group of ravers hunched over what smelled like fresh kills, their bodies writhing and moving like a pride of lions. Elish could see fresh body parts hanging from their frames by bits of twine. He knew from Jade's stories these were trophies that would eventually be made into more complex jewellery. Jade had been upset and put out when Elish had made him abandon his ear necklace in a rusted out car they'd passed, and had described with boasting pride the crown of finger bones he'd been given.

Then Elish heard talking, actual words being spoken instead of grunts and screams. He turned to his right and saw a cluster of five ravers, guns in hand. Past them, Elish could see a group of still alive townspeople.

The survivors were clustered together, huddled like sheep, weeping and whimpering, and most, if not all, of them bleeding from wounds.

"No, smaller knife." Elish heard the raspy deep voice of a raver. "Bucket for chips. Now."

Elish understood what he was witnessing just from those few words. These would be the new ravers. Their chips would be removed for a time, enough for their minds to succumb to the maddening yet preserving sestic radiation. And then they'd be put back in to work through the radiation but keep them as the new generation of ravers.

"Yes," the raver called. He was a male who looked to be older, though age was always hard to pinpoint with these irradiated creatures. He made the motion to say more before his milky eyes, with only small dots for pupils, shot to Elish. An enthusiastic hiss rumbled in his throat and guns clicked.

Elish gave one short whistle, and the sounds of guns clicking was soon replaced with them falling to the ground.

"I'm not here to hurt anyone," Elish called. He walked to the older raver and put a hand on top of his stringy grey hair. "Kah!" Elish spat then said calmly, "My husband created all of you. Where is the one who leads you?"

"Husband?" The man put his hand on Elish's head and said *Kah*, as well. "King Jade's husband? You're Big Shot?"

Elish gave him a flat look. "No. I certainly am not. Big Shot is not Jade's husband, but the man is safe in Skyfall right now. King Jade is…" The corner of Elish's mouth twitched. "…currently ill. I will be staying here for the time being. Where is the man who leads you?"

The old raver tipped his chin and made a sound that resembled a hacking cough and a screaming eagle. Elish turned around, and saw a large dark-skinned man who had been walking down the road turn towards the sound. He was tall, taller than Elish was and even Nero, with large muscles and dreadlocks that fell past his shoulders.

The leader of the ravers walked over, blood staining his lips and dripping down his chin. Elish saw that he had a bushmaster in his hand and a decapitated head in the other.

The man looked at Elish and his eyes narrowed, ones completely free of the white film that the radiation-crazed ravers had. "Where's King Jade? Is he with you?" the man asked.

Every time they mentioned Jade another javelin pierced Elish's heart. The boy would've been hanging off of his arm and running off in all directions like a puppy who just got off of his leash to play in the park. Oh, he would've been so pleased with what he was seeing.

Elish swallowed hard and shook his head. "The boy is ill and he wished for me to… check on your progress. What do you call yourself?"

"My arian name was Trent," the raver said. "King Jade called me Beast. A strong name. I am Prince Beast now. Who are you, King Jade's husband?"

Who am I? If only the raver knew just how complicated that question was now. It felt like Elish had died the precise moment that Jade did. Or perhaps the road to Elish's death had begun the moment Silas had told them Reaver was burning and Killian dead, and the boy was just the final blow… either way he wasn't Elish, and he no longer felt like James either. Even James the greywaster had more dignity than this vacant shell had.

"Make up something… I no longer have a name," Elish said dismissively, then he looked around. "You seem to have a good formula here. What is your end goal with this place? Are you taking over the towns to raze them, or are you trying to establish your own community?"

Beast crossed his muscular arms over a chest bare but for a necklace of fingers and… penises from the looks of it. "We want right to live with arians. They don't let us, we kill them."

"Fair enough," Elish replied. "Is this all the people you have, or is this only your army?"

"Our army," Beast said back. "We have three towns now: Jadetown, New Jadetown and…" As if almost comically, the raver looked around with his face creased in thought, much like the animated facial expressions of Big Shot. Then his dark eyes widened and he nodded. "New New Jadetown."

If Elish had ever had a sense of humour, or a bone left in his body to feel that emotion, he would've laughed, or at least shaken his head in exasperation.

"Why don't you call this place Shadowtown? That was… *is* his middle name," Elish said.

Beast seemed to turn this around in his head before nodding his agreeance. "Yes, that will do. Shadowtown. You will become honoured resident until you leave." Beast put a burly hand on top of Elish's head and *Kah'd* at him before turning and walking towards the huddled mass of arians, spits and snarls falling from his lips making the frightened livestock cower and scream. Most of them held heavy lacerations on their skin, and some were missing limbs or had them reduced to bone. Elish looked over them but from what he could see, none of them were from the caravan he'd been riding with.

"You... what's your name?" Elish asked the old raver.

"Louis," the raver replied.

"Did you see a caravan here? A woman was leading it with her son and four mercenaries. Possibly with legion."

The old raver's forehead wrinkled as he thought of this. "Ask stock." He motioned to the herded people.

"I – I saw them... Robyn, right?" a man suddenly spoke up. Elish walked past the old raver and towards the one who had been brave enough to speak up. The man was glancing around terrified as a female raver stood a foot away, with an assault rifle in her hands and a nasty-looking machete on her belt.

"That's right. Where's the caravan?" Elish asked coolly.

But to Elish's dismay, the man's eyes widened, and when he took a closer look he realized he was the barman who had served him and Reaver. Elish had asked him if they'd seen Jade, and as usual, Elish's purple eyes were quite memorable.

"They left three hours before the attack. They were going to spend the night but they seemed pretty spooked," the barman said, then he started to look uncomfortable. "They decided to go with a legion escort while they had the chance."

"What direction are they going in?" Elish pressed.

"Let me go and..."

"I wasn't negotiating, greywaster. What fucking direction are they going in?" Elish snapped and he took a step towards the man. The barman held up his hands defensively, the whites of his eyes glowing in the torchlight. The others behind them stood back as well, only to get yelled at and threatened by the other ravers keeping them clustered together.

"I just want to be let go," the barman said. "Just–"

"You're a fucking coward, Aiden," a woman with tied back dark hair suddenly snapped. "Saving your own fucking ass. What about the kids?

What about our old? Fuck you, Aiden."

The barman, obviously named Aiden, ignored her and took a step towards Elish. "They're heading back towards Mariano. Come on, I did my best to help you and the other guy when you were here a few months ago. Let me go."

Here with the other guy... Well, his fate was sealed then. Elish turned away from the barman and made eye contact with the female raver. "Kill him. I need to catch up with that caravan. I'll be back." The female raver nodded and said something to him, but it was drowned out by the shouting and cursing of the barman. Elish didn't turn around, but could hear the barman's terror-laced screams rise, before they stopped as if someone had pressed mute on a remote.

Elish stepped out of the town and looked to find the North Star, with that as his compass he started jogging towards the direction of Mariano, his gun still in hand.

All of the noises inside of the town fell to silence as he sprinted along the newly paved road, a road that he had travelled down many months before with Reaver by his side. With everything that had happened with Jade, his thoughts hadn't been with the man, but now he found himself almost smiling while he relived the adventures that they'd had. He had praised himself many times over for breaking through Reaver's shell, and had been looking forward to moulding that boy to be the king of the greywastes. He had always assumed he'd need to force himself to be civil to the boy who'd been such a disobedient little shit in his youth, but in all honestly... he'd enjoyed Reaver's company, and had been close to considering him a dear friend. It took a lot for Elish to allow someone into his small circle of true friends, and that boy had surprised him enough to warrant receiving the gift of trust.

It would've been perfect, everything had been coming together. Reaver would rule the greywastes and Killian would be his voice of reason. Caligula and Nico would have the Legion, and he himself would have Skyfall with Jade as a husband by his side. All of his seeds had been sprouting and flowering, the chess pieces positioning themselves nicely.

And then, one after another, everything caught on fire and burned to cinders right in front of him.

Fire had always been his enemy. And now the flames had not only symbolically burned his seeds and carefully laid out plans... but it had taken Jade from him, and Reaver and Killian too.

Elish felt his jaw tighten, and he realized the hand that was holding the gun was clenched. The more steps he took into the darkness, the more he found his anger bubbling to the surface. It wasn't fair and it wasn't right. He was close to having everything and now look at where he was.

He was in the company of filthy ravers, a drug addicted, alcoholic mess that couldn't make it one day sober without falling apart. What had once been a life of luxury, of control and comfort in his thick shell, had been shattered; one hammer blow after another. The world in which he had lived for over ninety years had been destroyed.

And what was worse? There was no one to blame this time.

No one but himself.

Elish picked up his pace, the sounds of screaming behind him rising like someone had poured gasoline on an already out of control fire. He hoped the people who were making those screams were in great amounts of pain. Elish's mind may be ablaze, but if there was one thing he knew he wanted, it was for the world to burn with him. Everyone should suffer; everyone should feel what he was going through in this moment. Why should they be left to live their lives as normal when his had been dismantled piece by piece? He was above every single one of them and they didn't have the right to be content when he was so miserable.

If I could release sestic radiation I swear I would find a laboratory and I would end this dead world again. I would take back two hundred years of healing, and rain pesticides down to kill the insects that crawl upon this necrotic flesh. I would rip their children from their arms. I would kill their lovers as they lay intertwined. I would show the world what happens when it dares not give me what I want.

Fuck them. Fuck every person who dares draw breath when my husband is forever silenced. It's not fair. It's not fair that I have to live for the rest of eternity when he's…

When he's…

Elish stopped and stared forward. For a moment he stood there in stunned silence, unable to accept what realization awaited him at the end of that train of thought.

Surely no… I'm different.

I loved Jade more than…

… more than Silas loved Sky.

I'm… different than Silas. It's not the same at all.

DON'T COMPARE ME TO HIM!

Elish let out an angry snarl, feeling disgusted and furious at himself for even daring suggest that what he was going through was anything compared to what Silas went through. It was different, entirely different. Silas was a mad man; Silas was insane. Silas enjoyed seeing those he loved hurt. He thrived on taking their loved ones away from them just because of his own… his own…

"You sound like Silas, you know." Garrett's faint voice weaved around his taunting thoughts.

"NO!" Elish suddenly bellowed. He whirled around to see Garrett staring at him, an expression of deep sadness creasing his face. "Don't you fucking say it!"

Garrett's thin lips raised in a smile, one that seeped pity. Elish kept shaking his head but no matter how much he tried to purge himself of the memory, of Garrett's voice, he heard it loud and clear.

"I bet you don't even see it, do you? You're becoming the very thing you're trying to convince us to kill. You give us our lovers… and if we don't do what you want… you take them back."

"Enough!" Elish roared. He turned from Garrett's image and walked down the road, but every time his boots hit the pavement he found his pace quickening, and soon he was running. Anything he could do to keep the realizations from mercilessly attacking his mind.

No. I was different. It was different. It was nothing like Silas and Sky.

"No…" the taunting cold voice said; his old self sounded amused, patronizing. "Because Silas and Sky were together for well over a hundred years. You only had Jade for three, and months of those were spent apart. You're nothing like Silas. Silas could withstand much more than you. Look at how easily your back broke. And you wanted to be king?"

Elish seethed; his insides felt like they were being actively yanked out of him, fury was baking into his bones and boiling inside of his skull. It was too much for him, the degradation and humiliation was more than he could stand. Even though his brothers and Silas were nowhere to be seen, nowhere near to witness his fall from grace, his worst enemy was drinking in every emotion, and watching every step.

Himself.

And at that, the cold voice laughed mockingly inside his head. Silas had been right all those years ago. No mutant could ever come close to being Sky. The evidence was right there in front of Elish. Chimeras were prone to insanity, instability, mood swings, sociopathic tendencies, and could become mentally psychotic as well. Chimeras were genetically engineered to be strong, fast, intelligent… but they all shared the same trait… the same trigger.

When they broke.

They broke.

Hard.

"I am not Silas!" Elish roared. He spun around, and this time he saw himself, his own cold violet eyes staring back with a frosted look that froze Elish to the ground.

"I am not Silas," Elish repeated, his own voice breaking under the mental weight he could feel pressing against his shoulders. "I wanted to… I wanted to…"

"Help the family?" his old self mused. "Golden boy. You don't believe it, why would you expect me to? You're more Silas than those three little raw clones you made. Isn't that funny?"

"I am not Silas," Elish said again. He realized his heart was palpitating; he was out of breath. "I would be better than him. Once I was rid of him, and I had my brothers… they could do whatever they wanted. I'd have Jade. What would I care?"

His old self laughed, and Elish could practically feel the ice roll from his lips. Was this what it was like when he talked to those below him? How bitter this medicine was.

"Yes, but you lost Jade and look what happened? You'd do better to just accept it. You did this because Silas shunned your love, and you decided to build a garden to hide in. Plant your tiny seeds and watch them grow, white spider. And then you watched them burn as well, and become infested by those who wish to take your place. Now what are you left with? Charred remains and a garden of spiders."

The words hit him, in every sensitive spot they hit him. And not satisfied with only humiliating him internally, they continued to draw up Jade's face, Silas's face, Reaver's, Killian's, even Perish, Lycos, Greyson, Lyle.

Ceph. Valen.

Julian.

And so many others.

"You're surely the most blind, foolish, and weakest chimera in existence," his old self chuckled. "Well, the first version of anything always has the most bugs. Too bad you can't just kill yourself. You–" Suddenly the voice changed tone, and Elish had to close his eyes and lock his fists when Reaver's voice hissed in his ear. "–weak piece of shit."

"Et tu, Reaver?" Elish said bitterly, and he started walking down the road again.

"Take your own advice," the dark chimera said, his voice a snake with its tongue flicking against Elish's ear. "What did you tell me to do when I would snap? You might be refined. You might be some elegant demigod with your flowing white robes, but you're still a fucking chimera. Stop embarrassing yourself, Elish. Stop acting like a kicked dog."

"Leave me be," Elish said, and without realizing it, he started picking up his pace. Soon he was back running, but still the voices followed him, sitting on his shoulders to spit their poison into his ears. They didn't stop, if anything they became louder and more assaulting the faster he ran. Insult after insult, ribbons of venom-laced words that flowed like beautiful poetry, but poisoned him with the intensity that only his own masochistic mind could generate. Only he could say such terrible things to himself, because he knew, above everyone else, that every word was true.

He was just like Silas… no, he was worse. He dismantled his family from the inside out, and not only that, he manipulated Silas like a puppet to make him worse. He was the one who kept giving him false hope that Sky could be cloned; he was the one who would dig the thorns of the man's memory into Silas's heart when his king looked too content with his life. It had been Elish all along ripping open those scarring wounds, and stuffing them with bacteria.

He had even taken two clones of Sky. The first one he lost, but the second he watched like a hawk, and when he had the opportunity to give this boy to Silas to make him happy, to stop the assault on the family – he wanted revenge more.

And now Jade was dead because of it.

I have no one to blame but my foolish self.

And it was because of those thoughts raping his mind, that he reacted the way he did when he saw a camp below a sheer ridge the road was winding down.

At first, the reaction was merely a jolt from his heart, but the quickened beat seemed only to fill him with a blackness that soon coated him like liquid hatred was being poured over his body. Instead of controlling these feelings as he had done for most of his life, Elish found himself embracing the hate. And when he recognized the caravan and its occupants below him, all sitting unaware around a campfire holding a pot of boiling soup, he used the feeling it brought as fuel.

And with a small smile, Elish lit that fuel on fire.

Elish clenched the gun in his hand and drew the blade resting against his hip… and he ran down the twisting road towards the unsuspecting caravan.

I will make the world hurt. I will set the world on fire.

I will kill everyone I can. Everyone I can get a hold of.

They will not live when my husband is dead. No one will live.

I swear on my immortal life the world will die beneath my hand. I do not care what it makes me. It doesn't matter if I am a hypocrite, I will take it gladly because nothing will stop me from showing the world how much I loved that boy.

Elish jumped onto a median and leapt off of the ledge of the ridge. He landed with a loud *thunk* right in the middle of the lit camp, and while he raised his gun and shot the first legionary in the face, he saw Robyn's wide eyes and Max sitting on the edge of the caravan.

The legionary's jaw blew off. Elish tossed the shotgun into the darkness that the campfire didn't reach, and grabbed the legionary's assault rifle. He turned around to see the second legionary raising his gun, but Elish was faster. He braced himself for the recoil and shot the legionary in the chest. The man screamed and stumbled forward, then a shower of sparks and hysterical shrieking sounded when the only thing to break the man's fall was the fire below.

Chaos ran circles around him. Elish heard a rattle and saw the caravan lurch forward. He looked and saw a leg disappear in front of the bosen cart, and ran after it.

Suddenly, the caravan shuddered and whined; a scream immediately followed and then a sickening crunch like someone had stepped on an egg. The bosen-pulled cart then rolled forward, two wheels rising up over a bump before slamming down to the earth. Elish looked down to see a mercenary, his head popped like an overripe berry, twitching badly, a dirty track mark down his back and over his skull. Pink brains and dark blue blood vessels in between the layers of hair, scalp, and skull could be seen, and they were still pulsing.

Then a crack sounded. Elish's head shot towards the noise, and though he was too inside of his own anguish to realize he was doing it, a growl sounded in his throat.

Robyn started taking quick steps backwards; her eyes were wide with terror, and the hands grasping the shotgun, trembling. It looked like she'd seen a ghost, and she very well was seeing one right now.

"Where's my pack?" Elish didn't recognize his own voice. It was low and full of tumbling gravel; he sounded more like Reaver than the man who'd grasped the brass ring in Skyfall. "Where are my things?"

"We – we shot you…" Robyn screamed, tears springing to her eyes. She raised the gun and pulled the trigger, but the bullet flew past Elish's shoulder. "I saw you die. I fucking saw you die!" She started to sob, the gun rattling so hard she almost dropped it.

"In the end, I will be the only man who lives," Elish growled, continuing to take steps towards her. "I will step over your disgusting parasitic bodies, and rid the world of your disease. I will exterminate all of you and let this condemned planet finally die." Elish sprung forward and wrenched the gun out of Robyn's hands and threw it into the night. "None of you will live while he is dead." Elish raised the knife he was holding and slashed it at Robyn, opening up her neck as the force spun her around. Blood splattered onto Elish's coat from the velocity of it, and when she landed more blood transferred from her dying body to the grey ground.

"Mom!" Max cried. He burst from the darkness and ran to her. He gave out a cry and took off his shirt to press it against her neck wound. It immediately soaked through, but determined, Max put pressure against it. "It's okay. It's okay." The boy's eyes shot to Elish, tears sprung to them.

"Why the fuck?" he screamed. "I thought we were fucking friends, James!" Tears rolled down his cheeks and he grabbed his mom's hand. "We helped you, you fucking asshole! I fucking helped you. I fucking felt sorry for you!"

Elish stood over Robyn and Max, only the moonlight above him shining down on the grisly scene below. He watched without blinking as Robyn lay dying; her blood coating the boy's hands and pooling below her head, with loose dirt and blades of yellow grass gathering with it.

Max kept speaking to her, his voice high and desperate, begging her, begging her not to leave him.

But the woman's eyes, fixed on her son's, only stared back at him, before, with a slight shudder followed by a relaxing of her body, her story ended.

"No! Mom? MOM!?" Max screamed; his face twisted in agony and desperation. He beat his fists against her, grabbed her and shook her, making his mother's blood fly everywhere. He shook her back and forth, screaming and screaming until he choked, and then threw up on the ground beside her.

"Why? Fucking why?" Max cried, his voice a desperate trill, begging Elish to give him any explanation for what he'd done. His eyes cradled a world of hurt and betrayal in their sockets, and his accusatory tone was none better. "She's all I have... she's fucking all I have."

Elish looked down at the knife he was holding, a thin layer of blood rimming the tip and making little islands on the stainless steel blade.

"Why?" Elish murmured to himself. He flashed the blade back and forth, and as the boy dissolved into agony at his feet; he turned the steel around to try and catch the moonlight.

Elish's purple eyes then shot back to the boy. He closed the small distance between them and kneeled down beside him. He rested a hand on the Max's shoulder and patted it, then gave it a gentle rub.

Then, in a flash, he was behind the kneeling boy. He pinned the boy's legs down with his knees and put his empty hand below Max's chin. He wrenched the boy's head back and drove the knife into his stomach. Elish felt the blade push against the skin before it gave way and slid into Max's guts like he was stabbing leather.

Max gasped. Immediately he tried to struggle, but Elish had him firmly held against his chest. With his gaze unfocused and his eyes staring off into the dark greywastes, Elish whispered kind and soothing words into Max's ears before he started sawing the knife through the boy's stomach, slowly slicing him and lacerating all of his internal organs.

When Elish had split Max open, he dropped the knife and wrapped the arm around Max's chest, and held the trembling boy in his arms. He closed his eyes and turned his hearing to the boy's heavy, desperate breaths, and like a low bass in the background, heard his heartbeat as well. Shock was preventing any more shrill screams and Elish was content with that; he wanted to enjoy the symphony in its purest form.

The heavy smell of blood and innards soaked into his surroundings, mixing in with Max's gasping breaths. Elish took in each sense and held it to him, and memorized them as much as he could. Every beat of the boy's weakening heart, every inflation of his lungs, Elish committed each to memory and promised himself never to forget.

And when the boy was dead he rose, the knife once again in his hand.

"Why?" Elish said out loud. He tested the knife against the tip of his finger and for the first time in months… he smiled.

A smile that would've made even Reaver do a double take.

"Why you ask?" Elish said again, and as those words left his lips the smile only widened. He looked at the blood-soaked knife and he held it eye level. Then, after turning it around several more times, he brought it to his lips. He licked it, coating his tongue with red before his tongue disappeared into his mouth.

"Because it made me feel better – that's why."

CHAPTER 28

Killian

"*AND THE NIGHT GOT DEATHLY QUIET, AND HIS FACE lost all expression. If you're gonna learn to suck me, boy, you better learn to suck me right,*" Ceph sang. Then he slapped his knees and clapped his hands as best he could with them being bound.

I sighed, and with Kiki joining in he continued onto the chorus. "*You gotta know when to blow 'em, know when to lick 'em. Know when to slow down, know when to speed up. You never count your cums, when they're playin' on your penis. If you're gonna learn to suck it, you better learn to suck it right.*"

I closed my eyes and leaned my head back until it hit the wall we were all lined up against, bound to office chairs. I was internally being destroyed by worry and fear being tied up. My head was throbbing from being beaten on continuously, my ear especially where I'd been bitten, and here I was listening to Ceph entertain himself from his own crippling boredom by butchering Kenny Roger's *The Gambler*.

It was like I was locked in a room with Reno, except a thousand times worse because at least Reno would've been worried with me. Ceph was taking this all in stride, making up lyrics to his favourite songs and using them to, not only drive me mad, but the two chimeras holding us prisoner.

"Come on, Killian. Join in!" Ceph looked over to where Adler, the undeniable clone of Sky Fallon, and in turn Perish, was sitting. He was on his laptop with his face tensed in concentration.

Ceph raised his voice and started singing the chorus a second time. Then when that drew no reaction from the born immortal chimera, a wry grin appeared on his face. "Hey Adi! This one's for you, kitten." He cleared his throat. *"I'm going to be a mighty king! So enemies beware!"*

"SHUT UP!" The second chimera burst through an open door leading into another area of the lab. The man, with blond hair gelled into long spikes and Sanguine-quality red eyes, kicked Ceph's chair and knocked him to the ground.

Ceph fell with a crash, the wheels of the computer chair still spinning. The chimera I now knew was named Spike, walked to the front of Ceph and dealt him a forceful kick to the stomach; but when he realized the nylon rope was absorbing most of the impact, he angled himself and kicked Ceph right in the groin.

Ceph howled, any man would have. His face twisted from the pain and his lips peeled back over his locked teeth. He swore and groaned, and because he was a fucking coward, Spike kicked him again.

"Next time I'll break your fucking jaw," Spike spat. He turned to Adler who hadn't even tilted his head to see what was going on. "Come on. It's going to get dark soon. You have to bring my chopper back or you're going to lose it again."

Adler, with curly dark brown hair falling over pale grey-blue eyes, glanced up at him, and like the first time I had seen him, his face wrenched my heart. Adler looked like Reaver, but that wasn't what was drawing out those emotions in me. He had Perish's eyes, and the first time I'd seen him, pointing a combat shotgun at me, I'd felt myself momentarily stunned.

Now whenever he looked at me, I just felt an overwhelming sadness. I'd done my best to ignore the sting I felt whenever I thought of Perish, and the hole that I equally had been avoiding acknowledging. Seeing someone who looked like Perry drew up feelings inside of me I wasn't ready to deal with… but ones I also knew had been building inside out for months now.

However, I was dealing with this inner pain differently than I would've before. Because I was using Perish's memory to fuel my bravery, and remembering one of the last words he'd said to me.

I was no longer going to let myself be abused by men. Perish had given me the tools to defend myself, and I could say with all honestly, I wasn't scared today. I was worried, but I wasn't scared.

"If… you're happy and you know it… spit up blood…" I looked over and saw Ceph, still on the ground, blow a raspberry which sprinkled blood

all over his face. I sighed, and shook my head as I tried to hide the smile. *"If... you're happy and you know it... spit up blood!"*

"Shut up!" Spike roared, and in his mouth I saw pointed teeth. He stalked back over to Ceph, and this time kicked him right in the face. Kiki cried out and looked away, but because I was watching the red-haired chimera I saw his head snap back, and a fresh flow of dark red spurt from his mouth, some of it staining Spike's red and black high-top sneaker.

The anger bubbling inside of me started to reach a boiling point. Even though he wasn't looking at me, I glared Spike down, and when I slid my locked teeth from side to side I heard an audible grinding followed by a shot of pain.

"Wow. What a big tough man!" I snarled, my voice overflowing with taunting. "Hitting someone tied up. You're such a strong man! Look at the tough man everyone!"

Spike whirled around, his red eyes two torches. I braced myself for it and because I knew it was coming I didn't take me eyes off of him. I kept glaring at the chimera the entire time he raised his hand, until the blow snapped my head to the side, wrenching my neck so hard the muscles spasmed underneath my skin.

"Are you done yet, Spike?" Adler said from the laptop. He glanced towards us and motioned for Spike to come over. "I see quad tracks but whenever they hit the road, the tracks disappear. It might be worth seeking out though."

"Just torture the information out of him," Spike snapped. He put a hand on my chin and puckered his lips at me. He had a nasty untreated cut on his forehead. I'd given him that by smacking him with a wooden statue. "I could get you to sing, pretty baby. I could get you to make all sorts of noises."

"He won't talk, I can see it in his face, and I'll kill him if he frustrates me." Adler locked eyes with me and we glared each other down. "Reaver will tell me what I want to know if the little shit's threatened."

Inside of my head I smiled at this. I flattered myself by trying to go over every encounter I'd had with Adler and Spike, to try and pinpoint just where he'd gotten this opinion of me from. I hoped it was my attitude, or maybe I was starting to look the part.

"I'm surprised Reaver would be dating some dipshit greywaster," Spike said. "He was obviously important enough for Perish to make radiation-immune. Maybe he's one of their slaves. Sigils."

"Sengils," I said coldly.

"Check his blood and log into the ACL," Adler said.

"I tried. An error code keeps coming up and I'm not fucking tearing Turris apart looking for the error code book. He's probably just some stupid greywaster."

"I still think he's a slave, one of the sex slaves."

"And I'm not a sengil, or a cicaro," I said curtly.

"Kick-car-oh," Spike said as he moved the words around on his tongue. "The sex slaves of the chimeras." Then he looked over at Kiki. "Mantis said almost all the stealths are sengils or cicaros because they're too wild to be on their own without a master to control them. Not until they're older apparently. You don't seem wild at all, you're quite docile."

Kiki smiled shyly and bowed his head to Spike. The kid had some horrible bruises and cuts on his face; he fought like I had. "I'm engineered to please my master no matter who that is. I love all my masters." He bit his bottom lip and I watched with disgust as he fluttered his eyes at Spike. "Is your real name Spike? I like that name." Kiki's eyes kept travelling around as he kept that dumb smile on his face. He must've had his head knocked around when they were capturing us because he was acting like a retard.

Spike beheld him with disdain and I did as well. I despised that kid. Ceph was bleeding and in pain several feet away and that little slut was batting his eyelashes and submitting to every authority figure he saw.

"It's my real name," Spike said. He hoisted himself up to a metal table that was beside Kiki. All three of us had been pushed against the wall in the far corner of the laboratory. Ceph, then myself in the middle, and Kiki with the table that Spike was now sitting on top of. In front of us was another long slab-like table with nasty-looking surgical instruments, put there while we watched as a means of intimidation, and past that to the right was a desk with Adler's laptop.

Then to the far left, beside the metal door leading to a set of stairs that was our exit, was a desktop with a flat panel monitor on a wooden desk full of plastic bins that held papers, folders, and CDs. There was a webcam on top of the monitor and a microphone. Adler had told us that could be used to talk to Reaver and Nero, or as he said 'would be a way for them to see us killed one-by-one' if we misbehaved.

We were all in this one room, but there was another wing of the laboratory. I knew Mantis was in there somewhere resurrecting, but what else could be found past that open door was anyone's guess. I was hoping it would lead to an exit but it wasn't like they were going to tell us if there was.

"My real name is Kincade," Kiki said cheerfully, and he looked to Ceph. "His is Cepherus. How old are you?"

"Nineteen," Spike replied. "Mantis says I'm a stealth chimera like you. Fifth generation with Reaver, Caligula, and Jade."

"I'm sixteen," Kiki said. Then his smile turned shy again. "I see you have a cut on your head. You know I'm trained to treat injuries. We seem to get injured a lot, and I'm pretty good at it."

"Spike. Come look at this," Adler called. Adler was clicking on a wireless mouse, the glow of the computer screen reflecting in his grey eyes. He had a unique voice, it was deep and raspy like a road with fresh gravel laid on it. I hated this clone of Sky, but this voice triggered something inside of me. I felt myself listening every time he opened his mouth.

Spike walked over and looked at the screen. "You've taken it too far from my tower. You're going to lose the signal, and the last time we ventured out that far we saw celldwellers and they almost got my chopper."

"I'm still seeing quad tracks." Adler shook his head. I didn't understand just what they were doing, or what they were looking at. I was assuming they were trying to find where Kiki's home base had been. But why? To take our Nong Shim noodles? There wasn't much there.

"What are celldwellers?" Kiki asked. I glared at him. He was staring with inquisitive eyes and was perked up and peppy. I looked over to see if Ceph shared my disgust at Kiki's submission, but Ceph was still on his side, staring up at the ceiling with no more fun songs spoken. I think he was getting tired, like I was.

"It doesn't matter if you see quad tracks. If their house is there it's too far for us to go. We just need to wait for Mantis to wake up."

Mantis to wake up? Then what?

"No. He's going to censor Perish's files, and I'm tired of him hiding shit from me. I have to see them. I don't fucking care how far away they are," Adler said. "I've been waiting months for that little shit to come here with Perish's quad, and I've been fucking cheated. You'll be fine."

"You're fucking sending me out there? Fuck you. If I get proxied I'm dead. You fucking go out, Angel Adler. It's your fucking crush you're after."

Perish's files? The realization hit me, and like smoke being cleared away from a colourful picture, I realized what I was watching. They were trying to find me and Reaver's plagueland house. They wanted all of the files, CDs, all of the things Perish had loaded on the quad. An immortal's life of information that he'd given me before he died. I barely even looked at any of these things. Perish's death had been too painful and raw, and my feelings for him too conflicting.

"You'll do as I fucking say, Spike."

Spike's already granite expression hardened further, and look of hostility became as clear as day, but then Adler whirled around. "I can see your reflection," he said coldly. "Don't you dare test my authority, boy."

Whoa. There were many cracks in this chimera faction. I watched with a new level of fascination as Spike turned from the laptop screen and stalked back over to the metal table he'd been sitting on; he shot me a hateful glare as he did, and I had one of my own to give him back.

And he called him boy? I guess he was thirty from the Blood Crow's timeline, but like Silas he'd stopped aging at twenty-four. Well, even if he didn't look that much older than Spike, he certainly felt like he was old enough to look down his nose at him. When I'd first saw Spike and Adler I'd assumed they were dating or something, but obviously not.

Spike deflected his gaze from me and instead looked at Kiki. The stupid cicaro was giving him back a smile, one that seemed like it was coming from someone with a few screws loose.

"Can I please have some water?" Kiki asked nicely.

Spike hesitated for a moment, then he nodded and jumped off of the metal table and disappeared out the door. While he was gone, I leaned down and nudged Ceph. "Want to try and get up?" I asked him.

Ceph's green eyes, previously disconnected, focused and looked at me. "Nah. I'm fine down here. Thanks though." Then his gaze returned to the ceiling. "I was in a dark place for a long time and I got good at kinda tuning everything out."

Spike came back with a cup of water and a straw. He held it up to Kiki, and the cicaro drank with a thankful smile. "Thank you," he said once he was done. "My throat was starting to burn."

And mine was too. "Can I have some... please?"

Spike's eyes flashed. "Tell me where the shit Perish gave you is and you can have some."

My jaw clenched and before I could stop myself I said something I immediately knew I would regret. Something drawn out from the area of my brain that stored everything I had learned being around Reaver. "Then I guess you can stick that glass up your ass, and you can go fuck your–"

Before I even got the last syllable out, Spike raised his hand and smacked me with the water glass. It shattered on my face, so close to my eye I saw bright lights shooting through my vision like a lit sparkler. I cried out from the pain, feeling like I had just been hit by a truck, and felt my head flop to the side.

Then I saw a fist, it hit my jaw before grabbing it and wrenching my chin up. Two blood-red eyes seared my own, and his grasp on my jaw tightened until my mouth opened and my face tensed; all of my efforts now concentrated on not screaming from the heavy pressure on my jaw.

"He's not fucking immortal. Don't kill him, you stupid fuck!" Adler snapped behind him.

Spike's lined face shook from rage and started turning bright red. He pulled my jaw before leaning down until he was nose-to-nose with me.

"I'm going to fuck you tonight, Killian," he said to me. His pointed teeth showing with all their glory as his mouth moved. "I'm going to fuck you in front of those two until they both get so hard they'll be dry humping the air."

"If you want to sow it, I'll make sure you reap it, asshole," I snarled, but my venomous words were only a mask, inside blood was gathering in my head, drawing out a heat that made me anxious. I knew I'd gone too far now, and for the first time since arriving here I felt a flicker of fear.

I couldn't handle someone doing that to me again… I just couldn't.

Spike yanked my jaw back and forth in a playful manner. "I'll be planting a lot of seeds in you. I'll–"

Suddenly, without me even fully realizing what I was doing, I jumped to my feet, taking the computer chair I was tied to with me. Spike jumped back quickly, bewildered at my sudden movements, and I did the only thing that jumped into my mind. I whirled around and used the back of the chair as a weapon, and felt it hit Spike, hopefully in the face.

Kiki gasped but Ceph laughed, fuelling me even more. When I was turned around and facing Spike again, I saw he was on the floor, blood now squirting from his nose.

Adler was running towards me. My mind raced, trying to think of something I could do, but in an instant he was in front of me.

Adler punched me in the side of the face, and like Ceph, I tumbled to the floor. My head smacked against the linoleum and haze overtook my senses, but I was with it enough to feel the impact of his boot on my stomach, and the pain that followed.

"If I catch you raping him, I'm proxying you," Adler snapped. "I told you, no sex. Not with them, not with Mantis, not with the Blood Crows, not with anyone! We're better than that! We're not like the Skyfall chimeras."

"You're the one that despises sex, Virgin Adler, not me!" Spike snapped, holding his bloody nose. "Don't knock it 'til you tried it." Spike then grunted as Adler, still reeling from my outburst, smacked him across the face.

"Mantis is going to fucking disown you when he finds out what you're doing to Reaver and Perish's little pet. You know Reaver's fucking Elish's prodigy. He's going to proxy *you*, this time." Spike jumped to his feet, and with a murderous glare towards me, he stalked out of the room, through the held open door.

"Yeah! Daddy's gonna beat your ass, Adi," Ceph called from the floor. "He's gonna fuck you until you call him Mantis." I looked down at Ceph, my eye now swelling shut and my head throbbing. He looked back at me, and I saw he was smiling. "Get it? Because if he already calls him Daddy… if he was fucking him it wouldn't be anything out of the ordinary so… he'd call him Mantis. Right?"

Blood was dripping down the back of my throat, and my head was pounding like it was being hammered on, but when Ceph laughed, still on his back with the computer chair tied under him, I laughed too and shook my head.

"It's really too bad you're married, Ceph," I said to him, and the smile turned into a goofy crooked grin. "I know a guy who you would've loved."

When evening turned to night, Adler eventually gave up on his mission to locate me and Reaver's plaguelands house and they both disappeared through the other laboratory door. We weren't fed or given any water, the lights were just tuned off and the door locked.

The side of my face had swollen up and the blood that had been leaking from my many wounds had clotted and dried. Now my face felt like it had a thin film on it that made it tight and itchy. Every time I would tense and flex my face, I could feel the coating break like I was wearing a mud mask. It was uncomfortable, and that on top of the throbbing pain that never seemed to fade, I wasn't in the greatest of moods.

Kiki might be awake to my left, but I wasn't sure. Ceph was obviously fast asleep from the ground-rattling sounds he was making. He sounded like a chainsaw trying to cut through metal. I had no idea how anyone could sleep next to that. If Reaver snored that loud, I would've smothered him with a pillow.

I sighed at the thought of Reaver. I glanced up at the ceiling and wondered just why he hadn't bombed the door yet. It had been long enough already.

Unless Nero had killed him. Kiki and I had both heard the music blasting and then the commotion. After that though, we'd been rather preoccupied with Adler and Spike.

I'd almost gotten away... I was so close I could taste it, but the two chimeras were so quick with their movements, they'd just been blurs.

What if Nero overpowered Reaver and had infected him with the worms? Reaver could be halfway to the plaguelands right now, and if he was, he would have the entire rest of the world to hide from me, or the parasite inside of him at least.

It seemed like Mantis was researching these parasites or something. It wasn't explained to me, but just through Spike and Adler's conversation it was as if Mantis was breeding them or experimenting on them. From what I heard they called it proxying, and Mantis regularly proxied both Adler and Spike, and once they came along... Nero and Ceph too.

It also was obvious Mantis had learned how to control the parasites, since Nero had been his puppet. Ceph, it seemed, must've gotten a different type because he was normal acting at the festival and his eye hadn't changed colour.

I jumped and looked towards the door as I heard a click. My remaining eye squinted from the pain of a flashlight being shined on it, but then the beam shone onto Kiki.

Footsteps followed, ones just tiptoeing towards us in a way that told me we weren't the only ones he wanted to hide his presence from. Sure enough, when the flashlight lowered I saw Spike holding food. He was shirtless, and wearing only white boxers with black designs.

His eyes hardened when he saw me, but they deflected to the cicaro. He put the flashlight down and directed the beam at the wall, casting long shadows of the four of us like we were actors on a stage.

Spike held out a bottle of water with a straw sticking out of it and brought it to Kiki's lips. I eyed a bowl of what looked like nuts mixed in with dried fruit, and felt saliva fill my mouth.

Kiki drank half the bottle and gasped when his lips broke the straw. "Thank you," he whispered.

Spike hesitated, his tongue poking out of his mouth. Then he laid a hand on Kiki's chin and began stroking his growing stubble gently. "If you want the food... I want something from you." Spike glanced at the dark hallway and started pawing his boxers.

I looked away from disgust and glared at the illuminated metal desk in the middle of the room, all of the torture instruments still laid out, but unused.

My nose curled like I was smelling something bad when I heard Kiki laugh lightly. "You don't need to bribe me. Adler might be in denial but I know you're not. We love sex. I get cranky if I don't get something every day." I glanced over and saw the moment Spike withdrew a thick cock, already hard. He was uncut, and the typical chimera girth and length. Kiki eyed it hungrily, and like the slut he was, he licked his lips while making eye contact with Spike.

"Come closer," Kiki whispered. Spike put a hand on the wall behind Kiki and leaned on it. He thrusted his hips up, but even with Kiki leaning down he still couldn't reach. Spike sat down on the metal table instead and spun Kiki towards him, and moments after that I started hearing light sucking, and Spike's deep breathing.

What a fucking whore. I wish Ceph was awake to hear this, but he was dead to the world. It was just me forced to listen to this blowjob in the cover of darkness. The quiet mixed in with one's enhanced senses in the middle of the night was amplifying the sounds, lapping and sucking and Spike's stifled moans, trying his hardest to keep quiet. When I looked again, I even saw a hand cupped over Spike's mouth, his other hand on Kiki's head as the cicaro bobbed up and down.

"Will you fuck me?" Kiki whispered in the middle of his exploits. "Please? I want it in me."

"I fucking can't!" I heard Spike hiss. "He'll hear, and you're fucking tied up."

"There must be some place we can go," Kiki said, and he gave out a moan and the sucking continued. "I know you haven't fucked someone in a while, I can feel it. I haven't either. It's in our genetics. Come on."

"I... no, no, just keep sucking," Spike groaned. I saw him with his hands now behind him to prop himself up, his hips jolting as he thrusted into the cicaro's mouth.

Then something occurred to me.

Just why am I watching and letting this happen?

"ADLER!" I suddenly yelled as loud as I could. "ADLER. SPIKE'S LETTING THE CICARO SUCK HIS COCK! ADLER!"

Spike shoved Kiki off of him. His hard cock, shining with saliva and with the head of it bright pink and swollen, getting pushed back into his boxers as it became flaccid. If looks could kill, even the white flames wouldn't save me from the glare of death that he was giving me.

He ran out of the room, but to my satisfaction, when he got to the end of the dark hallway, the flashlight in his hand, I saw him skid to a stop.

"He's fucking lying," Spike snapped. He pushed past Adler and turned a left. I couldn't see well with the flashlight's disappearing beam, but I saw the shadowed figure look down the hallway then back to where Spike had been, and then disappear.

Kiki leaned over and grabbed the bowl with his teeth. He spun around with the plastic bowl in his mouth like Deek after he'd fetched the stick we'd thrown, and rolled over to me. He leaned down and rested it onto his bound hands, and with it balanced, he placed it on his lap, close enough so I could grab the food with my bound hands.

"It's amazing how easy men are to manipulate," Kiki said with a proud smile. "Tuck in!" Then he looked over and laughed lightly. I knew why when we both saw Ceph, half-asleep, giving us both quizzical looks.

An insult was waiting in my mouth but I was too hungry to throw it at him, and I didn't want to risk the food getting taken away. I reached down and picked up a perfumy dried fruit, an apricot I think, and popped it into my mouth. All my hatred for Kiki, at least for the moment, disappeared.

And when I heard Spike shouting, followed by a loud impact of him getting hit, and even better... a *thunk* and a crash – I even smiled at the cicaro.

CHAPTER 29

Reaver

I WOKE UP TO THE SOUND OF SOMETHING FRYING, something that must've deposited a lot of grease into the pan because it was sizzling and snapping.

My awareness came back to me, slowly at first; but once my muscles began to react to my mental signals, everything began restoring. I felt as if I was a computer being booted up, and I was waiting patiently for the default programs to finish loading.

Then the sharp inhale of breath to expand lungs that were used to being dormant. I never got over how satisfying it was to feel my tight chest stretch to near bursting.

And with that inhale, I smelled greasy meat... bacon I believed. My stomach growled from anticipation, followed by a burn in my throat to remind me that I was starving, and hadn't eaten in possibly days.

Without realizing it, I put both of my hands to my face, then felt my own skin tense from my furrowed brow. I rubbed my eyes and opened them, my world blurry and my eyes stinging from the bright orb that was shining down above me. It was then I realized I was on something spongy, and when I took another deep breath, this time tasting as much on the air as I could, I smelled the microfiber scent of the couch, and the lingering odor of arians whose smell I didn't recognize personally.

I shut my eyes tight and squinted them to try and force them into focus, during this time my mind went back to its shifting, sorting through memories of what had happened to try and get as much information as I could. So far there were no blatant alarms ringing inside of my head, but that didn't mean there were none there.

Then plates could be heard clinking against one another. I winced at the noise and squinted again, this time my eyes focused and I saw in front of me a sliding glass door that revealed behind it, emerald green grass. So green it seemed deceptive, and planted in this grass, large trees with thick brown bark.

I sat up, realizing that indeed I was right and I was laying on the couch, and looked around the house. There was a coffee table in front of me, made of grey slate, with a red silk covering that had an ashtray resting in the middle, made out of the foot of an animal, and full of cigarette butts. There was also empty beer bottles beside an adjacent chair, and a groove from someone's ass in the seat of it.

Past the coffee table I saw a stone hearth with charcoal in the fireplace, and on the mantle, old photos, more artifacts, and a clock showing me it was two in the afternoon. Framing the mantle were black bookshelves full of books, and cabinets that I just knew was filled with more crap.

And then my memory started coming back. My eyes widened at the same time as my body crunched up like a crumpled piece of paper, and I sprung to my feet and whirled around to face who I now realized was in the kitchen.

Yep, standing behind the kitchen island, watching me with a half-smile, was Nero.

"Afternoon, Ducky. All healed and brand spankin' new?" Nero said. His cheerful voice drew up all sorts of malicious feelings inside of me. I hated myself for it, but the fact that I had been on a runaway train of PTSD, flashbacks, impotence, and psychosis, speeding towards a brick wall, and he was absolutely carefree and fucking jovial, tore at my infected wounds. The part that frustrated me the most was that I'd expect nothing more from this asshole, and yet my mind was flaring because of it, like I somehow expected remorse or an apology.

It didn't make sense that my brain would want something like that, and the very fact that it was an emotion hidden, but still making itself known inside of me, made me hate myself, absolutely hate myself.

Or maybe I was just frustrated that I was reeling from this still, unable to shake the effects of what he'd done, and everyone else around me had moved on. Even Killian had moved on, and had used his time with Perish to make himself stronger – and use my own weakness to fuel that campaign. So they were either moving on, or using my misery to strengthen themselves.

It was just me stuck in the past. I didn't want to be and I was doing everything I could to shake it, but though my will was strong and my desire to get over this was more powerful than every other drive in me... I couldn't control what was happening.

I wasn't used to not being in control. I needed to take back control, but I didn't know how.

A king in Aras – but a fucking psychotic pauper in the greywastes.

My ears burned as Nero looked at me. Inside my dark self was still screaming at me to attack him again. That killing him and torturing him would make it all better, but I'd done that, I had killed him, and I was still bursting with infection.

I'd know when the time was, I guess. Right now I had to keep the mumbled pact we'd made, and concentrate on getting the boys back. During this time I'd appease the need to get my revenge by analyzing my enemy and finding more weaknesses I could exploit. He had a husband and a cicaro, but both were out of my grasp at the moment. If I listened and stuck around him, maybe I would find out another weakness.

Or maybe find a way to deliver him back to the Legion. Then he could kiss the concrete some more with his husband, and I'd take custody of his cicaro and turn him against him.

"Yeah," I finally managed to mumble and I got up from the couch. I looked around, half-hoping Killian had already killed his way back to the surface. "How long were we out for?"

"I woke up yesterday evening and it's–" Nero glanced at the clock I'd just seen. "Two now. So you've been out for a day and a half. I was out a day. There's been no movement from the laboratory, and the blood slicks would've shown prints, so the kittens are still down there. Makes me think they don't have cameras here, but I don't know." He turned and took the hot pan off of the stove and flicked it off. I walked over and sat down on the stool and observed not just bacon frying in the pan, but mashed potatoes, already golden brown on the top surrounded by bubbling fat, and another frying pan with a yellow lake of what would eventually be scrambled eggs.

Smelled good enough and I was starving. I had barely had any of the Melchai fresh food, and there were a lot of things I wanted to try.

But I fucking didn't want to eat with Nero, my body simmered at the thought of it. Even looking at him right now felt like I was swallowing a hot iron bar.

I watched Nero, not taking my eyes off of him, as he turned around with a loaf of bread and plopped it down in front of me with a serrated knife, then he slid a toaster, so shiny I could see my reflection, towards me. "Cut up some bread for toast. They fucking have homemade marmalade here. Can you believe it? I've been eating that shit with a spoon." I stared down at the golden loaf of bread, already missing a quarter of it, and heard him open the fridge, grab something, then the sound of silverware. Nero turned around, and put a jar of something orange and yellow with bits of shit in it, beside the bread loaf and a spoon.

I couldn't stop staring at the knife, visualizing with crisp quality, sawing off his head. The serrated edges of the knife would be like I was using a chainsaw.

But I would go slowly.

"Try it. Ever had marmalade before?"

One of the things I always enjoyed was pinpointing the exact area of their vocal cords. It soothed my heart to hear those shrill, desperate screams before they were abruptly cut off.

A hand entered my vision and Nero snapped his fingers at me. "Hey. Ever try marmalade before?"

My head jerked back and I glanced at him before looking away. "Stop talking to me like we're friends," I said darkly. "Get me the fucking food, so I can figure out a way to get into that lab."

When my gaze turned back to Nero I made a point to not blink. I glared into his purple and blue eyes, both clear of blood and sparkling again, and watched his every movement, his every facial expression.

"Yeah. I know you're pissed at me, but you didn't kill Kiki so you must have some goodness in you, Reaper-boy." The left side of Nero's face scrunched as he gave me a half-smile; he looked like a fucking stroke victim. "You try marmalade or not?" He skidded the jar to me; it landed right beside the serrated knife and the loaf of bread.

I don't know why but I answered him. "Is it jam?" I asked. We had jam in the greywastes but it was full of sugar crystals from age. I looked down at the jar and picked up the spoon. "You spoiled fucks probably got this shit every morning." I unscrewed the mason jar and smelled it, the inside of my cheeks gave a jolt as I smelled the sugary citrus, the weird spasm you get whenever you anticipate eating something sour.

Nero snorted and started loading up two dishes he had out. "Yeah. I feel bad for you greywasters having to eat that old shit. I was kicking around the plaguelands with Ceph and Kiki for the first bit and there's a lot of food, but it all tastes like ass."

They were in the plaguelands too? This revelation drew up an entirely new set of questions. It was enough for me to want to keep conversing with him, for now. "You were in the plaguelands?" I asked. I took a spoonful of the chunky orange goop and popped it into my mouth.

I regretted it immediately. My entire face scrunched up as an overwhelming sour and sweetness exploded in my mouth and murdered every taste bud that I had, before raping my saliva glands. It was too much flavour, and I didn't know what to do with it.

Then Nero started laughing, undoubtedly at the expression on my face. I grimaced and spat out the remainders back on the spoon, that and a lot of spit.

"What the fuck is wrong with you, dude? It's just orange and lemon jam!" Nero howled. "It's fucking that sour to you?" He handed me a dishtowel and I started scraping my tongue with it to try and kill the sweet and citrusy flavour stinging my taste buds to the point of pain. When he offered me some water, I took it, and downed the entire glass.

"What happened to it?" I said, my face twisted in distaste. "There's too much flavour in it. Did science do that?"

"*Did science do that?*" Nero laughed harder as he said my question back to himself. "No, binky. That's just what fresh fruit is supposed to make marmalade taste like. I guess it makes sense though, you greywasters are used to everything being centuries old. Your mouth isn't used to real flavours, 'specially not citrus."

He slid me a heaping plate of food, steaming and smelling like angels had been sacrificed to make it, but I was skeptical of it now. I picked up the spoon of saliva and jam and tossed it into the sink nearby and poked one of the scrambled eggs. "I don't trust this fresh shit anymore. What else is citrus?"

"Nothing," Nero chuckled, and he took a stool and pulled it up on the opposite side of the island. "You recognize the rest of this at least? Come on, work with me. You know what the fuck eggs and bacon and potatoes are, right?"

"Yeah. We had that shit in Aras. Bacon we had a lot of but it was rat bacon, eggs we paid out the nose for and potatoes, the ones I grew, were small. We actually need to work hard to survive there," I replied. "Not like you."

"Oh, stop trying to pick a fucking fight, Reav," Nero said, his mouth already full of food. "This is entirely different circumstances. You're my little bro now, not my prisoner. Shit's different, so lighten the fuck–" Nero ducked just in time for the jar of marmalade to fly past his head before smashing into the wall between the counter and the upper cabinet.

I slammed my hands down on the stone kitchen island, my eyes blazing and my shoulders tensed together. Nero, who was looking behind him, slowly turned back to me with twin raised eyebrows.

"I am not your *little bro*," I said in a harsh whisper. My fingers scraped along the stone before my hand locked into fists. "You're going to stay the fuck away from me, understand? I have nothing to say to you. I want nothing from you. I'm only here for Killian. Do you understand me or should I dumb it down for you?"

Nero picked up his forkful of scrambled eggs. "I understand you." He nodded towards my food. "Just shut up and eat and like you fucking said, then we can start trying to find a way inside the lab."

The dismissive way he was handling this made a ringing come to my ears, but through some grace from some dead god I sat back down. I kept telling myself nothing would come out of killing him again, but my hand shaking back and forth like I had Parkinson's was making it too clear that it was going to take all of my self-control not to tie him up and torture him now.

Nero was right in front of me. Right – in – front – of – me. The fucking bastard responsible for so many things currently going wrong inside of me.

I just wanted to scream at him everything that was fucked up with me now. I wanted to take him by his thick neck, and shake it back and forth and tell him I had lost who I was, and I was losing Killian. Not only was I going into some weird fucked up state whenever a flashback took me, not only could I not have sex with my boyfriend anymore, but because of this Killian was climbing all over me in an attempt to push me down and stand on me. Fucking Killian, wimpy shit Killian was trying to dominate me now. That's how fucking screwed up I was, and I just wanted to scream it in his face.

As if... he'd have the solution for me to take my life back.

'I can help you, brosy. If you let me... I can help you. I can help you

make all your weaknesses your strength.'

To preoccupy myself, I ate. It tasted good which was a distraction. The bacon was my favourite part, the crispy fat melted in my mouth and was bursting with flavour but in a good way; the eggs were all fluffy and shit and I drowned them in ketchup cause I loved that stuff, and the potatoes were mashed with not just butter but milk or cream. Milk was even more rare than eggs since we had to get it from the bosen, and it was usually given to the kids so they wouldn't grow up to be runts.

The bread was fresh too. I popped the last bit into my mouth and decided I was calmed down enough to start asking him one of the many questions that had been burning on my lips. Beforehand I gave myself a stern talk and took several deep breaths to keep myself cooled down. He was the only one who had answers and I didn't have a variety of people to ask.

"How did Mantis end up infecting you with those worms?" I asked, setting my fork down. Nero had already polished off his plate, he ate like he was a vacuum cleaner, and had cracked open a beer. One was also set aside for me.

Nero got up and took his beer, and motioned for me to follow him. I picked up my own drink and we walked into the living room. He sat down on one end of the couch and I took the other.

Nero reached into his pocket and pulled out a purple tin. He opened it and my eyes lit up when I saw pills, small black bricks, and white baggies.

"You liked heroin, didn't you?"

My jaw locked and I nodded stiffly. He'd asked me what my preference was when I'd been tied to that bed. He remembered what I liked, how cute.

"You ever have china white before?"

I shook my head but I didn't trust myself to talk. Nero got out a baggy and started prepping a few lines of white powder with a black card that had raised silver writing. "It's powdered heroin. It's your new best friend now." He handed me the bag, with quite a bit of powder in it. "A present for you."

I took it without a word and after he'd leaned down and inhaled three lines, he handed me a metal sniffer and I obliged. It seemed wrong, but I was a drug fiend like probably all of my brothers were, and Nero knew that. He knew my currency, and I wasn't going to say no.

"There. That'll calm your ass down," Nero said when I'd raised my

501

head from icing three lines myself. I rubbed my nose and took in a long breath.

"They're called proxy worms or proxies." Nero explained. "We saw them in the plaguelands and barely escaped. We realized they couldn't survive without radiation and we booked it here. Unfortunately... Mantis is just as much of a crazy scientist as Perish, except, unlike Perry, he's more obsessed with utilizing the worms than feeding greywasters and creating splices. Mantis was all friendly and shit, but unfortunately he overheard me telling Ceph I wanted to tell Silas about Adler, as a way to get in his good books so we could go home and go back to our lives. Mantis got spooked and he put his special experimented-on worms in us."

"Experimented on?"

Nero nodded. "Apparently the worms function really different in immortals. Because the worms we see in the plaguelands kill their hosts pretty soon after they infect them, or proxy them as Mantis calls it. We can survive with them inside of us, and we immortals come back to life when we do get killed," Nero explained. "Once the worm is inside and implanted in an immortal, it starts to learn and become smarter and each life cycle has the worms evolving to learn its host. Mantis figured this out by implanting Adler throughout the years, and he's been breeding worms to obey him. What I was implanted with, was a higher generation of worms so I was a dumb puppet. For someone like Ceph, he was implanted with a different kind where they just kinda... wait patiently and learn you, I guess." Nero's shoulders shrugged. "They're pretty fucked up little creatures. I'd stay the hell away from the plaguelands if I were you."

Jesus fuck. Killian and I were lucky to get the hell out of the plaguelands when we did. Though being in the same house as Dr. Mind Control wasn't that much of a step up.

Then my eyes closed as the cold yet comforting rush of dopamine swept my body. I heard Nero chuckle before I think it hit him, because I heard a light moan. I remained still for a moment, knowing he'd know why I wasn't answering him back, and let myself enjoy it. There were many perks to being immortal and one of those perks was having my tolerance brought down to nothing whenever I resurrected.

Then suddenly I felt Nero's hands on me. My eyes snapped open, only to see the coffee table rush towards me before I was yanked back. Immediately anxiety burst inside of me like a popped blister, but I realized I had been about to fall forward, face first into the coffee table.

"Lay backwards, Ducky," Nero said in a calm, oddly doting voice. I was too high to feel anger at the tone he was speaking to me in. He got up and reached behind me and put the pillow against the arm of the couch and, too high to care, I obeyed him and leaned against it. I tucked my legs up and watched as Nero laid on the other side of the couch, his eyes also glassy.

"There. Your heartbeat is slowing down. You've been having mini-heart attacks the entire time. This is why I usually kill them after," Nero said, and his eyes slowly closed. "Did Kiki tell you why I'm out here?"

"Yeah," I said. The pleasure flowing through me was like someone had blended up an electric blanket, added the afterglow of an orgasm, and then, to top it off, sprinkled that comfortable relief you got after laying down to sleep after working the graveyard shift. That was drugs, and I hadn't had them hit me this good since Killian shot me with my first dose of black tar heroin back in my basement. "Sanguine broke you out, right?"

"He did. I fucking love that guy. The history we have is one for the books. I saved him. Hey…" I opened my eyes slowly and saw he was staring at me. "How the fuck did you two end up here? And how can the chicklet survive the radiation?"

"I'm not telling you shit," I said to him. "You're Silas's fucking slave. And–"

"I left the family." I was surprised at the sharpened tone Nero had. I looked at him and saw he was staring right back at me, a flicker of regret in his eyes but also solidarity. It looked like he might actually be serious. "If I go back, Silas will kill Kiki and encase Ceph at the very least, and probably me too. Ceph was in that concrete tomb for thirty years over bullshit, and I'm not letting Silas have him again. Until Silas promises me Ceph's safety and Kiki's immortality… I'm not returning to Skyfall." He picked up his tin and pulled out a cigarette. "So we're two of the same now, like it or not. We're both fugitives and we both don't want anyone to know where we are." Then Nero was quiet for a moment. "You can fuck me over just as much as I can fuck you over. You might want to consider just getting over what happened. We'd be better allies than enemies, Duckling. The two of us would be powerful side by side."

"Fuck off," I mumbled and busied myself with the bottle of beer. I noticed Nero wincing when I picked it up though, probably waiting for me to wing it at his head. "When I get Killian back, Mantis and his slaves, and you and your slaves, can get the fuck off of my property. I'm taking this place over."

Nero snorted at this, the flint of his lighter rolled and I smelled the sharp tang of his cigarette being lit. "That won't happen. You and I can run this place together though, peaches. I love you enough to do it with you. Fuck, you have no idea how wild you drove me. You – you I respect, brosy."

Then he handed me the cigarette.

My body started to tremble like I'd been picked up and placed into the arctic. I looked at the cigarette and saw him handing it to me after he'd fucked me. Telling me… he wanted to have real sex with me one day, that I probably fucked hard. I put it between my lips and when I didn't answer he backhanded me, the cigarette getting knocked out of my mouth and replaced with blood.

I got up, the drugs not able to kill the infestation of memories that were travelling all throughout my body like hatched spiders. I started walked away from him, the cigarette shaking in my hand and my breathing suddenly starting to catch and stall in my throat.

"Reav?" Nero called after me. I heard the couch shift as he got up. I walked through a hallway, not knowing where it would take me, and started opening doors. I found the bathroom, then the laundry room – then, finally, I found a bedroom with a large master bed, the sheets messed up and the grey carpet covered with the dirty clothes of a man. This must be Adler's room. I turned off the lights and shut the door, sharp wheezes coming from my throat now, and leaned against it.

I clamped my hands over my mouth and stared at my boots as my night vision adjusted and turned them into a glowing blue. I squeezed my hand over my mouth so hard my teeth dug into my palm. I couldn't let Nero hear this. Oh, fuck me, what the hell had happened to me? What had happened to me? Who the fuck was I?

I wasn't Reaver. THIS DIDN'T HAPPEN TO REAVER! How did this happen? Perish raped Jade, and Killian. Silas sodomized and tortured Killian, and still he recovered. Why couldn't I? WHY COULDN'T I?

I shot to my feet and a bellowed cry rushed from my mouth before I could stop it. I grabbed the first thing I could see, which was a flimsy table with a lamp on it. I picked up the lamp and threw it against the wall, another scream breaking my throat, and watched with satisfaction as it shattered. The reward of seeing it break made me pick up the side table and smash it over a wooden desk, the feet flying off of it and splinters bursting into the air before falling down like rain.

My body was heaving, anger coating me and lubricating my limbs, making every movement I made seem like it took no effort at all. But the penalty of it was that I was barely in control of myself. All I wanted was to hurt things, smash things, I was tired of rotting in my madness I had to fix this! I can't stand this. I can't stand this for one more day. I just…

I just…

Light flooded the room.

My body froze, and I was no longer able to move or speak. I realized I was standing like a deer in the headlights, keeled over, and with my breathing a heave like I was taking in my last breaths. There was something liquid dripping down my face, but I didn't know what.

A dark silhouette stood in the doorway. There was a blue-embered cigarette in his hand, the other on the door frame.

"Holy… shit," I heard him say. He pinched the cigarette's ember with his fingers and threw it away, then approached me. But when my eyes shot up to his, he paused and kept his distance. "I really fucked you up, didn't I? You did kind of make me lose control. You were such a badass, and it got me off having someone with so much fight. You gave me a run for my money, and it was the best couple weeks I'd had in years. You were a fucking devil."

I realized I was still staring at him, but my vision had receded in the back of my head. My eyes had been turned inside out, and now all I was seeing was Nero on top of me. And all I was feeling was his body pressed against mine. He was breathing into my ear, raising my ass up off of the ground so I was forced to see his cock thrusting into me, pulling out blood. So much of it was collecting underneath the rim of his head, and as he thrusted and thrusted it would congeal and stick to it.

I was a fucking devil? I had so much fight apparently.

"Reaver…? Shit. You're kind of reminding me of how Sanguine got. Now I really feel bad. Look, you were the family's enemy at the time. You killed Timmy, and we needed to know where Perry was. And like I said, I was pissed at you for being Sky's clone. He practically took my husband away from me, and having him in my possession, and Kess giving me the all-clear to torture info out of you… it wasn't anything personal, you know? You understand that, I know you've raped guys before. I kill 'em, or I get off seeing them all emotionally crippled after 'cause it's satisfying. But those guys are just random men, I wouldn't do it to a brother of mine. And… I don't know. I kind of feel attached to you now after all of that. All protective and shit."

It was replaying right in front of me. In front of my eyes, and I couldn't escape it. It would haunt me, terrorize me, stalk my footsteps and snap at my heels. Every moment I was in Nero's possession. Every sick thing he did to me and made me do to him, to Kiki. Having Nero and Kiki blow me, forcing me to cum, forcing me to betray Killian and fuck Kiki from the power of the ressin, or just when I'd attempted to kill him. All the times Nero raped me, made me sleep beside him with his cum dripping out of my ass. I remember his loud snoring, Kiki's head resting on his chest and rising up and down with Nero's breathing.

So clear it was. So clear I was sure that this… this was the false reality.

"Ducklin'? I'm sorry. I kind of really want us to be friends and bros. How about when we get Adler and Spike, we'll rape them together. Just you and me, and we can cripple them and laugh at their issues afterwards."

Then I saw Killian. I saw Killian glaring at me, challenging me with his blue eyes. Taking control and aiding me when I'd slip into the very psychosis that was ravaging me right now. I didn't know what was worse, having this experience constantly plaguing me or knowing I was losing my boyfriend.

"Reaver? Shit… bro, you're staring off like your mind broke, at least say something, or… you know, blink."

I was losing me. I needed help, but I didn't know who could help me. Elish was gone. There was no one in front of me but the very person who had snatched me out of the air to break me down for his entertainment.

And he was right in front of me.

Apologizing?

My vision focused. I looked at Nero. The brute chimera looked back, and through all the unwanted emotions ravaging me, I felt surprise to see genuine guilt on his face.

I knew it was real, because unlike Elish, Nero couldn't hide his emotions.

He actually… felt bad.

So he wouldn't hide his emotions when I kill Kiki in front of his eyes? When I pour the concrete over Ceph's body as I whistled happily to myself?

Good.

"I hate feeling guilty… you're an asshole," I heard Nero mumble. "I only feel guilty when it comes to my brothers. So I really do see you as one."

I will take away everything that he loves.

Just be patient.

Okay.

Suddenly there was a crackle of static all around us. It was enough to break me out of my state. Nero and I both looked above us to try and locate the speakers we were both hearing.

"Reaver?" My body locked in place as Killian's raspy voice, sounding weak and small, sounded over a loudspeaker we couldn't see.

"Killian? Did you kill them already?" I said, trying to sound positive. "Where are you?"

"In the hallway where the metal door is. On the right-hand side. Go into that room and turn on the flat screen computer monitor. The computer is already on. It's a feed to the laboratory. Adler wants to talk to you." Killian said weakly.

I exchanged glances with Nero and we both nodded to each other. "Are you okay?" I asked him. "How's Kiki?" The static continued as we walked into the living room. I couldn't locate the speakers but once the feed was over I was planning on combing through the entire mansion to find every embedded electronic. I should've done it sooner, another thing this manic state was taking from me.

"I'm okay, but don't get upset when you see us. We fought."

My throat tightened as those words sunk in, and I prepared myself for seeing Killian injured. They couldn't kill him at least, and I bet they didn't even know he was immortal. I could use this to my benefit. Give them more cards than they thought they had. If they thought they had a better hand, they'd be more likely to take risks with us.

Nero slowed down, and with a glance up he grabbed my shoulder and hissed in my ear. "I can see a little black coil in the recessed lighting. It's the same audio wires I've seen Silas use," he said in the chimera whisper I knew all too well. "There are no cameras. Once we talk to the dude, we'll go around the mansion and disable them so they can't hear our conversations anymore."

"Roger," I said to him. We walked through the kitchen and found the room Killian had directed us to.

It was an office, that much was obvious. The flat panel monitor was on top of an oak desk with stacks of notebooks, manila folders, hard drives, and other science stuff. There were also filing cabinets, three of them, a leather couch on the left-hand side, a standing lamp, and two credenza-type cabinets, one of them with the door ajar, suggesting it was also chock-full of science shit.

I leaned my hands down on the monitor and flicked it on, bracing myself for the worst.

But nothing could prepare me for what I saw, and even though Killian was immortal, I still felt nausea grasp me, and on its heels was anger.

The left side of Killian's face was swollen and black, with an angry red hue surrounding it and travelling down his neck like a rash. His left eye was completely shut with dried blood crusted into his eyebrows, and his earlobe had been severed and was hanging off like... it had been bitten.

Kiki was a bit better. The boy was behind Killian on a rolling chair which he was tied to. His head was hung low and there was flaking red blood and other fluids dripping from his nose and mouth. His face wasn't as swollen as Killian's but there were lots of bruises and several nasty cuts.

"YOU FUCK!" Nero roared beside me. He banged his fist against the oak computer table and I heard a loud snap. "Show me Adler! Where are you, you fucking cunt-sucking bitch? Fucking show yourself!" My ears ached from the booming bellow that filled the room.

Killian wasn't looking at me, but I realized he actually was. I glanced up and saw a webcam above me, Killian must be looking at the screen.

Ignoring Nero, I gave Killian a smile. "You did fight, Killer Bee. Did you get a few of them at least?"

Killian tried to smile back, but then his single blue eye shifted to the left and I saw him wince before nodding. He looked back to me. "Do what he says, Reaver," he said to me simply. Then he looked at Nero. I saw his lip, one of them split and blackened with caked blood, stiffen at the sight of him beside me. "You too." His tone completely changed at that.

"You look after Kiki. Understand me?" Nero said harshly. And when Killian only glared at him, he let out a hiss between his teeth. "Hey. Look at me. You fucking look out for him. This shit isn't his fault."

Killian only had one working eye but it flashed with hostility. The Killer Bee I despised was finally directing his dominance at the right guy.

"Since when do you give a fuck about what is someone's fault?" Killian said, glaring right into the cam. "I'd stay up there where you're safe, chimera. Because once I fucking get a hold of you, I'm going to skin you alive and make you fucking eat–"

Suddenly two hands appeared in the screen and they both roughly shoved Killian off of the chair. Killian flew out of sight, but I heard a crash and several bottles breaking.

"Hey!" I snarled, now it was my turn to lose my temper. I slammed my hand down on the table, wanting to jump through the screen to strangle whoever touched him. "Untie him and fucking try that with him then, you cowardly piece of shit. Come up here and face us!"

I saw a brown leather jacket, well-worn, and with a navy blue t-shirt underneath. I saw brown hair, curled into little spirals that fell slightly past his ears, but it was covering his face as the man leaned down and pick up the chair Killian had been pushed off of. He righted it, brushed the curls from a face and he sat down.

Wow. I was…

… staring at myself.

Adler had my face shape, my small nose and ears, and my lips as well. But his eyes… his eyes were Perish's through-and-through.

Or… Sky's rather.

Adler glared at the screen, he had blue eyes, almost grey and with a ring of dark blue circling the outer edges. There was no doubt in my mind this man was a clone of Sky, and the way he was glaring at me and Nero, told me he had more than a handful of chimera traits.

"There is a saying we have around here," Adler said coolly. He had a deep voice, coarse and almost raspy. I was half-expecting smooth tones like Silas but his voice was his own. "If you see a rat in your house during the day, rest assured you will see dozens once night falls." He looked at Nero and then back at me. "It looks like my home has become infested with rats. I warned Mantis about taking you in, Nero, but he did out of the goodness of his heart because apparently you two were friends in Skyfall. He was a fool, and when he wakes up he'll see I was right."

I heard a strange noise. I looked towards it and saw that Nero was grinding his teeth. "You need to come up sometime, Adler. It's best you start negotiations now."

"Negotiations?" Adler said in the same rough voice. "You come into my home, by invitation, and stay as our guest, then proceed to double-cross the man who has been protecting me since I was ten years old from the very king you yourself were running from. And then your slave boy alerts your family to try and take over my home? There are no negotiations, Nero. You may have not known me for long, but I assure you, I'm not a man to fuck with."

When Adler rose I felt the chair lean back as Nero clenched it. "Adler?" he called. Then he let out a vicious *Fuck!* when Adler walked towards Kiki.

"Hey!" Nero yelled. "What do you want not to hurt him? Hey!" I watched as Adler walked past Kiki and picked up something metal on a nearby table, a table that was covered in tubes and machines. He looked at the camera, the smug yet rancour smile still plastered on his face.

"What do I want? You betrayed us, I will take nothing from you," Adler replied. He walked up to the cicaro, who was bound tightly to the black computer chair, and grabbed him by his hair before wrenching his head up.

Kiki looked up at him, his orange eyes disconnected and far away, and his mouth slacked and open to help him breathe through what looked like a blood-filled nose.

"For your own future self-preservation I'd leave him be," Nero bellowed. "Immortality lasts a long time, buddy." My chair tilted back further, and then he slammed his hand down on it.

I knew exactly what he was going through. This was reminding me of when Killian and I had been Perish's prisoner. The feeling of being helpless while some batshit insane asshole was torturing someone you loved.

Killian was immortal, but Kiki wasn't. What bad feelings I felt over the little cicaro, who was a pretty nice kid, were lost however.

Because I was enjoying seeing Nero in misery. It was just another note to make in my book of Nero. I always knew I could use Kiki to get back at him, but the more information I got the better.

Kiki's lips trembled and his eyes focused enough to look up at Adler. But then they looked down at the device Adler was holding and he whimpered and started shaking his head back and forth in a way that told me he recognized what it was, and he was scared of it.

I saw a flicker of electric blue from the device and realized it was some sort of Taser, but a smooth cylinder, not one I had seen in merchants' caravans. Kiki gave out a frightened cry, like a scream a wild dog gave when you were beating on it, and got it into a corner, then Adler plunged it into Kiki's crotch.

I'd never heard a more horrific scream, but it was drowned out by Nero's bellow of rage. The poor fucking cicaro went rigid, his eyes so bugged out I thought they were going to pop out of their sockets. He went as stiff as a board, and when Adler pulled the electric prong away, I saw not only a growing wet spot from the kid's own piss, but more char marks and a hole in the crotch which showed blackened and red burnt skin.

Kiki let out a choked sob and he started shaking his head back and forth. "Master?" Kiki sobbed. He cried out again, more agonizing sobs breaking up his howls. "Master. I'm sorry!"

Another bellow came to join in with the screams, making a tempo between the two of them that, in the cockles of my heart, I did quite enjoy. Nero's lower registers mixed in with the tenor screams from Kiki did make a wonderful song, but unfortunately, I had to keep my poker face.

But I would make it my goal to draw out the same scream from Kiki. Perhaps with Killian underneath him, his cock already deep inside, and my own sliding in on top of it. We'd fuck him hard and bloody and we wouldn't stop until we coaxed the same alluring chorus from them.

"It's okay, Kiki-weeki," Nero choked, drawing my attention away from my fantasy. "I'll get you out of there. Okay, baby boy? Master'll save you, just hang on for me, okay? You know I'm good for it." He let out a frustrated cry. "What the fuck do you want, Adler?"

Adler chuckled. He grabbed Kiki's hair again and shook him with an amused cackle, before shoving him backwards. Kiki only sobbed quietly to himself, and Adler left him and sauntered over. He sat down in the chair, like he hadn't even gotten up in the first place, and smiled darkly.

"What do I want?" Adler said nonchalantly. He looked down, where I think Killian was, before he bent down out of sight.

Killian shrieked, a gut-wrenching shriek full of pain that soon became distorted from a build-up of fluid, blood or saliva I didn't know, I just knew he started choking and gasping.

Nero's angry cries were now mingled with mine before they were followed by the sound of the chair being thrown to the ground. I had jumped to my feet, unable to just sit here and watch this happen, and ran to the metal door.

I started pounding on it, blind rage seeping down and covering my eyes before muffling my hearing like I had been plunged into the deepest of oceans. "Open it up!" I screamed. I hammered on it and pulled on the handle, dried blood flaking off into my hand. "Open it up and fucking face me!" I kept yelling and continued my assault on the door. When Nero finally grabbed me and started pulling me away I was clawing at it so hard I was leaving streaks of blood where my fingernails had peeled back.

"Come on. We'll get him eventually, Ducky," Nero said to me, his voice harsh and determined. "We'll fucking get him. We'll torture him together. We'll..." Nero swore and dropped me. He wiped his hand down his face, before he turned and drove his fist into the wall. It went right through it like it was paper and when he pulled out I saw pink insulation and wires.

My body was heaving, and I kept looking around as if expecting something to magically appear that could help us. I found myself unable to concentrate, unable to answer him back. I wanted to run in every direction, but in the same vein I wanted to stay absolutely still so I could gather my thoughts back, find a way to sort this shit out.

"We just need to sweet talk," Nero whispered, "and once we gain his trust... he's ours."

I didn't know how but I managed to nod.

Nero clapped me over the shoulder. "We'll show him just what happens when he fucks with chimeras." And he turned and walked back into the office. Without wanting to, I trailed behind him... and Adler was waiting for us with a smile.

He was holding up Killian's head as Killian kneeled down beside him.

Killian's eye was glassy, and there was fresh blood trickling down his mouth. He was completely incoherent.

But now in the background I saw another man. It was obviously Spike, not just because he was the only other man in the mansion that Nero mentioned, but because he had blond hair gelled into spikes and a fucking spiked collar around his neck. On top of that, he had black eyeliner from the looks of it, anything else I couldn't see from the distance and the camera quality.

"You," Adler said, and he looked directly at me. "Let's play the honesty game. Let's see if you'll tell me the truth. What's your name, brother?"

"I'm not telling you anything," I spat. "I was here to rescue Nero. I didn't have a fucking problem with you. You and your asshole guardian tried to burn me and my boyfriend alive. You two were the ones to start this shit, not me. I was only trying to save him."

Adler's expression turned hostile. "We were the ones starting shit? We didn't know who the fuck you were. We were doing the same thing we do every festival and nothing more." He glared at me, and I fucking glared right back. "You were the ones to break into my fucking home. You're the criminals here, and you will get treated as such." He shook his head. "I'm a very nice man. But when you fuck with my home, you fuck with me; and you don't want to fuck with me, my friend."

The poker face was starting to wear as he continued to speak. I didn't know if I wanted to burst through those doors and shake him, calling him a fucking moron, or laugh until my heart gave out.

"What do you want, Adler?" I said to him. "If you want us to leave, give us Kiki, Killian, and Ceph and we'll leave."

Adler's expression didn't change. "I have no reason to trust you. Mantis trusted Nero and he was gearing up to betray us and let the filth King Silas know I'm alive. I was told all about him and what my destiny was supposed to be. If he had it his way, I would be turned into him and made into a sex slave. No. You will never leave Turris."

"We're not staying," I snapped at him, quickly reaching the end of my rope with this asshole. "Look, buddy. You may not know me, but you only have one fucking small window of time to talk to me before I fucking get pissed, and you don't want to see me pissed. For your best interest, you will send up Killian and the other two, and you will let us leave. You have one warning. One fucking warning."

Adler chuckled, and that laugh to me was like nails on a chalkboard. My teeth clenched and slowly slid from one side of my mouth to the other. Not only was I at the end of my rope with this bastard, he was lighting the end of it like the tightened tip was a fuse.

"I'm so intimidated," Adler hissed. "I'm fucking shaking with–"

"Reaver Dekker," I said, cutting him off. My tone was flat and without emotion, barren words coming from a dry mouth.

Adler smirked at me, his hand still wrapped under Killian's chin to hold him up. "Oh, I know. I know all about you, brother dearest. Are you as dark of a chimera as Elish says?"

"I am not just a chimera," I said to him. I averted my gaze from the screen and looked at the little black webcam. "I am the clone of Silas Dekker and Sky Fallon. A born immortal with every chimera enhancement, and almost every ability available to the family. I am the perfected version of you, who was sent away after being deemed defective. I am the end result of decades of research and I, unlike you, am the one created to be Silas's partner. I was raised in the greywastes where I trained to kill immortal chimeras from birth by my friend and ally, a man you apparently know, Elish Dekker, and my fathers Lycos Dekker and Greyson Merrik." I moved closer to the camera. "You have one chance, Adler Dekker, to release my property back to me, and release Nero's property back to him. I will not ask you again. And if you deny me what belongs to me, you will be smoked out of your lab like the rodent you are, and you will be killed."

I stared at the camera, and heard Nero give an impressed whistle behind me, then I turned back to the monitor.

There was no smug look on Adler's face. He was staring at the screen, his eyes narrowed and his jaw tight. His hand slid away from Killian's neck, and my boyfriend, dazed and out of it, shifted backwards so he was away from Adler's touch.

"If you threaten me again, this beautiful boy's brains will be painting my walls," Adler said coolly. "I call the shots here, not you. I have your partners and the slave boy, remember that."

"I was not engineered to love, merely dominate," I said back. "Kill him. I can find another." I motioned to Spike who was still standing in the distance. "I love them blond, maybe him?" I smirked when Adler's eyes narrowed just slightly, before he caught himself and they hardened back to granite. "I'm done shooting the shit with you. Either tell me what your end game is, or fucking rot down there for all I care. I have things to do."

Adler regained himself enough to laugh. "Spike... why don't you fuck Killian in front of this cam. Show the scary chimera just what we do to mouthy children. My eyes widened and my breath was taken from me.

He wouldn't fucking dare...

Adler laughed at my expression. "Oh, I have a great many things I plan on–"

Suddenly Killian's unfocused eyes shot to Adler, and a fraction of a second later Killian jumped to his feet, raised his bound hands, and threw them over Adler's neck. Killian pulled Adler backwards off of his chair, and I saw sneakers and jeans before he toppled onto the ground.

No way. No fucking way!

Killian went down with him and I heard Adler shouting and bellowing, calling for the blond one behind him who ran over and started trying to pull Killian off of him. I saw a flash of Killian's face – and it was coated in blood.

At the exact same time Nero and I burst out laughing.

"Go, Killian!" Nero hollered, and as he shook and slapped my shoulders I started cheering Killian on as well. I felt a rush of pride as Spike dragged Killian away, before Killian jumped to his feet, blood indeed coating his mouth, and swung his bound hands towards Spike. The strength behind the blow successfully threw Spike off of his feet.

"Get 'em, Killer Bee!" I yelled as loud as I could so he could hear me. Killian was pulled to the ground by Adler, and though I wanted to jump through the screen to help him all I could do was egg him on. "That's my boy! That's my Killi!"

Killian's head popped up, he looked at the camera. He managed a smile, but his eyes, heavy with worry, stole the joy right out from under me.

I kept my own smile for him, but already my heart was being weighed down. "I'll come get you as soon as I can, baby. I promise. Just–" I looked behind him when I saw quick movement, and saw Adler on his feet, his face twisted in rage and his eyes boiling in their sockets from anger. He had a gash on his neck and shoulder, staining his navy shirt purple as it flowed freely down his skin.

"Killi, duck!" I yelled, but it was too late. Adler swung the metal Taser-like cylinder, the width of a flashlight, at Killian's head, and it hit his skull with a sickening crunch.

"Fuck... FUCK!" Nero screamed beside me. "NO! ADLER!" Nero yelled, but all I could do was stare, seeing only the top of Adler's head, his bent over back, and the metal baton being swung again and again; each time it appeared on the camera's feed, it had more blood on it.

"NO!" Nero cried. I was shocked to hear real, uncensored despair in his tone. I couldn't believe what I was hearing. Nero was showing this emotion over Killian? "FUCKING CUNT! NO! FUCK!!!" Nero ran out of the room. I could see the blood flying up, it was sticking into Adler's hair.

And the sound... the sound of a blunt object fracturing a skull.

Thunk thunk thunk.

I knew that sound well.

Adler grabbed the webcam and pointed it down to the floor. I saw Killian, the impact had popped his left eye out, the one that had been shut from the swelling. It stood out as the only white thing on a face that had been beaten beyond recognition. His nose was crushed, his lips lacerated from his teeth going through them, and the side of his head was the texture of ground meat.

There was so much blood too, mixed in with bits of hair and scalp, and a lot of shattered bone.

And Killian was still alive. I saw his mouth struggle to open; his body seizing and twitching. There was a lake of blood inside of his mouth, with shattered teeth swimming around the red pool like debris after a flood.

Even though I knew he would come back, the fact that Killian was still alive physically hurt me.

Then the metal cylinder was swung down one more time. It hit his jaw and knocked it out of place, Killian made a small gurgling whine, the pooled blood now running down his mouth with the bits of tooth.

He blinked his remaining eye, then with a sharp, congested inhale… he died.

I looked away and reached down to the desktop… and turned it off.

With automatic movements, I grabbed the chair I had been sitting on and steadied it underneath the recessed lighting above the bedroom. I got onto it and pulled out the small black microphone and severed the cord. I left it dangling, and took the chair into the hallway.

I passed Nero, who was hammering on the metal door and screaming, fucking screaming his head off. He was manic with rage, completely in berserker mode, and that would be the last thing the laboratory, and all those in it, would hear.

I got onto the chair and pulled out the microphone in the hallway, and moved to Adler's bedroom and pulled that one out as well.

I found one more in the living room, Nero still screaming. None in the kitchen, none in the other hall. I found one in the entrance and pulled it. Then one in the hallway upstairs but none in the other rooms. I even paused and tuned my hearing, but once I unplugged the other electronics I could hear nothing. No secret video cameras, no more microphones.

There would now be no one eavesdropping on us inside of his mansion. I was alone with Nero while Adler, Spike, and eventually Mantis, crawled underneath my feet like roaming croaches.

And they were about to learn just what it meant to fuck with chimeras.

CHAPTER 30

Reaver

WHEN I CAME BACK DOWNSTAIRS ALL WAS SILENT. I walked into the living room, severed microphones dangling from my hands, and saw Nero hunched over on the couch, a cigarette being held to his lips.

I grabbed a cigarette from the tin on the table and lit it. I sat beside Nero and took a long, long drag. While filling my lungs with the taste of a BlueLeaf Recon Series opiate cigarette, a family favourite, I gave Nero a sideways glance.

Nero was staring at the cold fireplace. His indigo eyes were heavy, yet staring, and his face was holding no mask, only showing naked grief mixed in with rage. He wasn't moving, and the cigarette tucked between his pointer and middle finger had a half-inch of ash on the tip.

"Why do you care?" I asked simply. "You didn't know him."

Like my words were hot water thawing the ice that had frozen his body, Nero leaned over and dashed his cigarette into the urson paw ashtray.

"I don't like seeing my brothers sad," Nero responded and held the cigarette up to his lips. "And you kind of know when they found someone permanent. I'm protective of you fucks, especially the little ones. Always have been." His lips slowly pursed, and he blew the silver smoke out like his mouth was a vent. "You should probably just leave. I'm going to be calling Silas. I'm turning that cocksucker in to him, and we'll see what kind of song he'll sing then. I won't tell Kingy I saw you."

I took a drag of my cigarette and felt an inner struggle going on inside of me. The waves of rage that had vibrated through my body, until my flesh had become calcified, those feelings met with a fresh confusion that Nero's honest words brought with them.

Nero slapped my knee. "I'm not sorry for what I did to you. Because I can't say I wouldn't have done it differently, because I wasn't future me back then, I was past me." I had to shake my head, he certainly didn't have the linguistic talents that Elish had. "I had a great time even though I knew you didn't, and if I knew it would fuck you up so much I'd have toned it down. They just toted you as being this fucking demon monster, so I just went all out, and it was great, honestly. I can't get it out of my mind. I loved it."

The silence that came after tuned my mind back into what my body was doing. I was once again betrayed by my automatic physical responses because there was a cesspool of nausea bubbling under my skin, some giant ball of rot; like the decaying carcasses being controlled by the proxy worms.

"I wasn't raised in your family." My response betrayed the voice inside of me demanding for me to keep silent and let the rot continue to spread and taint me, but my mouth moved in defiance. Whether I could blame it on the opiate cigarettes, or the residue from what I just saw on the computer screen was anyone's guess. "I didn't get fucked by Silas at fifteen. I wasn't raised around skimpy-dressed cicaros, or whatever shit you idiots were undoubtedly exposed to too young. I didn't get my cock sucked until I was sixteen or seventeen, and I didn't start having sex until last year. I didn't care about that sort of shit, and unless it's Killian, I still don't. I never liked sexual contact or any physical contact."

I saw Nero look at me out of the corner of my eye. "Fucking seriously?"

My head nodded, even though my mind had already left the living room and locked the door to Adler's room. Why I was saying this to him, I didn't know. Maybe I didn't want Nero to think I was weak. He had an opinion of me beforehand, and it looked like I'd successfully convinced him I was some damsel bitch. There was something inside of me that felt compelled to defend my honour. I was the man in Donnely watching Nero rape Perish, feeling flickers of respect and awe, and an even deeper thirst to emulate the chimera I'd seen as a power figure.

And the cape I'd put in Aras when I was burning the convicts had manifested that desire into something physical.

"I was trying to fuck Silas as soon as my cock was big enough at thirteen and I started getting wet dreams so often I thought I was a pervert. He was locking his bedroom at night because he was tired of waking up to me sucking him off and beatin' my meat to it. Silas lied and told me my cock would fall off if I had sex before fifteen, and I believed him." I snorted at this and Nero chuckled. "If I didn't believe him so much I'd have taped Garrett's mouth shut and given him what for. Fuck. I'll have to show you the video of me on my fifteen birthday. Silas had his mouth on my dick for, I counted, bro, fifteen seconds before I came, huge gobs of it all down Silas's mouth, he couldn't eat it fast enough, and I was just moaning like I was in a porno. I came nine times that night. Nine times, Duck. In the end, Silas was fucking me so hard I thought I was going to die from the pleasure. I just wanted him to go faster. Oh man... fuck, I love that video."

I shook my head, and hid the smile with another drag of the cigarette. "The first time I entered Killian it was the same. I had to pause and just stay absolutely still but he was squirming underneath me from the pain and tightening himself, and I just wanted to tell him to stop it or else I was going to cum. I just couldn't believe I was doing it. I hated being close to people, even just hugging made me stiffen up and cringe, which sucked because Killian was just this face hugger from *Alien*, always on me. I got used to it though."

Nero's lips pursed and he nodded. Then he reached over and dashed his cigarette again. "I'm sorry, Reav."

"For what?"

Nero gave me a confused look before to my amusement his expression grew concerned. "You... what do you mean 'for what'?" He leaned back and his cheeks puffed out as he exhaled. "Okay. I'm going to prep you some china. I guess I've seen this shit happen to chimeras. We've got so many mental problems we block shit. I've—"

"Elish's right, you really are a moron," I said through the cigarette in my mouth. "You really think Killian could've survived ground zero and that much sestic radiation? Or being in the plaguelands? You really think I'd be sitting here shooting the shit with you after my boyfriend got his face smashed in? Or that I'd even bring him to this house in the first place after everything I went through to save him? He's immortal, you dumbass. I'm not leaving, you're not calling Silas. The two of us are going to show that pompous, delusional little cocksucker just what happens when he fucks with us. If Killian doesn't himself, because that kid has turned into a fucking psycho lately."

Nero's head snapped towards me, and a brief moment passed of him just gawking.

Then, with a raise of his hand, he smacked me upside the head, the cigarette shooting out of my mouth and landing on the table in a shower of embers and ash. I almost fell forward from the force of it and the room temporarily flashed white.

"That was a shitty thing to make me believe, you fucking bitch," Nero said as I rubbed my head with a smirk on my face. I leaned over and picked up the cigarette and heard him chuckle. "I was wondering why you hadn't gone Fallocaust, or started tearing out your hair like your brittle fucking mind would've done. Fucking weak little shit going batty over some hardcore sex, but acts all stone-cold monster when his boyfriend gets his head smashed in. I was wondering what the fuck was wrong with you."

Surprisingly, the smirk turned into a half-smile and I reached over and grabbed his tin of drugs. "He's resilient. You have no fucking idea. The past several months his balls have grown twice as big. Honestly, I fucking hate it though."

Nero tossed me his black card and a metal sniffer when I brought out the china white. I needed some right about now. The fact that I was talking civilly to the man who had caused all of these problems inside of me, while Killian lay dead and my two newest enemies slinked underneath my feet, was showing just how mentally fucked I was in that moment. Maybe my mind finally realized I couldn't save Killian while spinning my wheels in the same mud pit.

"Hate it? Why? It gets me off when Kiki shows dominance. The fact that he stole the Falconer and left the family behind to save me, then rescued the two of you. I love seeing the kittens cut their adult teeth," Nero said. "He's going to grow up to be a fucking chimera to be reckoned with and I can't wait."

I leaned down and did several lines of china white. I rubbed my nose with the back of my hand and handed the sniffer to Nero.

And as he sniffed his nose and rubbed it at the same time, no doubt to clear it. I watched this man who had become the sole vessel for all of my hatred. A chimera who had tortured and raped me for weeks, beat me down without mercy, who had made me chew through my own wrist to free myself.

"You okay? Bad hit?" Nero asked.

"P-prep me some more." To swallow the barb of humiliation being shoved down my throat, my breathing broke up my words, making them resemble a gasping plea. I clenched my teeth and mentally tried to force the anxiety down to my feet, but it kept rising up like I was trying to push down water with my bare hands.

I closed my eyes, and even though I knew it would make me look even weaker, the lesser of the two evils had me burying my face into my hands, my elbows resting on my knees.

Unfortunately that ended up only multiplying the intense feelings of anxiety that was lighting my blood on fire. Several seconds later I rose and started pacing behind the couch, unable to sit still for any longer.

Even though my eyes were wide open and staring, I saw inside the vivid pictures in my head, the image of my own colon and intestines coming out of my ass, the bright red shiny prolapse followed by light pink intestines, leaving streaks and patterns on the sheets like a morbid art project. Nero had fucked me so hard he'd pulled out my own guts, this was after he'd sodomized me with a knife.

I thought that was bad. I really thought that was bad. But what happened next was worse.

"Reaver… I've kind of been around Sanguine enough to know what's going on." I heard him get up. "I don't carry the shit on me, but I'm going to check Adler's stash for Xanax. Go outside and get some fresh air."

Like the obedient dog I guess I still was, I walked through the sliding glass door. It was late afternoon now and the sun was blazing, burning through the cloak of ashes to make the yard humid and stifling. I walked out and stayed under the awning where it was shady, and saw two of the bat-cats stretched out underneath a row of rose bushes dozing comfortably.

I stared at them, like one would do when feeling motion sickness. But not a minute later of laboured breathing that was doing nothing but spreading the tension, I ran to bushes opposite of the cats and started throwing up.

This petri dish of growing infection that I had become was starting to become too large for the colourless void to contain, and I found myself scared for my mind.

I had… never been scared for myself before.

I was immortal. What did I have to fear? Wasn't I stronger than that?

Again I threw up, sour bile that left a chalky taste in my throat and mouth splashing against violet roses, dousing them in yellow-tinged rain that beaded on it and dripped off into the bright green leaves. I had to inhale sharply in order to breathe through the heaving, and I soon found myself unable to catch a breath.

There was no doubt about it. I was having a panic attack, and I had to get away from here as quickly as possible. Nero couldn't see this.

"Hey, I found some."

I whirled around, and when he saw me Nero's eyebrows raised. He extended his arm and presented me with three blue pills. I took them and popped them into my mouth, more sour joining the already gag-inducing taste of the puke, and I started walking along the house to where I knew the dirt road was.

"Hey. Don't fucking leave, idiot. The cultists'll recognize you."

I kept walking and I heard Nero jog up to me.

"No, get the fuck away from me!" I suddenly snapped. "Fuck off."

"You're not blowing our fucking cover by prancing down to Melchai."

"You don't tell me what the fuck to do. Do I look chained up to you?" I whirled around and reached to my belt to draw my combat knife, only to have my hand graze an empty sheath. Nero must've taken it while I was resurrecting.

But then I remembered seeing it on the coffee table. He hadn't taken it, just removed it while I healed.

"You're not thinking straight, and I'm not going to let you march down the fucking road where they can see you. We have enough shit on our plates trying to get the boys back, dumbshit." Nero jumped back as I took a swing at him and roughly pushed me. I stumbled backwards, and my back hit a tree.   .

"Why the fuck are you getting all panic attack anyway?" Nero said, his voice raising. "Your boy is fucking immortal."

"Why? WHY!" I exploded. By now my head was throbbing, a migraine coming swiftly and quickly, and proceeding to saw my skull in two. "Because I'm a fucking idiot for sitting with the bastard who tortured me like a fucking subhuman. Who made me have to tell my boyfriend I fucked another man. Who's given me nightmares that have rendered me a babbling, sobbing idiot!" The higher my voice raised the more I felt myself lose control. Everything around me was turning hazy, and I was starting to think all of this might be a dream. It had to be a dream. This wasn't Reaver.

"Who keeps telling me I'm overreacting to almost a month of being fucked until my intestines spilled out of me. Who beat me senseless, who suffocated me from face-fucking me, who fucking drugged me, humiliated me, made me chew my fucking hand off and even then you couldn't let me go!" My voice was breaking. Oh fuck. Reaver, stop. Stop showing this side of you to him. Anyone but him. Anyone but fucking Nero.

"You made me unable to have sex with my boyfriend without going into a psychosis so real I hurt him, I killed him just last week from it. I ripped out his throat. I have become such a weak bitch in front of Killian, he's starting to try and dominate me... that little shit has been challenging me, talking back to me, trying to soothe *me* when I turn into a manic anxiety-plagued mess! My life has been destroyed. I don't even know who the fuck I am anymore because of this. Because Reaver Merrik doesn't act like this; Reaver doesn't feel like this! I didn't have weaknesses before this besides Killian being in danger, and he's immortal now. I'm fucking supposed to be stronger, unbreakable. I'm the born immortal killer. I am the Reaper who kills for fun, who manipulated an entire town to burn their own alive. I was unbreakable. I was fucking unbreakable!" Though no tears came I let out a sob, and at that, my legs became water and I fell to my knees.

"And you guys are looking at me like this wasn't a big deal, like I should be over it because I'm a chimera. But it's all I think about and no matter how many times I try and get over it... I can't get you out of my head. I can't stop seeing you whenever I try and be intimate with Killian; whenever I try and be half the dark chimera I was. I've lost myself... and I've lost the respect of my boyfriend... all because of you."

I looked up at Nero, and I saw a look of astonishment on him, as if someone had just ran up and smacked him across the face. He just stared at me like I had been uttering incantations, not a blink or a mouth twitch, just a fixed look.

But as he looked at me, I saw something different with him, a change in his normal visage. Nero looked unbalanced, off-kilter, like a painting of a man with slight enough facial changes for you to know that something was wrong, but not enough for you to put your finger on it.

"I'm like... your Jasper?" Nero suddenly whispered. He ran a hand down his face, staring off into nothing for a moment. He was acting like he'd come to a realization, but I didn't understand what he was saying.

Then my mind caught up with my mouth, and with cruel vigor embarrassment flooded me, making my ears burn with a heat that rapidly spread to my head. If this outburst was supposed to try and lance the infection that I was now unable to contain, it hadn't succeeded. Now I had only confirmed to my worst enemy that he had damaged me beyond repair. The humiliation from this was so strong I honestly felt like killing myself.

I got up to my feet and started walking away from him as quickly as I could.

"You know why this happened, Reaver?" Nero said.

My feet stopped and I paused. In front of me was the beginnings of the hill we'd scaled to get down here, brown dirt with bits of grey rocks and lumps of yellow grass clinging to the incline.

"It happened because you let yourself have a weakness," he said. I heard him start to walk towards me. "And your weakness is too much pride. You know my brother Elish...? He's so full of pride to the point of just seeping it, and we love him for it. He's just this dominant badass, all cold and unfeeling, and people gravitate to that since he backs up his shit with being so ruthless and completely frozen solid. You know what I haven't done to Elish in like... forty years?"

I saw Nero out of the corner of my eye stand beside me.

"I haven't fucked him. No one has but the one guy he can't say no to. Silas. And every time Silas fucks him, he's like raping Elish. Because Elish hates it, you can see it in his face. This disconnect like he's flying around in outer space and not in his own body, the same one I saw on your face at times. Kingy now only fucks him when he's mad at him, or needs to feel powerful and in control. It's not sex anymore, Silas actively rapes the dude and for days after Elish is just a fucking monster. You can tell it screws him up inside, but he'll never admit it, he just puts a few more bruises on Jade."

Was that true? I didn't even have to think about it, I knew it was true. Elish didn't tell me outright but the story he'd shared after I told him about Nero gave enough stock to Nero's words. An incident that happened between Silas and Elish that I suspect was a huge trigger in him deciding to kill Silas.

So the cold chimera had a weakness besides Jade. Even he couldn't absorb and compartmentalize having himself physically dominated.

"With me… I've never been raped before," Nero said, and then he let out a dry, humourless laugh. "I've been fucked against my will, but I've never been dominated or raped. Because I don't play the game that you prideful guys play. I don't see someone sticking their cock inside of me and fucking me as them being dominant towards me. I just don't play the sub-dom thing. I don't see the submissive partner in that sort of way. You saw it yourself, I let Kiki fuck me in front of you, didn't I? And I'd have let you, but I decided to save that for another time."

The time he was referring to jumped to the front of my head, pushing the other caustic, degrading thoughts aside. I'd been half-conscious, Nero already using my body thoroughly to the point where I'd been a crumpled heap. I remember him being on his back, not even on his hands and knees so he didn't have to look at the kid, on his back with Kiki's rapid panting filling the room to the beat of his thrusting hips, and Nero's groans and growls of encouragement.

"Reaver… I'm going to give you the most powerful piece of advice I can, brother to brother. You need to find these weaknesses, and make them your greatest strengths. Find them and fucking gild them in steel with a diamond coating. Pride will break you in this family, and if Silas ever does catch you, he'll do a lot worse than me, believe me, baby. You felt nothing towards me but you hate Silas, imagine Silas in place of me and what that'd honestly do to you. With the snap of his fingers not only he could rape you, Reaver, but I've seen disobedient chimeras get gang raped by the entire family, and I happily took part in it."

I felt a hand on my shoulder, and my mind was too full from his words to make any move to shake him off.

Because though the old, arrogant me would dismiss him because my own pride would deafen me to any sort of advice… I found myself actually hearing him and absorbing his words.

Nero was right.

"You want to know a secret?"

I looked at him and saw the corner of his mouth was raised in a smirk.

"I've raped a lot of guys, you were hands-down the best. You fought and fought. Where most kids your age would've crumpled and died, gone completely catatonic and dead to the world, you kept fighting it even when it did take you. I had you for almost a month and I was a thousand times harder on you since you were immortal, and I didn't have to worry about permanently killing you. I was that sadistic with you because I had to be, because you just kept on fighting, and not only that, outsmarting me. It was hot." He rubbed my shoulder. "And when you chewed your hand off and escaped? I was honest, I did want to let you escape just to hunt you down. Because I knew you'd keep fighting. You just didn't give up.

"Reaver-baby… do you have any idea how powerful you would be… if you got rid of those weaknesses and made them your most powerful strengths? If you got not just your old self back… but used this to fucking refine who you are, smooth off those damaged edges. Shit, brother. If you could turn it over in your mind… and make that experience make you harder, darker, more fucked up and psychopathic, then the next time it happens and someone ties you up and sticks their cock in you… you can laugh and tell them to fuck you harder."

Nero chuckled and shook his head. "Imagine the look on Silas's face? On anyone who makes the mistake of thinking they can dominate you in that way. Fuck, Reaver. You're this much of a psycho bitch just being twenty, if you can swallow that pride and learn this craft at twenty, you'll take their power away. Killian is immortal like you said, no one will have anything to hold against you, they'll have no power over you. You'll be unstoppable."

I'd be unstoppable.

His words sunk into me, and I realized that while I had been listening to him, my breathing had slowed, and the anxious knot that kept stealing my breath had started to loosen. For the first time in I didn't know how long… I felt better.

I felt hope. Light at the end of what seemed like an endless dark tunnel.

There had never been a time where I thought Nero would be the one to help me through what had happened. I had felt completely alone in facing this, the only man who had helped me far away in Skyfall dealing with his own crumbling life in the form of his dying pet. A man who I realized I was very similar to. Both with two weaknesses: the boys we loved, and our egotistical, sometimes arrogant, pride.

But I didn't have to be Elish. I didn't have to adopt the same weaknesses he had, whether he'd admit it or not. I didn't have to become solely Elish's protégé; I could learn from the man that, even with the hatred that had burned so deeply inside of me, I had respected and admired when I'd first seen him in Donnely. Respected his power and authority, and how he made Perish scream and cry underneath him as he dominated him with an iron fist.

And not only was Nero a force in himself, who had decades of experience on me. Someone who struck fear into the hearts of his younger brothers, and commanded respect; someone who talked openly about raping men and enjoying it, and made no apologies over what he'd done to me unless he actually meant it... I was realizing...

He would make a powerful ally, and perhaps the first act of cauterizing these weaknesses would be swallowing my pride and doing something I knew, deep down, would start me on the road of getting myself back.

No. Not getting myself back.

It would be my own rebirth. The dark chimera rising from the white flames like a phoenix, stronger, more ruthless, and ready to take on whatever was thrown my way.

"You're right," I said, after there had been silence between us for quite a while. "Everything you said, is right." I looked over at him and felt him squeeze my shoulder. "I'll make every weak flaw inside of me my hardest point. I thought I was created to be the worst, but I understand now I was only created with the potential. But I'll prove that I am who I thought I was, and actually be that chimera... with your help."

Nero smirked, his hand still squeezing my shoulder. "I'm going to fucking make you into a god." Then the smirk that seemed to fit his face like he'd been making it inside his steel mother, turned into a smile and then a laugh. He shook my shoulder before sliding his hand to my neck and pulling me towards him. He kissed my cheek, before slapping my backside hard. "Enough emotional shit, you fucking prissy bitch. Come inside and drink with me."

CHAPTER 31

Reno

I WRAPPED THE TOWEL AROUND SILAS AND HELPED him out of the shower. It was the biggest shower I had ever seen, but Silas also had the biggest bathroom I'd ever seen too. It was the size of my bedroom back home with a Jacuzzi tub that could fit six people, like as big as a hot tub almost. There were three sinks on a long white and grey marble counter top too, over a dark brown wood counter with flashy faucets. The floors were the same white with grey veins like the counter tops, and the walls half coffee brown tile, half lighter brown. And, my favourite thing, a painting, protected with a cover because of the steam, I guess, of Silas sprawled out in some kind of green jungly oasis, naked and exposing it all, with Sanguine on one end of him looking sinister with his hand sliding up Silas's leg, and Drake leaning against Silas with his hand on his inner thigh and a coy smile on his face. I recognized Jack's painting style by now, and knew this was another one of his masterpieces.

But fuck the painting, this bathroom was just amazing and I couldn't get over it. When you first walked into the bathroom all you saw was a glass door off to the side, then you opened the door and realized the shower was a small room in itself. It even had a bench built in (perfect height to prop up a leg, or to sit down and receive a surprise), and above it, recesses full of soaps and bottles of more soap. There were two giant shower heads that rained water down, three on each wall to shoot it at you, and a detachable hose with many power settings which I one day might want to play with. This shower made Garrett's normal walk-in shower look like my mouldy piece of crap in Aras. I was really going to have to speak to Garrett about a renovation.

I rubbed Silas's shoulders but realized he was starting to shiver bad. He was staring at the floor just shaking like a leaf, his lithe, grey body swimming in the black towel I had wrapped around him.

It had been day four of spending time with Silas, and it was morning. During the first full night I'd spent with him, Silas had woken up with a start at 3 am, and in his lucid, out-of-it-state, he had started rambling and babbling about everything from where Reaver was, to wanting to check on the babies. I wasn't sure which babies he was talking about. I kept telling him they were okay, but I couldn't convince him they were.

Eventually I called Garrett and asked him where the knock out pills were, he was up here in five minutes flat and we drugged the king pretty good. Silas slept like a rock after and it gave me and Garrett a couple hours to ourselves. We finished off the rest of the spaghetti and started making loose plans for our new royal holiday. Garrett was beaming and kept looking at me with those loving eyes. And surprisingly, his emotions didn't bounce off of me like they did previous. Before when he'd beg me to say something or show I was still in there somewhere, I couldn't do anything but stare at him and robotically say what he wanted to hear. It was the first time I could honestly say I felt a little bit better when I went to bed. And when Silas kept repeating these lucid, babbling moments every night after bed, it had started to become a routine for Garrett to come up, drug him with me, and we'd get our time together after.

There was still a gaping hole inside of me, one that I didn't think would ever be filled, but I noticed myself feeling Garrett a little bit more every night, enough to have a conversation and receive his affection.

Now I was trying to do to Silas what Garrett had done to me: attempting to draw out any reaction from him, anything to break him from the automated movements and his sad words that were so heavy you only had a moment to listen to them before they sank down to the infinite chasms below.

Four days and it was hit and miss... but I think I was making progress.

"Poor boy," I murmured as I rubbed his shoulders harder. I looked over and saw two blow dryers and smiled lightly to myself. I grabbed one and plugged it in and turned it up as high as it could go. Silas's eyes raised just slightly, giving me a look that was still the definition of depression, but with the faintest flicker of curiosity.

I started blowing the hot air onto his neck, then pulled back the black towel to warm up the grey skin underneath it. When I had taken his clothes off, I had to hide the grim look as I took in his thin frame. Every rib I could count, and he had a thigh gap so wide it made his legs look bowed. I almost thought it would be easier for him to die and resurrect to his normal weight, but then I remembered what Silas had said about the white flames.

"Hey, raise your arms," I told him. "So I can dry the rest of you off." Silas obeyed and he slowly lifted his arms, the corners of the large towel in his trembling hands. I waved the hair dryer over his chest and arms, then got an idea. I grabbed the other, plugged it in and pointed it at his arms, or more specifically the towels. The force behind the blow dryers made the towel start to blow just slightly in the double gusts of air.

"Na na na na na na na na, Bat Silas!" I sang.

Silas's heavy green eyes looked at me, and my heart absolutely burst when I saw a small twitch in the corner of his lip, before it hooked to the faintest, but still visible, crooked smile. Silas closed the towel back around him, and not wanting to push him, I started drying his hair.

I brushed it and fluffed it up all nice, and when he was dry, I walked him out to his bedroom. I was pleased to see that the sengils I had called up had cleaned his room, and had done so in record time. I wanted them in and out before Silas was out of the shower, so I had let in a team of seven of them. They had sheets in hand, a thin blanket since it was still August and sweltering outside, fresh pillows, and had vacuumed and picked up the trash and wiped everything down, and had even put little fabric ribbons on the charmander and the two stuffed cats.

Silas paused when he stepped into the bedroom. I was worried for a moment he was pissed I'd gotten it cleaned, then I realized he might've just been confused since I'd done this on the dial-a-sengil phone out of his earshot.

"Want me to order you some food?" I asked as he walked to the bed, smelling like Febreeze and holding purple sheets and a black comforter with purple pinstripes.

To my dismay Silas didn't answer me. He dropped the black towel onto the white chair and curled up naked on top of the bed, then hugged the charmander to him.

I sighed and sat on the foot of the bed and started rubbing his shoulders. "Want to watch some television?" It was like I was walking up a steep hill, every time I got a glance at the summit I slid right back down to the bottom. I'd see a hint of Silas, and I'd fool myself into thinking it would stick, but then he'd shut down like he was a laptop with a blue screen error.

Silas didn't answer.

"Want to go for a walk?"

I wasn't expecting an answer to that one. I knew he was a long way away from going outside into the sun, and, sure enough, he didn't answer.

"Want me to lay with you?"

I watched him and listened for any answer. I was about to suggest video games when I got a faint. "Yeah."

"Okay, I'm good at that." I slipped on some dry boxers. I'd been in the shower with him and I just didn't think it was right to bathe naked with him, stupid I know, but it just felt weird and inappropriate since I was taking care of him. I put them on, and laid down beside him and he turned away from me. I took a shot in the dark of what he wanted and became the big spoon, and he relaxed when I drew him to me.

I closed my eyes and started some rhythmic breathing, a thing Garrett had taught me when I was still in my hysterical crying stage of grieving, and was surprised and complimented when Silas started breathing in tune to mine. With every exhale I felt his body relax further, and I could even feel his heart through my hand start to slow, and I knew mine was as well.

Everything quieted down after that, and I felt my eyes start to become heavy.

"Reno?" Silas whispered. My body jumped; I hadn't even realized I had drifted off. I woke up, the unexpected nap no doubt from my late night time with Garrett, and realized that during my sleep Silas had gotten up and put on a new pair of grey drawstring boxers and a new undershirt.

I yawned. "Sorry, I'm up," I said, rubbing the sleep from my eyes. I squinted them and saw Silas's forlorn eyes staring at me, they looked red and puffy. I think he might've been crying.

"Aw, you should've woken me up so I could've been awake with you, mister," I murmured. I raised a hand and stroked his cheek with the front side of it.

"I woke up like this," he mumbled back. "I woke up crying. I... I dreamed I was back in Aras. When I opened my eyes and saw you, I was so sure for a moment..." Silas's face tensed, creases appearing in his forehead, and my own stomach knotted. I knew it was coming, I prepared myself for it.

"I was sure we'd both be heading to Aras, and he'd be there with Killian."

The sting hit me as expected, and in a two prong attack my throat tightened and throbbed. That kind of throb where you knew if you spoke you'd start crying. I didn't answer back, I couldn't.

"Why did he have to uncover my secret?" Silas whispered.

I wanted to tell him he fuelled that runaway car by practically raping Killian, but the remembrance of what he did to my now dead friend immediately hardened myself against Silas. I had to purge that memory and remind myself he wasn't the same man, that a different one was in front of me now. I didn't have clean hands. I lost my virginity as a top raping a legionary as Reaver held him down for me, and had raped dozens after him with no guilt whatsoever.

"You… raped Killian," I said back, as slowly and cautiously as I could. "So… him uncovering the secret was kind of because of that. Because you were trying to drug and get with Reaver."

Silas was still. "I forgot about that," he admitted. Then his gaze became slightly more aware. "Did you know Sanguine was there with me the entire time? He sneaked in behind Killian's back while he was throwing up, and dropped a maggoty scaver carcass behind him to scare him. My Sanguine was out of there before Reaver even noticed. He was so quick. We had a tracker on Killian the entire time, that's how we stalked him. Sanguine was wonderful; Theo dropped in too, several times. My stealths are so fast."

I didn't know how I felt about this. I wanted him to stop but my mouth was glued shut trying not to cry.

"I was so alive," Silas whispered. Then the awareness disappeared like the dimmer switch on a light had been turned low, and his eyes became dead again. A brief moment of life before it was extinguished by his own misery. "Yet no more happier, just content in tormenting my babies."

Silas choked and his face dissolved. Even though it felt like little needles were stabbing my heart, rapidly and without rest, I held him and shushed him as he cried. My feelings were overwhelmingly conflicting, and I decided once he fell asleep I would be self-medicating with some opiates. I just… whenever I was reminded of the hurt he'd caused my friends, the swells of hate rose and crashed against my surface, but then he became a puddle of sadness and I couldn't hold onto that hate.

Sadly the choking turned into full blown sobbing, and my soft hold became tight when he started to absolutely fall apart. I would be lying if I didn't secretly hope it was from guilt over what he'd done to us, but I could never ask.

Even after he'd calmed down I continued to pet his hair back. It was hard, his hair was blond like Killian's. Silas's was more golden and it had the waviness to it, Killian's was a lighter blond and straighter. Still, even with those differences it reminded me of the times I held that little guy. The time I remember the most was when he'd thought Reaver had been killed by Greyson. So funny knowing that he actually had killed Reaver; fucker'd just come back.

I wonder how Reaver would be when he came back, and what would he be coming back to. Garrett was adamant he wanted to make me immortal soon, I was twenty-three now, but... I don't know. Hearing Silas talking about how terrifying it was to be unable to escape his mental torture, made me not know if I really wanted to be.

If I wasn't... I'd be forty-three when Reaver came back. Damn.

"Tell me a story?" Silas croaked, his voice raspy and congested from a stuffed-up nose.

"Hm, okay," I thought for a second and tried to think of some old books I'd read. "There was a little kitten named... Guacamole."

"No..." Silas pulled away from me. "I want to hear a story about Reaver."

"Oh..." I swallowed hard. "That's going to hurt..."

"A funny one," Silas said. "I know you have them. You told me a lot of them when I stayed over at your house."

I took in a deep breath and exhaled slowly. I didn't know how to feel about this, but orders were orders, let's see if I can get through this without breaking down.

Then a recollection came to me, one that made me smile sadly. "This happened when he was eight and I was ten. This new kid came to live in Aras, ten like me, some snotty little asshole who was always trying to one-up us. I had a Game Boy Colour, but his dumbass father had scavenged him a Game Boy Advance. We had a stereo we'd play our Disney songs on, cause we acted them out and pretended and all of that, but he had a CD player. So he'd tag along, and he'd butt-in on whatever we were doing and tell us his daddy could make it better. His name was Jussin."

"Justin?"

I thought for a second. "Yeah, actually that was probably it. Well, at this time me and Reaver had this thing we'd do... we'd find anything big and we'd put wheels on it and sail it down this area of the red canyons that had this super flat slope that angled up before there was like a fifty foot drop off. Greyson was just happy that Reaver was leaving him alone, so he'd give him scraps to put wheels on and we had a way to get down to the canyons to collect the wheels if needed be, since it was a pain in the ass to find wheels to put on shit. For Reaver's eighth birthday Greyson and Leo even put wheels on a fucking fridge and a stove. They used the dolly and hauled it to the top of the ramp and sailed that shit down! It was great."

I saw Silas's mouth twitch, just the faintest hint of a smile like last time. "So we're scrounging around and Justin is following us, being annoying. And we find a huge score: a Barbie Power Wheels! Like one of those ones you could drive around, not working, of course, but the wheels move. Fucking Justin starts bragging about how his daddy is going to buy him a Power Wheels that does work, and it'll be black with a red racing stripe. All of a sudden this has been going on for weeks, his dad saying this shit to him. We knew it was bullshit, fucking little liar. Anyway... Reaver's getting real short with him. You know Reaver, and he was the same back then, he doesn't like people talking his ear off and I knew unless I had shit to say, or a joke to make, I kept my mouth shut when we were scavenging. Reaver hates noise and he wants to hear what's going on around him.

"So Reaver announces, all of a sudden, that we're going to sail the Power Wheels down the ramp. I suggest going to the Slaught House to see if they had some diseased rat babies we could stuff in there, to make it like a Thelma and Louise type of thing, but he just says nothing and we go to the canyons. Justin is following us around, bragging and talking and not fucking shutting up."

I paused and smiled when I saw that both corners of Silas's mouth were raised. His eyes were heavy, but he was smiling.

"I know what's coming," he said to me. I nodded, feeling pleased and successful that I was making Silas happy.

"So we get to the top of the ramp and all of a fucking sudden Reaver looks at me and says 'pin him down'. And I'm like 'fucking what?'. 'Pin him down,' Reaver says. I obeyed since I was whipped even back then, and Justin gets frightened and starts to cry. I was a strong kid, and stronger than Justin, even though we were the same age. Reaver jumps on him with fucking zip ties he had stuffed in his pocket, and wrenches his arms back and fucking zips him! Worse? He pulls out a spool of fishing line and starts wrapping his fucking arms! He has this shit planned out long before. So then he slips off the kid's shoes, which Justin also bragged about 'cause they were new, and Reaver stuffs a sock in his mouth which he ties off with a bandana he had been wearing over his hair. He tells me to put Justin in the Barbie car with this fucking wicked grin on his face, eyes just so bright." Silas was hanging on my every word, and now I did see he was smiling, it wasn't a big beaming grin but it was a smile.

"The kid's in the car and now he's gagged, and Reav tied his feet and legs with fishing line. Then we fucking rob him! Taking his Walkman, his Magic cards he kept tied with an elastic in his pocket, and a fucking gold slammer and five fucking Pogs. A goldmine for us! But when I realize Reaver's really going to send this kid off over the edge, I start to get so scared. Because I knew we would get in shit! Not even like banishment or anything, I was worried I would get a fucking spanking so hard I wouldn't be able to sit down. Not even a mom spanking, a dad spanking which meant the belt. That's when you knew you were in shit, am I right?"

Silas smiled wider. "I didn't really have parents but... I know what you mean. Go on."

"I start telling Reaver... 'Dude, Greyson will beat you to death.' Greyson was really hard on him, Leo was the mother of the two. But Reaver, in classic Reaverness, informed me that he wasn't scared of 'that shithead', and with Justin's muffled cries and his struggling, we start to push him towards the ramp. I keep saying 'Okay, Reaver. We scared him. We scared him, Reaver. We should let him go.

"Reaver just glares at me and says haughtily: 'If we let him go, he'll tell on us and then we definitely will get a lickin', which was Greyson for 'spanking'. And with a flashy grin, and his tongue sticking out of the corner of his mouth, he starts making a fucking speech!" I cleared my throat, fully riding this happiness that, even if temporarily, was vanquishing the depression and darkness that had rooted into both of us. "Since the beginning!"

"No way!" Silas said with a smile. "He didn't start it off like that!"

"He did!" I exclaimed. "He said 'Since the beginning, man has always wished for the flying car!" Silas put a hand over his mouth and laughed lightly, his eyes just shining. I went on. "We are here today to test out our patented flying pink car called the Justin Sissy Car! A very brave young man named Justin has volunteered to test this newest invention!" He then tells me to help him push it and by now Justin is howling and crying, thrashing himself around in the car and trying to roll himself off of it and the shithead is real close to doing it too. Scared he would run and tattle on us, I hit him over the head with a fucking rock! So now he's really fucking howling, and I'm getting so fucking scared someone is going to hear him. So with no more speeches, Reaver and I give the car a huge fucking push and we let go." I grinned and started making the motions of the car going down the ramp with my hand. "He fucking sails down the ramp, and he's shifting back and forth trying to tumble out of it, but it's too late... he reaches the end, sails in the air, and it's like... AHHHHhhhhhhh!!" I made my scream fade, and with my pointer finger in the air to mimic the car, I trailed it down and made a crashing noise at the bottom.

"So Reaver and I exchange glances and Reaver starts to laugh, of course."

"Of course."

"We both look down and see the kid ten feet away from the Power Wheels, fucking wheels still spinning, and you can see the kid's face is just bleeding and mush. We run down there to get a closer look, and holy shit, he's beyond dead. His head is smashed and his eyes wide open in terror, fucking limbs all splayed wrong. Totally dead! Reaver fucking takes out a hunting knife he always had strapped to his side... and fucking starts stabbing him! Just for the fuck of it! When he's done with that, I shit you not, he slits him from dick to neck, cuts open his rib cage like it was a rusty gate and starts pulling out his insides and identifying them!"

"That's a chimera alright," Silas chuckled. "Did he eat him?"

"We both did!" I exclaimed. "We ended up dismembering him and sneaking body parts into Aras, the guts, besides the liver and heart, which Reaver had to eat apparently, were given to the deacons, and we stashed his body in an abandoned house. We snuck out a hotplate and all the stuff we'd need and we ate as much as we could. Then when the search for him got too heated, we fed the rest to the deacons and no one ever fucking found out! Reaver told me once he was an adult that he knew that Greyson and Leo knew, but they loved their little monster. Makes sense now why they'd give him a pass. Fucking icing on the cake? Justin's dad gave us a lot of his old shit, since we were his buds!" I laughed and then sighed, and as my story came to an end my heart started to hurt. This happy story was just a reminder that I'd never have those times with him again. They were lost in time, I was the only one to remember them for the next twenty years, not even Leo and Greyson could recount Reaver as a child.

That brought me down, completely down to the ground from the small shreds of happiness I had been feeling while telling Silas this story.

"He'll be back," Silas whispered. I think he noticed my change in expression. "I will find a way to cool the flames and I'll bring him back... I'll find a way." His voice cracked and I shushed him and rubbed his side. "I will. I never fail."

How can someone feel so much hope and dread from a single sentence. I found myself scared and Silas sensed this. He seemed to be able to sense my shifts in moods. I didn't know if it was my facial expressions, heartbeat, or the head stuff he could do.

"Why doesn't that make you happy?" he asked me. His eyes searched me. The all-knowing, piercing gaze that looked so far past what a normal man could see, stripped me again and made me stand bare and exposed in front of him.

And I knew with his hold on my mind, that I couldn't lie. There would be no use in it, I could feel him inside of me.

"He's going to be devastated." My voice cracked and I shuddered. "Poor Tinkerbell..." It was my turn for my eyes to well. The world didn't know just what they had lost when Killian died. I think that boy was the last pure thing to walk this world, one that struggled every day to create light. He was a little ray of sunshine in the grey, a big smile and eyes that shone so brightly they seemed unnatural. Nothing alive was as sweet as him, and nothing ever would be.

When Silas's face darkened I shifted away from him, tears stinging my eyes. All at once, the invisible strings that had attached themselves to my brain became weighted down with black oil; and I could feel its poison pickle my brain, erasing the positive feelings that telling Silas the story had brought.

And his face reflected that, Silas's expression was of undiluted revulsion. He was the complete opposite of Killian, and that was obvious just looking at him. Silas was surrounded by darkness. He was both sadistic and masochistic, his inner demons switching from pleasuring each other to tearing each other to ribbons of flesh and pools of blood. Two creatures with black hearts to add to the endless demons holding masks to their faces. We had all heard the term mental shapeshifter by now, and the proof of that was in front of me as I saw the black flames burn behind the dark green eyes. Even the fire in him was a contradiction, clashing flares of energy that universally couldn't coexist, but had somehow found a loophole in the time-space continuum to be both black and white, hot and cold, light and dark, the Ghost and the Immortal.

So many emotions hanging from this man, heavy emotions that bowed his back like they were attached to him from wires. He was the puppet master, and yet, he was the one with string wrapped around his wrists, his neck, his feet, all leading to two hundred and fifty-five years' worth of living as King Silas Dekker.

Killian was a feather, light and innocent, but one that blew in the wind with no control over where he went or where he landed. He was used to having no control, so he took everything as it came; and though they stepped on him, crushed him, ripped the downy barbs from the quill, he still caught wind and floated on. Killian still floated on, and even at his worst, even emotionally crippled, that fucking boy still kept on flying.

Tears sprung to my eyes, and as my face dissolved. I made a break for the door and I quickly walked to it. I saw that boy's face in my memory. I heard his laugh, his voice, higher than mine and Reaver's, which was a stereotype of his innocent, shy nature.

No one realizes just what the world lost but me. Just like Reaver's childhood, only I will have the memories of Killian and who he was – until his boyfriend woke up, and saw that the world was now darker, crueller, worse with Killian gone.

I left the room and sat on the couch, I had a good cry and smoked a cigarette. I didn't want to go back into Silas's bedroom. If he said anything bad about Killian, I might punch him in the mouth.

But when I eventually came back, an hour and three cigarettes later, I saw that he had gone back to being the sad, haunted Silas I'd momentarily chased away. I sat beside him and rubbed his shoulders to show him I wasn't mad. I wasn't sure if that was what I was feeling, maybe I was just lonely.

An hour later there was a knock on Silas's door. I looked up, and then to Silas who hadn't even flinched. He continued staring off into nothing, his eyes heavy.

"Want me to get it?" I asked him. I received no answer but when there was a second, more hurried, knock on the door I patted his shoulder and got up. As I passed the coffee table I saw his phone flashing, it must've been on silent, and my eyes widened when I saw there were ten missed calls.

I opened the door and saw Ellis, Garrett, and Teaguae standing side by side. Their faces promised me no good news, and my heart started to plummet.

"What happened?" I asked, dropping my voice to hopefully give them the hint to keep quiet too.

I stepped aside as all three of them walked in. They looked around trying to spot the king, and I saw Garrett's apprehension increase when he realized that Silas was still in his bedroom.

"No... improvement?" Garrett whispered, his eyes looking to the closed bedroom door.

"There's improvement just..." I hesitated. "Right now is just a low point. It's up and down."

Teaguae sighed and brushed back his hair, the same wavy golden blond as Silas's but shorter. "Ellis... we need him. We need him," he said. It took me off-guard to hear the rapidness of his words, almost bordering on desperation. He turned, and at the same time Knight walked in holding a briefcase. Ellis's son looked around and his shoulders fell. "Papa's still in his bedroom?" he asked grimly. "Mom, it's worse than I thought. There were a hundred in attendance according to my source."

"A hundred?" Garrett said faintly. He took my hand and pulled me to the couch. "Luca, we'll all be needing drinks, smokes, drugs... you know where they are."

Luca was here too? I looked behind me and saw my sengil friend. The bruises had healed but unfortunately the poor kid lost all of the vision in the eye Jack shattered; he had a white patch over it now. Still a trooper though, he gave me a polite smile and inclined his head, then he disappeared into the kitchen.

"What's going on?" I said. My heart was already on the verge of having a heart attack, and I had to know before I passed out and died. I sat down with Garrett beside me, and Ellis and Knight sat opposite. Teaguae took the chair to my right.

"We think the Crimstones might have rallied again," Knight said. "We think... I... Garrett, it couldn't have been anyone else?"

I had to clamp my hand over my face to keep from swearing. The word *Crimstone* alone sparking an anxiety inside of me that seemed to now be conditioned.

But then I caught the last of Knight's sentence. "It couldn't have been anyone else? What happened?"

"There was a break-in in Black Tower yesterday, early morning. We didn't find out until two hours ago when Drake resurrected. Two masked men tried to steal Jack's body while Theo was out doing fuck knows what with one of the Falconers," Ellis said. My mouth dropped open, and a chill froze my muscles. "We thought they'd taken Theo and the Falconer, but luckily they didn't. Theo told Drake he was going out, but he didn't say what he was doing. However, it's because of Theo that Jack was almost taken. He was supposed to be guarding the library. Drake says he fended them off but he died of the wounds he sustained doing it. He doesn't know who they were, but it was two males." She shook her head. "Juni was out at the time, and we think that might've been what they were waiting for."

"Jesus fuck," I whispered. "So the only witness is Drake?"

Ellis's face darkened. "Unfortunately. He's adamant that Ares and Siris come and stay in Black Tower with him since he's scared. They've agreed but I'll be needing them to scout out what we're seeing happen in Moros."

That's right, Knight mentioned a hundred people in attendance?

"So a hundred Crimstones now? Is that what you're saying?"

Ellis shook her head, beside me Garrett got up and I saw him walk towards Silas's bedroom. I felt pulled to go with him. I was protective of Silas and the close connection we'd been sharing; but I knew I had no authority to do so, especially not in front of the others.

"There's a new ring leader but we don't know who he is. The hundred were the residents of Moros who gathered at an underground rally three days before this happened. He's recruiting, and he's getting more supporters than we thought he would. The personal issues that the family is going through has dropped public opinion on us. Silas, Elish, and Nero were our power heads; they were our backbone. Garrett..." Ellis glanced to the hallway, and when she saw that Garrett had disappeared into the bedroom she felt comfortable enough to say: "He doesn't have the same presence as them. He doesn't have what those three have, and right now we desperately need that. We don't even fucking have Kessler. We need to at least pretend this family isn't limping along like a sick dog."

Her teeth clenched and she looked to the bedroom door again. "We're going to have to give him some tough love right now. We need Dad to snap out of this. We have to come back at full force and squash this before it gets out of hand." She paused, but in that silence I could see her gather her confidence, and several moments later I knew why she had hesitated. "We need Sanguine back and we need Nero and Ceph back. Caligula has the northern greywastes swarming with legionary trying to find Kessler, and we have to find him quickly. It's been three months since he disappeared, three months since the explosion–"

Reaver and Killian have been gone for three months.

"– I already spoke with Caligula, and he's on orders to start looking for Nero and Ceph as well. I'm going to send Teag into the plaguelands with Grant in case they went there and start making it known that Nero will be welcome home. I'll use fucking skywriting if I have to. We're going to need Nero either way; even if we do find Kessler it could be three more months before he fully resurrects."

"Silas will never go for this," Teaguae said, shaking his head back and forth rapidly. "You know he won't, Ellis. Just like we know he won't go and get Sanguine. He's never gone back on his punishments. You know this, and if you ask he'll just leave him there longer."

"He has to!" Ellis snapped. She slammed her hand against the arm of the couch. "If he's too depressed to run Skyfall, he has to let us bring in the family members who can do it with the iron fist that Skyfall needs right now. I love Dad, and I understand he's going through a lot, but he can't have both right now. A hundred, Teaguae, a hundred people were at that rally, and now that the Crimstones were able to waltz into Black Tower and almost kidnap Jack... they're well-aware we're weakened right now."

Suddenly Garrett scrambled out of Silas's bedroom. He closed the door right in time for all of us to hear something break against it.

I shot up angrily. "What the fuck did you say to him?" I snapped. Garrett looked at me surprised. I'd rarely gotten angry with him, but I realized I didn't want to see Silas upset or under any more stress. I felt protective over him, like I was his guardian now or something.

"I – I was just requesting–"

"Requesting or manipulating him?" My voice continued to raise. "You just barge in there and start making requests of him without even asking me how he's doing, or if it's a good time? I told you he was at a low point." With a flare of my temper, I glared at Garrett and then the other three on the couch. "From now on, anyone who wants to talk to him has to go through me first. Understand?"

At precisely the same moment, I got three dropped looks that quickly turned hostile, Ellis especially. And when I looked to Garrett, I saw he was standing still like a prey animal trying to blend in with the scenery.

"Your fiancé is getting a bit too bold, Garrett," Ellis said coolly. "Telling me when I can and cannot see my own father?"

"If you want Silas to give you permission to get back Sanguine and Nero, barging into his bedroom when he's having a rough morning isn't going to do the fucking trick," I said to her. My tone was authoritative and firm, but inside I was fucking shaking and my ears were boiling hot.

"He's been having a rough three months!" Ellis hissed loudly and pointed to the door. "When he gets like this, Elish steps in and then Silas has all the time in the world to find himself, but Elish is gone, Nero is gone. We need at least one of them here!"

I understood that, and I didn't want the Crimstones to start causing shit, so I raised my hands. A part of me wondering where these big balls had come from. "Okay. Give me a day, give me twenty-four hours. I'll talk to him about it."

"We need Caligula to start looking for Nero a soon as possible," Ellis sighed. "And Sanguine. Sanguine will get those fucking Crimstones, and as horrible as it sounds, if Crow's fully taken him he'll be just as effective. Dad can fix his mind when the Crimstones are dead." Ellis got to her feet and took a shot of some brown alcohol; Luca was standing out of sight with a tray of shots and cigarettes laid out. "I need to do as much damage control as I can. Garrett, did you want a ride back to your office?"

Garrett looked at me. He looked dejected from me yelling at him, but unfortunately I needed to be alone with Silas. I pecked his lips and squeezed his hand. "I'll call you for our nightly chat when it's time. I need it to just be me and him if you want this to work."

Garrett let out a breath through his nose and nodded. He kissed me back and took a shot as well, then let out a hiss from the taste. "Okay, let's go. I look forward to tonight, lovely Otter."

And with several tense goodbyes, I was alone with Silas once again… with yet another weight added onto my crumbling shoulders.

I opened the door and saw Silas sitting on the edge of the bed, his elbows resting on his knees and his head slumped. I stepped in, but recoiled with an *ouch* when I stepped on a shard of porcelain. I raised my socked foot and swore. Nothing was sliced, it had just jabbed me.

"I liked that lamp," I said to him. "You broke the lamp I liked, jerk."

Silas raised his head and gave me a hollow look. "They can do whatever they want. I just want to be left alone," he said, his tone deader than ever. He deflected his gaze and laid back down on the bed. "You succeeded. Goodbye and lock the door behind you."

My head tilted to the side. It took me a minute, since I wasn't that bright, and I found myself feeling pissed. "You fucking think I'm here to try and get Sanguine and Nero back? Fuck off. You know me better than that, you dumb prick." I disappeared and picked up the tray of drinks, cigarettes, and on closer inspection, a little white bowl of powder and metal sniffers, and walked back in.

"I suppose I was the one to summon you first," Silas said in a low tone. He picked up one of the shots, whisky I think, and looked at it. "Why are you still here then?"

I got myself a sniffer and just took some right out of the bowl. I wasn't sure what it was, but the back of my throat wasn't going numb, so it wasn't coke. "I don't know," I said. "You know I've always liked making people laugh and shit, and make them feel better when they're sad. You're pretty sad, so you're kind of like... a happiness project for me. I want you to be happy again." I realized I could ask him the same question back. "Why did you ask for me to come here?"

Silas reached over and grabbed the sniffer from me. Doing drugs together was this family's thing, I've learned. It was the same as having a cigarette or a drink with them. Funny enough, Reaver had always been this way, long before he knew he was a chimera.

"You're the only man who treats me like a normal person," Silas said as he stared at the metal rod. He started weaving it between his fingers. "No one here does. I'm their king, their father, their papa, their master, or to Reaver I was something to despise and hate. With you, however, there's no layers of film you look through, distorting your perception of me like the others. You see me as I am, the good and the bad. You have no idea how difficult it is living a life where no one treats you like a person. My time in Aras was the best time I'd had in years... because I was just a normal greywaster, and I was treated as such."

I gave him a funny look. "You fucking acted like you enjoyed it at the time, walking around like you're gliding, and that silky, condescending voice. I've seen that smile as you're torturing your chimeras. You fucking almost had Sanguine kill me when you were trying to figure out where Reaver was, and you would've done it. You were happy as shit being a king, master, all of that."

Silas was quiet the entire time I said this, the sniffer still twirling in his fingers. Then he dropped the sniffer and laid back down on the bed. "None of it matters now that Sky's gone."

My mouth twisted to the side. "Silas... Sky's been gone for... how many years? Like way over a hundred, right? I know you loved him but... he's been gone for a really fucking long time."

Silas's face dropped. I hated my big mouth; I don't think I should've said that. "I'm coming in too, move over." I laid down beside him, and as his eyes filled, I put a hand on his head. "You told me he was a monster, that he tormented you. Why has it been over a hundred years and you're still like this? That you let your family fall apart because of your obsession with cloning him? Why him?"

"You wouldn't understand."

"Make me understand," I urged. "Come on... tell me a story this time. Make me understand."

Silas took in a deep breath. I was sure he was going to just fall back into silence, but to my utter astonishment... he started talking.

"Sky and Perish created Skytech and the two of them worked on just creating sustainable food for the people and also how to protect living creatures from the sestic radiation, which eventually would become the Geigerchip. When Sky died I shifted almost all of our focus on creating clones, genetically engineered humans which would eventually become my babies, but for me personally... I wanted to clone Sky. So I could put his O.L.S into the clone and it would be like he was back."

I nodded and started stroking his upper arm.

"It turns out that my DNA and mutations were easy to clone, but I didn't want a born immortal like me, I wanted one of Sky but his genetics were different... hostile almost. The child would die, his heart would stop and he'd die. I only had a finite number of tries from Sky's salvaged brain matter so I decided to put the matter to rest." Silas's eyes darkened. "Then Perish found some old files referring to a lab. An above ground one where our research from Germany had been transferred to when the Second Cold War started. He repaired a plane with some other men, and went on a trip. He was successful and my babies came several years later."

Silas smiled faintly. "Having my babies was such a breakthrough. It fuelled my belief that cloning my Sky was right around the corner." Then the faint smile faded and his lips stiffened. "When someone dies, you grieve them and eventually... you find yourself moving on. Even when in the throes of mourning, when you don't think you'll ever get over the pain... eventually you find yourself thinking of them less and less, and living your life. Is this correct?"

As much as it stung me because of my own recent loss, I nodded.

"But what if you could never move on because you were convinced you could bring him back? Not just a fool's hope... but you genetically engineered children with yours and his DNA. You had babies living to the third trimester who were identical to him. It was worse, or better, when my science chimeras grew up and the research accelerated. I always had Elish beside me, telling me just a few more years, just a few more years... so I never have that acceptance and that closure. Sky is always just several years away," Silas said. "And it became an obsession for me. The more time that passed, the more videos I watched, pictures I saw of us together... the more I missed him and yearned for those times with him. Then I just fucking spiralled, it got out of hand..." Silas reached behind him and grabbed the charmander and clung it to him. "It got so bad I couldn't stand Perish anymore, or his voice. He sounded just like Sky, that raspy, gravelly voice that was so unique to those twins. I altered his brain trying to make him as different to Sky as I could... and I got desperate enough to implant that poor man with Sky's O.L.S to try and make him my Sky. Perish was never the same since, even after it was removed."

I patted the charmander. "Was this dude Perish's?"

Silas nodded. "He loved his Char Char. Almost three hundred years old and he had loved that damn thing."

"Wait..." I raised an eyebrow. "I thought you guys were like twenty-four when the..." My voice dragged and Silas chuckled dryly.

"No. It was a miscommunication I suppose. I stopped aging at twenty-four and people just assumed that's how old I was when the Fallocaust happened, and I just went with it. It's easier that way and once you're as old as I am, age doesn't really matter anyway. They don't know I was created, not just someone with a random genetic mutation. I was created in Germany during World War Two, with a handful of other boys. We were supposed to be living bombs, immortal weapons who could take out entire cities at our whim. I was a part of a splinter group designed to have the mental abilities I have. I was one of the best," Silas explained to me.

I was in awe as he spoke this, and I realized with even more shock, that I might be the first person to hear this in centuries. "The war went on for many years, and we were smuggled to Canada and it was there we stayed when the war ended. But what we didn't know, was that our next prime minister was a sympathizer. So, yes, the war was over, but really, nothing was the same after that, things changed. It was so gradual at first that only the conspiracy theorists clued in, but the next thing we knew other countries were rising up, experiencing the same problems as us. Insane government control, human experiments, corruption. We didn't know this was going on, and we'd later realize no one knew because they were controlling the media.

"Years before the Second Cold War started, I was homeless after leaving an abusive boyfriend and I was drawn back to a town I had lived in, in my younger years. I met Sky there one evening at a convenience store. He took pity on me and brought me home to where Perish was. We didn't know the other ones' secrets, but we should have... born immortal attraction," Silas said. It looked like he was completely lost in recollection. "We eventually found three others living in a remote cabin a few miles inland. When the war got bad we took shelter in there... until all at once we started getting bombed, the world started collapsing, and the few born immortals the government had been able to find and capture, were destroying cities left and right.

"And then came Gage. Sent from the government to hunt us like dogs." Silas's level tone started hovering over dangerous. I waited for him to say more, but he was silent after that.

Curiosity got to me. "Who's Gage?" I whispered. "Why did the government want to hunt you guys down? Because you guys can explode and destroy stuff? Did he catch any of your friends? Or you?"

Surprisingly, Silas tensed up at the questions. "I will only forgive you once for asking me these questions," he said, and there was no mistaking the warning tone. It froze up my chest like it had been coated in liquid nitrogen. "If I find out that you have told any of my chimeras, including Garrett, or any soul about what I have told you... I will not just kill you, for I know you wish for death at times like me." Silas looked right at me, and those glaring green eyes pushed past my own eyes and into my brain. I wonder if he realized just how much he'd told me and regretted it. "I will make you immortal and I will put you in concrete, and you can spend an eternity in that darkness. Do you understand me?"

And there was that hammer being swung at my frozen chest. I nodded. "I know when stuff goes way beyond what I should be talking about. You know I'm good for it."

Silas's peering eyes narrowed, and he tilted his head to the side. "You're telling the truth to me…" he said slowly.

I looked at him dumbly back and cocked an eyebrow. "That's nothing new. I don't think I've ever lied to you."

Silas stiffened and nodded. I think more to himself than me. He slowly rose and nodded at me to get up as well. "Come with me to the living room," Silas said placidly. "I must take care of the home I worked so hard to build." Silas, with his shoulders slumped and his head hung low, entered the living room and picked up his remote phone.

"Bring Sanguine home. Find Nero." That was it. Silas pressed the end call button on the phone and his chest slowly rose, and fell, with a long sigh. "And we can now see just how well they function without me," he whispered, and the phone slipped from his hands and fell onto the carpet. "They have no use for me, Reno. They'd be better off without me."

"Si," I whispered. I walked to him and took him into my arms. "I can't stop you from believing that… all I can do, is suggest that maybe we can think of ways we can get them to love you even more. Think of ways we can repair the wounds. Garrett and I have been planning on a holiday for the entire city, maybe we can create a couple more babies to get some good press too? Everyone loves babies." I thought for a second. "Any chimeras wanting to marry partners besides me and Gare?"

Silas sniffed. "A few."

"We can marry them, hook a few more up with some soul mates, have lots of get-togethers and those famous chimera orgies. Why don't we put our heads together and do a bunch of awesome things for the family and Skyfall. That'll make you feel good inside, and everyone will see that you're just fine and still Mr. Badass." Then something occurred to me. "We can focus on Moros too. Throw some benefits at them, so when the Crimstone asshole holds his rallies he will have a few less followers."

I patted and rubbed Silas's back, and after a few moments, I felt him nod. "It usually makes me happier to exert my power over them, and control them with an iron fist. But I suppose we can try it your way."

I chuckled and pulled away from him, then I leaned in and kissed him on the cheek. "You'll love seeing your chimeras happy because of you, instead of miserable, I know it. You're a good guy, Silas, and I'm going to make you see it."

Silas's hands raised, and he put one on each side of my face. He stroked my cheeks with his thumbs before, to my surprise, he leaned in and pressed his lips against mine. Not just a quick peck either, he closed his eyes and instinctively I did too. I opened my lips, a heat collecting at the top of my head, and when I felt his tongue slip into my mouth I welcomed it. We kissed deeply, our lips moving and shifting to take each other in, in as many ways as possible, and I felt his hands on my cheeks travelled down to my neck, then grab my backside.

"We'll see, amor," Silas whispered when our lips broke apart. "We'll see just what you can draw from me."

CHAPTER 32

Jade

PHYSICALLY THE HOUSE IN FRONT OF ME WAS LIKE any other decrepit, single-level structure in the greywastes, but when I stepped off of the Falconer and onto the greywastes ash, dry and crunching underneath my boots, I could feel a darkness that seemed to radiate off of this unassuming building. It was bulging with fetid liquid, nose-curling stenches that embedded themselves in your nose, and yet in the naked world, without my empath abilities amplifying these feelings, it was just another broken building, long dead and succumbing to the slow, yet steady, elements of nature.

For the first time in my life, I was not alone in feeling these heightened senses. I heard another pair of boots hit the fine, but compacted dirt, and a moment later, the spike of an anxious heart followed by an audible gasp. I looked to my side and saw Gage's wide eyes staring at the house as if it was a monster about to eat him up.

"Bad things happened here," Gage said in a hushed voice. He looked around and his pupils retracted. I looked too and saw three crows sitting on a tractor coated with rust. "Horrible things."

I walked away from the Falconer and to a flat area in front of the house. Glancing up, I saw three more crows, one on the roof, and two more perched on a shed that had been reduced to a heap of refuse.

"All I know was that a man held him here," Theo said behind us. He jumped out of the Falconer, and glanced around with his copper eyes. "It's a family secret which has been kept close to the hearts of those who lived during that time. They only tell us it is a place of Sanguine's nightmares."

"And Silas sent him back here?" Gage stuffed his hands into his jeans and started walking around the front of the house with me, the unease was weighing down his shoulders; they were slumped but at the same time, tense.

Theo kicked what looked like old tracks, but on closer inspection I realized they were drag marks. I started walking to the porch, not wanting to admit I was dreading what I would find.

"Silas is in a deep depression right now," Theo said.

"I know, you said that..." Gage said slowly, "but that does not justify it."

"You'll understand one day," Theo replied, following my footsteps to the porch. "He's not well, and he's rather extreme at times. He can be..."

"... a monster," I said bitterly. I wanted Gage on my master's side so I held nothing back. We had to have Gage secured. He was powerful, extremely powerful, and he would be a formidable ally to have in my master's pocket. "He takes out his misery on us, and Sanguine was unfortunately in his crosshairs."

"Sanguine was in his crosshairs for freeing Gage," I heard Theo say defensively. "With all due respect, new friend, we have no idea who you are, or how dangerous you are. Silas does. I will not judge my master when we do not have the full story. Gage says himself that he's dangerous and we saw that from him burning down Olympus." I looked at Theo when I felt his eyes on me, and sure enough, he was giving me a piercing look. "You would do well to remember that, dead boy. There is no need to suck up to him. We see that he's a kind-hearted man, but if you're going to assume Silas encased him for no reason, you will only prove your own arrogance." Theo turned and nodded his head to Gage. "No disrespect intended. You're intelligent enough to see that this is no personal attack, aren't you?"

Gage put a hand on the splintered door frame, swollen to the point where it had separated from the nails and now resembled needle-like teeth in open jaws. "I do, Theo," he said simply. "But I just wish Silas helped me, not condemned me to that madness." He walked into the house and his hands stuffed his pockets again.

Theo and I both followed. The familiar stench of must and mould hit my nostrils, and because the roof had sunken in at the far side of the house, I also smelled that soured aroma of fabric and wood that had been continuously wet and re-dried again and again. This was a familiar thing to smell in Moros, and it brought me right back to my old home.

But even though Moros was a slum, with garbage clinging to the edges of the sidewalks, forgotten furniture left to rot in the alleyways, and old cars that had been stripped down to their frames, Moros's houses were nothing compared to this pit.

Maybe not a pit, maybe a radrat's nest. At the end of the hall, in what I think was the living room, were piles of what had once been boxes; some stacked against windows nailed shut and walls of warped panelling puffed out like broken piano keys. The boxes that were now so disintegrated their contents stood alone, some even keeping the shape of the boxes by re-hardening into a compacted cube. In between these rotting boxes was furniture, so rat-chewed and destroyed they were just rusted springs and gnawed wood, some with the occasional scrap of fabric, clinging to their frames like the shreds of clothing on a decomposing corpse.

I walked in and passed a microwave, the inside of it speckled with black and the bottom had a dried yellow stain of what I assumed was rat piss. My eyes rose when I caught a beam of light, and saw that the living room eventually led to a kitchen with a hole in the ceiling. The kitchen cabinets had fallen down on their faces and almost disintegrated, and the linoleum curled up like clawed hands, clenching in their grasp dirt and garbage, none of it recognizable but several broken plates and a fork reflecting in the light.

My nose wrinkled and I turned from it. When I saw Theo standing at the end of the living room looking down a flight of concrete stairs, I felt my heartbeat jump.

"He's down there, isn't he?" I said slowly. I scanned the living room, now also seeing a television underneath a fallen curtain, its gold rod now the home for multiple spider webs, and when I didn't see anything living inside this garish dump, I walked to him.

Gage was on the third step, and he wasn't moving. There was a white door at the bottom of the stairwell with a thick metal pipe held in between two metal hooks. That was what was keeping the door closed; no padlocks could keep a chimera inside.

"Are you going in, or…?" I glanced at Theo. "I know him and we're friends, but… I don't know if it should be me."

Like our glances were going in a circle, Theo looked back to Gage. "I'm not immortal and I've heard horrible stories about Sanguine's psychosis." Then he filled his lungs before letting out a long sigh. "But I love Sanguine and he loves me." And with that, Theo turned and started descending the stairs too. He even walked past Gage so he was in the front, and gently removed the metal bar from the door.

He tried the handle, and we all held our collective breath. When there was a click from the lock unlocking, the tension didn't dissipate – if anything it tripled.

Theo held the metal rod in his hand and cracked the door open.

"Sanguine?" Theo whispered. He peeked inside but, to my alarm, he gasped and shut the door.

Without a word, Theo started running back up the stairs, his face blanched and his copper eyes bulging. "I'm done," he called back to us. "I'm done. Fuck this."

My head turned to the closed door when I heard a low, demonic growl come from the other side of it. It sent a chill up my spine, and I exchanged collective looks of horror with Gage.

But I snapped out of it just in time to grab Theo. "No, you're staying," I hissed and grabbed the metal rod from him. I held onto him by the collar of his leather jacket and looked at Gage.

"You can heal him?" I asked.

Gage nodded. All of our heartbeats were messes, drums beating out of sync, each one trying to challenge the other to see who could rip out of our chests first. I tried to calm mine down but it was like talking down a rabid dog.

"What did you see?" I said to Theo. I took a step towards the door; Theo stepping too but his feet were dragging. "Is he… is he chained?"

"Yes," Theo said in a thin voice. "He looks chained." The chimera made a nervous noise when I grabbed the handle and pushed open the door.

"Sanguine? It's Jade," I called. "We have someone here to help you, okay? We're going to bring you home."

Another growl sounded, another threatening growl just seeping warning. It was doing what it was supposed to do, a hand felt like it was grabbing my chest and squeezing it. There was no way someone wouldn't feel fear from that eerie, animalistic sound.

I gathered up all of my bravery and pushed the door open. Then, with Theo and Gage behind me, I took a step in and was immediately hit with a wall of overwhelming stench, one of rot, sewage, and many more smells that made my eyes water. I mentally compartmentalized it and took one more step in.

Then Theo pushed the door all the way open… and the light illuminated what could only be a demon.

I'd never seen anything like it and I knew as I looked at him, that it couldn't be Sanguine. There was no way this thing could be Sanguine.

Two eyeballs with red irises lay bulging in a slab of red, marbled meat that was his face, the whites of them so prominent they looked painted on. They were staring at me, fixed with intensity on my face, above two slits where his nose should've been and pointed teeth stretched into a smile.

But Sanguine wasn't really smiling. Nausea washed over me when I realized that his lips were gone, his exposed red gums blending in perfectly with the raw flesh on his face.

He'd… picked off all of the skin from his own face.

Then his eyes moved, looking from me to the men who were cowering behind my body, and I realized that the reason why his eyes were bulging so much… was because he had no eyelids.

He'd torn off his own eyelids. They now glared, unblinking and seeing all, through a mop of greasy, stringy black hair.

When I looked down, the vomit rose to my throat and I had to force back the gag. His arms were resting on the corner of the bed on either side of him, they had been chewed, not just gnawed on, chewed like a beaver trying to bring down a tree. There was normal, pale skin on his elbow and several inches below, then mangled pink and red flesh, hanging tendons that hung like a curtain down two white arm bones shining as white as his lidless eyes. Both arms were like this, the left one even had bite marks on the bones.

"Kill him," I suddenly cried; the reality of what I was seeing suddenly hitting me, throwing me out of this temporarily paralysis over the horrible sight in front of me. This wasn't a monster, this was Sanguine, funny and loyal Sanguine who everyone in the family loved. What had he done to himself? What had Silas done to him? "Theo. Theo, you have a gun. Put him out of his misery!" Tears sprung to my eyes.

I turned around to snatch the gun I knew Theo had in his holster – but he was gone. Only Gage was behind me, and the look on his face was akin to the one I knew was on mine.

"Gage, get Theo," I yelled, unable to control my own voice. "Get–" Suddenly Gage gasped and recoiled. He grabbed my shoulder and tried to pull me to the stairs, and at the same time I heard a raspy wheeze and the sound of shuffling.

I looked just in time to see Sanguine lunge at me, his unattached chain trailing behind.

Sanguine grabbed my shoulders with his hands and I was thrown backwards; my head smacking up against the stairs and the concrete edges digging painfully into my back. My hands flew up and locked against his shoulders, and I tried to push him away, but then I felt him pull me up, only to smash my head against the steps again.

Sanguine screamed right into my face, his pointed teeth never more menacing and demonic than they were when shown through those lipless teeth. I found myself stunned, just from the horror of his appearance. I felt like I was in a living nightmare, something like this man couldn't exist in this reality.

No, no, it's Sanguine. Sanguine's sick.

"Sanguine!" I screamed. The demon chimera's bulging eyes focused right on me, his teeth separating to accommodate rasping, heavy wheezes, ones that smelled like the rot of the room he had been imprisoned in. "Sanguine, it's Jade!" I started to struggle madly, the fear controlling me and commanding me to get away from him at all costs. "It's me."

The visible muscles in Sanguine's face contracted, and the growl returned. His eyes flashed with insanity and I felt his hands on my shoulders tighten.

I knew what was coming. I didn't know how, but I knew, and it was what saved my life.

Because just as Sanguine's skinned face, teeth bared and open like a bear trap, lunged for my neck, my arm went up. I shielded my neck with it, and Sanguine instead sunk his teeth into it and clamped them down.

I didn't even feel the pain, the adrenaline coursing through my body temporarily disabled the receptors, but I could feel the pressure and the feeling of his teeth scraping against my bones. I pushed back, trying to get him off of me, but when the awkward angle he had me in prevented me from doing that, I instead punched him in the head.

Sanguine's crimson eyes rolled up to my own, so bulbous and protruding I didn't know how they were staying in his skull. He looked like a zombie, something that shouldn't be alive. With him closer I could see just how bad his masochistic injuries were. It looked like he'd skinned his own face off in chunks, there were shreds of flesh hanging off of it, some dried to leather, others red from still working blood vessels. This monster wasn't Sanguine, this wasn't the chimera who had taken me under his wing in Moros, who I shared a majority of my DNA with.

I broke our eye contact and looked to see blood trickling through his teeth and down my arm. I tried to wiggle out of his grasp, but suddenly Sanguine wrenched his head to the left, trying to take my arm with it, but he only succeeded in scraping his pointed teeth along the skin, like a rake scraping against soft dirt.

I screamed, the pain finally making itself known. I pulled my arm back and saw Sanguine bear his teeth at me. I scrambled away and tried to pull myself backwards up the steps. The demon chimera watched me, and slowly began to advance.

"Gage?" I yelled, desperately crawling backwards up the stairs. I tried to focus my empath abilities to stop him, but the panic that was a hurricane inside of me had my mind racing to remember how to do it. My mind had been crystal clear the night that Kessler ambushed us, but now it was in overdrive, madly off in all directions.

"Theo?" I was too scared to turn around and make a break for the stairs. He was too close to me and I knew he'd be on me in an instant. The way he looks added an entirely new level of fear. If he looked like normal Sanguine, I would've been able to fight tooth and nail, but I was face-to-face with a living, breathing ghoul, and it was tapping into the prey sides of my primal instincts.

"Get out!" I suddenly heard Gage yell, his voice shrill with panic. "Get the hell out of there. I… I can't control him. He isn't responding to me. Quick, go, Theo's coming with a gun."

Sanguine's eyes shot to the top of the stairs, and he snarled at Gage. Then, like Gage's words were the magic spell to switch my fight to flight, I suddenly was filled with a shot of liquid energy, and an intense drive to get the fuck away.

I shot up like a jackrabbit and started running up the stairs.

"Duck!" I heard Theo yell. "DUCK!" But I wasn't fucking ducking. I lowered my head and continued running, then to my horror, something slammed down on my back.

My senses were knocked out of me when I hit the stairs, the edge of the top step meeting my forehead, shooting stars and bright lights into my vision. And before I even got a chance to scream, I felt pressure and a stinging pain in my neck… and then gunshot after gunshot.

The sounds of the gunshots overwhelmed my brain. I shut my eyes, a throbbing pain pulsing in my head like my heart had been transplanted inside of it. Even with my eyes shut, however; I could still see flashing white lights, as if the pain currently pooling and multiplying to other parts of my body had manifested into a visual hallucination.

Then something I dreaded, and didn't even know was coming until it was too late. I felt the familiar pull on my body, followed by the light warning tremors that felt like someone was pinching small threads from my skin, and then the crescendo… a full-blown seizure.

What happened after was a blur of white-washed reality and the continued influx of pain, but I did recognize something familiar, the glowing staticy aurora that was Gage's healing abilities. I was more conscious of his presence this time, and I caught glances of his face, grave from intense concentration; but every word spoken and everything done to me seemed like it was happening on a movie screen, with the audio being played in an adjacent room.

Finally, I came-to on the floor of the Falconer. I felt warm hands remove themselves from my head. "He's waking up," Gage said, the relief palpable in his tone.

"His… his fucking injuries stopped bleeding just like that?" I heard Theo say, amazed. "You can heal people with that?"

I squinted and was still for a moment to try and get my bearings. "Stay still for a moment," Gage said, then he addressed Theo. "I can't really heal wounds… it's kind of difficult to explain. The radiation kind of… stops the wounds from bleeding out, it kind of cauterizes them I guess you could say. He's not healed and he needs to go back to Skyfall."

"No." I suddenly shot up, but I regretted it when a rush of dizziness and throbbing filled my vision with red. Gage steadied me, and so did Theo. "I need to get to Elish," I said. "I'm not going back to Skyfall." I managed to look at Gage, his expression was grave, his odd-coloured eyes full of concern and apprehension. "You said you would come with me."

"I think you should go with him, new friend," Theo said. He had a wrapped bandage in his hand and a bloodied towel. I was relieved to see a white sheet covering a body just three feet from me. Sanguine was dead, and he would resurrect and hopefully be okay. "You've been lucky that Silas has been too depressed to dispatch people to look for you, but that will change. I will not tell him I saw you, but if he asks… we have our loyalty and I am loyal to my king. It's best I don't know where you'll be going next. Jade, you said Elish might be in the northern greywastes?"

I had until I was told that Killian had died, and that Reaver was trapped under the flaming rubble of the plaguelands lab. Now it was just a theory I was putting too much faith in.

But where else could he be? Elish had many secrets and the few I knew about were in the northern greywastes and Aras. I think I knew Elish wouldn't go to Aras. Too many bad memories.

So the only one I could grasp onto, no matter how vague… was one of the last things he'd told me.

To go to a town called Garnertown and ask where the town Mantis was and to find the man who founded it.

I looked at Theo. "Can you drop us off at Garnertown. Do you know where that is?"

The relief I felt when Theo nodded shot what was left of my dizzy disconnection out of my body. I got to my feet with Gage's help and turned to him.

"Come with me," I said to him. "You'll be safe with me. I'll protect you. I've survived in the greywastes before, and we'll find my master soon." I turned back to Theo. "Give us a month and come back to Garnertown. If we're not there… we found him. Please, Theo, can you do this for me?"

Theo's mouth pursed and moved from side to side, then slowly, but hesitantly, he nodded. "For you, dead boy, I will keep your secrets. Jack may be awake by then and if I am back in Cardinalhall, chances are I will be deployed in the northern greywastes anyway to look for Kessler." Theo walked past me and the sounds of rusted gears soon followed, then a slam as he closed the Falconer door. "We'll be in Garnertown in no time at all. I would take one of the packs and fill it with supplies and clothing. I will be dropping you off but I will be staying in the plane for the night and leaving in the morning. I will be telling anyone who asks that I went to visit a friend of mine in Greenbase and it would be odd for me not to spend the night. He's quite attractive."

"But… we will be going back to Skyfall eventually?" Gage asked. He looked at the white sheet. "I don't want to be gone from Skyfall long."

I nodded. "I know you want to talk to Sanguine, but he's going to be resurrecting for possibly a month." This was a lie, it would probably only be a week or so, but I needed him to go with me. "How about you go with me now, and Theo can pick you up in a month? Sanguine will be awake by then."

Gage, still staring at the body, considered this. "As long as I am back within a month... I believe that will work. Sanguine is too weak now anyway and... I'd like to meet this Elish, this... powerful man I've heard so much about." He sighed and nodded. "Yes. I will go with you."

I was so full of hope and excitement I felt like I was going to burst, but in those happy feelings was the dark underbelly, one that held doubt, anxiety, and even apprehension. What if Elish wasn't there? For all I knew he could be in Irontowers, or the outlands. I could be way off.

But when I thought of Elish's last words, the hope returned. Mantis was a friend of his and it was entirely possible he'd be staying with him. If my master was in mourning over me and his failed plans, if he had left the family, he wouldn't be in any of the family's hidden apartments. He'd be nowhere where they'd be able to locate him.

I knew my master inside and out, and my knowledge of him was pulling me back to the area of the greywastes where our adventures had taken place. The last location we had been together before my brain had failed me. In a lot of ways, it was the last place where we'd been happy.

I just knew he was here, my heart told me he was close and we shared a bond, an invisible string, that would always draw us to each other.

In a matter of days, I would come back from the dead, and take my place beside my master... where I belonged.

The plane landed a mile from a modest settlement, with a wall surrounding it made out of sheet metal and bricks. I jumped off with Gage and two backpacks full of supplies. Thankfully in these backpacks, that were always kept in the crates, were a couple hundred bucks as well. It would be enough to live off of for the month, but barely.

Theo bid us goodbye and remained in the Falconer with the resurrecting body of Sanguine. It was just me and this strange new guy now, and I hoped that he didn't have any secrets he was keeping from me. So far he seemed nice, easily spooked and kind of timid, but I could tell he had a good heart on him and his aura reflected that opinion.

Gage was standing stiff and with his jaw set; he was looking around the area we'd been dropped off in. We were standing on a two-lane road, covered with gravel and dust that had been blown in throughout the years. Around us, the road framed blackened remains of houses. They were in all directions and stood out like we were in the middle of a freshly dug graveyard. None of them had been spared of the fire, but when my eyes focused on each individual one, I saw that they were in different stages of being claimed by the dead world. Some of them, the closest ones to us, appeared to have been burned during the last winter. The charcoal was fresh, and when I walked to a thick beam standing like a greywastes tree, the black rubbed off easily to stain my hands. But looking past the dark bones of the house's frame and burned contents within it, I saw other houses now covered in a cloak of dirt and dust.

Out of curiosity, I walked to it and started kicking away rusted cans, now brittle as paper and covering my shoes in flakes of brown, and nudged a couch that had been reduced to springs.

"I think they have been harvesting the houses for firewood and whatever they can salvage," I said to Gage. I bent down and picked up a children's book, its pages swelling the colourful book to three times its size. I put it back and walked out of the frame. Then I noticed that there were no trees in the vicinity, it was all flat and rocky; the only thing erupting from the ground were the burned frames that would eventually fall too. "I wonder what they'll do when the wood is gone."

Gage watched me walk by, then I heard him start to follow me. "Why don't they just grow more trees?" he asked.

Inside I just shook my head, amazed at just how little this man knew of our world. "Some do grow but it's really rare," I said. "The radiation is still strong. It's just survivable to humans if they're Geigerchipped. It gets rid of the radiation. We chip domestic animals too, but there isn't a way for us to keep it from the plants, plus..." I glanced up at the sky. "Even though we get blue skies and sunshine, the sun is still cloaked and it's not as strong as it used to be. So everything grows stunted unless you have a lot of human intervention. So we have it in Skyfall but in a place like this, literally on the fringes of the habitable greywastes... they can barely grow anything."

"Why would they live so far out here then?" Gage asked. He was now walking side by side with me as we walked to the town. "So far from Skyfall?"

"Some people don't like laws and authority," I replied. I led him off of the road, which would take us northeast and away from Garnertown, and we started walking around more charred houses. "If you want benefits from Skyfall, you live in what's called a block. For the residents of a block, you get Ratmeal to grow rats for consumption, those are subhumans not actual rodents. You also get Geigerchips for a reduced cost, and protection from the Legion but only for big things like invasions or something, the block has separate law enforcement. You also get grants, like you get a certain amount of money for each stray cat you have and for each pet cat, but you also get penalties if more than normal die. Fucking Silas loves cats." Then I laughed. "That's actually a quality we all share. I guess you might not, since you're an entirely different type of born immortal, right?"

Gage lowered his gaze. "I don't know," he said honestly. "I don't remember that much. I just remember walking for a long time. I died a lot. The world that is uninhabitable is a terrifying place with terrifying things. I don't want to go back there. I cannot go back to that place. There were terrible creatures out there… are there ones here?"

His eyes widened when I nodded my head. "I mean, it's safer than where the radiation is too lethal for humans but it's still dangerous out here. We have ravers, which are arians whose Geigerchips either broke, or they stumbled into an area with too high of concentration. It doesn't kill them, it just drives them insane, makes them unable to get infections so they have grotesquely deformed bodies and faces. They differ in intelligence but…" I smirked and decided to not tell him about what I had done to my ravers. "… but some of them can be pretty smart. We also have centipods, giant centipedes that eat humans, deacons, those are giant wolves, celldwellers, those are humans with horribly long limbs that are like nine feet tall, and the worst of all… the greywasters." I chuckled at my own joke, but Gage's already wide eyes bugged out at this. "Some are nice, but a majority of them are so starved, desperate for food and safety, they'll kill you if you so much as cough. My friend Reaver, he hunted and ate legionaries for sport, he was quite the murderer, but that's just what you have to be to survive here. It's a rough and unforgiving existence."

"Yes… you're all cannibals. I remember that," Gage said in a tone that I just knew was judging me.

"Cannibalism is a way of life here. The taboo of it went out the window during the Fallocaust," I said. "We don't have a choice, not with how skinny and stringy the animals are. We farm the subhumans, and eat convicts or the elderly who have finished their retirement time. We eat the ravers too."

I saw Gage turn a bit green, but he nodded. "I could have as well. I don't remember. I just know we didn't do that before the Fallocaust."

I had to laugh at that. "There were a lot of things we didn't do before the Fallocaust, but then the world ended, and in order to survive… we had to adapt. And we did." My laughter faded though and I started to get a prickle of doubt in my heart. "Gage… you're going to have to toughen up if you want to live in this world. This isn't dog-eat-dog, this is human-eat-human. Only the tough ones survive."

"I'm immortal," Gage said simply. "We survive anyway."

True… "Yeah, but if you don't toughen up, Silas will eventually find you and encase you again, right? You have that to worry about."

Right in front of me the nauseas expression on Gage's face faded, and it was replaced by a glint that I could only describe as both fear and solemn resolve. "He will not take us," he replied simply. "No matter what I have to do… Silas will not put us back in there."

The conversation died after that, and we both continued on our way towards Garnertown.

It looked like this place hadn't been taken by my ravers. The walls were intact and the buildings looked decrepit but in a greywastes way, not so much as a 'ravers came in and burned everything and ate everyone' sort of way. There weren't any crucifixions either, and that had really become our thing when we had taken over Velstoke.

While we walked towards the town, my imagination went wild thinking of what my ravers could be doing now and what would eventually come of them. The Legion was supposed to be swarming this place looking for Kessler's head, so that might spell bad news for my subjects. I hoped they would be able to fight them. I owed my life to the ravers, without them I would've died cold inside of an abandoned shack. Plus Elish might've never found me.

The two of us stepped onto the road that would lead us to Garnertown. This road had several vehicles on it, some pushed off of the road and others left where they'd died. I even spotted a camper, and amusingly enough, there was a clothesline attached to it and a rust-streaked white van. It looked to be occupied, so I decided to give them a wide berth, no need to talk to anyone who could be hostile. I wanted to check out the town, not have a conversation with a greywaster.

As we approached I started to hear the rumbling sounds of a generator but it was faint. I looked around the burned out frames, and found a detached garage hiding behind a two-level house that still had the upper level intact. When we got close enough, I could see an extension cord which laid on the ground like a large snake, and eventually disappeared into one of the camper's windows.

Then I saw the door of the camper open. We kept walking, but my fingers drummed against the pistol I'd borrowed from Theo.

When I saw a rifle in the man's hand, his eyes watching us as we walked along the road, I decided since we'd already been spotted, to give him a wave so he knew we weren't hostile. He nodded at us and by his legs a medium-sized black and white dog poked its head out and gave us a low *woof*.

"If you're going to Garnertown, I'd think twice about it," the man suddenly called, pushing the dog's head back inside with his foot. "They're on lockdown from a raver attack several weeks ago. They're not taking in anyone new."

Well shit. "Do you know which direction Mantis is in?" I called to him. "That's where we want to end up."

The man waved his hand in a beckoning fashion. "That's west," he called and pointed behind him. "Several days walk, two since you two look young and capable." He then motioned to me and his chapped lips disappeared into his mouth. "I can tell you a good place to camp for the night, but I want water for that information. Just a bottle."

If I could avoid a confrontation I'd take it. Plus we needed a place to sleep for the evening and night was going to be on us before we knew it. "Okay," I called. "But we're leaving it here and then going west. No offense but we're not in Skyfall, so we're not going to visit."

The man nodded and rested his rifle on his shoulders. "Do you want to trade smoked meat for more water? I have arian."

I paused. In my pack were just energy bars and a couple cans of fois ras and flaked rat meat. I wouldn't mind some fresher meat, and if Mantis was only two days away we'd have extra.

"Okay, but you leave your gun there."

Another nod. I heard Gage make a nervous noise in his throat, but I ignored it, and started jogging towards the man waiting for us in front of his rusty camper.

The man had the usual gaunt and half-starved look of any greywaster, with short curly dark hair and dark eyes. He had glasses on too that were being kept together with duct tape, and the rifle he left behind was so rusted I wasn't sure it would actually work.

I had learned enough from Reaver to not turn my back to him. I motioned for him to go ahead of us. He nodded, walked along the side of his camper, and disappeared around the corner.

We followed, and when I turned the corner I saw a small smoke house that had been hiding behind the camper. It looked to have been converted from an old shed, and there was smoke, faint and almost invisible from the heat, coming out of a tin-wrapped chimney.

"Smells good," I commented. I took off my backpack and started rummaging around. "So what's the trade? Two pounds for two bottles?"

"Sounds fair," I heard him say. "As for the location I spoke about. You're going to want to spend the night in Junction subdivision. You'll hit it in about three hours. The houses are intact, new builds that haven't had people in it. Good place to spend the night."

I nodded, looked up with the two bottles in hand, and watched him open up the shed door.

My eyes widened when I saw three small bodies hung up by their legs. Their skin was baked to a golden brown, in some areas holding small bubbles filled with grease, and their heads, genitals, and hands had been removed. Their feet remained however, to tether them easily to rusted hooks on the ceiling, shrivelled things that glistened with grease, with small toes that resembled little raisins. One of them was a toddler, the other two perhaps six or seven, but who knows how much their bodies had shrunk from the continuous heat.

The man brought out a knife he had resting on a stump and spun one of the older kid corpses so its back was to the front. I saw several chunks had already been carved out of its backside and the meat showing through had already started hardening to a dark red. The smell was alluring, however; and even though these were arian kids, my mouth started to water.

"T-those are kids?" Gage said faintly.

I shot him a look, and when we made eye contact I gave him a piercing glare. I didn't care if he had been encased for years, he had to learn the rules out here and I wasn't going to look a gift corpse in the mouth. Water for two pounds of kidlet was a good trade off. Who cares how they died?

Gage deflected his gaze and turned around. He started walking to the west, and since he was in the right direction, I let him go off to pout.

Then the man got up and gave his chest a funny look. "Weird, my Geigerchip is buzzing. Is yours?" He thumped his collarbone and glanced at me.

I swallowed, hoping that we weren't about to explode, but since it wasn't concentrated I think we would be okay. "No, mine's fine. There's a bit of a breeze today, maybe it's being carried on it." I walked to him with the three bottles in hand, two for the meat and one for the information, and licked my lips in anticipation when he offered me a slice of it on the flat surface of his blade.

It was delicious, sweet and tender and just bursting with flavour. "If you want to double that offer. I wouldn't mind going thirsty for the rest of the day just for another two pounds." The greywaster chuckled at this and nodded. He directed me to a sack with grocery bags inside, and with some small talk exchanged, I filled my bag with meat.

"I'd watch your ass going to Mantis," the man said. We were at the edge of his property under the clothesline now. Gage was still walking, and the man's Geigerchip was still buzzing. "The Jade Ravers are spreading like cancer. As soon as I get the camper fixed I'm heading as far west as I can before I can't take it any further."

Jade Ravers? I tried to hide my reaction, but I needed more information. "I've heard that there were a bunch of smart ravers who can shoot guns. Is that what everyone is calling them?"

The man nodded, cracking open one of the bottles and taking a generous drink. He sighed and closed his eyes for a second. I wonder how long it's been since he had fresh water. "That's what they call themselves. Apparently their leader was named Jade but I think he either died or has stayed in Velstoke, or Jadetown as they're calling it now."

I stood up a bit straighter, pride rushing through me and making me want to run to Velstoke just to say hello to everyone. Was the Beast still in charge? I wouldn't doubt it, he'd been fierce.

"Wow," I said with a shake of my head. "Well, keep safe, my friend, and thank you for the information." I shook his hand and continued on my way, my shopping bag full of aromatic smoked kidlet. It was a good haul, if I say so myself.

I was half-expecting a gunshot to ring, and for me to fall down dead, but none came. I jogged up to Gage who was staring ahead, not looking too happy with things.

"What's your problem now?" I said, a bit too dickish than I had intended. It was weird having a boy scout in the middle of the greywastes, and it made me wonder if he ever could become an ally to my master.

"I find it disturbing you're asking that when you have meat in a grocery bag that has been carved from a child," Gage said. I saw his Adam's apple bob as he swallowed hard.

I don't know if it was because I was just excited to be close to Mantis, or that this guy was starting to grate on my nerves, but I fished into the bag, pulled out a chunk of meat and ripped off a piece. I chewed it and offered him a bit.

Gage recoiled, his nose curling. "That's disgusting."

"That's the greywastes and if everyone thought like you, the human race would've died centuries ago," I said with my mouth full. "Kids have a rough time here. They probably got diseased or something. It doesn't matter, they're dead anyway and it's good food. Just try a bite, it's really good."

Gage's wrinkled nose tucked up further to the bridge. "I'm okay." He paused and stuffed his hands into his jeans. I was noticing he did that whenever he was stressed out. "My apologies. I know this is normal living for you," he said with a sigh. "I'm starting to wish they'd advised me to go back to Skyfall. I've been out here only several hours and already I've seen so much. I feel badly for Sanguine but I believe I can help him. Once he resurrects I will heal him."

I put the meat away and closed the bag. "Sanguine has some issues but he's a wonderful guy," I said. "Unfortunately what Silas did kind of regressed him, I think. The place that Silas put him into was where a man kept him prisoner for eleven years. I've never had it confirmed but I think the dude kept him down there as a sex slave. And we're talking little little, like eight until nineteen."

Gage's expression turned sorrowful. "His mind was fractured. I saw it for myself until I was forced out. I can understand why now. Why did he mutilate himself? He seemed normal for the few seconds I saw him when he'd broken me out."

"I'm guessing it's from the stress from being back there. Masochism kind of runs in the family." I went through a time of hurting myself to get Elish's attention. "We're self-destructive. We have a lot of issues but we're a close family. Silas is systematically trying to destroy us but my master has a plan to fix that."

In front of us, the road we were on joined onto a highway. The highway was four lanes wide, separated by medians, and on the other side of it there was a ledge that led down to piles of rusted cars.

I jumped up onto the median and started walking on top of it. I looked ahead, hoping to see Mantis already, but there were rolling hills in front of us. Eventually though, the highway wound around it, so there was nothing to see but grey and more dismantled houses. On the hill at least, I could see black trees, ones that hadn't been harvested yet.

"They don't like this place but they don't fully know why," Gage said after we'd been walking for an hour. "They're beginning to suggest I go back to Skyfall."

Shit. I was losing him already. I wanted to bring him to Elish. This kid was just too powerful to let slip through our fingers. Not to mention that even after healing me I was still having seizures whenever something hit my head. I kind of wouldn't mind him around just to heal me when I needed it.

"We won't be here long," I lied. I really had no idea how long Elish would want to be here for. "And, like I said, Sanguine will be resurrecting anyway. Less chance of Silas catching you."

"I suppose…" Gage said slowly. His face scowelled and he rubbed the back of his neck. "I don't know why they're so uneasy… and I still don't believe they know either."

I didn't know what to say to that, and I didn't want to draw attention to his multiple personalities, so the conversation died. We carried on in silence, only the occasional quip breaking through the empty air.

After a couple hours of walking, we spotted the subdivision the man had been talking about and settled into one of the houses that still had a good roof on it. It didn't stand out, and there were so many identical ones I knew it would be a safe place for us.

I ate my fill of kidlet, savouring each taste as it dissolved into my mouth from the smoke tenderizing it, and licking my fingers after I'd consumed an entire pound. Gage ate a Speedbar on a wooden chair I had brought up to the second level of the house, and read a book in silence.

This would be a good time to try a new different angle, a way to take his mind off of wanting to go back to Skyfall. It wasn't anything fancy, just some good ol' fashion fear. If he wanted to go back to Skyfall, he would have to be walking back to the Falconer in the middle of the night to catch Theo before he left; and to someone as timid as Gage, I could paint him some terrifying pictures.

I pulled up a plastic chair and put it by the window to sentry, then glanced over to Gage. "A lot of really dangerous animals come out at night, so I'll keep first watch," I said to him. "You don't have night vision, do you?"

Gage shook his head back and forth. This was excellent then.

"The ravers are starting to take over towns that border the radiation-filled plaguelands, and they're–"

Gage's head shot up from his book, and his heart spasmed with fear. "P-plaguelands?" he suddenly said. His mouth dropped open and his hand flew up to the back of his neck. "We're near the plaguelands?" I was surprised to hear fear in his voice. "H-how close are we?" He jumped to his feet and went to the window I was at.

I blinked. "I don't know, but it's definitely many miles," I said slowly. "We're not that close... why?"

Gage looked around, his heartbeat going crazy. He was scared of the plaguelands, terrified of it. "I can't go back there. We can't let them know we're out here." He scanned the dark greywastes, his eyes jutting back and forth as he searched. "That was what they were nervous about... that was what they sensed. There are others out there... they can hear them on the sound waves, they sense them. They're close."

Whoa. "What?" I said giving him a funny look. "No one can survive in the plaguelands but mutated animals. Who are you talking about?" Was this a head thing or a... real thing? I really wasn't sure.

Gage's upper teeth pressed down on his bottom lip, his chest was pulsing and he was almost hyperventilating. "I can't return there," he whispered under his breath, he said it with such silence I wondered if I was supposed to hear it. "We need to continue to make our home in Skyfall."

Then, like he had realized that he was speaking these crazy thoughts out loud, his eyes shot to me and he looked away. "Never ask me about this again. If you want us to be friends... you will never ask me about this. Can I trust you?"

Questions were burning me alive. I was so curious and intrigued about this I almost felt physical pain not being able to have them answered. What was he talking about? Or was he just batshit insane?

Maybe his time encased in concrete had permanently messed him up. I wouldn't doubt it for a second; he'd been in there for over a century. He didn't seem to remember much from it, and I wondered if he'd been able to put himself into some sort of stasis. One thing was obvious though, this guy was pretty messed up.

Unfortunately if I wanted to keep myself in his good books, especially since he did allude to us being friends, I had to respect his wishes... even if it was killing me inside.

"Okay," I said with a sigh. "I won't ask about them."

Gage, nervous and now sinking his teeth into his bottom lip, nodded, before he ran a hand down his face and turned from me... then went back to his wooden chair. He made no mention of leaving this place at least, and eventually we both fell asleep.

But our sleep would not be peaceful. I woke up in the middle of the night and realized there was something rummaging around downstairs. My chimera instincts quickly kicked in, and I jumped to my feet. I remained as still and as quiet as I could, and tuned my hearing to try and pick up what had decided to enter our temporary shelter.

I scowled and tilted my head, then closed my eyes to give my enhanced hearing as much power as I could. That scowl only deepened when I realized I could hear a dog panting, and while I was listening, I witnessed its movements change from scrounging around the house, to climbing up the stairs.

I drew my gun and looked down at Gage. My jaw set when I realized he was still asleep, and my soured feelings towards him got another fresh injection of bitterness at this.

I walked to the window, which I had left open, and looked down. But when I saw three men below me, all three of them holding rifles, I quickly stepped away from the window, and out of sight.

One of them I recognized as the man who I'd traded the water with.

Inside my head I swore, and tried to force my heartbeat not to spike, but just a moment later I heard scratching on the door... followed by a bark.

Gage woke up with a jolt and a gasp. I reached down and grabbed his shoulder, and to my absolute disdain, he let out a small scream.

"Shut up!" I hissed to him. I looked to the door and a growl started sounding from my throat. "There are three men outside, one of them was the man I traded with. Get out the knife I gave you." He might be immortal but I wasn't, nor was I his teacher. I turned from him, and when I heard footsteps start to climb up the stairs, I discreetly glanced out the window. I saw that there was only one man outside of the house now. He was looking into the greywastes, his rifle on his shoulders as he kept guard.

Channelling every stealth trick I knew, I climbed out of the window, and put my pistol back into its holder. I shifted to the left, my boots lightly pressing against the black shingles of the roof, and got out of the line of sight; so when the other two burst through the doors, I wouldn't be seen.

My heart was hammering, adding its own background music to the lucid and streamlined thoughts coming to my head. There was no fear, no desperation. I managed to keep myself calm and collected as my boots gradually crab walked me to the left; my back pressed against the exterior walls of the old house.

And when I got into the right position, I waited.

I didn't have to wait long. There was a crash as they kicked open the door, and without mincing words, they opened fire.

Which was exactly what I had been waiting for. With the shots shattering the hot summer air, I jumped from the roof and landed on top of the man with the rifle. I aimed for his shoulders and I hit my mark. He slammed to the ground with only a muffled cry that was drowned out by the thunder cracks of gunfire above me, and I drew my knife and stabbed him in the neck.

The blade went in easily from my force alone, and with the adrenaline using my blood as a highway, the knife slid in and out multiple times like my hand was the needle of a sewing machine. In and out, one after another, until I felt his body start to seize underneath me.

I picked up the rifle, and on silent feet, I ran back into the house.

The shots quieted down and I heard talking. I ran to the foot of the stairs and looked up to see the black and white dog. His head was lowered and his eyes were two flashing spheres, and when I stepped onto the stairs, I heard a menacing growl.

I chuckled. I fucking hated dogs; they had nothing on deacdogs. I held the rifle up and positioned the dumb mutt in the cross hairs and pulled the trigger. The noise blasted my ears, like a gong being hit right beside them, but as it faded I was treated to the sound of a high-pitched yelp and the dog flying backwards and stumbling. It scrambled to its feet while its pleasing screaming continued to tickle the inner sadism that was as a part of my DNA as my yellow eyes, before it fell to the ground in a heap of flailing legs. A dog's dying yelps were almost as satisfying as a pig's. Both were loud about it, like they had this built-in belief that somehow their dying was more important than a regular animal's death. And whereas any normal arian would find it heartbreaking to hear, I for one, had always enjoyed it.

"Moe?" a man cried. Without even looking down the stairs the man ran to his dog, his own yells of sadness mixing in with the chorus of pain-filled yelping.

I stepped into the shadows, leaned the rifle against a wallpapered wall with the paper now curled like an unravelled scroll, and waited with a content smile on my face.

I missed this!

"Where is he?" I heard the man who had sold me the food yell, then a *thunk* of a fist hitting meat. Gage being the meat. "Where is he, you mutant fuck?"

Well, I hadn't even thought of that. Was that why we'd automatically had targets on our backs? My deduction when I realized we'd been ambushed was just starving greywasters needing food in a time of raver versus arian warfare. But maybe we'd automatically been labelled as mutant defects because of our eyes.

I heard Gage cough, but there was no answer. I kept myself poised in my hiding place and was still, until the sounds of one of them descending the stairs could be heard.

Clunk, clunk... clunk, clunk...

My heart had always been racing, but with my body a statue against a wall, I could hear the heavy beating echoing inside of my own chest. It was exhilarating. I had missed this so much, I felt cheated that it had been so many months since I had gotten a chance to kill. It was like caging a lion and feeding him dinner scraps. A predator was meant to hunt, meant to kill and consume without mercy. That was what a chimera was.

And finally, I was getting the chance to live up to my engineering.

My eyes were fixed to the corner of the wall I had my back pressed up against. I could see the end of the railing, and past that was the foyer to the entrance. All of this was in light blue of every possible shade, illuminating objects that, to a normal arian, would be covered in darkness.

Then my target stepped onto the main level, and without wasting a moment, I grabbed him by his jacket and pushed him hard. His gun fell to the ground and he stumbled backwards, crashing into the edge of the railing. The railing had stood tall against time and the elements, but it crumbled from the man's weight, he tumbled to the ground with the broken and splintered wood.

I raised my fist and punched him in the face, and at the same time he grabbed my hair and tried to wrench my head back, I leaned down and sunk my teeth into the soft, vulnerable skin of his neck.

I had a style, all of my brothers had a style. Mine was ripping out necks, something that pleased and satisfied the bloodthirst inside of me. Kind of like Sanguine's love of fire.

My teeth pierced his flesh, and I had to fight against his hands desperately pulling my hair and grabbing the side of my face. I closed my eyes tight to protect them and tried to finish him off. Like a snake swallowing a mouse, I opened my jaw as wide as it could go, before I clamped it shut and started to thrash my head back and forth.

The man gasped and tried to scream. I felt a pain in the side of my head from his scratching and pulling, but it was shaken off by my head snapping back and forth. Finally, I freed the piece of neck I had been determined to bite off, and was rewarded by a gush of liquid hitting my face.

I opened my blood-covered eyes, the warm cruor stinging them, and looked down to see his neck quickly become covered by red. I leaned down to try and get in another bite, only to have his hands let go of my hair to clamp over the wound.

As I watched this man desperately try to stem the flow of the gushing blood, my chest rocked from the heat this act of killing was bringing to my body. It could only be described as orgasmic, it has always been orgasmic. And though this man was a disgusting parasite still walking along the rotting carcass that was the world, there was a momentary bond between us, like two lovers intertwined.

My mouth was open in a grin as I watched him try to save his own life. Under the filth he wasn't that bad on the eyes, and probably in his thirties. I would be lying if I said there wasn't burning elsewhere, and when I shifted myself onto his body, straddling him, I felt the tightness in my pants, and a hard cock against my thigh.

But the lust wasn't for him. It was for my master that I would be seeing soon. Just knowing that I was so close to seeing him again threw me into a frenzied excitement. In the daylight I wanted to see him because I loved him and missed him, but under the covers of darkness my body was aflame and aching with anticipation to have him inside of me. To experience our all-night sessions. I wanted him to take me, and draw out orgasm after orgasm. I wanted his cock in my mouth. Fuck, it had been so long since I felt that cock twitch and throb between my lips as he came.

And with those flames inside of me, I leaned down and took the still-alive greywaster's cheek into my mouth. While he grunted and gurgled, I bit down, the soft, stubble-speckled piece of meat tightening in my mouth before my teeth punctured it. I then pressed harder and pulled, until I severed the cheek and held it in my jaws.

The man had no more screams. He only looked at me with his eyes bulging; his hands clasping his neck while it shot blood out from in between his fingers. He watched as I dropped the piece of cheek onto his chest; then I tilted his head to the side, and with a smile, bit off the second one.

Then I sat on his navel, leaned down, and started eating the two pieces off of his own chest, consuming and enjoying the sweet and tender meat. I'd never had arian cheek before, not from the face anyway, but I do believe this would be something I'd be eating in the future. It would taste even better cooked, the fat, with some heat, would melt and tenderize the meat. Fried for sure, perhaps with mushrooms and shallots, or if I was feeling like really treating myself: seared and roasted in the oven.

When I was done I looked up at the man and saw that he was dead. His hands limp, and the blood that had been gushing with such vigor between his fingers, now stagnant. He had died with his eyes fixed on me; I had been the last thing he saw.

I rose, wiping my mouth with the back of my hand, and turned to find Gage.

He was standing only three feet from me, the expression on his face stunned and horrified.

"I'm leaving," Gage said. I was surprised that his voice, usually timid and unsure, like he never wanted to speak his feelings out loud, was hard. "I'm going back to the Falconer and I'm going back to Skyfall. If you follow me... I'll have no choice but to kill you." He walked past me, no bags or anything in his hands, and headed towards the door.

I threw my hands up into the air and dropped them. "This is fucking normal for this place, asshole," I yelled at him. "It's called the greywastes, and I'm what's called a chimera!" I started walking to him but when he heard me following he whirled around and he held out his hand.

"They realized something when I was sleeping... we're heading north." Gage's eyes flared. "We're heading towards the plaguelands, aren't we?"

"We're not going into the fucking plaguelands, Gage," I snapped. "So you and your multiple fucking personalities are fine. We'll be in Mantis soon…" I took a step towards him. "Just go–"

"Quiet!" Gage snarled. He glared me down; his stance showing me he wasn't fucking around. "I meant what I said. If you take one more step. I'll kill you. Let me go. We're not going near the plaguelands, and I will not be with someone of your ferocious nature."

I wasn't stupid. I had seen what Gage could do. I glared at him but said nothing, and after several tense moments, Gage nodded. He then turned around, and disappeared out the door.

I walked up the stairs, passing the dead dog and stepping on his blood. I went into the room we had camped in and saw the second dead greywaster. He was dead, but there wasn't a mark on him, only a great deal of blood which I could see had come out of his ears.

The mark of the empath. An empath who could do terrible things without the aftereffects that I suffered from.

And I think I'd just made him our enemy.

CHAPTER 33

Elish

THE SOUNDS OF SHARPENING STEEL FILLED THE AIR
and Elish tested the blade on his fingernail. He gently shaved it against the
flat edge and smiled to himself when he could see white flake off like he
was shaving a candle. Nero had taught him how to test to see if a knife
was sharp when he was younger, and that had always stuck with him.

"Big sharp," a raver who was passing by said. He walked up to Elish
and nodded his approval. "Big sharp. Stab, stab, stab!"

Elish glanced at him. "You would say, *very sharp*, not big sharp," he
said to the raver as the man, with a floppy fisherman's hat on to cover a
completely scalped head, continued walking to wherever his destination
was.

"Very sharp," the raver called, his voice fading as he disappeared
behind a building. "Very sharp, Quiet Man. Beast asked for you. Go to
Beast." And then he was gone.

Elish shook his head and continued sharpening the blade. When he
was pleased with it, he sheathed it into a scabbard on his belt, and drew
his dirty and stained grey long coat over his torso and tied it off. He got up
from the electrical box he had been sitting on and started walking towards
the center of town. On the way, he unscrewed a bottle of wine he kept in
his coat pocket, and after a long drink, he popped a cigarette into his
mouth.

When he got to the center of town he spotted Beast, who was standing
guard over two captured arians. The scared looking couple, a man and a
woman, were chained to the metal frame of a tipped over payphone box.

They were huddled together, looking terrified and trembling in their shoes, wild eyes going in all directions before focusing on Elish.

The man held up both of his hands as Elish approached, and there was a mark of relief on his face. "You're not one of them…" he said. And, sure enough, there was relief in his tone. "We're just travelling to Garnertown, that's all. We weren't here to cause any trouble." When he took the female's hand and squeezed it, Elish's eyes narrowed. "Let us go. Please, we're just trying to survive here like you."

Elish looked to Beast. The raver was standing several feet away, with his arms crossed over a chest holding two ammo belts and an assault rifle. The leader of Jade's ravers had started putting vertebraes into his long dreadlocks and was also sporting fresh, and rather ripe, ears and penises on his necklace.

"Are you not going to remove their Geigerchips and have them join us?" Elish asked Beast.

Beast shook his head. "Not strong enough, too weak, would die from radiation. We're going to eat them. You brought us much meat, honour goes to you, Quiet Man." Beast thumped his chest and laid a hand on Elish's head. Elish knew the custom and lowered his head as well in acceptance.

"No, no!" the woman suddenly sobbed. "Please. What do you want? We'll give you anything just don't fucking eat us!"

Elish was unfazed. He pulled the knife out and tested the blade against his finger. "You would have more luck bargaining with the raver," he said casually. "I have come to enjoy taking the lives of arians, especially ones who beg." His violet eyes flickered up to the couple. The woman, with short blond hair and pale eyes currently red from her wailing, was young, possibly twenty but not much more. The man had a short beard and black hair which was flattened from being hidden under a hat. "So any more whining from you and it will only feed my thirst even more."

"Come on…" the man said, his voice cracking. "The world is fucked up enough as it is. We'll never go back to being civilized people, like before the Fallocaust, if we keep doing shit like this to each other. Have some compassion."

This drew a chuckle from Elish. "Compassion?" He tilted the knife to catch the sunrays. It was hot out today. He was now wearing a cowboy hat he'd found on most days, but today he had nothing to cover his short blond hair, twisted in greasy locks and unbrushed. "The world is dead, love is dead, compassion is dead. Stop trying to force breath into a world that took its last strangled gasp years ago."

This made the man pause, though the female still cried into his shoulder. "You don't talk like a greywaster..." His forehead wrinkled. "Your eyes... you're a chim-"

Elish's jaw clenched, and his body tightened under the greywaster's words. He advanced on the man before changing his mind at the last second. Wanting to make the man suffer a little bit more, he turned to the woman and grabbed her by her short hair, just long enough to get a tuft of it.

Elish slid the knife over her throat, opening it up with ease. The woman's hands rose to her neck, her mouth open and sucking the air, and the blood began to flow. Elish then pushed her bound body onto the man as she struggled, no screams able to sound from the depth of the wound. And as the man looked down, gaping in shock but unable to bring voice to the horror he was witnessing, Elish stabbed him in the side of the neck and jerked the knife towards himself. The blood immediately shot from the wound like a main pipe had burst, and for no other reason than because he was curious, he put his hand in front of the flow to test the pressure.

As he felt the hot blood shoot against his palms, he heard Beast call the others. Elish retracted his hand after that and shoved the man to the ground. He held up a hand, hearing the thumping of feet against the pavement that were the other ravers running towards their meal time, and pulled the man's pants and underwear off of him. He sliced off a piece of cheek, one of the best cuts, and turned around with the meat in hand.

Over two dozen ravers were behind him. Elish could hear the orchestra of their quickened heartbeats, thumping with excitement over their dying meal. They stared at Elish with their mouths open like hungry dogs, their bodies twitching and pulling towards the food, but they wouldn't move without Beast's signal.

Elish turned to the leader and nodded to him. "I will be in my house for the evening," he said.

Beast nodded and with a loud *Kah!* the ravers ran past Elish, the sounds of growling and snapping filling the air to mix in with the heavy scent of blood.

He had decided on a rancher that was as far away from the center of town as he could possibly get. Only on windy days did the heavy stench of rot reach this place, and for the most part, once he was inside of the house he could pretend that the ravers didn't even exist.

The house had belonged to someone of a higher class, and it had been stocked with food and wired for electricity. The ravers had no use for gasoline, even with their healing brains they knew that explosive liquid was best left to the arians, so Elish had an endless supply for himself. The drugs were also something he had an abundance; once he'd told Beast what to look out for he'd been given bags and prescription bottles full of opiates, methamphetamines, benzoids, and baggies full of mysterious powders which he sometimes tested when he was feeling particularly low. The only thing he had to share was the alcohol, and after he'd shown several of the smarter ravers how to make mead from scavenged honey and a supply of yeast they'd found, the wine and hard liquors were mostly left to him.

Elish turned on the generator and sat down on a blue couch. He looked down at the white powder sitting in a small white dish, formerly for soy sauce when one ate sushi. He had no idea what they had used it for, obviously not the Japanese dish, but now it was for ground up Dilaudids.

He felt an affinity for those drugs. Just saying the word 'Dilaudid' had Reaver looking up from whatever he was doing like a gopher popping out of his hole. Jade had loved them as well, he said they gave him energy whereas the oxycodone had made him more loving and content, yet sluggish and tired. Jade had told him in detail what every opiate did; in truth Elish had already known, living with brothers who had a taste for drugs, and at one point being quite the consumer himself, he was educated on their effects and side effects.

Elish's shoulders slumped, and he looked down at his bloodstained hands. They were now dry and the blood was starting to flake off and fall to the ground like dust. His jacket was also showing dark stains and the smell had begun to saturate the room. He took the jacket off and dropped it into a bathtub full of water and soaking clothes, before indulging himself in a generous amount of opiates. Then, before they kicked in, he washed the cheek of meat and put it into a pot, dashed some onion soup mix on top of it and placed it into the oven. After waking up to a house full of smoke several days before, he'd scavenged himself a timer; so he wound it for an hour and placed it on the cluttered counter.

Around his kitchen were half-eaten meals, or ones not consumed at all. On the kitchen table there was barely any table left to see, just pots full of untouched macaroni and cheese, Bush's beans, or Chef Boyardee, dirty dishes, garbage, and fly traps. He always cooked, just to give himself something to do, but by the time the food was ready he was usually too drugged up and depressed to touch it.

But even if he knew that's how the night was going to go, he still did it. Elish exchanged his warm bottle of wine for a cold one and sat down on the couch and turned on the DVD he was watching. He settled in for another night of loneliness and drinking, only *The Lord of the Rings* trilogy, extended edition, to keep him company. He'd just started the marathon last night but he was starting from the middle, since the last half was a blur to him now.

And it looked like tonight wasn't going to be any better. The drugs, with the liquor as fuel, started to do their work on his body. He felt himself slip into the half-conscious, half-lethargic state Reaver had called 'zombieland', and soon his head was nodding until it hit the back of the couch. He let himself be taken by it, and the lucid dreams that would eventually find him.

His heart retracted like a touched sea anemone when the first thing he saw was Jade. The boy's face was as vivid as ever, and the smile that appeared on it when he spotted Elish, just as full of love.

But Elish didn't smile back. He looked and saw that his hand was outstretched towards the boy and immediately retracted it. Elish turned from the boy; his eyes inside of this dream trying to close so he didn't have to look at him.

"Why don't you look at me anymore?"

His voice... Elish bit down on the inside of his cheek and his hands clenched into fists. *I will never hear that voice with clarity. The closest that I will ever get is on VHS tapes, most of them showing him egging on Sanguine to fuck him harder. Or the half-dead creature that I held up when we had been married.*

Never to hear him say I love you, something that used to make me sigh and shake my head, disliking it when he'd force me to show him my own feelings. 'Why does he have to hear it when he knows it?' I'd say to myself.

I would say it every day now, if only I'd been given the chance.

"Well?" Jade said. "Why don't you look at me anymore?"

Elish looked into the darkness, feeling a physical pain inside of his chest. He tried to push it down but he knew it was no use.

"Master?" Jade said, more forceful this time. "At least look at what you've done."

What I've done? Elish turned towards Jade, confused by his words.

Elish's face twisted in despair when he saw what was standing in front of him, and took a step back.

Jade's naked body was covered from head to toe in bright red burns and patches so burnt they had charred to black. His hair had been seared off and was now resting like a destroyed nest on top of his head, and his ears and nose were missing, only blackened nubs remaining like the wing tips of a roasted bird. Strips of his skin were coming off of him too, like how the walls of the abandoned buildings shed wallpaper, and underneath that skin was dull brown meat, to which the taste would be little different than the very meat that was cooking in Elish's oven.

Elish shook his head back and forth. The boy raised a hand to him and an accusing finger was pointed at Elish's chest. He could see blisters on the tips of Jade's fingers, and as he looked closer, he saw that his arms were covered in them, raised opaque nodules bulging with fluid, some already burst and coating the area around it in glistening liquid.

"This is what I get for trusting you," Jade said bitterly. His lips were two slabs of raw steak, with pus dripping and trickling down his chin. "I was burned alive as I fucking called for you." He took a step towards Elish, his bright yellow eyes solar flares that threatened to melt Elish in his place. "You remember me calling for you? Before you ran to chase that man? You knew I was healed enough to call for you but, once again, it wasn't enough for you. Just like how you didn't make me immortal. It was never enough until you had exactly what you wanted."

Elish couldn't speak, the only movements his still body could make was to continue shaking his head back and forth.

"You wouldn't accept me as your husband until I was old enough to not be a boy to you. You refused to let the family acknowledge our marriage. You were embarrassed of me!" Jade snarled. As he stepped closer to Elish he could smell, with clarity, the aroma of Jade's cooked flesh. "You were humiliated to have an eighteen-year-old gutter rat as your fucking husband!"

"You? Don't give him all the credit."

A coldness hit Elish's body as the deep voice of Reaver sounded in the darkness. He saw the man he'd known since before he was born, step into the dim lighting around him, and beside him was Killian. Both of them just as seared and burnt as Jade, if not more so. Reaver's skin had almost entirely carbonized, and from head to toe there were deep fissures in the hardened skin where red and pink flesh peeked through every time the boy moved.

"He still has to answer for what he did to me," Reaver growled. As his mouth moved it widened two cracks in the thick blackened skin that had appeared on both sides of his face, clear liquid leaked from it, and when the boy smiled, two more large splits appeared. "What do you have to say for yourself?"

"Well?" Killian snapped, his tenor voice ringing, the accusatory tone making it all the more piercing. "Was it worth it?"

"WAS IT WORTH IT?"

"WAS IT WORTH IT?" Suddenly Elish could hear the ringing of a fire alarm, and the smell of the three's cooked flesh intensified. Then, all at once, he was hit with an overwhelming rush of anxiousness and despair. It made his chest tighten in on itself like a piece of paper being crumpled in a fist.

"It wasn't. I SAID IT WASN'T!" Elish yelled. He closed his eyes and let out a bellow filled with anguish. "IT WASN'T!" When he opened his eyes, all three of them were nose-to-nose with him, and with glaring eyes they grabbed Elish and pulled him into the darkness.

Elish's eyes snapped open as he hit the floor. He looked around, his heart banging and his breathing rapid, and realized he was back in the rancher. The house was now filled with the aroma of meat cooked and done, and the alarm he'd set was ringing.

For a moment Elish was still, the images of Jade, Reaver, and Killian still fresh inside of his mind. Then he rose and turned off the alarm, and took the roast out of the oven.

Elish leaned against the oven and shut his eyes. He drew up the faces of the three men he'd failed, and committed them to memory. Yet another terrible image he didn't want to forget, for no other reason than to punish himself.

Like he knew he'd eventually do, he left the cooked roast in the pan on top of the stove and went back to the living room; his steps wobbly from the drink and his mind swimming but not nearly as numb as he wished for it to be. With that thought in his head, he gathered his supplies for injecting heroin and started preparing himself a dose, knowing with solemn knowledge, that he would not be stopping for quite a while.

Jade

When I saw that ravers had taken over Mantis, I felt my heart crush like a mallet had been taken to it. I was too crestfallen to cry but my teeth were biting down on my bottom lip so hard I could taste copper.

In front of me were spray-painted buildings, but unlike the usual mosaic of colourful scrawl, like most raver-infested buildings had, these ones actually resembled things. They had shown off their claim of this place with trees, yellow suns, and bloodied corpse stick-figures being eaten by fanged stick figures. It was like a child had been given finger paint and told to paint a scene straight out of a horror movie.

Why I was still approaching this town I didn't know. I guess deep down I wanted to see a familiar place, and maybe I was stupid enough to believe that Elish might've been here. But my heart was now filled with doubt, and not only that, the knowledge that I had many lonely days ahead of me as I walked from town to town looking for my master.

I felt so disappointed in myself as I continued on this empty road into the grisly, and decimated, town. My gut feeling had been that he'd be in Mantis, but he wasn't here. There was no way that my Elish would stay in a place like this. Not only did he hate unclean things, but he hated ravers too.

My eyes took me to a pile of chewed bones rotting in the doorway of an old Subway restaurant; the doors and windows boarded up and crossed out with giant red X's. This place had such a stench to it, it was making my eyes water, and my ears were almost deafened by the loud buzzing of tens of thousands of flies. Both the smell and the sound were amplified by the sweltering summer day, and I could see heat waves coming off of the pavement.

I looked around but only saw more bones, some of them in the middle of the street with scraps of green flesh still clinging to them. The reason for that was spotted when I saw stray dogs and cats lounging around together, their ears flicking occasionally to dismiss a fly that had decided to land upon them.

Drowning in my own sadness, I inhaled a shuddering breath. I wiped my eyes, convincing myself it was from the smell rather than my own disappointment, and continued down the deserted street.

But it didn't remain deserted for long. I spotted a raver hunched over something. His head moving back and forth like he was eating. He was dressed in only pink shorts and sandals, and was growing a good amount of blond hair on his head.

It was a chipped raver. I glanced around to make sure I didn't have a sniper pointing a gun at me, and said a loud *Kah!*

The raver jumped to his feet and whirled around. I smiled when I recognized him. I'd named him Sunny because his mouth had been split open with a knife, making him look like he was smiling even when he wasn't. The name extended past his disfigurement, however; he had a great temperament and did actually smile a lot. I don't think I could've found a better raver to meet.

"KING JADE!" Sunny exclaimed; the scars still on his face and his excited grin giving him quite the disturbing appearance. "KING JADE! KingJadeKingJadeKingJadeKingJade!" He said this so fast my name became just one syllable, and with his arms open, he ran to me and threw them around me. He started laughing and jumping up and down in the air, and even though my heart was broken, I couldn't help but smile and let out a chuckle too.

"Hey, Sunny," I said to him with a laugh. I pried him off of me and put a hand on his head; he wiggled around in excited anticipation over me officially greeting him.

"Kah!" I said with a smile. Sunny looked up and beamed at me. His blond hair now long enough to fall over his brow. He had a foggy left eye that had never cleared up, so I guessed he'd always been blind in it, but the right one was brilliant and crystal blue.

"Kah!" Sunny greeted me back and grabbed my hand. "Come see Beast. Come say hello." Sunny started dragging me down the street, and by now other ravers had come out of alleyways and buildings to see what all the commotion was.

Some of the others were new, but a lot of them recognized me. While I was dragged down the street, the ravers shouted my name and the *Kah!* greeting and some even patted my shoulders and arms with smiling faces.

I saw ravers with assault rifles and semi-automatics on their backs, knives and handguns on leather belts. All of them were wearing clothes and a great deal of them had hair on their heads and grey rough scabs on their bodies from where their previously open wounds had calcified and hardened. It was incredible, and to think that I'd done all of this filled me with pride. I just wish my heart wasn't disintegrating at the moment so I could actually enjoy it.

Finally we reached what I believed was their town center. In all actuality, it was just an intersection but an intersection of the main road so there was a double-lane street and single lanes branching off to the north and west. In the middle of the road was a brick fire pit, heavily used and with scorched bones tucked in between the scrap wood, and a tipped over phone booth with chains leading to metal collars.

This town square smelled a bit better, but looking around I could see blood splatters on the pavement. I'd trained them as much as I could, but their manners still left a lot to be desired. Well, I'd need to stock up on supplies before I left so perhaps I would stay for a few days and teach them some new things. They never had to worry about catching diseases or infections because of the sestic radiation, but I'd guess they were more susceptible now with the Geigerchips.

When Beast spotted me, a wide and open grin, one that rivalled Sunny's, spread on his face. He thumped his chest with his left hand and walked towards me.

"King Jade! Finally here," he said, his deep voice echoing off of the tall buildings around us. All the ravers gathered in the square, talking excitedly amongst one another. I heard my name mentioned quite a bit.

Beast slapped a hand roughly on my head and *Kah'd*, and I did the same, then he hugged me to his chest and crushed me against him.

"About time!" Beast said when he let me go, my ribs ached so hard I had to rub them. I sure did love these guys. "We kill three men for you tonight. Big feast!" he exclaimed. Then he looked down the street and shook his head. "Quiet Man's been locked in house. So sad. Are you late or something? Acts like hasn't seen King Jade in ages. So sad."

My smile turned into a confused half-smile. I glanced in the direction Beast was looking in and gave him a funny look. I felt bad for not remembering who Quiet Man was, but it was flattering that he missed me so much. "I left everyone at the same time," I said to Beast. "That's nice that he missed me. Invite him over for dinner tonight. I have a few corpses I drained and hung, but they're a good day's walking away. They might still be good though if you want to send some guys out to get them."

"Oh, sorry, apologies." Beast bowed his head to me. "Quiet Man our name for him. Like you named me Beast but name was Trent. Is husband. Husband's sad you're late."

Beast said something else, but my ears had filled with static and pressure, so much of it it felt like someone was pushing against my forehead from the inside. It was as if I couldn't comprehend just what he was saying, and that rendered me absolutely senseless.

Elish was here? My… my master was here?

Beasts shocking admission played over and over again in my mind. Every time I felt my mouth move in a futile attempt to achieve verbal confirmation of what had been told to me, my tongue became a useless slab of meat. I was well-aware that I was looking at Beast with dumb astonishment, my mouth open and drying out and my eyes stinging from me forgetting to blink, but I was a robot who'd lost connection to its data servers.

"Okay?" he said confused. He looked past me, then to me again, and patted my head. "Seizure again?" He flicked my nose, something they all liked to do when I was recovering from a seizure, and then patted my cheek. "Poor king," he concluded.

"Elish?" I finally managed to sputter. I raised a hand and cupped my mouth, before I had to grab onto Beast's arm to steady myself. "Where is he? Show me where he is. Show me where my husband is."

Beast nodded, and turned around so his back was to me. I didn't understand why until I remembered that he'd carried me on his back a few times when I had first been taken in and had been too weak to catch up with the others. I'd regained my strength after a while and could more than look after myself, but he seemed to have remembered.

Then, as if my mind had stopped buffering and to compensate it was overloading me with all of the data I'd missed at once, what was going on hit me and hit me hard. I looked at Beast's back and let out a rather nervous and shrill laugh. I added another hand to my cupped mouth, unable to stifle the laughter that was rolling manically from my lips.

The ravers surrounding the square, perhaps unsure of what to do, or just seeing an opportunity to feel included in all of this, started laughing too. This only made me laugh harder, and with a shake of my head, I climbed onto Beast's back and locked my legs around his waist.

"Okay, Beast," I said through my laughing. I clung to him, feeling like I would float away if I didn't. "Take me to my husband."

In a matter of minutes, my master was going to get the shock of his life, and I was so excited about seeing him I didn't know how I was containing it. If there was an opposite to starting a Fallocaust, some way of making the world green again and alive I would've done it from the sheer happiness that was gathered inside of my body. No one could stop me after this day. I could take over the world one-handed right now and still be back in Elish's arms in time for evening tea.

And soon I would be in Elish's arms; I knew Beast's hug would be nothing compared to the bone-crushing embrace he would give me. What would Elish do? What would he say? I honestly wouldn't be surprised if he beat me senseless and then killed me himself for making him think I was dead. It had been a month now since Olympus burned down; a month of me being in Kerres's possession where he'd tortured and raped me. What had Elish been doing? I knew he'd never show his emotions, but deep down I hoped he'd at least cried a little on the inside.

I refused to have expectations, however. Soon I'd be bursting through that door and those cold eyes would meet mine. I'd smell that mint and nutmeg as he embraced me and then I'd get back to my job and make us both tea. I'd tell him about my adventures and he'd probably just shrug off my supposed death with a wave of his hand and berate me for losing my wedding ring and collar.

Oh, I missed that man. I missed my master.

Beast ran with me through the streets, and I was smiling the entire time. It looked like Elish had taken residence far away, where none of the other ravers lived. That was typical Elish. He might've even been here when the ravers took this place over, but refused to leave his house out of pride and dignity. He was an idiot like that – but my idiot.

When Beast pointed to a rancher, and I heard a muffled generator in the distance, my heart pushed away the excitement in my chest and poured in equal parts anxious anticipation. The catalyst translated into dizziness, and when Beast stopped and I slid off of him, I became worried I might throw up on Elish's driveway.

"He's in there, in there for days," Beast said to me. "Asked not to be disturbed. You drag him out for dinner tonight?"

I took in a few deep breaths but I found myself a dizzy, trembling mess.

It took me a moment to find my voice. "Give us some time alone tonight, Beast, or perhaps wait for us to come out. We haven't seen each other in quite a long time," I explained to him through chattering teeth.

"I'd like some time alone with him."

Beast looked disappointed but he nodded. "Okay. After done, you come and we'll have feast." He put a hand on my head and bowed his own. "Very happy, King Jade is back. Very happy. Come back to square soon." I bowed back and rested a hand onto his dread-locked head, and he turned and started jogging back towards the square.

I turned and faced the rancher, trying to keep all these physical symptoms in check. For a brief moment I just stood in the driveway and stared at the house in front of me. The curtains were drawn which was kind of unlike my master, who loved a brightly lit house, but I could see the faint glow of a lamp in the living room.

Oh wow, I was trembling so bad... I was shaking in my boots. When I started walking to the entrance, three stairs then a concrete landing with an iron railing for support, I half-expected myself to fall down. My legs were just jelly. I found it so funny I was feeling this much anxiety over seeing him.

I walked up the stairs and faced the door; the door's brown stain lifting off and peeling and the gold on the door knob flaked. Dumbly, I didn't know what to do. Do I knock? I laughed at the absurdity of my dilemma, but eventually I raised a shaky hand... and knocked on the door.

My legs wobbled. I was silent, listening for any movement; but when I focused my hearing to pick up his footsteps, all I could hear was the bass-like drumbeats of my heart and crickets and hoppers chirping in the yellow grass that made up his front yard.

He didn't come to the door... I knocked again and chewed on my lower lip. Did he think I was a raver? Was he sleeping? It was nine o'clock at night. I had been walking all day but the pain in my feet had disappeared with my excitement getting here. Elish had a pretty predictable schedule... he didn't usually go to bed until midnight and if he was in the mood, we didn't fall asleep until after three. Unless he'd been planning a night for us, then we'd go to the bedroom early.

I let out a long exhale, and not knowing what else to do, I put a hand on the door knob... and turned it.

It was unlocked. Like a dam was bursting, a new flow of anxious and excited energy flowed through me. I pushed the door open and stepped inside.

I looked around and was shocked when my senses were overwhelmed by the smell and sight of garbage and rotting food. I could see a kitchen at the end of the brown panelled hallway, pots and pans piled up and empty cans buzzing with flies. I stepped in, shut the door, and took a step towards the kitchen.

I walked down the short hallway and saw two other doorway arches before the hallway led to a kitchen. When I got to them, I looked to my right and saw doors undoubtedly leading to the bedrooms and the bathroom…

Then I looked to my left, to the living room – and I let out a strangled sob.

That couldn't be him.

No. No. No. That couldn't be him.

He was laying on the couch, wearing a sleeveless undershirt and cloth pants. His face was grey, and sunken in; his eyes, framed with deep black circles, glassy slits which stared off into space. I saw the faintest glimmer of purple in those faded eyes, covered by greasy blond hair that was cut shorter than I'd ever seen it. He had facial hair too, but it failed to cover the open sores I could see were littered all over his face, untreated and caked in dirt. Every part of him was squalid; his clothes just faded rags with blood and other stains.

And his arms… my mind stalled from the disbelief of seeing red puffy track marks and more dime-sized sores. It drew up in me excuse after excuse as to why I was seeing this, even telling me I was hallucinating, that Gage had killed me. That seemed more probable in this moment than the reality that my master had become a filthy drug addict. There was just no way someone I saw as such a personification of elegance could fall so far from grace.

This was Elish Dekker I was talking about. Gelus Vir. The cold chimera. There was just no way.

But the evidence was all around me. Orange caps and empty syringes were everywhere: on the coffee table, on the dirty, clothing and garbage-covered floor, and there was powder streaked on a wooden coffee table and small sniffers caked with white and yellow.

No… this wasn't Elish. This couldn't be my master.

I choked and took a step back. There was no way this could be him. This was a homeless vagrant, a greywaster who… who looked like Elish. Elish would never let himself get like this. There was no way my master would ever let himself stoop this low. Elish was a demigod, he was the end result of ninety-one years of refined dignity, of practiced grace and pride. This man wasn't the man I had fallen in love with in Skyfall. The chimera with hair like the sun that cascaded down his shoulders, with amethyst eyes that shone with cold intensity, and a formidable countenance that made everyone who saw him stand in awe.

This was not the man who I saw that night I ran into his study and hid beside the fireplace. This was not the man who read to me, who abducted me and broke me, then built me up again stronger than ever.

This person I was seeing was an imposter.

Unable to look at this false man any longer, I turned away.

"Why do you keep coming back?"

I froze in place, my back turned to him. My breathing stopped, the last remains of my inhale being held hostage inside of my throat.

I closed my eyes tight and felt my jaw lock; my lips started to tremble.

It was his voice.

Dear god, it was his voice.

"Have you not tortured me enough?"

My mind was screaming at me to not turn around. What I had seen lying on that couch had overwhelmed my emotions so much, I mentally felt like I couldn't handle seeing what I had seen again.

But even though this was the truth inside of my head, my body cared not, and turned me back around.

Two purple gems stared at me through half-open eyes. And my heart lurched when I saw the look of despair on his face. An expression I didn't even know he knew how to make, but in his rough, dishevelled appearance, it seemed like the only look that suited him.

I looked away, unable to meet his gaze, my tongue glued to my mouth. I didn't know what to say to him. I didn't even know what he was saying, or why.

This strange man took the thoughts right out of my head. "You never had trouble looking at me before," he said, his voice dull, lifeless. "In all truths… I don't hate it when you come to me. My greatest fear is forgetting his face."

His face?

My face?

All at once, the emotions that I had hastily hid from the shock of seeing him like this, rushed to me with an intensity that threatened to knock me off of my feet. It was as if his voice had infiltrated the barriers I had quickly erected, destroyed them like they were made out of matchsticks, then reached down and found the love I had for him, snatched it, pulled it from me and put it on display right in front of my eyes.

A sob broke through my lips, and I ran to him.

I got down on my knees in front of the couch, and as he looked at me with confused disconnect, I threw my arms around him and sobbed.

"I'm alive," I said through choking breaths. The strength of the emotions hitting me simultaneously were sending my normal breathing patterns into chaos. I pulled back and put my hands on both sides of his face and openly wept. "Master?" I choked. "Master? Look at me. It's Jade. I'm here. I'm here."

Elish's glassy eyes found mine, the sadness pouring from them. He looked deep into my eyes and I saw a small smile appear on his lips.

"I know you're here, Cicaro," he whispered. He drew his hand up and gently touched my wet cheek. "I do love it when you visit. Even though you yell at your master so many of those times."

"No. I'm here!" I sobbed. I looked down and touched his arm, an empty needle resting on his stomach where his hand had been. I could see a fresh track mark, still swollen and red. "If you didn't become a drug addict… you'd know I was here."

The corner of Elish's mouth rose, a weak half-smile that made his left eye squint. "If I don't do the drugs, love. I cannot see you." He gently wiped my eye with his thumb. "And then how will I get to tell you how much I loved you? How sorry I am… for failing you."

My face crumpled. I buried it into his neck, my body shaking as sob after sob shook me like an internal earthquake. All of my fear from seeing him washed away, replaced by a hollow sorrow, and love… so much love.

I never thought… not even in my wildest imagination…

"Oh, my Jade," Elish murmured. "I thought I could have the world. I thought I deserved the world and more. I thought that was what I wanted, my greatest wish." I raised my head as he brushed my hair away from my forehead, and as we locked eyes, he gazed deeply into my own. "When in truth, none of that mattered the moment I realized you were gone. Decades of plans, careful calculating." He wiped away another tear; I saw his purple eyes glisten as they filled. "None of it mattered in the end. All that mattered was you." As he said this, a tear slipped down his cheek, and it was my turn to raise a hand and wipe it away.

I stared at him, his words stealing the breath from my lungs. My body shook even more, and my teeth started to chatter, visceral reactions to words I knew I would never forget. I didn't know what to say back. He'd never spoken to me like this before. It was hard to even get an 'I love you' from him and now… and now he was emotionally exposed in front of me. Baring me his soul and entrusting it to me.

Elish reached his hand up again and he laid it on the side of my head.

"I love you," he whispered to me. "I only wish I realized just how much I needed you, before it was too late."

Another sob burst from my lips. "And… here I thought it was only me needing you."

That sad smile appeared again, then he shook his head and his hand slipped and fell. I watched his eyes slowly close, and I heard him mumble, just faintly: "You were always an idiot, maritus."

I stroked his cheek, looking at this man in front of me in a way I never thought possible. As he drifted off to sleep, I realized that I was feeling inside of me, an entirely new type of love.

Because I didn't think less of my master seeing him in this state. A state that was unprecedented for the cold chimera who I had come to worship. I found myself loving him even more, not just as a master, but as a husband.

I knew that when he woke up, sober and aware, he would be embarrassed, cripplingly humiliated, but that was just too bad for him. This moment between us would be one that I would always remember, because not only did it signal a shift in his feelings towards me, but also a change in my own emotions.

I felt like I had aged fifteen years in just a few minutes. Never before had I felt such a pull of responsibility towards him, so much love. Not the love of a cicaro to his master, but the love that a couple shares, a concrete mutual trust and understanding. I knew when he woke, he might beat me senseless to try and regain that power he'd know he'd given me… but eventually he would come to trust me with his heart. I was worthy of it.

And I was ready.

I was ready to be Elish's husband.

CHAPTER 34

Jade

I DECIDED, NOT TOO SOON AFTER ELISH HAD PASSED out, to kill him. What a weird thing to conclude but that was the reality of having an immortal as a husband. I knew just from the track marks on his arms, and the state that he was in, that he was physically addicted to the heroin and god knows what else, so now would be the best time to detox him. Because I myself was a pro at prepping heroin, I made two large doses and injected them into a vein in his arm. He didn't even flinch when I slipped the needle in, not even a mouth twitch.

Then I rubbed his chest and watched him, almost in fascination, and listened to his heart. It happened quickly and quietly; I think because I gave him such a large amount. In Moros I had heard when someone overdosed, they threw up and heaved, that it was messy, and I'd prepared myself for that. But my master slipped into death peacefully. His heart raced for just half a minute, beats out of sync and desperate like fish caught in a net, before it just… stopped.

Elish's face relaxed, his mouth opened just a little bit, and his body sunk into the couch. I smiled at him and kissed below his eye, a part that didn't have any facial hair, and got up.

I wanted to sleep beside him, but even though I was a chimera, I didn't have the strength to lift him. I sprinted to the square to find Beast, but on my way, I encountered two ravers I knew and enlisted their help. The two of them carried Elish to his bedroom and laid him down in an old mattress that I had thankfully found new sheets for. This place had been well taken care of before its occupants had been killed, and there were still clean clothing items. It looked like Elish hadn't cared enough to use any of them.

After the ravers left, I found myself alone in this garbage-strewn house. I believed that with so many other ranchers around us we'd probably just end up abandoning this one and moving, so I didn't bother cleaning it. I was hungry, however; so I found canned soup in the pantry, cleaned a frying pan which was in a horrendous state, and feasted on smoked kidlet in mushroom soup and had four packs of fruit snacks for dessert.

Then it was late enough for me to fall asleep; I was exhausted from a full day's walking. I raided the previous owner's dresser and was content to find clean boxers and a sleeveless undershirt, where Elish must've gotten his, then I curled up beside my master.

His body was no longer boiling hot, which I think meant he would be awake in the morning. When I examined him I also saw the track marks on his arms already healing, and the open sores had already been covered in a thin layer of skin, but the redness was still showing through.

I knew my excitement might prevent me from sleeping, so I swallowed a couple opiate pills to send me off to a comfortable sleep, and laid down beside Elish. My heart sang when I got in my usual position: on my side with my head resting above the crook of his arm, and my hand on his chest. I thought it would be impossible for me to feel any more happy, but falling asleep beside him after the two of us being separated had me so content I drifted off with a smile on my face.

Even with the drugs warming my blood, it was still hard to commit to sleep. I woke up several times with aching cheeks, from smiling, and a jumping heart. Whenever I would brush the fringes of consciousness my heart would leap with excitement and anticipation and I'd need to force it to calm down and let me sleep longer. I felt like I was a child again waiting for my first Skyday morning in Edgeview, knowing that I was going to wake up to presents unlike my previous Skydays.

Finally, I woke up and it was morning. I could hear the hoppers chirping outside and the sun beaming through the corners of the curtains. I squinted and cuddled into Elish more, the haze of sleep shrouding not just last night's events, but the past several months.

Then I heard his heartbeat.

My eyes opened and a pulse of shock ripped up my spine and centered in my chest. I raised my head and looked at my master.

I smiled when I saw that his chest was rising and falling; his heartbeat strong and greeting my hand like it was knocking on a door. Elish had resurrected fully, he was just sleeping now.

Slowly, so I wouldn't wake him, I sat up and shifted myself over. I sat cross-legged, my back against the wall, and ran a gentle finger down his arm. He was still dirty and bedraggled, but the sores had all healed and his face, though rather gaunt, wasn't as thin as it had been previously. This man sleeping so peacefully beside me still didn't look like my master, but I had helped him take the first steps.

I had waited long enough, if I made myself wait any longer I knew I would explode. I laid down beside him again and started caressing his soft warm cheek.

"Elish?" I said softly. There was no need for chimera hearing to hear my own heart; it was trying to break out of its prison to meet Elish's. I was so full of anticipation and anxiousness I almost felt like time was going to stop. "Elish?" I said a bit louder.

My lips pursed when I saw Elish's closed eyes tighten, and his ungroomed eyebrows draw close together. I rubbed my thumb against his cheek and leaned in to gently kiss his lips. "Wake up," I said softly.

I pulled away, and when I did I saw his eyes slowly open. My breath caught in my throat, and starting from the hand on the side of his face then spreading throughout my entire body, I froze in place, like his eyes alone had forbidden me from moving.

He looked at me through those partially closed lids, and I saw the confusion appear on his face.

"Good morning," I whispered to him. My voice cracked from the emotion pressing down on it, and I had to will myself not to sob and dive into his arms. "I... I missed you."

Elish's eyes widened, and I heard and felt his heart jump. Then suddenly, Elish pulled away from me, and stared at me with an expression on his face that told me he didn't believe I was real.

"Calm down..." I said softly. I held out my hand to try and take his arm, if only to keep him still, but Elish jerked away from me, and scrambled backwards.

And my poor master rolled off of the bed and landed with a *thunk*.

I got up, but he shot to his feet. He stared at me, and started walking backwards. His face was pale with shock, his purple eyes wide and staring at me like he'd woken up next to a whipwolf.

"Calm down," I said again. I stepped off of the bed and held out my hands. Elish took another hasty step back, like my hands were on fire, but his back hit the wall. He pressed up against it, and I witnessed the expression of pure shock on his face turn sorrowful.

"So my mind has finally broken I see," Elish said to me, and his eyes filled with grief. He gave me that same sad smile, a look of longing deeply implanted, before he turned and took a step towards the door.

I grabbed onto his arm and pulled him back. I briefly saw surprise before I slid a hand behind his head and drew him in for a kiss.

Elish's lips were tight from the suddenness of my actions, but after a moment of us joined, they softened. I wrapped my other arm around his waist and felt my body flush with electricity when I felt his hands grab my side.

And when he realized I was solid, that I was warm, breathing, alive… he pulled away from me.

I'll never forget the look on his face when our eyes met again.

He was staring at me in disbelief, his eyes wider than I had ever seen them, and overflowing with a perfect mixture of shock, awe, and overpowering love. His mouth was open; one hand still on my side, feeling the heat of my skin against his hand.

Then he looked at my neck, and saw the prong marks from the collar Kerres had had me in, and the bite from Sanguine's teeth; both hastily bandaged.

"H-how?" Elish croaked. His eyes jutted from one side to the next, looking me over and trying to take in as much of me as possible. I saw the moment a tremble came to him, and felt the tremor travel down his arm to the hand that was touching me.

I reached down and took that hand, and with a smile on my face, I brought it up to my lips and kissed it. "It's a long story," I said to him, and gently clasped his hand in mine. "I was below the explosion in Olympus. Someone, two people actually, pulled me out and… wouldn't quite let me go until I took matters into my own hands." My smile widened under his awestruck look, he looked absolutely frozen in that state. My poor master. "My heart told me where you were, and it was right. You should know by now, nothing can keep–"

Elish grabbed me and pulled me into his arms, and as soon as I felt his body against mine, the constricting embrace seemed to crumble my calmed countenance. With that single movement, I became a boy being reunited with the man he loved, and I started to cry.

My eyes closed as he held me, our bodies pressed so tightly against each other's I felt us become one person. Our hearts beat together, our lungs struggled for air together, and I even heard him let out the smallest sob, though drowned out by my own crying.

We stayed in each other's arms for quite a while, but I couldn't say how long. I just knew I had fully melted into them, and had let his presence, his being, soak into me again.

I had missed this master of mine.

When he finally separated our bound bodies, he cradled my head in his hands. He drew my face up and looked down at me, not even hiding the wetness on the corners of his eyes.

"Never in a thousand lifetimes..." he whispered. It was his turn to gently wipe my tears away with his fingers. "I will never let you go." He took me into his arms again, a little softer this time, and I heard him sigh. "I love you."

"I love you," I said back to him. "We'll always find each other. We're like two magnets, I think."

"Indeed," Elish chuckled. I smiled when I heard some lightness come to his voice. "I would kiss you, maritus. But as you can see... I'm quite the mess."

We pulled away again and I smiled at him, seeing him so happy brought a blush to my cheeks. "I have the generator on... you can have a shower, if you want."

Elish's brow suddenly furrowed. He looked at his arms and turned them, then gave me a suspicious look that was accentuated by his still smiling face. "I must've died before..." His eyebrows unknitted and raised, then his eyes rose to look at me. "That wasn't... a hallucination last night." He sighed deeply.

But that just made more tears start to come to my eyes. There was nothing I could say back, no words to explain just how much what he said meant to me, so I wrapped my arms around him again and buried my face into his neck and cried.

"Shhh," he shushed me, "don't cry."

"I'm sorry I put you through that," I sobbed. "I'm not worth it."

"I will decide your worth," Elish whispered to me. I felt his fingers run through my hair, then they found the bandage on my neck and the gouges from the collar's prongs. "But you're hurt. Is it bad?"

I shook my head. "No, they're not. They'll heal just fine with some attention."

"Those will be the last injuries you have," he whispered. He continued to caress my hair. "No harm will ever come to you."

I tightened my hold on him and felt him rest his chin on my head.

"You'll need to let go of me long enough to let me shower," he said. "Then we will leave this disgusting house and find ourselves a clean one. Once we're settled in, you'll tell me everything. The one next door was in fair condition and the families were using the same generator."

I pulled away from Elish and wiped my eyes. "You really suck at housekeeping."

Elish put a hand on my shoulder and directed me out of the bedroom. "I found there are a lot of things I'm not too good at doing." He took his shirt off and then slid his cloth pants down. I flushed and leaned against the doorway and looked at the warped frame. It had been so long since I'd seen him naked. I couldn't believe it, but I felt my ears burn with embarrassment. I wasn't used to seeing him this way anymore.

He didn't notice, or maybe he just didn't want to point it out. I heard the faucet get turned on.

"Would you like me to make you something to eat?" I asked him, still analyzing the wooden door frame.

"No," Elish said, and then he paused. "Just stay where you are… I don't want you to go far."

I wonder if he's afraid I'll disappear? That if he lets me out of his sight, I'll vanish, all this time only a figment of his imagination.

I heard him get into the shower and while he got clean I found the towels and laid one out for him. I wanted to find him some clean clothes but the last thing I wanted to do to my poor master was have him peek out of the shower curtains to find me gone. Instead I scrounged around the bathroom cabinet, and underneath the sink I found an electric razor and some shaving cream. I hadn't shaved in several days and I already had a good amount of stubble, so I shaved myself and, with several glances to the closed shower curtain, even trimmed myself downstairs too. I wasn't too overgrown but I usually kept it short, Elish did too.

Though if just seeing him naked brought a flush to my cheeks and a rush of coyness, I could only imagine what our first night being intimate would be like.

Elish had a long shower, a really long shower. I trimmed myself on top and on bottom while I waited, and even got my pits in too. I also rinsed us both some toothbrushes and brushed and mouth-washed. The toothbrushes were used which was kind of gross, but well, we'd live.

When Elish finally opened the curtain, his skin was once again the colour of cream, and his sun-coloured hair even looked a bit longer since it was wet. He was starting to look like my elegant master again, but he still really needed to lose that beard. I had laid out the electric razor on the sink, plugged in and everything, and hoped he'd take the hint.

I handed Elish a towel as he stepped out, then he motioned for me to get in. "I will get us both some clean clothes. The residents of Mantis were ambushed, which is a boon for us. I believe these ranchers were for their elites, or the closest one could get to an elite," he said as he wrapped the towel around his waist. I took off my shirt, and while I got naked I saw him reach for a toothbrush.

I jumped in and quickly showered. I even grinned happily and felt a shiver of excitement when I heard the razor turn on. It was silly and I felt silly, but knowing that when I stepped out of that shower, he'd look as close to my master as he could… it just filled me up with happiness. I felt like I was breaking some sort of greywastes law being this jovial. People were supposed to be half-starved and miserable in the greywastes, and here I was practically jumping up and down.

When I was done, I turned off the shower and stepped out. I saw clothing laid out for me on the sink and I had to smile at this thoughtfulness. He'd picked me out a blue t-shirt trimmed with black and black jeans, and had even laid out some Nike sandals too. I dressed myself and styled my hair, and did all the proper post-shower maintenance, and walked out to the rest of the house to find him.

I saw a beam of light and smelled fresh air. I got to the end of the hallway and turned towards the open door–

–and saw my master.

Elish was waiting for me in the doorway. He was leaning against it and looking in, wearing a dark purple button-down with the cuffs folded back, black trousers, and shoes.

Fuck, did he ever look stunning. His still-damp bangs were falling over shining violet eyes, the shirt he was wearing making them all the more intense and vivid, and his face was now clean shaven and without a single blemish or mark. His skin was pale and smooth, the black circles under his eyes gone, and his lips were rosy pink and the corners lifted into a crooked smile.

He looked so different with short hair, younger too. It was bangs in the front, but the back of it was just starting to touch his nape. It was clean and glowing in the sunlight. No more greasy locks, it seemed to steal the light around it like he was the living sun.

And he was.

With my eyes fixed on those drops of crystal, I walked down the hallway towards him. And to prove just how in sync we were, the moment I was close enough Elish put a hand to the side of my neck, and directed my lips to his.

As our mouths joined and our lips locked, I felt the blood rush to my head, filling me with a dizziness that made me feel drunk. I closed my eyes and felt him open up his lips, and in tandem to his movements, I did as well. Not just my chest was throbbing, but my head too. The blood that pooled was pressing against my brain, increasing the intoxicated bliss that threatened to spill me onto the floor. I wrapped my arms around his neck, just to keep myself from falling, but the more I tasted him, the more our lips moved and took in each other deeper and deeper, the more I felt like I was going to pass out.

When our lips separated, I stood there for a moment, my mouth open and my eyes closed. I could feel his hot minty breath against my nose, and then his forehead lean against mine.

Then a kiss, a slow kiss on the corner of my mouth, and like I was Sleeping Beauty, I opened my eyes and took in a deep breath.

"You look quite thin," Elish murmured. "And you're wrong, those bite marks look severe." He closed the door behind me and grabbed a single backpack, stained and covered in greywaste ash. "I won't be liking the story of how you escaped that fire, to when you came to me, will I?"

I shook my head as we walked down the concrete steps. "No, but you might like some parts," I said, thinking of Kerres and how his story had ended. "But I don't think I'll like yours either, huh?"

"No, you most likely won't," he replied simply. He led the two of us to the rancher next door and opened it. But when I followed behind him, he held out a hand and I stopped in my tracks.

I thought he was going to check it for hidden occupants or something, but he rested the dirty backpack against the wall and turned to me.

I yelped from surprise and laughed when Elish picked me up and carried me inside. I grinned from ear to ear, and when I saw that he was smiling too, I slid an arm around his neck and kissed his cheek. "Is this our starter home, Mr. Dekker?" I teased through laughter that had been reduced to giggles. I felt like an idiot, an absolute giddy idiot, but I couldn't help it. No one was here to see us but ourselves, and I was going to soak in and treasure seeing my master this happy.

"A starter home? Don't sell me short, maritus. This is our starter *town*. A prince of Skyfall would not just give his husband a mere rancher," Elish said. And when I let out a squeal, he actually laughed. "You're such the idiot. Did those filthy ravers tell you what this town is now named?"

I shook my head and looked around as Elish started walking us around our new house. It was the exact same layout as the old rancher, except, of course, much cleaner. There was still the belongings of the previous residents, since the ambush was apparently quick. But that was a boon as Elish had said, everything was already laid out for us.

"I named it for them," Elish said. "Shadowtown. After you."

"I love it." I beamed. He walked us to the window and nodded towards it. I knew what he wanted, and reached out and drew the blinds up, squinting as the bright sun flooded the living room. He walked me to every window and I did the same, each blind getting drawn making this place seem all the more like home.

Finally we reached the bedroom. I gasped and let out a surprised cry when he tossed me up into the air and onto the bed. I bounced up high, my arms flailing to keep myself from falling off and grinned when I settled down.

Elish kneeled down onto the bed, and when he lifted up my chin, I bit the bottom of my lip. He leaned in and we shared another kiss, and like the previous one, my head was overcome with heat.

Then Elish pulled away and stroked my neck. I shivered from his touch. "Yes, your collar did burn," he murmured, and when I opened my eyes I saw him looking down at my neck.

I touched his arm and felt my old collar still fastened around it. I remember seeing it on him during my lucid moments. That collar had been our bind since the very beginning, and I couldn't put into words how I felt knowing he kept it near him. "We can use this one for now," I said to him.

Elish shook his head. "No. I believe I have outgrown it."

I opened my mouth to protest that I hadn't outgrown it, when I realized just what he had said. "You…?"

He nodded, and I saw a solidarity come to his face. "I have seen many flaws in myself over the past year," he admitted quietly. "Weaknesses that were drawn up and put on display right in front of my face and my family's. You know me well, maritus, I am not a man who wants to have weaknesses. And when I do see them…" I froze when his purple eyes shot up to mine. I could see the coldness in him, the flickers of my old master shining through. "…I extinguish them."

I stared, my body trapped within that frigid gaze and unable to move. Elish ran a finger along my neck, and his eyebrows, still slightly pink from him grooming them, met. "I realized that a man who needs a collar and a leash on his pet, is a man who doesn't trust his property not to flee from him. You stopped needing that collar last year but I still bound you for my own personal need. I am not a weak chimera who needs reassurance of his dominance by beating on smaller creatures, or smaller chimeras. I am not some fool with issues of his own self-worth that needs to derive power from being a bully."

"I… I never thought of you like that," I stammered, shocked by his words.

But Elish raised a hand and I said nothing more. "I realized that I had been embarrassing myself by having to beat a fifteen-year-old boy, then a sixteen-year-old, then a seventeen-year-old. When I told you on our wedding day that I had learned more from you in those two years, than I had in my previous eighty-seven, I meant it, but I didn't realize I was still learning." He looked back at me, those cold eyes drawing a tremble from my body. They were eyes of a powerful man, who might've just exterminated his last weakness with nothing more than a chimera like Elish's greatest fear: complete self-awareness.

"Jade." He trailed his hand up and grasped my chin. "I no longer want you as my pet. I have no need for one. I have no need to embarrass myself further in front of you, or my family, by denying my feelings for you. I have been broken down to nothing, I have been humbled, and now I wish to return a thousand times better than the chimera I was previously." Elish rose from the bed, leaving me still sitting, entrapped within his powerful gaze.

He got down on one knee.

I swayed, my head pulsing and my face burning, when I saw him reach into the breast pocket of his shirt… and pull out my wedding ring.

"Marry me," he said. Those two words, unlike the ones gilded in steel previous, were softly spoken. "Let me make you immortal, and together we will become unstoppable. A force the world, living and dead, has never seen. And let me deliver to you, that very world, Jade Shadow Dekker."

I looked down at the ring, then back at him. My mouth was open, ready to speak, but all I could do was stare at him. I thought for a moment he was rubbing my hand, but when I glanced back down I realized I was shaking with such intensity my hand was tapping against his.

"Y-y…" I started to stammer.

But then, a cold calmness overtook me, coating me completely within its frigid hold, and extinguishing the dizzying heat. I felt myself rise above the raging emotions, making me stammer and shake, and with a deep breath, I centered myself and stood up straighter.

"I will marry you," I whispered to him in a calmed and level voice. I saw a look of pride flicker across Elish's face. I know he noticed. "But I will always worship you," I continued. "I will always look up to you. You're my keeper, my master, my entire world. You will always hold dominance over me." I smiled and let him take my hand into his.

I felt him slip the ring back onto my finger, then our lips joined again. We kissed deeply, and when I opened my eyes, I saw that I was surrounded by those opal hues, that crystally aura that was brighter than ever.

But there was something else. I saw purple and black ribbons swirling and twisting along the opaque auroras like chinese dragons, and it was then I realized I wasn't just seeing his aura. I was seeing colours that had used to be solely my own.

I pulled away and looked into Elish's eyes, and the expression on his face changed again. I knew he saw what I saw.

"They're no different," Elish whispered. He took my chin, his eyes fixed on mine as he saw our auras flicker in my eyes. "Remarkable."

"There's no denying it now, magnus maritus," I said to him with a smirk. "You're stuck with me until time ceases to go forward."

Elish looked down at our joined hands, our matching wedding rings shining in the sunlight.

"I'll live," he said simply.

CHAPTER 35

Reaver

"AMAZING, HUH?" I HEARD NERO CALL OVER THE sound of the rusty iron gate closing shut. "It's completely enclosed and they have everything here."

I didn't answer him back. I was standing on a rock twenty feet above him, staring out onto a valley that had more shades of green than I knew could exist.

There were trees with so many leaves on them you couldn't even see the brown branches, and some of them held bits of colour that I knew were fruit. In between these belts of trees were emerald fields that shimmered from the light breeze that was sweeping across it. I saw three cabins as well, and vineyards behind them, then more trees until you hit the sharp, impossible to climb, rocky ridges that cradled this oasis like two cupped hands.

"How did they do this?" I said. I was saying it more to myself but Nero heard me.

"Just like Silas cleared away Melchai's sestic radiation, Adler did the same to this place. It's free of radiation just like Skyfall," he called up to me. "I think it's past time for you to learn how to do the same. Don't you think?"

I turned and started climbing down the ridge I had scaled to get a better look at where Nero was taking me. He had a hunting rifle in his hand, and I had my M16. We had a reason for going down into this valley.

Some chimera negotiating was about to take place.

When I jumped back onto level ground, Nero and I started walking down a well-worn dirt path, grass that smelled good enough to eat was on both sides, mixed in with green bushes bursting with flowers. I even spotted a bee which I tried to swat with my hands.

"I did it once," I said to Nero, "the radiation thing. But only once, and I have no idea how to clear it. I never tried though." I walked towards a bush full of berries and picked a couple of them. But when I turned around, one halfway to my mouth, and saw a look of smirking anticipation on Nero's face, I lowered it. I didn't trust that look, that look meant I was about to make an ass out of myself.

"They're raspberries, you dipshit, but you puckered like a nickel hooker from just marmalade, so I know it's going to be funny," Nero chuckled. "You gotta get used to real food sooner or later, so have at it."

I popped one into my mouth and although my mouth twitched from the sourness, I worked past it; they were pretty good. "Killian is going to be in heaven with this place," I said. I looked around and saw a bird fly overhead. I could hear them too, tweeting and all of that. I'd only heard birds on television, we didn't have any in Aras. "I'm surprised he hasn't killed Adler and Spike yet with how Cujo he's gotten."

"It won't be long," Nero said. We got to a bridge with a river trickling underneath. I looked down to see if I could see any fish. The smells here were amazing, the water smelled fresh and the mud did as well. I could see bugs that weren't flies, and hear noises in the grass. There was no negotiating it, this place would be mine. "We have our plan and if it doesn't work, we'll up our game. The fucks can't stay down there forever, and Adler is naïve and stupid enough not to think long term." Then Nero raised his rifle and I saw him look into the forest.

I did too and spotted a little fuzzy thing with a long tail start to run up a tree. A second later, there was a crack of the rifle, and the little fuzzy thing flew off of the tree like we'd smacked it out of there.

"Yes!" Nero hissed. I'd never seen an animal like that, so I ran into the woods to get it, taking a moment to run my hand up and down the thick brown bark of a pine tree. This place was unreal.

As I walked in, I could smell blood. I followed my nose which brought me right to the creature. I picked it up and examined it. It was a squirrel! However, it was now missing most of its head. It was massive though, but not enough for us to eat.

"What we're looking for are their horses," Nero said to me. He took out a machete he had on his belt and started twirling it. I had one as well.

"They have four of them. We have irradiated ones you might've seen in the plaguelands, and they have them in the blacksands too, but the real ones are only here and the Dead Islands. They treasure them."

"At least they did have them here," I said with a smirk. Nero returned my ominous smirk and opened the sack he was carrying for the squirrel. "Have you ever eaten horse?"

Nero nodded. "Whenever exotic animals die we usually get to eat them. Kind of tastes like... I don't know, kind of like bosen. I don't feel like spending all night here gutting it. I just want the head and we can take as much as we can carry and leave the rest for the carracats, the wolves, and the lions."

"I think we should just kill everything," I said, my eyes now sweeping the trees as we carried on down the path. "I want to eat a carracat."

"Nah, we love kitties."

"Yeah, but Adler will squirm like a bitch if we threaten one of those bat cats in front of the cam. It'd be worth it."

"No. We love kitties."

I rolled my eyes. "Them loving cats just means it would get a reaction out of them." I narrowed my eyes and nodded ahead. "I think we're getting to one of the fields we saw. Any idea where the horses are?"

Nero shook his head. "No, but they'll probably be happy to see people. They haven't been fed in three days."

And I haven't seen Killian in two days. I'd been done playing Adler's game a long time ago and now I just wanted those assholes off of my land.

We hadn't turned the webcam back on and they hadn't tried to contact us either. We'd debated shutting the generators off, but for all we knew they had backup power for the laboratories so we didn't bother.

"Eventually Mantis needs to wake up and he'll do something about this," Nero said. I started sprinting ahead and he followed me. I wanted to get to the clearing. "But, then again, Adler could've shot him in the head knowing Mantis would tell him to stop acting like an idiot."

"Most likely. He's a real immature thirty-year-old." I shook my head and we both ran into the clearing.

"Hah!" Nero stopped and pointed a finger. I looked in the direction and on a bed of emerald grass and further on, stakes with vines propped up, I saw the horse.

"Wow," I said under my breath. I took my M16 out and stepped off of the trail. As soon as I started walking through the green grass I saw hoppers jumping around in all directions. "It's so big! What a majestic, beautiful, stunning creature, surely created by God." I raised my M16, clicked it to automatic, and pressed down on the trigger.

I could hear Nero's laughter over the sharp cracks of gunfire. The horse jumped, explosions erupting on its brown body with small craters being left behind. It reared back and started running away from us, but it only got four meters away before its back legs gave out. I started sprinting towards it with a grin on my face as it fell to the ground in a heap of thrashing limbs, a loud squeal coming out of it.

"You got the first shot. Lemme finish it off!" Nero called behind me.

"Yeah, fuck you!" I called back, and when I heard Nero run faster, no doubt trying to catch up to me. I poured on the speed as well, and before I even slowed down, I pointed the gun at the horse's head. Its eyes wide and rolling around in its head, the whites exposed from fear.

I shot it in the eye, but just as my finger pressed on the trigger, Nero barrelled into me and I flew off my feet. I landed on my back, the M16 in one hand, and as I got to my feet with a grin, a loud thunderclap sounded, and echoed off of the ridges.

"Bitch was already dead. You fuck!" Nero unsheathed a long machete, but when he turned to me I saw his eyes widen.

"Okay, Duck, you cut off its head," he said, and as he ran past me, he gave me a wink.

I turned around suspiciously. I looked past the running idiot and saw what he'd seen… another horse. This one was brown with white splotches and was nervously sprinting away from us.

I ran after him, no way was I going to let him have this one all to himself. I knew I could run faster than him, I was bred for it, so I drew up every stamina reserve I had and caught up with him.

Then I remembered I was a sentry, a sniper. I fell back and brought the scope up to my eye and got the horse into the crosshairs – just as Nero raised his hunting rifle.

I swore loudly when I heard the gunshot go off, and more expletives spilled from my mouth when the horse went down like a sack of bricks. I gritted my teeth, and because he was Nero, he held both hands up in the air, the rifle still in one of them, and *whooped*.

I aimed, not at the horse, but several feet from him. I let a single shot rip, and a chunk of grass flew up in the air, right behind the showboating brute chimera.

Nero flipped me off with a shit-eater grin, but when I brought my scope up to my eye and pulled the trigger again, he lowered it just in time.

"Hey, I felt the heat of that one, assfuck!" Nero called, and then he reached into his belt and pulled out the machete he'd been carrying. He waved it around in his free hand. "I got this one. You get the other one. We'll *Godfather* the fuck out of them. Get some meat too."

"Roger!" I called and turned around to head back to the horse I had killed. Admittedly though, my head was turning me in every direction trying to find something else to shoot. The field stretched on for a good half-mile in all directions. I could see the cabin off in the distance surrounded by fruit trees and even a little fence, I'm guessing to keep animals out of their garden. This place was unreal, literally unreal, this shit just didn't exist in our time anymore, unless you were in Skyfall, I guess.

I approached the horse and kicked its head with my boot. I sheathed my M16 and brought out the machete and poked its bulging stomach a few times. It looked like they had a lot of guts inside of them.

Because morbid curiosity would always be my downfall, I raised the machete and slashed its stomach. The razor sharp blade sliced right through, leaving a fissure of white tissue in the opening. I kicked it with my boot and slashed it again, and then a second time.

On the third time I saw a piece of pink intestine appear, gravity pushing it out of the slash. I was amazed with how big it was, I did one last swipe and had to quickly jump back when the laceration burst, spilling intestines and organs down onto the green grass, barely missing my boots.

The smell was alluring. There was something about the smell of something fresh and dead that got to me. I got down on my knees and started sifting through the warm intestines, enjoying playing autopsy as I identified each larger than life organ.

I found myself needing to close my eyes, my instincts were starting to get away from me. I had been too busy joking around with Nero to enjoy taking the life of this rare creature, and I wanted to satiate the bloodlust that was starting to parch my throat.

I swallowed and rose, then started hacking off the horses head. That didn't help though, every low *thunk* of the machete against the horse's neck, and the continuous flow of the perfumy blood, only made it worse. And soon I was looking behind me, and to where we had been to try and find something else to kill.

Something big, like the horse. I looked down, and with one last chop, I severed the last of its spine. I sliced through it and kicked the horses head to the side. Then I got down on my knees and ran my hand along the cooling red meat. I could feel my heart pounding now, pumping hot water through me, and pooling in all the wrong places.

Or the right places.

"Have you gotten to the meat yet?" I suddenly heard Nero call.

My head jerked towards Nero.

And as I slowly got to my feet, Nero stopped in his tracks, the horse's head balanced on his shoulders.

Nero's eyebrows raised. "Well, that's an interesting look on you..." he said and took a step back. "Let's go... find something else to kill."

I lowered my head and started walking towards this six foot five brute chimera. This challenge that would satisfy the uncontrollable instincts inside of me that was demanding for me to take a life in the most gruesome way possible.

My mind shot a direct feed of images into my brain, and I was once again reminded just who this chimera was. It made a grin come to my lips, and I broke into a run.

But to my anger, Nero didn't run. He dropped the machete onto the ground, raised his hands, and did the 'come here' motion towards himself.

I swung the machete at his head, but he was quicker than his appearance made him out to be, Nero ducked and grabbed the nape of my neck, and pulled me off of my feet.

I was brought to the ground with a snarl, and before I could flip myself up to standing, a boot slammed down onto my chest, and another one on the hand clenching the machete. He reached down and grabbed the machete and threw it, then removed his boot.

"Make it a fair fight," he said lowly, and stepped away from me as I jumped to my feet.

"Like you fucking did?" I snarled back, a growl now sounding as I slowly walked a circle around him. "Don't preach fair to me, Goose."

"Duck and Goose, I like it," Nero said, not taking his eyes off of me. He moved with me as I walked around him, his arms out and ready for my next attack. "Come on, bro, don't let all that bloodlust go to waste. Take it out on me. I–"

I ran at him, and when he reached out to grab me, I skidded like I was stealing third base, right underneath his swinging arms. In a flash, I was on my feet, and jumping towards his back.

My eyes fixed on his neck, partially covered with black hair starting to curl away from the nape. With it in my sights, I opened my mouth; and when I was close enough, I leaned down and bit into the side of his neck, my arms grabbing onto his shoulders to steady myself.

"What's with you fucks and necks?" Nero bellowed. I kneaded my teeth into the skin, and when the skin broke and the blood spilled into my mouth, my mind lit up like an exploded firework.

Chimera blood. I started gnawing at his neck, desperate for more. Timothy's blood was nothing compared to this, this was something else entirely. It was aromatic, bursting with a flavour that I felt an immediate addiction to. It had such a powerful hold on me, I completely lost my bearings. I forgot that I was in the middle of a fight, and my body did too, because I felt the spring of desperation quickly morph itself into lust.

And he knew – that fuck knew. Nero grabbed me by my hair and wrenched my mouth away from his neck. He pushed me off and turned around, my hair still in his hands, then he wrenched my head up and locked our lips together.

My body was overcome with lust, the blood mixing in with the chimera thirst making a dangerous concoction. Without a single prompt from his lips, mine opened, and our tongues picked up right where they'd left off several days ago on the top floor of the mansion.

Except he wasn't being controlled by a parasite, and I wasn't trying to distract him.

And, unlike now, I didn't have a hard cock pulsing with heat between my legs.

I closed my eyes, Nero's hands everywhere and mine were too. I slid them up his shirt and his slid down my cargo pants. I didn't feel him unbutton them, but I felt him grab my cock and pull it out. A moan resonated in my throat, the sound of it lost from his tongue deep in my mouth, and our heavy breathing accelerating with every minute. The next thing I knew he was sliding his hand up and down it, each stroke feeling like the antidote to a third degree burn.

Then, like what had happened many times before…

… my reality was taken from me.

"Make him cum, Kiki."

"That's right, my little fuck-boy." I could hear that taunting laugh, so close to my ears I cringed from the heat of his breath. Worse still, the burning lust controlling me like a puppet disappeared, and like an avalanche, the anxiousness, the shame, the humiliation came back. It stuck to me like a bad stink, sinking into all crevices of my skin and entering my body to contaminate all good feelings I had managed to cultivate since I'd escaped from that bedroom.

Then the climax, the feeling that I knew would set me over the edge, the pressure between my legs that lit the firecrackers that were strung throughout my body. The one that had woken me from the dead, and had sent me to the white flames.

"All virgins bleed," I heard him hiss in my ear.

I gasped, and when I felt his tongue still in my mouth, and the scent of him all around me, I wrenched away from him and stumbled backwards. My hand went to my chest as it tightened like drying leather, and I took in a sharp inhale.

But no air entered my lungs.

"Reav?"

My eyes shot up to him and I saw Nero standing over me. His jacket covered in blood, his hands too, and a glisten of saliva on his lips which I knew was my own.

I was hyperventilating, I knew what was coming. I had to get away from there as quickly as I could. I had to go somewhere, some place dark. I needed to fix myself. Why wasn't I fucking fixed yet?

After that was just flashes and blurs. I was running up the trail, then through the gate, but I didn't fully get a hold of reality until I was in Adler's room with the door closed and the lights off. By now I was drenched with sweat, taking in gasping wheezes, and feeling like I was going insane. The room was closing in on me – no, the world was closing in on me. It was becoming smaller and smaller, pressing up against my body and crushing me. I had to get fresh air, no, no, I had to stay where it was dark and enclosed. No, I needed, I needed… drugs, no, alcohol, no, no I needed to just fucking die.

This was it. I was broken. If I wasn't broken before, now proved it. I didn't know what I was more pissed at myself for: making out with Nero, or that fucking PTSD flashback ambushing me during the act, just like when I was with Killian, then sending me into another panic attack, another god damn tailspin.

I thought that asshole was supposed to help me fix this shit? If making out with me and pulling on my cock was his solution, then he was a fucking retard. Oh, what the fuck did I expect from Nero?

Killian is going to kill me, but at this rate I'll have killed myself first.

My eyes shut, and my teeth locked so tight that the familiar squeaking could be heard. I waited for the crack and the shard of tooth, but instead my mouth opened and I let out a scream so loud I was sure Melchai heard it.

I slammed my fists against the wall, and as scream after scream rolled from my lips, I trashed everything I could get a hold of that I hadn't already previously broken. I was done. I was so fucking done with this. I was finished with not being in control of anything. No wonder I couldn't control Killian, I didn't even know how to handle myself anymore.

Ever since Nero... ever since that asshole took my fucking power away. And what does he want me to do? Take it back? How the fuck can I take back what he stole? I don't even have enough of me left to hate him, and yet he still haunts me at every step. How can I take anything from him?

Well, what did he take from you?

I looked at the floor, the room echoing with the sounds of my ragged breathing.

He took from me something that... I didn't know was possible to take.

He made me feel violated, and no one had ever made me feel that way before. I hated myself because I felt like such a... little bitch for having such a reaction to some physical act. That was what he took from me, he took my ability to feel unbreakable.

You gave him that power to take.

I know.

Well, go get it back.

How? Kill him? He won't fucking care. Rape him? Still wouldn't fucking care.

Why does everything have to be solved with violence? Take it back a different way.

I laughed out loud at myself. "I'm a chimera," I mumbled. "Everything has to be won with violence. Even Elish's solution for me was to go and kill. Too bad killing just makes me horny, and I can't even satisfy that without seeing and feeling Nero fucking me."

Elish, as Nero pointed out, is just like you. He doesn't know any other way but manipulation and violence. Nero does.

I opened my eyes and turned to the closed door. My mouth went dry as I thought back to what Nero had told me yesterday, everything he had told me.

"Reaver baby... do you have any idea how powerful you would be... if you got rid of those weaknesses and made them one of your most powerful strength?"

Jesus fuck.
I know what I had to do.

I opened the door and walked out of Adler's room. My breathing had slowed sometime during my time in darkness but now my heart was racing. The mansion surrounding me was becoming dark as evening set in, but I could see a single light on in the living room.

My mind was screaming at me to not do it. What little was left of the prideful, yet weak, creature I had become was clawing at the inside of my brain, shrieking, no, begging me, begging me not to do it.

I have to do it.

I don't have a choice.

It was like an epiphany of foreboding. That grim gnawing in your gut that you get when you know the solution to the question that had been plaguing you, and the solution was the very last thing you wanted to do. But you knew, yeah you knew, it was the right one. The only one.
Killian.

*I don't want to do this, and please, fucking please, Killi Cat.
Forgive me.*

And you will. I know you will. Because who you remember me being, the man who pulled you from that factory, the man who crossed the northern greywastes to get you... will be the next person you see.

I promise.

I stood underneath the archway to the living room, and saw Nero sitting on one of the chairs, fucking playing a handheld poker game.

Last chance to back out.

BACK OUT!

Fuck you. You cowardly piece of shit, you bitch that would like nothing more than to see me suffer. Shut the fuck up.

And that screaming voice inside my head did just that.

"Nero," I said. A static electricity, starting from my toes and fingers, slowly travelled through my body, before gathering like a transformer on a power pole. It burned brightly inside of me, and took away the pounding heartbeat, the sweat gathering on my brow, and all of my doubts.

And it left nothing behind but a cold resolve.

Nero glanced up at me, but he only looked back down at his game for a split-second before he did a double take. "Yeah...?" he said slowly.

"Get up. We're having sex."

Nero stared at me, then looked past me as if expecting the people from *Candid Camera* to be hiding in the hallway.

"Are you serious?"

"I won't be in about three seconds if I don't see you on your feet and walking to the fucking bedroom," I snapped. "Do I have to spell it out for you? Are you really that—"

"Okay, okay!" Nero got to his feet. Both of his hands raised in his own defense. "I just needed to take a moment to make sure I didn't suffer a stroke." He then walked up to where I was standing and I saw a flash of a coy smirk. The look every man had, either internally or externally, when they knew they were about to get some.

I turned around and roughly shoved him, for no other reason than I was pissed off it came to this.

Nero paused, and right when I started walking past him, he put an arm around me and roughly drew me to his side. He kissed my cheek and licked it, before I managed to pull away.

I wasn't going to take the bait. I stalked into the bedroom and started taking off my clothes. When I saw Nero was as well, I turned around and stared at the curtain-covered window, absolutely seething.

"I've never had someone so pissed off after demanding I have sex with him," Nero said bemused. I heard his drug tin come out, then with purposely slow movements, he handed me a glass pipe with a small rock in the center. "Remember ciovi? It'll help."

I shook my head, still staring at the curtains. "I need to be sober for this," I said. "When you're afraid of heights, you defeat that fear by climbing up something high, not watching a movie of someone else doing it. I can't have anything blocking me from doing this, or it won't work."

"You sure?"

I nodded. "Weakness into strength."

"I have never fucking respected you more, brosy." And with that, I felt him slowly kiss my neck.

Automatically, I scrunched up and became rigid. Nero chuckled at this and kissed my neck again. "I'm not fucking Medusa; you don't need to turn to stone. Go lay on the bed."

I sighed and ran both of my hands down my face. I still had my boxers on, so I wasn't feeling nearly as freaked out as I would be in about ten minutes, but as soon as I sat by the head of the bed, my heart started to go insane.

And when Nero turned off the lights, leaving only Adler's lamp on his study across the room, the anxiety hit me.

I saw Nero approach and stand at the foot of the bed, also still wearing boxers, blue ones. He crossed his arms and chuckle. "You're so cute. You have no idea how cute you look." He crawled onto the bed, and as my ears started to catch on fire, he laid down beside me and slid his hand over to the side of my face.

Weakness into strength.

I closed my eyes and let him direct my face to his, without wasting a moment, he opened his lips, and I did mine, and the tongue that was now familiar to me, met my own.

And because it was something that was now familiar, in a sense that extended past that bedroom in Cardinalhall, I started to feel my tightly wound body loosen.

"There we go," Nero whispered when our lips momentarily broke. "Just keep those eyes closed." I knew why he was saying that when I felt his hand rest on my hip bone, before sliding down to my stomach, then to my navel. He started slowly stroking it with his hand, those lips and that tongue still distracting me.

I pulled away from him when his roving hand slipped underneath my boxers; the blowtorch on my ears got white hot and it acted like fuel being directly injected into my heart.

"Relax," Nero whispered. He took my hand which was digging into the sheets, and placed it on his neck. "You're not chained up, remember that." Then he slid his hand right where it had been previously, but this time he ran two fingers down my cock.

Fuck. I was hard. I don't know if I was expecting that. I took in another deep breath and tried to loosen my body and accept his touch. I hadn't started going into my own head, so, so far, so good.

Nero joined our lips again, and this time when his hand travelled out of my pants he put it on my shoulder and lightly pushed me down onto my back. I let him, but found both hands covering my face.

And I kept them on my face when I felt him slip my boxers off. The colder air hit my cock but a moment later... I felt his tongue lick the tip.

I sucked in a breath and let him separate my legs. At the signal that I hadn't snapped yet, the tongue I felt got bolder and started licking the rim of my head, then those familiar lips closed over the crown, and that even more familiar tongue started caressing and rubbing it in slow circles.

That... fucking felt good. I let a heavy breath fall from my lips as the feeling took me. It had been a long time since I'd felt any sexual pleasure. What small bits I had managed to get with Killian were soon ripped from me like I was getting a bucket of ice water tossed onto my body.

And he was doing it different than when he and Kiki were fucking with me. Nero was taking it slow, testing his tongue along every curve, tracing the slit and the sensitive skin underneath the head, then running his fingers along the shaft and grasping it with just the right amount of pressure.

It had been a long time since I had cum, not counting what had happened after Kiki rescued us since I was too in psychosis to enjoy it. Nero knew this, and every time my breathing started to quicken, and that tightening pleasurable tension began to gather, he'd slow down, before he stopped altogether and moved down to my balls.

Then he grabbed onto my legs with both hands and encouraged me to separate them. My throat went dry at this, but it wasn't what I was expecting.

"No, no!" I pulled back when I felt his tongue lick my left cheek. "You're not doing that."

I looked down and saw Nero smirking at me. "Lay back down."

"You're not doing that!"

"Lay back down. It'll make what's happening later easier. Trust me."

I swore and threw my hands over my face again. Nero chuckled, and I felt his tongue tease my hole.

I'd done this to Killian, but never – never – had I ever let him do it to me. It was another on my 'never going to let you do it' lists. No, I didn't have a solid reason why. I fucking loved doing it to him, it was just... not me.

And least it *wasn't* me.

"Why the hell does that feel so good?" I gasped. Every lap of his tongue against it almost had as much pleasure as when he was licking my cock. I didn't understand it, it didn't make sense. I knew Killian made the most sexiest of noises when I was doing it to him, but that kid made those noises at anything I did to him.

"See? Trust me," Nero said, and his tongue returned to where it had been. Honestly, I didn't want him to talk anymore, it felt too good.

I hated it, but wow. I soon found my hand resting on my inner thigh, the other one dug into my navel, and as the pleasure intensified with every lick, every tensing then loosening of his tongue, my fingernails burrowed into my own flesh.

And when it was too much for me, my hand slipped to my cock and I started playing with it.

Then that fuck smacked my hand away. I growled and clenched my teeth, but withdrew my hand without comment. I was relaxed and riding on cloud nine right now. I was happy enjoying the feelings drawing up pressure inside of me, I could be content with that.

But then I heard him suck on his fingers. I knew what was coming and I opened my eyes. "No. Lube. Give me that at least."

Nero, with his middle finger in his mouth, nodded and rose. He beelined it for Adler's desk and came back with a bottle of lube and a bottle of what looked like rum. He took a swig of the rum and handed it to me.

I was about to pass on it but one sip wouldn't fuck with me. I took a long swig of the throat burning liquid, and as it seared my throat... I felt him start to push a finger against my hole.

I distracted myself with the bottle and took a second shot, and right as I swallowed it down, Nero slid the finger inside.

He groaned. "Puppy, you're fucking tight. You're gonna kill me."

I didn't answer him. I had a bottle between my lips but I was biting down on the rim instead of drinking the alcohol inside. My breathing had quickened in a matter of seconds, the first spring of apprehension starting to take me.

I felt his mouth on the head of my cock, cold now from the alcohol. There was no teasing this time, he went right to work on me, one hand on the shaft to hold it up, the other sliding his middle finger in and out.

I didn't like the rhythm. It was making me uneasy. It was digging up too many buried feelings. I didn't like the back and forth, the in and out.

My body started to twist and my face became tight.

"You're going to snap my finger off. Ease up," Nero said. I felt his lips remove themselves from my cock and greet my neck instead. "Relax for fuck sakes."

"Shut up," I said through clenched teeth. Then, just to prove to me he was an asshole, Nero pushed in a second finger. I gritted my teeth, and without realizing it, I grabbed onto my head and gripped my hair. My body was writhing now, and the shallow pool of anxiety was starting to grow bigger. "You're not going to fucking get me to relax, just fuck me and get it over with."

He groaned at this. "Oh? Are you gonna beg me first?"

"I'm not playing this game," I snapped. "Just fuck me already!"

Nero grabbed the side of my head and drew me in for a kiss, then, with a forceful jerk of my right leg, he raised it up and bent it back.

My heart skipped and I pulled away from him, ice and fire both running rampant throughout my body. My face burned, my chest froze, and both of these sensations combined to make a hurricane currently destroying me from the inside out.

I immediately regretted my fucking mouth. Nero put a hand on my chest when I tried to raise it, and pushed it down like I was a kitten who'd just jumped onto the counter. He slid behind my leg until he was kneeling between them, and I saw a hungry look in his eye that smacked the recollections right back into my head.

And I realized sometime during all of this, he'd lost his boxers. Kneeling in front of me, completely naked, was who I now realized was the first chimera I actually feared. Not any more though, our time in this mansion had erased that fear, or it had... it had anyway.

But it was all coming back, and this wasn't some PTSD shooting into me and scrambling my hold on reality, this was fucking reality, this was happening.

"Hey." Nero grabbed my chin. "Don't put your hands on your head, you're not bound. I told you, put them on my shoulders were you can see them."

I don't think I could do this. I felt like he was telling me to hold my breath before he pushed me into the ocean with weights bound to my ankles, expecting me to somehow survive it. Time would fix me, this wouldn't, this was just going to fucking make me more–

"Hey!" Nero smacked my cheek. "Weakness into strength. You're fucking fine. Stop acting like a little bitch."

My eyes shot up to him, and for a moment the anger replaced every ounce of anxiety. I reached up and fucking smacked him right back. Nero's face flinched just slightly, but instead of dealing me a punch to the eye like I was expecting, he grabbed my hand and put it on his side.

He poured some lube onto his palm and slid it up and down his cock, just as long and thick as I'd remembered it being. I kept trying to steady my breathing, but I couldn't; it was grabbing me and dragging me where I didn't want to go.

Nero leaned over me and took my other hand, he put it on my leg and even though it was the last thing I wanted to do, I pulled my leg back. My chest was rising and falling rapidly, and my body both the surface of the sun and pluto – but I knew I had to do this.

Weakness into strength.

This is just some physical act which you let have power over you. So take the power back.

Become, not just the person you were before, but something better, something stronger. Don't just drain the infection, Reaver, gild the wound in steel. Take your biggest weakness, and make it into one of your strongest attributes.

I nodded, and with my teeth chewing the bottom of my cheek, I slid a hand behind Nero's back and drew him in. Our lips locked, and he lowered himself onto me. I could feel his strong, muscular body envelop mine, closer than I would've ever felt comfortable before. And as quickly as the sparks of unease came, I cauterized them, and used his lips as a distraction.

"There we go," Nero murmured when our mouths briefly broke apart. I closed my eyes so I didn't have to see how close he was to me, how his entire body was inches from my own, and prepared myself for what I knew was about to happen.

I drew in a deep breath when I felt his cock first push against the opening. I held it in my chest and dug my fingertips into his shoulders. I'd felt this mixture of pressure and pain with him many times previously, but this time it would be different. It would be different.

The breath slowly blew out of my mouth, and I forced my body to relax. I felt Nero drizzle more lube onto both me and him, and then the pressure returned.

Then the head broke through and he was in me. I was immediately assaulted by that fiery pressure and the overwhelming sense of girth. I threw my head back and gasped, but when I tried to inhale another breath, I found my chest had become a locked box. This brought more panic to me, and before I could attempt to calm myself down, I realized I was already pushing him off of me, and I was yelling.

I didn't even realize I had started yelling. In my head I was attempting to breathe but my mind was already ten steps ahead of me, screaming at him to get off of me.

"You're fine!" Nero said through heavy breathing. He pushed my chest down, and like a small elastic band being stretched too tightly, I felt another overabundance of pressure and on its heels: pain. Lots of pain.

"Get off!" I screamed. My arms were up again, pushing and pushing, desperation now fully soaked into my skin like the sweat I realized I was drenched in. "Enough. Stop!"

"Reaver!" Nero grabbed my chin and wrenched my head up. He locked his eyes with me. "Listen to me... are you listening? Shut up and listen. You're fine."

"Fuck off," I gasped, my face scrunched in pain. I looked around the dimly lit room just to keep reminding myself that I was in the mansion and not in Cardinalhall. It did something to ease the tremors rattling through me, but not enough to keep my mouth from opening in a soundless scream.

With one last push he was fully inside of me, but then almost immediately he pulled himself out. I closed my eyes with relief as the pressure suddenly dissipated, but then he slid it back inside, with ease this time.

This time the burning wasn't as extreme. I let Nero hold back my legs and put both of my hands around his back. I looked at the ceiling, seeing Nero's neck, ear, and his black hair in the left horizon of my vision.

"Relax," Nero groaned. "Or don't. Fuck, you're like a tight fist."

Relax? I remember telling Killian the same when I felt him tensing around my own cock during our first time. But it was hard to do when someone was skewering you with something that was three quarters the width of a coke can.

He slowly pulled it out and eased it back in, his heavy breathing in my ear like it had been before. But he was never this slow with me during my time as his prisoner, he was a relentless machine hammering into me with growls, grunts, physical blows, and the overpowering stink of cigars and cigarettes.

I didn't realize he'd lowered his head until he took my left pec into his mouth, and it was there, with the bud in his lips, that I felt my body start to slowly unwind.

"That's your spot, eh? We all have one," Nero said, before his lips tightened around the nipple and he pulled it. Then his hand removed itself from my leg and he pinched the left pec with his fingers.

I hated how good it felt and I hated how audible I was about it. I couldn't help it though, Nero knew his stuff and he was determined to find, and exploit, every one of my sensitive spots.

Even ones I hadn't even realized I had.

Something else was happening too. The pain of him inside of me, it was disappearing. The pressure was still there, but I no longer felt like he was trying to disembowel me.

And, maybe, it was actually starting to feel good.

A groan slipped from my lips, and more followed. Soon, with every push of his hips, I was making small noises.

"There we go," Nero whispered. He licked my neck and nipped it, and his thrusts started to accelerate. I had been worried that the rhythmic motion would trigger something inside of me, but the quicker his movements, the more I found myself enjoying the sensation.

I could do this. I am doing this.

Nero sped up, and the sounds of our skin smacking together was added to the groans now rolling from both of our tongues. The kissing had stopped and the verbal back and forths had too. We were now deep into it. Me with my hands on his shoulders and side, and Nero with my legs firmly in his grasp, legs that were being pushed further and further back as he tried to get more of himself inside of me.

I swore, the feeling an overwhelming mixture of pressure and pleasure. There was no more pain but the occasional sting, and I was almost ashamed with how much I was enjoying the feeling of having something inside of me. I never knew that being on the receiving end could be just as good as being the top. There was something inside of there that made it feel fucking amazing, and I think I might've been missing out.

Then I made the mistake of looking underneath his chest, to where we were joined.

And I saw the blood.

All of a sudden panic ripped through me, without any notification or sign of its coming. It hit me like a cattle prod to the chest, and my reaction was just as swift as its current.

"Get off of me!" I screamed. I tried to pull back with a loud bellow… but to my horror I only felt him wrap a hand around my neck.

"Stay still," Nero growled. It wasn't in the tone he'd been using with me before, it was low, hostile, and one that told me I no longer had a say in what was going on.

Terror flooded me.

"Get off!" I yelled. I tried to shift myself away from him but his hips kept relentlessly driving into me, forcing more pressure into my body. He didn't stop, no matter how much I screamed at him, and when I made a fist and punched him, he grabbed it and held it behind my head.

Nero chuckled and kissed my cheek. I squirmed and screamed so loud my voice broke. I inhaled, only to feel my lungs unable to accommodate the pressure and panic. It was building; I didn't know what was going to happen but…

What if I was releasing radiation right now? We didn't have Geigerchips, we wouldn't know.

"Nero… Nero… I'm going to blow the fucking mansion up if you keep this…. FUCKING STOP!" I shouted, but he kept my hands locked behind my head. I didn't even realize he was no longer holding my legs; I was too stunned and in a frenzy to do anything about it. "Nero!" I shouted.

"I said fucking stop! Something's happening." More pressure was gathering. I could feel it being drawn from the room and centering in my chest, each thrust bringing more and more into me.

I was an idiot, a fucking idiot for trusting Nero. This is what I get for being desperate enough to trust the man who raped me. I waved fresh meat in front of a chimera's face, and I was getting exactly what I deserved.

The pounding continued, faster and faster. I could smell blood now, and when I opened up eyes I didn't even realize I'd closed again, I saw the roof of Cardinalhall.

"Nero!" I yelled, my voice broken shards of glass. His body was drenched in sweat now, and so was I. All I could hear was the smacking of our skin and my own screaming, and all I could feel was pressure and gathering tension.

Then his laughing, his taunting – fucking – laugh.

All virgins bleed.

"Nero!" I screamed.

No, fight it, fucking fight it. Fucking, FIGHT IT!

But I couldn't control what was happening inside of me.

"What, puppy?"

What? What!?

I let out a scream of frustration, but it was no longer directed at Nero, it was directed at me. My confusing storm of emotions was filling me with many feelings, but the one that kept rising to the surface was one of unbelievable anger. I was angry that I was trying to quit. I was angry that I'd taken it this far only to back out now. I was angry that I even had to do this.

But I was doing it, and I had to force myself to make it to the end. I was stronger than this. I would conquer this as I had conquered and perfected so many other faults I had inside of me.

This is only one stop on my never ending road, one bump, and ten thousand years from now I'll look back at this time and laugh at myself for being so weak.

I might be many things – but I was not weak.

I was the one in control.

I was the fucking one in control!

I let out what could only be described as a battle cry, and then through clenched teeth, I grabbed onto the sanity trying to slip from me, and I didn't let it go.

"Fuck me harder!" I cried. I found my lips tensing and I realized I was grinning. I don't know why. I didn't know if it was because my mind was breaking. All I knew was that I wasn't going to let this fucking bullshit take me any longer. I controlled my own mind. I controlled my own body and I controlled what I reacted to.

Not Nero.

Not the psychosis inside of me.

Or the wussy bitch I'd become.

"Fuck me!" I yelled again. I sunk my teeth onto Nero's shoulder, and as I heard him bellow, his thrusts increased.

And the pressure inside of me suddenly reached critical, and with a gasping, loud groan, my hands went between my legs and I started stroking my own cock.

"Fuck!" I cried. I looked down, my eyes wide open and my breathing heavy, and I saw the first spurt of cum fall from my fully hard cock. I didn't even realize it was hard until I was viciously pumping myself between my legs.

I dropped my head onto the mattress and cried out, suddenly and swiftly feeling the confusing pressure that I'd felt building, translate into orgasmic pleasure. A different type of orgasm, this one was rooted deep inside of me, one that had me bearing down instead of tensing up. It felt… oh fuck, it felt good. I let it roll through me like an earthquake, and when it finally started to fade, I was panting and desperately trying to catch breath in my burning lungs.

Nero was groaning heavily in my ear, and I felt his cock tense and contract as he came. We became one sweaty body in that moment, two men who at one point hated each other, now locked together and sharing the weirdest of bonds.

When both of our orgasms had faded, Nero slowly pulled his cock out, just a small amount of blood on it, nothing like what it had been before, and then laid down on his side with his head propped up by his hand.

I kept staring at my now half-hard dick, the corners of my vision shining. "That was intense." I shook my head and laid my head back down onto the bed, and wiped my hands down my face. My breathing was still catching in my throat, my lungs on fire, but the anxiety… the anxiety had disappeared with the pressure from the orgasm.

I think… I think I felt… better.

I did. Holy fuck. It wasn't that bad… I actually don't think it was that bad. I could do this, even with Nero's stamina I could do this. I could survive it if I was ever dominated again.

This hadn't been a mistake – I might've just found myself a golden ticket.

"Nero…" I said. I looked over at him, he was looking pleased with himself.

"Yes, Ducky?"

I found the side of my mouth rising into a smirk, and through a pounding heart I said to him:

"Is that really all you got?"

CHAPTER 36

Killian

THE FIRST INHALE I TOOK DURING MY THIRD TIME resurrecting was one that filled my lungs with frigid cold. The shock of it made me gasp and cough, then my eyes opened to figure out just what the hell was happening.

It was dark, it was dark and my body was freezing. I shifted around and felt ice underneath me and when I tried to sit up my head smacked up against something hard.

Panicked, I put my hands up against the ceiling only five inches above my head. The first terrifying thought was that I had been buried, but although my mind was on a runaway road, careening fast and picking up terror like speed, my mind allowed me to come to the actual conclusion:

I was in a fucking freezer.

I started pounding on the cold plastic, claustrophobia rooting itself deep inside of me and drawing out a phobia I hadn't had a minute ago. My lungs took in another cold breath and I opened my mouth to scream.

Then suddenly I saw light, and the scream in my throat disappeared, replaced by shock as the bright lights above me stabbed my eyes.

"Well, that's rather unexpected," I heard a man say.

Without wasting any time, I jumped out of the freezer, and as I did I felt a hand grab a belt loop on my pants and help me out. I fell onto the floor and inhaled warm, stuffy air.

My eyes shot up before they widened.

In front of me… was Mantis.

He was still wearing the robe Reaver had shot him in, with a blue beater shirt and blue plaid boxer pants underneath – and he was looking down on me with a peculiar expression on his face.

Mantis looked to be in his mid-thirties, with dark hair several inches long, and a strong jaw and chin. He had vivid but narrow grey eyes and light stubble, and even though he looked unkempt I knew from just how he carried himself, and from our brief interactions at the festival, he was a strange yet proper man.

And not a chimera.

"So Elish has dispatched yet another tentacle into my home. In hopes for what?" He watched me intently as I got to my feet, his eyes analyzing every detail of my face.

He didn't look that happy to see me, that was for sure. "I am not one to divulge sensitive information freely. So though I suspect who you are, I will not say it out loud in case I am mistaken. So I will ask you this… who made you?"

"I'm not a chimera," I said flatly.

"I know," Mantis replied back, his tone cold. "I asked who made you, boy."

Already he was rubbing me the wrong way. "Kristin and Jeffrey Massey made me," I said, throwing his tone back at him. I braced my feet and steadied my stance as his eyes travelled around me like a spotlight. "I'm a Tamerlan factory worker's son, and now a greywaster."

Like someone had clicked *smile* from a list of facial features for a robot, the corners of Mantis's mouth turned up, and with that new expression, the eyes that had been simultaneously digging out every detail of my face and body, became brilliant.

"Killian Massey. Yes, I suspected it was you, but I did want to make sure… such a pleasure to meet you." Mantis held out his hand. I stared at it for a moment before I took it and we shook.

But when I tried to retract it, he held on, and turned it so it was palm up.

Instinct told me to snatch it back and get it out of his firm grip, but I found myself too shocked at what he was doing. Because when he stared down at my palm I only saw Perish when he had done the same to Reaver's. A moment that would become burned into my memory, because we'd later find out that Perish wasn't a chimera at all, but Sky's twin brother.

And my boyfriend above me had the same palms as his.

My eyes closed for a brief moment when I felt Mantis trace his finger along my palm lines, but opened them when I heard a low laugh, then his release. "So many hidden gems embedded in this dead world and all you colour blind fools see is grey."

His words hit me, and an off-kilter feeling started to raise the hairs on the back of my neck. I took Mantis's own palm and looked at it, then at my own.

"No, Kaiser, you'll find no answers in my hand, unless you've defied the laws of science and have taken up palm reading," Mantis said, amused. He pulled back his hand and gave me a lip curling smirk. "I should've been paying more attention when I looked into those eyes at the festival. So Perish was successful then? You have broken free of the shackles that bind even the most strongest of men and have become an immortal?"

"Yes," I said. I glanced down at my own palm and wondered what he saw.

"And you're now immune to radiation too? Prolonged Concentrated Exposure was successful?"

I nodded, a brief recollection was gathered and delivered to the front of my mind as I remembered Perish mentioning Prolonged Concentrated Exposure. It was exactly what it sounded like, doses of concentrated sestic radiation right into your body until you develop an immunity. I suspected the ravers must have some sort of version of that, but with Jade's ravers maybe it was different.

"Fascinating," Mantis said with an odd smile. "So..." He took a step towards me and I took one back. "... tell me, Kaiser–" Why was he calling me that? "–who is above us? Was that Reaver who shot me?"

I glanced up at the ceiling and then to the closed metal door. I had been so distracted talking to this man that I hadn't even got my bearings.

I was still downstairs apparently. At least Mantis was awake, which meant an adult who knew chimeras could put a muzzle on the two bitches that had kept me, Ceph, and Kiki prisoner.

"He'll talk to you, he won't talk to Adler..." I let out a sigh of relief and walked to the metal door, I put my hand on the lever and turned it.

It was locked.

My attention shot back to Mantis and I saw his smile was gone, but when he saw the expression of fear on my face, he shook his head slowly.

"You're not locked in here with me, Killian," Mantis said in a tone

626

starting to dip into impassiveness. "We are locked in here together."

"Adler locked you in here?" I said. I gave the door handle one more try before sighing and walking back to the freezer. I sat on top of it. "Why would he do that to you?"

Mantis pointed to the ceiling. "I suspect it has something to do with the feet thumping around my mansion. Confirm it for me like I asked. Elish has come for my clone, hasn't he? I see no other explanation as to why his science experiments and the thick-headed brutes would show up at my doorstep for no reason."

"No," I said with a shake of my head. I drummed my feet against the side of the freezer. "We came to Melchai to escape the proxy worms." Mantis's gaze shot to me again, one that filled with even more interest. "We started hearing about Man on the Hill and Angel Adi. Reaver and I aren't stupid, we knew you guys were chimeras or similar. We got curious and went to the festival, and you know what happened next. Kiki begged for our help to free Nero and Ceph, and that's where you got shot and I got captured and killed by Angel Adi and his pitbull. Elish is back in Skyfall, apparently Jade is really ill and Elish won't leave his side. Elish doesn't even know..." I caught myself, but my politeness had died some point along the way and I didn't even try to make up a false trail as to where I was going with those last words. I let them hang and die on the air, then said, "You can keep Nero and Ceph, I don't give a flying fuck. I just want to leave with Reaver. We don't care about Adler, or what you're doing, or who you're hiding from."

Mantis fell silent but the expression on his face was loud enough to make up for it. It scanned me for any falsifications in my statement, but even though I wasn't lying, if I was he wouldn't know. I'd become quite good at the poker face and this man was no chimera, with no enhancements, or–

"Your heartbeat remained steady. So you're telling the truth," Mantis said amused.

Wait, what? "You're not a chimera," I said to him suspiciously. "How the hell would you know? You're just some Skyfaller Silas made immortal, right?"

Mantis leaned against the wall of the storage room we were both locked in and crossed his arms. "I suppose since you were nice enough to freely give me information, I will do the same to a point. I was the first artificially-created immortal. I was the one who Silas performed the first operation on, and after I was deemed a success it was done to the first generation. The same thing happened every time we had a breakthrough in implanting enhancements. I was their experimental specimen, and my reward was those very enhancements and an immortal life as a chimera psychiatrist. The only thing that differentiates me from chimeras are my genetics."

That was interesting, but it led to another question: "Why are you this far away in the north? And... with Sky's clone and a chimera?"

"And why are you?" Mantis smiled thinly. "Perish told me he was leaving you a quad full of his research. I assumed when you never arrived that you had been trapped inside and were burning. But no, not only are you safe, but you still remain near the explosion. Why is this?"

"Hiding from..." My words trailed and I realized he'd basically tricked me into answering the question I'd just asked him. "... from Silas."

"And Elish?"

"We're not..." I sighed and looked at my boots, streaked with wetness now from the freezer I'd jumped out of. "... we don't hate Elish. We just wanted to be..."

"... dead?"

"Just at peace and... to have some quiet."

Mantis nodded at this. "Some people love to play games, Kaiser, others would rather unplug the system and go outside for a while."

Unplug the system? I had to deflect my gaze as he said this. I'd said close to that in my own head many times when Asher the game player had come to Aras. It looked like Mantis had reached a conclusion that I'd come to rather quickly when I'd been forced into Silas's games. But... didn't that just mean...?

"We're not that different from the sounds of it," I said to him slowly, then I looked at the locked metal door. "It's too bad we got off on the wrong foot. A lot of this could've been avoided if we'd had this conversation before that festival. Maybe I could've convinced Reaver to let you keep those meatheads instead of him needing to settle a score."

"Settle a score?"

I knew then I'd said too much, but there were many reasons to hate Nero. I would never tell him what Nero did to Reaver, but I also didn't have to lie either. "Nero was the one who pulled the trigger on Lycos," I said. And it was true. It might've been Silas's orders but he was the one who shot his own brother. Reaver never mentioned hating him for that, but I'd never forgotten. "We weren't here to save him... we were here so we could have him to ourselves." Then I thought back to the festival. "What are you doing with proxy worms? You... were able to have Nero under your control. We were ambushed by them in the plaguelands."

Mantis's eyes brightened. "You were? Tell me everything. Where did you see them? How many?"

"Why are you implanting chimeras with them?" I asked first. "And what else are you doing here in this lab? I lived with Perish, I saw his splices. I know what you guys can do."

Mantis's brow furrowed at this before he raised a single dark eyebrow. "You catch on quickly. Very well, information for information. The worms' migratory patterns are of great interest to me. You must've found Calgary then?"

"Calgary? In what used to be Alberta?" I said, surprised. "That's hundreds of miles from where we were. I saw my first one in an old Wal-Mart off the highway, maybe fifty miles from the border, and we got swarmed by them that..." My voice trailed when Mantis's face dropped. "... that... that night."

He let out a nervous laugh that automatically stirred up an anxious feeling inside of me. "You must be mistaken... the radiation is too weak along these lines. They cannot survive unless they're implanted into immortals."

"They... followed us to our house, a few hours from Melchai. We saw them infect a whipwolf. Reaver says he saw this huge mass, two-storey's high, of dead animals moving south..."

Mantis paled, then he gave me the weirdest, stressed out smile. "Will you indulge me for a moment and get back into that freezer?" he said through pressed teeth. "I won't be long."

I knew just from his expression that what I'd just disclosed was something major, and though I didn't trust this man, I realized I wasn't at risk of being locked in the freezer; there wasn't even a lock on it.

And I think I knew what he was about to do...

So I opened the freezer, which I saw was full of meat wrapped in brown paper, and slid back in.

As soon as the door closed, a loud and extremely pissed off voice rang out.

"ADLER GET THE FUCK OVER HERE!" Mantis screamed.

I opened the freezer door. "How are you going to even explain how you know?"

"I've been lying to that little brat since he was ten. Close the damn freezer!"

I shut it with an eye roll, and waited to see if Adler would actually come. I was looking forward to Mantis getting a hold of him. He was a normal build, not strong and muscular like Greyson, but I'd seen Leo verbally rip Reaver's face off many times.

"What!" a faint voice could be heard, one I recognized as Adler.

"This is no longer about our issues. I must be let out now to deal with something imperative. You've made your point, Adler. Let me out," Mantis said sternly.

"Are you going to show me Perish's files?"

There was silence, but I think I could imagine the expression on Mantis's face. "We will discuss Perish's files when I take care of pressing matters."

"Then no."

"This isn't about those files, Adler."

"Then tell me who he is. Tell me where he is and why we can't go get him?"

"I told you, Adler. He's dead."

"Fuck you, Mantis."

"ADLER!" Mantis shouted. "This goes beyond your god damn delusions! He's dead and even if he isn't, he thinks you are!" This was fucking intriguing. I couldn't wait to tell Reaver what I was listening in on. I had no idea how all of these tidbits of information fit together but I had a feeling it all wound together into a really interesting tapestry. I wonder how much I could get out of Mantis, and more importantly, if we could use it as a future bargaining chip or blackmail.

"Adler!" Mantis yelled louder. "I... fine. Let me out, and I will look at Perish's files myself and tell you if–" I heard something slam against metal, once, twice, and a third time. "What the hell do you plan on doing? Keeping me down here forever? If my god damn horses starve or they hurt our cats, I swear on the Fallocaust I WILL WEAR YOUR FUCKING SKIN!"

Everything went silent after that, and then a minute or two later he lifted up the freezer door and stalked away from it.

"Who's he want information on?" I asked as I crawled out of the frozen coffin.

"None of your business," Mantis said in a flat tone. He kicked the door again before letting out a long string of expletives, followed by threats, towards Adler.

"Why don't you just lie?" I said as I got back onto the freezer. "You said you've been lying to him since he was ten. So lie some more."

"He's gotten smarter. I made the mistake of taking in a sick chimera and the fool has been teaching the boy logic and filling his head with intelligence ever since. The exact opposite of what I've been trying to do since finding him. Both Spike's teachings and my own un-teaching has recently come back to bite me in the ass. You idiots barging into my house has just been the icing on the cake that is my life currently."

"You've been purposely keeping him stupid?" I said slowly. I thought back to my boyfriend. Reaver was super intelligent when it came to surviving in the greywastes and fixing things, but he had trouble getting through books that didn't have pictures in it. "But why? The only reason I can think of is that you don't want him to know he's Sky's clone and he already knows about that, and he knows about the Dekker family."

"Long story," Mantis said acidically.

"Well, I don't see anything else for us to do."

Another look. "I trust you about as far as I can throw you, Kaiser. Your genetics will make you inclined to betray me, I'm sure."

"Yeah, those Tamerlan genetics are deadly."

Mantis said nothing, he only kicked the door again.

"For a scientist you're certainly not following scientific method very well. The experiment of *kicking the door* isn't producing results. So research why and come up with a new hypothesis instead of repeating your failed procedure," I said casually.

Mantis stopped and gave me a heated glare. I couldn't help but stifle a laugh. "Sorry," I said with a half-smile. "According to Reaver immortality has turned me into a 'huge bitch'. I've been enjoying not being terrified all the time a little too much."

"I remember the feeling," Mantis muttered, and he slid down to the cold linoleum floor. The searing look I had earned faded and one of concern took its place. "I have horses, slaves, carracats, lions, and my felicos, and two sociopaths who are probably torturing them as I speak to you. I've spent twenty years making Turris a paradise, and if that boy destroys my work I will bury him head first into the ground and sodomize him with a katana."

"I think Greyson and Leo both made threats like that," I said. I looked around the small freezer room, about seven by ten, but all there was was an air vent and even I wouldn't be able to fit through it. "Chimera kids seem to be impossible to raise."

"Which is why they started sending them out into the greywastes and surrogating them," Mantis mumbled. He started rubbing his left temple, looking exasperated. "My job in Skyfall was trying to curb their mental issues. I had some success. Skyfall would be in ruins without my psychological guidance."

"My chimera could use some psychological guidance," I said, and sighed over my own words. "I wouldn't be surprised if the reason Reaver hasn't blown up the house is because he and Nero keep killing each other." I leaned back and looked up at the ceiling. "How long was I resurrecting for?"

"I'm not sure. You were in the freezer when I myself woke up and I don't know what extent my own injuries were. I'm guessing two, maybe three, days," Mantis said.

We both looked up when we heard footsteps above us, and then a door slam.

My heart jumped when I heard the muffled sound of screaming, not just anyone's screaming…

"Reaver?" I cried. I jumped up onto the freezer and put my hands to the ceiling. "That's Reaver! He sounds…" I paused and my heart dropped. "He sounds like he's…"

Like he's going through another one of his… states.

My eyes brimmed and when I heard a crash, followed by another scream I started slamming on the ceiling. "Rea-" I yelped when suddenly Mantis grabbed the rim of my jeans and pulled me off of the freezer.

I was thrown off-balance, but before the floor met me I was caught and steadied. "Be quiet! Adler and Spike think you're dead and it's going to remain that way. You need to suffer in silence." I pulled myself from him and shoved him away, then climbed back onto the freezer, just so I could be close to Reaver.

I held onto myself enough to not cry out again, but the tears were running down my face. "Where are we below?" I whimpered.

"Adler's bedroom," Mantis replied, then he winced when we both heard a crash. "I decorated that room from furniture I recovered from a god damn mansion in Edmonton." Another crash, followed by a sigh from Mantis. "And there goes my China vase."

"This is more important than your vase!" I cried, before clamping a hand over my mouth to keep myself quiet. "He's been going into these... crazy states lately after something bad happened to him, and I'm not there to calm him down! Only fucking Nero, his worst enemy, is!"

"Crazed states, you say?"

I looked at him, he sounded interested in this. I nodded and wiped my eyes. "I can't tell you what happened, but something bad and he's been unstable ever since."

"Would you call it... a psychosis?"

"That's what he calls it."

"And... what caused this?" Mantis's eyes went bright again.

"Why does Adler want Perish's files?"

The brightness disappeared from Mantis's eyes and he leaned against the wall of the storage room with a defeated sigh. "We could have many interesting discussions if we each didn't have so much to lose from a betrayal of trust."

"Indeed," I said, and sat back down on the freezer. I heard another frustrated scream and more tears sprung to my eyes; I wiped them away quickly. "I'm so worried about him."

"You should be," Mantis said airily. "I've counselled a lot of chimeras after traumatic events. One completely fractured himself into two people, required implants and Silas's own mental abilities to repair him. He's still half-mad to this day."

"Who?" I asked, glancing up.

"Sanguine," Mantis replied. I was surprised he answered. "He was kept captive in a dark basement for eleven years by a pedophile, from eight until nineteen. He was starved and tortured, raped and left alone with no one to talk to. He ended up creating an imaginary friend and that friend eventually became his other personality. A peculiar man named Crow."

I tried to stop the horror washing through me, telling myself that that wouldn't happen to Reaver, but I found that my heart had already assumed that it would – if it wasn't already.

I stifled a sob, but when I saw a knowing smirk come to Mantis's face, it quickly dissolved and turned into anger.

"Rape was it? I thought as much. That really is the only thing that gets them, that and losing what you'd call their soul mate. Since you are here for him, I assume it was Nero doing what Nero does best?"

"Shut up!" I cried. "He won't turn out like Sanguine. Once he kills Nero… he'll be fine. He just needs to get some revenge…"

"Didn't help Sanguine," Mantis said nonchalantly.

"What did?" I sniffed.

"He's never fully recovered," he said back to me. "Scars are scars, memories are memories. This will change him forever, whether he likes it or not."

"Not Reaver," I whispered. "Nothing can change him."

"You two are going to be together for a long time. I suggest you get rid of that notion. It's false for arians and it's false for chimeras, and it is all the more false for the dreaded born immortal chimera."

I fell to silence… I had nothing to say to that.

But once our mutual loneliness became greater than the silence, we started talking again. Heavy topics were avoided and we settled for neutral conversations. We talked about everything from the felicos, the bat cats we'd seen outside, to exchanging cooking recipes and tips. I'd noticed that, thankfully, Reaver had stopped yelling above me, and that everything had gone silent.

Adler and Spike didn't come back which I was surprised about. I thought they'd at least feed Mantis but there was no movement outside. I didn't even hear anything when one of them turned out the only light we had in here, and in the pitch black, we bid each other good night and I slept on top of the freezer, Mantis on the floor.

I woke up in the middle of the night to a weird sound. I opened my eyes to darkness and sat up, my brow furrowed and my head craned. At first I couldn't make out what I was hearing until I realized…

"Someone's having sex on Adler's bed. He's going to love that," Mantis mumbled sleepily. I looked over at where I'd seen him last, and realized he could see me perfectly well.

"Ceph and Kiki will be thrilled," I said and stifled a yawn. Even though I couldn't see anything, I closed my eyes to try and listen better. I think I heard groaning.

"Get off!"

"REAVER!" I screamed, then suddenly I felt hands over my mouth. I bit down, my mind going insane from what I knew I'd just heard.

Mantis pulled back with a hiss. "Shut up. If you want out of here them thinking you're dead is the way to do it," he snapped. "What you think is happening, is not happening."

"Yes – it – is!" I snarled. I started pounding and kicking on the door. "Nero has him again! He fucking–"

"And it was silent until that one scream? It's rough sex, they're chimeras, certainly you know this by now," Mantis said back. He pushed me away from the door and I fell to the floor, the darkness making it impossible for me to find my bearings.

"He'd never sleep with Nero. Don't be an idiot," I said.

"Then Reaver walked in on something and he's pissed off. Either way, shut up," Mantis said back. I heard another muffled yell. Something was going on up there. I felt like I was going mad being locked in this fucking dungeon. There was no greater torture than to be forced to witness the love of your life being hurt, and you not being able to do a damn thing about it.

More muffled sounds were heard, and groaning too. I bit my bottom lip and shut my eyes tight. I wasn't sure how much more of this I could handle. "Get me out of here!" I demanded. "You said them thinking I'm dead is the fucking key... well use it. Get me the fuck out of here, I don't care what you have to tell that idiot."

"You need to wait until morning. Now be quiet!" Mantis hissed. The anger was growing in his tone, but he didn't fucking understand. If Nero had Reaver... fuck, I had to save him. This could be what permanently breaks his mind. I fucking had to save my baby.

"REAV–" Suddenly I felt something made of fabric around my neck. It got pulled back tightly, cutting off my air flow.

My hands shot to my neck. I tried to grab the cloth as it tightened around my neck but my fingers grasped nothing but my own skin. Mantis grunted behind me, and I felt him torque the bind. I opened my mouth to try and plead with him, tell him I would be quiet, but soon my head was filling with a painful red pressure, one that was pushing my eyes out of my socket, and my tongue from my mouth.

He was fucking strangling me with the arm of his robe.

I clawed at my neck, my mind launching me into survival mode, but soon I felt the cold floor greet me with a painful impact. Even then I wasn't spared, Mantis began strangling me again and soon after that, I experienced my fourth death.

When I finally forced the first gasp of air into my lungs, and my eyes snapped open to the bright lights I had been seeing as red through my closed eyelids, I realized I was wrapped in Mantis's robe and tucked into the corner of the storage room in between the wall and the freezer.

Mantis was watching me, leaning against the wall and looking bored.

"Reaver? Did you hear anything else?" I asked. I held a hand to my throat but there wasn't even a muscle ache from Mantis strangling me. I wasn't going to bother chewing him out for killing me, in my time engulfed in flames I'd come to the conclusion he was justified in doing it.

Mantis shook his head and shuffled himself up so he was sitting straighter. I think he had been sleeping. "No." He got up and handed me something that was resting on top of the freezer. It was a Ziploc bag of something red and white. I opened it up and saw it was strawberries and cake, a bit frozen still but not much. It looked wonderful. "You've been out for about eight hours. Four for the resurrection and four for just sleeping. Eat. Adler or Spike will be coming in with a bucket which they expect me to relieve myself in. When they do, you're going to be hiding behind that door."

I stopped, a piece of white cake with strawberries frozen into some whip cream halfway to my mouth. "What?" I said.

Mantis nodded towards the door. "This is why you needed to keep quiet. I can sense the tension building and everything is going to come to a head soon. I need to quell this before it does. You'll be hiding behind the door, and as soon as Spike or Adler's back is turned you're going to ambush them. I'll be right behind you and we'll escape together and calm these rabid beasts they call chimera teenagers."

I jumped to my feet and started sizing up the door, my mouth now full of sugary sweet food. I took a step back and nodded. "That's a perfect idea. Spike's mortal, right?"

"Yes," Mantis replied. "He's my assistant to a lot of important research. I'd appreciate you not killing him. As for Adler, I only want him alive so I can murder the little bastard myself."

"I think Reaver will be wanting that honour. He had to see me get beaten to death," I said. I walked to the freezer, opened it, and started sifting around until I found a pack of ground arian. I weighed it in my hand and liked how it felt, this was going to be my bludgeoning weapon.

"We can all have our turns," Mantis said and he got to his feet. "It's almost afternoon and I need to use the restroom rather badly. I'm going to try and expedite this. Get into your proper hiding position and keep a good grip on that meat."

My pulse spiked at his words and I took in a deep breath. The thought of getting out of this fucking room was one that filled me with both calm and adrenaline. Not only did I have to get out of here, I had to see if Reaver was okay. Why was he shouting up there and why the fuck was I hearing sex? If Mantis's words were right, maybe Nero was fucking some hot Blood Crow or one of Mantis's slaves, and Reaver got pissed off but... why 'Get off'?

The increased tempo in my pulse continued to eat my adrenaline stores. I didn't want to admit it to myself, but Reaver was right with what he'd been yelling at me about... I was looking at him differently. I was starting to not trust him to take care of himself. But how could he blame me? I'd seen his spiralling descent into what he, and now Mantis, called psychosis. I had every right to be worried about him. I loved him, and I'd been through a lot of what he was going through. He needed to let me help him.

There was no way Nero got him again. It was an impossibility. Mantis was right, and even if Reaver had changed since his time in Cardinalhall, it wasn't feasible he'd let Nero get the drop on him again. There was just nothing more to it. No one would do that to Reaver again. He'd blow up the plant the moment Nero put a hand on him.

But why there was still a tightness in my throat, I didn't know.

"Adler!" Mantis suddenly yelled. I pressed my back against the wall, the metal door a couple inches away, and waited with my heart in my stomach. "Adler! I need to piss. Get the fuck over here before I piss in your fucking frozen strawberries."

There was so much Lycos in that man, it made me smile just a little inside. I really missed Leo and Greyson. I wish I'd gotten to have a conversation with Leo as Lycos, just to talk to the real chimera who had come from this family.

And I wish Greyson was here to handle Reaver.

"It's me. Adler's... just out for a moment. Stand back, you know the drill." Spike, eh? Good enough. The adrenaline was rushing through me like a white-hot current, and once again, the knowledge that I didn't have to worry about being permanently killed acted like an accelerant.

I was going to make that bitch a little less pretty.

The calmness dashed away any nervousness I had. I made my stance but kept my face void of expression. I waited patiently, my eyes locked on

Mantis, and heard footsteps approach.

Then a click, and in that click, my heart jumped.

Mantis stayed against the wall with his arms crossed. There was a glare on him that was his poker face, because Spike would expect nothing else from him.

"Adler's upstairs. It looks like Reaver knows where Adler's crush is," Spike said. I inched towards the edge of the open metal door, and saw the back of Spike's head and his shoulder.

And then he took another step inside. "So he'll be gone soon and when he is… I can–" In the same moment that I lunged at Spike, the brick of frozen meat in my grasp, the chimera spun around and I saw his red eyes widen with surprise.

I bashed him right over the head, a good amount of force behind the blow too. Spike stumbled backwards with a surprised scream, then Mantis grabbed him and held him up.

Needing just one more hit, I raised the pack of frozen meat and gave him another hard smack. That was for almost raping me, and for being a fucking piece of shit in general.

"The door!" Mantis barked. I whirled around and caught the handle right before it closed, then I held it open and Mantis dropped Spike. He ran through and I followed.

Then I doubled back. I walked over to Spike as he lay groaning on the floor, blood dripping from his mouth – and I kicked him right in the balls.

"Killian!" Mantis called. I turned and nodded, then kicked him one more time. That was for Ceph.

I shut the door, locking Spike inside, then I trailed behind Mantis. The scientist was stalking down the narrow laboratory hallway, towards the room I'd been held in.

I was greeted with two gasps of surprise.

"Killian! You're fucking immortal?" I heard Ceph's voice first. It was vibrant and full of life. I looked over and saw him and Kiki still tied to their chairs, now looking extremely dishevelled and smelling like they'd reached their past-due date.

"Surprise, guys," I said and jogged over to them. I glanced at Mantis. "You need to make it really clear to Reaver that you were imprisoned too. Actually… untie them, I want to go up first." I gave Ceph and Kiki a smile before I ran across the room, grabbing a machete and a handgun on the way.

"No. I need to see that man face-to-face," Mantis said bitterly, and he disappeared up the stairs. I turned away from him and doubled back with a half-shoulder shrug, and started slicing through the binds with the machete.

"You guys okay?" I asked. Ceph wiggled out of his binds and started flexing his hands. I moved onto Kiki.

"Yeah. I'm swimming in my own piss though," Ceph said, and then he gave me a goofy smile. "I'm so happy you're immortal. You –"

"FUCK!" Mantis suddenly shouted.

All of our heads turned towards Mantis, and a split second later the fucking stairwell exploded. I turned around, and not knowing why, an automatic reaction I guess, I shielded Kiki from the debris the explosion had caused. I closed my eyes, feeling Ceph grab onto me too to create a human shield, and felt, thankfully small, impacts against my back.

I turned around, smoke filling the laboratory, and groaned when I saw Mantis laying at the bottom of the stairwell, shrouded in dust. I ran towards him, my ears throbbing from the blast, but skidded to a stop when I saw just how badly he'd been injured.

No, not injured.

He was dead, impaled many times over with wooden shards and... fucking nails, I think. I looked to where the staircase had been, and saw that it was now almost completely blown to smithereens, but... the door was open at least.

I smelled the smoky air and found it familiar; this explosion had been done with C4. "Reaver," I whispered under my breath. I turned and saw Ceph, now on his feet, untying Kiki who appeared unharmed. "They hotwired the stairs... but how Adler got out then I don't know." I looked up the stairwell and squinted my eyes to try and see past the smoke. "I... yeah, we can still get up the stairs just be careful and... Ceph, put Mantis into one of the lab rooms."

"Roger. Be careful," Ceph said.

The entire left-hand side of the stairwell was collapsed and could collapse further, but I was skinny and could contort my body like a ferret. I weaved myself around the shards of wood and slunk up the stairs. During my careful ascent I saw nails embedded in the walls, confirming my theory that they'd manufactured a nail bomb. Reaver was always my creative killer, but his fucking nail bomb came dangerously close to killing me, and possibly his precious little *Kicky*.

The entire hallway on the main floor was destruction. I'd figured it had been detonated with C4, but there wasn't as much fire as I thought there would be, so I wasn't sure. Whatever it was, it had destroyed the hallway wall which had the kitchen on the other side of it. I could see right through the pink insulation, now coated with drywall dust and smelling like gunpowder.

"Kiki…" I called down when I saw smoke billowing from a couple places. "Grab a fire extinguisher and make sure nothing's burning. It's hard to see in this smoke and dust."

"Okay, I'm just coming up right now," Kiki called behind me.

I nodded and coughed into my hand. "Reaver?" I called, but I knew if he was around he would've been down here already. But then where was he?

My gaze took me to the kitchen, past that would be the hallway where Adler's bedroom was, and underneath that bedroom was where me and Mantis had been held prisoner.

And where I'd heard those noises…

Then I was moving, my legs taking me, almost without my consent, towards the bedroom. I ignored the voices in the hallway, ones belonging to Ceph and Kiki as they tried to get through the smoking debris, and continued on my way.

I pushed the door open, and my eyes widened when I saw the destruction I'd heard. Broken furniture, tossed clothes, vases, files… the entire room had been trashed. I could even see holes in the walls, obviously from fists, angry fists.

I took another step in and my nose twitched. It smelled like… sweat and lubricant.

Like I was walking my own path of damnation, my boots took me to the bed. At this point I had no thoughts inside of my head, only tunnel vision to observe the evidence I was starting to see gather.

Blood speckles on the sheets…

I pulled a blanket back and saw streaks, and the tinged outlines of dried cum. I put the blanket back where I had found it and walked to the other side of the bed.

Nero must've brought a man here, like I'd thought.

I nodded to myself. I looked down at the front of the bed and my boots crunched down on porcelain. I looked down and saw that right beside the vase was a bloody machete. I picked it up and used it to push

640

the pillow away. There was more blood underneath the pillow, but no binds or signs of anyone being tied up.

I turned to walk out of the room, but then I stopped. Still without a thought in my head or a quiver in my heart, I looked down and saw a pair of black boxer briefs. I picked them up, and looked down at them.

They were Reaver's.

Reaver who never slept naked, not unless we'd just had sex.

And especially not with… Nero here.

I looked down and realized there was another pair of boxers beside the ones I'd just picked up.

A larger pair.

Brute chimera size. And whereas all the other clothes had been covered in plaster dust, debris, dirt from the room being trashed, these ones had been placed on top of the mess and recently.

Like last night.

Calmly, I placed the underwear down onto the blood-streaked bed, then picked up the blue pair and did the same. I laid them out nicely, and folded them; my pulse steady, my breathing calm.

So Reaver slept with Nero.

My boyfriend, who had been falling apart for the past several months… had sex with the man who raped him.

Reaver had sex with someone else, and not just anyone else…

"Killian!" I heard Reaver's voice exclaim, sounding excited and out of breath. I heard the door slam against the wall. "You fucking broke out? I knew you could…"

I slowly turned around and saw Reaver smiling at me. He was sweaty and his hair was messed up. He was injured too, his shirt was blood-soaked with a tear on the shoulder that looked to have been a stab wound.

But that wasn't what I was focused on.

It was the hickies all over his fucking neck.

The emotions that had been too extreme and damaging to hit me initially, flooded me with such a force it felt like the world was ending again. It was a dam bursting when there was only a small hole for all of the water to escape through. It overwhelmed me, electrified me, and filled me with such a blind rage I announced it with a manic scream.

And as Reaver stared at me blankly, I raised the machete and charged him.

CHAPTER 37

Reaver

Earlier That Day

I RESISTED THE SMIRK WHEN I FELT NERO'S LIPS LOCK onto the side of my neck. The seal broke with a pop, and was replaced by his tongue. "He can wait one more minute," Nero whispered in my ear. "Bend me over the desk, give it to me."

I batted him away, the room we were in heavily saturated with blood. "I've been waiting too long for this," I said to him, but when he kissed my neck the heat returned to my already exhausted and sore body.

But then I shook my mind clear of it. No. I was already feeling on top of the world. I was already feeling my old self flow through my veins. Anything after this would be sex with Nero and I wasn't a cheater. It was going to be bad enough explaining why I had to do this to Killian without him turning homicidal.

Another kiss. I leaned down, both to get my neck out of the way of his mouth and to turn on the desktop computer. When I rose, I looked behind me and smiled at the two horse heads propped up on coat racks behind me. I'd wanted to add some of the Blood Crow's heads to the mix but Nero had talked me out of it. We'd use that ace for later.

"Come on! At least let me suck it one more time. I put up all your fucking duct-taped nail bombs on the lab door for you," Nero said, his voice trailing a whine. "Come on! You didn't tell me when the last time would be. I didn't get to savour it."

"It wasn't for your enjoyment – it was therapy."

"Does that mean I get to charge you money?"

"It means you broke it, so you fixed it," I muttered, and the Windows

XP screen came into view. "Alright, shut the fuck up. I don't know how they have this computer wired."

I started clicking around but I saw Nero's finger come into view. "Remote access," he said. "Team Viewer, click that. We use it all the time in the military. If he has it set up that it syncs automatically, if his computer is on it'll fire up."

I nodded. "Good. I hope they get a good fucking view of what we've done."

"Teach him to piss off the Don, eh, Corleone?"

I smiled when I saw the Team Speak program icon. I glanced at the webcam and back at the screen, wondering what I'd see.

"Indeed... I think I'm about to make him an offer he can't refuse." I moved the mouse over to the Team Speak icon, but paused when another window automatically popped up and started to load.

It was an email system.

"This is Mantis's email..." Nero murmured behind me, and as it started to load the emails inside of it, I paused when I saw a familiar name.

Perish Dekker.

A lot of Perish Dekker emails... all of them sent within days of each other.

Backup files 1/100.

RE: Last wishes.

To be forwarded to my family.

To be forwarded to Silas.

For Skytech's future.

Back up of my video to Killian.

Back up to my video to...

My mouth went dry.

... to Reaver.

"None to Nero? What an asshole."

"Be quiet," I whispered. I swallowed hard and decided to tell him what had been on my mind. "Killian told me before Perish made him immortal... that Perish put something inside of his head. It was some sort of thing with wires coming off of it..." I let out a tense breath and the cursor hovered over the email. "We'd been meaning to go to the plaguelands house after this to look through Perish's stuff... to see if he put something in him to make him act... different."

Nero shifted his weight. "Well, click on it then."

"Get out of the room first… I don't want you around for this. Go make some more nail bombs for the door."

He let out a growl before clasping a hand on my head and shaking it. Then he turned and left the room, leaving me alone with an email in front of me that I wasn't sure if I wanted to read, and a video attached that I wasn't sure if I wanted to watch.

But if this meant my answer to what had been making Killian act differently… this would be the best time to know. I was starting a new life today, and if what was on this computer was what I thought it was… maybe Killian could be starting his old life right along with me.

Plus we were with a scientist who could take out whatever the implant was. And if Mantis refused… Kiki mentioned Sid.

I clicked on the email and it opened up. The email didn't hold anything groundbreaking, just 'second copy' and Perish's name. I clicked the video and let Windows Media Player pop up, and I held my breath.

And there was that bastard. He was sitting down on a chair in a laboratory, the laboratory he'd eventually die in.

Perish looked groomed and bathed, but he also was hollow-faced and haggard. The journey he'd forced Killian to take with him had done a number on his body. But he'd hid it as much as he could with a crisp new lab coat and a shaved face.

"*Reaver…*" Perish glanced at what I guessed was the computer screen before looking at the webcam. "*This video is for you, and only you, so please… tell Killian to leave and make sure he's not listening to this.*"

Perish paused and leaned back in his chair. He let out a long breath and pulled another laptop onto his knee and clicked around on it for a solid minute.

"Okay, that's enough time… pause this if you're still fighting him tooth and nail."

I smirked and at the same time Perish did too. We both knew Killian… really well.

"*Okay, Reaver…*" Perish took in a deep breath, and I could tell right away I was face-to-face with the real Perish, not the damaged one that had been created through Silas's abuse and the fact that he was missing a chunk of his brain. This was Perish Fallon, who he used to be.

"*First off, I want to apologize for what I had to do to Killian to get him to this point. I knew from an early time that this was what I'd eventually have to do, but I didn't know what Sky would make me do in exchange for the information on PCE. Prolonged Concentrated Exposure. In order to get the information from Elish's laptop, I had to play Sky's game, and yeah, he was no better than Silas... worse actually."* Perish ran a hand over his short black hair and rubbed his nose. *"What I'm about to tell you... you have to know. There is just no two ways around it, brother. You have to know this. You need to know what to look out for... and just who you're dealing with now."*

The bottom dropped out from under me, and nausea and dizziness both took their place inside of my churning stomach.

I tried to push it down. This was just confirmation... this was a good thing.

Perish reached to the table the laptop he was speaking to me was on, and I saw him get out two small vials with a quarter inch of blood in each of them. He held up each one to the screen and I saw a KM on one and a RD on the other.

"This is Killian's blood," Perish said, and to the other: *"This is yours. I got it while we were in the greyrifts apartment."*

Why does he need mine?

"This laptop is one that is wired to the ACL, the Arian Compliance League, and it has admin privileges... I want to show you something, Reaver. Something I... didn't even think was possible." Perish opened the vial of my blood and unwrapped a dropper that looked like one diabetics' used. He dipped it into the blood and slid it into a machine out of sight.

I heard a beep and Perish picked up the laptop again – and he turned it towards the screen.

It was a smiling mugshot of him, and his information beside it. There was also a gold stripe above it with CHIMERA below.

"Your blood shows up as mine." Perish put the laptop back down. I shrugged at this, wondering if that was the big news, but my dead brother seemed to read my mind. *"So what, right? You have a lot of Sky's DNA, more than I think you realize, but you have Silas's DNA in you too. Okay... so once again, you're thinking... why do I care? This is good, I hate Silas, right?"*

"Yes," I said to the screen.

Perish nodded at me. I couldn't help but get the feeling we were talking to each other live, like Adler and I had. *"Okay, I agree. Hi, brother."* Perish smiled, but then he let out a long breath. *"Now... here is the twist, Reaver. Here is the problem I was confronted with when I tested your blood... Reaver. Do you remember when I told you the reason why Silas found you... was because I had sent your blood in? What Lycos had been trying to avoid had happened, a lost chimera had been found through his blood."* An electric chill shot up my spine, and suddenly I began to feel cold. *"But Reaver..."* Perish dipped the tester strip into Killian's blood and slipped it into the tester. *"... it wouldn't have mattered. It would've just shown up... as Perish Dekker."*

What?

He was right... but what the hell was he saying?

"Only... it wasn't your blood that alerted Silas..." I stared at the screen. I felt like my body had frozen up, that I had been gutted and my insides now lay on the floor.

Perish... stop talking.

"I wish I knew this long ago, Reaver."

I looked up, my breath now catching in my throat.

The laptop screen that Perish was holding... had a picture of Silas, and on his face was the slightest of smirks.

"Every ACL accessible by the Legion and almost everyone else, would show an error code if they scanned Silas's DNA, a special code. Not my personal laptop, however. This error code would get noted and sent directly to one chimera to personally check – and one chimera only... guess who?"

"Elish," Perish and I said at the same time.

"Now, first I need to say this... please don't bash the computer or my laptop. I know you're probably mad, but listen to this. Killian isn't, and never was, immortal, nor was he immune to radiation. Reaver, Killian isn't a born immortal and he isn't a chimera. He's basically the stripped down foundation we use as a base to create chimeras. Killian is what's called a raw clone and Elish has two more out there. Killian is Silas's DNA, but his DNA only with nothing else mudding it up but that also means... he's got the exact same brain as he does. Unaltered by chimera genetics."

The exact same brain... as Silas.

"As you know by now... I made him immortal, and I made him immune to radiation. I also implanted him with something else, something extremely valuable." I just stared, my mind shutting down and going numb. I didn't know what else I could do; I was afraid if I moved I would

smash the computer monitor.

How could this be true…? My Killian?

"I implanted him with something called a spiderwire. It'll make him still age, so he's not trapped as an eighteen-year-old. Don't take it out until he's at least twenty-four. A man's brain stops growing when he's that age and, Reaver, you're going to need these six years to make him not turn into a monster – not turn into Silas." I stared at that man, and the look he was giving me back seemed to know what I was feeling right now.

My worst enemy wasn't myself after all. I wasn't the one who had Silas's blood flowing through my veins.

It was the monster I'd been seeing kill my boyfriend right in front of me.

I was hoping for an explanation. To tell me it wasn't just me seeing this change… but I didn't want this.

"Once the spiderwire is taken out, the brain will stop growing," Perish said. *"Reaver. When I found out this information about Killian… I wanted to take him then and there, far away from you and Skyfall. But then I realized… I had to trust you to do what's right for your boyfriend, your boyfriend, not mine. If I thought you couldn't do this, I'd be in California right now and you'd never see us again."*

Perish dropped his gaze and I saw his shoulders rise and fall. *"I saw Silas and Sky together, and, Reaver, they were something. They destroyed the world together and they rebuilt it together too. They were two sides of the same coin, the light and the darkness, the sword and the shield, but you could never pinpoint just which one was what. Just like I could never figure out who was more toxic to who."* He looked back up to the screen, his face heavy. *"You have a chance right now, to mould Killian, to create a better version of what his genetics tell him he is. I can't stress this enough, Reaver, if you don't you two will tear the world apart with your love and hatred for each other. There is no breaking up, there is no being with anyone else, you two will always be attracted to each other. You two will always come back, even if you're on opposite ends of the earth. I've seen it happen. I've seen thirteen born immortals from three continents end up in one small town. There is no escaping Silas and Sky. Which brings me to one more thing…"*

Perish's lower lip tightened. *"This is a request from me to you, brother. Forgive Silas for what he did to you, and give him what he deserves."* My eyes widened when Perish held up an O.L.S. *"This is my*

O.L.S, it's empty now. I used it to make Killian immortal. I will be instructing Killian to take Sky's out after I am gone. I need you to go to Melchai—" My eyes closed. *"—find a man living in a mansion, his name is Adler. He's your older brother, a backup plan by Elish. The O.L.S will work flawlessly. Implant Adler, just cut his head open above the brain stem and put it in, and then give him to Silas. Let the family be at peace, and use this time to keep Killian, Killian."*

"Reaver..."

My eyes opened, and I saw that Perish was staring directly at me. *"He's still Killian..."*

No, he isn't.

"... but I've studied psychology for over two hundred years and I've seen firsthand how immortality changes people. I fear with everything that Killian's been through... he might have trouble at first finding his stride. You need to help him. No one is born evil, and Killian is a testament to that. Please, love him. Because I..." I saw Perish's light blue eyes start to well. *"... because I love him, and now I understand why. He's who Silas could've been, if Silas had just been given the chance."* Perish wiped his eyes and took in a deep breath. *"Be good to him, and let him be good to you. And if he's ever unsure, let him know... I was ready to go and wherever I am... I am finally at peace. Goodbye, Reaver. I'm sorry we never got a chance to properly meet."*

The video ended.

For a long time I just sat staring at the computer monitor. I didn't want to move, or speak, or even breathe. I was afraid if I made any sort of movement it would disrupt this fragile state of null that Perish's words had put me into. Like I was walking along the razor's edge but had frozen in the middle of my shaky stride.

I wish I could say deep down I knew... from Elish's hints, from Killian's actions, even Killian declaring himself a chimera magnet earlier this year. I wish I could have that small chunk of life preserver to grab onto, that told me maybe I was prepared for this information.

But I wasn't.

This... I didn't expect.

I turned on Team Viewer but all I saw was dark. I picked up what I thought was a computer microphone and spoke into it. "Adler," I called.

There was a snap from the speakers and static, then I could hear muffled noise. I turned up the volume and saw something get taken off of the cam.

Adler glared at me through the webcam, behind him I saw Ceph and Kiki, still bound and looking greasy and dirty, but alive. "Ready to meet my demands?"

"You never told me your fucking demands, you stupid piece of shit," I said to him. "Where's Killian?"

Kiki's face fell and Ceph looked away from the cam. That told me a lot. And when Adler's hostile expression held no out of place emotion, that told me even more. They'd probably butchered him already.

I remained calm but closed my eyes for a moment. I took in a deep breath, my eyes shut so tight I could see lights gathering on the corners.

"In the freezer where he belongs," Adler said.

"Did you butcher him?"

"Maybe I did, maybe I didn't."

He didn't then. I let out the breath and opened my eyes, the pricks of light fading into the glaring LED's that illuminated this room. So Killian was still intact, and if he was in a freezer he might even be alive already.

"I want his body. It's my block's custom to eat their loved ones," I said to Adler. "Tell me what this is all about... and give me Killian's body, and Kiki and Ceph. This is the only chance you will get to resolve this without bloodshed. You will not receive another one, and I caution you on throwing my civil attitude back into my face."

Adler leaned back in his chair and crossed his arms over his chest. "I want Perish's files," Adler said.

He rubbed his nose after saying this.

So he was nervous and uncomfortable. His resolve was wearing down. I knew he was a weak shadow compared to me and Silas, and this was the proof. Adler wasn't as strong as us, which made me excited. I would have a lot of fun destroying him.

"Why?" I asked. I looked to the corner of the computer screen and saw Mantis's email still up and running. "Mantis got a copy of almost everything."

Surprisingly, he spoke. "Because I need to find someone that Mantis is determined to hide from me. A brother I met long ago. He didn't know I was immortal and he thinks I'm dead. Perish has one of the only admin laptops that can access everything, including chimera records. I want him found."

Interesting. I analyzed this brother of mine's face and saw all of the signs of discord. They were like the swords of Damocles dangling over him, swinging back and forth on rusted wires just waiting for the slight breeze that would have them breaking free to stab the man below. The look filled my mouth with saliva and I found it easing a smile to my face.

"So this is all about love, is it?" I said in an amused tone. Adler's nose twitched at this and he rubbed it again. I found it funny that he wasn't more cautious of me. In all respects, he did kill my boyfriend, but perhaps his chimera engineering had stunted his abilities to have empathy, much like it did mine.

"It's about finding someone who was my... best friend and... someone I care deeply for," Adler said. "He didn't know that I was a born immortal and when I died he buried me and I never saw him again. He doesn't even know my real name. He... Mantis told me he most likely thinks I was Spike, since Spike got fostered near where I met him. This guy knew I was a chimera and... he helped me. He did a lot for me." Adler's lips tightened and I saw a flash of anger illuminate his grey eyes like a lightning strike during a storm. "Mantis has no right to keep me from him. So go get me that laptop, get me Perish's shit so I can find out where he is and I can tell him I'm okay. I don't want to fucking go to Skyfall. I don't want anything to do with you, or that insane piece of shit Silas. I'm not like you."

I laughed lowly. "You are like us, whether you want to admit it or not. It's your genetics and you can't escape it. No matter how much Mantis tried to make you into a pussy."

"I'm not fucking like you," Adler spat. He shook his head, visibly upset. "Just get me the admin laptop so I can get the hell out of here and find him. I'm fucking tired of living in this shithole. I'm thirty, it's time I leave the fucking nest. I spent ten years out in the greywastes and three years when I took off the first time. You want this place? Take it, but I want to know where Asher is first."

Wait.

Back the fuck up.

"Asher?" I exclaimed, and I started coughing when the spit got stuck in my throat. I slammed my hand against my chest but found the next outburst I had was a barking laugh. I looked at the screen and saw Adler glaring at me, but he looked shocked and all the more uncomfortable. "Asher? Fucking *Asher*. Are you serious? You're fucking *serious*?"

Adler's face drained of all colour. His eyes were saucers, and so wide

I could see the blue ring that framed the grey irises. His shocked features seemed out of place for the rugged, gilded steel look he'd had the previous time we'd met.

My laugh was reduced to a smile, a smile that further killed the born immortal looking back at me, because he knew… yeah, he knew.

I fucking had him.

"You don't know who he is," Adler said, his words coming too quickly for them to hold any truth. "You're a fucking liar, like all chimeras."

"Two inches shorter than you, large eyes so green they seemed to have stolen it from the living earth," I said. My head tilted to the side, and my ruthless smile gave way to a full grin when I saw Adler's eyes jump back and forth. He was watching me and looking for lies, but I was going to serve him nothing but cold, hard honesty.

Reaver-style.

"Triangle-shaped face, small nose and ears. Three earrings in each earlobe. Did he dye his hair auburn? Or was he his natural wavy blond?" I asked nonchalantly. "I'm not sure about that, but what I do know, is that he walks with such stealth and grace, it's like he's gliding. When he talks, you drop everything and hang on his every word. Everything he says feels like it's important, and you have this quiver inside of your gut that tells you to listen to him. That you can learn the world while walking in his shadow."

My words were pulled directly from the mouth of Jade talking about Elish to me. The lovesick devotion I saw on the pet echoed what I knew was inside of the clone of Sky. I'd never felt that way for anyone, including Killian. My boyfriend I loved for entirely different reasons, but I wasn't stupid… I knew chimera love.

And the terror on Adler's face, so perfectly mixed in with the longing, told me I couldn't have been more right.

"Where is he?" Adler stammered. When he saw my smile get all the more sardonic, he jumped to his feet and slammed his hand down on the table. "Tell me!"

I smirked and slowly shook my head. "Shouldn't have killed my boyfriend. Well, eye for an eye. Later, Adi." I shut off the desktop with our parting words a scream on his end, and a laugh on mine.

I got up and ran to the metal door and switched off Nero's detonator. Then, as I heard boots slamming on the steps, I grabbed the machete resting on the table and eyed Nero who was eating a sandwich.

"I'm going to go play for a few hours," I said to him as I swung the machete around. "After I think we'll be able to get the boys."

Nero looked up from his eating. "Cool," he said with his cheeks full of food. He looked like a squirrel. "Good news, then?"

"No, a lot of shit news actually," I said to him casually. We both turned towards the lab door when we heard it slam against the wall, this was quickly followed by Adler screaming my name. "But there was a silver lining. Switch the detonator back on and join me outside if you want. Maybe if I'm lucky we can kill Spike."

Suddenly Adler burst out of the hallway. He was holding a handgun which was pointed at me and wearing the most wildest of expressions on his face. The little bitch looked absolutely insane right now. He kind of reminded me of me, except not nearly as crafty and conniving.

"Where is he?" Adler screamed. The gun was shaking in his hand. "I told you, I'm leaving once I know. You can have Turris, I don't fucking care. Where is he? Where did you see him?"

His eyes deflected from mine, and I heard Nero rise to his feet.

"You killed my boyfriend. I'm not telling you shit," I said. I sauntered up to him and he raised the gun as if thinking that would stop me.

I mock advanced on him, and when he flinched, I took that opportunity and lunged for the gun.

He held on tight and tried to wrench it back. We struggled, but I had been wrestling guns from my fathers since I was five. I pushed the gun down and twisted it to the right, using Adler's own grip against him. It worked and Adler's hold weakened. I snatched the gun away, but to make sure he wasn't going to try anything wise, the moment I had the gun in my possession I punched him in the side of the head.

Adler stumbled from the blow but he recovered quickly. With fast movements, faster than I thought he was capable of, he grabbed my shirt. Then, with a frenzied scream, he made the motion to punch me.

Thinking he was aiming for my face, I ducked, but I was wrong, not only was he not aiming for my face... he hadn't been about to punch me either.

It was a mistake, and one that would cost me. I felt an impact on my shoulder and a cold, dull pain. I looked down and saw a knife firmly in his hand, then watched him retract the blade and raise it in the air to stab me again.

Then I saw a flash of black and Adler suddenly disappeared. I watched with satisfaction as Nero lifted him up into the air, then threw him down onto the ground like he was a wrestler performing his special move.

And with a scream, Adler hit the floor hard, the force of the slam making the artifacts on the shelves rattle. The idiot lay there, stunned and injured, then he curled himself up like a squashed bug.

Nero came over to me but I was fine, I think. "Turn on the detonator," I said to him lowly. Nero nodded and disappeared into the hallway. Temporarily leaving Adler where he was I walked into the main bathroom and grabbed a first aid kit. I walked back to the main living area and started roughly, and probably rather badly, stitching the wound. It didn't take much, five stitches, but I was doing it as the blood continuously poured out of the wound.

When I was finished I turned around to see Nero standing with Adler below him. He had Adler by his curly dark brown hair, with his face wrenched up so he was forced to look at me.

When we made eye contact, Adler's expression became all the more desperate. "Where is he?" he gasped, blood now freely flowing from his nose. He spat and sputtered, and it started dripping down his chin.

"We have a garage don't we?" I asked Nero.

"With a back room too." Nero nodded.

"Excellent. Help me bring our brother there, Goose."

Nero's expression turned gleeful. "I love you, Ducky."

I grabbed a machete leaning up against the couch and slid it between my belt and pants, then we both grabbed Adler and started dragging him outside. Adler, of course, didn't like this, but surprisingly his only way of showing his objection was to whimper. I think the blow to the head had been a money shot, it might've knocked a few senses out of him.

I wrenched Adler to his feet but his legs gave out like they'd become pipe cleaners. From how his mouth was moving, I think he was trying to speak, but it became apparent that he was struggling to get breath and talk at the same time.

"We're going to have so much fun with you, kitten," Nero said in a tone dripping honey. He jerked Adler up when his feet started to drag but that just made him struggle. I tightened my grip on his jacket to keep him steady, and held him as Nero opened up the garage door. My shoulder was wet, and with every movement I felt a dull gnawing pain, but however bad the stitched stab wound was, I wouldn't be stopping what I knew was going to be some good ol' fashion redemption – with just a nice dusting of revenge for flavour.

When I saw the garage in front of me, I laughed. "Oh, this is fucking perfect!" I said as I held Adler's hands behind his back. He fell to his knees and I let him. I couldn't believe what a nice little set up this was.

There was a Land Rover-type truck to the left, and quads, dirt bikes, trikes, and just normal bicycles everywhere else. Every one of them appeared to be in good shape, and I couldn't look in any direction without seeing metal tables and power tools.

But that wasn't what caught my interest. At the far end of the garage was the back room Nero had mentioned, and not only was it a room… but it had a bare mattress on the ground and shackles and chains that appeared to be mounted on the walls. There was also a door in the same room but it looked like it hadn't been opened in a while, it might've even been barred.

Well, wasn't that just perfect.

"This is where Mantis held you, isn't it?" I asked Nero as we dragged Adler across the garage. He was resisting and pivoting his feet, but they easily gave out from under him.

"That's right," Nero said cheerfully. He yanked Adler's hair, making the kid groan from pain. "Fucking held me there when I was out investigating. He beat the shit out of me and tased me when I was tied, and then implanted me with a fucking proxy. One of the ones he could fucking control." And with that reminder fuelling his thirst for vengeance, he yanked a fistful of Adler's curls and made him look at him.

"Isn't revenge awesome, puppy?" Nero growled. I know he was talking to me but his indigo eyes were glaring down the brother in front of us.

"It's been a while since I've been able to pay back some owed debts," I said. I closed the garage door and walked behind Nero as he dragged Adler to the garage's back room. I took out the machete I'd slipped between my belt and cargo pants and trailed behind. "Shackle him."

Nero roughly shoved Adler onto the mattress, and pressed his boot against the small of Adler's back.

"I'm immortal, do whatever you want," Adler coughed. "I'm not afraid of you assholes." Then he looked directly at me, and his face twisted like a snarling dog. "I'll eventually find him. You? I took your fucking toy away forever. So do whatever you want. I took something you can never get back."

I exchanged amused smiles with Nero, the sounds of chains now gracing my ears. "And where is my boyfriend?" I asked him. I held out the machete and pressed it against his chin. "Did you eat him?"

"I put the little bastard in the freezer," Adler sneered. "Mantis is probably eating him as we speak."

Nero and I laughed. Adler's eyes flickering back and forth. He was confused, but too angry to show it on his face.

"You locked Mantis in the freezer room, didn't you?" Nero asked. He grabbed Adler's head and pushed him towards the outstretched blade. I saw a drop of blood appear and trail down to join the additional injuries we'd inflicted on him. "So you put Killian's body in the freezer... with Mantis locked in too? Interesting. I bet Mantis is pissed at you too, eh?"

"Fuck him and fuck you two," Adler's tone tuned bitter. "I'm immortal. Do whatever the fuck you want. I've been tortured before. I really don't give a shit."

Nero's eyes shone and so did mine. "Reav... he sounds like someone familiar... doesn't he?" Nero took Adler's t-shirt into his hand and brought out something black from his pocket, there was a *shink* and a knife appeared. Nice-looking switch blade.

"He does," I said lowly. I got down on my knees, Adler glaring up at me through his brow, with curls of dark brown framing his blue-grey eyes. They were such an interesting colour, the grey seemed so steeled, but then wrapped around the monotone like a blanket was this beautiful sky blue.

I quickly snatched Adler's chin and raised it. I smiled at him and heard cloth rip as Nero cut his shirt off of him.

Then, to my own surprise and joy, Adler's gaze broke from mine, and when he saw that Nero had cut his shirt off... his eyes widened and his face dropped. I followed his gaze and realized what had induced this expression... Nero was hard.

Adler started backing away from Nero. I tuned my hearing and was further pleased to hear his heartbeat spiking. It was now an intense and steady thumping, one that made my own heart give a flutter of excitement.

That fucking idiot didn't have a clue what we'd been implying this whole time. This retard was such a sheltered little bitch it didn't even occur to him what we'd been planning all the while.

"What the fuck...?" Adler croaked, his throat sounding dry and constricted. Then, when Nero reached down and tried to grab the front of his pants, he recoiled and started hyperventilating.

I knew I shouldn't be taking so much enjoyment from this. I knew it was fucked up and I wasn't in denial about that. I was this kid earlier in the year. I'd had gone through hell with what Nero had done to me, and I knew I was about to put my genetic clone through the same thing.

But honestly...

There was something so fucking gratifying about it, so validating. I wanted to break him. I wanted to take this sheltered, fragile little creature into my hands and gently snap every bone he had. I thirsted to see his face twist upon penetration, thirsted to hear his heart pound desperately against his chest. I wanted to watch his eyes glass over then smack him back to awareness, and hear scream after scream shoot from his lips like an automatic weapon.

Was it the saying that misery loves company? Or perhaps I was more depraved than even I realized. All I knew was that I had suffered more than I'd ever had before, and I couldn't explain it, but there was a powerful dark force that wanted me to inflict the same trauma on Adler.

Unable to stop myself, I kneeled down and grabbed Adler's chin then kissed the corner of his mouth.

Adler jolted away and looked at me with terror in his eyes. It was like he was a preppy daddy's boy who'd stumbled down the wrong alley. "Don't do this," he said, his voice faint. He looked at Nero, and the terror turning to pleading. "Mantis took you in... he only proxied you because you were going to fucking kidnap me. What the fuck, Nero?" He let out a cry and tried to kick me away when I attempted to steal another kiss.

Nero laughed, and in a flash, he grabbed onto Adler's pants and started pulling them off of him. Of course, Adler let out a horrific scream and began to struggle. I got up from my kneeling position and slammed a boot down onto his stomach to keep him from moving, and allowed Nero to finish removing his pants. Nero threw the pants behind him, a brightness on his face that I was quite familiar with, and then leaned down to start slicing off Adler's underwear.

"Oh, he has the cut gene," I said. I kneeled back down, my knee pressed against Adler's stomach, and checked out the goods. "And he doesn't even trim himself. Nero, you don't want to fuck him all hairy and disgusting, right?" I motioned to his switch blade. "Shave some of that off." Then I pressed the tip of the machete into the base of Adler's cock and twisted it. Adler sucked in a desperate breath and let out a shuddered cry. "Cut him a few times for me, Goose. I want to taste him, see if he tastes like me."

"You're going to fuck him too, right?"

I reached over and started unbuttoning Nero's pants. He was kneeling over Adler now, pinching dark pubes, quite long too, between his fingers before slicing them clean off with the blade.

I had no intentions, I could never do that to Killian, but I didn't want Adler to know that. "We'll see." I pulled out Nero's cock, solid and ready, and felt a rush when I heard him groan from my touch. This hot feeling had long since gone to my head, and there was no part of me that was in control of the dangerous hot energy jumping from me to my brute chimera brother. I'd love to say that I didn't know what was coming over me, but I did, and I was enjoying finding Reaver again too much to start touching on any moral grounds.

I wasn't a moral person, and I never had been, but I was faithful to Killian and I'd never do anything he wouldn't allow me to do if I explained why I needed to do it.

Having sex with Nero was something I knew I'd had to do, and Killian would understand, but doing this to Adler was nothing more than me needing revenge and wanting to see him suffer like I had. This was for me, the sickest most depraved part of me, and it was because of that I wouldn't do to Adler what Nero was planning on doing. That would be cheating, and that wasn't me.

But even though I was strong... I wasn't strong enough to not let my hands wander.

I ran my hand up and down Nero's dick, and let the thick member rest on my palm. I could feel it twitching and I could smell the blood rushing through the thick vein he had on the side of it. That cock fucked me all night last night – and I'd liked it.

And now... it was going to get quite the treat.

"We need to free the boys and let them have a go with him," Nero said through groans. "Fuck, I want to see Killian fuck him, really bad."

I smirked at this. "He might." The thought that I could have a go with Adler, if Killian was beside me, filled me with even more excitement. "We had plans on raping Kiki in front of you once we freed you anyway."

Nero gave me a surprised look. "Fucking HOT!" he said, before slicing off another chunk of pubes.

And this is why it's better to join the maniac, than try and beat him.

"Stay the fuck down!" Nero snapped when Adler tried to move away from him. The little bitch was scrunched against the concrete wall, as far away from us as he possibly could be. He was shackled with his wrists above his head now, and that chain was embedded in the wall. There were no chains for his legs though. I had one hand on his leg and the other had removed itself from Nero's cock and was now rubbing my own crotch.

"There see? I cut ya, I told you to stay still," Nero said. He laughed when Adler said nothing back, still staring at us like he couldn't believe what was happening. I loved these reactions, and I felt spoiled for choice right now. I could do anything and everything to him. I could draw out the most agonizing of reactions.

I love life.

"Go on, Reav. Give it a taste. Dare him to kick you." Nero removed his shirt, showing off his washboard abs and toned stomach. He had tan lines on him too, I bet I did as well.

I looked down and saw a shine of blood in the now short black strands of pubic hair. It was gathering around the base of his cock, the usually grand chimera dick now tucked up close to his body. His balls were too, timid and afraid and huddling close to their host.

I leaned down and put my mouth over the wound, but the moment my lips tasted the blood Adler pulled away with a spastic gasp, and I heard chains tighten before a frustrated and fearful cry sounded.

"What do you want...?" Adler wheezed. "I told you, you can have Turris. Mantis can... he can create another Killian."

I licked the blood, and just to taunt him further I ran a tongue up the deflated piece of flesh. Nero liked this. I felt him unbutton my own pants like I had his, then warm hands withdrew my cock.

"I don't need another boyfriend, one is enough." My tongue devoured the blood, and I felt Nero's lips greet the tip of my cock. "The man you killed was no greywaster. Killian is an immortal just like us. You really think I'd have let you continue to play this game if you killed my partner?" I smirked and petted Nero's hair back as his mouth went up and down on my cock. Adler just stared at me, tucked up like a boy after Daddy gave him a beating. "No. You didn't kill my boyfriend. You don't have a single card against me, Adler Dekker." I rose and tried to kiss his neck but Adler jerked his head away. And just to prove how fast he was, Adler snapped his head towards me and managed to get my chin into his teeth, I felt the spring of pain and flinched away out of reflex, but laughed when I saw flecks of my own skin in his teeth.

"Tsk, tsk, bona mea," I purred. I slid a hand around Nero's neck and pulled my cock away from his lips. "Biting his master. Goose... why haven't you started fucking this little bitch yet? He's ripe and ready, wouldn't you say?"

Nero groaned. "Fuck, Reav. I fucking love you." He licked my chin before our lips joined again, this time my tongue meeting his to taste the copper it was laced with. "I'm divorcing Ceph," he said when our mouths broke apart. "We're running away to Florida. We'll ride crocodiles."

I chuckled. "Make him scream, puppy," I whispered to him.

"Fuck you!" Adler suddenly cried. As he thrashed and kicked, I grabbed onto his leg and held it back. I had a perfect view of what was about to happen, and not just visually, every sense I had was about to be indulged. It was taking the breath away from my lungs and replacing it with fire, an unquenchable thirst.

Teach him to fuck with me. Teach him to fucking taunt me with my boyfriend's life. Even if Killian was immortal, Adler didn't know that. He'd taken my soul mate from me. He'd brutally beat Killian, and this was after ordering Spike to rape Killian in front of me. I don't give a shit how much he was screaming, how much he was pleading... his hands were soaked in blood.

Adler was no fucking innocent victim; he was a little shit finally getting what he deserved.

So why would I feel empathy for someone so willing to take all that I loved from me?

Or maybe you're just acting this extreme because then you don't have to think of Killian being Silas's clone?

For a split second, all of the hot desire inside of me disappeared, like cold water had been dumped onto my head. This threw me into a panic, and I found myself desperate to take back the intense feeling I'd felt only moments ago.

And this made me break the rule I'd given myself minutes before. The one where I said I wouldn't touch Adler. But at this moment, I didn't care. I didn't even care if that inner voice was right about why I was doing this.

I licked my middle finger, and without warning, I shoved it inside of Adler's ass.

Adler screamed, then his hips jutted up and his torso twisted. I saw Nero grab his right leg and bend it until Adler's knee was on his chest.

Our victim was now crushed against the wall of the garage, his face pressed against the concrete and his hands tucked up by his chin. He gave out a desperate whine, his eyes shut tight – and then he started to beg.

"No... no... no..."

A second finger was pushed inside of him, and I was rewarded with another wonderful shrill scream. And as he screamed, he tried to get away from me, but he was already pressed up against the concrete wall, there was nowhere for him to go. Because of this, I was able to keep my fingers inside of him.

He was tight, so fucking tight. His hole was a wound elastic band and I could feel it contracting and stiffening as his tense body went even more rigid.

"He seems so stressed," I purred to Nero. "Why don't we make him cum? Loosen him up a bit."

"Yes, sir." Nero kissed my neck and took Adler's flaccid dick into his hand. He put his mouth over the cowering cock and started sucking on it. I adopted his rhythm and began finger fucking Adler.

Nero withdrew his mouth for a moment, and licked his lips. "Curl your finger up and find his prostate," he said. A tongue stuck out and swirled around Adler's head, our victim's confused breathing filling the small room. "Hit it with the tips of your finger, match my rhythm."

"I remember that trick," I said. And I did, because he used it on me. I curled my finger up and felt around for the root. It was apparently just the end of a man's dick and was a wonderful source of pleasure. I'd discovered just how wonderful it was last night when Nero was pounding against it. It had opened up my world to orgasming as a bottom.

Adler gasped. His face scrunched and went red, and once again, he attempted to pull away from us. But there was just nowhere to go, nothing he could do but contort his torso and try to move his legs. Nothing me and my brother couldn't handle.

"Is he getting hard?" I pushed my finger against the hidden area inside of Adler and heard another strangled gasp.

Nero withdrew his mouth and cackled. He was holding a hardening cock in his hands like a trophy fish.

"He likes it. He won't fucking admit it, but he likes it," I taunted. I reached up and brushed Adler's hair back. "Don't you, sweetcakes?"

Adler reared up and tried to take my finger off. I laughed and started batting his cheek while he snapped at me like a wild dog. Eventually he gave up and instead started throwing his chained arms forward in an attempt to break the links, or at least rip Nero's head off.

"Fucking enough!" Adler roared. He kicked his legs and twisted himself around so his ass was exposed. I dug my finger in, feeling his hole tighten and contort in a desperate attempt to get me out of him, but he didn't have far to go and all he succeeded in doing was baring more of his ass to us.

Adler realized this and sat down again, scrunching himself into the far corner of the hall, hyperventilating breaths coming from his mouth and his eyes bulging.

"What do you want?" Adler suddenly screamed. He tried to cover himself with his hands but the chains stopped him.

"I want to add another notch to my bed post," Nero said sweetly. He ran his fingers through Adler's hair and leaned his hand against the wall. I drew Nero's pants the rest of the way down and then his boxer briefs. He raised his knees and I managed to take them all the way off.

And then I took off mine and started playing with my cock. I'd gone multiple times last night but he was throbbing and ready to go. What I'd fucking do to have Killian beside me right now. The next time I saw him I was going to bend him over, no matter where he was, and make him fucking see oblivion. It had been too long since I'd fucked him, and I wanted to prove to him that I was okay. I was finally fucking okay.

"We don't have any lube. I'm going to fucking kill him," Nero chuckled. He reached over and started stroking my dick. I groaned and thrusted my hips to get myself in further.

"I have some in my cargo pants," I said through my quickened breaths. I stroked his prickly chin and the side of his face. He was talented with that mouth. I was going to make Killian take some lessons, and maybe let him experience a blowjob from Nero.

Oh the shit you fantasize about when you're horny. I knew very well that I'd be feeling embarrassed and ashamed after I'd cum, but for now? I wanted to appease every perverted fantasy in my head.

I dug into the pocket of my cargo pants and tossed Nero the lube.

"Fuck off!" Adler snarled. It seems the reality that it was go-time had hit him. "I swear to fucking god, I'll have all of the fucking Blood Crows behind me and I'll let every one of them fucking gang bang you, you fucking dirty faggot!"

I raised my hand and backhanded him, so hard his head smashed against the concrete wall.

"Yeah, do it again. I fucking dare you!" Adler screamed. He spat blood at me and tried to hit me but the chains stopped him. "Unchain me and fucking try that again! You fucking pussy. Do that when I'm free and see what fucking–" I hit him again, anger suddenly erupting inside of me. His words, words that had come from me not too long ago, hit me where I didn't even know I had sensitive flesh exposed.

"Ah, don't let him get to you, precious," Nero purred. But I got to my feet and snatched the small silver key we'd placed beside the mattress, out of Adler's reach.

Nero let out a surprised whistle, and without saying a word, I unshackled Adler's neck, and then both of his wrists.

Adler wasted no time. He grabbed me and pushed me, but that was all he got in. I punched him in the face and he fell backwards. Then I grabbed his leg, pushed it back, and without even telling him to, Nero got into position.

Adler howled and screamed, more alive unchained than he was when we had him bound. A new energy coursed through me, adding a vigour to the horniness that was burning my flushed body alive. What had been play just seconds ago had reached a threshold, a snapping point that I hadn't even realized I'd been edging. But I hit it, I not only hit it, I broke it and had bathed in the blood and fluid that it had sprayed onto me.

"Scream louder," I growled. I smacked him again and laughed when Adler's mouth opened and a scream rang out. Not just any scream, this one felt like it had been carried from the darkest pits of hell. Cradled in the arms of demons and fed with nothing but pain and terror. He knew what was coming, and I knew what was coming.

I was in control. I was the dominant beast. I was a demon taking this angel's power away. A sheltered little shit used to being pampered and worshipped. Thirty years old and as green as the grass outside. A fucking virgin who hated sex, who wanted nothing but to find the very man Mantis and Elish were trying to keep him from.

And he was mine.

I wrapped one hand over Adler's neck, the other one pinning his wrists above his head. Nero was between his legs, and, boy, was he ever smiling.

"Fuck him," I growled.

The room was electrified, it was thick and seeping energy, hot and sweaty electricity that made the fine hairs on my body stand on end. I could feel it in my chest, just fucking glowing like an orb, like the sun itself had been stolen; I hadn't felt this alive in a long time. Since I'd left Aras. I had been dormant for too long. I had been a weak wraith of the man I had once been for too – fucking – long.

And seeing myself finally coming back, breaking through the hardened but broken shell...

I fucking felt like singing.

I laughed instead. I laughed, and when I saw Nero position his cock over Adler's hole, I grinned.

"NO!" Adler screamed at the top of his lungs. His voice broke, and when he sucked in a shuddered breath, he started coughing, blood sprayed onto Nero's chest and chest hair. "NO!" he screamed again, my ears ringing from his song. I watched intently as Nero push the tip against the opening, and felt further satisfaction when Adler let out another howl.

It was tight though, of course the little virgin was tight. I spat on my fingers and rubbed the saliva onto Adler's hole.

"Break him," I said to Nero, my voice low and dangerous. "Fucking break him."

Nero winked at me, then looked down, and with Adler's screaming and thrashing highlighting the act, Nero pushed himself against Adler's ass... and I saw the head disappear inside of him.

Oh did Adler ever fucking scream.

As soon as Nero broke through, he jerked his hips down and made Adler take his entire length. Adler shrieked, his eyes closed and his face blistering red. He started thrashing like an animal in death's jaws, so I rested a knee on his chest and leaned over him to keep his wrists firmly in my hands.

I couldn't see what Nero was doing because of the angle, but I wasn't interested in that. I wanted my attention focused on Adler, I wanted to take in and enjoy every facial movement, drink in every scream. I might never get the chance to do this again and I was going to enjoy it.

I was no longer the victim, and I wasn't doing this to someone innocent either. I was paying back the bitch who killed my boyfriend, the fucking piece of shit who'd ordered his brother to rape the boy I loved more than anything in the world.

And it was just so satisfying.

Adler's eyes began to bulge, at the same time that Nero started to roughly fuck him. The back room was filled with the sounds of Nero's heavy panting, skin smacking up against skin, and Adler's screaming and crying. The smell was enjoyable as well, blood, sweat, and terror. A smell that had once made me nauseas, but now... fuck, if it was a cologne I would wear it every day.

Adler let out yet another scream, but unlike the others, this one broke into a sob. His attention shifted down to where the action was, and I saw a look of horror cross his face.

I looked down too.

Nero's hips were flying, there was no slow rhythm, no gentle movements, he was fucking him hard and fast with no signs of rest in the future. My brute chimera brother was a relentless machine, and just like he had with me, he was showing it.

But it wasn't me.

I was no longer the victim.

And I fucking never will be again.

I make victims, I don't become one.

This thought inside of my head made me smile.

And riding the emotions that these thoughts drew up in me, I leaned down and licked the blood that covered Adler's face.

He didn't move away from me this time, little bitch only whimpered.

"Poor boy," I murmured and indulged myself with another taste.

Adler's grey eyes rolled up to mine and he stared at me as if pleading for me to stop this, but if he thought I'd stop this now... well, he obviously didn't know who I was.

I kissed the corner of his mouth, and with a smile, I gently caressed his cheek. "All virgins bleed," I whispered to him. "Whether it's some arrogantly confident greywaster, some pure born immortal with a god complex, or my sweet little Killi Cat the first night I took him. They all bleed just the same."

"Fuck, Reaver..." Nero groaned and then he let out a laugh. "I swear, you're gonna kill me."

Suddenly there was an explosion outside.

CHAPTER 38

Reaver

NERO AND I LOOKED BEHIND US AND MADE EYE contact.

"The door," we both said at the same time. I looked down at Adler, and swore violently. "It's either Spike, or the boys got out. Fuck!"

Nero was already pulling himself out of Adler. "We need to take care of this."

Yeah, fun time was over, at least for now. "Let's go get the boys. If it was Spike, we can bring them back and let them have a go at our little prince." I leaned down and patted his cheek. Adler stared at me, his left eye now bloodshot and his nose trickling with fresh blood.

"I fucking love you," Nero groaned. When I stood up he handed me my pants. "You better have a go at his ass after we break Killian on him."

I laughed, I don't know why, but I laughed. Maybe I was just fucking happy to finally feel happy again. To have my control back, to have *me* back.

"You're beautiful," Nero said with a grin. He kissed my cheek and smacked my ass. "Now get your fucking clothes on, you dirty whore. We got boys to save."

"Yeah, I'm the whore. Me with my two sexual partners," I said as I nudged Adler in the small of his back. He was being quiet. I'd rather stuff and tie a rag around his mouth but it had already been several minutes since I'd heard the explosion. "How many men have you fucked?"

Nero whistled as he buttoned up his shirt. I quickly got dressed too. "Like a thousand, maybe? I've done every single legal age brother. I even fuck my nephew if he asks nicely. Then all the sengils and cicaros, any boy with a pretty face. Yeah, over a thousand, way over a thousand, I bet."

"You're probably swimming with disease," I said. I laced up my boots and Nero did as well and we crossed the garage, closing the door behind us.

"I probably have had every disease known to man, but once I die my body gets rid of it. Yours too." Nero slicked his hair back. "So are you going to tell Killian or does this get to be our dirty secret?" We walked outside, the sun was shining down on us and the smell of C4 was heavy in the air. I could see smoke wafting out of the sliding glass door but it wasn't enough to suggest the entire house was about to go up. Our nail bombs weren't meant to explode the house, we just wanted Spike or Mantis to get impaled. Bonus if it blew the door open but those doors were meant to be bomb proof. Perish had covered all of his bases when it came to these underground labs.

"I will never keep anything from him," I said honestly, but then I remembered me and Elish's kiss. "What he doesn't know is only because I've been going through shit and it just hasn't come up, but I'd never lie to him. I'm not a cheater. This just… I needed this."

"You carry yourself better and you just radiate now," Nero agreed. "See what Dr. Nero is capable of doing? If Silas ever gets a hold of you, he'll have nothing on you. Whereas before me… you'd just be all crippled and broken. So you're welcome."

"Yeah, go fuck yourself," I said back, and Nero laughed.

"I'm going to quickly go to Melchai," he said, and he glanced down the winding road to his left. "If I don't calm the cultists, the Blood Crows are going to come here to make sure everything is okay and we can't have them seeing us. Are you going to be okay handling Spike and Mantis?"

I nodded. I hadn't even thought of the Blood Crows below us. Nero was right, that explosion would be heard in the town and the last thing we needed was them seeing all of us with Angel Adi raped and beaten and the Prophet missing.

"Don't worry about it. I can handle this easy." And with that, Nero sprinted towards the entrance of the house and I crossed the yard towards the sliding glass door. The intense smell of burning stuck in my nose, and razed my nose hairs like a forest fire was sweeping through it.

I walked inside and looked around, my lungs stinging with the toxic fumes, and made my way towards the lab door.

Then I stopped. I looked down the first hallway by the living room and saw that the door to Adler's bedroom was now closed. I sprinted to it and opened it up to see if someone had made it through the door alive.

I couldn't believe it. "Killian!" I exclaimed, unable to stop a smile from spreading on my face. Killian looked great from what I could see, fully recovered and with all of his parts. He was standing in front of Adler's bed looking down at something.

Fuck, I was so glad he was okay. I know he wouldn't permanently die but I didn't want to be without him for five or six months. I wanted him to see me at my prime again.

"You fucking broke out? I knew you could..." My voice trailed as Killian slowly turned around, before it died in the air. His eyes were glaring and unrecognizable, two wide and staring orbs that called for nothing less than an exorcism. I'd never seen this expression on his face, and my heart crushed at the suggestion that he'd been violated down there and had slipped back into that state I now understood all too well.

But then I looked past him for a split second and saw me and Nero's boxer briefs neatly laid out on the bed, and then I saw the shine of a machete held tightly in his hand.

A gut-wrenching scream broke through Killian's lips, filling the chemically air and shattering the silence that had fallen upon us – then, with a flicker of light, Killian raised the machete... and charged right at me.

"Killian... calm..." I swore and stepped backwards into the hallway. I held up my hands, never thinking he would use the machete on me, but to my shock, Killian swung the weapon with a scream and only missed me by an inch. The machete embedded itself into the door frame with a crack, and Killian wrenched it free. His face was twisted in grief and bright red, his breathing hyperventilating and being exhaled through teeth clenched tight.

"Calm down!" I shouted. I started taking quick steps back as he stalked towards me, looking like the fucking dude from *The Shining*. "Killian. Put the fucking machete down."

"You fucking piece of shit!" Killian screamed at me. "You slept with him, didn't you? You fucking slept with Nero? How could you?!"

I kept backing away, I was in the living room now making my way towards the sliding glass door. "I'm not talking about this with you when you're holding a fucking weapon. Put it down and stop acting like a maniac."

"FUCK YOU!" he roared. There wasn't a single tear on his face, no hairline cracks in his visage. There was nothing on his boy's face that hinted to the sweet naïve boy I'd fallen in love with in Aras.

I just saw Silas.

My chest tightened at my own internal words.

"How could you? How could you do this to me?" Killian cried. He swung the machete again and hit an oscillating fan on a side table. It flew into a bookshelf where it crashed onto the ground. "Who are you? Who the fuck are you?!" He charged at me and I jumped away, this time the tip of the blade grazed my shirt. I saw a slit appear and a thin red line form across my chest. I looked down and suddenly felt a burst of anger go through me.

"Put the fucking machete down, you fucking psychotic bitch!" I snarled.

"Don't you dare talk to me like that!" Killian screamed. "I don't even know you. I don't even know who you are. Admit it. Tell me you fucked him!"

My vision turned red, the outrage at his words, the attitude I'd been hating seeing on him was palpable. I locked my fists, and felt my body start to tremble like I had jumper cables clipped to my fingers.

"We're not having this fucking conversation now!" I snapped. "Now put the machete down and stop acting like a fucking psycho. NOW!"

"Fuck you!" Killian yelled. His voice now becoming broken and scratchy from his screaming. "I'm done. I'm done with you! I'm done with this relationship, you fucking cheating whore. So fuck off!"

I laughed. Before I could even stop myself, I laughed. Killian's manic eyes stared at me, full of discord, the machete still in a white knuckle grip.

"I'll tell you when this relationship is over," I said to him, and though my voice was low and threatening the smile remained on my face. "You really think you can get rid of me? You must not know chimeras."

Killian's eyes seared mine, and he stood his ground as I stepped towards him. Deep inside, through the rage igniting my blood, I was surprised that he was.

"I don't listen to you... I only listen to one man," Killian said to me coolly, and dropped his gaze, "and that man is dead. Somehow, somehow even though he's immortal, he managed to destroy himself." When I took another step towards him, shifting my head to try and force him into eye contact with me, he stepped back. "Don't come any closer to me."

I took another step.

"Don't – come – any–" When I closed the last foot of distance, Killian raised the machete and swung it at me.

The cold blade bit through my shirt sleeve and embedded itself into my skin. I stood my ground and maintained my piercing gaze, even though I could feel the steel grinding against the bone in my arm.

"Do it again. Do it as many times as you want until you're done with your fucking tantrum," I growled at him. Killian wrenched the blade away, and I heard the tip scrape against the floor. "Then when you're done acting like a fucking drama queen, I can tell you why I let him fuck me."

"I don't care why," Killian said, his voice hollow. "Why would I care what a stranger does?" He looked up at me, and our eyes locked. I saw Silas in those eyes.

For the first time since the day he came to Aras... I saw Silas in those eyes.

He was Silas's clone. He was the clone of my greatest enemy. The boy I had fallen in love with... had the blood and bones of Silas, the brain of Silas.

And as I looked into those eyes, I saw no love in them for me... and I knew he was seeing none in mine. Killian, the boy I would burn the world for, looked at me with such a scathing hatred it was as if he was looking at Silas too.

Perhaps we had both turned into the people we hated the most.

"You're the stranger, not me," I said to him. "I fixed myself."

Killian shook his head, before saying to me in a steeled voice coated with hatred. "No... you're just a fucking chimera's whore now."

His words made me see red, and as the crimson enveloped my vision, I felt a scalding heat pour through my body, boiling my blood and melting my bones. It was overwhelming, to the point where my body began to shake.

But it was no tremble of despair, no tremble of sadness. What he'd said to me fuelled up such a violent rage, I felt myself step out of my physical body.

That was the only way I could explain, or justify, what I did next.

Before I could stop myself, I raised my hand... and I backhanded him.

I hit Killian so hard he flew backwards and slammed down onto the ground with a cry. He grabbed onto his cheek and looked up at me, stunned and crushed.

When I stalked towards him, he let out a fearful cry and started scrambling backwards. I then raised my boot and slammed it down on his chest and put my weight on it.

"You want to be a little badass now, huh?" I hissed. Killian started gasping for air, whimpers falling from his lips, outwards signs of submission that the inhuman anger I was feeling promptly dismissed. "You think you can run with the fucking big boys now, Killer Bee? You think you can fucking talk to me like that? You must think I'm a fucking joke now, don't you? Some weak little bitch who'll just take the horse shit spilling from your mouth?"

"No…" he whimpered.

"Oh, don't fucking backtrack now, Killian," I snarled at him, his submission directly feeding my rage. "You think you're top dog now? I have a rough few months after being brutally raped and all of a sudden I now have to deal with you trying to dominate me? And now you're giving up at the eleventh hour? Where's the badass Killian, huh? Where is he?" Tears started to well in his eyes but I was having none of it. I smacked him in the side of the face and grabbed his chin. "Look at me when I'm fucking talking to you!" I yelled. "You tried to chop my arm off with a fucking machete and now you're crying from a fucking slap? You want equal partners–" I smacked him again. "–then you'll get treated like an equal, tough guy!" I took my boot off of his chest and stood back. "Get the fuck up."

Killian wiped his nose and shook his head.

"GET UP!" I screamed. I picked up the machete and flung it through the open sliding glass door. "If you think I'm the type of person to cheat on you, to let Nero fuck me just because, you're a fucking idiot!"

I turned back to him, he was on his feet now and trembling. "I did it because I saw no other fucking way. Do you have any idea what I've been going through? How much I've felt like I've lost myself. How I didn't even recognize myself anymore? And on top of that, having to deal with you trying to dominate me when I'm at my weakest. Do you have any fucking idea how that feels? I've been going through hell, fucking utter hell, and unlike when you went through it, I didn't have a supportive partner… I had some little shithead bitch taking advantage of me! NO LOOK AT ME!" I screamed when he tried to look away, tears were streaming down his face now. "I did the hardest fucking thing I've ever done, Killian. I took the offer of the man who had crippled me to make my weakness into a strength. I did the hardest fucking thing I've ever done and I let him fuck me. I let him fuck me in a place where I had control. I let him do it so I could get used to it, so it wouldn't be my fucking kryptonite anymore. I, Reaver-fucking-Merrik, did it because I was so broken I knew there was no other way. And guess what? It fucking worked. It fucking worked and this morning I felt the first flicker of myself come back. But you don't care do you?" I turned and picked up the nearest thing I could find, the dish Nero's sandwich had been on, and I threw it. "You don't care because you didn't even let me fucking explain it to you. Whatever, you think you don't know me? I don't even fucking know you."

"You know me," Killian said quietly.

"No. I fucking don't," I snapped, but then I shook my head. "Actually, you're right, maybe I do. Maybe I do fucking know you." I grabbed his arm and started pulling him towards the sliding glass door. "You do seem familiar now. Now that I know who you fucking are." Killian made a nervous noise and tried to pull away from me, but I only clenched his arm harder and dragged him towards the garage. "You wanna see just how weak I am now, Killian? You want to see how I'm nothing but some fucking pussy unable to fuck his own boyfriend?"

"I – I know you're not that."

"Like fuck you don't." My nails were breaking his skin but I didn't care. I continued to drag him towards the garage, and towards where we'd left Adler. "I'm just some coward now, am I not? You're the dominant chimera, you're the big man. Remember my promise to you, Killian? How you wanted to rape Kiki? You wanna prove to me you're a man, Killer Bee?"

"Reaver... stop," Killian cried, and suddenly he jerked away from me, freeing his arm. "You're really scaring me. Please, stop."

When I advanced to try and grab him, Killian jumped back with a cry of fear and turned to run from me, but I snatched him by the collar of his shirt and pulled him backwards. Killian screamed and started sobbing.

I dragged him to the closed door, then I kicked it open so hard it slammed against the wall, raining debris and dust onto us.

I grinned, clenched Killian's shoulders, and walked him to the back room.

Through the plumes of disturbed gyprock dust we both saw Adler, chained and bound, laying on his side with his grey-blue eyes shell-shocked and terrorized. He was naked and trembling, the blood on his body a bright contrast to his white skin... especially the blood that had pooled in the crack of his ass, and had dripped down to form a bright stain on the grey mattress.

Killian gasped and put his hands up to his mouth.

"Nero did that," I purred in his ear. "I'm not a cheater, so I decided to wait for you to do it with me. I want to watch you break him in. I want you to lose that last shred of virginity on him. It's just the two of us now... do it, Killian."

Killian didn't move. I took his shirt and ripped it off of him, and when he tried to run to the door, I slammed it shut and leaned against it.

"Prove to me that you have the balls to back up the attitude," I demanded, a snarl in my tone. "You wanted to rape Kiki. I have better than that. I brought you prey that just lost his virginity not even an hour ago. I held him down for Nero, it was amazing watching it happen to this pathetic piece of shit, the fuck who almost had his brother rape my boyfriend in front of me. It made me feel on top of the world to inflict on him what had been inflicted on me." I pressed a boot against Adler's ass, it left a mud print on the white skin. "And now, he's yours. That's just how fucking awesome I feel now, Killian. How much I fucking missed dominating. No worries now. I fucking feel GREAT!" I turned Killian around and pushed him towards Adler. "Go on! I'm cured; I can fucking handle your attitude now. So you might as well start off on the right foot and show me what you have in store for me. Show me how grown up and dominant you are."

Killian turned away from Adler, and I saw his lower lip stiffen. He stood there, half-naked, thin and gaunt, and his entire body started to shake, not just tremble, but shake like a petrified kitten.

Then his face dissolved... and as he stood there in the cold of the room... he started to sob.

Not just cry... sob.

For a moment I was still. I stared at him with the anger still controlling me, but when I saw the look of utter devastation on his face, the intense sadness that made him look so tiny and helpless, it dissipated like the fire in my blood had been turned to ice.

Once again... the anguish on his face brought me down from my own madness.

"Fuck..." I whispered.

I walked towards him, but to my horror, Killian let out a scared cry and started backing away from me, as if I was a master and he was a beaten animal. I let him dodge me, I didn't want to scare him more, and watched as he ran for the door.

Killian opened it and ran out, I followed. I closed it behind me and watched as the poor boy took several steps before his trembling legs gave out and spilled him onto the ground. He was sobbing hysterically now, and at the same time trying to crawl away from me.

My eyes burned, and the guilt of what I'd done to him hit me and hit me hard.

"Killi..." I cried. I ran to him, and when he started screaming I held out my hands. He was looking at me with such terror my heart felt like it was being shredded.

How could he look at me any different? I had been terrorizing him.

"I won't hurt you... come here," I pleaded. "I'm sorry. Please, baby, come here."

Killian's head shook. He wrapped his hands around the back of his neck and clenched them. He was in such a state he was having trouble breathing, he just kept choking and gasping.

I got down on my knees in front of him. "Please, baby blue. Come here," I whispered. I held out my arms again and lightly touched his shoulder. When he didn't recoil away I rubbed it, and slowly, I pulled him into my arms.

I thought he had been crying hard before, but when I squeezed him to me, the poor boy completely broke apart. I'd made him cry lots of times, but never to this extent. His frail body shook like an earthquake was happening underneath his skin, and his breathing was so laboured and hard I was afraid he was going to pass out from lack of oxygen.

What the fuck did I do? What was wrong with me? I was so fuelled by just feeling like myself I had forgotten who I was for him. Killian didn't need the Reaper... he needed me.

My eyes stung. I was so ashamed of myself. I got caught up in it... it was a high in itself to finally feel powerful again.

"Baby... I'm sorry," I whispered. I started rocking him back and forth. "I love you. You know I'd never do anything to hurt you. I was desperate when it came to Nero. I was going to tell you everything when I got you back. You know I'm not a cheater, I'd never do that to you." I rubbed his back as he continued to sob uncontrollably. "You know how pathetic I've gotten, how weak. I just couldn't go through another day like that. Another day all psychosis and miserable. It worked... a little too well. I'm sorry I got crazy with you, baby bee. I'm sorry I hit you."

Killian's hyperventilating breaths sounded like gasping screams, one after another rolling from his lips and each one of them lanced me. This wasn't Silas doing this to him, or Perish... it was fucking me.

I don't care what his genetics were, or whose blood ran through his veins. He'd never once looked at me different for being Silas's clone... and neither would I.

"Shhh..." I soothed. Killian clutched me and unleashed another wail. "It's okay. It's okay. Come on, honey bee. Let's go inside the mansion and lay down together."

"You smell like him!" Killian suddenly cried. "You smell like Nero."

My throat burned. "Killi... I had to do it. You don't..." The burning travelled to my eyes and I shut them. "You don't understand how much I was scaring myself. You know I hate sex... you know me enough to know I was in a desperate place."

"What about him!" Killian pulled away and pointed to the door, his face anguished.

I deflected my gaze. "I didn't fuck him. Honestly, that was just me on a power trip and I wanted to pay him back. You said you wanted to do it too."

"Fuck you!" Killian cried. He shoved me away but he ended up clutching my shirt and letting out another heartbreaking wail. Then he collapsed into my arms and started crying again. I squeezed him tight to me.

But then, as if what else I'd done had dawned on him fully, he once again shoved me away, hard. "So you let Nero fuck you... and then you kidnap and hold Adler down while Nero raped him?" Killian yelled. He staggered to his feet, his chin shaking from his chattering teeth. "How can you fucking tell me it was therapy when the next fucking morning you're cheating on me again?"

"It wasn't fucking cheating!" I said, raising my voice. I got up too. "If you fucking think that's cheating, you don't fucking know me. I'd never do that to you."

"Then why did you hold down Adler for Nero?" Killian screamed. He walked over and kicked the door open. He walked up to the bloody, out of it born immortal, his boots stepping in Adler's blood. "Was that fucking therapy too? Letting Nero do to Adler what he did to you? When you know how much that broke you? Where is Nero? Did you send him on some sort of fucking shopping trip so you could have Adler to yourself?"

"He fingered me, tried to kiss me." I felt like a bucket of cold liquid was dumped on me when Adler's weak voice croaked. "Nero sucked his cock too. D-don't play innocent, you d-disgusting p-pervert."

You could hear a fucking pin drop.

Killian's eyes slowly travelled up to mine, and when there was no denials on my lips, I saw the turmoil drain from his face... and nothing else remained.

Killian walked out of the back room, past me, and towards the exit.

"Killian, fucking come back. I'm tired of explaining this shit to you," I called after him and I followed his steps. "I've been real fucking understanding of your shit and your psychosis and it's starting to piss me off that you're not showing me the same."

Killian whirled around, several feet from the exit of the garage. "You fucking cheated on me!" he screamed. Behind him I saw a flicker of black and realized Kiki was standing in the shadows, a surprised look on his face. I don't even know how long he'd fucking been there.

"How can you think I'm dumb enough to give you a pass with Nero, and then this shit with Adler? Plus Nero sucking you off? Are you fucking kidding me?" Killian continued to yell. Kiki's eyes widened. "Who's next? You going to suck off Kiki too? Oh no, sorry *Kicky*. He's Kicky!" The corners of Killian's eyes welled. "You give the fucking chimera pet a cute little nickname and let him hang off of your fucking arm. Then you let Nero, the man who raped you, put his cock inside of you. And now... and fucking now... you helped Nero do to him, what he did to you? And you fucking FINGERED HIM?" Killian turned around and picked up a wrench laying on a wooden table full of tools and power tools. He flung it at me but it was too far away for me to have to duck.

"You know what, Killian?" I raised my voice. "I did what I had to do, to get myself back. Alright? I did what I had to do to get my power back, and I fucking did. I fixed myself. So if you're looking for an apology, you're going to be looking for a long fucking time. I'm not sorry. I feel great, and quite frankly, I'm fucking insulted that you keep insinuating that I cheated on you, that I somehow love or respect you less."

"YOU DON'T LOVE ME!" Killian screamed, his voice bouncing off of the high ceilings and echoing back to my ears. He picked up a screw driver and flung it too. I saw it coming but I didn't move, I let it hit my chest and fall to the ground.

My stance became rigid. "Too far, Killian," I said flatly.

"FUCK YOU!" he sobbed. "You don't fucking love me, you're not capable of it. You don't respect me, you haven't respected me for months. I watched you become an emotional wreck who pushed away all of my help and did mental gymnastics until he convinced his delusional fucking mind that I was somehow dominating him. Which I never fucking was! I just wanted to be treated like a man! Then I watched you flirt with that fucking cicaro, and you get pissed at me for being bothered by it. And now I get to hear about how you let Nero fuck you, cum inside of you. And then, to top it off, you had a fucking threesome and help Nero rape your fucking brother! And what have I gotten? You killed me the last time you tried to be intimate with me, and yet you can easily sleep with your fucking brothers? You don't love me, your chimera engineering forbids loving some dumb greywaster. You love your family, you love the chimeras, just like you'll love Silas when he comes for you. You'll never love me like you love them. I see that now."

"That's fucking enough!" Kiki's voice rang out. He burst out of the shadows and was suddenly nose-to-nose with Killian. "Just because you're too selfish to understand our family doesn't give you the right to speak to him that way!" the boy shouted. "He did what he knew was right. Master Nero is a great man, and I bet he did a better job fixing Reaver than you ever could!"

"YOU SHUT THE FUCK UP!" Killian shrieked. He picked up a wrench, but with a swift movement, Kiki slammed his hand down on Killian's upper elbow and the wrench dropped to the ground. "You fucking little whore! Stay the fuck away from me!"

"You stop yelling at him!" Kiki yelled, matching the intensity of his voice with Killian's. "Stop yelling. He's had a long day. He's had a long fucking year!"

"YOU'RE NOT HIS PET! HE'S NOT YOUR MASTER!" Killian cried, tears running down his cheeks. He looked at me, anguish on his face, but his words to me had rendered me speechless. I wouldn't admit it to myself... but they'd hurt me.

I had done so much for him. From the moment he'd stepped foot into Aras, to me sleeping with Nero. He'd never listen, but I'd gone to bed with that chimera for Killian, as fucked up as it sounds.

I'd sacrificed my own dignity for Killian. I'd given that boy a piece of my soul… and this is what he has to say to me? I loved him, even if he was Silas's clone… I loved him.

This is what he thought?

"Fuck you, fuck all of you," Killian sobbed. "You're a real chimera now, Reaver Dekker. You sleep with who you want, you do whatever you want without care of how it affects others. You're a selfish bastard and I'm done. I'm just done. Go suck Kiki's cock for all I care. I don't stand a chance when it comes to your family, and I don't want to be in a relationship where I have to always wonder just how strong of a hold they have on you."

He looked at me for some sort of reaction but I couldn't move. I didn't even know if I was breathing or not. I felt like I was being violated again, but this time it was my heart that was the target.

I just wanted to get myself back.

I just wanted to… feel like myself again. Have some power again.

And he was leaving me because of that?

"You're a piece of shit, Killian," I heard Kiki say.

"Yeah. I know he'll make this my fault. He's good at that." I heard footsteps, but I still hadn't looked up. "You win, *Kicky*. The Dekker family wins. Goodbye." I heard a sniff, and the footsteps got farther away.

My gaze was fixed on my boots, the bloodstains now dusted with grey ash. I could see outlines from the footprints, ones that travelling all around the garage.

And I could hear a pounding. *Thunk – thunk – thunk.*

It was my own heartbeat, but it sounded like it was in my head, pushing and throwing its entire weight against my skull. *Thunk – thunk – thunk.*

Did… did Killian just break up with me?

My Killian?

"Talk to me…" I could hear that weak voice so clear inside of my head, the frail, pain-filled tones only broken up by the pounding in my head.

"I don't know what to say!"

"I… I have to get you out of here. Killi. I know it hurts but…"

"Tell me about…" He'd sucked in a breath so hard, he'd started to

cough. I almost cried out when I saw blood sprinkling my hand. I was so terrified… I was so heartbroken. *"Tell me the story about… about when we first met."*

His pulse was slowing… his pulse was slowing. I could feel it. I was so scared. I'd never been this scared in my life.

Killian was dying in my arms.

"Oh, Killi…"

"Don't leave me here. You can't"

"I've barely had you."

"We've been apart for months. You can't, Killi Cat… you can't."

You can't.
You can't leave me.

I won't let you.

"Greywasters just can't be with chimeras," I heard Kiki say. His voice was beside me and I heard him light a cigarette. I took it from him when he offered it. "They're just not compatible, they say. I think you should join us." His heart skipped at the prospect. "Master Nero's a craftsman. I love him so much." Another skip. "And I think… me and you could be really good friends." He held out his hand, wanting me to take it, but all I could do was stare.

There were no more footsteps. Killian had left me. I'd done everything I could to explain myself. I said I was sorry. I wasn't a cheater… I wasn't.

I never loved you? I loved my family more?

Killian, I'd kill for you.

I… I'd end the world for you.

My eyes narrowed, and I looked down just in time to see the cigarette crush in my grip. I didn't even feel the sting of the ember but I smelled my own flesh burning as the small flame smouldered against my skin.

"R-Reaver…?" Kiki said slowly. I heard shifting and a new noise, buzzing, intense buzzing.

"Those are… that's a box of Geigerchips…"

I walked towards the shelf of tools and heard Kiki's breath catch in his throat. "Radiation…" he whispered, and he let out a shuddering gasp. "Reaver! You're releasing radiation! Reaver… you need to–"

I looked down at the spread of tools and picked up a handheld circular saw.

"–you need to get outside before the garage blows up!" Kiki ran over to me and pulled on my arm. "Hurry, Reaver."

I turned around, and locked eyes with the cicaro, and as the sounds of hundreds of Geigerchips going off filled the garage like a disturbed hive of bees, I smiled at him.

And I didn't stop smiling.

The next thing I knew… my world was collapsing around me; the knitted fabric of the universe that kept everything together had torn apart right in front of my eyes. I could see the fibres; I could see little black holes that sucked in the white flames like vacuums before consuming themselves and disappearing as quickly as they came. This was my world as I walked to where I knew the garage door was. Just white, just white and a roaring from the explosion that was bringing the garage to its knees.

Then I raised my head, and raised my hands to the air. One of them carrying something heavy and dripping. I took in a deep breath and observed a white glow radiating off of my limbs as I poured sestic radiation into this small oasis in the dead world. They weren't on fire, but they were one of the only things that weren't. The entire world seemed to be coated in these opal, crystal-like flames, but they didn't burn me, and I walked out of the garage safely.

"Reaver!" I heard a distant voice scream. He screamed my name again and again, each time more desperate, and more shrill, than the one previous. I looked forward but only saw white, or what I thought was white. I realized, as my sense of smell came back to me, that I was seeing smoke.

I kept walking, clutching what was in my right hand hard so I didn't drop it. My feet hit grass but I only knew from my boots sinking into it.

Then finally, I saw the silhouette of Killian, his hands balled in front of him as he sobbed my name. A stance that showed agony, pleading to a dead god for me to not be in the garage, even though he'd been the one to leave me there.

My heart didn't flinch, my body was numb and allowing no other emotions to come forth. I had reached my breaking point, and the evidence of that was clutched in my hand.

The smoke cleared, and I heard Killian let out a cry of relief. I could see him, sobbing and hysterical.

Then he saw what I was carrying, and he stopped. Like the world had frozen, he paused mid-cry, and instead gaped at my hand with his mouth open in shock.

I walked up to Killian, and the boy stared at me. His bloodshot eyes wide and his lips moving to find words I knew he'd never speak.

I raised my hand, Kiki's head dangling from the tuft of hair I was clenching, and I pushed the cicaro's severed head into Killian's chest.

Then, and as a thunderous sound of the garage roof collapsing shook the ground underneath our feet, I leaned in… and growled into his ear.

"Never doubt my commitment to you again."

End of Volume 1

A NOTE FROM QUIL

Wow, is it ever great to be back! I missed my boys and it's been just amazing to be back writing The Fallocaust Series. This is where I belong and whenever I'm away from the boys I feel a piece of me missing.

So volume 1 is now finished, I hope you enjoyed it. Volume 2 and the conclusion to The Suicide King will be available soon (if it isn't already), so check my website for updates on when that will be.

I loved writing this book, even if it did give me a few extra grey hairs. When I first started Fallocaust our characters spent most of their time in Aras, but now the world has expanded and with each release you get to see different areas of the greywastes, different areas of Skyfall, and the plaguelands. I'm looking forward to discovering more of the Fallocaust world, introducing new characters, and seeing just where everyone ends up, and their journey getting there.

I'll leave it at that since this is only the end of volume 1, so I'll save my spiel for volume 2. But I would like to thank you for coming with me as I traverse around the greywastes, and for making my dreams of becoming an author come true. I also must thank my amazing beta readers who also happen to be just as amazing friends: Mare, Kristie, Chad, Brent, Lewis, and Matt. You guys are awesome, thank you for helping me make Fallocaust as great as it can be.

And as usual for updates on book releases, to view excerpts, or to watch me slowly slip into psychosis, follow me on Twitter @Fallocaust, also find me on Facebook /quil.carter, and of course, my website: www.quilcarter.com. I'm also found on Spotify, where I have playlists for all of my books. In those playlists are songs mentioned in the series, songs I think suit the book, and ones I listened to while writing.

Be good, everyone! Actually, no, be bad, bad is more fun.

Sincerely,

Quil Carter